CHASING THE DREAM

The Complete Series

ELIZABETH BRIGGS

More Than Music

CHASING THE DREAM #1

Chapter One

Tonight was going to be epic, I could feel it. I edged closer to the stage, pushing past emo kids with sweeping black hair and girls in fishnets and combat boots. Julie and Carla followed, our hands linked so we wouldn't lose each other while I searched for the perfect spot. Not right in front so we looked like obsessed groupies hanging all over the band, but close enough to get a good view of the stage and feel the music vibrating under our skin. After some maneuvering, the three of us wedged into a space in the crowd and clinked our beers together.

"Here's to the end of finals," Julie shouted, over the noise of a hundred conversations going on at once. "And the end of our junior year!"

"I still have a final tomorrow morning," Carla shouted back. "What time are they going on again, Maddie?"

"Any minute now," I said. "Don't worry. Kyle's band only has one album. We'll be out of here in an hour." I had a final early, too, and normally I'd be studying right now and then going to bed at a reasonable hour to make sure I got an optimal amount of sleep. But it wasn't every day a friend's band got a gig like this in a club on Hollywood Boulevard. Besides, I was a music major. This totally counted as research.

I rocked back and forth on my feet, full of that intoxicating mix of excitement, anticipation, and longing I always felt right before a concert started. The club was dark except for the spotlights highlighting the equipment on stage, poised and ready for the band to come out. People with dyed hair and tattoos and piercings pressed all around us, and I felt more out of place than ever with my black-rimmed glasses, red flannel shirt, and jeans.

Julie fit into the crowd better with her knit panda beanie, despite it being approximately the temperature of the sun in here. She'd made the hat herself and on anyone else it would look stupid, but with her long black hair and red lips, she somehow managed to pull it off. Combined with the skater dress with stars and planets that she'd also made, she was really rocking her sexy nerd look tonight. Sort of like an Asian version of Zooey Deschanel.

Carla looked gorgeous as usual, like she'd walked straight off the runway and into the club, which she probably had—she modeled on the side while pursuing her theatre major. She was half-Portuguese and half-African-American, and casting agencies went crazy for her smooth dark skin, head full of wild curls, and tall, thin frame. It was a shame Julie and I were the only ones who knew she'd rather fix old cars and play video games than do a photo shoot.

The glow of Carla's phone lit up her face as she checked her texts yet again. Probably another string of annoying questions from her boyfriend.

"Is that Daryl?" I asked.

"He just wants to know where I am."

"Don't tell him," Julie said, slapping the phone away. "He'll show up uninvited."

It wouldn't be the first time he'd crashed our girls' nights looking for Carla, convinced she was with some other guy. Probably because he knew she could do way better.

"He won't. I told him we're leaving right after the show."

A cheer went through the crowd as the band walked onto the stage, and I stood on my toes to get a better look. Hector, a Latino guy with curly hair tucked under a baseball cap, sat in front of the drums. He was followed by Becca, a blue-haired pixie in a dress with safety pins all over it. She stumbled across the stage like she was drunk, but managed to pick up her bass and slip it over her neck. Next came Kyle, his black hair hanging in his eyes and the gauges in his ear flashing under the lights. He moved behind his keyboard, but my gaze left him as soon as his older brother Jared appeared.

The crowd's cheering took on more of a screaming sound, and one girl even yelled, "Jared, I love you!" I rolled my eyes. Not that I blamed the girl. With dark hair that always stuck up like he'd just gotten out of bed, a perpetual five o'clock shadow, and blue eyes that could charm any girl into giving him his phone number, Jared was impossible to resist. I wanted to, believe me, but every time he opened his mouth and sang it was all over.

Jared gave the audience a wicked grin while he grabbed his guitar, a black Fender Stratocaster almost identical to my own except for the color. Like Kyle, he had tattoos running up and down his toned arms, and I couldn't help but wonder if they continued under his shirt.

The entire club buzzed with excitement, every one of us poised on the edge, holding our breaths and waiting for the plunge. In this moment, right before the music started, it felt like anything could happen—and I was ready.

Hector yelled out, "One, two, three, four," and the band launched into their first song. Jared's hard guitar riffs filled the small club, matched with the deep pulse of the bass, the fierce beat of the drums, and the eerie moan from Kyle's keyboard. The music ripped through me, touching the wild, dark part of my soul I kept locked away. My fingers itched to form the chords myself and play along, but I kept my hands in fists at my sides. Instead I nodded my head to the music, picking out each note Jared played and feeling it in a way only another musician could.

When Jared leaned into the mic and sang, his smooth voice washed over me like a soft caress. It was like the last, decadent bite of a chocolate-covered strawberry. The smoky burn of whiskey as it slipped down your throat. The final night of passion before your lover left forever. I sang along to the words, feeling each line strike me deep inside. I understood exactly what he was saying, like he'd written every word just for me, like somehow he understood me in a way no one else did. Of course, every other girl in the club probably felt the same way I did. And a few guys, too.

I tore my gaze from Jared to watch the rest of the band. Hector was a blur as his muscular arms flew across the drums. Becca swayed while she played bass, her movements sluggish and her eyes half-closed like she could barely keep herself awake. Lately Kyle had been complaining about how she kept coming to rehearsals wasted, but I couldn't believe she'd do that tonight, not for their biggest performance ever.

Kyle was bent over his keyboard, head bobbing along while he played, and I loved seeing him in his element. We'd met as freshmen, and since we were both music majors who played piano, we always ended up in a lot of the same classes. We didn't hang out much outside of school or anything, but whenever we had a group project or a duet to perform we always paired up. Over the years, we'd bonded over a shared love of movie scores, superheroes, and other geeky stuff, even though he was covered in tattoos and never wore anything other than black and I thought staying up past eleven was living on the edge. Somehow we'd just clicked—but never in a romantic way.

The song ended, and the audience cheered. Jared flashed the crowd a smile full of dark promises. "Thank you," he said. "We're Villain Complex."

Julie whistled loudly beside me, and Carla covered her ears from the piercing sound. I blinked at them, coming out of a fog. I'd been so lost in the music I'd completely forgotten my friends were with me.

"They're so good!" Carla yelled.

"And the guys are so hot!" Julie added.

"I told you!" I shouted back at them. And then the next song started and I was swept away, falling under Jared's spell again.

Villain Complex had won the UCLA vs USC Battle of the Bands a month ago, securing the win for UCLA and making Kyle an instant celebrity around campus. Before that they'd only done a handful of small gigs and parties, playing both covers and songs from their own self-produced album. They were so talented it was only a matter of time until they really took off, and I'd be able to say I knew them before they were famous.

When the show ended, most of the audience crushed toward the exit like a herd of sheep. I was one of the few people crazy enough to move against the crowd and head for the stage, losing Julie and Carla somewhere in the fray. I finally made it to the front, next to a bunch of groupies gazing at Jared while he bent over to unplug something. I struggled not to stare along with them, but was saved when Kyle spotted me.

"Maddie, you came!" He jumped off the stage and grabbed me in a hug.

"I wouldn't miss it for anything. You were amazing!"

"Yeah?" He brushed hair away from his face, the tattoos on his fingers spelling out LIVE LOUD. "I was so nervous. You have no idea."

"It was a great show. Seriously. I was impressed."

"Thanks. That means a lot, coming from you." His face broke out into a grin. "Hey, I didn't get a chance to tell you the news. We have a live audition for *The Sound* on Friday!"

"What? No freaking way!" *The Sound* was a reality TV show where different rock bands competed against each other while being mentored by a famous musician. The winning band got a recording contract with a major label, and the top four bands were sent on tour together across the country. Plus, the show had millions of viewers, so even the bands that didn't win picked up a ton of new fans just from being on it.

"I know. Crazy, right?" He laughed like he couldn't believe it himself. "Jared sent in a video of us performing, plus MP3s of all our songs and a bunch of other shit. I didn't think anything would happen with it, but yesterday a producer called out of the blue and invited us to come on the show to audition."

"Wow, this is huge! I'm so happy for you." I gave him another hug and meant every word I said—but I was prickling with a touch of envy, too. I wanted Kyle and his band to win, of course. And it's not like I wanted to go on *The Sound* or anything, hell no. It's just that, for once in my life, I'd like to do something bold like that, too. No more standing in the crowd and cheering for others, no more hiding in an orchestra or behind a piano, but on stage, living the dream out loud and in front. But that wasn't me.

A girl with hair the color of fruit punch slammed against Kyle, wrapping her inked arms around him. They kissed for the longest, most awkward moment ever while I stood next to them like a creepy voyeur. Finally they remembered I was there and broke away, grinning like two beautiful misfits in love.

"Hey, Maddie!" Alexis said with a big smile. "Wasn't Kyle incredible up there?"

"He really was," I agreed.

"I'm so proud of you, babe." She kissed his cheek, and he smiled at her like he was the luckiest guy in the world. They'd been high school sweethearts but had broken up when she'd gone to Princeton. Now that she'd transferred to USC, they'd reconnected at the Battle of the Bands and had been inseparable ever since.

"Hey, I got some killer photos of the show," she said. "I can't wait to get them on the website."

"Cool. Send them to Jared so he can put them up." He jerked his head toward his brother, who was talking with one of the groupies. "Jared!"

Uh oh. So far I'd managed to avoid all interactions with Jared for my own safety. Kyle had warned me that his brother had a new girl every week, and I knew they definitely weren't geeky girls like me. If we never met, then Jared could remain the version in my head, the guy who wrote songs that made me feel less alone in the middle of the night and who grinned at the audience like he knew their darkest secrets. Once we met, he would be a real person. But I couldn't exactly run off now, not with him walking over to us, even though the voice in my head yelled, *Go, go, go!*

"What's up?" Jared asked, smiling at us. It was a different smile from the one he used on stage, a private smile for friends that made him look even more like Kyle. I saw the real him for the first time, and it was even better than I'd imagined. I was doomed.

"Kyle talks about you all the time," Jared said to me, after we were introduced. "Great to finally meet you."

He hopped off the stage and spread his arms, moving in like he wanted to hug me. This wasn't all that shocking since Kyle was a hugger, too, but I stood there, frozen and tongue-tied for an excruciatingly long pause. It should be criminal for a man to be so good-looking. How were normal girls like myself supposed to touch the sun without getting burned?

"You too," I finally said and stepped toward him.

As his strong arms circled me, a little tremor ran through my body, like a static shock jolting right through my chest. He was the perfect height for me to press my face into the curve of his neck and breathe him in, but I restrained myself. The hug was brief, but even that second of contact was enough to leave me breathless. I quickly pulled away and took a few steps back to a safe distance.

"We're having a party at our place after this," Kyle said. "You should come, Maddie."

"Thanks, but I should get home." I had that final in the morning, and Carla would kill me if I kept her out all night. Besides, Kyle and I didn't exactly run in the same crowd, and I wouldn't know anyone at this party other than him and Alexis. And Jared now, but he was dangerous to be around.

"At least stop by for a few minutes," Jared said, giving me that warm smile again. I practically melted all over the floor, like a chocolate left in the sun. So unfair.

Alexis glanced between me and Jared with an amused smile, like she could tell how he affected me. "Yes, you have to come."

Kyle nudged me with his elbow. "C'mon. You can check out our studio while you're there."

Well…I supposed it wasn't that late yet, and I *had* been dying to check out the band's studio. It would be a good friend-gesture if I made an appearance, and if the party was crowded, I'd probably be able to avoid Jared the entire time. A few minutes couldn't hurt, right?

Chapter Two

By the time I showed up with Carla and Julie in tow, the house the brothers shared in the Hollywood Hills was completely packed. We squeezed our way inside a room that smelled of pizza and beer while music pounded in the background. I immediately spotted Jared leaning over a stunning blonde in the corner, twirling her hair in his fingers. No surprise there.

I'd never been to Kyle's place before, and even though he'd hinted about his family having money, it was still a shock to walk through the piece of prime LA real estate the brothers somehow managed to afford. Not that it was fancy or anything—it was actually pretty sparse, a typical bachelor pad with few personal touches. But it was two stories, with a pool and an amazing view of the city sparkling with a billion lights, and that didn't come cheap.

"We really should head home soon," Carla said as we stepped into the kitchen, where it was slightly quieter.

Julie grabbed some drinks from a cooler and passed one to each of us. "Relax. Have a beer."

"Fine. One beer only." But Carla promptly ignored it and started texting again.

"I'm fine with leaving in a few minutes," I said. I didn't know anyone here, the music was super loud, and I had no desire to watch Jared hooking up with one of his groupies. I'd say hi to Kyle, check out his studio, and then we could go. My duty as his friend would be done, and I'd still get enough sleep for my final tomorrow. Win-win.

"Speak for yourself," Julie said. "I had my last final today, and I am a free woman for the summer. Tonight I plan to find a guy who will make me forget all about molecular biology."

Julie was on the pre-med track with plans to apply to medical school next year, but it was no secret she hated it. Her true love was designing clothes, but she said that was just a hobby, not a career. Or maybe that was her parents speaking. I was never sure.

She nudged me with her elbow. "And you should talk to Jared."

"What?" I nearly dropped my drink. "No!"

"Seriously, you've been undressing him with your eyes all night. Make a move already."

"I have not been undressing him!" The words came out way too loud, and the people next to us glanced over. Even Carla looked up at me with raised eyebrows, like she didn't believe my protest. I flushed and lowered my voice. "It doesn't matter. He's a total player, and besides he'd never go for someone like me anyway."

"Why not?" Carla asked. "You're beautiful and smart, and you play guitar, too. That already puts you ahead of these other girls."

"I don't really play guitar. I mean, I do, but only for you two…"

"Hey, you don't have to marry the guy," Julie added. "Just go talk to him. Have some fun."

"Or ask Kyle to set you up," Carla said.

"No. Definitely not." There was no way I'd ask Kyle to hook me up with his older brother. Ick.

"Fine, but you have to do something about this," Julie said. "You're practically obsessed with the guy."

Carla gave me a sympathetic smile. "You do listen to his music a lot…"

I hated when they ganged up on me like this. "Hang on, just because I think he's talented—"

"And hot," Julie butted in.

"And because I like his band's music doesn't mean I'm 'obsessed' with him."

Julie rolled her eyes. "Fine, then let's find you another guy to get your mind off him. How long has it been since you got laid?"

I rubbed a hand across my face, more than ready to go home now. "I don't know."

"When did you break up with Chad? Six months ago?"

"Something like that," I muttered, hoping she'd drop it already. Chad was a communications major who said "dude" too much and spent most of his time at the beach. He'd been easy on the eyes and pretty good in bed, but he didn't get me at all. The final straw had been when he'd bailed on one of my big recitals to go drinking with some friends. Music was my life, and if he couldn't understand that, then there was no point dating him anymore.

Julie opened her mouth to push me again, but I held up a hand. "Fine, I'll talk to Kyle, okay?"

"Yes! Go forth and conquer!" She raised her beer to me while Carla patted my arm and wished me luck before going back to her phone.

I returned to the living room and found Kyle in the crowd, dancing close with Alexis. "You made it!" Kyle said when he saw me. "Want to check out the studio now?"

"Sure." I'd promised Julie I'd talk to Kyle, but I hadn't actually agreed to bring up Jared, after all. "Or I can find it myself. Just tell me where to go. I don't want to interrupt."

"Nah, I'll take you. I locked it so no one can steal our gear." He paused to smile at his girlfriend. "You coming?"

Alexis kissed Kyle on the cheek. "No, you two go ahead."

"You sure?" He pulled her in by her waist and gave her a ridiculously long kiss while I stared pointedly at the floor.

"Go," she said, laughing and shoving him away. "Get your music geek on."

Kyle started to lead me through the crowd, but a bottle smashed near us, loud even with the music blasting. In the corner, beer and green fragments of glass dripped down the wall above Jared while Becca glared at him from a few feet away. Conversation died as everyone turned to watch the scene.

"*Another* girl, Jared?" she yelled, her words slurred. "How many tonight?" She reached for another bottle to throw, but Hector appeared at her side and yanked her back.

"What the fuck, Becca?" Hector asked. Jared slowly wiped beer off his face like he couldn't believe she'd just done that.

"Don't touch me!" She flailed her arms to fight him off. Hector immediately released her, but she stumbled into someone behind her. "Stay away from me!"

"Shit, not this again," Kyle muttered. "Here—the studio's at the end of that hallway." He handed me a key and then darted over to grab Becca's arm and help steady her. "Hey, let's get you sobered up."

"I'm fine," she muttered. Her eyes closed as she swayed next to him.

Jared stepped forward, fists clenched at his side. "Becca, this has to stop."

Kyle shot his brother a sharp look. "Let me handle this."

"Then handle it! We can't have her on *The Sound* like this. Either she gets her shit together, or she's out of the band."

Becca's eyes snapped open, and she jerked away. "I'm done anyway! Done with you, done with your band, done with all this shit!"

She stormed out the front door, and Kyle raced after her. Jared started to follow, but Hector held him back and they started arguing in low voices. Kyle had been right about Becca being a mess, and I knew they'd been through a few other bassists before, too. Hopefully he could get her straightened out before their audition.

Conversation around the room picked up again, but I slipped down the hallway and found the door Kyle had mentioned. It clicked shut and locked behind me, and the noise of the party faded to a dull thrum. The studio seemed to be a soundproofed garage with cheap carpeting that peeled up in the corners. The far wall had the Villain Complex logo and a bunch of quotes painted in black, including: "You don't know the power of the Dark Side," from *Return of the Jedi*; "You either die a hero or live long enough to see yourself become the villain," from *The Dark Knight*; and "One lab accident away from being a supervillain," from *The Big Bang Theory*. Under the quotes was a couch with an acoustic guitar flung across it and a small table covered in empty soda and beer cans. The rest of the studio was filled with microphones, headphones, pedals, amps, and cords crisscrossing the floor to connect it all.

I stepped carefully through the room, like I was walking on hallowed ground, and inspected the instruments on display. Kyle had a top-of-the-line keyboard that

I wanted to run my fingers across, but I held back. I didn't see the bass Becca had used earlier—maybe she'd taken it before her dramatic exit. The drums were here, though, in pieces, waiting to be set up again.

Jared's black Fender sat in the middle of the room, propped up on a stand instead of in its case. It was already plugged into a small amp, like it was just waiting for someone, anyone, to play it. I glanced around the room—stupid, since I was obviously the only one in it—and took a step closer. I just wanted to look at his guitar, to figure out why it was plugged in when no one was here. Maybe Jared had been checking it after the show and had been interrupted. Or maybe he'd planned to sneak away from the party to be alone, just him and his music behind the sound-proofed walls. If so, I could relate to that. Music had always been my way to escape and deal with the world on my own terms. I just didn't think of Jared as the kind of guy who needed to escape, too.

The guitar was beautiful, with a smooth white faceplate, gleaming struts, and a shiny fingerboard. My fingers itched to touch the silvery strings, to form a chord and let it ring out through the amp, to hear what it sounded like without all the other instruments accompanying it. And if I was honest, I wanted to close my eyes and pretend I was on stage, playing for a crowd, hearing them scream for me. The longing I felt every time I went to a concert stirred up in me again. It wouldn't hurt if I played one chord, right? That was it. One chord, and I'd put it back. No one would ever know.

Before I could stop myself, I picked up the guitar and threw the strap over my head. It settled against my shoulder, and with one hand on the fret board and the other on the strings, I was home. I closed my eyes, picturing Jared when he was on stage and how his talented fingers had moved across the guitar. I imagined him singing my favorite song of theirs, "Behind the Mask," and the words and notes melted together in my head. I strummed the guitar, the sound ringing from the amp, the vibrations traveling up the ground and into my feet. God, I loved this guitar. It sounded just as good as my own, if not better.

Now that I had the guitar in my hands, the compulsion to play was irresistible. What was one more chord, right? I was alone and the room was soundproof. The door had locked behind me. Kyle was dealing with Becca, and he'd given me permission to come in here anyway.

I knew it was a bad idea. I knew I should put the guitar down and walk out of the room. But I started strumming anyway.

I was hesitant at first, but once I started, I couldn't stop. My hands found the chords automatically, and the words flowed out of me with the music. Exhilaration swept through me with each note, and I closed my eyes and let the song take me away. Soon I was belting out the words, shredding the guitar like I was on stage playing for a massive crowd. I'd never do this in front of anyone else, but here, alone with this guitar, I could pretend. I could let myself go.

And then I opened my eyes and wanted to die.

Jared stood in front of me, his eyes wide and mouth open slightly. He must have come in while I was playing. How much did he hear? Or worse, *see?*

My fingers slipped off the strings with a screech, and I nearly dropped the guitar. Thank god for the strap. "I'm so sorry. Kyle gave me the key and I was just—"

There was no way to explain what was going on, so I shut up. I'd been singing his lyrics, playing the song he'd written. Not to mention, I'd been using *his* guitar. That was like wearing someone else's underwear. You didn't just play another person's guitar without their permission.

I yanked the guitar off and tried to put it back, but knocked the stand over instead. Hands shaking, it took me two tries to right it again, all while Jared stood there, gaping at me. Why didn't he say anything? Was he so angry he couldn't speak? I set the guitar down carefully, then backed away like it was on fire—and ran straight into the drum set. Cymbals crashed as I fell against it, knocking the equipment all over the floor. Great, now he must think I'm a stalker *and* a complete klutz. I jumped up too fast, and my legs were so unsteady I started to topple over toward the table. Jared caught me before we had another disaster, his hands gripping my arms to balance me.

"You okay?" he asked, his blue eyes holding mine and making my heart pound even faster. If I stared into those eyes too long, I'd fall into them completely.

I jerked away from his touch and stumbled back. "I'm sorry, I—"

"You were playing one of our songs."

"Was I?" I asked with a forced laugh, trying to edge toward the door to make a quick escape. "I mean, uh, yeah. I was. Obviously. But it's not a big deal. It's not like I listen to your songs a lot or anything. I just have that kind of ear where I hear something once and can play it back and uh…" *Stop talking*, I shouted at myself. *STOP.*

The thing about music was true. I could usually play anything just from listening to it a few times, but I'd also listened to Villain Complex's album about three thousand times and practiced the songs in my room with my guitar hooked up to my headphones. I wasn't obsessed or anything. I just liked their music a lot. But he didn't need to know any of that. This was humiliating enough as it was.

"Really?" he asked. "I wish I could do that."

Not the reaction I'd been expecting. I thought he'd yell at me to get out of his house or think I was another of his swooning groupies. Okay, maybe he wouldn't think that. I didn't look the part with my boring glasses and plain brown hair and flannel shirt. No, he probably assumed creepy stalker fangirl. I had to get away, out of this room, as far from Jared and his guitar and this nightmare as possible.

He started to say something else, but I blurted out, "I have to go."

I escaped through the door and back to the party, slipping into the anonymity of the crowd. Once away from Jared, I could finally breathe again, but the urge to flee was still strong. I found Alexis and gave her Kyle's key and told her to say goodbye to him for me. Now all I had to do was find my friends and get the hell out of his house.

Julie was flirting with a guy with a fauxhawk, but I grabbed her arm. "We need to leave. Now."

"What?" Julie looked back at the guy and pouted. "Right now?"

"Yes. Trust me on this." As I spoke, Jared appeared at the edge of the room, his head swinging around like he was looking for me. "Oh, god."

She craned her neck to follow my gaze. "What's going on, Maddie?"

"I'll explain when we're in the car. Now can we please go?"

She nodded, and we made our way out the front door, where we found Carla arguing with Daryl. I knew he'd track her down. Unbelievable.

"I told you, I was just about to leave!" she said to him.

"We're going now." I didn't wait to see if they followed me. I started down the hill toward where my Honda was parked, anxious to get away from the house, away from Jared, and away from the most embarrassing moment of my life.

I could never go to a Villain Complex show ever again, that was for sure.

Chapter Three

Despite a restless night of sleep, I somehow managed to forget about the disaster with Jared and focus on my music history final for two hours. With that done, my junior year at UCLA was over, and I was ready for an entire summer interning with the LA Philharmonic. I'd beat out hundreds of other people to get it, and even though I'd probably spend my entire summer doing boring stuff like filing and pouring coffee, I couldn't wait.

Last night was in the past, nothing but an embarrassing memory. I'd put it behind me, and with any luck, Jared had gotten so drunk after I'd left he'd forgotten the moment had ever happened. I was over it. Really.

Except when I walked out of class, Jared was there, leaning against the wall in a black leather jacket. He stood up straight when he saw me and I skidded to a halt, breath catching in my throat. Someone crashed into me from behind, and I stumbled forward and dropped my bag. Because I couldn't have just *one* embarrassing moment in front of Jared, no, not me.

"Hey, Maddie." He picked up my bag while I moved out of the way of the students streaming into the hallway.

"Um, hey." What was he doing outside my class? He'd graduated from UCLA a year ago, so there was no reason for him to be here. I conjured up all kinds of horrible scenarios: He wanted to yell at me for touching his guitar. Or I'd broken the drums and now he wanted me to pay for them. Or he just wanted to see what kind of freak played his song from memory.

Calm down, I told myself. Maybe he wasn't here for me. Maybe he was waiting for Kyle. Yes, that made a lot more sense. Except…Kyle wasn't in my music history class.

"What are you doing here?" I asked, taking my bag from him.

"Looking for you." He rubbed the stubble along his chin, like he was thinking. "Kyle told me you play piano, but I had no idea you played guitar, too."

No one did, other than Carla and Julie. To everyone else, I was geeky Maddie who played piano—and sometimes violin or clarinet—but that was it. Only my roommates knew I practiced guitar for hours in my room, losing myself in the sound of the strings buzzing from my amp until my fingertips were sore and my hands cramped.

"And you can sing, too," he continued.

All the mortification from the previous night came back and set my cheeks aflame. I couldn't believe he'd heard me singing one of his songs.

"I'm so sorry," I said, clutching my bag to my chest. "I shouldn't have touched your guitar. I don't know what I was thinking—"

"You're really good. Do you know all our songs?"

"Yes." No, wait, why did I say that? Backtrack time. "No. Maybe. I mean, I might." I tried to shrug casually, like it was no big thing, but I wanted to melt into the linoleum floor, seep into the cracks, and disappear. I prayed for an asteroid to hit the spot I was standing in and wipe me off the face of the Earth, but no such luck.

"I need your help," he said, fixing an intense gaze on me. "We have a live audition tomorrow for *The Sound*. Problem is, our bassist quit last night, and we need a fourth member of the band."

"What?" Was he saying what I thought he was saying? No. Impossible.

"I know—worst timing ever. Can you play bass by any chance?"

"No..."

His face fell for an instant, and some reckless part of me wanted to lie and say yes or promise him I'd learn. How hard could it be to learn the bass if I knew how to play guitar, right? Though I immediately realized how dumb that idea was because a) I could never learn bass in time for an audition tomorrow; b) I shouldn't care about making Jared happy, even if his disappointed face broke my heart; and c) none of that mattered because he couldn't possibly be asking me to join his band anyway.

"That's okay," he said. "I can play bass, and you can play guitar. It'll work." His smile lit up his face again, with a look that could charm any girl lucky enough to bask in it. Right now, that girl was me. "So what do you think?"

Jared was asking me—*me*—to play guitar in his band. In an audition on live TV. In front of four of the greatest musicians ever, plus millions of people at home. Mind. Blown. Somehow I'd been handed my secret dream on a silver platter. Next up, Jared would ask me out, too. Yeah, and then we'd ride off into the sunset on a rainbow unicorn with our million-dollar record deal.

"You want me to join your band?" I asked slowly, studying him for any sign that this was all a joke.

"Just for the audition. That should give us enough time to find another bass player to take Becca's place."

Ah, there was the catch. I would only play with them for one day, giving me a tiny taste of their lifestyle, and then they'd drop me as soon as the audition was over. No, better to never know what it would be like to play guitar on stage, to be part of a band, to make music with Jared and Kyle. Besides, I couldn't play guitar in front of the world. Guitar was my secret, my fun escape, and nothing more. My internship started on Monday, and I needed to focus on that—not on silly dreams of being a rock star.

"I'm sorry, but I can't." I spun around and rushed toward the exit before he could respond. I didn't want him to see my face and how much I desperately wanted to do it.

"Wait!" He ran after me, but I kept going, past other students who watched us with curiosity. "Maddie, wait!"

Damn his long legs. He caught up to me, practically jumping in front of me to stop me in my tracks. I kept my face glued to the floor, to the contrast of his black combat boots and my green Converse. I couldn't look up at him or I'd be tempted to say yes to anything.

He lowered his voice. "Please, you're the only person who can help us. You're an amazing guitarist, and you already know our songs. We need you."

I shook my head, looking anywhere but at him. Hearing him say he needed me with his whiskey-chocolate-sex voice made my legs a bit shaky, but what he was asking for? It was too much.

Jared got down on his knees, right in the middle of the hallway, and everyone stopped to watch us. He raised his hands like he was begging. "Please, this is our one chance, but without a fourth member, we can't do it. You're perfect and it'll only be for a day, and then I'll owe you. I'll do anything you want." He topped it off with a grin. "Help me, Maddie Taylor, you're my only hope."

Damn. How could I say no to a *Star Wars* reference from a hot guy on his knees? The word slipped out before I could stop it. "Okay."

"Yes!" He jumped to his feet and hugged me, making my head spin. "Thank you, thank you, thank you. I really owe you one."

The students around us clapped, like he'd just proposed to me or something. I gave the crowd a faint smile, feeling sick to my stomach. Jared quickly rattled off all the details about the audition tomorrow and told me to meet the band for practice in a few hours. And then he left, before I could come to my senses and change my mind.

———

Julie and Carla were watching *House Hunters International* when I walked into the apartment we all shared.

"You can just repaint the stupid room!" Julie yelled at the TV.

I collapsed on the sofa beside them and threw my head back with a groan. Now that Jared was no longer in front of me and the glow of his smile had worn off, the reality of what I'd agreed to do was sinking in. I couldn't go on the show with the band, but I seemed to be physically unable to say no to Jared either. Maybe I could pretend I was sick. Or break my arm. Yes, I had to injure myself. That was the only way to get out of this mess.

"Was your final that bad?" Carla asked.

"Maybe she needs to eat." Julie handed me a box of crackers, which I waved away. Eating was the last thing on my mind right now.

"My final was fine, except Jared was waiting for me outside my class."

Julie dropped the box, spilling crackers across the hardwood floor. "He what?"

"Was he mad about last night?" Carla asked.

I'd told both girls the entire embarrassing story on the drive home from the party. They'd thought it was hilarious naturally. "No, he wasn't mad. Even worse—he asked me to join his band."

"WHAT?" Julie and Carla both blurted out together.

"I know! But it's only for their audition on *The Sound* tomorrow, and then they'll find a new bassist. It's not a permanent thing." I sucked in a breath and then spit the rest out. "And I said yes, but now I need to tell him no because I can't do it. I just can't."

My two friends looked at each other, and something passed between them. Julie turned back to me. "You *can* do this, and you will," she said in her fiercest voice.

"Julie's right," Carla said. "This is what you've been dreaming about forever. You have to do it."

"But I'm not a guitarist!" I protested. "I've never played live before or on stage or in front of…well, anyone." At least, not since my mom had flipped out on me all those years ago.

"You've played guitar for us a million times," Julie said.

"And you play piano on stage all the time," Carla added.

"Yes, I play piano on stage, and sometimes I go wild and play the violin in an orchestra. But playing guitar in a band in front of millions of people is completely different!"

"You'll be fine," Carla said. "Besides, it's only one performance. Just pretend you're playing for us."

Julie nudged me with her shoulder. "Plus this gives you a chance to get close to Jared."

"I don't want to get close to Jared!"

"Why not?" she asked. "Everyone wants to get close to Jared."

"Yes, that's *exactly* the problem."

"Do it for Kyle then," Carla said. "You've known him for years, and now he needs your help."

I hadn't thought of that. If I backed out now, they probably wouldn't have time to find another guitarist or bassist before the show. I couldn't do that to my friend. "You're right…but then, why didn't Kyle ask me to join the band himself?"

Julie shrugged. "Maybe Jared didn't tell him about your little solo performance last night."

That could be it. Kyle didn't know I played the guitar. Or maybe Jared had told him, but Kyle didn't want me in the band. I didn't exactly fit their image after all. Or even worse, maybe Kyle was upset I'd never told him I played guitar and that his brother had found out before him. Even if Kyle didn't know yet, he'd learn the truth in an hour when I went to rehearse with them. I dreaded the look on his face when he realized I'd kept this from him for three years.

"I don't know." I took off my glasses and rubbed my eyes. "I mean, look at me. I don't belong in their band. They're all so edgy and I'm so…not."

Julie faced me and put her hands on my arms, her amber eyes drilling into mine. "Stop it. Those guys would be lucky to have you in their band."

Carla wrapped her arms around both of us in a big group hug. "If you'd like, I can do your hair and makeup tomorrow before your audition, and Julie can help with your clothes. We'll make you look amazing."

I gave them the biggest smile I could muster up. "I don't know what I'd do without you two."

"So you're going to do it?" Julie asked.

I tried to think of any other protests, but when it came right down to it, I couldn't find another reason to say no. "Yeah, I'll do the audition."

Julie and Carla immediately started planning what they were going to do to me in the morning, but I wasn't feeling as optimistic. As much as I loved these girls, there was no makeup or wardrobe in the world that could make me a rock star.

Chapter Four

An hour later, I parked in front of the Cross brothers' house and grabbed my gear from my backseat. I'd brought my own electric guitar and matching amp, though I wasn't sure if I would be playing it or Jared's for practice or the audition. I'd almost brought my acoustic guitar, too, but left it behind in the end. Villain Complex wasn't an acoustic kind of band.

The studio's garage door was open, and Jared spotted me as I came up the driveway. He walked over and grabbed the handle of my guitar case.

"Here, let me help you." He took the amp, too, leaving me with empty, sweaty hands, which I rubbed on my jeans.

His leather jacket was gone, and he wore a T-shirt that said, "It's Good to Be Bad." For the first time, I got a close look at the tattoos on his arms: bars of music surrounded by spider webs, black stars, and roses with thorny vines. Like Kyle, he also had a triangle tattooed on the inside of each wrist, one dark and one light. I'd never realized a guy's forearms could be sexy, yet somehow he managed to pull it off.

He set the guitar case on a long table and popped it open. He whistled when he saw the vintage sea foam green Fender Stratocaster inside. "Wow. Where'd you get this?"

"I bought it at a pawn shop, along with the amp." Both were chipped and dented, but I loved them. They were the only instruments I'd ever bought with my own money, right after I'd left for college. The grand piano back home, my violin and clarinet, and even the keyboard crammed next to my bed were all guilt presents from my father. My acoustic guitar had been my mom's once, back when she did things like play music. But this guitar—it was all mine.

"May I?" he asked, and I nodded.

He ran a hand over the body and neck of it with the gentle caress of someone who understood how precious it was. I watched his fingers touch each string and imagined what it'd be like if he touched me that way.

Stop it. I forced my eyes to the floor. *He's not for you.*

"Very nice," he said. "You can use your guitar for the audition or use mine if you want. Whatever works."

"I'll use mine, I guess." Even though I'd played Jared's guitar last night, it seemed too intimate now, too much of a reminder of that embarrassing moment when he'd caught me. It was bad enough being alone with him in this studio again. "Where are the other guys?"

"They should be here soon. You can start warming up if you want."

Warming up was a little too close to playing guitar, which was the entire reason I was in the studio, but that didn't mean I was ready to do it. I hadn't played in front of anyone but Julie and Carla in years. And Jared, but that had been an accident. Now he expected me to play again, and the thought made me want to run straight back to my car.

I picked up my guitar and started to tune it, mostly to give myself something to do. My hands shook while I adjusted the knobs, and I took deep breaths, trying to force myself to be calm. If I didn't get control of my fingers soon, I'd never be able to play. I couldn't decide if I was more worried about that or more hopeful.

Jared opened another case and pulled out a deep blue electric bass I hadn't seen before. Soon the studio was filled with the sound of us plucking strings as we tuned our instruments. We stood only a few feet apart but didn't speak, and an awkward cloud hung between us. Or maybe that was just me; Jared seemed oblivious to it.

"So you play bass?" A dumb question, but I had to say something to end the tension.

"Yeah, although it's been a while." His gaze swept across the studio. "I can play everything in here to some degree."

"You can?" My voice sounded a little too eager. I cleared my throat and dropped my eyes to the frets on my guitar. "Were you a music major also?"

"Nope. Philosophy. Something my brother never lets me live down."

"Philosophy?"

"Yep. And now I'm a bartender who writes angsty songs, which I'm pretty sure is what everyone does with a philosophy degree."

I couldn't help but laugh. "The job market for professional philosophers does seem to have dried up these past few years."

"Tell me about it." He adjusted his mic and raised an eyebrow at me. "And what lofty plans do you have for your music degree?"

"I'm hoping to get into USC for graduate school. They have a degree in music scores for movies, TV, and video games."

"Ah, joining the enemy," he said, referring to the rivalry between UCLA and USC.

"Maybe. There are good programs at NYU and Berklee College of Music, too, but I'd rather stay in LA."

He studied me for a moment, his bass momentarily forgotten. "So what's your favorite movie score?"

"I don't know. There are so many great ones." I adjusted my glasses as I considered. "Pretty much everything by John Williams—he did *Star Wars* and *Jurassic Park* and *Indiana Jones* and about a million more. I also love the *Lord of the Rings* scores and *The Dark Knight* and, oh, the *Tron Legacy* score by Daft Punk is amazing, too…" There I went, babbling in front of him again. His eyes were probably glazing over by now. "Sorry. I could talk about this stuff for hours."

In response, he started singing "The Imperial March" from *Star Wars*. "Dun dun dun…"

"That's the ringtone on my phone," I said with a laugh. "Wow, that probably makes me the biggest geek ever, huh?"

"Nah. I approve." He gave me a smile that sent a rush of warmth from my face down to my toes and to everything in between. "Who do you think picked all the quotes for our wall?"

"That was you?" I glanced at the wall behind us with all the quotes by or about villains. I would have guessed Kyle had chosen them, not Jared.

Kyle and Hector arrived at that moment, interrupting us. They stopped just outside the open garage door and stared at me like I was a weed in their garden. Jared must not have told them I was joining the band.

"*This* is the new guitarist?" Hector asked.

Ouch. I knew I didn't look the part, but it still hurt to hear it out loud.

"Maddie?" Kyle's mouth dropped open, and his eyes swept over my guitar and back up to my face. "You play *guitar*?"

"Not really," I said, and then realized that probably didn't help matters, since I would be auditioning with them tomorrow. "I mean, I know how to play, but…"

Kyle turned to glare at his brother. "How did *you* know she played guitar?"

"Relax, it's not what you think," Jared said, which instantly made me flush. Great, they assumed I was one of Jared's flings. But to my surprise, Jared didn't reveal how he knew. "She told me last night at the party."

Kyle's eyes narrowed, like he found that hard to believe, but Hector cut him off. "Forget it. We all agreed—no more girls in the band. Not after what happened with Becca."

"Hector's right," Kyle said. "Sorry, Maddie. It's nothing against you."

"We don't have any other option," Jared said. "Unless you can find someone who can play guitar or bass and knows our songs before tomorrow morning."

"How do you know she can actually play?" Hector asked. "She probably just said that to get in your pants."

"Hey—" I started to protest.

"She knows our songs?" Kyle asked and then tilted his head back to the ceiling. "Actually, that doesn't surprise me. Maddie is some kind of musical genius. She can hear a piece one time and then play it back perfectly."

"That's a bit of an exaggeration," I muttered, but no one was listening to me. Maybe I should leave and let them sort this out on their own. I glanced at my guitar case and wondered how quickly I could pack up and flee to my car.

"Shit, I don't know." Hector removed his hat, spilling his dark curls, and then shoved it back on again. "We should forget this audition and wait for the next one."

"The next show won't be for another year," Jared said. "We can't wait that long. And what if they don't want us next year? No, we have to do it tomorrow."

"I need to talk to Maddie alone," Kyle said.

He led me down the driveway, far enough that the others couldn't hear us. I swallowed hard as I waited for him to speak, preparing for the worst. He stared at the guitar still around my neck and then sighed and swept back the black hair that was always falling in his eyes.

"Why didn't you tell me you played guitar?"

"Um…" I stared at the ground. I hated that I'd kept this from him for so long and that he was hurt now because of my omission. But how could I explain that guitar had been my secret all these years? Something that had just been for me. Not my parents. Not my teachers. Not even my friends. I didn't think Kyle would understand somehow. He wore his entire personality on display and didn't care what other people thought. It was one of the things I admired most about him.

"I only play when I'm alone, and not seriously or anything," I said. "I used to play more, but my mom…she didn't approve. Told me to focus on piano, on violin and clarinet. 'Real instruments,' she called them. Probably because she used to play the guitar and that's how she met my dad…" I trailed off, but Kyle nodded. I'd told him all about my family before. "When I was a kid, she caught me playing her old guitar and nearly smashed the thing. She was drinking, of course. It scared the crap out of me, and after that, it was easier to keep that part of myself hidden. But I'm really sorry I didn't tell you."

"It's all right. I get it." He sighed again. "Are you sure you want to do this?"

"No, I'm terrified." I choked out a little laugh. "But I also want to help you."

His face softened a little. "I appreciate that. I really do. But I don't think that's the only reason you're here."

"Of course it is." I tried to keep my face blank. Was my attraction to Jared so obvious that even Kyle could see it? I didn't plan to act on it or anything.

"Is it really? Because we can't have another Becca situation."

"What happened with her anyway?"

"She and Jared hooked up about a month ago." He scowled at his brother, still in the garage. "They both admitted it was a mistake the next day, but it was never the same after that. Becca started drinking more, and she got crazy jealous any time he was with another girl. They'd fight, and then I would smooth things over and then it would happen again. We all hoped she'd get over it, but then she started showing up to rehearsals drunk—if she showed up at all—and well…you saw what happened last night. I don't think Jared actually expected her to quit the band, but none of us really want her back either."

"Nothing like that is going to happen with me. Trust me." Becca's situation hit a little too close to home, and I was definitely not following in her—or my mother's —footsteps.

"I know, but…I just don't want you to get hurt. I love my brother, but he doesn't do relationships. Promise me you won't get involved with him, okay?"

"I won't, I promise." I gave him a smile that was more confident than I was. "And I'll only be in the band for one day anyway."

"True…" He gave a reluctant nod, and we went back inside.

"Everything okay?" Jared asked.

"We're good," Kyle said. "Let's hear her play."

They all looked at me, and I froze. "What? No."

"Great, a guitar player who won't play guitar," Hector muttered.

"Don't be an ass," Jared said, hitting a button that lowered the garage door, locking me in with them. "Of course she'll play."

The time had come. They were all waiting, and if I was going to be their guitarist tomorrow, I had to show them I could actually do it. There was nowhere for me to run now. I flexed my fingers and placed them on the guitar. They hadn't told me what to play, and I felt too self-conscious to perform one of their own songs for them, but nothing else came to mind either.

I remembered Carla and Julie's suggestion earlier, to pretend I was playing for them if I got nervous. If we were sitting on our couch right now, what would they want to hear? Something mellow. Something fun. Something they liked to sing along to. My decision made, I tapped out a beat and started Incubus's "Wish You Were Here." It was a perfect choice because right now I did wish they were here with me.

The song was off at first, every chord sounding like it was being ripped from my hands instead of flowing smoothly. Turns out, playing for three hot musicians in their garage-turned-studio was nothing like playing in my apartment for my two best friends. But once I got into it and stopped thinking so much about how they were watching me, my fingers knew what to do. The music poured out of me as it always did, from my body into the guitar, out the amp, and then back to my ears again in a perfect cycle. I never felt this way when I played the violin or clarinet or even the piano. With those instruments, I was precise and controlled and didn't get lost in the music. Those were work, but this—this was like breathing.

When I got to the chorus, Jared sang the lyrics, more to himself than anyone else, and I caught the other guys nodding along, too. Eventually I'd played enough, and Hector raised a hand to stop me.

"Okay, that wasn't bad," he admitted. "But do you actually know *our* songs?"

Not bad? I'd take it. Kyle gave me a reassuring smile, too, so he must not have thought I was horrible either.

"I know them," I said.

"Told you she could play," Jared said, moving in front of the mic. "We're doing 'Behind the Mask' for the audition. Let's run through it and see how it goes."

I nodded, relieved. Jared had already heard me playing that song and must have approved, or he wouldn't have asked me to join them. All bands performed one of their original songs during the audition, even though the bands used cover songs during the actual show. "Behind the Mask" was a good choice because it demonstrated the band's sound, plus it showed off Jared's impressive vocals and had a catchy beat.

Hector started us off, but I was too slow jumping in and then had to miss a few notes to get back on track. Things started getting better, but once Jared started singing, I missed a chord again. As the song progressed, I found it hard to keep time with them. I'd never played guitar with anyone else before, and I was always just ahead or behind the guys. That made me even more stressed out, and then I missed more notes and so it continued. My only consolation was that Jared wasn't doing so hot on bass either. The song ended, and the garage dropped into silence. I knew what we were all thinking—we were terrible. Less than an hour with the band and I'd ruined them.

"Well, that was a disaster," Hector finally said. "She may know the song but that doesn't mean she can play it."

"It wasn't *that* bad," Kyle said.

"Give her a break," Jared said. "Maddie's never rehearsed with us before."

My heart beat a little faster hearing him defend me, and I had to remind myself that he needed me for the audition and that was it. Once it was over, I'd probably never hear from him again. But still, it was nice to know he didn't think I was a complete failure.

"Sorry," I apologized to all of them. "I'm just nervous. I'll get it right this time."

"Anyway, the real problem was me," Jared said, his forehead creased as he checked the tuning on his bass again. "I'm so out of practice with this thing, there's no way I'll be in shape for tomorrow."

"You'll be fine," Kyle said. "You wrote the bass line in this song. You know it better than anyone."

"Yeah, but that was a long time ago." He rubbed his face, wiping away the frustration. "Let's try it again. If we have to rehearse all night to get it right, then that's what we'll do."

We practiced the song for hours. Any time I lost my place, I focused on Hector's drumming and got back on track, and when I wanted to throw my guitar pick in the trash, Kyle's encouragement kept me going. Playing with them wasn't as scary as I'd thought it would be in the end. And standing beside Jared while he sang was even better than listening to his voice in my headphones or through my computer, even better than seeing him perform live. Because this time, I was playing *with* him.

"All right," Jared finally said. "That was good. I think if we go any longer, we'll have nothing left for tomorrow's audition."

"Thank god," Kyle said. "I was about to pass out here."

Hector stood up, twirling a drumstick in one hand. "You were right, Kyle, Maddie does pick things up quickly."

"Told you. It's freaky, right?"

I bowed my head, but couldn't hide the small grin on my face. My arms trembled with exhaustion, my fingertips throbbed, and my hands had cramped up, but I felt whole, like I'd been missing a piece of myself all my life and finally had it glued back on. And I never wanted to lose it again.

Chapter Five

The guys picked me up bright and early in their van, their gear already packed inside. I squeezed my way into the backseat next to Kyle, who wore a faded black T-shirt and a studded belt. He gave me a quick once-over as I got inside. "Perfect."

I said a silent thanks to my two best friends. Julie had picked out a black baby-doll dress with a hint of lace and loaned me some ropey chain jewelry and knee-high boots. Carla had given me smoky eyes, dark red lips, and a hint of curl to my usually limp brown hair. Somehow they'd made me look fierce, but still like myself, too. Even my black-rimmed glasses looked more ironic than nerdy now.

Hector gave me a nod, too, which I supposed meant he approved. He was dressed similarly to Kyle, except with his usual baseball cap with the Villain Complex logo.

Jared turned from the driver's seat and looked me up and down. It might have been my imagination, but his eyes seemed to linger a little longer than the other two guys' had.

"You look great," he finally said, making my heart skip a beat. "We don't have much time, so let's go."

The van's door slid shut with a *thunk*, and we were off, driving along the sleepy Saturday morning streets of Los Angeles toward downtown. I picked at the hem of my dress, the whole situation surreal. I was in a car with three guys in a rock band, going to audition for a TV show I'd watched for years. It was hard to believe this wasn't all a dream.

The guys didn't talk much, and the closer we got, the more nervous I felt. This was really happening now. I couldn't back out. Well, I could, but I'd completely screw the guys over and I would never do that. Kyle was my friend, and Jared had taken a chance on me. Yes, it was only because he needed me for the audition, but I still appreciated his faith in my skills.

We soon reached LA Live, a giant plaza with restaurants, movie theaters, and clubs, plus the Staples Center, where basketball games were held, and the Nokia Theatre, where *The Sound* was filmed. The auditions were taking place across the street, at the LA Convention Center, and a huge crowd was already lined up along the sidewalk to be in the audience. We parked the van, and some guy with a headset and a clipboard checked us off and had us unload and tag our gear. He gave us a card with a 93 on it and said they'd call our number when they were ready for us.

"Are there really ninety-two bands before us?" Jared asked him.

"Nah, we hand the numbers out randomly," the guy said, before waving us into a huge room with a bunch of other people.

Judging from the wild assortment of clothes and hairstyles and the way everyone stood in groups and eyed each other with a mix of thinly veiled curiosity and contempt, these must be the other bands waiting to audition. I took in the vast crowd, and my stomach did summersaults. From the guys with long hair and motorcycle jackets, to the punk rockers with mohawks, to the country princesses who looked like Taylor Swift clones, all of them belonged here much more than I did.

"I need coffee," Kyle said. He took our orders—coffee for me and Hector, tea with honey for Jared (for his voice, he said)—and then joined the very long line at the coffee stand. All the tables and chairs were already taken, so we found a spot by the wall and leaned against it. There was nothing to do now but wait.

While Hector sat on the floor and drew in a sketchbook, Jared surveyed the room with a line of worry across his forehead. He wore a black button-down shirt with the sleeves rolled up to his elbows, showing off his inked arms. His face had the perfect amount of stubble brushing his chin and framing his mouth, and even in this crowd, I couldn't help but be drawn to him.

"You okay?" I asked, after he sighed for the fifth time.

Jared ran a hand through his hair, making it stick up more. It made him look even better somehow. "I didn't think there would be so many people here, you know?"

"Yeah." I didn't mention that there were probably dozens more on their way or auditioning on other days because I understood how he felt. This was his chance to follow his dream, to make it big with his band, and now it seemed impossible in the face of all this competition. Villain Complex was good, but we'd only spent one night practicing together, and there were so many bands here, and oh god, the more I thought about it the more I might throw up.

"How about you?" he asked.

I pressed my hands to my stomach, willing it to be calm. "Honestly? No, I'm not okay."

He laughed and sang my words to the tune of "I'm Not Okay (I Promise)" by My Chemical Romance. He continued with the next lines in the song for a minute, and some of the other people around us turned to watch him serenading me. It should have been embarrassing, but instead it made me smile and some of the tension in my shoulders relaxed. It wasn't every day a hot guy sang to me, after all.

He finished with an exaggerated bow, and I laughed. "Yes, that song popped into my head, too," I said. "Unintentional song reference, I promise."

"It got you to laugh, so my work here is done," he said, and I melted even more.

Kyle returned and shoved coffee cups at us. "Rumor is, none of the mentors have filled up their teams yet. Sounds like we still have a shot."

He leaned against the wall next to Jared while they sipped their drinks. When they were side by side, it was obvious they were brothers, with the same deep blue eyes, perfect mouths, and striking jawlines, but Kyle was like Jared with the volume turned to full blast. Kyle showed the world he didn't conform—with his dyed-black hair, multiple piercings and ear gauges, and tattoos crawling up his neck and down his fingers—but Jared was more restrained. Only the tattoos on his arms hinted at his darker side, like his true self couldn't quite be contained and had bled ink across his skin. If he wore long sleeves, you'd never know what lurked underneath.

Perhaps that's why Jared was the one who took my breath away. I could relate to that restraint, to keeping a piece of yourself hidden at all times and feeling like everything had to be under control. There was a part of me—the part that played guitar in my room every night and felt more at home at a rock concert than in an orchestra—that I kept hidden away, too. Problem was, I wasn't sure I wanted to keep that Maddie locked up anymore.

At one point, Jared made his way around the room to talk to the other bands. He was a natural at it, with his easy charm and charisma, but all I saw were the beautiful women placing their hands on his arms and the way he stood too close to them, laughing at whatever they said. He was supposed to be checking out our competition, not collecting phone numbers. I hated that seeing him flirt with other girls bothered me so much. Kyle had warned me, after all, and it's not like anything would happen between me and Jared anyway.

"What'd you find out?" Kyle asked when Jared returned.

"Some of these people have been waiting for two hours already." He sighed and leaned back against the wall. "We're going to be here forever."

Hector grunted. "Unless the mentors pick all their team members before we even get in."

"Don't even say that," Jared said. "Just don't."

"Relax, that's not going to happen," Kyle said.

Other bands got called up and then disappeared, never to return. It was impossible to know from this room what happened to them or what our competition was like. The longer we waited, the more I was convinced that Hector was right and the mentors would fill up their teams before we got a chance to audition. No, that'd be too easy. It was more likely we'd get on stage and I'd screw up horribly, and it would be my fault the band wasn't picked for the show. How could the other guys trust me with something this big?

Our number was finally called thirty minutes later, and we all rushed to the desk at the front of the room. A woman with a high ponytail and a polo shirt with the show's logo on it grabbed four clipboards and shoved them at us.

"This is the show's contract. Each of you need to print your name and the date and sign it at the end."

I tried to read the small print, but there was just so much of it. Pages and pages of legalese I didn't understand. The guys looked just as baffled, except Jared, who was actually reading the thing like it was interesting.

"It's all pretty standard stuff," the woman said, sounding annoyed that we weren't signing it immediately. She started ticking things off on her fingers. "If you're selected during the audition, you agree to be on the show for the next five weeks. The show will pay for your hotel, plus a small living stipend. Any songs you record for the show will be sold on the website, and you'll receive ten percent of the profits. If you're one of the final four bands, you agree to go on tour in August, and if you win, you receive a recording contract from Mix It Up Records."

"Um, should I sign this if I'm only a temporary member of the band?" I asked while I flicked through it.

"No changes in band members for the duration of the show, including the audition," the woman snapped. "It's right there on page four."

"No changes?" I nearly dropped the clipboard. If I did this audition, I'd be stuck with the band for as long as they were on the show. Or even longer, if we made it to the final four and were sent on tour. That would be the entire summer —and my internship started next Monday. There was no way I could do both.

"What?" Kyle asked and then spun to face Jared. "Did you know about this?"

"No! I would never trick Maddie into joining the band. I swear, I didn't know."

Kyle tossed his clipboard on the table. "That's it then. It's over. Let's get our gear and go."

"I told you we should have waited until next year," Hector muttered.

Jared scanned the contract again. "This can't be it. There must be some other way."

Kyle sighed. "Should we call Becca? Maybe if we begged her…"

"No. Definitely not. We can't trust her to keep it together for the next five weeks."

"I know, but—"

While the guys argued, I stared at the contract in my hands. The decision I made here could impact the rest of my life, and the two choices weighed on me, heavy with their uncertain futures. I could leave the band now without any hard feelings and go back to my normal life and the internship I had worked so hard for. That was the safe path, the one I'd been traveling on for the last three years. Once I washed off the makeup and returned the clothes to Julie, I'd be regular old Maddie again, who only practiced guitar in secret and had her future figured out.

Except…I didn't want to go back to my normal life anymore.

I'd joined the band thinking it would only be for this one audition. But now that I'd played with them, I wanted more. I wanted to compete with them, to perform their songs on stage, and maybe even have a shot at winning this thing. I wanted to fight for my dream—my *real* dream—for once in my life, instead of standing in the audience and cheering for someone else.

"I want to do the show," I said, my pulse racing with equal parts fear and excitement. "If you'll have me in the band, that is."

"Are you sure?" Kyle asked. "You were so excited about your internship."

"I was, but when I practiced with you guys last night, it just felt…right. Like this is what I'm meant to be doing. I don't want to look back years from now and wonder what if, you know?"

"Yeah, I get that." He turned to the rest of the band. "Well, I'm happy to let Maddie join the band permanently. What about you guys?"

"I'm cool with it," Jared said.

"Of course you are." Hector rolled his eyes. "But yeah, let's do this."

Jared grinned and draped an arm across my shoulder, sending another spike of heat through me. "Welcome to the band, Maddie."

———

After signing the contract, we were taken to a small waiting room and told we'd be going on in ten minutes. Hector stretched his neck and arms while Kyle texted someone, probably Alexis. Jared ran through some vocal exercises and paced back and forth, like he was about to burst through the door and take on the crowd by himself.

I sank onto the couch, the room suddenly spinning. Now that the big moment was almost here, I didn't know if I could go through with this. My stomach threatened to bring up everything I'd had today—which, granted, had been only a small coffee. Maybe I should have eaten something this morning. Great, I was going to blow this entire audition because I hadn't thought to grab a muffin before I left.

"How are you doing?" Jared asked, sitting next to me. "Still not okay?"

"Very much not okay." I took off my glasses and cleaned them on my dress, my movements quick and shaky.

Jared placed his hand on mine, and I nearly jumped off the couch. But then his hand was gone, so fast I almost questioned whether it had actually happened, except that his touch left a lingering warmth on my skin.

"Relax," he said. "We're all nervous, but we nailed it during last night's practice. We've got this."

I nodded, but I had no doubt the rest of the band would be great. They'd all performed on stage together before, many times. I'd played with them in their garage for a few hours. Not the same at all.

Kyle dropped onto the couch, squeezing me between the two brothers. "I don't blame you for freaking out, Maddie. This whole thing is terrifying. But I've seen you perform a dozen times, you'll be great."

"That was different," I said. Today I'd be playing guitar in a rock band in front of hundreds of people and the four amazing musicians we needed to impress to get on the show. Musicians from bands I'd grown up listening to and had fangirled over for years. And if we got on the show, our audition would be aired next week for the entire country to watch. Including my mother.

"Just don't screw up and we'll be fine," Hector said.

"Gee, thanks for the pep talk," I said, and the other guys laughed. Even Hector grinned, and that sense of belonging—that feeling that this was right—struck me again. I was a part of this band now. I could do this.

Our ten minutes were up too soon, and we were directed down a brightly lit hallway and into the backstage area. *The Sound* used a special kind of rotating stage that I'd also seen at music festivals, with a platform on each side so bands could set up and break down their equipment while another band was performing. Then the stage rotated, and it began again. This saved a lot of time with so many bands playing back-to-back.

I couldn't see the band currently on stage, but their music pounded under my feet as the crowd cheered for them. We were about to be in the exact same spot, in front of that same crowd, with our music blasting through the speakers. No, I couldn't think about that or I'd run straight back to that waiting room.

We rushed onto the back side of the stage, which had already been cleared by the previous band. Our gear was waiting for us, and some roadies helped us get it unpacked quickly. After hours of waiting, everything was happening so fast. I didn't have time to think; I just shoved my earpiece in and grabbed my guitar to check the tuning while the other guys handled their own instruments. I got my distortion pedal and mic set up just as the band on stage finished their song. I heard the mentors commenting but couldn't tell if the band had done a good job or not. Either way, it meant we had to hurry.

Kyle got behind his keyboard, Hector sat at the drums, and that left me and Jared up front. My sweaty fingers dropped my guitar pick, and when I went to grab it, my knees nearly gave out from under me. When I straightened up, Jared stood right in front of me, his bass hanging from his neck.

"Ready?" he asked.

"Um, as ready as I'll ever be." Which was to say, hell no. I smoothed my hair and yanked the bottom of my dress down, wishing I had a mirror to check how I looked one last time.

"Just have fun. It'll be over before you know it." He brushed a finger against my cheek, making me shiver. "Stray eyelash," he explained. "You look amazing, by the way."

Our eyes locked, and for a second, it was only the two of us on stage, about to make music together. He offered me one of his heart-stopping smiles, and it gave me the strength I needed to go through with this.

The stage began to turn, ending the moment. Jared and I moved back to our positions in front of our mics as the roar of the crowd grew louder and spotlights flashed in our eyes. My heart pounded as an entire sea of faces stretched before me. And in front, the four musicians who would decide our fate.

This was our one shot to change our futures forever. Our one moment to lose ourselves in the music and hope we brought the audience along with us. Our one chance to turn our dreams into reality.

I was ready.

Chapter Six

I sent off a silent prayer to the universe that I wouldn't screw up just as the stage finished rotating. Hector started us off with the snap of his drumsticks, and we all jumped in with the opening to "Behind the Mask," exactly like we'd practiced. My guitar rang out across the giant theater, louder than I expected but blending with the rest of the band's sound. Jared began to sing, his voice like heartbreak and salty tears, and the crowd pulsed with each word. In seconds, he'd captivated them, like I'd seen him do to the audience at the shows I'd been to.

My fingers danced across the frets, and my pick pounded against the strings. I tried to lose myself in the music like in our rehearsal, but this time there was a crowd watching my every move. My chest tightened at the sight of the four mentors eyeing our performance, judging everything we did. Was I looking at my guitar too often? Or not enough? Should I move around the stage? Look out at the crowd? No, that would only make me more nervous. I should probably move though, instead of standing like a statue. But what if I moved too much and knocked something over? Or, worse, crashed into Jared? No, moving was out, too. Safer to stay in one place. *Just focus on the music,* I told myself. *Also, don't pass out.*

At the chorus, Jared gave me an expectant look. Right, backup vocals. I leaned into the mic in front of me and joined in, but my voice was too quiet at first. Probably because I didn't actually want anyone to hear me sing. I raised my voice and hoped Jared was hypnotizing the crowd enough that no one paid any attention to me.

Near the end of the song, the music quieted down and only Jared's vocals filled the room, haunting and pained as he sang about how no one saw the real him. His words hit me right in the gut, like they always did. When he finished the verse, I jumped back in with the killer riff he normally played, kicking the song up a notch. The other guys joined us, a bonfire of Kyle's synth and Hector's drumming and

Jared's bass. The crowd went wild, and a red light lit up in front of us with a loud buzz.

I missed a note in my surprise, but the other guys never lost their place. One of the mentors had picked us! Surely the other guys were freaking out as much as I was? Hector's steady beat immediately got me back on track, but then another buzz sounded—a second mentor wanted us! Followed by the buzz of a third! I'd been scared we wouldn't even get one, and now we had *three*? I couldn't believe it.

And then it was over. With one last note, the song ended, and the crowd roared. Somehow that had been both the longest three minutes of my life and the shortest. Sweat dripped down my face—it was freaking hot under all these lights— and adrenaline raced through my veins, making my arms tremble, but I felt more alive than ever before. *This is it,* I thought. *This is what I want to do with my life.*

The audience continued to scream, and Jared raised his arms, basking in the crowd's love and in our victory. Kyle and Hector came out from behind their instruments to stand next to us, grinning like drunken fools.

Three of the mentors had red lights in front of them: Angel Reese, the former singer of the '80s glam metal band Dark Embrace, still sporting bleach blonde hair and a spiked leather jacket despite her age; Dan Dorian, the long-haired bassist and singer of Loaded River, a '90s grunge band that had played with Nirvana and Pearl Jam; and Lance Bentley, a young pop star who personified tall, dark, and handsome. He'd won the last three years of *The Sound,* but rumor had it that he'd slept his way through all the women on his team. No thank you.

The only one who didn't buzz for us was Lissa Cruz, a beautiful brunette country singer who was known for being the sweetest mentor on the show. That was okay—we needed a coach, not a cheerleader.

The host of the show, Ray Carter, joined us at the front of the stage. He was probably in his late 40s, with overly gelled black hair, skin that screamed "spray tan," and a flashy white suit.

"That was one of the best things I've heard all day," he said into his mic. "And the audience clearly loves you. Who are you and where are you from?"

"We're Villain Complex from here in Los Angeles," Jared said, and the crowd cheered even louder. I couldn't believe they were making this much noise for *us.*

"That was killer," Angel said. "I need you on my team! I—"

Dan cut her off. "Yeah, I loved the way you—"

"Hey, I was talking!" Angel snapped. "Wait your turn."

Dan rolled his eyes but gestured for her to continue. This was normal for the show; part of the draw was seeing the mentors bicker between each other. Still, it was crazy that two musicians whose songs I'd listened to for years were fighting over us. Was this really my life? How did I get here?

Angel started again. "As I was saying, I love your sound, I love your look, and I think you'd be perfect for my team. With my help, you could definitely win this thing."

"Are you done with your sales pitch yet?" Dan asked her and then continued before she could answer. "Look. You've got the raw talent. You've got the skills. You've also got some things you need to work on, but I can take you to the next level."

"No, this band is mine!" Angel said, slamming her fist on the table. "I buzzed in first!"

"That doesn't mean anything," Dan said.

"But I want them. I want them *so bad*." She practically fell out of her seat saying it, and the crowd went wild.

"Okay, you've heard from two of the mentors," Ray said. "Lance, you want to chime in?"

Lance leaned forward, his dark gaze slowly taking us all in. "Listen. I've won *The Sound* three times already. Join me and we'll win."

"That's it?" Ray asked, after a brief pause.

Lance shrugged and sat back. "That's all I need to say. They know what the right choice is."

"All right then," Ray said and turned to us. "It's up you now. Whose team do you want to be on? Take a moment to talk it over."

The crowd erupted with shouts, and we huddled together next to the drums. "What do you guys think?" Jared asked. "I think we should go with Angel."

"I don't know," Hector said. "She hasn't won before. Lance has won three times. Seems like a sure deal."

"That's why he won't win again this year. Viewers are tired of it. They want someone else to win, with a new sound."

"What about Dan?" Kyle asked. "Loaded River was my favorite band as a kid."

"I don't know. He didn't seem that excited about us," Jared said.

Kyle snorted. "He was more excited than Lance."

"Maddie, what do you think?" Jared asked.

The three of them looked at me. I'd kept quiet until now because I wasn't sure I'd get a vote. I was brand-new after all.

"Um." I turned back to check out the mentors again. Definitely not Lance, but I couldn't decide between Angel and Dan. Both of them thought we could go far in the competition, and both seemed to be good mentors from what I'd seen on previous seasons. The crowd chanted names, but it was hard to tell which name was the loudest.

"Time's up," Ray said. "Who do you pick?"

"Angel," I told the guys. "I'd go with Angel."

Hector rolled his eyes. "You only picked her because Jared did."

"*No*, I picked her because she seemed the most enthusiastic. We need someone who will fight for us 'til the end."

"My thoughts exactly," Jared said.

"Fine," Hector said, and Kyle nodded.

We turned back to the mentors and the crowd, and Jared grabbed the mic. "We pick Angel."

"And Team Angel gets another band!" Ray yelled.

One of Dark Embrace's songs started playing through the speakers while Angel jumped up and cheered. She rushed onto the stage and hugged each of us before I knew what was happening. Her hair smelled of cigarettes and very strong perfume, and I nearly gagged.

"I'm so happy! Welcome to my team," she told us before going back to her seat. She stuck her tongue out at Dan, who just shook his head.

The stage turned so the next band could audition. Bright lights flashed in my eyes as we were taken into another room, and as soon as the door shut, we all erupted.

"We did it!" Kyle wrapped an arm around Jared and Hector's necks, bringing them in for a squeeze. "We actually did it! Alexis is going to be so jealous. She loves Angel."

"I can't believe it," Hector said, his eyes wide. "Did that really happen?"

Jared laughed and clung to the other guys. "I told you we'd make it!"

I stood apart from their guy-bonding moment. It was fine—they'd been together for years, and I was the new kid. But then Jared pulled me over with an arm around my shoulder. "Get in here. You're a part of this band, too."

His touch sent sparks through me, as it always did. I had so much I wanted to say to him—to thank him for taking a chance on me and convincing the others to let me join the band. To tell him how much it meant that he'd believed in me. But this time, words failed me. Kyle looped his arm around my other shoulder, and the four of us stood together in a huddle, grinning ear to ear.

"That's cute," Ray said, speaking to a camera guy. "Make sure you get a shot of this."

We pulled apart at the reminder they were still there. I'd completely forgotten about the interview they did with everyone who got on the show, when they asked how the band got started, what kind of music they liked—that kind of stuff. Hopefully one of the other guys would do all the talking since I'd been in the band for, oh, less than a day now.

Ray arranged us so that Jared and I stood in front, with Kyle and Hector slightly behind us and to the side.

"This will be quick," he said. "I'll ask you some questions and you'll look straight at the camera when you answer. Don't worry if you mess up, we'll edit it together so you look good. Ready?" He launched right into it without waiting for a response. "I'm here with Villain Complex from Los Angeles, who just joined Angel's team after a fierce battle between her, Dan, and Lance. Tell me, why did you pick Angel as your mentor?" He shoved the mic in Jared's face.

"It was a tough decision, but she seemed like she wanted us the most."

"You're the singer, yes? Can you each state your name and what you play in the band?"

"Sure. I'm Jared Cross, and I'm the lead singer and bassist." He flashed his stage smile, and Ray thrust the mic at me next.

"Oh, um." I yanked at the bottom of my dress, worried the camera was getting a view. "I'm Maddie Taylor, and I play the guitar."

"And sing backup," Jared added, much to my dismay.

The other guys said, "Hector Fernandez, drums," and "Kyle Cross, keyboard."

"Great," Ray said and then asked Jared, "So what does Villain Complex mean? Who came up with that?"

"I did," Jared said. "It's a play on the phrase 'hero complex,' which is when someone always wants to save the day and get recognized for it. I figured someone with a villain complex would crave the opposite—they'd want to be noticed for the bad things they do. Fame through villainy and all that." He laughed. "Basically, we all love comic books, and villains are cool."

I studied his face and wondered if there was a personal reason he'd chosen that name or if they really were just comic book geeks. His comment reminded me of the lyrics in "Behind the Mask," about presenting a certain image to the world but no one seeing the real person underneath.

Before I could ponder it further, Ray continued with his next question. "Can you tell us a little about how long you've been together and how you formed?"

"Sure. Kyle and I started playing music together when we were kids. Our mom's a songwriter and our dad's an entertainment lawyer, so it must be in our blood. Hector was my best friend in high school, and I convinced him to learn the drums so we could start a band." He stopped and glanced at me. "And Maddie joined us…recently."

Ray quickly rattled off a few more questions to Jared about the band and what we hoped to get out of the show while the rest of us just stood there like we didn't exist. Hector and Kyle kept trying to butt in, but Ray never let them have the mic.

"One last question," Ray said. "Maddie, are you and Jared together?"

"What? No!" He hadn't addressed me for the entire interview and now he asked *that*? Where had that question even come from?

"So no hidden story there?" he asked, and I shook my head. "C'mon, there has to be something. Look at this guy. You like him, right?"

My god, what was this guy's problem? As the camera focused on me, I coughed, trying to find the words to make this moment end.

"No, we're just friends," I finally managed to say. Jared stared at the floor, like he wanted to be anywhere else. Me too, Jared, me too.

"Too bad. Okay, that's it," Ray said, and the interview was over. He left the room without another word, with the camera crew trailing behind him.

"What the fuck was that?" Hector asked. "This isn't the Jared Cross band."

"Huh?" Jared asked. "I didn't ask the questions."

"No, you just answered all of them. And this isn't the Jared and Maddie love story either."

"I didn't—" I started while Jared said, "There's nothing—"

"Whatever," Hector said. "Just keep it in your pants, man."

Jared's face darkened. "What the—"

"Enough," Kyle said, getting between the two of them. "The show is just trying to find an angle they can work. Don't worry about it. Besides, Maddie already promised she won't hook up with Jared."

Wow, thank you, Kyle. As if this moment wasn't embarrassing enough. "Can we please drop this?" I asked.

Jared raised his eyebrows at me and Hector snorted, but no one else said a word after that.

The show gave us all the information about what would happen next, and we were finally sent home. I still couldn't believe I'd made the choice to do this, to give up my internship to join a rock band and compete on a reality TV show. Who was I and what had I done with my former self?

Chapter Seven

Quitting my internship was harder than I'd expected. Let's just say the LA Philharmonic wasn't pleased to have their carefully selected intern back out at the last minute. I'd definitely burned some bridges there, not to mention with the professor who'd sponsored me. I came pretty close to calling the guys to tell them I couldn't join the band after all, but Carla and Julie assured me I was doing the right thing. God, I hoped they were right.

On Monday, I met the band at the high-rise hotel in LA Live where we'd be staying as long as we were on the show. We were only allowed two rooms, and the guys decided it would be best if they shared one, giving me a room all to myself. I think they just didn't want to argue over who would have to share with me.

I dropped my luggage off in my nice big room and ran into the guys again in the elevator—their room was a few floors up. As the door closed, a voice said, "Going down," and immediately the Fall Out Boy song "Sugar, We're Goin' Down" popped into my head. As if on cue, Jared started singing the chorus of that exact song.

"I heard that, too," I said, and he grinned at me.

"I thought of Aerosmith's 'Love In An Elevator,'" Kyle said.

"Also a good one," Jared said, and belted out the lyrics.

Hector shook his head. "Not me. I heard that Nelly song 'Country Grammar.'"

"What?" Kyle gaped at him. "I think we might have to kick you out of the band."

"No kidding," Jared said. "I'm not sure our relationship can survive such fundamental differences in musical taste."

"Please, we all know you'd be lost without me," Hector said.

"True." Jared grabbed him, and they wrestled until the elevator door opened. I rolled my eyes. *Guys.*

The lobby was all smooth bamboo and stainless steel trim, and my shoes squeaked loudly as we walked across the shiny floors. Some of the people checking in or sitting on the couches were business people or tourists, but the rest had to be musicians on the show, with their dyed hair, faded band T-shirts, and guitar cases. Many of them were sizing us up, too.

"What do you think the other bands on Angel's team are like?" I asked the guys.

Kyle shrugged. "Who knows? Last season she had all kinds of music."

"Yeah, but she tends to go for harder stuff usually," Jared said. "Punk, emo, heavy metal."

"Last season she had one pop band that almost won though," I said.

"True. I just hope she picks a good song for us to play in the battle."

After the auditions, the next step was *The Sound*'s Battle of the Bands. Basically, the mentors paired off the six bands on their team and had them compete against each other by performing the same song. The mentors chose the winners and also got one rescue that they could use on any band eliminated from one of the other teams—leaving four bands on each team for the next show.

Usually there were two battle rounds, but this season had been shortened to only six weeks and moved to the summer instead of the spring, probably because ratings had been dropping steadily. Maybe they hoped a shorter season would keep everyone on the edge of their seats the entire time, or maybe they thought the show would have less competition in the summer since there was nothing else on TV.

We found the meeting room for Team Angel just as four guys with skinny jeans and identical shaggy haircuts walked over. They had that combo of nerd-meets-hipster down, and two of them even had black-rimmed glasses to complete the look.

"Are you on Angel's team, too?" one of the guys asked. He had a boy-next-door kind of face, with broad shoulders and sandy blond hair. Definitely the best-looking one in the group.

"Yeah, we're Villain Complex," Jared said, and we all made our introductions.

"Sweet name," the cute guy—whose name was Sean—said. "Wish we'd thought of it. We're The Static Klingons."

I couldn't help but laugh at the *Star Trek* pun. "That's awesome."

Sean grinned at me. "Yeah? I think you're the only person who's gotten it so far."

"We probably should go in now," their bassist said, scowling at us like we were the enemy. Technically we were, even though we were on the same team.

Sean opened the door and stepped back, waving me inside. "After you."

I smiled at him and entered. The room had identical chairs lined up in rows, facing a podium at the front. A camera crew was already set up so they could film clips for next week's episode. Judging by the clusters of people in the chairs, three bands had already arrived. That meant one more had to show, and Angel was nowhere to be found either.

I picked a spot in the fourth row, and Kyle and Hector filed in next to me, with Jared going around to sit on my other side. The Static Klingons sat two rows in front of us, and Sean turned around and grinned at me before saying something to his band.

Jared leaned closer to me. "He likes you."

"What?" I said it a little too loud, then blushed and lowered my voice. "Why do you say that?"

"I saw the way he looked at you."

"This is the real reason why having Maddie in the band is a bad idea," Hector said, smirking. "Now we're going to have to fight off hordes of horny guys going after her."

"Thanks for the offer, but I think I'll be okay," I said, but I was secretly pleased Hector thought I would attract so much attention. Or that he would actually fight them off for me. Not that he'd need to because one boy smiling at me one time did not equal "hordes of horny guys." Nor did it mean that this one guy was interested in me that way. Sean just seemed friendly.

Jared didn't seem to think Hector's comment was amusing at all. "You said it was a bad idea to let Maddie join because I'd—how'd you put it?—'bone her and then break her heart?'"

"Oh, god, you said that?" I asked Hector.

His face turned almost purple. "You have to admit that is your style."

"Give me a break," Jared said. "One time with Becca and—"

"Knock it off, you two," Kyle interrupted, giving them each a warning look. "This is so not the time for this."

"I wouldn't do that to Maddie anyway," Jared muttered.

"We'll see," Hector said, leaning back and crossing his arms.

Jared turned away but didn't say anything else. Tension created a concrete wall between them, with me and Kyle stuck in the middle. I was relieved Jared wouldn't do that to me, but also a tiny bit disappointed he didn't see me that way, even though I knew it was for the best. I didn't want to mess up anything with the band, and getting involved with Jared would do exactly that.

The last band arrived, with hair spiked into mohawks and chains hanging from their leather jackets. Definitely Angel's type. The one girl in the band wore a chain-mail bikini and very short shorts, and I recognized her as one of the people Jared had talked to before our audition. She caught his eye and winked, and I almost threw up in my mouth a little. The rest of her band glared at everyone and sat down.

While we waited, Kyle and I quietly discussed the other bands and tried to figure out what kind of music they played. I started to wonder if Angel would ever show or if we'd all been given the wrong time or what.

Hector was lost in his sketchbook, and I leaned over to ask, "What are you drawing?"

"Just working on ideas for my next graphic novel."

"Can I see?" Kyle had once mentioned Hector went to art school, but I didn't know much else.

"Sure." He passed me the sketchbook, and I flipped through it. There were lots of random doodles, but also rough sketches of comic panels with lots of action.

He was good—like professional-level good.

"Wow, this is awesome," I said. "What's your graphic novel about?"

"It's called *Misfit Squad*, and it's about a group of teens who have really uncool superpowers, so they band together after the other superhero groups won't let them in. Like the main character accidentally breaks things, and at first it seems like a curse, but then she learns to control it." As he talked, Hector's face lit up in a way I'd never seen before, even when he was drumming. "The first one just came out, and we're planning to do two more."

"Okay, I definitely need to read that."

"I'll give you a copy later."

"Hector designed the Villain Complex logo, too," Kyle added. "And did the quote wall in our studio. He's amazing."

Angel finally walked in, nearly an hour after our scheduled time, with her stringy blonde hair and caked-on makeup trying to cover up her wrinkles. Back in the day, she'd had a voice that could go from screaming to sweet to sexy in an instant. But after one of the band members committed suicide, Dark Embrace had broken up, and she'd started bouncing in and out of rehab. Now she was just a washed-up celebrity trying to relive her former glory days. Still, my mom had played her songs all the time, and I'd grown up with her raspy voice and scratchy guitar, so I was a bit star-struck being in the same room with her. Almost enough to forgive her very late arrival.

"Good, you're all here," she said, like she hadn't made *us* wait. "Let's get this over with." She gestured to the two assistants who had walked in with her, and they began passing papers out to all of us. "Here's your schedule, blah blah blah. Read it, whatever."

She leaned against the podium and started playing on her phone. Jared and Kyle exchanged a look, the kind siblings give each other that say an entire sentence without a word, and I got the feeling they were not impressed. I had to admit it was odd how the Angel at our audition had been so excited while this one seemed like she couldn't wait to get out of here.

We spent a few moments looking over our band's schedule for the week. After this meeting, we had to take photos together, but then we were free for the rest of the night. Starting tomorrow we had a six-hour rehearsal slot every day at a local studio. On Friday, we'd record the song so people could buy it on the show's website, and on Sunday, we'd be filming the actual battle round, which would air Monday night.

Angel finally put her phone away and stood up straight. "Are we rolling now?" One of the camera guys nodded, and she tossed her hair and put on a big smile. "Welcome to Team Angel. I'm so thrilled you're all here!"

Silence from all of us. Maybe we were supposed to cheer or applaud or something, but none of us could be bothered. She looked annoyed for an instant and then continued. "All six of your bands were chosen because I believe you can win this thing. I'm confident that this year I have the most talented group of musicians on the show, and I know Team Angel is going all the way!" This got a tiny bit of forced applause. "Unfortunately, only one of you will make it to the final four. You all have talent or you wouldn't be here, but to make it to the end, you need to work hard and want it more than anything. I want you all to ask yourselves: How bad do you want this? What are you willing to do to win?"

Angel had been doing this show for four years, and she gave the same speech every season. I wondered if she knew from the very beginning who had the best shot at winning, if she could tell, just by looking in our eyes now, who wanted it the most. As I glanced around the room, it hit me that we might not be on the show after this week. Out of six bands, only three of us would be staying with Angel. Any band she eliminated might be picked by the other mentors, but there was no guarantee that would happen.

Beside me, Jared's eyes took on a fiery determination I'd never seen before. Jared was in this thing to win it, no doubt. He'd do anything for that chance, but would I? How much did I want it? Or was I only doing this for Kyle? For Jared?

No, I wanted to win, too. Maybe not as much as Jared did, but after hearing that roar of the crowd, feeling the music blasting from the giant speakers, and playing with the band at my side, I wanted to do this for the rest of my life. I wanted that record deal and the tour and the future as a part of Villain Complex. To get that, we had to win *The Sound*.

After an appropriate pause for her words to sink in, Angel continued. "This week we have the battle round, which will be fun." I couldn't tell if she was being sarcastic or not. She waved at her assistant, and he passed her a sheet of paper, which she squinted at while he disappeared against the wall again. "Okay, let's see here…. First up, The Static Klingons will compete against Villain Complex."

I groaned softly. Why couldn't we have been up against any of the other bands on the team? Of course we would be paired with the one band that seemed sort of nice. Now there was a strong chance one of us would be going home next week.

"You're both going to perform 'Somebody Told Me' by The Killers," Angel said. "I think it'll be a good song for your different sounds."

An interesting choice. I liked the song, but I worried it was a bit too peppy for our usual vibe. Maybe that was more of The Static Klingons' thing.

She paired off the other bands and then said, "I'll see you all at your rehearsals." She flicked a hand at her assistants, and they left the room.

"I haven't played this song before," I said to the guys. "Have you?"

"No," Jared said, as the other two shook their heads. "Which means we need to work our asses off this week."

Chapter Eight

We spent the next couple hours having photos taken of us, both individually and as a band. After that, another camera crew had us walk down a long red carpet outside while they filmed us. Like in the interview the other day, they had me and Jared up front, and the other two guys behind us. We did this multiple times, walking toward the camera and trying to look cool with the wind blowing our hair back, like we were a Serious Band Doing Serious Music. Mostly, I felt ridiculous.

When I returned to my room, my phone was flashing with a bunch of texts from Julie and Carla asking how my first day was and another from Jared telling me to come to their room to watch the show in an hour. I'd forgotten that the first episode of *The Sound* was tonight, and there was a good chance we'd be on it. Even if we weren't on until tomorrow's show, we needed to check out the other bands and see what we were up against.

I wrote the girls and told them my day was crazy but exciting and that I would update them more later. After a quick shower, I pulled on some yoga pants and a tank top, but one glance in the mirror told me that wouldn't work. The tank top was too tight on its own, and this wasn't like hanging out with my roommates in my apartment. I barely knew these guys—other than Kyle anyway. I switched to jeans and threw a flannel shirt on over my tank top. Much better.

When I got to the guys' room, they already had two pizzas sitting on the desk, and my stomach growled. Hector was hogging an entire bed, Jared was on the other, and Kyle took up the only chair, leaving me no place to sit. I hesitated just inside the door, trying to figure out a way to solve the seating problem without it being super awkward.

"Grab some pizza and come sit," Jared said, patting the bed next to him. None of the other guys said anything, so I guessed that was my spot then. Thanks a lot, guys.

I got some food and a beer and sat next to Jared, careful to stick to my side of the bed so we didn't touch. With my luck, I'd probably drop pizza all over his white sheets. Why couldn't they have ordered something less messy to eat? But soon the warm smell of cheese and pepperoni hit me, and I was digging in, too.

"Oh my god, this pizza is the greatest thing I've ever eaten."

"I know. I thought I was going to chew my arm off earlier," Jared said.

"Maybe the show is starving us so we'll lose those ten pounds the camera adds."

He laughed, and I loved the sound of it, how honest and real it was. "That must be it. Though I think you look perfect the way you are." His voice dropped so the other guys couldn't hear the last part, and I swear the room temperature jumped by at least ten degrees.

"Quiet, it's starting," Kyle said and used the remote to raise the volume.

For the first few minutes, the show explained the premise and how it worked and then introduced the mentors. They made a big deal about how Lance had won the last three years in a row and then showed a quick preview of the bands performing tonight, including a one-second shot of us, before it cut away to commercials. I nearly dropped my pizza when I saw it. I knew our audition would be aired one of the nights, but it was still a total shock to actually see us on TV.

"That was us!" Kyle said, slapping his hand on the desk.

"We must be on tonight's show," Jared said.

He got up and dropped his empty plate in the trash and then sank back on the bed. His elbows brushed against my side as he opened his laptop, making me tense up, but when I tried to look at him without actually looking at him, he didn't seem to notice. Had he purposefully sat a little closer to me this time? Or was I imagining it?

The show returned with the first audition from an alternative band I didn't recognize. Lissa was the only one who buzzed for them, which explained why I hadn't seen them yet. The auditions continued, and we all made comments about who was good and who was probably just filler while Jared took notes on his laptop. There were always a few bands that would obviously get weeded out early on. They weren't bad, but they didn't have the skills or experience yet for the show. I really hoped we weren't one of those bands.

I finished my pizza and tossed the plate. This time, my thigh touched Jared's when I sat back down, but he didn't react. I settled against the pillows and watched the show, but left my leg there to see if he'd do anything and—if I was honest with myself—because touching Jared woke up every inch of my body in a way I couldn't resist. He didn't move his leg, but he didn't make any *other* moves either. I must have imagined that he'd sat closer to me earlier. And now that I wasn't eating, I didn't know what to do with my hands. I tried different positions—crossing my arms, leaving them at my sides, and finally settled on lacing my fingers in my lap.

After an hour, we were finally on. We all sat up straighter and Kyle said, "Shh!" even though no one was talking. They showed part of our interview first, when we all introduced ourselves, and then they cut to a clip of us waiting before the audition with the other bands. I hadn't realized they'd been filming us, but there was Jared singing to me in front of everyone and the look on my face of pure longing made me cringe. Was I always that obvious? They followed that clip with the interviewer asking if there was anything between me and Jared and my quick denial and then went to commercials.

"Wow, you looked horrified by his question," Jared said.

"I know!" Kyle said. "Did you see her face when he asked that?"

"Yeah, hilarious," I said, trying to make light of it so they would move on as soon as possible.

"Is the idea really *that* bad?" Jared asked.

"No!" I said, a little too loudly. "I was just surprised when he asked me that."

"I love it." Hector cracked up. "Maddie's the one girl disgusted by the idea of dating you."

"Ha fucking ha." Jared threw a crumpled–up, oil-covered napkin at Hector, who tossed it back at us. Naturally, it landed on my lap. I threw it at Kyle, and it bounced off his head and hit the floor. He gave a mock-growl, and we all laughed.

Our laughs cut off instantly the second the show was back on. The stage turned, revealing me clutching my guitar like it would protect me from the audience somehow, and Jared looking confident and sexy as usual, a man born to be on stage. Hector started us off, and he was an animal on the drums. His muscular arms pounded away while sweat dripped down his forehead, and his energy fueled the rest of our performance. Meanwhile, Kyle bobbed his head to the music, sometimes playing the keyboard one-handed and getting the crowd going. I hadn't seen either of them when we performed, and it was fun to watch them now.

And then there was me. Stiff. Wide-eyed. Looking like I was about to bolt off the stage. It was obvious who the weak link in the band was, and even worse, this was on TV for the entire country to see. I might have been playing the song, but I just wasn't bringing it.

The mentors began buzzing for us, and on the bed, my fingers dug into the sheets, itching to get back on stage with my guitar and relive that moment. Jared's hand slipped between our bodies, and he tangled his fingers with mine, sending a jolt under my skin. I wanted to look at him, to see his face when he squeezed my hand, but then it would make the moment too real. Instead, I kept my gaze on the screen while Jared's thumb brushed against the spot on my wrist where my pulse raced, making my lips part with a silent sigh. None of the other guys noticed, too busy watching the mentors fight over our band on TV. They showed the clip of the guys all hugging after the audition, with Jared pulling me in to join them, before the show moved on to the next band.

Jared finally released my hand and put his fingers back on the laptop, allowing me to breathe again.

"That was pretty good," he said. "Even though I sucked at bass, and my voice was too pitchy on the third verse."

"You were fine," Kyle said. "I screwed up the bridge though."

"You were both amazing, and Hector, too," I said. "I'm the one who stood there like a deer in the headlights the entire performance. And I was so shocked when a mentor buzzed for us that I lost my place."

Jared leaned against me, nudging me with his arm. "You did great, really."

A conflicting mix of feelings rushed through me. I wanted to rest my head against his shoulder. I wanted the other guys to leave so I could be alone with him. I wanted to escape to my room and forget about Jared completely. That was definitely the safest option.

"That was your first live show," Kyle said, bringing me back to the moment. "You'll do even better next time."

Hector nodded. "Don't stress about it, Maddie. You were really good."

I gave them all a weak smile. "Thanks. I just don't want to let you guys down."

"You won't," Kyle said. "You just need more practice on stage, that's all."

Jared sat up straighter. "Look, it's The Static Klingons."

The four of them wore matching shirts made to look like they were crew members on *Star Trek*. Sean spoke for the group during their interview, describing how they practiced in an old barn in Nebraska.

"Ha! Your boyfriend lives on a farm," Kyle said.

"He is *not* my boyfriend." Sean was cute, but he was so…vanilla. So bland. He reminded me of my high school boyfriend—nice and boring and safe.

Hector smirked. "But he'd like to be."

We quieted down as the band took the stage. Their song got the audience going, though not as much as our performance had. Sean played guitar and had a catchy, high-pitched voice—a little nasally but in a good way.

"They're not bad," Hector said.

"Yeah," Kyle said. "They sound sort of like if Weezer had a love child with Daft Punk."

"They're really good," I said. "And unfortunately for us, their sound is perfect for The Killers' song."

Jared sighed. "I wish Angel had paired us with that punk band. We'd crush them."

"But then you wouldn't have the chainmail bikini girl to flirt with," Kyle said.

"Eh, she lives in Boston anyway."

Hector snorted. "Like that matters. You're not going to *date* her."

"Hey, I already told Jared he's not allowed to bring girls up here," Kyle said.

"Yeah, but that means you can't bring Alexis either," Jared said.

"I'll make that sacrifice to not have to deal with your women the morning after." He made a gagging sound.

Thanks for reminding me, Kyle. And soon, Jared would have even more groupies, more screaming girls who would love to invite him to their rooms for the night. I couldn't let myself forget the kind of guy Jared was, no matter how he made me feel. Especially since he seemed to make *every* girl feel that way.

The guys kept bantering until the show ended. When it was over, Hector went into the bathroom and Kyle went onto the balcony to call Alexis. Leaving me alone in a bed with Jared, our bodies much too close and my hands way too tempted to reach for him again.

"I should go," I said, jumping off the bed. "Early morning and all that."

"Right." He walked me to the door. I stepped outside, and he lingered in the doorway. "Maddie," he said, and I turned back, wanting something I wasn't ready to name yet. But all he said was, "Goodnight."

Chapter Nine

The next morning I downloaded "Somebody Told Me" and listened to it on repeat as I got ready. During my elevator ride to the lobby, I got so into picking apart the guitar chords that I nearly crashed into Jared when I stepped out.

"Hey," Jared said, giving me a quick once-over with a smile. "You look great."

"Thanks." I flushed, but reminded myself that Jared always said things like that. It didn't mean anything. He was just a flirt.

Julie had helped me get my wardrobe ready for my time on the show, including an all-day shopping event over the weekend. Everyone had to be prepared to be filmed at any time, so I had to keep up my rocker look for the next few weeks. Today I was wearing a long, one-shouldered top over black-and-white-striped leggings and ankle boots. But I was more surprised by what Jared wore; over his black jeans, he had on a T-shirt with the classic Joker and Harley Quinn on it.

"Oh, wow, I love your shirt," I said.

"Yeah? They're my favorite Batman villains."

"Mine too! They're like the Bonnie and Clyde of comics." I paused before revealing the next bit since it might cross the line, but I decided to let my geek flag fly. "I'm actually dressing up as Harley Quinn for Comic-Con next month."

"Really?" he asked, as we moved to a spot near the revolving doors to wait for Kyle and Hector.

"I know, it's pretty nerdy, but my friend Julie is making all the costumes. She's going to be Poison Ivy and my other friend Carla is going to be Catwoman."

"Gotham City's most dangerous women. I like it."

"That's the idea."

"You know, we're all going to Comic-Con, too. Maybe I'll dress up as the Joker." He winked at me.

That wink was dangerous. It could get a girl in trouble. And was he saying he wanted to go as a couple? Or was I reading too much into that comment? "You're all going to Comic-Con?"

"Yep. Hector's going to promote his graphic novel, and he got me a ticket, too. Kyle is going with Alexis, who's taking photos for the website she works for. I've never been before, so I'm excited."

"We went the last two years. It was amazing."

I told him about it as we waited for the other guys—waking up at 3 AM to get in line for the biggest panels, eating nothing but pretzel dogs and mini-pizzas for days, the unbelievable number of people crammed into the exhibit hall, plus all the incredible costumes and free swag. Jared listened intently and asked questions, and in return, I asked all about Hector's graphic novel. Hector had done the artwork, inking, and coloring, but someone he'd met online had written the script. The band really *did* live up to their geeky name.

Jared's phone buzzed, and I stood close enough to sneak a peek when he checked it. The text was from someone named Michelle and said, *"hey sexy wanna get 2gether 2nite?"* He shot me a quick glance and shoved the phone back in his pants without answering. He probably didn't want me to see what he wrote back. It had to be from one of his many groupies or maybe someone he'd met on the show. One of those girls from the audition perhaps? The girl with the mohawk and chainmail bikini? Did she seem like a Michelle? Whatever. Jared's sex life was none of my business.

When the other guys arrived, we walked the three blocks to the address we'd been given for the studio, and Jared told us how Villain Complex's social media sites had all gained thousands of followers overnight. More people had visited our website in the last day than ever before, and many were even buying the album. It was crazy to think we now had fans all over the country, rooting for us and anxious to see our next performance. Even more pressure to do a good job on this week's show.

We stopped at a brick building that looked like it had once been a factory or something. The windows were all dark so we couldn't see inside, and there was no sign or anything—just a number on the black door.

"Is this it?" I asked, checking the address again on our schedule.

"Must be," Kyle said.

We stepped inside and found a lounge with dark couches scattered around the room, plus an attached kitchen area with coffee and food. A guy at a reception desk directed us to room four, where our gear was waiting for us in a soundproofed studio. Someone from the show had dropped off sheet music, and I studied the guitar tabs, mentally replaying the song in my head. I was already familiar with "Somebody Told Me," but singing along to it on the radio and playing it with the band was a totally different story. I hadn't been lying to Jared, though—I did have an ear for this stuff. I set down the papers after a quick once-over and tried out the opening guitar riff. It was easy but very catchy with the way the chords got higher and higher.

The other guys tried some things, too, testing out their own parts of the song. After a few minutes, Jared turned to face all of us.

"Before we do anything else, we need to figure out a way to differentiate our version from whatever The Static Klingons do."

"Good idea," I said. "They already have a similar sound to The Killers, so they probably won't change the song very much."

"What if we made the song darker?" Kyle asked. "Drop the tuning, make it almost an emo cover of the song."

Jared rubbed the stubble along his chin as he considered. "That could work, and it would sound more like our own stuff, too. Let's try it."

For the next three hours, we worked on getting our version of the song figured out, experimenting with different ways to make it our own. The guitar on the song wasn't hard, but the bass was trickier and Jared had a tougher time with it.

After a particularly bad play-through, we decided to take a break and stretch our limbs before the next three-hour block. I headed to the kitchen to grab lunch and found Sean in there, pouring some coffee.

"Hi," he said. "Crazy day, huh?"

"Very. I'm still trying to catch my breath."

"Me too." He watched as I grabbed a plate and piled on some salad. "I hate that our bands are competing against each other."

"I know, it really sucks." I examined the mini-sandwiches, trying to figure out what they were, and then grabbed two turkey ones and a soda. I was just thrilled the show wasn't starving us today.

"So how's it going for you?" Sean asked, resting his hip against the counter in front of me. "With the song?"

"We've got it figured out I think. Just need to practice more. How about you?"

"We've done covers of 'Somebody Told Me' before at shows, so we feel pretty good about it. What kind of spin are you putting on it?"

"Um…" I wasn't sure what to tell him, and then I was distracted by the sight of Jared in the lounge, talking to a girl with long copper hair. Was this Michelle? She gave him a flirty smile and put her hand on his elbow, and I wanted to dump my plate of food on her head. Jared flashed her his devilish grin, but when he looked at me and Sean, something crossed his face. He ditched the girl and walked over to us.

"Hey," he said, standing close to me and glaring at Sean. "What do you think of the song choice?"

"We're happy with it. It's a good song for us. You?" Sean's sunny disposition had vanished, and he eyed Jared with an openly hostile look. I wasn't really sure what was going on between them.

"We'll make it work."

"Cool." They stared each other down for a long, painful moment, and then Sean turned back to me. "Hey, it was great to see you, Maddie."

"You too." I pulled my shirt down to better cover my leggings, suddenly self-conscious. The mood had turned frosty ever since Jared had arrived, like they both wanted to stake their claim on me or something, which was ridiculous.

"What was that about?" I asked Jared once Sean had left.

Jared turned to make himself some tea with honey. "He's trying to work you to get info on what we're doing."

I rolled my eyes. "He's just a nice guy, and you're being paranoid."

"Okay, then he wants to get in your pants."

"I highly doubt that." Yes, Sean was the sort of guy I usually dated, but he was also our competition. He lived in Nebraska anyway. "And if he does, what do you care?"

It was a loaded question and Jared's eyes widened for second, but then his cool exterior took over again. "I don't. Just be careful what you say to him."

"God, Jared, I'm not going to tell him anything."

I walked away before he could reply. Did he actually think I would betray the band just because some cute guy smiled at me? And why did it sting so much that Jared didn't care if Sean wanted me? Like the other guys, he only saw me as a little sister. While I found this charming in Kyle and amusing in Hector, when Jared acted like an overprotective big brother, I kind of wanted to kick something.

———

According to our schedule, Angel was supposed to show up during our final two hours of practice, but she never did.

That night I told the guys I was tired and watched the second group of auditions alone in my hotel room. I couldn't handle another night of awkwardness next to Jared, especially after our conversation earlier.

For the next few days, we spent most of our time in rehearsal, and Angel still never appeared. I was starting to think she was a mentor in name only. Were the other bands on her team being ignored, too, or was it just us? I thought about asking Sean, but Jared's warning echoed in my head. I didn't think Sean was using me for info, but it wouldn't hurt to be careful either.

In the evenings, many of the bands hung out in the lobby of the hotel, mingling and gossiping and flirting, but I didn't join them. I had zero interest in seeing Jared slipping off to some hotel room with another girl. Besides, I felt like an imposter around the other bands, like as soon as I opened my mouth they'd realize I wasn't really one of them. I didn't want them to think, *Why are you on this show, you hack?*

Instead, I retreated to my room and ate alone every night. Being around the guys all day was exhausting anyway, and I needed some alone time to recharge. I sent updates to Carla, who was in New York on some fashion shoot, and Julie, who had returned to the town in Northern California where we'd grown up to see her parents.

On Thursday night, she called me while I was watching TV and painting my nails a dark burgundy. "Hey, Julie, what's up?"

"I saw your mom today, and she asked how you're doing." Julie paused, and I could feel her judgment in the silence. "You didn't tell her about the show?"

"No, I haven't spoken to her in…" Honestly, I wasn't sure how long it had been. "A while."

"Maddie!"

"I know, I know. I should have told her." I sighed. Everything with my mother was so difficult, it was easier to just ignore that part of my life sometimes. "What did you say?"

"Nothing, and it was seriously uncomfortable. You need to tell her."

"I'm sorry. I'll call her tomorrow." I blew on my nails, debating whether or not to ask the thing I really wanted to know. "How's she doing? Is she…"

"She looks good. Better. She said she's been sober for three months now."

I closed my eyes, relieved. I didn't think it would stick, but at least she was trying. Again. "Where did you see her?"

"At the store. She was buying cigarettes."

"Of course." The only two things my mom would leave the house for: booze and cigarettes. "How's your family?"

"Ugh, all they want to talk about is my sister and how wonderful she is. They'd trade me in for a clone of her in an instant."

I laughed and started painting my toenails while Julie told me all about her time back home. It should have made me homesick, but it didn't. When I'd turned eighteen, I'd gotten out of that place as fast as I could, and I had no regrets.

———

On Friday, we went to a different part of the studio to record our version of the song so *The Sound* could sell it on the website. The more songs a band sold, the better they did in the live shows; though for this episode, they'd just earn us some extra cash. Angel was supposed to attend the recording session, but, surprise surprise, she never showed up.

The other guys had rented a recording studio before to make their album, but I'd only recorded music for school so a lot of it was new to me. The sound guys advised us from the control room while one of the producers watched—a guy named Steve who wore the biggest watch I'd ever seen, along with a suit that probably cost more than my car.

In the live room, we played through the song together a few times, and then we each recorded our part of the song alone, too. When it was my turn, I played my guitar with the headphones on, just me and the music, the sound clear and beautiful while everything else faded away. Jared went last, recording the vocals while the rest of us watched, his eyes closed as he emptied his soul into the lyrics. I'd never seen someone who could channel emotion like he did every time he sang, like each word was being ripped out of him. His voice stirred something deep inside me, a longing that was almost painful, a desire I couldn't ignore. I ached to pull him into my arms and press my lips to his, to feel him pour that same passion into me.

Saturday was our last practice before the battle, and it was starting to look like Angel would be a no-show for that, too. I grabbed some coffee during our break and prepared to settle in for our last three hours of rehearsal. We'd gotten the song down, and now it was only a matter of practicing until we felt confident we wouldn't make any mistakes tomorrow.

We still had about ten minutes to relax before we started again, so I sipped my coffee and played with my guitar picks. Hector was sprawled across the floor drawing in his sketchbook while Kyle and Jared talked quietly, heads ducked close together. Brother stuff, I guessed.

The door banged open, and a stream of people entered with cameras and other equipment, followed by Angel and her assistants. The four of us just gaped at them as they set up around the room.

"All right," Angel said. "Let's hear what you've got." When none of us moved, she snapped her fingers a few times. "I only have a few minutes, so hurry it up."

Unbelievable. She didn't show all week, and now she acted like we were wasting *her* time? Still, we each scrambled up and got in place while she grabbed a stool and sat in front.

"Any day now," she said.

Jared scowled, but he adjusted his mic and we started the song. We were all off this time, the pressure of the camera crew and of Angel's gaze making us each mess up. When she turned to me, I lost place of where I was in the song, and I had to make my mind blank for a second to find where we were so I could jump back in.

"Stop, stop," Angel said, waving a hand at us. "You on guitar, what happened there?"

"I—I just got distracted, sorry."

"Whatever, just get it together. And you," she said to Jared. "You need to step it up." She flicked a hand at the camera crew. "Okay, let's film this one and get this over with."

Jared gripped the mic so hard I was surprised it didn't break, but he said nothing and we started again. Angel let us finish this time and then plastered on her fake cheer now that the cameras were rolling.

"That was great!" she said with a little clap. "I love the way you've twisted the song and made it darker. I'm so happy you chose me for your mentor!"

Kyle snorted and then covered his mouth with his hand like he couldn't believe that had escaped. Angel's eyes narrowed at him, but then her phone rang—playing her band's most popular song, of course. She held up a finger to us as she raised the phone to her ear.

"You've got to be kidding me," Jared muttered.

My thoughts exactly. Since there was nothing to do but wait for Angel, I picked up my coffee and took a sip, but it had gone cold now. Yuck. I moved across the room to dump the plastic cup in the trash.

"No, you tell him that doesn't work for me. All or nothing!" Angel yelled at someone on her phone, pacing across the room like an angry jungle cat. She waved her free hand as she spoke and backed right into me, knocking into my arm. Coffee splattered all over both of us, and time seemed to slow as Angel looked down at herself and then up at me.

"You stupid bitch!" She wiped coffee off her leather jacket. "Look what you've done!"

"I'm so sorry!" I looked around for some napkins or something, my face burning. All of this was being filmed by the camera guys, who were probably thrilled to have captured some drama. I could only pray some kindhearted producer cut this moment so the entire country wouldn't laugh at me. Kyle ran over and handed me some napkins, but Angel waved him off when he offered her some.

"I don't have time for this shit," she snapped and turned to the door.

"No, you don't seem to have time to be a mentor at all," Jared said.

She spun to face him. "What did you say to me?"

"You heard me." He moved to stand in front of me, like he was going to protect me from her wrath. "And you need to apologize to Maddie."

Angel pointed a finger at Jared. "You ungrateful little shit, you're lucky to even be on this show!"

Seeing her shout at Jared upset me even more than her calling me a bitch. "We should have picked one of the other mentors."

"No kidding," Hector said. At some point, he'd moved to stand beside us, fists clenched at his sides.

Angel looked like she might strangle one or all of us. I was surprised the show didn't intervene, but they probably loved this stuff. "You're done," she yelled. "Tomorrow you're all gone!"

She stormed out, followed by her entourage, who either gave us looks of sympathy or ignored us completely. The door closed, and we were alone again.

"This is all my fault," I said, my shoulders slumping. "She's going to send us home because of me."

Jared ran a shaky hand through his hair. "No, if anything that was my fault. Shit, what have I done?"

"I can't believe you said that to Angel," Kyle said. "Even if it was true."

He sighed. "I know, it was stupid. I just can't stand bullies, and when she yelled at Maddie, I lost it."

There he went, being my big brother again, but this time I didn't mind as much. I placed my hand on his arm. "Thanks."

"What do we do now?" Hector asked. "We're screwed."

There was only one thing we *could* do. We had to nail this song and hope for a miracle.

Chapter Ten

We arrived at the Nokia Theater early on Sunday for a quick soundcheck, followed by an hour of hair and makeup. We got to pick our own outfits for this show, and of course we all wore black. I had on a low-cut top with leather pants, of all things, and after about ten minutes, my crotch was sweating and I was cursing Julie in my head. But I had to admit, I did look pretty hot—and we needed every advantage we could get tonight.

We filmed a clip about what it was like being mentored by Angel, and we'd forced smiles and lied through gritted teeth about how great it was. We'd decided being honest wouldn't help us if the show was trying to cover up what she was really like. Now that our battle with The Static Klingons approached, I found it hard not to bite my dark red nails and tear out my extra-volumized hair. We already knew Angel was going to pick The Static Klingons no matter what happened today, and our impending doom hung over us through every step of our prep work.

Our gear had been transported to the theater and carted away, and it made me realize how much we left it in the hands of others. I hated giving up my guitar to strangers and trusting they wouldn't mess it up or misplace it, but bands on tour did it all the time and *The Sound* had this down to an exact science after so many years.

We were shuffled into a waiting area for Team Angel's bands, where we could watch what happened through giant TV screens. The battle rounds weren't live and didn't use the rotating stage; instead, the two competing bands were both set up on opposite sides of the main stage. As the first competitors went on, I found myself munching non-stop on the chips and cookies they'd put out for us while trying not to watch Jared flirt with the mohawk girl from the punk band. The only way to distract myself was to eat my anxiety away, until Sean appeared next to me at the food table.

"You're getting crumbs all over your shirt," he said, trying hard not to stare at my cleavage and failing.

"Ugh, thanks." I brushed off my chest with a sigh. "I thought eating would help, but now I just feel sick."

"Me too. This whole week has been overwhelming. Very different from life on a farm, trust me."

"I bet."

For a few minutes we watched the screen, where two country bands from Team Lissa took turns performing "Need You Now" by Lady Antebellum. The first band was good, but they were missing a certain spark, while the second one, Fairy Lights, was led by a pretty blonde teenager with an amazing voice. When both bands finished and Lissa chose Fairy Lights, it wasn't a surprise at all.

Sean cleared his throat, reminding me he was still there. "So I saw your audition. Your band is really good."

"Thanks, but you don't need to be worried. The song is a much better pick for you." I left out the part about how Angel wanted to kill us, too.

"Maybe, but I'm curious to see what you'll do with it."

Was he trying to get info out of me or just being nice? Hard to tell. Maybe I'd try the same tactic on him. "What do you think of Angel?"

"You mean when she actually shows up?" He laughed but then looked around like he was worried someone had heard him. I didn't think they were filming us now, but you never knew. "She's…okay."

It sounded like The Static Klingons hadn't gotten much more mentoring than we had. Of course, they probably hadn't dropped coffee all over Angel and turned her into a screaming banshee either, but what could you do?

Jared laughed at something Mohawk Girl said, and jealousy sliced through me like a sword to my gut. I shifted my gaze back to the screen as two other bands went on stage, but that only reminded me that we were going up there soon. The walls in the stuffy room began to close in around me, and the urge to bolt grew strong. I desperately needed some air right away.

"I have to go," I said to Sean. "Good luck today."

"Thanks. You too."

I stepped through a door to an outside area, where a few people were smoking, and found an empty spot by the chain-link fence separating the space from the parking lot. I kicked some trash away, sank to the ground, and closed my eyes. My leather pants would probably get all scuffed up, but at this point, I didn't care.

I'd thought I could handle all of this, but the paralyzing fear had crept back in and this time it was mixed with dread. Did it even matter if we performed today? We already knew Angel would never let us stay on her team, even if we blew The Static Klingons away. And odds are I was going to mess up and embarrass the band during our show. I couldn't even remember how the guitar went in "Somebody Told Me." What had been simple in practice now seemed impossible. I'd given up my internship for this show, and now we'd be going home in the second week. It didn't seem fair.

"Hey." Jared's voice made me snap my eyes open. "Are you not okay again?"

His reference to the song he'd sung for me before our audition made me smile

—barely—but I wished it had been Kyle or even Hector who had found me. Jared looked especially handsome today, with his hair spiked up and the barest hint of eyeliner making his blue eyes pop even more. Being alone with him was a delicious agony.

"I just needed some air," I said.

"Sorry. Should I go?"

"No," I said, a little too quickly, and then cursed myself for it. It would be better if he left, but I also wanted him to stay. I was a hot mess.

He sat next to me on the ground, his long legs stretching in front of us. "I always get stressed before shows, too."

"You do?" I found that hard to believe. Jared was always so confident on stage, so sure of himself. "You make it look easy."

"That's all an act, but it does get easier every time. You'll be a pro soon, too."

"Assuming we don't get kicked off this week, you mean."

He leaned his head back against the fence and stared up at the clear sky. "Trust me, I'm still beating myself up for that."

"It wasn't your fault."

Jared was silent for a minute, picking at a rough spot on his black jeans. "So you and that Sean guy, huh?"

"What? No. I mean, he seems nice and all, but that's it." I nudged Jared with my shoulder. "You jealous?"

He flashed me a smile that made my toes curl. "Maybe."

"Don't be." The words slipped out, and I wanted to cover my mouth the instant I said them. I'd meant it as a joke, but it had come out a lot more serious. But he didn't respond or brush it off with another joke. His eyes searched mine, like he was looking for answers in them.

I dropped my gaze. "We should head back in."

"Yeah, Kyle's probably tearing the place apart looking for us."

He jumped to his feet and reached down to help me up. I slid my hand into his, but as I stood, I stumbled into him a little, still unsteady on my new heels. I braced myself on his chest, our hands still entwined, almost like we were dancing and just as close. My eyes caught on the patch of skin just above the buttons on his shirt, and I itched to undo them and see what was underneath. His free hand rested on the curve of my hip, and my gaze traveled up to his mouth, to lips that begged me to kiss them.

"There you are," Kyle called from the door to the theater. "I've been looking for you two everywhere."

I jumped back, hoping Kyle hadn't seen how close we'd been a second ago, and Jared shoved his hands in his pockets. I was equally grateful to Kyle for saving me and annoyed with him for ruining my moment alone with Jared.

"Sorry," I said. "Jared was just giving me a pep talk before the show."

Kyle looked back and forth between us, like he didn't believe that was all there was to it. I'd promised him I wouldn't get involved with his brother, but I wasn't doing a very good job of staying away from Jared. No matter how much I tried to fight it, I was attracted to him. Unfortunately, so was every other girl who laid eyes on him. Being in close proximity to him all week had definitely not helped me get over it either—if anything, it had only made it worse because now I knew Jared a little better. He'd stopped being an impossible fantasy in my head and become a real person I actually liked to talk to, and that was even more dangerous. If I wasn't careful, I'd get my heart broken or get kicked out of the band. Or both.

Kyle informed us were scheduled to go on in fifteen minutes. Commence panic mode. I ran to the bathroom to check my outfit and makeup, and then the band was directed to the edge of the stage to wait for our cue. The Static Klingons were taken to the other side, and Sean waved at me as he walked past. Jared raised an eyebrow at me, but I ignored him. I didn't have time for any more guy drama, not with so much riding on this next performance.

Ray Carter walked onto the stage, this time in a dark red suit, and it was time. "Now we have a battle between two bands on Angel's team! First up, from Nebraska, The Static Klingons!" The band walked out from their side of the stage while the audience cheered. "Versus…Villain Complex, from right here in Los Angeles!"

We rushed out, smiling at the crowd of 7,500 before us—yes, last night I'd looked up how many people the Nokia Theatre held. It was hard to see anything with the bright lights blinding me, so I focused on getting to my spot without tripping. As I threw on my guitar strap, I caught Angel eyeing us from her chair with a smirk, no doubt plotting our demise.

Once both bands were in place, Ray continued. "They're both performing 'Somebody Told Me' by The Killers, and now we'll flip a coin to see who goes first." He flicked it dramatically. "And the first one up is…The Static Klingons! Here we go!"

He hustled off the stage while the lights over us went out, leaving our band in darkness while The Static Klingons were illuminated. Sean gave the audience a boy-next-door smile before starting the opening guitar riff. As the band rocked out, we stood on the other side of the stage and watched, knowing we would be next, performing the same song for a mentor who hated us. And the worst part was… The Static Klingons were good. They'd barely tweaked the song at all, but it worked for them. Basically, we were screwed before we'd even started playing.

The song ended, and everyone cheered. I clapped along too because it seemed like the polite thing to do, and the other guys joined in with me. Sean gave a little bow, and from the center of the stage, Ray said, "And now, Villain Complex!"

The lights flashed over to us, and my heart pounded as I looked out into the theater, at all the faces staring at us. They'd already heard this song once, and it couldn't possibly be as exciting to hear it a second time. Going first definitely would have been better.

Jared grabbed the mic, pulling it close as he surveyed the crowd, and the theater went quiet. "Somebody Told Me" had a killer opening with great build-up, and we nailed it. Our version was darker and edgier, and when Jared sang, he twisted the lyrics into something beautiful and tortured, full of longing and regret.

My focus narrowed down to the guitar in my hands, and the rest of the world faded away until it was just me and the music. We got to the bridge and Jared held the last note, turning it into an anguished cry that rang across the room. We let it hang over the crowd for a heavy pause and then dove back into the chorus, with me singing backup behind him. I loved this song and the way we'd made it our own, and once again I felt like I belonged here, on stage, with these three guys. Playing with them gave me an energy I'd never experienced anywhere else.

We ended strong, and the sound of the audience's cheers washed over us, like a blissfully cold wave on a hot day, but I couldn't tell if they screamed more for us than they had for The Static Klingons. The mentors clapped, too, but it was hard to know what they really thought. None of them had used any of their rescues yet, but that didn't mean they'd use them on us either. Even though, in my opinion, we'd totally owned this song.

Ray Carter moved to the center of the stage again. "That was great! I love that song, and tonight we had two amazing performances of it. Dan, what did you think?"

"I thought both bands did a really amazing job. The Static Klingons got the crowd going, but Villain Complex has such a killer sound and they did something really unique with the song. I'm glad I don't have to pick one as the winner."

"Thanks, Dan," Ray said. "Lissa, what about you?"

"Like Dan said, both performances were strong. I do think the song was a little better for The Static Klingons and their sound, but Villain Complex held their own, too. I'd probably go with The Static Klingons myself, but definitely a tough decision."

Damn, guess we weren't getting a rescue from Lissa tonight. Still, we only needed one.

"Lance?" Ray asked.

"I agree. They're both talented bands. I wouldn't want to let either of them go."

As usual, Lance kept it short. Ray turned the mic over to Angel. "Well, these are your bands. It's your decision, Angel."

"I know," she said with a dramatic sigh. "I shouldn't have paired these two together. They're both so good!" She was really playing it up tonight, like we didn't already know who she would pick. I wished she'd just get it over with already.

"It's time to make your choice, Angel," Ray said. "Which band stays on your team?"

"I don't know." She tossed her bleached hair, her brow furrowed like the decision was really difficult. "This is just *so* hard."

Here it came. Our final moment on the show. I took Jared's hand for support, then realized everyone would see that on TV and quickly reached for Kyle's hand, too. Jared grabbed Hector, and the four of us all stood linked together on stage, united against our mentor.

Angel's eyes narrowed at the sight of us together, and then she plastered on one of her big fakey smiles. "I choose The Static Klingons!"

I squeezed my hands into a death grip around the guys' as the audience cheered. It was over. Our fifteen minutes of fame were up, and now the entire country would see us get kicked off on week two of the show. If only I hadn't spilled coffee all over Angel, if only Jared had kept his mouth shut, if only we had picked a different mentor at audition, if only we'd practiced more.... I wanted to rewind the last week and do everything all over again.

Ray went over to The Static Klingons, who were all jumping up and down and smacking each other on the back. The mic was thrust into Sean's face, and he grinned at the audience. "Thank you, Angel!"

They left the stage, and Ray made his way back over to us. "Any last words for our mentors and the audience?"

He shoved the mic in my face, but when I opened my mouth, nothing came out. I was frozen, blinking back tears, wishing this wasn't the end. What was I going to do now? I'd given up everything to be on this show, and now we were going home.

Jared leaned in, saving me. "We're really happy for The Static Klingons. They're great guys, and they deserve to be here."

A loud buzzing rang out, and something around us flashed red and blue. The audience erupted into frenzied cheers. What was happening?

"A rescue from Dan!" Ray yelled into the mic.

Dan wanted us on his team! We weren't done yet! I started laughing and wiped at my eyes. Kyle shouted, "Yes!" while Hector grinned and thumped Jared on the shoulder. Jared just looked shocked and squeezed my hand harder. We were still holding on to each other, even though the other guys had let go.

"I think this band has a lot of potential," Dan said. "I wanted them from the beginning, and now that Angel was dumb enough to let them go, I have my shot."

"Hey!" Angel said, glaring at him.

"What? You made the wrong choice." He shrugged, and I already loved our new mentor. "Anyway, they're really talented, and I'm excited to have them on my team."

"Thank you so much!" Jared said into the mic.

"And that's Villain Complex, the newest member of Team Dan!" Ray said, and our time on stage was over.

We ran backstage and had another group hug with lots of laughter, the relief making us all giddy. We had no idea if things would be better or worse on Team Dan, but at least we were still on the show for another week.

Chapter Eleven

Monday morning we took a shuttle to our new recording studio, which was a bit too far to conveniently walk to. This studio was a big, boxy concrete building, with tiny slits for windows and no other distinguishing features. They sure didn't like to advertise these places. Inside, the lobby was sparse except for modern white furniture and a display of all the awards Dan's band Loaded River had won —Grammys, MTV Awards, and many others I didn't recognize. Along the wall were photos of the band, plus shots of Dan and his husband, who was the drummer in another grunge band.

There were three other bands already there: a folk band with a bazillion people in it, a Christian heavy metal band, and a reggae band. They all gave us the side-eye when we entered. I got it—we were the new kids, the outsiders, taking the spot of someone else on their team. Even though the show liked to pretend there was camaraderie between team members, the truth was, we were competing against each other. With each episode, one band went home from every team, so in a way these people were more a threat to us than anyone else on the show. Until the final episode anyway.

"Tough crowd," Jared muttered while we sat on the last remaining couch.

A camera crew was already set up around the room, and Steve, that producer from our recording session with the giant watch and expensive suits, supervised everything from the side. It still creeped me out that everything we said or did here could be aired on the show.

Dan arrived and handed out our schedules himself. "Everyone welcome our newest team members, Villain Complex." The other bands grunted or let out a weak hello. One older woman with dreadlocks from the reggae band gave us a warm smile, but she was the only one. "Make sure you check your schedule for the week," Dan continued. "You'll notice you have a lot more interviews and all that crap, so don't miss those or the producers will be on my ass. The live shows start next Monday, and each week has a theme. This first one is 'Sick of It All,' whatever that means, so start thinking about your song choice."

"He lets us pick the song?" I whispered to the guys. I thought the mentors always chose.

"Remember for the live shows, it's all about appealing to the audience at home," Dan said. "If you have any problems, let me know. I'm going to meet with Villain Complex now, and I'll see the rest of you in rehearsal tomorrow."

The other bands took off, and we stared at our schedules while Dan talked to Steve for a minute. I could already tell that being on Dan's team would be a very different experience from Angel's. Dan was friendly but direct and acted like a real person instead of a diva rock star. He also smelled like pot and had long hair that looked like it hadn't been washed in a month, but hey, no one was perfect.

"He seems a lot more involved than Angel," Kyle said.

"Let's hope so," Jared said. "Either way, the mentors don't have a say anymore in who stays. From now on, viewers vote for whoever they like the most."

"So we just need to appeal to all of America somehow," I said with a sigh. "Piece of cake."

"All right, let's head into the studio," Dan said, waving us over. We followed him into a soundproofed room where our equipment was already waiting for us, like magic. "This will be your room for the rest of the time you're on the show, so go ahead and get settled in."

"Thanks for rescuing us," Jared said. "We really appreciate being given a second chance."

"Hey, I wanted you on my team from the start." Dan grabbed a stool to sit on. "Besides, I heard you got in a fight with Angel, and I'm a fan of anyone with the balls to stand up to her."

"Maddie threw coffee on her, too," Kyle said.

I scowled at him. "I didn't throw it. She bumped into me."

"Yeah?" Dan asked. "I need to hear this story."

Kyle told him all about it while we got set up, and Dan laughed along with us. "Damn, I knew she was neglecting her team, but I had no idea how bad it had gotten." He shook his head. "Well, you're on Team Dan now, so forget all that. Today we'll pick your song for the next episode, but mostly I want to talk about who you want to be as a band and how you can be better at that, both on stage and off."

For the next few minutes, we all brainstormed a song for that week's theme of "Sick of It All." Ultimately, we decided on "Uprising" by Muse, since it would give viewers a good idea of our sound and the kind of band we wanted to be. Even better, I already knew how to play it.

"That song has already been approved by the producers, so you're all set," Dan said, as he put on reading glasses and checked some papers in front of him. "I'll have the sheet music sent over tonight, but for now I'll give you some tips I wrote down after watching your other performances again. First, Jared, your voice is incredible, but your bass playing could be better. Did you start out on guitar, by any chance?"

"Yeah. I know I need to work on it."

"It's obvious to anyone who primarily plays bass, but you're not terrible either. Just remember that your job is to bridge the drums and the guitar. You need to provide the groove and the pulse for the entire song. Bass isn't as showy as the guitar, but it's just as important."

Jared exchanged a look with his brother like, "What is happening?" Dan was the bassist in Loaded River, so it didn't surprise me he had tips for Jared. Still, I was impressed Dan knew our names already and that he'd done his homework on us. Five minutes in and he was already a better mentor than Angel. We might actually learn something from him.

"Maddie, you're a strong guitarist," Dan continued. "In fact, from a technical standpoint, you might be the best guitarist on the show. But let me guess—you're a classically trained musician?"

I nodded, still reeling over him saying I might be the best guitarist here. That was so far from the truth I couldn't even consider it.

"I figured. You're too stiff when you play, like you're focusing too much on hitting the right notes and not on the emotion the music is conveying. You have the skills and you know the songs, but you don't *feel* them. You need to work on your stage presence and bring a little passion to your performance. I'll help you with that."

"Thanks." Everything he said about my stage presence was true, and I was eager to improve. I'd take any advice he had.

He gave the other guys some tips, too, and then said, "All of you need to remember, sometimes less is more. You need to learn to listen to the rest of the band and react to them, instead of just focusing on your own playing. This is what makes the strongest bands: cohesion. We'll work on that this week. But cohesion and raw talent aren't enough to win this show, especially since you're not exactly what the producers or record label are looking for."

"What do you mean?" Jared asked.

"Do you remember Addicted to Chaos? The last rock band that won *The Sound*, two seasons ago."

"They broke up after they won, right?" I asked. "When the singer and drummer got a divorce or something?"

"I remember that," Kyle said. "Didn't one of them get arrested, too?"

Dan nodded. "It was a total nightmare for the show. The divorce ripped the band apart, and they stopped showing up for the tour and bailed on recording their album. When the show sued them for breach of contract, they really went off the deep end, trashing concert halls and hotel rooms, getting in fights in bars.... The bassist even got hit with sexual assault charges. The show had a pretty bad rep for a while because of them, with the network threatening to cancel *The Sound* entirely. Ever since, the producers have wanted a nice, no-risk, low-drama winner. That means, no edgy rock bands and no bands that have any sort of romance angle at all."

"There is no romance angle," I said quickly. "We're just friends."

Jared shot me a sharp look, but said nothing.

"That's good," Dan said. "I know the show has been trying to feel out what kind of relationship you two have. They don't want another repeat of Addicted to

Chaos, so don't do anything to fuel those rumors about the two of you being together."

I nodded. Being part of the band and winning the show were the only things that mattered, and I couldn't let my attraction to Jared mess that up. I'd just have to stay away from him as much as possible over the next few weeks.

"Fine," Jared said, though he didn't sound happy about it. "But do we even have a shot at winning if they don't want another rock band?"

"Yes, because it's up to the voters who wins. No matter what the producers want, your band is one of the most popular ones this year. I think you can make it all the way to the end, but you'll need to keep winning the viewers over and not just when you're performing. I'll be coaching you on what to say in interviews, what to wear for the live shows, and how to act when you're in public. You have an image to keep up now. You're not just a band anymore—you're a *brand*, too. "

I wasn't sure how to process all of this. We could work on cohesion and I could try to avoid Jared, but I'd never thought about our "brand" before, other than how I dressed to fit in with the other guys. Now it sounded like everything we did from this point on would be scrutinized, especially if we didn't fit with what the producers wanted.

Dan checked the papers in front of him again. "Jared, from the rumors I've heard and things I've read online, you seem to be something of a playboy, right?"

Jared coughed and stared at the floor. "I guess so."

"Good. Play up that angle for the show. Stay single, flirt with women, make everyone at home think they could have a shot with you. That will prove you're not with Maddie and might get you more votes. Ladies love a bad boy."

Hector smirked. "Shouldn't be too hard for him."

Jared nodded, but his hands were clenched at his side. Dan's advice made me want to punch something, but I didn't know why it would bother Jared since it was the same thing he was already doing now.

"The rest of us don't have to do that, right?" Kyle asked. "Because I have a girlfriend."

"Nah, you're fine," Dan said. "In fact, you should mention that. You have the edgiest look in the band and having a steady girlfriend will make you seem more relatable. And Hector has the diversity angle covered, which is good for attracting a wider audience."

Hector scowled, and I didn't blame him. There was more to Hector than just being Latino.

"Hector's an artist," Jared added. "He has a graphic novel that just came out."

Dan wrote something down. "Okay, we'll see what we can do with that." He turned to study me again. "And to attract the male vote we'll have to make sure Maddie looks hot every week."

"Should I wear my contacts instead of my glasses?" I asked with a sigh.

"No, keep them. The glasses make you seem more relatable, more real, especially to other girls."

I hated this. For the live shows, it wasn't just about being musicians anymore; now we had to look and act certain ways to get votes. I just wanted to play my guitar, not worry about manipulating the viewers to like us, but I had no choice but to go with it for a few weeks. It was a game, and if that's what it took to be on the show until the end, so be it. And unfortunately, my contributions seemed to be "looking hot" and "not getting involved with Jared."

———

The next few days went by in a blur of practice, and Dan actually showed up for every single one of them for at least an hour while the camera crews filmed from the sidelines. We'd been working on everything he'd told us, and I could already tell we were improving a lot. One day Dan even had us switch instruments to try and give us a better understanding of each other. Turns out, I was terrible at drums (though they were fun), not too awful at bass (maybe I'd learn it next, once this was all over), and playing keyboard was as easy as guitar for me, even if I wasn't familiar with Kyle's setup. Hector was a disaster with anything other than the drums, while Kyle could scrape by on every instrument, even if he obviously never practiced them. Jared was good at everything, of course. It shouldn't surprise me, since he wrote most of the band's music, but it'd be nice if he were bad at something for once.

Our rehearsals were interspersed with photo shoots and interviews about what it was like to work with Dan now that we were on his team, along with questions like why we chose this song and why we wanted to win *The Sound*. Dan had coached us each on what to say, and we repeated his sound bites until they lost all meaning. The show especially loved to ask me and Jared about our relationship status. We both chimed in that we were single and, yes, we would definitely date a fan. Those lines sounded fake when I said them, but Jared was much better at pulling them off than I was. I avoided him entirely outside of rehearsal, which was easy since I kept to my room a lot…until Kyle insisted I come to their room to work on my stage presence.

Jared opened their door, wearing nothing but a towel around his waist. His wet hair hung in his face, and water dripped down his long, toned chest. I'd always wondered if Jared's tattoos continued under his shirt, and the answer was no, except for the word "VILLAIN" inked across his chest, just below his collarbone.

"Hey," he said. "I didn't know you were coming."

"Um…Kyle told me to stop by." Damn, it was really hard not to stare at him. My eyes followed the dark hair that trailed down his stomach and under the towel. *Please let that towel fall*, I thought. I'd never wished for something so hard in my life.

"Ugh, go put some clothes on," Kyle said from behind him.

Jared stood back to let me in, and I was careful not to get too close to his steaming, naked body as I walked past. He disappeared into the bathroom and shut the door, and I remembered how to breathe again.

Kyle rolled his eyes. "Sorry. I thought he was going to the gym with Hector."

There wasn't much room to practice, so we moved the desk and made space in front of the sliding doors to the balcony. Once that was done, I pulled out my acoustic guitar and checked the tuning. It wasn't as exciting as my electric guitar, but it would have to do since my Fender was still in Dan's studio.

Jared emerged from the bathroom wearing black jeans and a T-shirt with

Darth Vader that read, "Choking Hazard." If there was anything that could make him sexier to me, it was a geeky shirt. Dammit.

He sat on the bed beside Kyle, and they waited for me to start. I put my hands in position on my guitar, but still I hesitated. I'd played in front of the brothers dozens of times now, but for some reason, I was more nervous than ever today. Maybe because they were both watching me intently instead of playing alongside me. It was like my first night in their garage all over again. Except now I was in their bedroom, which made it even worse.

Jared must have sensed my reluctance because he grabbed his own guitar and plugged it into a small travel amp. I hadn't realized he'd brought his Fender to the hotel, the same one I'd played at his party all those nights ago. He started the opening to "Uprising," and with his music to concentrate on, I joined him on my own guitar. The mix of acoustic and electric sounded odd, but it didn't matter for this exercise.

Kyle examined me for a minute and then jumped up. "Your body is too stiff." He grabbed my arms and shook them a little. "You need to loosen up."

I dropped my guitar pick and then grabbed it off the floor. "I'm not that stiff."

"You look like you've got a piece of wood jammed up your ass," Kyle said.

"You *are* pretty stiff," Jared said. "Try moving your hips when you play. Like this."

He stood behind me and put his hands on my waist, and I sucked in a breath as he showed me what he meant. Heat rushed through my body as I imagined him sliding those hands lower, across my bare skin. He stepped back, and I remembered Kyle was still there, too, which cooled me off a little.

Jared took off his guitar and passed it to me. "Here, use mine. Playing with an acoustic guitar isn't the same."

I flushed as I put it on, remembering the previous time I'd used it. I started up again, trying to keep my arms loose and swinging my hips along with the beat, but I was so focused on moving that I missed notes and got all messed up and had to stop playing. Or maybe I was still flustered from Jared's hands on me.

Kyle squinted. "Well, that was terrible. You looked like you were in pain or something. This time try not to look like you've been set on fire and are trying to put it out."

I sighed and played the opening again, moving less and forcing myself to smile, but Kyle shook his head. "Nope. You look like a creepy doll with that grin."

"Ugh!" I flopped onto one of the beds, dropping the guitar next to me. "This is hopeless. I'm never going to be any good at this."

"We have to find something that works for you and doesn't make you look psychotic or like you're dying. Maybe—" Kyle stopped and fished his phone out of his pocket. "Shit, Alexis is here early. I've got to run. Sorry. We'll continue this tomorrow, okay?"

After his brother left, Jared sat on the edge of the bed near me. "Kyle's only trying to help you."

"I know. I just suck. I'm going to ruin everything for us." I threw my arm over my face. This bed was comfortable. Maybe I could just lie here forever, and then I'd never have to perform again. A perfect solution to this problem.

"You don't suck." He jumped up and grabbed his guitar again. "C'mon, maybe I can help. Kyle spends all his time on stage behind a keyboard anyway."

I sat up to watch him. I was willing to try anything at this point, and let's be honest, I always enjoyed seeing Jared perform.

"For me, the trick is to feel the music and move along with it. Tap your foot, nod your head, whatever feels natural." He started the opening again and leaned back, stretching his long body as he played. I stared at the spot where his stubble trailed off on his neck, yearning to press my mouth there. I imagined the way it would feel to slide my fingers under his shirt and across his toned stomach. I wanted to see that tattoo on his chest again.

He stopped and frowned at me. "What?"

What was *wrong* with me? I dropped my gaze and grabbed my own guitar. "Nothing."

This time I tried to feel the music as I played, but it didn't come as easily for me as it did for him. The truth was, I was still too distracted from picturing all the things I wanted to do to him. It was like avoiding Jared had only made my desire for him increase, and now that we were alone—and now that I knew what he looked like without any clothes on—I found it even harder to resist him.

"That was better," he said. "But I can tell you're still holding back."

No kidding. If I was in this room with Jared for one more second, I might not be able to stop from touching him. Where was Hector? Shouldn't he be back from the gym by now?

"This isn't working," I said. "Maybe we can try again tomorrow." Tomorrow, when the other guys were here, too, and I could focus on something other than being alone in a hotel room with the hottest guy I'd ever met.

"Hang on, I have another idea."

I sighed. "I don't know…"

"Let's try playing something together, something just for fun."

"Like what?"

"Do you know this one?" he asked and then started up "Blitzkrieg Bop" by The Ramones. It was one of those songs most rock guitarists learned since it was simple but a lot of fun to play. I reluctantly joined in when the chords repeated again. When he got to the chorus, I sang along too, and he grinned at me.

As the song went on, I loosened up and let myself get into the music with him, tapping my foot to the beat. We jammed on our guitars and grew louder and more ridiculous, not caring if the people in the rooms next to us complained. It was the kind of song you could easily be silly and over the top with, and by the end, we were bouncing around and belting out the words like we were drunk.

When it ended, I fell back on the bed and laughed, my pulse racing. Playing with Jared like this, banging on our guitars and singing at the top of our lungs without caring what we sounded like, it was different from playing alone or with the band or even in front of Julie and Carla. With one song, Jared had reminded me why I loved playing guitar in the first place.

He crashed on the bed next to me, and we stared at the ceiling as we caught our breath. After a minute, he propped himself up on one arm to look at me. "I'm impressed you could sing all the words to that one. Who knew piano player Maddie had this hidden punk rocker inside her?"

"No one. Before I joined the band, guitar was a secret, a guilty pleasure. Something I only did when I was alone in my room."

He raised an eyebrow. "And yet you picked up my guitar at a party and played one of my songs like you had written it yourself."

I covered my face with my hands and groaned. "I knew you'd bring that up eventually."

"Hey, I'm flattered. Besides, it worked out in the end." He trailed a finger across my arm, his touch soft, making me shiver. "I saw the real you that night, and just now I saw her again. That's the trick. When you're on stage, play like you do when you think no one's watching."

I dropped my hands to stare up at his face, so close to mine I could smell the shampoo he'd used. I wanted to kiss him so badly my body ached with it. It wasn't just how his hair was still wet, framing his blue eyes and dark lashes, or the way the tattoos on his arms stood out against his otherwise flawless skin or how his voice made me forget everything but him. It was the Jared I discovered every time we were alone together, the one who somehow found the real me and set her free.

His hand cupped my face and his head dipped lower, lightly brushing his lips across mine. Little warning lights flashed in my head. What was I doing, lying on a bed with Jared, about to kiss him? This couldn't happen. Not only because of what Dan had said about the producers and the show, but because I knew if I fell for Jared, I might never recover.

I pressed a hand against his chest. "I'm sorry. I have to go, um, to dinner. With my friends. Right now."

He stared at me while I jumped up and stuffed my guitar back into the case. "Maddie—"

"I'll see you tomorrow." I ran for the door before he could even get up.

Once outside the elevator, I pushed the button a hundred times until it arrived. Only when I stepped inside and the door shut did I allow myself to relax. That had been way too close. Kissing Jared could only lead to heartbreak, and it would ruin everything with the band and with the show. But how was I supposed to resist him for another three weeks?

Chapter Twelve

The crowd screamed as the lights went up and the four mentors walked to their seats, waving at the audience. Ray Carter appeared on stage, his black hair shining, and he flashed a big smile.

"Welcome to *The Sound!* This is the first live show, and tonight's theme is 'Sick of It All.' Starting now, your votes will determine who stays and who goes, and ultimately, who wins *The Sound*. We have some amazing performances lined up, so let's get started! But first, let's talk to the mentors about their bands and what they're hoping to see from them."

I watched from the screens in the lounge and then turned away to get some coffee. After a full day of hair, makeup, wardrobe, and soundchecks, I was already exhausted—and we still had another hour before we went on stage.

Mohawk Girl was filling up on coffee, too, wearing a green plaid skirt with a studded corset and matching choker. "Hey," she said as I grabbed a cup.

"Hey." I wasn't sure what to say to her. We'd never really talked before. I didn't even know her name.

"You're a lucky girl."

"Huh?" Had I missed something? Maybe I was more out of it than I'd thought.

"You and Jared," she said, nodding to where he sat with Kyle. He looked over at us, as if he'd somehow heard his name, and winked.

"Oh. We're not together." I dumped a bunch of sugar and cream into my coffee and stirred it, hoping this conversation would end already. She was not helping with my plan of thinking about Jared as little as possible.

"Yeah?" She leaned against the table, with no intention of leaving. "I tried to get him up to my room the other night, but he wouldn't go for it. I figured it's 'cause he's with you."

"Nope. We're just friends." I was tired of repeating that phrase, but maybe if I said it over and over, I'd start to believe it, too.

She nudged my side with a bony elbow, which kind of hurt. "Uh huh. He can't keep his eyes off you. If you're not tapping that now, you need to get on it before someone else does."

I was sure my face had turned bright red, despite the layers of makeup on it. "Um…thanks for the advice."

"No problem. Good luck tonight."

"You too."

She went back to her band and I sipped my coffee, going over her words. All the rumors I'd heard about Jared made it seem like he would sleep with any girl who offered, and Dan had told him to encourage this reputation. But to be honest, I'd never actually *seen* Jared do anything beyond flirting, and hearing he'd turned down this girl who had thrown herself at him was a huge relief. But even if Jared *was* interested in me, he and I had to stay apart as long as we were on the show. Besides, I doubted he wanted anything beyond a quick fling, like his former bassist had been.

Bands moved in and out of the lounge as they waited for their sets or recovered afterward, and I admired all of their costumes. Compared to some of them, our band's sleek, futuristic, black-and-red military uniforms looked almost tame. Of course, mine had a short skirt and a low-cut jacket with nothing underneath, while the guys got pants and a jacket that completely covered them. Dan said it was necessary for the "young male vote," but the blatant sexism still made me want to set my costume on fire, even if I did look pretty hot in it—especially with the tall black heels that made my legs look longer.

The Static Klingons took the stage and performed "Pumped Up Kicks" by Foster the People, which the audience seemed to enjoy. When they were done, Sean ran over to me with a giant smile. "Maddie!"

"Hey, Sean. Great performance!"

"Thanks!" He reached out a little, like he wanted to hug me, but then pulled back when I didn't respond. "I'm so sorry about the Angel thing. I just feel horrible about how it all went down."

"Don't worry about it—really." Not this again. I'd seen Sean a few times in the hotel lobby since our battle, and he always apologized for getting us kicked off Angel's team. Truthfully, I should be apologizing to him, since we now had a better mentor and he was still stuck with Angel.

"Are you doing something tonight after the show? Do you want to get something to eat or…?"

While Sean talked, Jared watched us with a scowl on his face. Probably worried I was giving away all our secrets again.

Hang on, was Sean asking me out on a date? I must have waited a little too long to answer because then he added, "You know, to talk strategy and stuff and, uh, just hang out… "

Now I was even more confused. Did he actually like me or was he trying to get info out of me? I couldn't tell, but it didn't really matter because I had no interest in going out with him. "Sorry, I can't tonight. I have a meeting with the band."

"No problem. Maybe later this week?" His drummer called his name, and he turned to wave at him. "I've got to run, but we'll talk later!"

He bounced off to join his band, saving me from further conversation. I'd need another excuse to avoid a date with him later, assuming we both lasted that long on the show. Who knew if either of our bands would still be around after tonight?

The Quiet Battles, the folk band on Team Dan, went before us with a song I didn't know, and there were so many of them they barely fit on the stage. Did they even have enough instruments for all of them to play? I saw a harmonica, a violin, and a banjo, and one guy even "played" a plastic bag, if you could call it that. I'm not sure crinkling it in front of a microphone counted as playing, but I was trying hard not to judge. They also had two complete drum kits. Who needed *two* drum kits? If The White Stripes could be the loudest band ever with only two members, there was just no need for that.

Next it was our turn. Our equipment was already set up on the back of the revolving stage, and we quickly got in place and waited while The Quiet Battles got comments from the mentors. The thrill of going on stage made every nerve in my body tingle. I wasn't scared this time; instead, I was anxious to get back out there and perform again. Playing on stage was my drug, and I was an addict now.

The stage began to revolve, and the crowd swelled in front of us. As red lights flashed behind us and smoke filled the air, the guys started playing. I waited, tapping my foot along with the beat, and then my fingers took off across my guitar with the eerie opening notes. Hector's steady rhythm centered us and Kyle clapped along to get the audience going while Jared's voice filled the theater. I nodded my head with the music and leaned into my mic to sing the backup chant at the end of each verse. The bass line Jared pulled off was almost hypnotic, and as his fingers moved up and down the fret board, I imagined those same fingers playing across my skin. I watched his lips caress the mic as he sang and pictured him doing the same to me. And as his voice rang out from the speakers, I wondered what it'd be like to hear him cry out my name instead.

Damn, I needed to get a grip. I stomped on my pedal to change the tone and forced myself to focus. Jared's advice about playing like no one was watching came back to me, and I tried to let myself fall into the song. Dan and the guys had told me to move more, so I started walking across the stage toward Jared, as if his words were pulling me to him. But when I neared him, I tripped on a cord in my stupid tall heels. I tried to catch myself to prevent a complete face-plant but ended up stumbling off the edge of the stage, on top of a very large security guard.

The audience gasped, and Jared's voice choked on the lyrics. For a second, I just sat there, stunned and horrified by what had happened. I couldn't tell if I was injured or not, my body still in the post-fall adrenaline shock. I got to my feet quickly, the audience pressing around me, on my level now with only the security guards keeping them away. Sweat dripped down my back, under my clothes. I had to escape, from the cameras, from the crowd, from this complete disaster of a performance. I glanced around, looking for an exit, but there was no way out.

Behind me, tiny explosions went off on the side of the stage, and the band kept going. No, I couldn't run. I couldn't abandon the guys, who were still trying to keep it together without me. No matter how embarrassed I was, the show had to go on.

I waved to show I was okay and then hopped up to sit on the edge of the stage. Kyle had filled in for me, but now it was time for the guitar solo. All I could do was go for it and try not to think about how I'd just ruined everything. With my legs hanging into the crowd and the security guards holding people back, I played my heart out. The high notes squealed as my fingers flew, and I blocked the world out, closing my eyes and letting the song take over. Just me and my guitar and an intimate performance with 7,500 of my closest friends. And somehow, it worked.

After the solo ended with the last hard riffs, I jumped back on stage with a little help from the poor security guard I'd tackled, and the crowd went crazy. I returned to my mic and joined in with Jared on the last chorus, and we ended together in perfect harmony.

The audience's cheers shook the theater, and even the mentors looked shocked by our performance. Jared threw one arm around me, holding his other arm out to the audience like I'd just won a prize or something. He whispered in my ear, "Are you hurt?"

"No, I don't think so." I leaned against him while Kyle and Hector joined us, adrenaline still pumping through my veins. Soon we were all holding onto each other, feeling the audience's enthusiasm like tremors coursing under our feet.

Ray sprinted across the stage. "Wow, what an…unexpected performance! That was Villain Complex on Team Dan. Angel, they used to be on your team and you let them go last week. Are you regretting it now?"

"Sure." She shrugged and inspected her nails, like she was bored with it all. Whatever, Angel.

"Lance, what did you think?" Ray asked.

"Great song choice. What I want to know is, what happened with that fall?"

The host shoved the mic in my face, and I froze. This was all live and Jared was so much better at this stuff, but I decided to be honest.

"That was an accident, but I thought, whatever, I'm going to own it. Sometimes I fall down, but I get back up again and keep going. That's life, right?"

The crowd screamed again so I must have said the right thing, and Jared squeezed me tighter

"Very wise words," Ray said. "Lissa, what did you think?"

"I thought it was brilliant how you turned an accident into a triumph. That's so important in this line of work because things do go wrong sometimes, and you just have to roll with it."

"Very true. Dan, they're the newest member of your team—how did they do?"

"All I can say is, I'm so glad I rescued them from Angel. What were you *thinking*?" He leaned over to smirk at our former mentor, who huffed and crossed her arms. When she didn't respond, he sat back and continued. "They've already improved so much in the week I've been working with them, and I can't wait to see what they do next week. I'm really proud."

My heart swelled at Dan's words, and it sounded like he actually meant them, too. He must think we weren't completely doomed if he was already talking about next week. I prayed my screw-up tonight hadn't cost us our spot on the show.

"Now it's up to you at home," Ray said, staring at the camera. "If you like

Villain Complex, download their song and vote for them on the website or by texting or calling this number."

The stage turned so the next band could play, and roadies ran around us and broke down our gear. Kyle wrapped me in a big bear hug as soon as we were out of view. "Are you all right? Are you injured?"

"No, I'm not injured," I muttered into his shoulder, which was pressed against my face. I tried to pull away, but he had me in a death grip. "Really, I'm fine!"

"Are you sure?" Jared asked, when I finally broke apart from his brother. "Does it hurt anywhere?"

"I can't feel anything, but that might be the adrenaline. Tomorrow I might wake up with a broken leg or something, but at the moment, I feel great."

Hector thumped me on the back, knocking all the air out of me. "That was hardcore, Maddie. Not sure I could have done that."

"Um, thanks."

The show had a medic check me out before they let me do anything else. She said one of my ankles was twisted and told me to ice it and stay off my feet for a day or two. Someone found me some flip flops, and then we had another interview with Ray about how we felt about the performance. He said I was really brave, but I replied that I just didn't want to let the other guys down. When he asked them what they thought, Jared leaned into the mic and said, "I nearly had a heart attack when she fell off stage, so I'm just happy she's okay."

We had to return to the stage with all the other bands on Team Dan one more time to wave while Ray reminded everyone at home how to vote, and the other musicians all patted me on the back and asked if I was okay. I may have fallen, but this felt like a victory.

Chapter Thirteen

By the time we got back to the hotel, I didn't think I could keep my eyes open even a second longer. Plus my ankle had started to throb now that the buzz from the performance had worn off. Even breathing seemed tough. Maybe I was more beat up from the fall than I'd thought.

I wanted to crawl right into bed, but the guys said we should check the Internet and see what people were saying about us. I was too tired to argue and soon found myself in their room again, sitting beside Jared on the bed while he opened up his laptop.

"Don't forget to vote for us, too," Kyle said. "And remind everyone to vote by 10 AM tomorrow."

I checked my phone and saw that Carla and Julie had been sending me panicked texts for the last hour or so. I texted them back that I was okay and reminded them to vote for us. I'd call them both tomorrow and give them the full scoop when I wasn't so tired. That reminded me: I'd never called my mom like I'd promised Julie I would. I'd meant to do it, but things had been so busy these past few days and I'd completely forgotten. Yet another thing to add to my to-do list.

"Holy shit," Jared said, staring at his screen. "Our Twitter account shot up to thirty thousand followers tonight."

"Thirty thousand?" I asked, choking out the words. Last I'd heard, we were at ten thousand. Kyle and Hector crowded around us to see the screen, and Hector whistled.

"That's good, right?" Kyle asked. "That means we're going to get enough votes to stay this week?"

"Maybe," Jared said. "Some of the other bands have fifty thousand. We should post more photos on Instagram and Tumblr. That might bring in more fans."

"I can ask Alexis to take photos of us rehearsing one day," Kyle said.

"Good idea."

"Thirty thousand," I repeated, still in shock. "We have *thirty thousand* fans?"

"Probably more actually," Jared said. "There's a huge segment of older people who watch the show who aren't on Twitter. I'll make sure our Facebook page is updated, too, and the website…" He rubbed his face, looking tired, and for the first time, I appreciated how Jared ran the entire business side of the band by himself. I had no idea how he kept up with it all on top of the rehearsals and other things we had to do for the show. I could barely find time to eat, sleep, and shower.

"What are people saying about tonight?" Kyle asked.

"I don't want to know," I said, biting my nails. "Unless it's good. No, don't tell me. Oh, god, it's probably all over YouTube already."

"Some people seem to think what happened was cool," Jared said. "One girl tweeted, 'I love how she kept playing, she's so fierce!'"

"I don't feel very fierce, but that's nice of her to say. What else?" I leaned over again, trying to get a glimpse of his screen.

"Nothing." He quickly yanked the laptop away, but not before I saw "four-eyed cow" and "she only did that to get attention."

"Is that what people really think of me?" I tried to reach for the laptop, but he passed it to Hector on the other bed.

"Only stupid people who shouldn't be allowed on the Internet," Jared said. "Besides, we're trending on Twitter, so I think your fall off the stage might end up being a good thing."

"The world is full of haters," Hector said. "Don't let them get to you."

"I guess so." Those comments stung, but I was too tired to stress about them right now. I yawned and checked the time. "I should get to bed."

As soon as I stood up, my ankle went out from under me with a sharp pain. I yelped and slammed into the side of the bed, bracing against it for support.

Jared was at my side instantly. "Do you need help?"

Kyle jumped up, too. "Should I get some ice?"

Talk about embarrassing. I didn't need both brothers hovering over me like this. I stood up a little slower this time, balancing on one foot. "I'm okay. I just got up too fast. I'll be fine after I get some sleep."

Jared slid his arm into mine, and every nerve in my body woke up. "Come on, I'll take you back to your room. I need to walk off some of this energy before bed anyway."

"You don't need to do this," I said as we moved to the elevator together. "I can get back by myself."

"I'm not going anywhere until I make sure you get to your room safely. I can't have my guitarist injuring herself again." He winked and hit the elevator button while I leaned against him, taking comfort in his strength. His breath ruffled my hair as he quietly added, "Besides, I'm worried about you."

The elevator door opened, and we stumbled in. "Really, Jared, I'm fine. It's just a twisted ankle, not that big a deal—"

The door shut and his lips were on mine, cutting me off mid-sentence. His kiss was tentative and searching, a question he wanted me to answer, but I was so surprised I just stood there while my brain caught up to what was happening.

He pulled away and ran a hand through his dark hair. "Sorry. I've wanted to do that forever, and when I saw you fall…"

My mouth opened but no sound came out. I swallowed and tried again. "You've wanted to do that forever?"

"I know it's a bad idea. We have to stay single while we're on the show, and the guys would kill me if they found out, and you're into that Sean guy anyway…" His voice trailed off, and he looked away.

I'd never seen Jared be anything but cool and confident, and it sent a thrill through me, knowing I'd done that to him. The elevator didn't move, waiting for us to hit a button, but suddenly I didn't want to go back to my room anymore. I grabbed the collar of Jared's jacket and pulled him down to my mouth, kissing him hard, showing him that he was the one I wanted.

We broke apart long enough for me to whisper, "It *is* a bad idea, but I don't care."

"Good. Because I can't resist you any longer." And then our mouths met again.

We kissed like we were drowning and our only hope of living was each other. He devoured my mouth with his tongue and lips while I tangled my fingers into his thick hair, drawing him closer. Knowing we shouldn't be doing this only gave our passion a desperate edge, a recklessness that had us gasping and clawing at each other, like we had to cram everything into this one brief moment we were alone. His hands slid down to cup my butt and lift me to his height, my back slamming against the side of the elevator, my skirt riding up to my hips. While he pinned me to the wall and teased me with his mouth, I smoothed my hands across his rough jaw, down his neck, along his broad shoulders. After weeks of fighting my desire for Jared, I needed to touch every inch of him, with my fingers, with my lips, with my entire body.

The elevator started moving, though neither of us had pushed a button. It said, "Lobby," and reality came crashing back, like a bucket of water had been tossed on us. We broke apart to opposite corners, breathing heavily. I yanked my skirt down just as the door opened.

Lacey, the blonde country singer from Fairy Lights, stood there wearing the sexy school uniform she'd performed in when she'd sung "Mean" by Taylor Swift tonight. Her eyes honed in on Jared as she sauntered in and hit the button for her floor.

"Hey there," she said, her voice accented with a Southern twang.

"Hey." Jared's hair was messy, but otherwise you'd never be able to tell he'd just been kissing me.

She touched his arm with a pink fingernail after the door closed. "I heard you're the guy to see if a girl is lonely at night."

Her words spread like ice in my blood, cooling my passion instantly. Did Jared get this a lot? How many girls' rooms had he visited in the few weeks we'd been here?

"That's me," Jared said, but he sounded tired. "How old are you anyway?"

"Seventeen."

He took her hand off him. "Sorry, we only serve eighteen and up here."

"Don't worry. I won't tell anyone." She flicked her hair and looked at him from under her long, fake eyelashes. "It'll be our little secret."

"I'm sure your mother would love that. She has to be here while you're on the show, right?" He moved around her to stab the button for my floor, like he couldn't wait to get away. I accidentally let out a faint chuckle, and she glared at me. Oops.

"Whatever." She crossed her arms and turned her back to us, and it was a very long ride to her floor.

After she got out, Jared let out a long breath. "What she said…just ignore her. That's not me."

I met his eyes but didn't respond. Jared had a reputation he had to maintain for the show, but I couldn't tell how much of it was based on truth and how much was an act. I didn't know what to believe anymore. Was the real Jared the one I saw when we were alone or the one I saw flirting with other girls and getting texts from them wanting to hook up? And now that I'd stopped kissing him, all my reasons for staying away from him came back to me. There could be no *us*; there could only be me and Jared, two separate entities, as long as we were on the show.

We made it into my room, and he leaned against the doorframe, not stepping inside but not leaving either. He dipped his hands into his pockets, fixing me with a smoldering gaze as he waited for me to make the next move. I could invite him in, but I knew where that would lead. Despite how much I wanted him, we couldn't let things go any further tonight.

"Do you need anything else?" he asked, with a quirk of his lips that hinted at a hidden offer behind his words.

"No, I think I'm okay. Thank you." But I couldn't stop myself from moving until our bodies were only an inch apart, his breath on my skin as I looked up at him. He drew me to him like a magnet, and there was only so much attraction I could resist.

He dipped his head, crossing the space between us. His mouth brushed my ear as he whispered, "Don't forget to ice your ankle."

God, he drove me crazy in the best way when he got like this, the way he was always looking out for me. "Yes, doctor."

His hand slipped into my hair, and he kissed me slow this time, tender, tilting my head back to explore my mouth without the frenzy of before. He teased one finger under the bottom hem of my shirt, burning a line across my skin, and I gasped. Our kiss grew deeper, and I pressed myself against him, gripping his jacket to draw him closer. I couldn't get enough of him, of the taste of his soft lips, of his masculine scent, of the way he felt under my hands.

"I need to go," he whispered between kisses. "Kyle is going to wonder why it's taking me so long."

I sighed. "I know."

He kissed me one last time, and I clutched his jacket and held him there, not wanting him to leave but unable to ask him to stay. I dreaded the reality of tomorrow, when we'd have to face what had happened and what it meant for the band. But finally, I let him go.

Chapter Fourteen

The next morning I was bruised and sore all over, my ankle was the size of a small country, and my mouth felt like it had been rubbed with sandpaper. All signs pointed to last night not being a dream, which meant today I had to deal with the aftermath of what I'd done.

Okay, technically Jared had kissed me first, but then he'd given me the chance to end it right there. I could have walked away and laughed it off later, but instead I'd crossed the line, passed the point of no return, and all those other clichés. There was no going back to the way things were before unless we both admitted it had been a mistake. Except…it hadn't felt like a mistake. It had felt like fate, like every moment since I'd met Jared had led me to this surprising, yet inevitable, conclusion.

I never wanted to get out of bed because then I'd have to face him again and figure out what to do about us. Luckily, the show's medic had told me to rest with my foot elevated until we had to be at the Nokia Theatre for the results show. The bands didn't perform tonight, so we only had to show up and pray we'd gotten enough votes to move on. They'd probably want to interview us again, too, because they never seemed to have enough interviews of us saying how great being on the show was.

I called Julie and then Carla to give them the update, but I didn't mention kissing Jared. I'd tell them eventually, but for now it was too new, too raw, too uncertain. Maybe last night had been a fluke, a one-time thing. Maybe today he'd regret it ever happened. Maybe tonight he'd be with someone else.

I shoved those thoughts to the back of my head. There was one other call I couldn't put off any longer, no matter how much I dreaded it.

"Hey, Mom," I said when she picked up.

"Madison, I was just thinking about you. How are things?" I heard the TV on behind her, with noises that sounded like a game show.

"Things are…good." I wasn't sure how much she knew about, well, anything. Even when I told her something important, she often didn't listen or forgot it soon after. It was easier to keep silent about my life most of the time. "There's something I have to tell you. I'm not doing that internship I mentioned before. I'm actually um…in a band. And we're on that TV show, *The Sound*."

She sighed. "I know."

"You know?" Why hadn't she called me? Never mind—that would have taken effort on her part.

"Of course. I watch the show. I didn't realize you still played the guitar."

"Oh. Yeah." I paused for her to say something else, to tell me how I was wasting my talent and how guitar wasn't a real instrument, but it never came. "I'm sorry I didn't tell you sooner, about the band and the show and…everything. It just happened so fast and everything got crazy and I've been so busy…"

"Hmm. I saw you last night. Looked like a bad fall."

"I twisted my ankle, but otherwise I'm okay. I'm icing it now."

"Good, good." Another pause. She sounded far away, like she was barely listening. Probably distracted by her show and her cigarettes. This is why I never called her; neither of us knew what to say to the other. "How's school?"

That was it for her interest in the show, aka the biggest thing that had ever happened to me. No words of encouragement, questions about how it was going, or good luck wishes. Why was I even surprised? And this question sounded like something she felt obligated to ask, rather than actual interest. "School is good. One more year and all."

"Is that all?"

"Yep, just one." Did she really not know that? Mother of the Year, for sure. I adjusted the ice on my ankle, but I needed a new pack. Perfect—an excuse to hang up. There was one last thing I needed to talk to her about, but I hated this part. Julie had said my mom looked better, but I had to hear it for myself. "How are you doing? With…you know…"

"I'm not drinking again, if that's what you're asking," she snapped. "Sober for three months now, thank you very much."

"That's great, Mom."

"Yes, well, it's not a big deal." There was another long pause. "Did you tell your father about the show?"

My fingers dug into the side of my phone. She always did this. I'd ask her about her drinking, and in return, she'd bring *him* up. Even though I'm sure it brought her just as much pain to talk about him. "No, and I don't plan to."

"He's your father."

"Tell that to his real family."

She huffed into the phone. "Suit yourself."

Neither of us said anything for a minute, and I tried to think of a way to end this on a better note. Nothing came to mind.

"I voted for your band last night," my mom said.

"You did?" It was a small gesture, and yet, for a mother who thought anything more than changing the channel was a chore, it was huge. Maybe it was her own way of saying she supported me. "Thanks, Mom."

After we hung up, I found my father's contact info in my phone. I probably *should* tell him about the show at some point. But as my finger hovered over the CALL button, I just couldn't do it.

———

By the afternoon, my ankle was good enough to walk on, so that medic did know what she was talking about. I headed to the lobby to meet the other guys, my stomach heavy with dread. I hadn't heard anything from Jared since last night. Not that I'd contacted him either, but still. He was the one who'd initiated this mess. He could have texted me at least.

I spotted him the second I walked out of the elevator, sitting at the lobby bar with a blonde leaning close to him, hands pressed against his chest. Typical. He met my eyes and something crossed his face, but I'd seen enough. I walked out of the revolving doors and stood under the warm summer sun, hoping it would burn away the jealousy swirling through my veins like poison. What had I expected really? That's who Jared was—the guy with girls all over him, who slept with one and then immediately moved on to the next. Kyle had warned me, and Dan had encouraged it, so I couldn't even say I hadn't known what I was getting myself into. I was mostly angry with myself, since I'd let myself fall for Jared's easy charm and good looks. Last night I'd been drunk on the moment, still high from the performance, half-asleep and delirious, but during the light of day everything was clear again.

I checked the time. The other guys were running late and Jared might walk out any moment, and I wasn't ready to deal with him yet. Screw it, I'd walk to the theater by myself. They could catch up. It wasn't far—just a short walk across LA Live past the restaurants, shops, and the Staples Center. It was empty this time of day with most of downtown's population still at work, and a faint breeze blew my hair back, helping cool me down by the time I got to the theater.

Even though we weren't performing, we still had to go through hair and makeup, plus a brief run-through so we'd know where to stand on stage at various points. The winner of last year's show was performing tonight, followed by a duo between Angel and Lance, along with recaps of last night's show and eliminations from each team. That gave us a lot of free time to sit around and wait for Team Dan to be called up.

As the night went on, I managed to steer clear of Jared by hiding in the bathroom whenever we might be alone together. Kyle must have noticed something was off though because he cornered me when I finally came out.

"Everything okay?" he asked.

"Just checking the ankle and all that." It was throbbing a little from all the walking around, but not too bad. Still, it was the only explanation I had for spending all night in the bathroom.

"That's not what I meant." He combed his black hair back, forehead creased. "Did something else happen last night with Jared?"

"Nope. Nothing happened." I hated lying to him, but I couldn't tell him the truth about me and Jared. Best case, he'd say, "I told you so." Worst case, he'd want me to leave the band when the show was over. Besides, kissing Jared had been a brief moment of weakness, and it wouldn't happen again. There was no reason to bring it up.

"Are you going to be able to rehearse tomorrow?" he asked.

"Yeah, but remind me to not fall off a stage ever again."

"I thought that would be obvious, but sure." He grinned, and my shoulders relaxed. I didn't want anything to be weird between us. Before I'd joined the band, we'd been the kind of friends who always sat next to each other in class and did homework together, but we'd never hung out much otherwise. Everything had changed that night after his show, and even if this thing with Jared was a mess, I was still happy I'd gone to that party.

"I'm really glad you joined the band," he said, echoing my thoughts.

"Me too." And there was the guilt again.

I was this close to spilling everything, but he led me back to the lounge. "C'mon, it's almost time for the Team Dan elimination."

Jared frowned as we entered together. "Everything okay?"

"Fine," Kyle said, shooting his brother a dark look. He must suspect I wasn't telling him everything, but there was no time to worry about that now. We had bigger things to stress about, like whether or not we'd still be on the show after tonight.

We joined the other bands backstage and waited until it was time for Team Dan to go on. Team Lissa went before us, and when Fairy Lights was saved, Ray yelled, "And America's sweetheart continues to the next round!" Ugh, when had they started calling Lacey that? She gave a pageant wave and dashed off the stage, where she was met by an older woman with big Texas hair. Her mother, I guessed.

When Team Dan was up, the show's people arranged it so Hector and Kyle would walk out first, with Jared and me behind them. Ray's voice echoed from onstage, preparing for our arrival.

"Maddie, can we talk?" Jared whispered, his mouth close to my ear.

I flushed with the memory of those lips on me. Dammit, I wanted to kiss him again. Must. Resist. "Later."

"How about coffee after the show?"

"I can't. My ankle—" I started.

He raised an eyebrow. "Would you rather I come to your room?"

"No!" They started waving us onto stage, but Jared didn't move, still waiting for my answer. I couldn't think of a good excuse, and I couldn't avoid him forever either. "Fine, we'll have coffee. Now can we go?"

We followed the other guys on stage, waving and smiling at the audience. This was the real trick to being an entertainer: pretending everything was great while your life was falling apart around you. Our lives were covered in gold foil, but if you scratched hard enough, you'd see the rust underneath.

We lined up with the other bands just as we'd practiced earlier, and Ray opened an envelope. "The first band to be saved is…The Quiet Battles!" Everyone clapped, and the many members of the folk band hugged each other. The wait was killing me, and I nearly grabbed Jared's hand but restrained myself. Instead I wrung my hands over and over while Ray took his sweet time announcing the next name.

"The second band is…As We Die!"

That was the Christian heavy metal band—leaving us and the reggae group for the elimination. *Please don't let us go home yet,* I silently prayed.

"And the final band is…Villain Complex!"

Relief swept through me, and I almost jumped up and down, except that would be bad for my ankle. Instead we cheered and hugged each other, and the three bands still on Team Dan left the stage in a whirlwind of applause and bright lights while the reggae band said their goodbyes behind us. We were safe, for one more week anyway.

———

Jared and I agreed to meet three blocks from the hotel at a small hole-in-the-wall coffee shop where no one would see us. He was already sitting at a table in the corner when I arrived, playing with the lid from his cup and gazing out the window. I ordered a coffee and sat across from him. I didn't know what to say or think or even what I hoped would come out of this conversation. When his blue eyes met mine, I was torn between wanting things to go back to the way they were and recklessly wanting to kiss him again.

"Maddie, about last night…"

In that pause I heard it all. I clutched my cup so hard the lid popped off and coffee spilled over the edge and onto the table. Jared handed me a napkin, and I mopped it up.

"Sorry," I said. Did these kinds of things happen to other girls, or was the universe just mocking me now?

"It's okay." He sucked in a breath, but I cut in before he could start again.

"I already know what you're going to say, and it's fine." If I said it, it would feel less like he was rejecting me and more like I'd decided this myself. Which I had. Really.

"You do?"

I nodded while I formed a pile of wet napkins on the table. "And I agree. Last night was a mistake, it can't happen again, and we should just be friends." His eyes widened and he opened his mouth, but I went on. "It's fine. Really." I gave a short laugh that sounded more like a choking sound. "We both got caught up in the excitement from the show. Don't worry about it."

"Yeah." He fidgeted with the heat protector on his cup and cleared his throat. "Kyle and Hector would lose their shit if anything happened between us anyway."

"I know, right?" This time it was easier to laugh.

He ran a hand through his hair and stared out the window. I thought he'd be relieved, but he looked as tortured as I felt and it tugged at my heart.

"Not okay?" I asked, trying to keep it light, yet also hoping it would remind him of all the times he'd asked me that.

"Of course I'm okay." He smiled at me, but it was missing the normal luster.

We both played with our cups and looked at anything but each other. Our usual easy banter had vanished, and my chest ached with everything I really wanted to say. I didn't know if I could go back to being friends with Jared. Just being near him made me sick with longing, and every time I saw him with another girl, I felt violent. But ending it now would be better for both of us and for the band.

After a few minutes of uncomfortable small talk, we finished our drinks and walked out. The late summer sun had set while we'd been inside, and now the streets were packed with cars and bathed in the glow of headlights. Jared kept his hands shoved in his pockets, and neither of us spoke. I just wanted this night to be over already. Why was the hotel so far away?

We passed between the thick pillars of a tall office building, and Jared stopped. "Maddie, wait." I turned to see his eyes pleading with me. "Back there—that wasn't what I was going to say."

"It wasn't?"

"No." He moved closer, and my breath caught. "Last night *wasn't* a mistake. I *want* it to happen again. And I *don't* want to be friends." His head bowed, and his lips hovered near mine, tempting me with how close they were. "Do you?"

"No, I don't want to be friends." Lady Gaga's "Bad Romance" popped into my head as I said it. That's what happened when you thought in music. "But what about the show? And…your reputation?"

"We'll figure something out. But Maddie, I swear, you're the only one I want."

I'd been dying to hear those words for weeks. Our mouths met, forced together by the unstoppable release of pent-up desire. He pressed me back against a pillar, using one arm to shade us from anyone who might see. With his other hand, he gripped my hip, digging his fingers into the fabric of my dress while he kissed me long and hard until I was practically moaning for more. I slid my hands down his chest and under his shirt, running my fingers across his bare stomach like I'd fanta-sized about for weeks. He tugged at my bottom lip with his teeth, driving me crazy, making me forget all the reasons we couldn't be together. I didn't know what we were doing or where this would lead, but I didn't want to stop.

"We should go to the hotel," I said, breathing heavily.

"I like the sound of that."

We walked side-by-side, stealing glances and smiles whenever we could. I still found it hard to believe that, out of all the girls he'd flirted with, he'd chosen me. He was just so different from the normal guys I went out with. I usually dated guys like Sean—friendly and nice, safe but not particularly exciting. But I was done with safe.

Suddenly, Jared belted out the chorus to "Bad Romance," which was still playing on a loop in my head, too. I laughed, and when he continued with the next line, I sang along with him, right there in the middle of the street while cars drove past and people in suits walked by. They probably thought we were crazy or drunk, but whatever. Jared was the first guy who truly got me, who understood that music coursed through my blood and crept into every single thought—because he was exactly the same way.

"Singing Lady Gaga might be the sexiest thing you've ever done," I said.

"Is that so?" He pulled me close, singing the next line of the song against my lips.

I pushed him back with a smile. "Stop or we won't make it back to the hotel."

"Is that a promise?" he asked, his arms circling my waist.

We turned the corner and froze when we saw Kyle and Alexis walking out of the hotel, on their way to dinner. We ducked out of sight and broke apart, returning to a friends-only distance. The magic vanished, leaving us with only questions and doubts.

I leaned against the wall and combed my fingers through my hair until my heart slowed down. "What are we going to do? We have to stay single for the show, and the guys will kill us if they find out."

Jared frowned in the direction of the hotel, rubbing the stubble on his neck. Finally, he sighed. "We'll have to be careful. Keep this under wraps until the show is over."

I bit my lip, considering. I didn't want to lie to the others, but I had to be realistic, too. Staying away from Jared for the next few weeks would be impossible. We couldn't ignore our attraction while spending almost every waking moment together. If we tried, eventually we'd combust from the sparks. Even now, with the threat of discovery so close, I wanted to touch him. But if anyone found out about us, it could ruin everything for the band.

"This is a really bad idea," I said.

"I know." He fixed me with an intense gaze that took my breath away. "But I can't think of any other way."

"Me either." We were really going to do this, to carry on a secret relationship under the other guys' noses and try to fool the entire world that we weren't together. And meanwhile, Jared would continue flirting with other girls in front of me. But the only other choice was to end it now, and that wasn't an option. "We should return to the hotel separately to avoid suspicion."

"Do you want me to stop by your room later?"

God, yes. But I shook my head. I might have agreed to a secret relationship, but I wasn't ready to go further with it tonight. And as much as I desired Jared, I didn't want to be just another hook-up either. If we were going to do this, I'd want something real. Problem was, I didn't know if Jared could give me that.

Chapter Fifteen

People thought being in a rock band was glamorous and exciting, but in reality, it was often pretty tedious. We spent most of our time rehearsing or doing other business for the show, and finding a moment alone with Jared was near-impossible now that I badly wanted one. Hector and Kyle were always around, and when they weren't, the cameras were.

Alexis showed up to a few rehearsals to take photos of us for the website and make out with Kyle between songs. It was torture watching them be so open with their love, not caring who saw them together. Meanwhile, Jared and I were forced to duck into closets, sneak into empty studios, and steal quick kisses when no one was looking. It was hard to keep the charade up, but I couldn't invite him to my room yet. I knew where that would lead, and I wanted to take things slow for now. Something had shifted between us when we'd moved from friends to something else, and we were still figuring out the rules of this new situation.

This week's theme was "Neon '90s," which meant we had to pick a song from 1990 to 1993. We settled on Depeche Mode's "Enjoy the Silence" after listening to the remix Linkin Park had done, along with the covers by Breaking Benjamin and Anberlin. There wasn't much for me to do during this song, but maybe that was better—less chance of falling off the stage and making a fool of myself again. Instead, it was Kyle's turn to shine on keyboard.

During our final rehearsal before the live show, Jared wore a T-shirt with a bunch of X-Men villains on it, like Magneto and Mystique. Seeing him embrace his inner geek made me want to rip his clothes off right there in the studio. He kept grinning at me like he knew exactly what I was thinking, but the other guys were too busy practicing to notice.

After we finished, the guys headed back to the hotel, and I made an excuse about wanting to check out the piano in one of the other practice rooms. I'd hoped

Jared would stay behind, too, but unfortunately, he left with them. Oh, well. Just me and the music. But I was used to that after a lifetime of practicing alone.

It wasn't completely an excuse either; I'd been itching to get back on the piano. I hadn't touched one since I'd joined the band, except for that brief moment with Kyle's keyboard. Guitar had completely taken over my life, and while I didn't regret it for a second, I did miss other instruments, too. Okay, not so much the clarinet.

I sat in front of the piano and ran my fingers along the smooth black-and-white keys. Without thinking, I slipped into my usual warm-up routine, as if I was practicing in my old living room or in one of the music rooms at school. The nostalgia should have been comforting, but instead it made me feel trapped, like I was shoving my true self back in a box.

I shook off the feeling and placed my fingers back on the keys. I wouldn't play anything I'd practiced in school. If I had only a few stolen minutes with a piano, I would play the music I loved most: movie scores. I'd lose myself in an epic piece, letting the melody paint a scene in my head, from romantic to action-packed to bittersweet.

To get into the mood, I played through a few different themes, from *The Godfather* to *Harry Potter* to *Inception*. Jared walked in at the end of the *Jurassic Park* theme, and I barely managed to keep my cool while I finished the piece, trying not to show how much his presence affected me. He could have returned to the lobby to flirt with other girls and keep his reputation going, but instead he'd come back to me.

He slid onto the bench, fitting against my side in a way that was deliciously distracting. "I should have known you'd sneak off to spend time with John Williams."

"I can't help it. He's just so dreamy," I said with an overly dramatic sigh.

"There you go, making me jealous again."

"How about this instead?" I started a fun piece while Jared watched my fingers dance across the keys.

"I know this," he said. "*Nightmare Before Christmas*, right?"

I nodded. "Danny Elfman is my hero. He sang for Oingo Boingo—"

"Who did the best '80s song ever, 'Dead's Man's Party.'"

"Yes! He also writes movie scores, like for all the Tim Burton films. I basically want to be him when I grow up."

"He does make some great Halloween music." He nudged me with his elbow. "Kyle told me you're from the Bay Area. Why didn't you go to the San Francisco Conservatory if you're such a musical genius?" My hands froze over the keys, and he said, "Sorry if that's too personal a question…"

"No, it's fine." I took a moment to consider my next words. "I picked UCLA so I'd be far enough away that I couldn't go home all the time, but close enough to hop on a quick flight if there was an emergency."

His eyebrows shot up. "Everything okay?"

"My mom's an alcoholic. Sober at the moment, but she's told me that before, so who knows. She's also just…a mess. It's a rare day she gets out of bed. And my father…" I used my sleeve to wipe fingerprints off the music rack, keeping my eyes fixed in front of me. "He had an affair with my mom. She had no idea he was married and had kids, a whole secret life he kept from her, but when she got pregnant, he confessed everything."

"Damn. That's messed up."

"Yeah. Most of the time I forget that part of my family entirely, until he does something like buying me a guilt car for my sixteenth birthday. He paid for all my music lessons and instruments as a kid, too, like he thought he could make up for not being a real dad by throwing money at us." I tried to shrug it off. "What about you? Kyle told me you both grew up in LA, and I know your mom is a songwriter and your dad a lawyer, but that's it."

Jared stared at the keys and didn't answer, and I worried I'd crossed some line by asking him something personal, even though I'd just spilled something myself. Finally, he said, "My parents split up when I was seventeen and Kyle was fifteen. Nasty divorce."

"Oh, I'm sorry."

"They'd fought for so long I was relieved at first—until they started trying to get information out of me and Kyle, using us like pawns in their never-ending battle. They even wanted us to testify that the other parent was 'unfit' to get custody of us, too."

"That's horrible." All these years, Kyle had never mentioned any of this. Though, in retrospect, he'd never mentioned any of his family except Jared. I could understand why.

Jared trailed his fingers along the keyboard, staring at nothing while he spoke. "When I wouldn't play their games they focused on Kyle, and it really messed with his head. He started doing drugs, he was sent to therapy—it was bad. I was supposed to go to Columbia but switched to UCLA at the last minute and rented us a place so Kyle could live with me while he finished high school. He got better once my parents gave him some space, and I think being in the band helped a lot, too. Since then it's just been the two of us, except for the obligatory holiday dinners with one of our parents."

No wonder the brothers were so close. I'd never known Kyle had such a dark past—he'd always seemed like the most balanced one in the band. I placed my hand over Jared's, entwining our fingers together. "You're a good brother."

He was silent for a moment and then cleared his throat. "So have you started applying to grad schools yet?"

"Not yet. But now, with the show…I don't know." I removed my hand from his. My future used to be crystal clear and I'd known exactly what I wanted and how to get there, but joining the band had changed everything. Something had shifted in me over these past few weeks. I still wanted to write movie scores someday, but I wanted to focus on being the guitarist for Villain Complex, too. If we managed to win the show, there'd be tours and albums to record, and I didn't know if there was room in that life for grad school, too. But I didn't want to quit the band or leave behind this new part of myself. Or Jared.

"If you wanted to focus on school, we'd understand," he said, as though he could read my thoughts. "I mean, we'd all cry and eat a lot of ice cream and listen to 'Everybody Hurts' by REM for days, but we'd eventually find *some* way to keep going."

"Good to know." I leaned against him, his body warm and comforting at my side.

"Don't get me wrong, I don't want you to leave." He brushed hair away from my face, his touch gentle. "But you can't let anyone hold you back. Not your parents, not the band, and definitely not me. In the end, all we have are our dreams."

"What if I don't know what my dreams are anymore?"

"You'll figure it out."

I thought he would kiss me, but he turned back to the piano and started playing something. I became transfixed by the sight of his long fingers moving across the keyboard and his perfect wrists and tattooed forearms arching over it. When he started singing, his voice raspy and full of emotion, I recognized the piece as "Stay" by Rihanna. Was he singing this in response to what we'd talked about? Or was I reading too much into it?

I needed to kiss him, but his voice was so beautiful I didn't want him to stop either. Instead, I pressed my lips to his collarbone, just above his shirt and his hidden VILLAIN tattoo. While he played, I trailed kisses along his neck, his skin humming against my mouth as he sang the chorus. I nibbled his earlobe and slid a hand along his thigh, trying to see how much of a distraction I could be. But still he kept playing.

As soon as he finished the song, he yanked me against him with a groan and pressed his mouth against mine. I moved to straddle him, my knees on either side of the piano bench, pushing my hips against his hard body. I didn't care that anyone could walk in and see us. Knowing how wrong this was, how dangerously close to being caught we were, only made this more right. I clutched his unshaven face as we kissed, and the rough feel of his stubble against my fingertips made me wild. His hands dipped under my shirt and traced patterns along my back, sending shivers down my spine.

Now that we were finally alone, we couldn't get enough of each other. His lips kissed down my neck like he needed to taste every inch of me, and the way he pressed his mouth against my pulse made me gasp. I tilted my head back, arching against him, digging my fingers into his shoulders. His hands smoothed up my stomach, along my ribs, inch by inch until he found my breasts. He circled my nipples through my bra, and I closed my eyes, losing myself in his touch. I couldn't focus on anything but Jared and how badly I wanted him, without all these clothes in the way. But when I moved my hands to the button of his jeans, he stopped me.

"We can't. Not here," he whispered, glancing at the door.

I sighed, remembering there was another life outside of this room, outside of us. "I know."

He pressed his forehead against mine while we tried to regain control of our breathing. "Trust me, I want to. God, you have no idea."

"Oh, I have some idea," I said with a slight smile. "But you're right. And we have that interview with that website tonight, too."

He groaned. "Yay, another interview."

"You know you love them."

"Maybe a little." He gave me one last lingering kiss. "But I'd rather be alone with you."

We reluctantly broke apart, and I knew I wouldn't be able to go slow with Jared any longer.

———

The show really was trying to starve us. By the time we finished the interview, it was close to midnight, and no one had fed us since lunch. Once we got back to the hotel, the four of us immediately piled into the band's van and headed out to find a late-night drive-thru. We ate burgers in the backseat, shoving food in our faces and laughing at the stupid questions we'd been asked earlier. "Which mentor would you want to date?" (Dan, obviously) and "what color would your music be?" (duh, black) were our favorites.

Once we were stuffed, we drove to the nearest supermarket, since we'd been living in a hotel for weeks and needed to stock up on basic things like toothpaste and deodorant. We stepped into the harsh fluorescent lights and I reached for a shopping basket, but Kyle stopped me.

"You'll need a cart for this," he said with a devilish grin. Wait—how much stuff were we getting?

"All right," Jared said, rubbing his hands together. "Time for another round of Supermarket Treasure Hunt."

"What's that?" I asked.

"Only the greatest game ever," Kyle said. Hector nodded solemnly, like this was serious business.

"Since Maddie's new, I'll go over the rules," Jared continued. "We each grab a cart and split up. You have ten minutes to find three bizarre items anywhere in the store, and bonus points if they all follow a theme. The person with the most ridiculous treasures wins."

"What do we win?" I asked.

"Bragging rights, of course," Hector said.

"Um, yay?"

"Meet in front of the bananas in ten minutes," Jared said. "Okay, go!"

The guys all shoved each other out of the way as they grabbed their carts. I followed behind them at a slower pace, laughing as they rammed their carts into each other's and made race car sounds before darting down the aisles. I studied the signs and chose the pet supply section, figuring this downtown supermarket probably catered to all sorts of rich people living in lofts with their pampered pets. Luckily, the place didn't let me down. I grabbed the three oddest things I could find and rushed back to the produce section.

Kyle and Jared turned a corner ahead of me, racing to get in front of each other and nearly knocking stuff off the shelves. Kyle arrived at the finish line first and seized a banana in each hand to do a victory dance, making me laugh.

"You totally cheated," Jared said.

"Did not."

Jared grabbed his brother and wrestled with him, their unshaved faces squished together while Kyle stuck out his tongue like he was dying. They had such a strong bond, and I loved seeing my two favorite guys being silly like this.

"Ow, beard friction," Kyle said, rubbing his cheek.

"We're so hot we're starting fires with our faces." Jared ran a hand along his matching dark stubble, and it took all my effort to not reach for him, too. Sometimes this secret romance thing was pretty damn frustrating.

Kyle grinned. "Hey, that can be our next song."

Jared belted out, "Fire in our beards / Ice in our hearts / You'll get seared / Here in the mart."

I laughed. "Sounds like a hit."

He gave a dramatic bow while Hector wheeled his cart over. Once we were all together, Jared announced, "Time to see what we all got. Kyle, as reigning champion you go first."

"My theme is 'candy fail,'" Kyle said and held up each item to show us. "Lollypops with spiders in them. Bacon-flavored breath mints. And mushroom-shaped gummies that look like dicks. Bam!"

"Ew," I said, not sure which of those things grossed me out the most.

"Nice finds," Hector said. "But I'll see your dick gummies and raise you my Crunchy Nude Balls." He held up a box of Korean rice candy with that name.

"Hector, there are ladies present," Kyle said, in an overly shocked way.

I held my hand over my heart. "It's true. I'm a delicate flower who is easily offended."

Hector snorted. "Of course you are. I also found these." He showed us his other two items: a Tea Bag Buddy for mugs and a bottle of something called Head Lube. For shaving, maybe?

Jared nodded. "The 'unintentional sexual innuendos theme.' Always a good one."

"I knew you'd approve."

"My turn," Jared said. "The theme tonight, ladies and gentleman, is 'strange things in your bathroom.' First up, garlic shampoo, so you can ward off vampires at all times and probably everyone else, too. Next, men's grooming wipes in 'boardroom scent,' for when you need to feel both clean and extra-manly down there. And finally, drumroll please…lightsaber-shaped lip balm."

"Um, I kind of want that," I said.

"I figured." He grinned and tossed it into my cart. "You're up, Maddie."

"This theme is 'crazy pet owners,'" I said, as I pulled each item out of my cart. "Number one: fruit smoothies for all those health-conscious dogs. Number two: water for turtles and tortoises, for the ones too spoiled to swim in regular water. And number three: a book called…*Crafting With Cat Hair*."

"What the shit," Hector said, taking the book to page through it. "I think you win with this alone."

Kyle leaned closer to look inside. "Agreed. Nothing can top fingerless gloves made out of fur balls."

Jared grabbed my arm and raised it over my head. "I'm proud to introduce our new champion, Maddie Taylor!"

"Woo!" I yelled, and the other guys applauded and hooted. Thank god the store was empty at this hour.

"Good job, everyone," Jared said. "Let's put this stuff back before the people who work here kick us out."

We split up to return our treasures and grab the things we actually needed. While I was deciding which snacks to get, Jared's arms slid around me from behind and he placed a kiss on my neck.

"Hey, stop that." I glanced around quickly, but we were alone in this aisle. It was only the thought of Hector or Kyle walking over that kept me from kissing him back.

"I couldn't resist." He let me go, and we pulled apart to an innocent distance but did the rest of our shopping together.

While we grabbed some beer, a girl about our age with bright pink extensions swayed down the aisle and stopped in front of us. She stared at Jared with narrowed eyes and then asked, "Are you famous?"

"Nope."

"You look like that guy on that show. Um, that one show on TV, you know? In that band?"

He waited for her to get it out, smiling the entire time. "Oh, yeah?"

"Wait, you *are* that guy! Right? You're, like, totally famous!"

He laughed. "Yeah, I am that guy."

"Oh my god, I love you, I love your band. Can I have a hug?"

"Sure." He held his arms out, and she rushed into them. Over her shoulder, he raised his eyebrows at me, an amused expression on his face. I covered my mouth to suppress a laugh. This was just too surreal, being attacked by a drunk fan in the middle of the night in a supermarket. I wondered if this sort of thing happened often to Jared. The girl didn't even seem to notice I was standing there, too, but that didn't surprise me. Jared was the face of this band for good reason.

"My friend is never going to believe this. She knows, like, all your songs," the girl said. "Can I get a photo so I can make her jealous?"

"Of course. But you have to include my lovely guitarist too." He dragged me in, though I scowled at him, and took a selfie of the three of us with her phone. "There you go."

"Oh my god, thank you, I love you!" She grabbed him again, pressing her face against his shoulder. I'd be jealous if this wasn't so hilarious.

"This has been so much fun, but we have to run," Jared said when the girl wouldn't let go of him. He mouthed, "Help!" but I shook my head and grinned.

As soon as we managed to escape across the store, we burst into laughter. "Does that happen a lot?" I asked.

"No, that was new. And very weird. I kind of want a shower actually."

"Better get used to it. You're 'famous' now. Soon you'll have fangirls ripping off your clothes every time you go out."

He moved closer, a teasing smile on his lips. "The only one I want ripping off—"

He cut off as Kyle and Hector rounded the corner and joined us, but I knew what he meant. We returned to friend mode and told them about the girl, and the other guys all laughed with us. It was a new kind of agony, being near Jared but being unable to actually *be* with him. But at the same time, I didn't want to do anything to jeopardize this new family I'd become a part of either.

Chapter Sixteen

arla hopped out of her '67 Mustang and grabbed me in a hug, and Julie dashed around to join us. With Dan's help, I'd been able to score VIP tickets for tonight's live show for my two favorite ladies, who were both back in town.

"I'm so happy you're here!" I hugged them back hard. After being surrounded by nothing but testosterone for weeks, I really needed my girls again.

"I demand to see everything," Julie said. "Dazzle me with your rock-star lifestyle."

Carla shook her head, her dark curls bouncing. "She's been talking nonstop the entire drive over. I kept turning the music up, but she just got louder."

"What? I'm so freaking proud of Maddie I could scream." She shrieked to demonstrate, and it echoed across the open-air parking lot.

"How are things going?" Carla asked me.

"Things are great. The show is amazing, and I've improved so much in these last few weeks, and playing with the band and on stage…there's nothing like it in the world."

"You do seem a lot happier than you've been in months. Maybe years."

As we headed toward the Nokia Theatre, we passed the massive line of people hoping to get into tonight's show.

"Thank god we don't have to wait in that mess," Julie said.

"Nope, you get the VIP treatment tonight. Backstage tour and—" I slid to a halt when I saw Jared ahead of us, near the front of the line. Groupies surrounded him, taking pictures with him and having him sign everything from their phones to their bra straps to their bare skin. He wore dark sunglasses and a black leather jacket, and with his hair spiked up, he looked every bit the bad boy rock star. A girl in a slinky dress pressed her red lips to his cheek, and he never dropped his smile. I wondered if any of his groupies could tell it was his stage smile and not his real one or if I was the only girl who knew that.

"Maddie?" Carla asked. She followed my gaze and then said, "Ah."

I tore my eyes away after another girl squeezed her body against him for a photo, and he whispered something in her ear. It was actually really cool of Jared to take the time to meet our fans. I didn't know of any other musician on *The Sound* who did that, and there was no doubt all those people would vote for our band now. But these women were so much more aggressive than the one in the supermarket, and I wanted to shove them all aside and prop a big sign on him that said, "MINE." I knew he had to keep up his reputation for the show, but god, it hurt to see him do it in front of me.

Julie clucked her tongue at me. "Still obsessed with him, I see."

"I'm not obsessed." Okay, maybe a little. For good reason. "Besides, we're just friends."

She nudged me with her hip. "Yeah, but you'd like to be more, right?"

"So nothing's happened with him?" Carla asked.

"No," I said, and my chest tightened up at the lie. I never kept anything from them, but there was too much at stake with the show and I didn't know if the girls would be able to stay quiet tonight if I told them what was really going on. Especially Julie. She meant well, but she was terrible at keeping secrets. I'd tell them when our time on *The Sound* was over, assuming my whatever-this-was with Jared lasted that long.

I led my friends around the crowd, away from the Jared Cross Fan Club, and into the backstage area of the theater. I hoped giving them a behind-the-scenes tour of *The Sound* would keep all our minds off of my love life, but no such luck.

Near the rotating stage, Sean was talking to one of the roadies, and he perked up when he saw us. "Hey, Maddie. Are these your friends?" He held out his hand to each of them. "I'm Sean. Nice to meet you."

Both Carla and Julie grinned at him like he was a giant chocolate cake, and I introduced them. "They're here for the show tonight," I added.

"You're in The Static Klingons!" Julie blurted out. "I love you guys!"

He laughed and turned to me. "You didn't tell me your friends were not only beautiful, but had great taste in music, too."

I grinned. "They're here with me, isn't that obvious?"

"Good point. Hey, do you want to grab that bite to eat sometime this week? Assuming we're both still around after tomorrow, that is."

The girls nodded frantically at me, and I plastered a smile on. "Um, sure. Let me get back to you on when I'm free."

"Great! Good luck tonight." He saluted my friends. "Ladies, have fun."

He walked off, and the girls checked him out from behind. "Holy hotness," Julie said, with a low whistle.

"He seems to like you," Carla said to me. "He asked you out in front of your friends—that's pretty bold."

"I know. He's cute and nice but…" I shrugged. "He just doesn't do it for me."

"How is that possible?" Julie asked.

Carla set her hand lightly on my arm. "Maybe you're so focused on Jared that you're ignoring the guy practically throwing himself at your feet."

"I'm not—" I started to protest. Was she really giving me guy advice when she was *still* with Daryl? I took a deep breath and started again. "Sean's just not my type, that's all."

"He's exactly your type, and he seems like the perfect guy to help you forget Jared," Julie said.

"You're the one who told me to go after Jared in the first place!" I blurted out, and then I glanced around quickly, hoping no one had heard me. Here they were, teaming up against me again. I loved my friends, but not the way they always wanted to run my life for me. I'd definitely not missed this over the last few weeks.

"Yeah, at the party. But you've known him for weeks, and if he hasn't seen how amazing you are by now, he's hopeless."

"But—" I bit my lip. I couldn't very well tell them the truth about Jared now. They'd just say he was going to hurt me, that this was only going to end badly, and a dozen other things I knew in my head but didn't want to hear in my heart. "Let's just drop this, okay?"

Carla gave me a pitying look. "We just don't want you to get your heart broken, that's all."

I assured the girls I wasn't interested in Jared and resumed the tour, but I didn't think they believed me. And a nagging feeling in my gut told me they were probably right about him. This thing between us could only end badly, but when I was alone with him, I didn't care.

———

For this week's show, some of the other bands had completely embraced the "Neon '90s" theme, but we'd decided to go in a different direction, with all white outfits for the guys and a short white dress and matching boots for me. The makeup people had gone a little overboard though, and my eyes were watering so much I darted into the bathroom to check them. I set my glasses on the counter just as Lacey walked out of the stall behind me.

"Nice dress," she said, in a tone that implied she meant the opposite. She wore a sparkly hot pink dress with a neon green cowboy hat and matching boots, so she wasn't really one to talk.

I dabbed at my eyes with a paper towel, but stayed silent. The producers loved to parade her around like she was some sort of Disney princess, and on the Internet, her band Fairy Lights was already an early favorite for the win. The only other band with as much attention was ours, but I suspected that was due to Jared's sex appeal more than anything.

"Don't think I'm not on to your little game," she said with her strong Southern accent. "Winning the audience over with your 'fall' and all those lies about how you and Jared aren't seeing each other. Soon all of America will know what you're doing."

I blinked at her. Was she threatening us? "I'm sorry?"

"I'm going to win this thing. You'd best be staying out of my way."

She left the bathroom before I could come up with a witty comeback. I didn't know what that was about or why she suddenly had such a problem with us. Was it because we were potentially her band's biggest competitors? Or because I'd seen

Jared shoot her down in the elevator? Whatever, I couldn't afford to let her get into my head before I got on stage.

I reached for my glasses, but they were gone. I checked the floor and then looked in all the stalls, in the sinks, even in the trash and the toilets, but my glasses had disappeared.

No, not disappeared. Lacey must have taken them.

I ran out of the bathroom to go after her and crashed into Jared. "Hey, it's almost time for our set." His eyes swept over my face. "What's wrong?"

"Lacey stole my glasses. I can't see anything. I can't play. We have to find her, we have to delay the show, we—"

"Slow down." Jared placed his hands on my elbows, holding me steady. "Are you sure she took them?"

"She was the only one in the bathroom with me, and I had them when I went in, and I've looked everywhere but they're *gone*." I closed my eyes to stop the hallway spinning around me. I couldn't deal with this right now, not when we were about to go on stage. Not when my friends were in the audience, ready to cheer me on. Not when our entire future rode on how we did tonight. "I'm going to kill that sparkly cowgirl."

"We'll tell the producers and they'll deal with her. For now, do you have another set of glasses or contacts you can use?"

"Back at the hotel, but we don't have time to get them."

"How bad is it without your glasses?"

"Um, bad. I can barely see anything." I covered my face with my hands, trying not to cry. I didn't need my eyeliner to be even more of a mess than it was. "This is a disaster."

He pulled me into his arms and kissed the top of my head. "It's not that bad. You don't even need to see to play the guitar. You could do it blindfolded. And maybe it'll be better if you don't walk around the stage. Less chance of falling off, right?"

"Very funny." But his calm demeanor was helping a little, and his words made me think. He was right; I didn't *need* to see. Maybe I *could* play the guitar blindfolded. "I have an idea."

———

When our stage turned, I was already standing in place, my guitar hanging from my shoulder, my pick clutched in my fingers. I couldn't see anything —not the rest of the band, not the audience, not even my guitar or the mic right in front of me. All I could make out were the lights shining on us, tinted red from the strip of fabric across my eyes. Hector had a matching one across his mouth, Kyle had one covering his ears, and to make our group complete, Jared had one tied around his neck. The red was a sharp contrast to our white outfits, and hopefully got across the Hear No Evil, See No Evil, Speak No Evil message we were going for.

The audience cheered as we rotated in front of them, and my nerves kicked up to high alert at all the sounds without the visuals to accompany them. As Kyle began, I thought my skin might jump right off me, and I prayed I could pull this off. What if I was wrong and I couldn't actually play blindfolded? In theory it didn't seem too hard, but I'd never actually tried before. I was doing it for the first time in front of a huge crowd, plus everyone watching live on TV.

But once I started, my fingers knew what to do. I forgot seeing and focused on hearing, feeling, being. On Hector's steady beat and Jared's baseline vibrating through my bones. On Kyle's clear tones tying it all together. Our version of "Enjoy the Silence" sounded like we'd dipped the original in black ink and razor-blades, and Jared's voice was perfect for it. And with nothing in the world except me and the music, I could easily imagine he was singing the words only to me.

When the song ended, his arm took mine to help me move across the stage to the center. I pushed my blindfold back, grateful for his help since everything around me was a blurred mess of faces and lights. By the roar of the crowd, I could tell the audience loved our version, and I knew Julie and Carla were some-where out there, cheering me on. The mentors praised our unique take on the song and on our interesting performance, and I hoped Lacey was watching this moment. *Suck it, cowgirl.*

The stage turned for the next band, and as soon as we were backstage, they wanted us to do an interview right away. On the way to the interview area, I stopped to ask producer Steve if they'd found my glasses yet.

"No, but we're on it." He had a rapid no-nonsense way of talking. "Don't worry. Let us handle this, and we'll get your glasses back to you in no time." He checked his massive shiny watch. "Now if you could just hurry to your interview, that'd be great. Ray has to be back on stage in six minutes."

Thanks for being no help at all, Steve. I rejoined the band, and we were hustled over to speak with Ray.

"That was a fun performance," Ray said. "And what a statement! Dan said it wasn't his idea—whose was it?"

"It was Maddie's," Jared said, leaning into the mic. "Her glasses vanished right before we went on, and she came up with this solution."

"Talk about quick thinking." Ray shoved the mic in my face. "We've never had anyone play guitar blindfolded on the show before."

"It was really Jared's idea," I said, blushing like crazy, like I always did when the focus was on me. "He said he knew I could play even if I was blindfolded, and a light bulb went off."

"You two are a great team." He grinned at both of us. "And it seems like there's some chemistry there, too. The fans want to know: Is there anything between you?"

"No!" we both said, too fast.

"We're just friends," Jared added. My least favorite phrase these days.

Ray laughed. "That's too bad, though you'd both break some hearts if the fans knew you were off the market."

"Don't worry. Jared is still available," I said and hated myself.

When the interview was over, Hector said, "He didn't even look at me or Kyle. All they care about is the Jared and Maddie will-they-or-won't-they bullshit."

"Sorry," I said. "I didn't mean for that to come up."

"It's not your fault," Kyle said, shooting Hector a look. "It's the producers trying to test us again."

"I just wish they'd remember we're part of the band, too." Hector shook his head. "Forget it. I need to get some air."

He took off down the hallway, and Jared frowned. "I should talk to him."

"He's pissed at you right now," Kyle said. "I'll handle it."

He left us alone or as alone as we could be backstage with other bands and people who worked on the show. Jared rubbed the back of his neck, and even without my glasses, he was beautiful. I wanted to press my mouth to the stubble along his jaw and trace his tattoos with my tongue. I licked my lips and his gaze lingered on them, and I knew he was thinking along the same lines.

"Let's get out of here," he said, his voice husky.

"Where?" We didn't have much time before we had to get back on stage at the end of the show, but a few minutes alone with Jared were too tempting to pass up, even if it was risky. Or maybe, *because* it was risky.

"Anywhere. I don't care, as long as we're alone."

We sneaked out the back door, and Jared took my hand as soon as it closed. I still couldn't see much without my glasses, but he guided me through the parking lot for the trucks with the show's equipment until we found a secluded spot against a chain-link fence between buildings, where it was unlikely anyone would see us.

I leaned back against the fence and slipped my fingers under the red sash at his neck, using it to pull him to my mouth. He yanked my blindfold down to cover my eyes, and I gasped into his lips.

"Do you have any idea how hard it was not to kiss you on stage tonight?" he asked, as he grabbed onto the chain-link fence above me, fitting his body against mine.

He claimed my mouth with his before I could answer. With the blindfold on, my other senses exploded with Jared. The taste of his skin, slick with sweat and desire. His smell, like soap and leather and something unmistakably male. The feel of his stubble against my cheek, his hard chest pressing against my breasts. His voice as he groaned my name, like I was chocolate and he wanted to take a bite. My entire world was Jared's lips and hands and breath and body.

"Jared, you're making me crazy."

"Tell me what you want," he said against my neck.

"I want you," I whispered. "Here. Now."

Jared gripped my hip with one hand, the other still holding the fence. His fingers slid lower, inching down my dress and then under it, moving along my bare skin and igniting a fire within me. Without warning, he lifted one of my legs, hooking it around his body. I clutched his shoulders for support while his hand smoothed up my leg and eased between my thighs. He teased along the edge of my panties in a way that made me moan and beg for more. No more going slow. After weeks of pent-up desire, I needed him now.

When I thought I'd die if he didn't touch me where I burned, he pushed my panties aside to slip one long finger inside me. I gasped and arched against him, but his mouth covered mine and swallowed my wordless cries. He slid his finger in and out slowly and then added another while he began to rub me with his thumb, circling my sensitive skin in a way that sent flames through me. He kissed me the entire time, his tongue matching his fingers as they darted into me, faster, harder.

Anyone could walk out and see me blindfolded against a fence and catch him fingering me, but that only made it hotter, knowing we could be discovered at any moment. Jared's touch wound me tighter and tighter, his mouth never leaving mine as my cries grew more desperate. My fingers tensed around the sash at his neck, holding him close as he brought me to climax, my every nerve springing free. He didn't stop touching me, and the pleasure went on for an eternity while I trembled against him. If not for the fence behind me and his body holding me up, my knees would have given out. Jared made my body weak in the best way possible.

"I'd love to continue this," he said, pushing up my blindfold so I could see again. "But we need to get back."

I nodded, unable to speak, my whole body warm and fluid from what he'd done to me. I wanted to return the favor, to make him as delirious as I was, but we didn't have time. We made our way back to the theater, and I was already counting down the minutes until we could be alone again. He'd brought me release, but instead of satisfying me, it just made me want more. I craved Jared like an addiction, and I was starting to wonder if I'd ever get enough.

Chapter Seventeen

I wanted to invite Jared back to my room that night, but I had dinner with Julie and Carla after the show so we could catch up and we ended up drinking too much for them to drive back. They crashed on the extra bed in my hotel room, and I spent the night tossing and turning, partly stressing about whether our performance would be good enough to keep us on the show another week, but mostly replaying those stolen minutes against the fence with Jared.

My friends didn't have tickets for the results show, so I returned to the theater alone the next afternoon. I'd slept in late and hadn't spoken to the guys at all, so I had no idea what kind of reception our song was getting online. It was actually nice being oblivious; people on the Internet could be pretty damn cruel sometimes. But at the same time, it made my stress levels shoot through the roof. Had anyone liked our version of "Enjoy the Silence" or was it too different from the original? We'd picked such a classic, well-known song, and it was hard to know if people would love or hate our darker take on it.

I met the rest of the band in the lounge. Jared wore his black leather jacket again, and the wicked smile he gave me filled my head with naughty thoughts.

"Tonight," I whispered to him as we walked to the stage. "After the show, my room."

In response, he set his hand on my back, moving lower to rest on the curve of my butt. I sucked in a breath, heat building between my legs at his touch, but he released me before anyone saw. Or so I hoped.

We waited while Dan and Lissa finished their duo, their two distinct voices meshing surprisingly well, and then our team was rushed on stage. I held my breath as Ray called the names, but our band was saved first, followed by The Quiet Battles, leaving the Christian heavy metal band to be kicked off this time. Safe for another week, and now we were in the semi-finals. I never expected to get this far, and it only made me want to work even harder to make it to the finals next week.

We all ran off the stage and hugged, and when Jared's arms wrapped around me, I had to restrain myself from kissing him in front of the other guys. It was getting harder and harder to keep up this friends-only charade in public, and I worried we were too obvious with all of our secret looks and quick touches. How could anyone miss the fire smoldering between us every time we were in the same room?

The show continued with a performance from a pop band whose song played every five minutes on the radio, followed by Team Lissa's elimination. Naturally, Lacey and Fairy Lights were still safe. Ray talked about how sweet and wholesome she was while she ran off the stage, and I wanted to gag. I had a few choice words for the viewers about the real Lacey, not that anyone would believe me over her.

Last night, my glasses had been waiting for me on top of my guitar case at the end of the show. When I asked producer Steve, he said he'd talked to Lacey but she'd denied everything, and there was nothing he could do. I couldn't tell if he was lying or if he thought I'd just misplaced my glasses. But I knew it was her.

Team Angel went up next, and The Static Klingons were safe, too, which meant I'd have to deal with Sean sometime this week. Instead, the punk band was kicked off her team.

Mohawk Girl and I ran into each other in the lounge after the elimination.

"I'm sorry," I said. "I can't believe you're going home."

She gave a one-shouldered shrug, like it wasn't a big deal. "It's fine. We knew we wouldn't win."

"You're not upset?"

"Not really. I'm thrilled we got this far. I mean, a punk band with mohawks and spikes? No way the producers would let us win the show. But we knew we'd get more exposure and bring in a lot of new fans, maybe even get some gigs out of it. That's all we wanted."

I was impressed by how calm she was. If we'd been kicked off tonight, I'd be hiding in the bathroom and sobbing. "I hope things work out for you."

"Thanks." She leaned close and lowered her voice. "We never had a shot at winning this thing, but you do. Don't let that Lacey bitch win, even if the show is practically handing it to her."

"I'll try." I was floored she thought we could actually win. But beating Lacey, America's sweetheart? That might be tough.

———

Thirty minutes after I got back to the hotel, there was a knock on my door. I opened it to find Jared leaning against the frame. His eyes drank me in, skimming up and down my body, and then he gave me a slow smile. "Room service."

He definitely looked good enough to eat. I shut the door behind him, and he pushed me against it, digging his fingers into my hair while he kissed me. I slid the leather jacket off him and ran my hands across his broad shoulders, down his hard back, along his strong arms. I pushed his shirt up, splaying my fingers across his stomach. Last night had given me a taste of how good it would be with Jared, and now he was wearing far too many clothes.

He pulled his shirt off, and I paused to stare at his toned chest and the dark hair trailing down into his jeans. I dragged a finger across his rough jaw and lower, tracing each letter of VILLAIN inked below his collar. When I saw him like this, tattooed and gorgeous and forbidden, I couldn't believe he was real and in my room and taking his clothes off for me.

He unbuttoned my shirt slowly, like he was savoring each new reveal of skin. When it fell to the floor, he pressed his lips to the hollow of my neck, making me gasp. He tugged down my bra straps and his mouth moved to my shoulders, kissing a line along each one. I threw my head back as he continued lower, down my chest, to the spot between my breasts. He unhooked my bra with one easy gesture, reminding me again how experienced he was. As his eyes swept over my chest, I had to resist the urge to cover myself. He'd been with so many other girls—how could I possibly measure up? And was I just another in his long list of flings?

"God, you're so beautiful," he whispered, and then his mouth was on me again and all my worries were forgotten. He took his time with each breast, circling and licking each nipple, while I tangled my fingers in his hair and whimpered for more. His fingers dipped into the waistband of my jeans, tugging my hips to him, while his lips and tongue continued their exploration of me. He moved slowly, worshipping my body, and I couldn't decide if I wanted to savor every second of this or if I just wanted to rip off his clothes and devour him.

He unbuttoned my jeans, his knuckles brushing against my waist. When he pushed them down, I stood before him in nothing but the lace panties I'd worn on purpose, knowing he might see them. He took me in with hungry eyes, lightly trailing his hands along the backs of my thighs, making me shiver.

"Beautiful," he whispered again.

His mouth moved lower, across my stomach and the curve of my hips. He tugged my panties down slowly, until I stood naked in front of him. Completely exposed and on display while he still had most of his clothes on. And somehow that brought back all my worries, all my fears, all my insecurities about the two of us.

I dug my fingers into his shoulders. "Jared," I said, my voice hesitant.

He pulled back to scan my face. "What's wrong?"

I bit my lip and looked away. Kyle's words came back to me: how his brother didn't do serious relationships, how I'd promised not to get involved with Jared. Next came Lacey's proposition to Jared in the elevator, followed by that text message from the girl wanting to hook up, and a never-ending stream of other girls I'd seen flirt with him. Jared might be mine tonight, but would he be mine tomorrow? And if not, was this night together worth the risk when it could cost me everything with the band and cost us all the win?

"We don't have to do this," he said when I didn't answer.

"No, I want to. It's just…" I tried to figure out how to word my thoughts without sounding completely lovesick and pathetic. If we weren't in my room, this would be the point where I would run away. Instead, I moved to the bed and pulled the covers up to my chest, so I wasn't quite so bare in front of him.

I took a deep breath and tried again. "I know you've probably been to a dozen other girls' rooms while on the show and that you don't want anything serious, but I don't know if I can do a casual hook-up, and I don't want this to ruin things with the band and the show and…"

He raked a hand through his hair, his mouth twisting. "Is that what you think this is? A casual hook-up?"

"No!" This was spiraling out of control fast, but now that it was out there, I couldn't take it back. "I don't know. You're always surrounded by girls, and there are so many rumors, plus that whole thing with Becca… Even Kyle and Hector joke about all the girls you sleep with. What am I supposed to think?"

"All of that is an act, just part of the image for the band. I know what other people say about me, but I thought you saw past all that shit." He shook his head, his voice pained. "Maddie, I haven't so much as kissed another girl since I met you."

"You…what?" Warmth rushed through me, a relief so strong it almost knocked me back.

Jared sat beside me on the bed. "Yes, I used to mess around a lot. But that's over now. That's not me anymore."

I wanted to believe him, I really did. Maybe I was too damaged from my own parents or maybe it would be different if Jared and I could be together openly, but it was just so hard for me to trust him. He said he'd changed, but how could I know for sure?

He must have seen the hesitation on my face because he sighed. "In freshman year, I caught my girlfriend in bed with our first bassist. Between that and the thing with my parents, I just lost it. I did whatever I could to forget, to feel nothing, to escape myself. I slept around, I drank too much, I got in fights. It was so much easier to be the villain, and after a while, everyone just expected me to be that guy. Girls started coming to our gigs or hiring us for parties because they thought I'd sleep with them, and the band grew more popular as long as I kept up that image. But after Becca, I knew I needed to get my shit together."

He'd never mentioned any of this before, and it made me ache for him. Suddenly I understood his obsession with villains and the meaning of the band's name and the lyrics in "Behind the Mask." He was wrong; the band wasn't popular because of his image, but because of how much passion he put into everything he did.

I wrapped myself around him, dropping the covers, my breasts pressing against his bare chest. "Jared…"

He touched my lips to silence me. "That night at the party, when I saw you playing my guitar, there was something so raw and honest about the way you sang my lyrics, like you really felt them. Not like the girls who came up to me after a show and said they loved my music but didn't know what any of it meant. You got it." He circled his arms around my back, holding me tight against him. "From that moment, you were the only one I wanted."

His words ignited something deep inside me. I did understand his lyrics. I knew all too well what it was like to keep a part of yourself hidden for years, pretending to be what everyone else wanted while you died a little inside. Jared had freed me when he'd invited me to join his band.

I lightly traced his forehead, his dark eyebrows, his jaw with its permanent five o'clock shadow. He was so beautiful, and I couldn't believe he'd had feelings for me all this time.

"Jared, I've been crazy about you since I saw you perform at the Battle of the Bands. Or even before that, from the first time I heard you sing, when Kyle gave me your album. That's why I know how to play all your songs."

His eyebrows jumped up. "Really?"

"Oh, god, does that make me sound obsessed?"

"No, I'm just surprised. It always seemed like you were avoiding me. You've known Kyle for years, and yet we somehow never met. And once we did, you kept running off, like you were scared of me or something."

"Of course I was scared of you. You're the bad boy rock star, and I'm the awkward piano player who likes movie scores and geeky stuff."

"I like geeky stuff, too." He cupped my face in his hands and whispered, "I like everything about you."

Our kiss was slow and tender, a caress instead of a demand. I poured everything into his lips, all the pent-up frustration, jealousy, and longing, all the misunderstandings and worries. With this kiss we wiped the slate clean. The past was over, and all that mattered was us, here, now. Together.

As our kiss grew deeper and more intense we sank onto the bed, our limbs tangling together. His chest pressed me down, and I loved the feel of him on top of me, the weight of his body, the brush of his soft hair against my breasts. He was still wearing far too many clothes though. I reached down and ran a hand along the front of his jeans, trying to unbutton them with fingers clumsy from lust. He stood up, and I watched with hungry eyes as he slid his jeans down his hips and off. His boxers fell next, leaving him as naked as I was, giving me a view of his entire, delicious body. And damn, it was a nice view.

I pulled him down on the bed, on top of me, and there was nothing between us now. Our bodies fit together, skin to skin, and it hit me that we were really, finally doing this. He kissed my neck and slipped a hand between my thighs, touching me where I ached the most. That fever overtook me again, the madness that Jared always brought out, making me want more and more of him. I was already so turned on by everything he'd already done to me, it didn't take long before his talented fingers created a frenzy in me.

"I need you," I breathed into his neck. "Please."

"Are you sure?"

"Very." I grinded my hips against him, and he groaned. I couldn't wait another minute. I'd lose my mind if I didn't have him inside me this instant.

He pulled a condom from his jeans, and after it was sorted, I wrapped my arms around his neck and pressed my lips against his, showing him without words I was ready for this. He spread my legs wider and pushed inside me, and I moaned from the satisfaction of finally getting what I'd been craving. He moved slowly at first, a delicious torture as his long length glided in and out, inch by wonderful inch. I lifted my hips to meet him, urging him faster, sliding my hands down his back to his butt to pull him deeper into me. We were as close as two people could be, and yet it wasn't enough. I wanted Jared to own me completely, to capture my body just as he'd already captured my heart.

"More," I breathed into his shoulder.

He grabbed my hips and rolled us over, pulling me on top of him with a teasing smile. "Show me."

I sat up and took a moment to appreciate the way he filled me completely in this position. He watched me, eyes drunk with desire, while I began to move, rolling my hips and making us both cry out. He let me set the pace, and I moved against his body at the perfect angle to drive me higher and higher. His fingers smoothed along my thighs, up my stomach, to coax my nipples in a way that sent pinpricks of pleasure to my core. My back arched while I rode him, my movements growing faster and more frantic, our breaths turning to gasps. Waves of pleasure crashed through me, and he gripped my hips and bucked under me while every part of my body trembled in sweet release.

When the tremors passed, he rolled us over again in one smooth gesture. "My turn."

I couldn't believe he was still going. All the other guys I'd slept with would have been done by now, but clearly all of Jared's experience was paying off. With one hand, he took my wrists and forced them above my head, holding me down while he rocked into me, hard and fast. He crushed my mouth with his and tugged at my lower lip with his teeth until I was whimpering for more.

"Yes," I cried, "Yes, yes, yes." This was what I'd wanted: a frenzy, a bonfire, a torrent of Jared pounding into me and claiming me as his own.

I wrapped my legs around his hips, drawing him deeper into me, and with his powerful thrusts he brought me close to the edge again. It seemed impossible so quickly after my last climax, but my entire body tensed up, from my fingers down to my toes. It was too much, it wasn't enough, and I never wanted it to end. I let go, losing myself in Jared the way I lost myself when I played guitar, when the music took over and made me whole. I broke apart into a million pieces, and he shuddered inside me, emptying himself with a few last thrusts.

We clung to one another, our naked bodies rising and falling in sync with each breath. His face was so close I could count the gold specks in his blue eyes, the dark lashes above them, the rough hairs on his chin. I was sure he could even feel the pounding of my heart through his skin.

He brushed sweat-soaked hair off my face and then kissed me, soft and gentle this time. "That was amazing," he said in a sleepy, content voice I'd never heard before. I hoped I'd soon come to know it as well as his real smile.

"Mmm…" I kissed him softly. "Even better than I imagined."

He raised an eyebrow and grinned. "So you thought about this a lot? With me?"

"Oh, stop." I covered my face with a hand. "As if that's a surprise. You know what you do to me."

"Nope, maybe you should show me." He nuzzled my neck, and I wanted him all over again. Jared really had become my addiction.

"When do you need to get back?"

"I told the guys I was seeing someone tonight, so I'm yours as long as you want me."

"Good." I wrapped my arms around his neck, kissing him hard. I didn't plan on letting him leave for many, many hours.

Chapter Eighteen

Jared kept me up most of the night, and even though I arrived at Dan's studio the next morning bleary-eyed and barely coherent, it was totally worth it.

As I headed into the kitchen area, I overheard Hector say, "I was starting to wonder if you'd lost your game, man."

"Me?" Jared asked. "Never."

The guys all greeted me, and when I met Jared's eyes, my pulse raced, knowing the secret we shared. I felt like I was wearing a giant neon sign that said "SLEPT WITH JARED LAST NIGHT." He'd returned to his room early this morning, and now wore a T-shirt with a stylized outline of Loki's helmet from *Thor* and *The Avengers*. He must have a never-ending closet full of villain shirts.

"What are you talking about?" I asked innocently while I poured my coffee into a disposable cup.

"Jared spent the night with someone," Hector said, in a singsong voice. Whoever said guys didn't like to gossip clearly had no idea what they were talking about.

"First time since we've been on the show," Kyle added. He raised his eyebrows at me, but I couldn't tell if he was suspicious or giving me a warning or what.

I focused on adding sugar and cream to my coffee. "Good for him."

"It's been so long I was worried about him," Hector said, slapping Jared on the back. "Thought he was getting soft in his old age."

Jared coughed into his cup of tea. "Do any of you find it odd we're standing here talking about my sex life? No?"

"Nah, everyone talks about your sex life."

Jared flipped Hector off, and the guys all laughed. I felt bad that he had to keep up this act with his two closest friends, but they'd also just confirmed that he hadn't been with anyone else in weeks too. Thank you, guys.

Jared caught me yawning and gave me a knowing grin. "Tired?"

"I'm just stressed about the show, that's all."

"I hear that," Kyle said while he refilled his coffee. "Hard to believe there are only two weeks left."

Two weeks and two bands per team. We'd made it into the semi-finals, and win or lose, soon all of this would be over. This week's votes were crucial, though, since if we made it to the finals, we'd get a spot on the tour across the country. But the competition was also stronger than ever, since only the best bands remained at this point.

"The Quiet Battles are pretty popular, so we really need to bring it this week," Jared said.

"Can we beat them?" Kyle asked.

"I think so, but it'll be close."

Hector grunted. "We've come this far. We are *not* going home now."

I hoped he was right. Being sent home now, when everything we wanted was within our grasp, was impossible to consider. It just couldn't happen; my brain rejected the idea completely. Of course, The Quiet Battles probably felt the exact same way, but only one of us would be on Team Dan a week from now.

We finished up and headed to our practice room to get started. My hand brushed Jared's hip as I walked past him, and it sent a little thrill through me, touching him right under the other guys' noses without them knowing. Even though I wished we could be open about our relationship, I couldn't deny that having a secret romance was pretty damn hot, too.

Dan was already waiting for us, reading something on his phone.

"Oh, hey," he said, when we entered. "Great job on Saturday. I just heard from Steve that your version of 'Enjoy the Silence' was the most downloaded song this week, so congrats on that."

"No shit?" Hector asked, and the rest of us made similar, shocked comments. Being number one was huge. Not only did it mean more money in our pockets (granted, not much after the show took its massive cut, but still better than nothing), but all the downloads translated to votes. That made our chances of staying to the finals even better—assuming people loved this week's song, too.

"We'll have to find some way to top it for the next show," Dan continued. "The theme is, 'Tainted Love,' so I guess they want some messed-up love songs. Any thoughts?"

"Bad Romance," Jared said immediately.

"The Lady Gaga song?" Kyle asked, looking at his brother like he was crazy.

"We can do a rock version of it, make it dark and twisted." He grabbed the mic and sang the chorus, his voice rough and sensual. The same voice that had cried out my name only hours ago. It nearly turned me into a molten puddle right there in the studio, and when he winked at me, I knew he'd intended that.

"Interesting choice," Dan said. "It will definitely stand out."

"I like it," I said, and Jared gave me a smile full of naughty thoughts. Yes, he was definitely doing this on purpose.

Not that I was complaining.

Hector tapped a drumstick against his hand. "I don't know…"

Dan pulled up the song on his phone, and we discussed how we could tweak it for our style. There was no actual guitar in the song, so we could interpret it in different ways. I played the main melody for them with some heavy distortion on my guitar, and that finally convinced Kyle and Hector.

"One other thing," Dan said. "For this week's show, the mentors have to do a performance of one of our songs with each band still on their team. Pick a Loaded River song you want to cover, and I'll join you for practice every other day."

We let Kyle choose, since he was the biggest Loaded River fan. He wanted "Nothing Breaks Me," a song I'd heard a million times growing up, with grungy guitar riffs and gritty vocals that would sound great with Jared singing them. It shouldn't be too hard to learn, but now we had two songs to perform, not one. Dan bumped our rehearsal time to eight hours a day, and combined with all the added publicity we had to do for the semi-finals, that meant we'd barely have any time to breathe this week.

———

We spent the rest of the day rehearsing the new songs and then dragged ourselves back to the hotel. We had tonight off for a rare change, and I couldn't wait to take a nice, hot shower and relax. Preferably with Jared.

As soon as we walked into the lobby, we could tell something was wrong. Everyone turned to look at us and not in a friendly way.

"What's going on?" Hector asked.

"I don't know," I said.

Laughter broke out at the bar, the kind you could tell is laughing *at* instead of *with*. The source seemed to be Lacey, who sat with the banjo player from The Quiet Battles and the busty singer of Brazen, a pop band from Team Lance. They stopped and gave us fake smiles as we passed by and then started giggling when our backs were to them.

"Why do I feel like I'm in middle school again?" Kyle asked after we got into the elevator.

"Oh, shit." Jared stared at his phone, and the expression on his face worried me more than anything.

"What is it?" I asked.

He waited until we were in their room and then held his phone up to show us. There, on his tiny screen, was an image of me in Jared's arms, my face pressed against his shoulder as he kissed the top of my head. We were in our white outfits from the last live show, the photo taken after my glasses went missing while he was comforting me. It was an intimate, private moment when we'd thought we were alone—and someone had plastered it all over the Internet.

Lacey. It had to be her.

"What the fuck is that?" Hector asked.

Kyle's head snapped back and forth between me and his brother. "Are you two together?"

I opened my mouth to confess everything, but Jared said, "No! This isn't what it looks like."

"Then who were you with last night?" Hector asked, crossing his arms.

"Just some groupie I met after the show. I don't even remember her name."

"Maddie, is this true?" Kyle asked, looking me right in the eye.

Behind him, Jared shook his head at me. I was torn between the two brothers, one a friend and one something more. I'd have to betray one of them no matter what I chose. I didn't want to keep this a secret from the guys, but I couldn't call Jared on his lie in front of them either. And, if I was honest with myself, I was afraid to admit the truth to them, too.

"He's right. It's not what it looks like. This was taken right after my glasses were stolen, when I was having a panic attack. Jared was helping me calm down, that's all." That part wasn't a lie, at least.

Hector poked his finger into Jared's chest. "Swear to us. Swear right now you're not together and we'll drop it."

Jared raised his hands and said, "I swear."

I nodded and kept my face blank, but inside I was breaking in two. When the show was over, we'd have to tell the guys the truth, and I could already imagine how angry they'd be.

Kyle frowned, but he blew out a breath and nodded slowly. "Well, how bad is the damage?"

"Bad," Jared said. "The photo's all over the Internet, and they have quotes from Becca saying I do this kind of thing all the time."

"That's because you do," Hector growled.

Jared glared at him, and I jumped in before this got any worse. "Lacey must have done this," I said. "When she stole my glasses, she threatened me, something about how we shouldn't get in her way or else."

"We have to tell Dan," Kyle said. "She can't get away with this shit."

Jared sank onto his bed and grabbed his laptop. "It doesn't matter. We're screwed. No one is going to vote for us now. The producers will make sure of it."

I wasn't sure I agreed with him. Just like he thought the band had only become popular because of his bad boy image, now he thought we were doomed because of one photo of us together. Still, we couldn't afford to lose even a single vote at this point in the show. I just hoped there were no other photos of the two of us floating around. We'd been so stupid and hadn't been careful enough, and now our reckless passion was coming back to haunt us. God, what had we been thinking?

My phone buzzed, and I was almost too afraid to look. Messages from Carla and Julie, asking if the photo was real, asking if I was okay, asking more questions I couldn't answer.

"Damn," Jared said. "Do not read any of these articles. Especially the comments."

"What?" I leaned over his shoulder to read his screen. The photo was on one of the most popular blogs about the show with the headline: "*The Sound*'s Secret Affair." Below, the article called Jared a playboy and made him out to be some horny asshole who slept with women as some sort of power trip. They described how this had led to Villain Complex losing their bass player, with a few harsh quotes from Becca to back it up, and compared our band to the show's former winner Addicted to Chaos—exactly the thing we'd been trying to avoid.

According to this article, I'd abandoned my internship with the LA Philharmonic to chase after him like some sort of star-struck groupie. They brought up how my father had cheated on his wife with my mom and my mom's subsequent alcoholism, like that explained everything about me. Like I was just reliving her mistakes all over again with Jared. I couldn't believe they would post stuff like this, shedding light on all the things in our past we tried to keep hidden. Things no stranger had a right to know about us. How did they even get all this info about me?

In the comments, I caught a glimpse of, "I knew it," and dozens of people calling me a slut. One even said I was probably sleeping with every guy in the band. Another said we'd only been rescued by Dan because I was screwing him, too. My eyes watered with tears, and I barely managed to blink them back. How could people be so cruel? And what was with these double standards—Jared could sleep with dozens of women and no one batted an eyelash, yet one photo of me hugging a guy and I was a slut? I hated the Internet.

Jared clicked away to a different screen with a sigh. "I told you not to read them."

I knew I shouldn't take the attacks personally, but it was hard. I wanted to ignore the slut comments, but the underlying sentiment behind every word was that I didn't deserve to be in the band or on the show. That I was a talentless hack, I'd gotten in the band by accident, and I was bringing the rest of the guys down with me. And it killed me because, deep down, I suspected all of that was true.

"I have to go," I mumbled, stumbling to the door.

Jared opened his mouth like he wanted to say something but then shook his head and dropped his eyes. I fled their room and ran down the stairs to my floor. No elevator this time. I couldn't risk running into anyone from the show right now. I had to get away—from the guys, from the show, from this life.

———

An hour later, someone knocked on my door. Jared stood outside, hands shoved in his pockets. He didn't move to kiss me, and any hope that things would be the same between us quickly slipped away.

"Not okay?" he asked softly.

"Not really." I stepped back to let him in, and he checked the hallway to make sure it was empty before he entered. He stood just inside the door—close but not close enough—and every inch of my body strained to throw myself into his arms. I needed him to kiss me and tell me everything would be okay, but he didn't make a move.

"We talked to Dan. He said the photo was no big deal and that we shouldn't worry about it."

"No big deal? Has he seen what people are saying about us?"

"He says this kind of shit always happens and it will blow over soon. He doesn't think it will hurt our chances on the show."

"I hope he's right."

"Me too…but maybe we should cool it for a while. Stop seeing each other, at least until the show is over. We don't need any more bad publicity."

How was I supposed to cool it with Jared when I saw him every single day? He was the guy I thought about when I couldn't sleep, whose touch set my nerves on fire, whose voice haunted my every step. The guy who always believed in me and made me want to reach for more. I didn't want to give him up. And maybe the article had struck a nerve or something because for the last hour all I'd been able to think about was my father and what he'd done to my mother and how I refused to become her. I didn't want to be Jared's secret anymore.

"Can't we just tell everyone the truth?" I asked. Yes, the producers didn't want us to be together, but it wasn't up to them who won the show. People liked our music, and some of the viewers might even be happy we were together.

"You already saw what they're saying online about us after one innocent photo. If we admit that we've been lying and sneaking around, the backlash could be huge. Not to mention, the guys will completely lose their shit, and you know what Dan says about cohesion and all that." He shook his head, his face pained. "We're so close to the finals and the spot on the tour. We can't afford to mess things up now. If nothing else, we owe it to the other guys to focus on the band for the next two weeks."

I wanted him to pull me into his arms and tell me he didn't care what anyone thought, that he was tired of the lying and sneaking around, that he'd do anything to be with me. But he was right; the truth would only make things worse right now. If we could just get through the rest of the show, win or lose, we might be able to have a real future together when this was all over.

"All right." I stared out the window at downtown LA sparkling with lights, at the Hollywood sign cresting the hills, at anything other than his pleading eyes and the lips I longed to kiss.

He cleared his throat. "Maybe you should go out with that Sean guy, too."

"You want me to date someone else?" I'd spent the night in his arms, and now he was pushing me toward some other guy?

"No, of course not." He drew a ragged breath. "I can't stand the idea of you with him. I just think it might throw people off, make them less focused on the two of us."

Maybe or maybe it would just fuel the slut rumors about me. I didn't want to lead Sean on, but I supposed one dinner couldn't hurt, as long as I was up front with him about only wanting to be friends. But Jared would have to keep up his reputation, too, and the thought made me sick.

"Fine." *Only two weeks*, I reminded myself. I could do anything for two weeks.

"I'll see you at rehearsal tomorrow." He hesitated and leaned in a little, like he was about to kiss me. I held still, waiting, wanting, anticipating, but he pulled back and slipped out the door without another word.

I wrapped my arms around myself and went over his words again. No matter what he said, I couldn't help but wonder if this was more than a temporary split. Suddenly our secret romance seemed a lot less sexy and a lot more like a mistake.

Chapter Nineteen

At the crack of dawn, we went on a national radio show and assured everyone that the photo was just an innocent moment of one friend comforting another. The entire band laughed off the bad headlines, acting like everything was normal, but I didn't know if anyone would buy it. Especially when the fracture in my heart got wider every time I looked at Jared.

After that we went straight to rehearsals, and I suffered for hours hearing him sing "Bad Romance," followed by a photo shoot with The Quiet Battles where we pretended to be one big happy family on Team Dan. When I finally collapsed into bed, I was too exhausted to stay up all night missing Jared, though I couldn't shake his ghost from my sheets.

The next two days were a repeat, with different publicity events and long hours rehearsing and recording both songs while the producers and camera crews watched us like hawks. Being on a break with Jared was easier than I'd expected since we never had a free minute alone together. Hell, if we got a chance to sit down and eat a real meal, we were lucky. Was this how musicians on tour lived? Sprinting from one thing to the next, pushing their bodies to the limits, giving up a normal life for one in the spotlight…. I almost questioned if I really wanted it that bad. Almost.

"We have a problem," Dan said on Saturday morning when he showed up for rehearsal. "I just talked to Steve, and he said the producers have changed their minds about 'Bad Romance.' Now they're saying you can't use it after all and have to choose something else."

"What?" I must have misunderstood him. No way could we have worked on this song for all those hours and now be unable to use it. Not with only two days until the live show. Nope. Not happening. Denied.

Jared gripped his bass so hard his knuckles went white. "But we've been practicing it all week. And we've already recorded it!"

"Did Steve say why?" Kyle asked. "Is there anything we can do to change the producers' minds?"

Dan shook his head. "He just said there was a problem, and no one can use that song anymore. It really blows, but they've done this before in previous seasons. I'm bummed, too. Your version sounded great."

"Shit. What are we supposed to do now?" Hector asked.

"How are we going to get another song ready by the live show?" I asked, breathless and jumpy, like the walls were closing around me.

Dan yanked over a chair and put on his reading glasses. "We'll pick another song right now, and I'll give you the keys to the studio so you can practice as much as you need. I'll cancel your interview tomorrow, too, so you can use that time to record the new song. I'm really sorry, but that's the best I can do."

He suggested we cover another pop song, something unexpected that we could do a rock version of, but none of us knew what to choose. We were still too excited by our version of "Bad Romance," too in love with the changes we'd made to think about any other song. With that thought, Carla's words came back to me about how I was so obsessed with Jared I couldn't think about another guy, and they sparked an idea. She adored Bruno Mars and I'd learned some of his songs to play for her, and I could definitely relate to one of them right now.

"What about 'Locked Out of Heaven' by Bruno Mars?" I suggested. The guitar in it sounded like something by The Police and I demonstrated for them, busting out the twangy chords from the verses and then the faster chorus riffs.

"That's a good one," Hector said. "It has almost a punk rock beat to it at times."

"Perfect," Dan said. "And the ladies at home will love Jared singing it, too."

Jared scowled, no doubt thinking of why I'd chosen this song. Maybe it was cruel, but I hoped every time Jared sang it he thought about me and what he was missing. He might have argued for a different song, but Kyle and Hector loved it. Dan got it quickly approved by the producers, and it was decided.

We worked late into the night and returned early Sunday for another long day, rehearsing in the morning and recording in the afternoon. By the evening, we all wanted to kill each other.

"The vocals in the second verse are still not right," Jared said, as we listened to the recording for the hundredth time. "I need to redo them."

"They're *fine*," Kyle said. "We don't have time to do them over."

The sound guys were taking a break, and Dan had left an hour ago. I rested my head on the table, too tired to move. When you played the same song nonstop for that many hours, it became like a word you'd repeated too many times: It didn't make sense anymore. That's the point we were at.

Jared continued on as if he hadn't heard his brother. "And the beat in the pre-chorus is off, too."

"Are you kidding me?" Hector asked. "I've recorded it three times already!"

"Well, do it again. We need to get this right."

"There's nothing wrong with it!"

Jared played the section again. "Right there! How can you not hear that?"

"Why don't you go in there and play it then?"

"Maybe I will!"

"Right, because this is the Jared Cross band, and you can do *everything*!"

"You want to trade places? You think it's so easy, getting in front of thousands of people and baring your soul on stage? Or answering the same stupid questions over and over again in interviews? Please, be my guest!"

"Guys, stop," Kyle said, raising his hands between them. "We need to call it a night."

"Seriously," I said. "We've been here since 7 AM. I can barely see straight, I'm starving, and my hands are killing me." Not to mention, this was starting to get ugly. Hector and Jared often bickered and then quickly made up, but never quite like this.

Jared rubbed his face, visibly exhausted. "No, the song isn't done until it's perfect. You can leave if you want, but I'm staying."

I had no doubt he would, too. Jared was not only a perfectionist, but he was hardest on himself. If we didn't stop him, he would work on this all night, and then he'd be a wreck at the live show.

"Jared, please." I placed my hand on his shoulder. "The song sounds great. If we stay any longer, we won't have any energy to perform tomorrow."

"She's right," Kyle said. "Your voice already sounds like you've been swallowing glass. You need to rest more than any of us."

"One more hour," Jared said. "Let me tweak a few things, and then I'll be done."

"Whatever, I'm out," Hector said and banged through the door. So much for our band's "cohesion."

I sighed, resigning myself to a long night in this cold, stuffy room. "I wonder if there are any more of those sandwiches in the kitchen."

"I already checked. There aren't," Kyle said. "Go get something to eat. I'll stay with him."

I hesitated. I didn't want to abandon them, but Jared had already put his headphones back on and was in the zone again, and there wasn't much I could do at this point. All my parts were recorded, and I didn't have the energy to do them over another time. Kyle had studied sound mixing in school, so he was more of a pro at this stuff than me anyway. Besides, Kyle knew how to handle his brother better than anyone.

"All right, but I'm going to check on you both later to make sure you get some rest. Don't let him burn himself out."

"I won't." Kyle gave me a quick squeeze, and I left. Jared never even looked up.

———

Sean ran over to me the instant I walked into the lobby of the hotel. "Maddie!"

"Hey," I said, with as much enthusiasm as I could muster. Naturally I'd run into him when I hadn't slept, showered, or eaten anything other than coffee and bagels over the last forty-eight hours.

"I saw that whole thing with the photo. I can't believe what people said about you. Are you all right?"

"Oh, yeah. It's just a big misunderstanding." I hadn't even had time to think about that drama, not with the new drama of the song change, but his words reminded me I was supposed to go out with him. I wanted nothing more than to pass out in my bed, but eating real food sounded pretty good at this point, too. And maybe Jared was right, and being seen with Sean would dispel some of the rumors about us.

"Hey, do you want to grab that dinner I promised you?" I asked.

"Yeah, totally. Right now?"

"If you're free," I said, and he nodded. "But before we go, I want to be up front with you, so this doesn't get weird. We're just going out as friends, okay?"

"Of course." He burst into laughter. "Oh, did you think I was asking you out on a date before?"

"No! I mean, I wasn't sure, and I think you're great and all, but with the show and…" This was getting super awkward. Time to shut up.

He grinned. "Hey, I'd totally be interested, but I have a girlfriend back home."

"Oh, okay. Good." It was a relief to know I wouldn't be leading Sean on and that he didn't expect anything from me other than a friendly dinner.

"Besides, Jared would kill me," Sean added.

"I doubt that," I muttered.

"You're really not together?"

"Nope." And this time, it felt like the truth when I said it.

We went through the revolving doors and debated the merits of the different restaurants at LA Live, finally settling on a brewery that blasted rock music and had good burgers. Perfect for a casual dinner with a friend, and since it was popular with people from the show, we'd definitely be seen together. A part of me hoped Jared would stumble back from the studio and catch me with Sean, run to my arms and kiss me in front of everyone, and say he didn't care who knew about us as long as we could be together. Yes, that level of cheese actually ran through my head. What could I say—I was running on four hours of sleep.

Though Jared never showed up to offer declarations of love, I still had a good time with Sean. We laughed about what a bad mentor Angel was, and he told me she'd shown up completely wasted for all her rehearsals this week.

"I have no idea how our song with her is going to go tomorrow," he admitted.

I whined about how the producers had changed our song at the last minute, but he didn't seem surprised. He said they'd denied his band from doing "Some Nights" by fun. for the first live show and that he'd heard about bands having other problems, too. Recording times getting switched without notice, interviews getting cancelled at the last minute, photo shoots that just never happened. We were lucky we had Dan keeping on top of these things for us, but it sounded like the other mentors weren't quite as hands-on.

Sean and I argued over which band on Team Lance would make it to the finals, since it was obvious Fairy Lights would be the last band on Team Lissa. I told him all about how Lacey had stolen my glasses and probably leaked that photo of us, but I wasn't sure he believed me. She'd been perfectly friendly with him, so maybe it was only me she hated for some reason.

Being with Sean was easy, and there was no need to sneak around or lie to anyone about spending time together. I had zero romantic feelings for him, but it was a relief to talk to someone going through a lot of the same things I was. I hadn't realized how much I needed to spend time with someone who wasn't in my band either. I loved the guys like family, but after spending every waking minute with them, I also kind of never wanted to see them again.

After our meal, we walked back toward the hotel but were stopped by a small group of people.

"Oh my god, you're the guitarist who fell off the stage!" one of them said, and the others chimed in with, "Yeah!" and "Whoa!"

I was taken aback for a second. No one had ever recognized me in public before; it was always Jared who got mobbed by fans. Would they call me a klutz? A slut, especially since I was with Sean? Or one of the other horrible things people were saying on the Internet?

"You're so cool," the first girl said. "I freaking love Villain Complex."

"Me too," the guy with them said. "Your band is killer."

"Can we get a photo with you?" a third girl asked.

"Um, yeah. Of course." That was not what I'd been expecting to hear. I wasn't anyone special, and these people acted like I was a celebrity. I couldn't wrap my head around it. But Jared was always friendly with the fans, and I needed to follow his example even if the whole experience was really strange.

They each gave their phones to Sean to have him take photos of us. I hoped he wasn't upset that they didn't seem to have a clue who he was. I posed with the group, smiling for a dozen shots, and then signed random pieces of paper for them. I'd never signed anything for someone in my life before that wasn't a legal document. It was amazing to meet real live fans of our band, but it was also a bit unsettling how they all acted like they knew me when they really didn't.

After they left, Sean said, "Wow, you're really famous now."

"I guess?" I shook my head. "That's never happened before."

"Clearly I need to cause some sort of drama, too, to bring in more fans."

I laughed. "If you do, make sure you never Google yourself. You can never unsee those things."

Chapter Twenty

On the day of the live show, my nerves were so frayed I was barely hanging together. I hadn't been this anxious about a performance since the Battle of the Bands round. We'd practiced "Locked Out of Heaven" as much as we physically could, but it was still not as smooth as we'd like. We were at a disadvantage from the other bands who'd had all week with their songs, and even if we nailed it tonight, I didn't know how many people would vote for us after the photo disaster. Clearly, we still had fans who liked our band, but would they be enough?

Tonight we'd gone for a classier look to shake things up from our normal hard rock image. I wore a strapless, black-and-white sheath dress, while the guys all wore black suits, thin ties, and white shirts. Each of them looked striking, from Kyle with his black hair slicked back and tattoos peeking above his collar, to Hector with his dark curls and broad shoulders filling out his jacket. And then there was Jared, looking almost—but not quite—a gentleman tonight. His blue eyes had a touch of dark liner, his shirt was open just enough to give a glimpse of his neck, and his tailored pants showed off every perfect angle. He looked amazing in a suit, and it killed me that I couldn't have him.

Our Loaded River song with Dan was the first performance of the night. Our mentor played bass, and though he normally sang "Nothing Breaks Me," he only chimed in on the chorus and let Jared take over. Without an instrument, Jared was free to flirt with the crowd and make love to the mic, and it took all my effort to not throw my guitar down and drag him off stage so we could be alone together. I knew what Jared looked like under those clothes, how his touch felt on my bare skin, how it sounded to hear him moan my name. Being so close and yet so far from him was pure torture.

I focused on the audience instead, and as they sang along with each word, I realized how lucky I was to be there, standing on stage with Dan Dorian of

Loaded River. No matter what happened tonight, playing beside one of my idols would always be one of the greatest moments of my life.

After the song, Dan returned to his seat in front of the stage with the other mentors. We all glowed with sweat and excitement, like some of the dark clouds hanging over us had dissipated. Maybe, just maybe, we'd make it into the next round.

The guys went to the lounge to relax before our next song, but I needed to cool off away from Jared. On stage, The Static Klingons performed their song for the "Tainted Love" theme of the night, Gotye's "Somebody That I Used to Know." Sean's vocals and the band's faster tempo made it a bit more upbeat than the original version, but I liked it. I cheered for them with the audience and waited for Sean backstage when they finished.

"There you are!" he said. We moved out of the way of the roadies setting up for the next band, and a camera crew followed us. Never a private moment, not this close to the end of the show.

"That was so good," I said. "You're definitely getting into the finals."

"Thanks, Maddie."

He placed his hands on my shoulders and kissed me, right in front of the camera. For a second I could only stand there, so shocked by his soft lips on mine, while my mind screamed that it was all wrong.

I pushed him away and choked out, "What are you *doing*?"

He shot a glance at the camera crew. "What? I thought we had a great time last night."

Wait—had I not been clear that I only wanted to be friends? I replayed our conversation in my head, and yeah, I'd been pretty damn clear. "You said it wasn't a date! You said you have a girlfriend!"

"I do, but…" His voice dropped, like he hoped the cameras wouldn't catch his words. "I thought if I kissed you I might get some extra attention for my band, get a few more votes, you know? And maybe make my girlfriend back home jealous at the same time. She, uh, didn't really approve of me going on the show."

"So you were *using* me? I can't believe you!" If I had something in my hands, I'd have thrown it at him. Maybe I could find something. A glass of water. One of my shoes. His guitar.

He ruffled his sandy hair, looking embarrassed. "I guess I thought you'd be okay with it."

"Why would you think that? Because of what everyone is saying about me?" Did he think I was a slut, too? Forget throwing something, now I wanted to punch him in the face.

"No! I don't know. Gah, I'm really sorry."

I shook my head and walked away without another word. Jared had been right about Sean all along. Even if the specifics had been wrong, Sean did have ulterior motives for spending time with me. Yes, technically I'd been using Sean, too, but he'd crossed the line by kissing me when I'd said I wasn't interested. And even worse, he'd made me the other woman against my will, just like my mom had been. If people thought I was a slut before, I couldn't imagine what they would call me now.

Jared stared at me from the other side of the revolving stage, where he must have seen everything. He disappeared into the crew unloading gear for the next performance, and I sprinted after him.

"Jared, stop!"

He halted, fists clenched at his side, and I caught up to him. His face was a blank mask, but pain flickered through the eyes I knew so well. I couldn't stand to see him like this, but there were too many people around to talk safely. I took his elbow and led him through the back of the theater to the out-of-the-way women's bathroom no one used, where I'd had my glasses stolen. We slipped inside, and I checked under the stalls to make sure they were empty and then locked the door.

Jared leaned over the sink, his head dipped down as he stared into the mirror. Under the dim fluorescent lights, he looked like a black-and-white photo—dark hair and smoldering eyes, white shirt and fair skin, black jacket and tie. I wished he would say something. I smoothed my hands down my dress to stop myself from reaching for him, fighting the invisible tether pulling me to him at all times.

"He kissed me against my will, I swear," I finally said to break the silence. "We went out last night, but I told him from the beginning it wasn't a date. Nothing happened."

He closed his eyes and drew a long breath but still didn't answer me, and a flicker of frustration made me continue.

"I don't know why I'm even explaining this to you. You're the one who wanted to cool things off until the show ended. *You* told me to go out with him. *You* flirt with other girls every single day. You have no right to be upset!"

He spun around to face me. "What do you want me to say, Maddie? That hearing you went out together makes me want to strangle him? That it nearly killed me to watch him kiss you? That every time I see you, I want to fuck you until you forget all other guys?" He spread his arms wide. "There, are you happy now?"

The passion behind his words nearly undid me. I slipped my fingers around his black tie to pull him to me. "Yes, that's exactly what I wanted to hear."

Our mouths and bodies crashed together, and after being denied Jared for days, his kiss started a riot within me. I dragged my teeth along his bottom lip and scraped them across his neck, making him gasp. His fingers tightened in my hair, tugging my head back so he could return the favor. The other night we'd taken our time together, discovering and savoring each other's bodies, but not now. We only had a few stolen minutes before we had to perform again, and our kisses had a frenzied, reckless edge, two addicts desperate for their next hit after going through days of withdrawal.

I gripped the lapel of his suit and searched his eyes. "You said we should take a break."

"You know we have to," he said, before pressing his mouth to mine again.

"Then why are you kissing me?"

"Because I can't stop myself."

He bowed his head to show me, tasting the curve of my neck and my bare shoulders. I arched my back, and he flicked his tongue between my cleavage, darting inside the top of my dress. When I moaned, his lips brushed against my nipples, already straining through the thin fabric. There was too much clothing between us, but we didn't have time to remove them. We shouldn't even be doing this here, in the middle of a show, when so much was on the line, when the producers and everyone else were only a door away. But we couldn't stop ourselves either.

His hands slid under my dress and along my thighs. I reached for the front of his pants to free the top button, urging him on without words. With one quick movement, he lifted me onto the bathroom counter, putting me at exactly the right height. My knees parted to straddle his hips, and I drew him closer, fitting him against my body. He bent down to drag my panties off me and placed a rough kiss on the curve of each knee. I gasped and tangled my fingers in his hair while his lips burned higher up my legs, along the inside of my thighs. He pushed my dress up to my hips, spreading me wider, kissing me everywhere except where I needed him most.

Only when I whimpered his name did he finally press his mouth to my core. He teased and licked and sucked every inch of me, driving me crazy, darting his tongue inside me. His mouth devoured me, his expert strokes making my entire body weak, and I threw my head back and planted my hands on the counter to steady myself. It was too good, the pleasure too intense, but his strong hands held me in place so I couldn't move away. I strained toward him, never wanting it to end, and he brought me right to the brink. But then he pulled back, leaving my body a spark about to burst into flames.

"Jared, please." I was so painfully close. He couldn't leave me like this.

He moved up my body again, mouth nuzzling against my neck, hands sliding along my waist. A condom wrapper crinkled, and then I felt him, hard and smooth against my sensitive skin. With one smooth thrust, he was inside me, and I groaned, digging my fingernails into him. As he drove into me, I wrapped my legs around him, my bare skin brushing against the back of his pants. I yanked open the collar of his shirt, needing more of his skin on mine, burying my face in his chest to breathe him in. No matter how close we were, I could never get enough of him.

He thrust in and out at a relentless, feral pace, like he was claiming me as his own. I was already so close, but he shifted angles to move deeper, making me cry out and completely lose control. I clenched around him as the orgasm ripped through me, but he didn't let up, pounding harder and faster, making the ripples of pleasure continue on and on. He gripped me tighter and moaned my name into my hair and then joined me in oblivion.

For a few minutes, we could only hang on to each other, hot and wet and shaking from the aftermath of our frenzy. When we could move again, he kissed me tenderly, stroking my cheek with his thumb.

"I missed you," he whispered.

I'd missed him too, so much. I sighed and pressed my forehead against his. "I don't want to go back out there."

"I know. But we have to."

Once we left this room, we'd have to turn off our feelings for each other again, put on our stage personalities and continue on like nothing had happened tonight. People were probably already wondering where we were, and our next performance was the most important one so far. As much as I wanted to stay with him, the charade had to continue.

I slid to the floor, and in silence, we fixed our clothes. We had another song to perform.

———

When I returned backstage, our gear had already been set up on the back of the revolving stage while Brazen played Maroon 5's "Wake Up Call" for the audience. One of the roadies rushed over to me with a horrified look on his face. "Maddie, there's an issue with your guitar."

I blinked at him. "What do you mean?"

He started to speak but then shook his head and gestured for me to follow him. There, inside my guitar case, was my beautiful sea foam green Fender, the one I'd bought with my own money when I went to college, the one I'd lovingly strummed every night in my room, the one I'd used for each performance on *The Sound*. It was the one instrument that was solely mine, and I knew every dent and chip on it. Only now its neck was snapped, too.

My mouth hung open, tears pricking my eyes, and I carefully lifted my guitar out of the case. The head dangled back, the wood completely splintered, held on only by the strings still attached. It was my baby, and now it was broken. Unplayable. Dead.

"It was like this when I opened the case, I swear," the roadie said, his words hushed. He knew how bad this was. "The other guys can vouch for me."

I clutched the guitar against my chest and sank to the floor, choking back a sob. I'd played it less than an hour ago, so someone must have done this while I was with Jared. If only we hadn't sneaked off...but how could we ever imagine this would happen? And who would do such a thing? We were all musicians here, our instruments were practically sacred to us.

"Maddie, what—" Kyle asked and then kneeled beside me. "Oh, shit. What happened?"

I held it out to him, unable to form words. He took one look and gathered me in his arms. I cried against his shoulder, and he just held me on the floor without saying anything. That guitar had become an extension of my body after so many hours playing it, and a part of me had been destroyed with it. And with only minutes before our next performance, we were screwed.

"Kyle, what am I going to do? The song—"

"It's okay. We'll get you another guitar."

"Where?" I gave a bitter laugh. "Who would let me use their guitar?" The only person I'd feel comfortable asking was Sean, except that was out of the question now.

"Maybe the show has one you can use?"

"It won't be the same, I won't know the guitar, and we've barely practiced this song as it is, and oh god, we're doomed. We're going home now, I know it."

Jared and Hector showed up, and Kyle and the roadie explained what had happened while I tried to pull myself together. Lacey must have done this. She'd stolen my glasses and leaked the photo, and now she'd broken my guitar, too. I knew she hated me for some inexplicable reason, but I still couldn't imagine she'd stoop so low. But I couldn't think of anyone else who would do this either.

While the guys argued about what to do, I rose to my feet, set my guitar back in its case, and stormed off. After a quick search, I found Lacey in makeup, wearing a poofy red dress and cowboy boots. One look at my face and the guy touching up her lipstick split. Lacey, to her credit, stood her ground.

"Why did you do it?" I asked, hands clenched at my sides.

"Pardon?" she asked.

"You broke my guitar. How *could* you?"

Her big blue eyes widened a fraction. "Your guitar is broken?"

"Don't play innocent. I know you did it!"

"Honey, I would *never* lay a hand on another girl's guitar. Not in a million years. I'd sooner steal your wallet or kiss your man."

"Is *that* what this is about? That time Jared turned you down in the elevator?"

Her nostrils flared a little. "I didn't touch your guitar, but maybe this is a lesson that you should keep an eye on your things instead of making out with every guy on the show."

It took all my control not to murder her right there under the vanity lights. "So you admit you stole my glasses?"

"I borrowed them for a few minutes." She gave a little shrug. "Just a bit of harmless fun between competitors, that's all."

"And the photo? Was that you, too?"

"Sorry, but no. Though I'm flattered you think I care that much."

My gaze swept over her for any hint she'd broken my guitar—chips of wood in her clothes, a broken fingernail, a bit of sea foam green paint—but there was nothing. I didn't want to believe her because that meant someone else was intentionally sabotaging me and the band, but unfortunately, I did. She'd been surprised when I'd mentioned my guitar, and no matter how horrible she was, I truly didn't think she would do something like this.

"Shouldn't you be on stage now?" she asked, twirling one of her blonde ringlets.

Did it matter? Without a guitar, we wouldn't be able to do the song. And even if we could find another guitar, I was too rattled to perform. The show might as well send us home right now.

Back at the revolving stage, Kyle and Hector were arguing with Steve, but I didn't see Jared anywhere. No one was performing up front, which was a bad sign. They'd probably had to cut to commercials or something to delay, but that would only give us a few minutes before it was do or die.

Dan rushed to my side. He never came backstage during the live shows, so this must be really serious. "Maddie, I'm so sorry. This has never happened before, but we're going to get to the bottom of this, I swear."

"Thanks," I said with a sigh. "Is there a guitar I can borrow for the song?"

"We can get you a Gibson, I know it's not the same, but—"

"No need," Jared said behind me, sounding out of breath. Sweat beaded across his forehead, his suit jacket was missing, his tie hung on for dear life, but he held his guitar case at his side and he'd never looked more handsome in his life.

"Did you go to the hotel?" I asked.

"Yeah. I figured this was better than some guitar you didn't know." No wonder he was out of breath. He'd gotten back so quickly that he must have run the entire way. Without even asking, he'd instantly jumped into action and known exactly what I'd need to get through this next performance.

He popped open the case and handed me his guitar. His black Fender was nearly identical to mine in weight and shape and felt almost as natural on my shoulder as my own guitar did. Plus, I'd already played it twice before.

"Thank you." I placed my hand over his for a brief moment, and when he gave me his real smile, it hit me: I was in love with him. And not like before, when I'd loved the idea of Jared, the tattooed rock star who could have any woman he wanted. Now I was in love with the *real* Jared, who sang to me in public, raced through supermarkets with his brother, and had a different villain T-shirt for every day of the week. Somehow that made everything worse because I had no idea if he felt the same for me, and either way, I still couldn't be with him. *One more week*, I reminded myself.

"Good thinking," Dan said, bringing me back to the moment. "Now get out there and win this thing."

The four of us looked a bit ragged, our hair and clothes messy like we'd just had sex (for good reason), but that worked perfectly for "Locked Out of Heaven." Jared made every girl in the audience swoon with his sultry vocals, and I stalked across the stage, my feelings for him making it all too easy to connect with the emotion in the song. It wasn't our best performance, but it was still pretty damn good. I just prayed it was good enough to get us into the finals.

Chapter Twenty-One

The results show was the longest hour of my life. In between performances from some of the previous seasons' winners (minus the band that had caused so much trouble, Addicted to Chaos, of course), the different teams were called up for eliminations. Team Angel was first, and everyone was shocked when The Static Klingons were sent home. I wasn't that sad to see Sean go, though The Static Klingons were a lot more talented than the remaining band on Angel's team, Not Too Calm. The show hadn't aired our kiss last night, thank god, so I'd never know if it would have helped Sean's band get more votes or not.

And frankly, I didn't care.

Fairy Lights was picked for Team Lissa, of course, and Lacey blew kisses at the audience when she strolled off stage. I still wanted to strangle her a little, but I knew in my gut she hadn't broken my guitar. It was back in Dan's studio now, but I had no idea if it was fixable. Not only had the producers been unable to find who had done it, they'd said it wasn't their responsibility to pay for the repairs, even though it happened while my guitar was in the show's care. Dan knew a guy who would look at it, but I wasn't optimistic. It would be expensive to repair, enough that I could buy a new guitar for the same price or less—but that was *my* guitar. I *had* to get it fixed.

Brazen won the final spot on Team Lance, and then it was Team Dan's turn. We stood on stage with the many members of The Quiet Battles (I finally counted them—eleven!), and I rocked back and forth on my heels, unable to stop moving. Kyle linked his arm with mine, probably to get me to stay still, but then we dragged the other guys in, too. *Please, please, please,* I chanted in my head as the band clung to each other. We couldn't go home now, not when we were so close to the end.

"And the band representing Team Dan in the finals is…" Ray Carter opened his envelope at sloth speed. "Villain Complex!"

The audience roared and lights flashed around us. Did Ray really say our name? Oh my god! We were in the finals! The four of us exploded with a burst of jumping, hugging, and laughing. We'd made it, we were going on tour, and we were one step closer to winning the record deal. My arms were shaking, and I could barely catch my breath. I wanted to let out a happy scream and kiss the guys and tell them I loved them. Hell, I loved everyone in the entire theater right now. And when Jared picked me up and spun me around, I grabbed his face and kissed him.

He stepped back, yanking his hands off me like he'd been burned. "What the hell, Maddie?"

Behind him, Kyle and Hector both stared at us like they weren't sure what they'd just seen. Oh god, what had I done? I hadn't meant to kiss him, I'd just been so caught up in everything, and with his arms around me, my body had taken over and done what felt natural.

"Wow, that was some reaction," Ray said. "We'll talk to Villain Complex in a minute. Let's give a hand to The Quiet Battles, who did a great job, too. We'll miss them."

We hugged the other band and said, "Good luck," but the entire time I was thinking about how I'd just kissed Jared in front of all of America. The show rushed us straight into an interview with Ray, so we didn't even get a chance to talk about what had happened before we were back on camera.

"Congrats on making it into the finals," Ray said. "Are you surprised you made it this far?"

"Definitely," Jared said, perfectly calm and collected again. "I mean, we hoped we would, but we never expected this to happen. We're so thankful for our fans who voted for us and downloaded our songs. We wouldn't have made it to the finals without them."

"Well, it's definitely well-deserved. 'Locked Out of Heaven' was a great song choice." He leaned a little closer to Jared, like he was going to let him in on a secret. "But there's something we have to discuss or the fans will kill me. That kiss." The crowd screamed, and I realized this interview was being shown on TV right now and on screens above the stage. "Now be honest—is there something going on between the two of you?"

Here it was. The moment it would all come out. I found myself strangely relieved. No more secrets, no more lies, no more sneaking around. After we came clean, this thing between us could finally be real.

"No, we're not a couple." Jared said, without any hesitation. He even gave a little laugh. "I was just as shocked as you when she kissed me."

"Maddie? Any response?" Ray shoved the mic in my face, but I could only stare at Jared with my mouth open. Was he really going to keep pretending? Even though our kiss had been live on TV in front of millions of people?

When I didn't answer, Ray turned back to Jared, ignoring Kyle and Hector like usual. "Everyone saw that photo of the two of you together, and now the kiss—but you're still saying you're *not* a couple?"

"No, I'm very single." He gave the camera a little shrug. "I can't help it if Maddie is into me though."

"You do have a reputation of being a ladies' man…"

I couldn't take it anymore. I walked away, not caring that my sudden exit was on camera or that everyone backstage was staring at me. The instinct to flee took over, and I shoved the back door open, stomped past the roadies on their smoke breaks, and ducked around the corner of the theater for some privacy. Only when I was out of sight did I lean against the wall and take big, gasping breaths of cold night air.

How dare he act like our relationship was all one-sided, like I was some groupie obsessed with him, following him around and begging him to love me. He'd been the one who had kissed me first, after all. The other night he'd held me in his arms and told me I was the only one he wanted, yet he still wouldn't admit to being with me. No matter what he said to me in private, he would continue to tell the world he was single and flirt with every girl in sight. I thought I'd uncovered the real Jared, the one behind the stage smile and the player reputation, but that was all a lie. Maybe Kyle had been right all along; Jared didn't want a serious relationship and this was a way for him to keep his options open while sleeping with me. He was just like my father, living two different lives, destroying everything with his secrets and lies.

"I think she went out here," Hector said, around the corner.

I stiffened, straining to hear if they were coming closer. There was nowhere for me to escape, and I didn't want to talk to any of them at the moment.

"Leave her. She needs some time to cool off."

Thank you, Kyle.

"This is what she does," Jared said. "She runs away when she's upset."

"You *are* together," Hector said. "I knew it!"

"No—"

"Then what was that back there?" Kyle interrupted, his voice quiet but sharp as a blade.

"I don't know. *She* kissed me. Why don't you ask her?"

"I don't need to ask her. It was written all over her face when she walked off!"

"It's nothing, I swear. Can we let it go already?"

"Stop lying to us!" Kyle suddenly yelled. I'd never heard him yell before, and it made me jump. Kyle *never* got upset. He was always the one who kept the peace, who calmed the other guys down, but not tonight.

"Fine, we hooked up!" Jared said. "Happy?"

"I fucking knew it!" Hector said. "First Becca and now Maddie!"

"This is *nothing* like what happened with Becca!"

"No? You slept with her and then dumped her, nearly breaking up the band in the process. How is this *any* different?"

Wow, when Hector put it like that, it was obvious I really had become a copy of Becca. Despite what Jared had said, he hadn't changed one bit.

"How could you do this?" Kyle yelled. "She's my *friend*!"

Jared said nothing in response. I peered around the corner and saw him staring at the street, head down and hands shoved in pockets, while his brother raged at him.

"I knew this would happen! Why do you think I didn't introduce you to Maddie for *three* years? Girls throw themselves at you every day, but no, you had to go after the *one* girl I said was off-limits! And it's my fault, too, because I knew Maddie was into you from day one, and I *still* let her join the band!"

I hadn't realized Kyle had kept me away from his brother for so long. I assumed we'd just been school-only friends who didn't really move in the same crowd. When we did hang out, it was always on campus or in a coffee shop or something. Once I thought about it, it made perfect sense. It must be tough having Jared as your brother sometimes. And I'd done the one thing I'd promised Kyle I would never do: fall for his brother.

"I said from the very beginning this was a bad idea," Hector said. "Not because of Maddie, but because of your inability to keep your dick in your pants. And the worst part is, you went behind our backs and lied to us for *weeks!*"

Jared finally spoke up again. "Only because we knew you guys would be pissed, and with Dan's talk about the producers and—"

"Don't give us that shit!" Hector shouted. "We're supposed to be a team! This isn't the Jared Cross band, despite what the show thinks, and you don't get to make decisions for all of us!"

"I'm sorry, okay?" Jared replied, his voice strained. "The whole thing was a mistake, and if I could go back and redo it, I would."

Was that how he really felt? It was all clear now. I was nothing more than a mistake, another notch in his bedpost he'd like to erase, another girl whose heart he'd broken. I squeezed my eyes shut, but a tear trickled down my face anyway and I swiped it away.

"I can't even look at you right now," Kyle said. "I'm going inside."

"Great, now we'll have to find *another* guitarist or bassist," Hector muttered.

"I know," Kyle said, as they went through the door.

I covered my mouth to hold back a cry. They were already talking about replacing me. I was going to be kicked out of the band, and the life I'd come to love would be gone forever. Jared was right—this had all been a mistake.

I waited a few more minutes in the hope I could escape to the hotel without running into any of them. But when I rounded the corner, Jared was still there, holding onto the chain-link fence and staring at the street.

He heard my footsteps and turned, face falling when he saw me. "Maddie…did you hear all that?"

"When you called me a mistake? Yeah, I heard it." I'd wiped away my tears, but my eyes watered all over again. No, I would not cry in front of him. I refused.

He sighed. "I didn't mean it like that. And what I said to Ray in there, that was all part of the act, you *know* that. We both agreed we had to do this."

"But when will the act end?" I asked. "When the show is over? What about the tour? What if we win? When will I be good enough to not be a secret anymore?"

"It's not like that! The show—"

"It's *always* the show or the band or some other excuse! How am I supposed to believe anything you say? You had no problem lying to your brother and your best friend for weeks. As far as I know, everything you told me is a lie, too, and you just don't want to give up your infamous player lifestyle!"

He stepped back, like I'd punched him in the chest. "Wow. I thought you saw the real me, but I guess I was wrong. I've been with no one else since I met you. No one!"

"So tell everyone right now that you lied, that you do care about me, that we do have something between us. Tell the whole world we're together, and I'll believe you."

He was quiet for a moment and then said, "You know I can't do that."

"Then I have nothing else to say to you." I started to walk away, but he moved to block my path, pleading with his eyes for me to listen.

"Maddie, you don't understand. This band is my *entire* life. It's all I have. If we fail, you and Kyle will go back to school and on to other things, and Hector has his graphic novels and his art. Me? I'm a fucking bartender. Oh, wait, I'm not even that anymore because I quit my job to come on the show. I put everything I have, everything I *am*, into this band. We have to win, or all of that is for nothing."

"How can you say the band is all you have? Even if we lose the show, you're talented, and you have money and connections. You have a brother who would do anything for you, you have a best friend who sticks beside you no matter what… and you have *me*. Isn't that enough?"

"That's not what I meant," he said, tearing at his hair. "Music is the only thing I've ever been good at, and if I don't succeed at that, I'll have nothing, I'll *be* nothing. I thought you, of all people, would understand that. And if I have to pretend I'm single and that I'll sleep with every girl in the world to keep people voting for us, to keep them coming to our shows and buying our albums, then that's what I'll do."

I did understand, on some level, because that same passion for music and that same drive to succeed urged me on, too. But Jared's words made it clear that this would never stop. Not even when the show ended because there would always be something else: the tour, the album, future shows. As long as we were *this* band, with Jared's "villain" image, we could never be together.

"I love you, Jared," I said, my voice breaking. "But I can't do this anymore. I can't pretend we're just friends and sneak around and watch you flirt with other girls. I just can't. And you're wrong—people will buy our albums and come to our shows because they like our music, not because of your stupid reputation. But if this is what you think the band needs, then I'm done and this is over." The words were torn from my chest, burning my throat on the way out, but I couldn't stop them.

His mouth fell open, but he didn't answer. I supposed his silence *was* my answer. I darted around him as the tears burst free. I couldn't look at him, couldn't be near him, couldn't hear another word from his mouth. I'd bared my heart to him, and he had nothing to say in return.

"Maddie, wait!" he called. But it was too late, and I was already through the door. Because that's what I always did when life got to be too much for me: I ran.

I dashed inside the theater, tearing past the roadies and other bands, heading for the exit so I could return to my hotel room and sob my heart out in private. But before I could get to the door, I bumped into Steve.

"Maddie, everything okay?" he asked.

I wiped at my eyes but couldn't answer him. No, everything was very much not okay. I'd just lost everything, and I didn't know what to do now.

"Let's talk somewhere private." He led me to his office, with a desk and a computer and a mountain of paperwork. I didn't know what he wanted, but at least there was no one watching me here.

He sat in his desk chair and gestured for me to sit. "I saw the interview, and I heard the band had a big fight outside. If there's a problem, I can try to help."

I sank into one of the chairs. How could he help me? He couldn't fix things with Jared or the band. God, how was I supposed to face any of the guys again after tonight? They'd already been talking about replacing me. I'd turned out to be exactly what Hector predicted, and even worse, I'd probably destroyed my friendship with Kyle in the process. And Jared…I couldn't even think about Jared right now.

I dropped my head. "I just…I can't do this anymore."

"I completely understand. You've been through a lot. This can't be easy for you." He folded his hands on the table. "We don't usually do this, but in light of everything that's happened, maybe it would be a good idea for you to leave the show." My eyes widened, and he quickly added, "I'm not saying we're kicking you off or anything, don't worry. Just that if you felt you had to leave, we wouldn't stop you."

Would they really let me leave? It was tempting, more tempting than I wanted to admit. Being on the show for weeks, trying to keep up a certain image while putting everything into the band and our performances, only to have it all fall apart tonight…. I was just exhausted. I wanted to go home and sleep for the rest of the summer.

"What about the contract? It says I have to stay for the duration of the show."

"It has a provision that band members can leave in emergency situations. Say, if they're injured or ill or if a family member passes away, things like that. This doesn't technically qualify, but I'm willing to bend the rules a tiny bit. We don't want you to be miserable, after all."

"But what will happen to the band? Who will play guitar for them?" Even if the guys were mad at me, I didn't want to screw them over.

"We'll find someone to fill in for you, don't worry." He gave me a sympathetic smile. "Trust me, they'll be fine. Let me handle everything. And if you change your mind and want to come back, that's okay, too."

I didn't *want* to leave, but I couldn't continue in the band either. That was clear after everything Jared and the other guys had said. Maybe the best option *was* for me to go home. Besides, it sounded like they would be okay without me. They could still win the show, and they could find a new bassist when they were ready, one who wouldn't sleep with Jared and ruin everything.

I made my decision, and that night I packed my bags and left the hotel for good.

Chapter Twenty-Two

My apartment was empty when I returned, and the mail had piled up. Julie and Carla must both be out of town again. They'd probably told me at some point, but I'd been a terrible friend to them. We'd barely spoken more than a few words in weeks, and when we had, I'd lied to them.

I'd lost myself in the show, in Jared, in the impossible dream and the beautiful lie. No more. Rock Star Maddie had been a total failure. Time to return to Normal Maddie. I'd been a fool, thinking I could be anything more than that. I'd been perfectly happy with my life and my plans for the future until Jared had invited me to join his band and gotten me off-track. He'd tempted me to want a louder life, one where he and I could be together, but we'd been doomed from the start. That life was over, and now I remembered who I really was: the geeky piano player who dated safe guys, practiced guitar in secret, and watched from the sidelines while others went after their dreams.

Maybe if I begged the LA Philharmonic, I could get my internship back for the rest of the summer. No, that would be impossible. But there were plenty of other things I could do until school started. I had enough laundry to last a lifetime. I could start applying to graduate schools. I could lie in bed all day and get really, really drunk.

Guess which one of those I did.

The less that's said of the next few days, the better. I turned off my phone so I wouldn't have to deal with the outside world at all. I raided our alcohol supply and forgot about personal hygiene entirely. I ate nothing but ramen and ice cream and watched a ton of Netflix.

In my darkest moments, I watched videos of us performing on the show and cried about how I'd never be on stage with the guys again. In my rush to leave the show, I'd left my guitar at Dan's studio, not that it mattered since it was broken anyway. Besides, it held too many memories now. It would be a long time before I could touch a guitar again.

I tried to watch some of the interviews we'd done, but all I heard were our lies and all I saw was Jared's fake stage smile. Even worse, someone had recorded the entire fight between the two of us with their phone and posted it online. One of the roadies, it had to be. I watched it over and over, alternating between regretting everything I'd said to Jared and getting angry at him all over again. This time I didn't read the comments under the video though. I'd learned my lesson on that at least.

But the videos that hurt the most, and the ones I watched a thousand times, were the ones capturing behind-the-scenes moments of all of us. The guys joking around in rehearsal, being silly on our breaks, wrestling and grabbing each other for goofy man-hugs. That time when we'd switched instruments and I'd banged on Hector's drums. Dan coaching me on my stage presence and my wardrobe.

And Jared—laughing at something Kyle had said or bent over his bass with a look of concentration or practicing the same lyric a hundred different ways to get it right. Those videos were the only ones that showed the genuine Jared, and I couldn't stop torturing myself with them. I missed the way his true smile lit up his face, the way his real laugh burst out of him like it was a surprise every time. But I doubted I'd ever see that Jared again.

———

I heard one of the girls wheel her suitcase into the apartment, but I couldn't get out of bed. What was the point? Besides, moving sounded like a lot of effort, and my head pounded like someone was kicking me in the skull over and over. Last night I'd discovered a secret stash of vodka in the kitchen and might have gone a little overboard. Not that it mattered, since I had nowhere to be anyway.

"Maddie?" Julie called.

"Here," I replied. Ow, too loud, so much pain.

"Why are you here? Isn't there a week of the show left?" Her voice got closer as she moved through the apartment. "Hey, since you're home, I need you to try on your Harley Quinn costume so I can do the final adjustments. Comic-Con is only in two weeks. Can you believe it?"

I covered my face with a pillow and groaned. I couldn't wear that costume now; it would only remind me of Jared. Not to mention, I was never getting out of bed again.

"Maddie?" She knocked on my door. "Can I come in?"

I gave a noise that sounded like "unngghh," and she opened the door and sat beside me on the bed.

"Wow, you reek. Have you been drinking?"

I moaned under the pillow. "I'm never touching vodka ever again."

"Hang on." She left and returned a few minutes later with some water and pain meds. "Take these."

I did as she said and then closed my eyes, leaning back against the headboard. Julie smelled faintly of vanilla, and her familiar scent gave me a small amount of comfort. She'd been my best friend since we were in eighth grade, but I'd barely seen her this summer. I missed hanging out with her. I even missed her getting on my case all the time.

"What's going on?" she asked.

"Didn't you see the show?"

"No, I was flying back from Seoul. What happened?"

Oh, right. She'd been visiting her grandparents. I should have remembered that. Further proof I was the worst friend ever.

I sighed. "It's over. The show. The band. Jared. Everything."

"What? Tell me."

I spilled everything, and she listened without judging or interrupting, letting me vent and cry. When it was over and I'd let it all out, she wrapped me in a tight hug. "Maddie, I'm so sorry."

"I ruined everything," I said, grabbing a tissue and blowing my nose. "My place in the band, my friendship with Kyle, my relationship—or whatever it was—with Jared, and even things with you and Carla. I've ruined it all."

"Okay, now you're being silly. You definitely didn't ruin your friendship with us. We'll be friends forever, no matter where life takes us, so don't worry about that. And I'm sure Kyle feels the same, too."

"I guess." I pulled my knees up and rested my head on them.

"Maddie, you know I love you, but when things get hard, you always run away. You ran from your mom and her drinking, you ran from Jared when he invited you to join the band, and now you're running from this, too. Maybe it's time to stop running and fight for what you want."

"I don't know what I want."

"Don't give me that. You know *exactly* what you want." She stood up and moved to the door. "Think about it. I'm going to unpack, but I'm here if you need me. And take a shower. You're disgusting."

She closed the door behind her. I sat there, digesting her words, until my headache faded enough that I could move again. I took Julie's advice and got in the shower, and the hot water slowly washed off the gloom of the last few days. My god, what was I doing? I'd turned into my mother, staying in bed all day, drowning my life in a bottle, and giving up guitar because a guy had broken my heart. That wasn't me. I didn't want to become her. My life didn't have to be one big repeat of her mistakes.

What did I want? I wanted Jared, but I wasn't sure I could ever have him the way I wanted. But even if we could never be together, I wanted to be part of the band again. I wanted to be *myself* again—my true self, the one I'd uncovered these past few weeks, who went after her dreams, who played guitar blindfolded, who fell off the stage and got back up again.

I wanted to fight.

Chapter Twenty-Three

I t was Saturday, which meant the live show was in two days, and if I wanted to perform with the guys, I had to patch things up with them and learn the new songs as soon as possible. I found them rehearsing at Dan's studio, but I couldn't face them all yet. I texted Kyle and asked him to meet in the room where The Quiet Battles used to rehearse.

When he walked in, he immediately grabbed me in one of his bear hugs. "Maddie, I'm so glad you came back."

"I'm sorry, Kyle," I said into his shoulder, fighting back tears. "For lying, for sneaking around behind your back, for breaking my promise, for quitting the band, for being the worst friend ever. For everything."

"It's okay. Did you get my messages?"

"Yeah. Eventually."

After I'd sobered up, I'd turned on my phone and found both texts and voice-mails from Kyle, Hector, and Dan, all begging me to come back. There'd even been one from my mom, asking if I was okay. And four from Jared that I still couldn't face. I'm not sure I'd ever be able to listen to those. But I'd checked all the others and had slowly come back to the world.

Kyle sighed. "I was really mad at first, at both of you, and I couldn't believe you just left like that. But I don't blame you for what happened, and I'm over it now. And since you left, Jared's been a wreck. He spends every waking moment rehearsing this week's songs, even long after Hector and I are done for the day. On those rare moments he does take a break, he just listens to this one My Chemical Romance song over and over."

I sucked in a breath. I knew exactly which song Kyle meant: the song Jared had sung to me before the audition, the one he still referenced all the time. "Is it 'I'm Not Okay'?"

"That's the one, and I swear if I hear it one more time I'll shoot myself." He tugged at the gauges in his ear, like he was annoyed.

The door opened and I froze, worried it was Jared, but instead Hector slammed into me. It was like being hugged by a mountain, squeezed between his hard chest and his muscular arms. "Maddie!"

Hector had never hugged me before, except when we'd been celebrating our on-stage victories, not like Kyle and Jared who gave their hugs freely. I held him for a minute, my eyes watering up again. It seemed like the guys had missed me as much as I'd missed them.

He finally let me go. "Thank god you're back. I've been barely keeping this band together without you."

"It's true," Kyle said.

I laughed at the idea of Hector, of all people, keeping them together. "You're okay with me staying in the band?"

Hector grinned. "Hell yes. We need you."

My shoulders slumped with relief. "I wasn't sure after the other night…"

He groaned. "Jared said you heard all that. Listen, I didn't mean I *wanted* to replace you. I just assumed you'd leave like Becca did."

"And you were right."

"Yeah, but you came back."

Someone knocked on the door, and Kyle slipped out to talk to whoever it was, leaving me alone with Hector. Was Jared on the other side? I wasn't sure I could deal with him yet.

"I'm really sorry about everything that happened," I said.

"Don't worry about it." He grabbed a drumstick from the back of his pants and twirled it in his fingers. "You know, I wouldn't be in this band if not for Jared."

"Oh, yeah, he made you learn the drums in high school?" I remembered Jared saying that in our first interview for the show. Why was Hector bringing this up now?

"Sort of. He and Kyle were always playing music, and one day I tried out their drums and was hooked. I spent every day at their house after that, just so I could play with them. When we started the band, I was living with my grandmother and we didn't have much money, so Jared bought me a drum kit for my eighteenth birthday."

"Wow, that's a pretty big gift."

"It was nothing to him. Changed my life though. And you know their mom is this famous songwriter and their dad is a big shot lawyer for, like, every big musician out there, right? But Jared refuses to let them pull any strings for him. He said if we succeed, he wants it to be on our own, without any handouts. He wants to know we earned it. That's just the kind of guy he is."

A lot of things about Jared clicked into place. How hard he worked, how much he pushed himself, how he would do anything to make sure we won. Not that it excused his actions, but I understood him a tiny bit better. "Why are you telling me this?"

He rubbed the back of his neck. "I know I get on his case a lot and complain about this being 'his' band and all that, but I honestly couldn't do all the things he does for us. Jared makes me crazy sometimes, but he's also the best guy I know. Don't give up on him yet, okay?"

I wasn't sure how to answer that. I didn't *want* to give up on Jared, but I couldn't continue with things the way they were either.

The door opened, and Kyle returned. "That was Dan. He wants to know what's going on."

I drew a long breath and stood up straighter. "Well, I'm back, and I'm ready to rehearse. What songs are you working on this week?"

"The new one is 'Radioactive' by Imagine Dragons. Dan chose it because none of us could agree on anything after the results show."

"What's the theme?"

"No theme since it's the finals. We also have to play our song from the audition again."

I nodded. I hadn't practiced "Behind the Mask" in weeks, but that song was branded on my soul. I'd never forget how to play it. I didn't know "Radioactive," but I would learn the guitar for it by Monday even if I had to stay up all night tonight and tomorrow.

"Who's been playing guitar?" I asked. "Or did you get someone to play bass?"

The guys exchanged a look. "Jared's kind of doing both," Kyle said.

"What do you mean?"

"On Wednesday we all assumed you'd come back after you blew off some steam, so Jared learned the bass for the song. But by Friday, it was clear you were gone for good, and Jared switched to the guitar."

"He learned *both*?"

"Yep. And recorded both parts himself, too."

No wonder he was spending all his time here; he was doing the work of two musicians instead of one. "Didn't the show get someone to fill in for me?"

"They did, but the guy was terrible, and Jared flipped out and scared him off. Dan's been filling in as needed until we figured out what to do."

I hung my head. "I'm so sorry I bailed on you guys. I just went a little crazy, and I couldn't deal with anyone. But I won't abandon you again, I promise."

"Hey, we all lost ourselves a little that night," Hector said. "But that's over now."

"Have you talked to Jared at all?" Kyle asked me.

"No." I glanced at the door again. Jared must be in this studio somewhere, only a few walls separating us. "I'm not ready to face him yet. I know I'll have to, but I just need a little more time."

Kyle nodded. "I'll tell him what's going on. For today, why don't you practice in here while you learn the song?"

"That sounds good." At some point I'd have to talk to Jared, but no matter what happened with him, I was a part of this band and I deserved to be on the show with them. I wanted to be by their side whether we won or lost and for everything that came after.

———

By some miracle, my hotel room was still mine. I'd never checked out, but I'd assumed the producers would cancel it after I'd left. But Dan wouldn't let them give it up because he kept telling them I'd come back. Even after I'd walked away, he'd still believed in me.

I set my bags down and fell onto the bed I'd slept in for the last few weeks, and it felt as much like returning home as going back to my apartment. Except this room was much cleaner at the moment. I pulled out my acoustic guitar to play through "Behind the Mask" again so I wouldn't be rusty on Monday, but as soon as I picked off the first chord, someone knocked on my door. I knew who it was before I even opened it.

Jared was holding his guitar case, and today's villain shirt said, "Moriarty Was Real," from BBC's *Sherlock*. He had dark circles under his eyes and looked like he hadn't shaved in days, but he was still every bit as handsome as I remembered. You'd think after spending nearly every waking minute with him for weeks I'd be immune to the shock of his blue eyes, his perfect lips, his kissable neck, but no.

"Not okay?" he asked softly.

"Not okay." Very much not okay, especially now that he was here. "But I will be."

"Did you get my messages?"

"Yes, but…I couldn't listen to them."

He gave me a hesitant smile. "Probably for the best. They were pretty pathetic. There was a lot of groveling and begging. Some drunken singing. It wasn't pretty."

Now I wished I had listened to them. Maybe things would be different now. Or maybe I still wouldn't believe a thing he said. Jared was a master of words, of using his voice and looks to manipulate people, and I didn't need any more empty promises.

He looked past me into the room. "Can I come in?"

I nodded and stepped back, quickly putting distance between us. I didn't trust myself being so close to him. But he didn't move toward me; instead, he set his guitar case down on the bed, and I realized it wasn't his case—it was mine.

"What…" I held my breath and popped it open. My beautiful green guitar had been repaired, and you couldn't even tell it had been broken except for a small ring of lighter wood on the neck. I ran my hands over it, my eyes tearing up. My guitar was scarred, but it was whole again. Like me. "You got it fixed?"

"I wanted you to have your guitar, even if you didn't come back."

"Thank you." Jared knew how much this guitar meant, and my heart softened a tiny bit, knowing he'd done this for me. I closed my eyes and strummed a chord, enjoying the familiar weight in my arms. This must have cost a fortune, especially to have it done so quickly. "How much was it? I can repay you…" Eventually. Somehow.

"No, definitely not."

"But—"

"Please, I want to do this for you. Let me try to be a hero for once."

I dropped my gaze. "All right."

He stood there a long moment, looking anywhere but at me, and our unspoken words hung between us. I felt like apologizing, but for what? For being honest about how I felt? I'd told him I loved him, and he'd let me walk away.

"I should go," he said, clearing his throat. "I just wanted to bring you that and to say I'm sorry for everything that happened and everything I said the other night."

"I'm sorry, too." Because I was, even if I wouldn't take back anything I'd said. I hated hurting him, but I couldn't let him keep hurting me either.

"I'm really happy you're back," he said. "And I know I might not be able to fix things between us, but I'm going to try."

I waited for him to say more, but he slipped out the door without another word. I wasn't sure how he planned to fix things. Nothing had changed between us since that night, even if he had gotten my guitar fixed. He obviously cared for me, at least a little, but that wasn't enough. He was still the guy who would do anything to win, who flirted with other girls, who flashed his stage smile for the audience and kept his real self hidden away. Maybe he wanted to fix things, but I refused to be his secret anymore.

Chapter Twenty-Four

It was time. One last day of performances, with four bands competing for the prize: a contract with Mix It Up Records, plus all the opportunities that came with it. Spots on late night talk shows. Songs on the radio. Performances on future seasons of *The Sound*. Plus, the headlining spot on the tour next month.

Somehow, despite the odds, despite all the roadblocks thrown in our path, our band had made it to the finals. When I'd agreed to help the guys with their audition, I never in a million years dreamed we'd get this far. And yet, I knew we deserved to be here. I knew we had a chance at winning.

I'd only spent a day practicing "Radioactive" on my own, followed by one day with the rest of the band, but for once, I wasn't too worried. I could admit it now: I was a damn good guitarist. I had the song down, and what I might lack in practice, I'd make up for in energy. I wouldn't let anything hold me back tonight.

We did our soundcheck in the morning, and then had an hour break for lunch before we had to start getting ready for the live show. I headed for the food table with the other guys, but Jared stopped me.

"Come with me," he said, a slight smile on his lips.

I'd finally listened to all his messages the night before. He'd apologized a dozen times and pleaded for me to come back—if not for him, then for the other guys. He'd even sung me a drunken rendition of "Stay" that had morphed into "I'm Not Okay (I Promise)" halfway through. It had broken my heart all over again, but hearing how upset he'd been had mended it a tiny bit, too.

"Where are we going?" I remembered all too well the other times we'd sneaked off during a show. Not that I wasn't tempted, of course, but nothing like that was going to happen today.

"I want to show you something."

He led me out the side entrance of the theater and past the security guards to where the line for the audience wrapped around the block. People stood when they saw us approaching, and some cheered or shouted our names. I slowed, uncomfortable with all these people looking at me. This wasn't like on stage where I couldn't really make out faces in the crowd, where there was some distance between us and the fans. And it wasn't like when we'd met fans before, one at a time or in a small group. There were *hundreds* of people here. Maybe thousands. But Jared walked over without any hesitation, and I tailed behind him.

"Hey," he said, to the group of girls at the front of the line. They didn't look a day older than thirteen and had one very patient parent with them.

"Oh my god, you're Jared Cross! And Maddie Taylor! We love you!" The girls all shrieked and bounced and flailed, and I couldn't help but laugh. They were so enthusiastic, so excited to see us. *Both* of us.

"Thanks," Jared said, with a warm smile. "We love you, too."

"I'm freaking out. I can't believe you're really here," one of the girls said, fanning herself.

"Where are you from?" he asked.

"Portland. We've been camped out here all night."

"Wow, thank you for coming to see us. We're truly honored."

"You're, like, my all-time favorite guitarist," a girl in glasses told me. "I totally want to be you when I get older."

Her words hit me hard, right in the chest, and my throat closed up. "Thank you," I managed to get out. "That means so much to me."

"She *is* pretty amazing," Jared agreed.

"Please tell us you're together," the first girl said, looking back and forth between us. "Please!"

"You…want us to be together?" I asked. Is this what Jared wanted to show me? Even though I'd wondered if some fans might want us to be a couple, I didn't expect this reaction after all the nasty comments about us online and everything that had happened between us. But these girls looked like they might mash our faces together and force us to kiss in front of them.

"Yes! You *have* to be!" my fangirl said.

"You're just *so* perfect for each other!" the third girl added.

"I agree," Jared said and smiled at me. "We're trying to figure things out right now. But I'm hopeful."

The girls all clutched their chests and said, "Aww."

I stared at him, completely speechless. For the first time ever, Jared wasn't denying his feelings for me. He wasn't saying he was single. He wasn't saying we were just friends. Was he giving up the act finally? Or was he just joking around in front of these girls?

They all wanted photos with us and asked us to sign things, and the crowd around us grew. We carried on down the line, talking to all of the people who'd come to see our band, and encountered the same thing over and over. The fans loved our music, and they didn't care about Jared's player image. They wanted the fairy tale, the epic romance, the story of the reformed bad boy who fell in love with the good girl. Some people even had signs that read "Jared + Maddie" with hearts all over them, while others had drawn the Villain Complex logo on their arms and cheeks like tattoos. We even ran into some people wearing Villain Complex T-shirts.

"I didn't even know we *had* T-shirts," I said to Jared.

"News to me, too. How do I get one of those?"

"Here, you can each have one," the woman said. "I made them."

I held the shirt up to my chest. "Thank you, I love it."

Jared and I both pulled them on over the shirts we were already wearing, and I thought the fan might faint on the spot.

We spent our entire lunch break there, and I was sad when we had to go back inside but also more alive than I could ever remember being. Talking to the fans made every single thing we'd gone through worth it and gave me even more motivation to do my best tonight. That was the dream, right there—not winning the show or the recording contract or even the tour. It was knowing our music had touched other people's lives, that people had come to see our band, that they were rooting for us. And finally, Jared realized that, too.

——

Our special guests arrived just before the show started. Hector embraced his grandmother and his three little sisters, speaking to them in Spanish, while Kyle planted a huge kiss on Alexis. And behind them all stood Julie and Carla, along with my third guest: my mom.

"Mom, you made it!" I said, and ran to her arms. There was nothing like being hugged by your mother. Even if things between us had been weird for a while, it was still the most comforting feeling in the world.

"I can't wait to see you perform," she said into my hair. "I'm so proud of you, Madison."

I'd called her right after I'd rejoined the band, but I hadn't been sure she would actually come to the show. Getting out of the house was a challenge for her on most days, but she'd flown down to LA to see me, and that was huge for her. Even if she didn't approve of me playing guitar, she was trying and she was sober, and I was going to do my best to keep things good between us from now on. And maybe, someday, I'd even call my father, too.

Jared stood to the side, the only one who didn't have any family or friends waiting for him. We'd each been given two tickets for family members, but he'd given his to Hector, while Kyle had given me his spare. Jared's family—the only people he really cared about anyway—was already here.

Julie gave me a fierce hug and whispered, "I'm glad you decided to fight."

Carla hugged me next and wished me luck, and then I brought my mom over to meet Jared. "Mom, this is Jared Cross."

"Ah, yes. I've heard a lot about you."

Jared flashed her his most charming smile. "Only the good things are true, I promise."

"I'm not sure I believe that," she said but smiled back. When he went to say hello to Hector's family, she leaned close and whispered, "He's very handsome in person."

I laughed. Yes, yes, he was.

Our guests left to find their seats, and Dan called us over for one last pep talk.

"I know things haven't been easy these past few weeks, and some of that was my fault. I pressured you too hard to worry about what the producers wanted and about winning votes, and I apologize for that. Your brand and your image are important, but this industry can drag you down and turn you into someone you're not. Don't ever lose sight of who you are—both individually and as a band."

He nodded at each of us in turn, and I knew he was referring to what had happened this week. Dan had never questioned my departure or my return; he'd just accepted it, and I was so grateful to him for that. He'd given us space to work out our issues, and we were stronger because of it.

"You may not be what the producers want, but I know you can win this thing," he continued. "You're the most talented, most original band on the show, and the fans love you. And no matter what happens, I'm proud to have been your mentor."

He hugged each of us and wished us luck and then took his place with the other mentors in front of the stage. Yes, Dan might have given us some bad advice, but he truly cared about us and wanted us to succeed. We'd learned so much from him in the past few weeks, and I was really glad I'd spilled coffee on Angel that day.

The lounge was mostly empty with only three other bands still on the show. While we waited for our turn to go on stage, Jared did his vocal exercises, Hector stretched his neck and shoulders, and Kyle paced back and forth. I flexed my wrists and fingers, trying to loosen myself up a bit. Tonight we'd gone for the full-out rock star look after Dan had pointed out that we were the only true rock band left. Black clothes and boots. Studded belts. Silver jewelry. Leather jackets. And Hector wore his normal Villain Complex hat, of course.

On the screens, we watched Brazen do a Katy Perry cover and Not Too Calm perform their song from the audition, which I barely remembered. Finally, it was our turn with "Behind the Mask."

When the stage rotated and we were hit with the lights and the roar of the crowd, I didn't know how I'd ever thought I could give this up. That familiar rush of adrenaline and endorphins swept through me, like a hit of my favorite drug, and I clutched my guitar, ready to begin.

We usually jumped right into our songs when the stage finished turning, since the producers were such crazy sticklers to the schedule, but Hector didn't start us off. Was there a problem? I turned to look at him and heard Jared speak into his mic.

"Before we start this song, there's something I need to say."

I spun around. What was he doing? The producers had a firm no-talking-to-the-audience rule. He was going to get us in trouble. I glanced at Kyle and Hector, but they were both grinning, so I knew they were in on this, too.

"It's amazing how a single moment can change everything." Jared smiled at me, a private smile hinting at all the things only the two of us knew. "This next song certainly changed my life."

The audience cheered, probably thinking of our audition. But from the way he looked at me, I knew he was referring to that moment when he'd caught me playing this song on his guitar, when he'd heard me belt out the lyrics like they were my own. The moment he'd said he'd first started to fall for me.

He pulled the mic from the stand and crossed the stage to face me. "Maddie, all my life, music's been the only thing that's ever made sense—until I met you. I know I messed up, but I'll do anything to get you back." He sank to his knees like he was begging, and the audience screamed, but they hushed when he spoke again. "You're the only woman in the world for me, and I don't care who knows it. I want to be with you and only you." He stopped and took a deep breath, staring up at me. "I love you, Maddie."

The crowd was silent, waiting for my response, but I was too stunned to speak. I couldn't believe he'd done this in front of everyone, on live TV. He loved me, and he'd just announced it to the entire world. No more lies. No more secrets. No more sneaking around or acting for the camera. No more watching him flirt with other girls and pretending I didn't care. Jared had made it possible for us to finally be together, for this thing between us to be real.

"Kiss him!" someone in front of the stage yelled, and I laughed.

I grabbed the collar of his jacket to pull him up to my lips. He wrapped his arms around me, and we kissed under the lights, in front of the crowd and the cameras, in front of the guys and my friends and even my mom.

"I love you, too," I said while the audience went wild.

Hector snapped his drumsticks, reminding me we were on stage for a reason. Jared moved back to his position, and I scrambled to control my racing heart so I could focus. Jared loved me, and he'd told everyone about us. I couldn't stop smiling.

We launched into "Behind the Mask," the same song we'd performed for our audition, but it sounded different now. Jared's bass playing had gotten much better, thanks to Dan's help, and I was no longer the terrified, awkward girl on stage. We'd all improved so much in the last few weeks—not just individually, but as a group. We'd learned how to work together as one cohesive unit.

I moved across the stage, letting the song pour out of me and into the guitar, feeling every note and every word deep inside me. And when Jared sang, his face twisting with the emotion behind the words he'd written, the audience sang along, too. I could even see some of the fans, the ones near the stage, swaying and shouting out the lyrics, holding their "Jared + Maddie" signs. The song took on new life, becoming a collaboration between us and the fans, an experience we all shared together. When we hit the bridge and the music went quiet to focus on Jared, the way the fans' voices echoed through the theater sent shivers down my spine. I joined in again with my guitar, and the rest of the guys rushed back in, and we finished the song even stronger, bolstered by the love from the crowd.

As soon as the stage turned around, Jared grabbed me and lifted me up, kissing me hard, sending flashes of heat throughout my entire body.

He set me back down, and I smiled up at him. "I can't believe you did that. I thought you would do anything to win, anything to make sure the band succeeds."

"I changed my mind." He ran his fingers through my hair, staring into my eyes like he hadn't seen me in years. "Don't get me wrong—I still want to win. But after you left, I realized winning the show wasn't worth losing you. Besides, you were right. I don't have to be the villain anymore for the band to succeed."

"You two are disgusting," Hector said, making gagging noises.

"Seriously, get a room," Kyle said.

"Oh, I plan on it." Jared kissed my neck in the spot he knew made me crazy.

Kyle opened his mouth to say something else, but his words died when we heard Fairy Lights start playing. Because they weren't doing the song they'd been scheduled to perform—they were doing a country version of "Radioactive."

Lacey had stolen our song.

Chapter Twenty-Five

At first, we all stood there and listened, like we weren't sure what we were hearing. Maybe this was a joke. Maybe they were messing with us, and they would switch to their own song any second now. But when they got to the chorus, we knew this was really happening.

"What's going on?" I asked. "Is she…. Are they…." I couldn't even finish the sentence. It was too big, too horrible, too unbelievable.

Hector took off his baseball cap and tore at his hair. "Shit, what are we going to do? We can't do this song now!"

Kyle pulled the crumpled schedule from his pocket. "It says right here they're supposed to be covering 'Jesus Take the Wheel' by Carrie Underwood."

Jared grabbed the schedule and studied it. "This must be some kind of mistake."

"How can it be a mistake?" I asked. "They're doing *our* song! And they've clearly been practicing it. Lacey did this on purpose!"

Kyle shook his head. "She couldn't have done this alone."

"He's right," Jared said. "The producers must be involved with this, too."

"We need to talk to Dan," Hector said.

We moved to a spot where we could see the audience while Fairy Lights continued their country version of our cover song. Normally the mentors sat and watched the performances from their chairs, but Dan was standing next to Lissa and arguing with her. We couldn't hear what he was saying, but judging from his frantic gestures and wild eyes, he was pissed.

The guys left to find one of the producers to ask what was going on, but I waited backstage for Fairy Lights to finish their song. This was the kind of disaster that would have sent the old Maddie running, but no more. I was ready to fight.

When her band finished, I was all ready to go off on Lacey, but before I could, her mother stalked up to her and dragged her off the stage. The woman lightly smacked Lacey on the back of the head, making her wince.

"What was that? That was awful! I've trained you better than that!"

"Mama, stop, please," Lacey said, smoothing her hair. "I did the best I could."

"The best you could? You were way too pitchy in the chorus. We went over this yesterday. I thought you got it, but clearly we should have rehearsed it more!" When Lacey's head dropped, the woman grabbed her chin and tilted her head up. "Hey, do you hear me?"

Lacey nodded, and I actually felt bad for her. Dammit.

Her mother huffed. "You have one more song tonight, and you better not mess it up. You are *going* to win this thing. Don't embarrass me out there."

The woman walked off, glaring at me as she passed by. Lacey took a moment to compose herself, wiping at her eyes, and she looked so young. I'd forgotten she was only seventeen, since she seemed so much older when she was on stage. And now I couldn't yell at her because I related all too well to having a difficult relationship with your mother, even if mine seemed nowhere near as bad now. No, I had to remember why I was here. I cleared my throat, and she turned, eyes narrowing at me.

"You stole our song," I said.

"Have you come to gloat?" she asked, as if she hadn't heard me. "That was a nice publicity stunt back there. I knew all your 'we're just friends' crap was an act."

I clenched my fists. She was just trying to distract me. "You stole our *song*," I repeated, louder.

"I don't know what you're talking about."

I shoved the schedule in her face. "You were supposed to be doing a Carrie Underwood song."

"I covered Carrie Underwood last week. Why would I do one of her songs again? Besides, that's the song you're supposed to be doing."

She handed me her own schedule, and there it was. "Radioactive" was listed as Fairy Lights' song, and "Jesus Take the Wheel" was listed as ours. We'd been given completely different schedules. As had the rest of the show, I was sure. The world seemed to close in on me, tighter and tighter, pressing against my chest, and no matter how much I gasped for air I still couldn't breathe.

"Did *you* choose 'Radioactive'?" I finally got out.

"No, the producers suggested it. I thought it was a weird choice, but whatever."

Everything clicked. The leaked photo of me and Jared. Our last-minute song change in the semi-finals. My broken guitar. Steve encouraging me to leave the show. And now this. It had never been Lacey or any of the other contestants on the show; it had been the producers all along. They'd been sabotaging us for weeks, either for more drama and higher ratings or because they wanted America's sweetheart to win the show. Or both.

They would never let us win.

I rushed off to find the rest of the band. In the lounge, Dan argued with Steve, waving the schedule in his face, while the guys watched it all unfold. I joined them, too stunned to tell them what I'd learned. I needed to hear what Dan said first.

Maybe I was wrong. Maybe there was some other explanation for all of this. Maybe there was a possibility we could still win.

Dan threw up his hands and stomped over to us. He dragged us out of the room and into a corner of the hallway, away from the cameras, where no one could hear us.

"This is bullshit. The producers fucked us over. I can't believe it."

I closed my eyes. It was all true. I explained what I'd learned from Lacey and what I'd just figured out—that the show had been sabotaging us for weeks; that we'd been doomed from the start and could never win the show. For a minute, the guys were silent, taking it all in, their faces frozen in horror. And then Hector erupted with a long stream of obscenities in both English and Spanish.

"I can't believe this," Kyle said. "This is so unfair."

"How could they do this?" Jared asked, his voice anguished. I'd known he would take this harder than anyone.

Dan paced back and forth, his movements stiff and jerky. "I'm so pissed I can't even tell you. They did this last season to Angel's team, but I was never sure if it was her incompetence or if the producers were actually manipulating things. I guess now I know."

Kyle rubbed his face. "What are we going to perform? We don't know 'Jesus Takes the Wheel' but we can't do 'Radioactive' now either."

"They're probably hoping you'll still do 'Radioactive' and that you'll look like you were copying Fairy Lights," Dan said. "Or they think you'll choke and not even go on stage."

Neither of those was an option. Jared and I looked at each other and something unspoken passed between us, the same idea popping into both of our heads at once.

"'Bad Romance,'" we said together, but the guys just stared at us.

"We have to do 'Bad Romance,'" I repeated. "We already know how to play it, and we even recorded it the other week before they changed the song on us."

"Exactly," Jared said. "They didn't want us to do that song before, so we're going to do it now as one big middle finger to them."

Hector rubbed the back of his neck. "We haven't practiced that song in over a week. But I guess it's the only song we *can* do."

Kyle nodded. "We might be a bit rusty, but we can make it work."

"Do it," Dan said. "It's the last show anyway. What are they going to do—kick you off?"

We were scheduled for the last performance of the night, and we spent every minute until then brushing up on the song while Dan discussed the changes with the sound and lighting people. We didn't tell the producers what we were planning in case they tried to stop us.

As we waited backstage for our cue, Jared pulled us all in for one final group hug. We laced our arms together, facing each other in a huddle, holding on to each other for support.

"The producers might not want us to win, but we're going to make it damn hard for them to stop us," Jared said. "And even if we don't win, look how far we've come in the past few weeks. A little over a month ago, we were lucky to get a gig, and now we're going to be touring the country and playing in giant concert halls. We have thousands of fans, who make signs and T-shirts and camp out all night to see us. As far as I'm concerned, we've already won."

I smiled at him, warmth spreading from my heart to the rest of my body. He really had changed since last week. But there was something I had to say to all the guys before this was over. "Whatever happens tonight, I'm really thankful you all took a chance on me. It was a huge risk letting me into the band, and I have loved every second of it."

"We couldn't have done this without you," Kyle said.

"I love you guys," Hector said to all of us, sniffing.

"Hey, don't get all weepy on us now," Jared said, shoving him a little. We all laughed, but we each choked up a little, too. Win or lose, our time on the show was over, and it was bittersweet.

We broke apart and took our places on the revolving stage, ready to face the audience one last time. Jared grasped the mic, his blue bass around his neck, looking dangerously sexy with his black leather jacket. I stood beside him, running a hand along my sea foam green guitar, the one the producers had tried to destroy. Behind us, Kyle hovered over his keyboard, and Hector twirled his drumsticks. My new family, all preparing to go to battle together.

When the stage turned, Jared spoke into the mic again, his voice soft. "This is for all of the fans who believed in us, who voted for us and downloaded our songs and came to see us tonight. Thank you."

The crowd cheered and waved around their signs, and he started the opening to "Bad Romance." We let his voice carry the song alone at first, hypnotizing every person who heard it. I joined him on the guitar when he started the first verse while Hector provided the steady beat that kept the rest of us in sync and Kyle added the perfect atmosphere. Our version was harder and darker than the original, promising a night of leather and lust, of pleasure and pain. Jared imbued the lyrics with all of his passion, giving them almost a desperate edge, filling each word with yearning and need. He sang to the audience, but in my bones I knew he was singing this for me, another reminder of what we'd shared and what was to come. And when the song ended, he grabbed me for another kiss, leaving the audience with that one final image of us.

Jared was right. Whatever happened with the show, we had already won.

Chapter Twenty-Six

At the results show, when Fairy Lights was announced as the winner of *The Sound*, we weren't surprised. Disappointed, yes. Angry. Sad. But not surprised.

In the morning, we would pack our bags and leave the hotel forever. The show was over and it was back to reality—except everything had changed since that first audition and our lives would never truly be the same. We had Comic-Con next week and the tour right after that, and then Kyle and I would start our senior year at UCLA in the fall. I still wanted to write movie scores, but I was going to hold off on graduate school for now and see what happened with the band first. One day I would find a way to do both, like my hero, Danny Elfman.

But before we left the theater for the final time, our mentor asked us to meet with him in an empty dressing room.

"I quit the show," Dan said.

"You *quit?*" I asked.

"I'm done. The producers put your cover of 'Bad Romance' on the website too late so the downloads couldn't be counted as votes. Or that's the excuse they gave me anyway. Such bullshit. Everyone knows you should have won." He gave a bitter laugh. "The Internet is going to go crazy with this one. You have some pretty devoted fans out there."

"But why?" Jared asked. "Why go to so much trouble to make sure we didn't win?"

"The record label wanted Fairy Lights from the beginning, so they pressured the show to make it happen. They plan to turn Lacey into some new Taylor Swift or something. And after the headache with Addicted to Chaos, the producers thought your band was too risky. With the network threatening to cancel the show, they wanted to make sure they had a winner who would keep out of trouble. And someone they could easily control, too, I'm sure." He shook his head, disgusted. "But forget about the show. That doesn't matter anymore."

Kyle exchanged a glance with his brother and asked, "What do you mean?"

"It's actually better that you didn't win because the show's contract is shit. Fairy Lights will be their slave for the next seven years, making no money and giving up all their rights to their music. But you're still free, and everyone wants you. My phone has been ringing off the hook since last night."

"Everyone?" Jared asked, raising an eyebrow.

"All the big record labels. Trust me, you're hot right now, and they want to sign you fast. Which is why I have a proposition for you: let me be your manager. My band is retired and I'm done with the show, but I know the industry, I know who you are as a band, and I've actually come to enjoy this crazy mentoring thing. Let me get you the best deal I can, and I'll make sure you become the next big thing. What do you say?"

We all looked at each other as we processed what he'd said, a hundred emotions flickering across our faces. Finally, I laughed. "Well, I vote yes."

"The lady has spoken," Jared said. "I vote yes, too."

"Yes!" Kyle said. "Hell yes!"

Hector slapped Dan on the back. "C'mon, was there any doubt we'd say yes?"

———

We went out and celebrated, just the four of us. After the live show, we'd gone out with Dan and his husband, plus our families and friends, but tonight's dinner was only for the band. We laughed about everything we'd been through, we ate off each other's plates, and the guys teased me and Jared about our relationship. Jared held my hand the entire time, not caring who saw us together, like he was afraid I might run away if he let go. But he was done pretending, and I was done running.

I don't know how we made it back to my hotel room without burning the entire building down. We were kissing and pulling at each other's clothes as soon as we got off the elevator, stumbling to my door and fumbling for the key to open it.

When the door shut, I tugged off his shirt and slid my hands along his chest, down his arms, kissing the VILLAIN tattoo and the dark and light triangles on his forearms. One day I'd ask him what all of his other tattoos meant, but later. We had time.

He let me explore him, like he sensed I needed to touch every inch of his body and mark him as my own. I removed his pants to worship his calves, his thighs, his hips, teasing my tongue along the dark hair trailing down his stomach, lower and lower. I tasted his entire body, kissing and licking and learning what drove him crazy, branding him with my mouth.

When he couldn't take it anymore, he spun me around and unzipped my dress, removing the last of my clothes. He trailed kisses across my shoulders and down my back, all the way to the curve of my butt and then up again. He wrapped his arms around me from behind so we stood naked together, skin to skin, him hard and ready against me. In the mirror, I watched as his mouth caressed my neck and his hands cupped my breasts, and for the first time, I agreed with the fans: Jared and I *were* perfect for each other.

He pulled me onto the bed and kissed me until I was begging him for more. We broke apart for him to put on a condom, and then he was on top of me again, between my legs. He held my face and stared into my eyes.

"I love you," he whispered.

"I love you, too," I gasped and clung to him as he stretched me, filled me, completed me.

For a minute, he rested his forehead against mine and held me, one body now instead of two. We moved together, slowly at first, savoring the feel of each other, but then picked up speed. I lifted my hips to meet his thrusts, digging my nails into his back. He ran his talented fingers down to that spot that drove me wild, playing my body like he played his guitar, and I swore I heard music.

I rolled us over so I was on top, and he grinned up at me. I grabbed his wrists to pull them above his head and ran my tongue along the lines of music tattooed around his arms. God, I loved his arms, whether they were holding a guitar or wrapped around me, and seeing them above his head like this, seeing him give himself over to me completely, made me even more excited.

I rolled my hips, sliding him in and out of me, the crescendo building as skin glided against skin. Our fingers entwined as we moved faster, the friction of our bodies lifting us higher, like an orchestra harmonizing and swelling just before the climax. He buried his face in my neck, his fingers tightening around mine.

"Maddie," he moaned, and I knew he was close, too, and that sent me over the edge. I gasped his name against his skin, rocking against him, tightening around him, dragging us both into bliss.

I released him, and he wrapped me in his arms and held me close. We lay together, breathing heavily and slicked with sweat, but complete. Whole.

"Not okay?" he asked with his real smile I'd come to know so well.

"Not okay," I agreed, tracing a finger along his lips. "I'm *much* better than okay."

Even though the show was over, this was only the beginning for us. I didn't know what would happen with the band, but I knew we'd get through it. Because what we had together was more than music. It was love.

Bonus Content

I hope you enjoyed More Than Music! Read on for a deleted scene from the book plus two scenes from Jared's point of view - exclusively in this box set!

―――――

Deleted Scene from More Than Music

This scene takes place on the morning of Maddie's audition for The Sound *(between Chapter 4 and 5).*

My bedroom door slammed open, jolting me awake. My two roommates burst inside and flipped on the light switch, blinding me. I groaned and pulled the covers over my face.

"Time to get up," Julie said.

"But it's so early." I squinted at the two girls at the foot of my bed. I'd barely slept and the sun wasn't even up, and they wanted me to get ready *now*? Two hours before the guys in the band showed up? Surely this was a mistake.

Julie crossed her arms. "Today's the day of your big audition and we're going to make you look so hot the judges will have no choice but to pick you for a team. Now get your ass out of bed so we can get to work."

"Sorry, Maddie," Carla said. "But Julie's right, we really need to get started."

I yawned. "Fine, fine. Just…give me a minute to wake up."

"What are you planning to wear?" Julie held up the cute black and green dress I'd pulled out. "*This?*"

"Yeah." I yawned again. Couldn't they have brought me some coffee at least?

"What do you think of this dress, Carla?"

She tilted her head. "It's…nice?"

Julie threw the dress on the bed. "Exactly. Nice. Do you want to look *nice* today, Maddie?"

I sighed, wishing I could find the snooze button for my two friends. "I feel like the answer you're looking for is 'no.'"

Julie rolled her eyes. "Obviously! You don't want to look *nice*! You want to look like a sexy rock goddess!"

I covered my head with a pillow while she rummaged through my closet and pulled out things to show to Carla. But none of my clothes met their approval, and after a few minutes Julie yanked me out of bed and into her room. While she went through her own closet, I sat at her desk and waited for her whirlwind to die down, knowing it was pointless to get involved when she was like this.

Julie's room was a study in organized chaos. Biology and chemistry textbooks had been shoved into the corner next to a sewing machine with baby blue fabric piled on top of it. Clothes hung from every spot around the room—a red plaid skirt on top of the closet door, a green sweater with elbow patches on the windowsill, and a trio of vintage dresses on the ceiling fan. Some of them even had strings hanging off or were only halfway finished.

"Maddie!" Carla called, from the bathroom we all shared. "Come in here!"

"Go on," Julie said, examining a black dress. "This might take me a while."

I shuffled into the bathroom. More makeup than I'd ever seen before was arrayed across the counter, in every possible shade. Carla also had a curling iron, hair spray, three kinds of gel, and who-knows-what-else spread out in front of her.

She smiled at my reflection in the mirror. "This is going to be so fun. You never let me do your makeup."

"Because I never look like me after." When she'd fixed me up before I'd always looked like I was trying too hard or something. She'd made me stand out, when I usually wanted to do anything but. She was a model, she was used to being in the spotlight–I wasn't.

I started to say more, but Julie dragged me back into her room and started holding clothes up to me before discarding them on the bed. "No, no, hell no," she muttered to herself. I didn't even get a chance to see the outfits she decided weren't good enough. I opened my mouth to argue that the original dress I'd picked was fine, but Carla attacked my face with some sort of cream, spreading it onto my cheeks.

"Wait. Stop." I held up my hands, and they both paused. "I know you want to help and I do need it, but can we not go *too* crazy here? I still want to be…me."

"We just want you to look perfect for your audition," Carla said.

"I know, but I'm already scared enough. I don't want to feel uncomfortable, too. Which I will if my boobs are hanging out and I have five inches of makeup on my face."

Carla patted my arm. "Don't worry. We're not turning you into someone you're not. You'll just look like the rock star version of you."

"Exactly," Julie said. "You need to relax. Just trust us. We know what we're doing."

I bit my lip but nodded. They always got carried away, but right now I needed them. I'd never look as sexy-cute as Julie or as flawlessly gorgeous as Carla, but maybe they could somehow make me look like a badass guitarist for one day.

Julie held up a tight red dress that would barely cover my ass. "How about this?"

Nope, I was doomed.

She burst into laughter. "Look at your face! I'm kidding! I'd never put you in this dress."

"Not funny. I've seen *you* wear that dress."

She held it up to herself in the mirror and grinned. "I'm shorter than you. I can get away with it." She tossed it aside and grabbed another dress from her closet. A tight black babydoll with a hint of lace, not too revealing but still sexy. "This is the one."

"Perfect," Carla said. "Now all she needs are some boots and a little smoky eye…"

"I love it." I had to admit, Julie *was* pretty good at this stuff. And Carla was an expert, too. They were right—I needed to trust them. "Okay. Do whatever you need to do."

To their delight, I gave myself over to them completely. They spent the next hour working on me, getting my outfit, hair, and makeup perfect. And at the end of it, I *did* feel a tiny bit like a sexy rock goddess.

Bonus Scene from Jared's Point of View #1

This scene takes place at the party after the Villain Complex concert (Chapter 2).

The music pulsed around us and people chatted over it, crowding together in my living room, sipping beers and eating pizza. I loved the energy of a group like this, the buzz of everyone having a good time, and knowing I was part of the reason for it. Hosting a good party was like being on stage – it was all about keeping people entertained.

The blonde ran a finger up and down the tattoos on my arm. "So you, like, write all the lyrics?"

"I do." I never dropped my smile, but inside I was debating how fast I could get out of the conversation. But part of keeping people entertained meant keeping our female fans happy, too. That was my job.

She licked her lips. "Wow. That's *so* hot."

I laughed, but I had to force it. I didn't even remember the girl's name. They all started to blend together after a while. I was tired from the show and just wanted to crash, but a part of me said I should do whatever this girl wanted. We'd just had our biggest show ever, we were auditioning for *The Sound* in two days, and a beautiful blonde was practically begging to crawl into my bed. What was the problem, really?

The problem was that I'd told myself I wasn't going to do that anymore. I wasn't going to be *that* guy anymore. And I really did want to change…but damn, sometimes it was hard to resist. Especially when she moved closer, giving me a nice glimpse down the plunging neckline of her very tight dress.

No. After the mess I'd made with Becca I swore I was done sleeping around. I still had to keep up my player appearance for the band, but that didn't mean I had to actually do anything with these girls. I just had to make them believe I would.

I leaned close to the blonde like I was going to kiss her, and her eyes fluttered shut, her lips parting. I whispered in her ear, "I'm going to grab another beer. You want one?"

She nodded and I turned away. Suddenly glass exploded against the wall above my head, drenching me in beer. For a second I could only stand there in shock as alcohol dripped down my face. What. The. Hell.

"*Another* girl, Jared?" Becca yelled. "How many tonight?"

I was too stunned to speak. I wiped beer out of my eyes and heard Hector say, "What the fuck, Becca?"

He yanked her back before she could throw another beer at my head, proving once again why he was my best friend. She yelled at him and he let her go, only so she could fall into Ted and his new girlfriend.

I could not believe Becca would pull this shit here, tonight of all nights. I'd almost lost it on her before the show when I could tell she was drunk. Now she was causing trouble again, after she'd promised she was over what had happened between us. One night, one stupid drunken mistake, and I would keep paying for it again and again.

She'd almost left us at the Battle of the Bands. Kyle had convinced her to stay, but she was getting worse every day. Drinking more. Missing practices. She couldn't even keep her shit together for one show. How was she supposed to go on *The Sound* with us? She couldn't get wasted every day and flip out every time I talked to another girl.

Kyle popped out of the crowd, grabbing Becca's arm before I could give her a piece of my mind. "Hey, let's get you sobered up," he said to her.

Of course my brother would try to intervene. He was always riding in on his white horse to save the day. But this was my problem, not his.

I moved closer, clenching my fists. "Becca," I said, trying to keep my voice level and not go off on her in front of all our guests. "This has to stop."

Kyle gave me a look that clearly said, *back off.* "Let me handle this."

"Then handle it!" Kyle always thought he could fix things with Becca – but some things couldn't be fixed. I couldn't take any more of this shit, not now, not when we had all our dreams within our reach.

"We can't have her on *The Sound* like this," I said. "Either she gets her shit together, or she's out of the band."

"I'm done anyway!" Becca yelled, spit flying at my face. "Done with you, done with your band, done with all this shit."

She yanked away from Kyle and stormed out the door, past the crowd gawking at us. I sighed and jerked a hand through my hair, needing to do something with all this angry energy rolling around inside me. Kyle shot me another *thanks for fucking everything up like usual* look – one I knew all too well – and ran after her.

I should probably follow them and try to mend this. As bad as Becca was these days, we needed her. But when I stepped forward, Hector blocked me with a stern look. "Don't."

"But—"

"You'll only make it worse," Hector said, glancing at the door and then back at me. "You really fucked up this time."

"No shit," I muttered. Another bassist I'd messed things up with. Granted, she'd been the only one I'd slept with. Over the last month I'd tried to patch things up with her, but obviously I'd failed. Now my entire band was pissed with me and we risked missing out on the opportunity of a lifetime.

I shook my head and walked off, the crowd parting around me. It's not like I'd been the only one involved in the screw-up. Hell, Becca had been after me since the day she'd joined the band. I'd done a damn good job of resisting her too, despite the way she'd thrown herself at me night after night.

Finally, I'd given in. I'd had a terrible fight with my mom about money, just before our show. She'd threatened to cut us off again, despite the fact she knew we needed that money to pay for Kyle's tuition at UCLA. But whenever she wanted to mess with my head she threatened to stop the monthly payments, until I gave in to whatever she wanted. That time she'd wanted us to agree to go to her 4th of July party instead of our dad's. Like we gave a crap about either one.

I'd gotten drunk after the show because that was the only way to get my mom's nagging voice out of my head. And there had been Becca, also drunk, taking her clothes off, climbing in my lap. Before I knew it we were both naked, and then we were in bed, and then it was the next morning… and everything went to shit after that. Once we sobered up we both agreed it had been a mistake and that we'd never do it again. But she couldn't seem to let it go, even months later.

I went out by the pool to get some fresh air but immediately spotted Kim, one of the regulars. She came to every show and tried to get in my bed after each one. Sometimes I let her. But I was done with all that, and I didn't want to deal with her tonight, not with Becca's words running a repeat in my head and her beer drying in my hair.

I made my way around the pool and slipped into the other entrance to the house, through the kitchen. A bunch of people greeted me and I smiled and pretended everything was great. "Having a good time?" I asked them, playing the good host. But as soon as they answered I took off. Only to be stopped by another blonde.

"Jared, I've been looking all over for you…"

Holy shit, how hard was it to get a moment of peace in my own damn house? I made an excuse and brushed past the girl, heading for the one place I knew I'd be safe: our studio. It was locked, so no one from the party would be in there. With my guitar I'd be able to work off some of this frustration. I could practically hear the music writing itself, nearly bursting out of me, a new song churning in my head. Strong emotions always turned into the best songs.

I used my key to open the door to the studio and slipped inside. But as soon as I did, I heard music – not the music playing at the party, but *my* music.

In the middle of our sound-proofed studio, Kyle's friend Maddie rocked out with my guitar in her hands. She was playing "Behind the Mask," the song closest to my heart.

And she was singing it, too.

At first I was too stunned to do anything but watch and listen. Her eyes were closed and she moved with the music, feeling each chord as she played it, living each word as she sang it. She had a beautiful voice, sweet but not too high. And damn, the way she played the guitar…it was magic. She was better than me, that's for sure.

I'd never heard anyone perform my own songs before. Not like this, anyway. Girls sometimes sang my lyrics back to me, usually when we were in bed, and I'd heard Kyle butcher this song on guitar before. But I'd never heard anyone play it like *this*. Almost like I was watching myself play it.

If it was anyone else I would have been pissed that she was using my guitar. But Kyle must have let her in, maybe even told her she could use it. He'd talked about Maddie so much over the past few years I felt like I knew her already, even though we'd never met before tonight. I'd invited her to the party because I'd wanted to talk to her, to get to know this girl that my brother had kept a secret for so long.

Kyle had never mentioned that she played the guitar though. And god, she looked hot doing it. She was beautiful, with long chocolate hair and cute black-rimmed glasses that made her look like a sexy librarian. Her hands were small but fast and lithe, her hips swayed as she played, and her lush lips moved with the words I'd written. The guitar strap was tucked between her round breasts, drawing my eyes to them. I could watch her like this forever.

How had Kyle been friends with her for so long and never tried to turn it into more? Or never introduced me to her until tonight?

Maddie opened her eyes and spotted me, and the perfect moment ended. Those big blue eyes widened and her mouth fell open. The guitar squealed as she jerked her hands off it, and her face went red.

"I'm so sorry," she blurted out. "Kyle gave me the key and I was just—"

She tore off the guitar and tried to put it back, before I could answer her. I was still in shock anyway, but that was nothing compared to how shocked she seemed to be. I felt a little bad actually. I had clearly walked in on something I shouldn't have seen and embarrassed her. But she didn't have to be ashamed of anything.

I started to reply, but then she backed up into Hector's drum kit and knocked it over. I rushed forward to help her up, catching her in my arms before she fell again.

"You okay?" I asked. We were close, touching, and something sparked between us. I'd hugged her briefly after the concert, but now she was looking up at me and she was so soft, so feminine, I didn't want to let her go. I had the strongest urge to kiss her.

She pulled away before I could act on that urge. "I'm sorry, I—"

She kept saying sorry. She didn't need to apologize, not when she'd just blown me away with the way she'd handled my guitar. "You were playing one of our songs."

That only made it worse. Her cheeks got even pinker and her eyes squeezed shut for a second.

"Was I?" she asked with a short laugh. "I mean, uh, yeah. I was. Obviously. But it's not a big deal. It's not like I listen to your songs a lot or anything. I just have that kind of ear where I hear something once and can play it back and uh…"

Kyle had mentioned Maddie was a musical genius before, and now I had proof of it. "Really? I wish I could do that."

She stared at me and I got the feeling she didn't like me. Great, what had Kyle told her? She'd probably seen me talking to the groupies and assumed all the rumors about me were true.

Okay, yes, they had been true once. But I was trying to change.

I wished she would relax so we could chat without her looking like I might assault her or something. I'd heard so much about her from Kyle that she already felt like a friend of mine, but I wanted to know more. Maybe even get her to play something with me. I'd love to hear what it sounded like when we made music together. Or did other things together…

I opened my mouth to ask her what other songs of ours she could play, but she bolted toward the door. "I have to go."

That was new. Girls didn't usually run away from me.

I let her leave, but as soon as the door shut I knew I had to go after her. There was something about her that intrigued me, and not just because she was one of the few girls who didn't fall all over me. She was a big part of Kyle's life that he'd kept from me all these years, and if she was such a good friend of his I wanted to know her, too. But mostly it was because when she'd played my song I'd felt a connection to her, like she experienced the music and the lyrics the way I did when I performed the song. Like she understood. I wanted to know how.

I checked my guitar and Hector's drums to make sure they were okay and then raced out after Maddie. I didn't know what my plan was. I just knew I wanted to talk with her a little while longer. To convince her to come back to my studio.

But once I got back to the party, she was already gone.

Kyle found me in the crowd. "Becca's gone for good this time. I tried to reason with her, but she said she doesn't want to go on *The Sound* with us. So we're basically screwed."

"Damn," I said. How were we supposed to find a new bassist in two days?

I pictured Maddie playing guitar and had an idea. A crazy idea, but one that just might work. "Are you going to see Maddie tomorrow?"

Kyle frowned. "No, why?"

"She just ran out of here all of a sudden. I wanted to talk to her."

"Oh, she has a music history final tomorrow. She wanted to get home to get some sleep."

"Music history with Mr. Walsh? Ugh, I remember that class." A plan formed in my head. I knew where Mr. Walsh's class was. I didn't want to tell Kyle my idea yet, in case Maddie said no and because there was something about that moment we'd shared together. It had been private. Secret. *Intimate.*

"Yeah, that guy is a hard-ass." My brother studied me, like he suspected something was going on. "Why do you want to talk to her?"

I shrugged and gave him my best smile. "Just wanted to get to know her little better."

His eyes narrowed. "Maybe it's good she left."

"Ouch." I shook my head. "It's not like that. I just know she's a good friend of yours and I was excited to finally meet her."

"Uh huh." He shot me one last warning look and then slipped into the crowd to rejoin Alexis.

I hadn't been lying. I had no intention of seducing Kyle's friend or doing whatever else he thought I was planning. Even if Maddie was ridiculously hot.

For a second I let myself picture that moment when she'd been in the studio, the way her lips had moved with my lyrics, the way her fingers had strummed my guitar, the way her hips had swayed to my music. I imagined what it would sound like if she was saying my name, if those hands were on me, if those hips were grinding against mine.

I banished the image and took a deep breath. Maddie was Kyle's friend and I couldn't get involved with her. He would kill me. Besides, I couldn't have a repeat of the Becca situation. All I wanted was a way to get on *The Sound*.

People from the party tried to talk to me, but I waved them off and headed back into the studio to pull out my old bass guitar. I had a lot of practice ahead of me if I wanted to be ready in time for our audition.

If I could pull this off we might be able to make our audition on *The Sound*, even without Becca. And Maddie was the key.

———

Bonus Scene from Jared's Point of View #2

This scene takes place at the battle round show, just before they go on stage (Chapter 10).

I pushed open a door leading outside from the backstage area of the theater. Maddie had disappeared this way a minute ago, her long hair flying behind her and her face pale, and I needed to make sure she was okay. Or as okay as any of us could be.

Tonight was our first performance on *The Sound* and everything was riding on what happened with it. In a few minutes our band would be competing against The Static Klingons and only one of us could move forward. All signs pointed to it not being us.

I didn't blame Maddie for wanting to get the hell out of the place. Winning felt impossible, like there was no point in even trying at this point. But if there was even a small chance that we might make it to the next round I was going to fight for it. And right now I had to make sure my guitarist could go on stage.

A couple guys were smoking along the wall, but I spotted Maddie sitting against a chain-link fence blocking off the parking lot. Her head was tilted down, her knees drawn up to her chest, and she wore these tight leather pants that made it impossible for me to take my eyes off her.

"Hey," I said, and her eyes snapped open from behind her black-rimmed glasses. "Are you not okay again?"

She gave me a faint smile at the reminder of our shared little joke—a reference to when I'd sang that My Chemical Romance song to her at our audition—but she didn't seem especially pleased to see me.

"I just needed some air," she said.

"Sorry. Should I go?"

"No."

She shook her head and her dark hair fell in silky waves down her shoulders. For a second I could only take her in, this girl who had completely turned my life around in only a few short days. Five minutes ago a girl with a mohawk had been hinting to me about hooking up later tonight, yet the entire time I'd only seen Maddie. The Jared from a month ago would have taken the punk girl back to his room with no hesitation and no regrets. But these days the only girl I wanted to spend time with—in or out of my bedroom—was Maddie.

She had no idea how she slayed me without even trying, how her soft lips, lithe hands, and lush breasts made it hard for me to think straight around her. But I'd sworn to my brother that I wouldn't touch her, and I'd meant it. After the drama with the last girl in our band I knew better than to get involved with Maddie. No way in hell would I ruin our chance of winning *The Sound* by hooking up with her.

Besides, she was *way* too good for me.

I could tell from her body language and the tight expression on her beautiful face that she was upset. Nervous about the show, no doubt. She was still new to all of this, and I remembered how stressed and anxious she'd been before our audition.

I sat beside her on the concrete, leaning back against the fence. "I always get stressed before shows, too."

"You do? You make it look easy."

"That's all an act, but it does get easier every time. You'll be a pro soon, too."

She sighed. "Assuming we don't get kicked off this week, you mean."

I stared up at the sky, a heavy pit of doom settling in my stomach at the reminder. If we went home this week I'd never forgive myself. "Trust me, I'm still beating myself up for that."

"It wasn't your fault."

It really was, but there was no sense in talking about it. What's done was done. I needed to distract her, to find a way to calm her before we went on stage – and distract myself from the fact that I couldn't have her.

Before she'd run out she'd been talking to Sean, the singer from The Static Klingons, who'd always rubbed me the wrong way. I kind of wanted to punch the guy's face in, but maybe that was cause I saw the way he looked at her. I tried to tell myself that it wasn't jealousy, that she was my guitarist and I had to look out for her and that Sean guy had asshat written all over him. But a part of me just wanted to know if she was into him.

"So you and that Sean guy, huh?" I asked.

"What? No. I mean, he seems nice and all, but that's it." She nudged me with her shoulder and smiled. "You jealous?"

I grinned. She saw right through me. "Maybe."

"Don't be."

Her voice softened with those words and I searched her gaze, trying to tell if she was joking. I didn't think she was.

She dropped her eyes. "We should head back in."

"Yeah, Kyle's probably tearing the place apart looking for us."

The last thing I wanted to do was go inside, but I jumped to my feet and reached down to help her up. She wobbled on her tall heels as she stood, pressing one of her hands against my chest to get her balance. I caught her, touching her hip, her other hand still in mine. The rest of the world froze around us.

We were close, only a breath apart. Her gaze lingered on my chest and she slowly raised her eyes, taking in every inch of me with the same hunger I felt for her. When they stopped on my lips I desperately wanted to haul her against me and capture her mouth with mine. From the way she looked at me I knew she wanted the same thing.

"There you are," Kyle called from the door to the theater. "I've been looking for you two everywhere."

Maddie jumped back and I shoved my hands in my pockets. Dammit, Kyle! My brother had the worst timing ever. Or maybe I should be thanking him, since I'd been about one second from doing something I would regret. Something that would only screw everything up for the entire band.

"Sorry," Maddie said. "Jared was just giving me a pep talk before the show."

Kyle looked back and forth between us, and I could tell he knew something else was going on. "We're on in fifteen minutes."

Maddie shot me one last look before following my brother inside. I ran a hand through my hair, trying to get control of myself again.

I wasn't sure how much longer I could resist her.

More Than Comics

CHASING THE DREAM #2

ONE

Tara

____

A trio of Ghostbusters bumped my shoulder, knocking me into a group of Disney princesses. I muttered a quick apology and continued through the mob, ignoring people at booths handing out flyers, swag bags, and free comics. I could barely breathe with so many bodies packed tight around me, at least half of which were in costume.

Welcome to San Diego Comic-Con, aka nerd paradise. Four days of shameless geekiness and a celebration of every fandom you could possibly think of. If you could watch it, read it, or play it, someone was probably cosplaying as a character from it.

I was in heaven.

Or at least I would be in heaven if not for the butterflies in my stomach.

Ugh. Butterflies in my stomach, seriously? Talk about a cliché. As a writer I shouldn't even be *thinking* in clichés. But I was about to speak on a panel about my graphic novel, followed by my first ever book signing. At Comic-Con, of all places. It was both my dream come true and an introvert's worst nightmare. Nothing had prepared me for the sheer enormity of the four-day event, or the chaos created by hundreds of thousands of people packed into the convention center. I couldn't decide whether I wanted to jump up and down and cheer, or curl up in a dark corner and rock back and forth until it was all over.

But, if I was honest with myself, the real reason for those damn butterflies was the fact that I was about to meet Hector, the artist of my graphic novel, in person for the first time.

I wasn't sure *why* I was so nervous about meeting him, either. I shouldn't be nervous. We'd been friends for years, after all. But…what if it was weird when we met face to face, without computer screens and thousands of miles between us? What if we didn't know what to say or how to act around each other? What if the connection we had online didn't translate into real life?

What if we just didn't click offline?

I forced my way through the crowd toward the Black Hat Comics booth. As the third largest comic book publisher, after Marvel and DC, they had a huge booth right in the middle of the exhibit hall. It could be spotted from anywhere inside thanks to the giant black wizard hat stretching all the way to the ceiling, covered in hundreds of little twinkling stars.

There was no sign of Hector yet, but I spotted the trim, dark goatee and wire-frame glasses of our editor Miguel, who stood behind a table with free post cards, buttons, magnets, and sample comics.

"Hey, Tara," he said, giving me a quick hug. "Good to see you again. Are you ready for your panel?"

"I hope so."

"I know you'll do great. We're just waiting for Hector now and then we'll head up to the room."

I shuffled out of the way of someone carrying a huge box of action figures into the booth. I stepped back and the crowd swallowed me up, blocking my view, and I had to fight my way through.

When I emerged, Hector stood beside Miguel, shaking hands and making their introductions. His mouth curled into a slight grin as our eyes made contact. My heart skipped a beat at the sight—another cliché, but given the circumstances, could anyone blame me?

He was so much *bigger* in person than I'd imagined. Not just tall, but broad and muscular, too. I'd seen him through a webcam, in photos, and on *The Sound*, but I had never seen the full package up close like this.

Nothing had prepared me for how large and masculine he'd be in real life.

Or how insanely hot he would be.

He'd always been good looking, of course. But in person he was mouth-water-ingly gorgeous, the living embodiment of tall, dark, and handsome, with curly hair peeking out from under his Villain Complex baseball cap, smooth, bronze skin, and warm, brown eyes I could fall into forever.

And his arms! His arms deserved sonnets written about them. They were huge —probably as big as my thighs, and all muscle. I had the strongest urge to wrap my hands around them and see if they were as hard as they looked. For a brief moment I imagined him sliding those arms around me and lifting me up, and how good they would feel as they brought me to his lips…

Hold on, where had that image come from? I'd never thought about Hector in that way before. We'd always just been friends. That was it.

"Great, you're both here," Miguel said, bringing me out of my trance. "I have to talk to someone for a minute, and then I'll take you both to your panel, okay?"

He disappeared into the booth and I stared up at Hector, unable to speak. I didn't know how to react now that we were together. Should I hug him? Shake his hand? Kiss him on the cheek? I had no idea what the correct social protocol was when you met an online friend in person for the first time.

"Hector…" His name was the only thing I could manage to say. Words, usually my closest friends, seemed to have abandoned me completely. Maybe it was those arms that were making me crazy. I'd always had a thing for guys' arms. Not to mention those broad shoulders and that toned chest, wow. His black t-shirt did nothing to hide the contours of his abs, and all I could think about was what he would look like without that thin fabric in the way.

Okay, those thoughts? They had to stop. This was just a silly rush of emotions from finally meeting him in person after so many years. Nothing more.

"Hey, Tara." He'd been checking me out, too. It was like we both needed to drink in the sight of each other before we could process that this was real life and not a dream.

I gave up on trying to figure out the correct social protocol and threw myself against him, into that hard chest and those incredible biceps. He wasn't really a hugger, from what he'd told me anyway, but I couldn't stop myself. I was just so happy that we were really together, face to face, after so long.

He didn't seem to mind. His arms circled my back and he pulled me tight against him, his face pressing into my hair. I heard his heart pounding as he held me and he smelled so good, like pine or something equally masculine. I could have stayed like that for hours, but I pulled back before it could get awkward.

"It's so good to meet you in person," I managed to get out.

His hands lingered on my arms, like he didn't want to let go of me either. "Finally."

"I know, I can't believe it took us three years." I studied his face, so different in three dimensions, yet nearly as familiar as my own reflection. Something about him looked off, like he didn't quite line up with my mental image of him, but I couldn't tell what. "It almost doesn't feel real. It's like I know you so well, but at the same time, I don't know you at all."

"It *is* strange. But you do know me. Better than almost anyone."

He looked so serious when he said that, so intense, that I wasn't sure how to respond. Instead I hugged him again. This time he didn't return it quite as hard.

"Sorry," I said, pulling away from him. "I know you don't like hugs."

"I'll make an exception for you." He had yet to take his eyes off me, even in the middle of all the chaos around us, and it made me feel warm all over. I couldn't stop smiling.

"Where's the rest of the band?"

"They're around somewhere." He finally looked away as he said it, like he was scanning the crowd for them.

"I can't wait to meet them. I feel like I know them already, after hearing so much about them over the years and watching you all on *The Sound*."

"That reminds me." He fished around in his pocket, and then shoved something into my hand. "Here."

"What's this?"

"A ticket and backstage pass for our show tonight. If you want to come, that is. You don't have to." He pulled off his Villain Complex baseball cap and ran his fingers through his hair. "You probably already have plans, huh? With Andy?"

"No, no plans." I played with the edge of the ticket, my stomach clenching at the thought of Andy. "I'd love to see you perform in person. I'll be there."

"Cool." He shoved his baseball cap back on, and I realized what was different about him.

"You cut your hair!" It was much shorter, trimmed close to his head now, though a hint of his glorious dark curls remained on top. It was a good look on him. A little more mature. I wished he'd take his hat off again.

He shrugged. "It was getting really long. Thought I'd get it cut before the tour."

"I like it. Although I loved your hair when it was long, too."

"You did?" Surprise flickered across his face. After years of video chatting I knew his expressions well.

"Of course. You have gorgeous hair." Oops, I'd probably said too much, but oh well. It was the truth.

Miguel returned and clasped us each on the arm. "All ready for your panel? Let's head on up."

I reluctantly tore my gaze from Hector and smiled at Miguel. "Ready."

Miguel led us out the exhibit hall and up an escalator to the second floor of the convention center. He gave us a quick run-down of our schedule for the next four days and I nodded and asked him a few questions. Hector didn't say anything, but he wasn't much of a small talker. He was the kind of guy who didn't waste words or speak just to fill silence, and when he did speak up it was honest and direct. I'd always liked that about him.

"This way," Miguel said, leading us past different meeting rooms with long lines outside them, composed of hundreds of people sitting along the walls and chatting with each other, playing on their phones, or reading comics. Hector and I walked close behind him through a surging crowd that moved like a herd of sheep, mindlessly pushing forward in either direction. It was all we could do not to get lost in it, and I clutched my Comic-Con badge tightly, worried it would fall off in the commotion.

A group of Assassin's Creed cosplayers stopped to pose for a photo and Hector had to dodge them. He bumped against my side, making me jump. "Nervous?" he asked.

"A little." I forced myself to let go of my badge. "I've never done a panel or anything like this before. I'm worried I'll say something stupid or just freeze up entirely."

"Nah. Won't happen. You'll do great."

We were forced to stop and wait while the Comic-Con volunteers ushered a massive line into Ballroom 20, blocking our path. "Are you nervous?" I asked, as the stream of people rushed past us.

He gave a little shrug. "Not really."

"No, you never seem to get nervous. Not even when you're on stage in front of hundreds of people, or on TV for the entire country to see."

"I get nervous. Just not on stage. Maybe if I was up front I'd get nervous, but when I'm in the back, behind my drums, I just…zone out. My hands know what to do and as long as I shut my mind off I'm fine. Same with this kind of stuff. The less I worry about it the better. That might work for you, too."

"Maybe." The volunteers capped off the line and let us pass, and we chased after Miguel down the long hall. "So when *do* you get nervous?"

Hector glanced over at me. His mouth opened, but then he looked away and scowled.

"Oh no," I said, punching him lightly on the arm. "Now you have to tell me."

His eyes dropped to the spot I'd touched him, still frowning. "I was nervous today, but not because of the panel." He raised those dark eyes to meet mine again. "Because I was meeting you."

"Really?" Hearing that made me feel a lot better. All those butterflies in my stomach vanished. "I was nervous, too."

"Yeah?"

I laughed. "Well, you *are* a famous rock star now."

"Not true. And you knew me long before all that."

I nudged him with my shoulder. "Then I guess neither of us had anything to be nervous about."

He gave me a rare smile, making him even more handsome. "No. I guess not."

TWO

Hector

Tara kept touching me. Normally I didn't like people touching me, but when she did it I wanted more. Only problem was it made it hard to focus on anything but her.

She was even hotter in person, in dark jeans and a tight *Firefly* t-shirt that showed off her large breasts, curvy hips, and delicious ass. Soft and feminine, yet without being so small I thought I'd crush her. With a body like that it was hard not to stare, but the rest of her was fucking amazing, too.

Her long, golden hair fell around her shoulders and I wanted to see if it felt as silky as it looked. But the thing that rendered me completely helpless was the way her blue eyes lit up when she smiled. No, not just blue, but sapphire. Cobalt. The color I'd use to paint a dark sky.

And the sound of her laugh—damn, I wanted to do whatever I could to hear it again. It was a reminder that she was warm and friendly and everything I was not. I was a dark cloud and she was the ray of sunshine that somehow managed to break through.

Maybe that's why I'd been in love with her for as long as I could remember.

"Here's the room," Miguel said, stopping in front of an open door with a long line next to it. A quick glance inside showed that the room was completely packed, too. It wasn't a huge one, especially compared to some of the others we'd passed, but there were a few hundred people inside at least.

"Are all those people here for us?" I asked.

"Yep. Great turnout, huh? I asked them to switch us to a larger room, but they couldn't do it."

"Oh shit." I knew our graphic novel had been doing pretty well, especially after my band was on *The Sound*, but I had no idea so many people would come to hear us talk about it. I thought we'd get maybe ten people, tops.

I hadn't been lying to Tara—I wasn't nervous before, but now that I saw the massive crowd I realized I wasn't prepared for any of this. Fuck, what if people asked me questions?

I should have asked Jared for advice or something. As lead singer for our band, he'd handled all the interviews and publicity stuff when we'd been on *The Sound*. At first it had pissed me off when he'd completely hogged the camera and made it seem like the band was all about him, but eventually I'd realized it was better that way. He was good at that shit and the rest of us hated it. And it's not like I wanted to be in the spotlight either. That's why I was a drummer and not a guitarist. Well, that and because beating the shit out of drums was way more fun.

"Wow, this is so overwhelming," Tara said. Her gaze swept across the crowd of people waiting for us, taking it all in—but I only had eyes for her. She turned to me, catching me staring, but I couldn't look away. I was held hostage by her flushed cheeks and kissable lips.

I'd memorized her face and heard her voice a thousand times, but seeing her up close, in real life, was different. All those feelings I'd tried to bury came rushing back to the surface and made it hard for me to breathe. I'd hoped meeting her would make me get over my stupid crush, but instead it had only gotten worse. The real Tara was so much better than even my best fantasy of her.

Christie, the moderator for our panel, arrived and introduced herself to us. She ran a comics site focused on diversity and was about the same age as Tara and me, with long black hair streaked with pink and a little stud in her nose.

We shook hands and she grinned at us. "I'm so excited for this panel. I begged them to let me moderate it cause I'm a huge fan of *Misfit Squad*. I'm dying for the next one to come out!"

"I remember the feature you did on it," Tara said. "We're so grateful for your support."

We walked into the room together and the crowd hushed. Christie, Tara, and I each took a seat at a table on a raised platform in front of a wall plastered with the Comic-Con logo. Name placards were placed in front of us, each of which had something on the back about watching our language because there were members of the audience under eighteen.

"They're talking to you here," Tara said, pointing at the warning.

I gave her my best innocent look. "Hey, I can be good."

"Uh huh." She scanned the room again, taking it all in with wide eyes. "I still can't believe we're on a panel at Comic-Con. This has been my dream forever and now it's real. It's all happening!"

Damn, she was so beautiful it was almost hard to look at her. I loved seeing her this happy and watching all her hard work pay off. "*You* made this happen."

Her smile got even bigger, bathing me in its glow. "We made it happen together."

"Nah, all I did was draw a few things."

"Oh, stop being so modest," she said, swatting at my arm. More touching. Yes, please.

I wasn't good with words—I left that to her and to Jared—but I had the strongest urge to pull out my sketchbook and draw the way she'd looked when we'd first seen each other in person, to capture her eyes meeting mine and her face brightening when she recognized me. I never wanted to forget the way she'd looked in that moment. For a brief second I'd thought it possible she could love me back.

And then it was over.

She'd never once hinted that she wanted to be more than friends, and I knew she never would—she'd been dating Andy for the past year and she was about to start a job in New York. Meeting in person wouldn't change anything between us.

Which is why she could never know how I felt about her.

Miguel propped up the first book of *Misfit Squad* on the table between us, gave us a thumbs up, and disappeared into the back of the room.

"Welcome to the *Misfit Squad* panel," our moderator said, into her mic. "I'm Christie Yamamoto from the *Diversity In Comics* website. This is one of my favorite graphic novels ever, and I'm so happy to be here with the writer, Tara McFadden, and the artist, Hector Fernandez."

The audience applauded and all the hundreds of faces blurred together, like when I was on stage at a show—except for four familiar ones in the back of the crowd. Jared sat there in a t-shirt with a bunch of classic villains on it like Dracula, Frankenstein, and The Wolfman. His arm was around his girlfriend Maddie, who was also our guitarist. Next to them was his brother Kyle, our keyboardist, along with his girlfriend, Alexis.

I shook my head at them, but a grin slipped through. I'd told them not to come to the panel because if I messed up royally I didn't want them to see it, but their smiling faces actually made me feel calmer. I'd never admit it out loud, but I was secretly glad they'd ignored me.

Christie held up a copy of the first book and the room quieted down. "*Misfit Squad* is out now and if you haven't read it yet, it's about a teenage girl whose power is breaking things. When she's rejected by her city's superhero group, she and some others with equally undesirable or 'useless' powers form their own group instead. Together they have to learn to control their powers and resist turning into the villains people *think* they are, while saving the city from the so-called super-heroes, who turn out to be the real villains."

She launched into our bios next, explaining how Tara had worked on different comics at Black Hat before writing *Misfit Squad*. It was pretty impressive that she'd done so much already, considering she'd just graduated with her English degree a month ago.

Next Christie described how I'd also worked on various comics while in art school and mentioned I was the drummer for Villain Complex, which had come in second on the reality TV show *The Sound* a week earlier. That got lots of cheers and I ducked my head a little, wishing I hadn't worn my Villain Complex hat. I hoped people in the audience were actually fans of *Misfit Squad* and not just the band, especially for Tara's sake.

"Tara, let's start with you," Christie said. "Where did you get the idea for *Misfit Squad?*"

Tara gave me a wide-eyed look, but leaned into the mic and started speaking. "I always loved comics, but had a hard time relating to them because the heroes in them were so much cooler than me." That got a little laugh from the audience. "One day I joked to a friend that if I was a superhero my power would be something no one would want, like breaking things. Then I started thinking about how that could actually be a pretty cool power, if you could learn to control it…and began coming up with other powers that at first seemed stupid or useless, but weren't. I pitched it to the guys at Black Hat and they loved the idea, and that's how *Misfit Squad* all began."

"Very cool," Christie said. "I think one reason *Misfit Squad* has such a huge following already is because it's a true underdog story. So many people relate to your characters and how they're outcasts, both among normal people and other superheroes, until they find each other and start their own group and become almost a family. Was that something you wanted to write about specifically?"

Tara relaxed a little, smiling at Christie. "That's definitely one thing I wanted to emphasize because I think if you're a little weird growing up, or something of an outcast, like I imagine all of us here are…." That got another chuckle from the audience. "Then you never *really* feel comfortable around most people. Especially your family, who probably never seemed to understand you. But as you grow up you find others like yourself, people who support you, embrace your weirdness, and love you for who you are—and they become your new family." She looked at me with this last line, and my heart constricted in my chest. She was killing me here.

"Comic-Con is definitely one big, crazy family," Christie said, with a laugh. "Hector, how did you become involved in the project?"

Shit, that question was for me. I focused on my band's faces in the audience—my own second family—and tried to relax. "After Tara wrote the script for the first book she put out feelers all over the Internet, in artist forums and places like that, looking for someone who might be interested in working on it. She had a random page's script…I think it was page 33 or something?"

I looked at her to confirm, and she laughed. "I don't think that page even exists in the final version. It got cut."

"Oh yeah, I forgot about that. Anyway, it was a good way in, with some fun action and dialogue. I loved the premise and the characters immediately from that short bit of script and knew I had to draw it. I put together a full page panel and submitted it." I shrugged. "I guess she liked it, because she chose me."

"There were a lot of good entries, but I knew Hector was the one the moment I saw his art. It was just so perfect for what I had in mind."

"The artwork is truly remarkable," Christie said. "It really brings the story to life. But tell me about your working relationship. I heard the two of you had never met in person until now. Is that true?"

"That's true," Tara said. "I live in Boston and Hector lives in Los Angeles, so we did all our work together online, through video chats and email, stuff like that. But we talk just about every day, so I feel like we've been friends forever."

"What was it like working with each other?"

"Tara's great to work with," I said. "She has a strong vision for her series but is also open to any suggestions I have."

"And Hector has some brilliant ideas, too. The books all changed a lot—for the better—thanks to his input. They became a true collaboration between the two of us. They're not just my books, but *our* books."

Tara gave me that brilliant smile again and I wanted to kiss her so bad. It meant a lot to me that she thought that about *Misfit Squad* 'cause I loved those books almost as much as I loved her. I'd put a lot of blood, sweat, and tears into them, and it was easily my best work. I was proud of what we'd created together.

"Another thing I love about *Misfit Squad* is how diverse it is," Christie continued. "There are characters of all different races, queer characters, even overweight and disabled characters. You don't see those too often in comics."

"That was really important to both of us." Tara glanced at me and I nodded. "We wanted to tell a story that had characters who weren't typical superheroes, and that included some who weren't white or straight or didn't have ideal bodies."

I leaned in to the mic and added, "And we wanted to make sure lots of different people could read the book and see themselves in it. That's something I never had when I was growing up and reading comics as a Mexican kid."

"Great point," Christie said.

Over the next few minutes she continued to ask us about the books and what was next for the series, before opening the panel to questions from the audience. In the middle of the room dozens of people scrambled to get in line in front of a microphone. Who knew so many people would have questions for us?

One of the Comic-Con volunteers waved a guy in a Green Lantern t-shirt to the mic. "Hey," he said. "Big fan of both *Misfit Squad* and Villain Complex. My question is for Hector. How do you balance being both a successful comic book artist and a drummer in a popular band? Is there one you consider your focus and the other your hobby, or are they both equal to you?"

"Good question," Tara said, turning to me. "I'm curious about this, too."

Damn, these people didn't mess around. They couldn't have started me off with an easy one?

His question was something I'd started to worry about with the band going on tour this month and preparing to record our second album soon. Tara and I hadn't discussed it, but with her starting a new job too it was something we'd have to address at some point if we wanted to do more than three books.

"They're equally important to me. I don't consider myself a drummer first and an artist second, or vice versa. I'm both all the time. Sometimes it's tough to find time to do both, and maybe it'll be even harder now, but I'll always find a way to make them each a priority. If you love doing something, if you feel drawn to it above everything else, nothing can stop you from pursuing it. I'm just weird because I feel that way about two things." I rubbed the back of my neck. I hadn't meant to talk so much, and worried I'd sounded stupid or boring. "I hope that answers your question."

"Thank you," the guy said, and was replaced at the mic by a girl in a Villain Complex shirt.

"Hi Hector! I just wanted to know, what is Jared like in person? And is he here, by any chance?"

In the back of the room, Jared sank lower in his chair and covered his mouth, trying not to laugh. Of course he would love that question, damn egomaniac. I wanted to roll my eyes but I kept my expression as neutral as I could while I answered. "Jared is a great guy and a very talented musician. Next question."

The girl looked disappointed but the Comic-Con volunteer shuffled her off and brought up the next girl, this one in a *Sailor Moon* costume.

"So now that Jared's taken, you're the only single guy in the band, right?" She batted her eyelashes at me suggestively, and a few people in the audience hooted.

I stared at her for a beat. "Is that really your question?"

She giggled. "Well, if you *are* single, do you want to go out later?"

I had no response to this. I wasn't used to being hit on like Jared or Kyle. My eyes found my friends again, who all looked like they were trying not to die of laughter. Yeah, laugh it up, assholes.

Tara patted me on the arm while smiling at the audience, as though she was amused by the question. "He's single and he's quite a catch, but I suspect you'll have to fight off a lot of girls for him."

I stared at her, wishing she hadn't said that. I didn't want to be single. I didn't want girls fighting over me. I wanted to be *hers*.

Sailor Moon was replaced by a girl in a tight, colorful dress. I couldn't tell if it was a costume or just how she dressed. "My question is um…what was it *really* like being on *The Sound?*"

Give me a fucking break.

I leaned forward, close to the mic. "Okay, I'm going to answer one more question about my band and that's it, so listen up. Being on *The Sound* was an amazing experience and did great things for our band, but it was also the craziest and most stressful and exhausting month of my entire life. It's awesome that so many of you are fans of the band, but this panel isn't about that. We're here to talk about *Misfit Squad*, so no more questions about the band or the show or my fucking personal life. You can come to our signing and ask me whatever you want there. But right now, someone needs to ask Tara a question."

So much for not swearing. I sat back and crossed my arms, and Tara gave me a reassuring smile. A huge chunk of the line left and went back to their seats, which made me even more annoyed. I hated that they'd made this about me and not about her, or what we'd created together.

"Yes, please keep your questions focused on the book," Christie said. She turned to the two of us, with a teasing smile. "Though I think we're all wondering —*is* there something going on between you two?"

Oh, shit.

THREE

Tara

"Sorry about that," Hector said when the panel was over and we were leaving the room to head to our signing. "I didn't realize they'd just want to ask about the show and all that."

Oh, thank god. I thought he was apologizing for that *other* question. But if he was ignoring it, then so was I. Especially after he'd so quickly denied that we were anything more than friends.

Which was true, of course.

"It's okay," I said. "I don't mind. Your success with the band sold lots of copies of our book, so I can't complain."

"Yeah, but I don't want people to see *Misfit Squad* as 'that graphic novel by the drummer in the band on *The Sound*.' I want them to see it as this kick-ass book you wrote and I happened to do the art for."

"Why can't it be both? If your band's popularity introduced more people to our book, then that's great. Really, I don't mind. I think it's good for us. It might mean we can do a fourth book, thanks to you."

He stopped in the middle of the busy hallway and turned to face me, his expression serious. "I just don't want to steal your spotlight. When Jared and I were on *The Sound,* the show made it all about him and it drove me crazy. I don't ever want to take this away from you."

I placed my hand on his forearm and smiled up at him. "You're not. I promise."

His body relaxed and he nodded. I wasn't sure why he was so worried about this, but it touched me that he cared so much. That he wanted this to be special for me. He had no idea that just meeting him in person had already made it special.

We caught up with Miguel and he led us through a giant, bright room packed with people in costumes rushing around or taking photos of each other. Our signing table was against one wall and there was already an enormous line beside it. I should have expected it, with the huge turnout for the panel, but I was still blown away seeing so many people waiting for us. There had to be hundreds of them there, all waiting for our signatures.

One end of the table had boxes with copies of *Misfit Squad* in it, ready to be sold to people in line. I'd brought special pens for our signing, pretty metallic ones in different colors, but Miguel also provided some boring, black Sharpies. As we sat, Hector picked one up and twirled it, like I'd seen him do with his drumsticks. He didn't even look at the pen, as if he didn't realize he was doing it. Under the table his left leg bounced, very close to my own. I had the sudden urge to put my hand on his thigh, to see if it would relax him. Or to see if it felt as muscular as it looked. Luckily the first people in line rushed forward before I could do it.

A girl in a Captain Marvel shirt shoved a well-read copy of *Misfit Squad* at me with a smile. I opened it to the title page. My first signed book. How mind-blowing was that? It still shocked me to see the book in person, this thing that Hector and I had spent three years working on together. It was even more incredible seeing actual proof that strangers were reading it and not just my friends.

"I love this book so much," the girl said. "When's the next one coming out?"

"Thanks! The second one's out in September." I finished signing my name, with a signature I'd practiced for a week to make sure it looked cool and was different from the one I used on checks and stuff. I pushed the book over to Hector and his arm brushed against mine as he signed. I watched his wrist flex as the pen moved, momentarily stunned by how he could make something so basic look so sexy.

He was left handed. How had I never known that before?

The line continued forward, until a guy with black-rimmed glasses and blond hair poking out of a beanie slid a book in front of me, along with a business card. "Hi Tara. I work for Giselle Roberts, the producer. She'd like to set up a meeting with you during Comic-Con, if you have time."

I blinked at him, wondering if I'd heard him correctly. Giselle Roberts was the biggest female producer and showrunner around. She was known for bringing diverse TV shows to the major networks and then dominating the ratings with them. She'd also created many popular reality TV shows like *Behind The Seams, American Supermodel,* and *Road Trip Race.*

"I'd love to," I said. "Do you know why?"

He pulled out his phone, checking something on it. "She didn't tell me, but I know she's a fan. Can you sign the book to her? And are you free tomorrow at all?"

"Sure." I raised an eyebrow at Hector, who shrugged. We both signed the book while the guy set up a meeting before walking away, leaving me completely baffled.

"What was that about?" Hector asked.

"Your guess is as good as mine."

"Hmm. Maybe she wants to turn *Misfit Squad* into a TV show?"

"No, then she'd want to meet with you, too." I couldn't figure it out, but the line moved at a brisk pace and I didn't have any more time to ponder it.

For the next hour we signed so many books my wrist began to throb. By the end of it I could barely move my hand and we'd run out of books to sell, although many fans had brought their own copies, too. And though some people were there because they'd seen Hector on *The Sound*, others seemed to genuinely love the book and were excited for the next one.

When it was over we said goodbye to Miguel and headed for the lobby of the convention center. "That was crazy," Hector said, running a hand through his short curls before covering them with his hat again. "I never expected so many people to show up."

"Me either. It was such a rush." I flexed my wrist. "Except now my hand hurts."

"It does? Mine seems okay."

"You're always using your hands, what with drawing and playing the drums. This was probably nothing to you."

He offered me his hand. "Let me help."

I rested my palm flat against his and little tingles shot through me. We were so close to holding hands. Touching like this was still in the realm of friendship, but at the same time, so incredibly intimate.

"Your hands are so tiny," he said, examining them.

"Or yours are just really big," I teased.

It was true, his were much larger than mine and his long, rough fingers completely dominated my own. What did they say about guys with big hands? Or was that feet? A quick glance down showed that those were big, too. I had to forcibly stop myself from checking the front of his jeans next.

He began to massage my wrist and his touch was firm but gentle. It was all I could do not to melt into a puddle right there. Time seemed to slip away, the crowd around us vanished, and I never wanted him to stop what he was doing.

"How's that?" he asked, releasing my hand and jolting me out of my trance.

I flexed my wrist and the pain was gone. His fingers were magic. I briefly wondered what else they could do. God, I needed to get my mind out of the gutter. "Much better. Thank you."

He nodded and glanced around the lobby, but didn't take another step. This was where we were supposed to split up and go our separate ways, but I got the feeling we were both stalling. I didn't want to say goodbye to him just yet either.

"Do you want to get coffee or something?" I asked. "A late lunch?"

He gave me another of his elusive smiles. "I'd like that."

We exited the convention center and joined the sea of people outside. The Gaslamp Quarter of downtown San Diego was almost as packed as inside the exhibit hall, with people hanging out in front of bars and restaurants, walking down the sidewalk to get to their hotels or one of the many off-site events, or standing around handing out flyers or trying to sell water bottles. The sun beat down on us, and I wasn't envious of anyone in costume in this heat.

We didn't talk much as we walked through the crowded streets other than to point out some of the things we saw, like cops pretending to make arrests for charity so people could take photos to send to friends or post online. Or the hundreds of ads and billboards for movies, TV shows, and video games that covered everything from the sides of buildings to the pedicabs and taxis in the street. Or the restaurants that had been completely taken over and transformed for the week, such as a café that had been redone for an upcoming zombie TV show, complete with undead servers and food made to look like brains and other mangled body parts. The menu alone made me want to gag. Needless to say, we decided not to eat there.

Every time I glanced at Hector, he met my gaze and his lips twitched into a small grin. Nope, we'd definitely had nothing to be nervous about. Being with him in person, even if we weren't saying a word, was just as easy as being with him online.

"How about here?" he asked, stopping outside a restaurant that looked fairly empty, possibly because it hadn't bothered with a fun theme. "Thai food is your favorite, right?"

"It is. How did you know?"

"You always eat it when we're on deadline and all stressed out, so I figured...." He shrugged.

"Huh. I never realized that, but you're right. It *is* my go-to comfort food." I tilted my head, smiling at him. "I'm impressed. But hey, *I* know you're allergic to seafood and you hate bananas and coconut. Oh, and your favorite food is your grandmother's tres leches cake."

His eyebrows shot up. "That's true. But I know *you're* addicted to Diet Coke."

"That's an easy one. Everyone knows that."

"Okay, how about this: you love chocolate but hate chocolate-flavored things. Chocolate cake, ice cream, milkshakes—all of those are out. The one exception is hot chocolate. Oh, and brownies. Can't forget those either."

I couldn't help but laugh. "Fine, I admit that you know me pretty well, too."

"Damn straight I do."

We got a table and ordered some food to share—he let me pick, since it was my favorite—and then launched right into easy conversation. He told me all about being on *The Sound*, since we hadn't been able to talk much while he was on it. It had only ended a week ago, and now he gave me all the behind-the-scenes scoop—how the producers had manipulated the results so Villain Complex couldn't win, how Jared and Maddic had carried on a secret relationship that nearly broke up the band, and how even though they hadn't won the show they'd gotten offers from multiple record labels for their second album.

"Dan is handling the negotiations now," he said, referring to the band's manager, who had been their mentor on *The Sound*. "But we've basically locked in a two-album deal with one of the labels. We plan to start working on new songs as soon as we get back from the tour."

"Wow, that's wonderful. It happened so fast!" I took a sip of my Diet Coke. "I'm *dying* to see you perform live. I watched the show on TV, of course, but it's not the same."

He picked up a chopstick and twirled it like one of his drumsticks. "So you're coming tonight?"

"Definitely."

"You probably need another ticket, huh? For Andy?"

I played with my napkin, avoiding Hector's gaze. "No, just one. I'm flying solo for a change."

"No? I thought you'd be here with him."

"He's at Comic-Con somewhere, I think, but not with me…" I'd been hoping to avoid talking about Andy. Or thinking about Andy. The wound was still so raw. But Hector deserved to know the truth. "We broke up a few days ago."

The chopstick hit the table with a soft clatter. "I'm sorry."

"Thanks." I sucked in a breath, trying to keep my voice steady. "It was a mutual thing. We both figured it was time to end it now that we've graduated. He's moving to Dallas and I'm moving to New York, so it's for the best, really."

Hector was silent for a moment, and I couldn't read his expression. "You were together for a year. That must be rough."

"Yeah." I sighed. "It's weird not talking to him anymore. I know we both have to move on with our lives, but it's hard saying goodbye to someone who was such an important part of mine for the last year."

I dropped my gaze to the table, wishing I hadn't said so much. I'd always been pretty open with Hector about my personal life, but now it felt wrong, like I shouldn't be discussing my ex with him. "Anyway, it's over and I'm ready to move on. What about you? You *are* single, right? Or did I mislead your fans at the panel?"

"No, I'm not seeing anyone."

Of course not. Hector had been single for the entire time I'd known him. I wasn't sure why, but I knew it had something to do with his past. If he hadn't told me by now then I figured it wasn't any of my business. Still, I couldn't help but wonder…

The food arrived, steaming plates of pad thai and prik king. We changed the subject back to work, to discuss ideas for a fourth *Misfit Squad* book. Miguel wanted a proposal with the first few pages and an outline for the rest, which I'd already written up and sent to Hector so he could start on the artwork.

"I put a few rough sketches together," he said. "If you like them, I'll get to work on them ASAP."

"Do you have time? You're on tour for the next month…"

"I'll make time."

He pulled his sketchbook from where he always kept it—tucked under his shirt in the back of his jeans—and flipped it open. He angled the page toward me, careful not to get it too close to the food.

"Wow, this is perfect." I slid the sketchbook closer to me. Hector always brought my scripts to life in ways I never expected, that were even better than I had imagined. He took my ideas, my story, and infused himself into them with his artwork, so the final version was truly a collaboration between us. Each book of *Misfit Squad* had both of our souls in it.

A waiter carrying a tray of food bumped my elbow and I dropped the sketchbook on the floor. Hector and I both reached for it but I managed to grab it first. Except now it was open to a different page.

This one had a drawing of a beautiful girl. It was in black and white and more realistic than his comic book art, and you could see the care Hector had taken with it. The girl was smiling, her head slightly tilted, her long blond hair (or I assumed it was blond, from the shading) flowing around her shoulders. Pieces like this reminded me just how remarkable of an artist Hector was. How he could capture someone so perfectly with just a charcoal pencil and infuse so much emotion and beauty into a simple drawing.

And then I realized the girl was *me*.

Hector reached across the table and snatched the sketchbook out of my hands. My eyes jumped to his face, and he looked pained. Like someone had just punched him in the gut. Was he worried I wouldn't like it? How could he possibly think that?

"Hector, that…that was stunning."

"It's nothing," he said, shoving the sketchbook back in his jeans.

"I didn't know…" I stopped, taking a breath. "I mean, I never realized you'd drawn me before."

He shrugged and took a long chug of his water. "I draw everyone," he finally said.

Maybe that was true, but I *knew* Hector's artwork. I'd seen hundreds of his drawings, both art for *Misfit Squad* and random sketches he did for fun. There had been something different about that picture of me. Something special. Something more…intimate.

"Hector, do you…" I faltered, trying to come up with a better way to ask the questions threatening to burst out of me. "Is this…" No, that wasn't right. I tried a new approach. "Why didn't you ever show me?"

He still wouldn't look at me. "It's not a big deal."

That didn't answer the question at all. My fingers tightened around the chain at my neck, the metal biting into my skin a welcome distraction from how uncomfortable this moment was. "Are there others of me in there? Can I see?"

"No!"

His harsh response made me jump. I banged my knee against the table, causing the silverware and plates to rattle, and he cringed at the sound. The ease of our conversation had vanished and tension had built a brick wall between us. But the more he evaded my questions the more my curiosity grew, and the more I *needed* to know the answers. Why wouldn't he just tell me?

"It's just, I know your art," I said, before I could stop myself. "And that drawing seemed like it *meant* something."

He visibly tensed and one of his chopsticks snapped in his hand. "Jesus, it's just a fucking drawing. You're reading way too much into it."

"Am I?"

He tossed the broken chopstick on the table and pushed his plate away. "It doesn't mean anything. I draw lots of people. Friends. Family. Random people on the street. That's all."

God, this had all gone horribly wrong. Hector was closed off about his emotions on even the best days, but I'd never seen him like this before. I had to back off. I didn't want to—I wanted to get *something* out of him. But I cared about Hector as a friend before anything else, and I could tell he desperately wanted me to drop this.

I plastered on a smile and made my voice light. "In that case, you should draw that guy over there in the Halo helmet and pink tutu and nothing else."

Hector laughed. I could tell it was forced, but at least things returned to some semblance of normality between us. Even if I couldn't shake the feeling that he'd been lying.

FOUR

Hector

In our dressing room, Jared bounced up and down on his heels and shook his hands out while doing his vocal exercises. I wanted to yell at him to sit down and shut up because he was making me crazy, but I couldn't mess with his pre-show ritual. That would only fuck things up for the entire band, and we were already on edge as it was.

Tonight was the first concert on *The Sound* tour, featuring the top four bands from the show. Our first performance in a giant stadium in front of over ten thousand people. We'd been rehearsing for the past week, from the minute *The Sound* had ended, but we'd had a lot to practice. Not just the songs either, but things like the order we played them in, the transitions between them, where Maddie and Jared stood on stage, even what Jared said to the audience—it was all scripted down to the second. We had so much to learn in a very short period of time, and that had resulted in some serious growing pains. We were used to that after the whirlwind that was *The Sound*, but I didn't think anything could really prepare a band for something as massive as this.

I wasn't nervous about tonight's show, not exactly. The waiting was what killed me. I wanted to get out there and play already, not sit around on my ass while two other bands went on before us.

Knowing Tara might be in the audience only made it worse.

I stretched my arms and neck, forcing myself not to check my phone again. It was almost time for our set and, as far as I knew, Tara still hadn't arrived. I had to accept that she wasn't coming. Not after what had happened at lunch.

After our fight—or whatever the hell that had been—I'd insisted on paying the bill, despite her protests, and told her I had to head to the stadium for the sound check. She'd promised she was coming to the concert, but I hadn't heard a single thing from her since then.

Thank god she'd only seen the one drawing. If she'd flicked through the rest of my sketchbook she'd think I was a stalker or something. I *did* have pictures of my other friends in there, too. Hell, I'd just done one yesterday of Maddie playing the guitar that Jared wanted to keep. But I had more drawings of Tara than anyone else. And like she'd said, they were different.

Whenever I missed her, or after we video chatted and her smile was still fresh in my mind, I had the urge to sketch her. Any strong emotion made me want to draw, to let it out through my art. Jared told me it was the same for him when he wrote music. And Tara always made me feel more than anyone else—no matter how hard I tried not to let her in.

But I'd never shown the drawings of Tara to anyone. There was something more…private about them. They were for me and no one else. She wasn't supposed to ever find out about them.

I broke down and checked my phone again. Nothing. Dammit.

"You okay?" Maddie asked from her spot on one of the couches, where she idly strummed her acoustic guitar. With her low-cut red top, black leather pants, and geeky glasses, she looked smoking hot, like some kind of sexy librarian.

"Yeah," I said, shoving the phone back in my jeans.

Jared sank beside Maddie, sliding an arm around her waist. The two of them had been joined at the hip ever since they'd officially become a thing during the finale of *The Sound*. Now they were completely unbearable 24/7, like five minutes apart would kill them. Don't get me wrong, I was happy for them. I just didn't want to see them making out every single minute of the day.

I'd been kind of a jerk to Maddie when I'd first met her. After Jared had nearly broken up our band by sleeping with Becca, our previous bassist, I'd told him I didn't want another girl to replace her. I'd thought Maddie was just another of his groupies, looking for an excuse to get in his bed. And like I'd predicted, the two of them had hooked up and nearly ruined our chances on *The Sound*.

But Maddie surprised me by being a great guitarist and, even with the drama, I grew to really like her. Not to mention, I realized how much Jared had changed because of her. He was better when she was around, happier than I'd seen him in years, and he obviously loved her. Now I couldn't imagine not having her in the band.

"Is Tara here yet?" Maddie asked.

"No. I don't think she's coming." I shrugged. "Whatever."

Jared arched an eyebrow. "I think Hector's not telling us something."

I glared at him. "*I* think you're annoying as hell."

"Aha! That means I'm right."

"Ooh," Maddie said, setting her guitar aside. "What do you think he's hiding?"

"I'm not hiding anything!"

"Something must have happened when they had lunch," Jared said. "He pouted all through the sound check."

"I did not."

Jared was usually so wrapped up in himself that it always surprised me when he noticed shit like that. Then again, he knew me better than anyone, even Tara. Best friends were such a pain in the ass sometimes.

"No? You kept coming in a measure early on the 'Somebody Told Me' bridge. That's not like you."

Unfortunately, he was right. I'd been totally distracted during our sound check and it had thrown off the entire band. I needed to get my head together before we went on stage.

"Nothing happened."

"Is that the problem?" Maddie asked, her voice concerned. "You *wanted* something to happen with Tara?"

"No!" The way she looked at me implied she knew my secret, but until this week I'd never even mentioned Tara to Maddie. Not even Kyle knew how I felt about her. Only one person did. "Let me guess. Jared told you."

She gave me a sympathetic smile. "I think it's cute that you've loved her all this time. It explains a lot, too. Like how you never talk about girls. Or seem to notice they exist at all."

"I can't believe you," I growled at Jared. "That was private. You've broken the bro code, man."

He gave a slight shrug. "She figured it out. What was I supposed to do?"

"It was kind of obvious," she said, her fingers tangling with his. "How was it meeting her in person for the first time?"

"Weird."

"Uh huh…"

"And good." I looked away, my teeth grinding together. Why were we still talking about this? "But mostly weird."

The door opened and Kyle came in, wearing a hoodie over his dyed-black hair. His sleeves were rolled up, showing off the tattoos on each arm. He passed a bottle of water to each of us and plopped down on the other couch.

"Where's Hector's girl?" he asked.

"Shit, does *everyone* know?" I muttered.

"Pretty much."

"She's not coming."

"No way," Maddie said. "I saw how she smiled at you during your panel. She'll be here."

I grunted and crossed my arms, hoping that signaled the end of this conversation. Jared opened his mouth and I knew he was going to continue bugging me, but I was saved by a knock on the dressing room door.

Kyle hopped up and opened it. A security guard stood on the other side, one finger on his earpiece. "There's a blonde with a backstage pass who says she knows you guys, but she's not on the list."

I jumped to my feet before I realized what I was doing. "That must be Tara. You can send her in."

Maddie smiled. "Told you."

I paced back and forth, too restless to sit again. Now that she was here I wasn't sure what to say to her. How long would it be awkward between us after what happened at lunch? Maybe if I didn't bring it up we could both forget about it.

But when the door opened it wasn't Tara who stood there, but Becca, our former bassist.

After the way things had ended, Becca was just about the last person I'd expect to see in our dressing room. She looked better than she had the last time I'd seen her, when she'd gotten drunk, thrown a bottle at Jared's head, and quit the band. Her blue hair was light blond now, like she'd bleached it, and she seemed more awake or something.

Jared stood up quickly, his eyes narrowing. "What are you doing here?"

"Hey," Becca said, closing the door behind her. "I wanted to talk to you. Well, to the entire band."

Shit, I hoped she wasn't here to cause trouble. I glanced at Maddie to see if she was okay, but she looked more curious than upset. Even so, I stood up straighter, getting ready for a fight. Not a physical one, of course, but mentally preparing myself for whatever was about to go down. "Spit it out then."

She rolled her eyes. "Relax. I just came to say sorry. That's it."

"You want to say *sorry?*" Kyle asked.

Becca ruffled her short hair, looking at the floor. "Yeah, I'm sorry. For every-thing that happened with us, and for quitting the band when you needed me. Oh, and for what I said to that reporter while you were on *The Sound*. I was drunk and didn't realize he was recording it, and… yeah, that's no excuse. It was still shitty of me even if I was drunk."

"You drove all the way to San Diego to apologize to us?" I asked. It was a two or three hour drive from LA, where we all lived. Probably even more with Comic-Con traffic.

"I've been staying in San Diego with a friend since I got kicked out of my apartment last month. When I heard you were doing a show tonight I thought I'd stop by." We still must have looked skeptical because she sighed and continued. "Look, I stopped drinking and doing all that shit and I'm trying to get my life together. In a few days I'm heading to Dallas to live with my sister, maybe go back to college and start over. So I wanted to make sure we were cool before I left."

Jared didn't look convinced, but Maddie placed a hand on his arm. "It's all in the past," she said to Becca. "Don't worry about it."

The two of them stared at each other for long beat, and then Becca nodded. If there was any lingering resentment between them, neither of them showed it. I was surprised Maddie would be so forgiving, until I remembered her mother was a recovering alcoholic, too.

"We're cool," Jared said, all traces of hostility gone.

"Thanks for the apology," Kyle added.

I reluctantly nodded. She did seem sober, for once. I'd forgotten what sober Becca looked like. And if the other guys were over the whole thing, then so was I.

"Good." Becca's shoulders relaxed. "Sucks that you didn't win *The Sound*, but it seems like the band is taking off anyway." She flicked a thumb at the door. "I'm going to head out and watch the show."

"How'd you get a backstage pass, anyway?" I asked.

"I hooked up with one of the security guards a week or two ago. Guess he's still into me." She shrugged. Jared laughed, and the tension in the room eased.

He grabbed one of the flyers off the table and held it out to her. "We're having a party Saturday night. You should stop by."

If it were up to me, I'd suggest we all go our separate ways and never speak again. But maybe Jared still felt bad for what had gone down between them. Another sign that he'd changed; the old Jared would have kicked her out of our dressing room by now.

She pocketed the flyer. "Maybe I will. Thanks."

As soon as she left, we got the fifteen-minute warning. Time to exit our dressing room and head to the stage—but first, Jared pulled us all in for a band huddle.

He sucked in a deep breath before starting. "Tonight we're playing a sold out show in our biggest venue ever. Thousands of people are waiting for us to go on stage. Can we just let that sink in for a minute?"

We all went quiet and the enormity of what we were doing really hit me. "Oh shit," I said with a short laugh. "We are so screwed."

"We're still figuring some things out," Jared admitted. "But this tour is our dream. And for us to achieve it so fast…of course there are going to be some rough spots along the way."

"We practiced our asses off," Kyle said. "We've got this."

"I still can't believe this is really happening," Maddie said, with awe in her voice.

A slow smile spread across Jared's face. "It's happening. A few weeks ago we were playing frat parties, parking lot shows, and small clubs. Now we're playing massive stadiums across America. Somehow, we've become an arena band almost overnight."

Kyle shook his head, like he was shocked by it, too. "It's been an amazing journey, and it's only the beginning."

"I'm so happy I could be a part of it," Maddie added, sniffing.

"You guys are cheesy as hell," I said, grinning at the three of them.

"Admit it, you love our cheese," Jared said.

"I admit nothing." He was right though. I loved Jared and Kyle like my own brothers, and Maddie already felt like a little sister to me, too. Even if they got a bit sappy sometimes and made me want to roll my eyes at them.

They all looked like they expected me to say something too, to finish up our little bonding moment. I wasn't good at that stuff, but I cleared my throat and gave it a shot anyway. "Whatever happens, tonight will be great 'cause we're together. We're more than a band, we're a family."

"Aww," Maddie said, her big eyes watering behind her glasses.

"See? I knew you had some cheese in you, too." Jared slapped me on the back. "You big softie, you."

I donned my toughest face. "Hey, there's nothing about me that's soft."

"Is that so?" His eyebrows shot up as he glanced at my jeans.

Maddie laughed. "Tara is one lucky girl."

I groaned. Of course they'd bring this back to her again. "Nothing's going to happen with Tara. We're just friends."

"Hmm, where have I heard that before?" Kyle asked, looking pointedly at Maddie and Jared. They'd given us that line a dozen times before finally admitting that they were, in fact, much more than friends. But this thing with Tara was different.

"Nah. She's not even here."

"Oh, she's here," Kyle said, with a grin. "Alexis texted me a few minutes ago."

"What? She is?" Hot damn, she'd come to see me perform after all. Maybe the sketchbook incident hadn't freaked her out as much as I'd thought.

"Perfect," Jared said. "Now, let's get out there and put on the best show we can, and try to have some fun, too."

We broke the huddle and headed toward the stage. Knowing Tara was in the audience gave me a burst of energy. I couldn't wait to get out there and do this thing. With the others at my side I felt like we could take on the world together, one song at a time.

Shit, maybe I *was* just as cheesy as they were.

FIVE

Tara

A s soon as I arrived at the stadium the clichés came back in force. My heart raced, my hands were clammy, and my inner goddess—whatever that was—awakened, all in anticipation of seeing Hector again. I'd become one of those girls I'd once mocked in books, who met the hot guy and instantly lost all common sense. Never again would I scoff at them.

I checked my face in my phone's camera. Was I too done up? Did I look like I was trying too hard? He'd seen me in pajamas and no makeup many times before. He'd seen me when I was so busy with school and our books that I forgot to take showers for days. He'd even seen me when I'd had the flu. Maybe I should take off some of this makeup. The eye shadow at least. I wasn't going on a date, after all, I was just watching my friend perform with his band. Not a big deal.

But it was too late, because I was already at the entrance to the stadium. Like everything at Comic Con, there was a gigantic line to get in but I skipped past it using my backstage pass—thank you, Hector—and the security guard waved me inside. The crowd was massive, with high energy and excitement you couldn't help but feel under your skin. People cheered, music blared from the stage, and the air smelled vaguely of beer and popcorn. Everyone was with a group of friends or part of a couple. And then there was me, all by myself.

I checked my ticket and headed for my seat while Brazen, the band that had gotten third place on *The Sound*, did a Maroon 5 cover on stage. I wanted to find Hector backstage, but Villain Complex would be on soon and I couldn't miss their performance. My spot was crazy good too, right in the center of the front row. So close I could see up the Brazen's singer's skirt as she danced around.

My phone buzzed in my pocket. A text from Andy: *Want to have dinner?*

The sight of his name made my stomach clench. I reread his text over and over, surprised he'd contact me this soon after our break-up. We'd agreed to try to stay friends, but I wasn't sure either of us were ready for that yet.

I texted him: *Sorry, busy tonight.*

He wrote back: *Tomorrow?*

I hesitated with my fingers over the screen. Tomorrow Hector and I had a Black Hat Comics party, but after that he would probably be busy with his band. It might be uncomfortable to see Andy so soon, but it *would* be nice to not have to eat alone. Like me, he was by himself at Comic-Con and I could understand why he wanted to hang out. When you're surrounded by so many people it's even more noticeable how alone you are.

And the only reason he'd even come to Comic-Con was because of me. We'd bought the tickets months ago, and when we'd broken up it had been too late to refund them or cancel his flight. Instead, he'd found a cheap hotel room for himself since he couldn't stay in mine anymore.

OK, I replied. *Have party in evening but will text when over.*

Perfect, he wrote back. *See you then.*

I hated admitting it, but I was sad that Andy and I had broken up *before* Comic-Con instead of after. He'd been my plus one for everything for the past year, and before that it had been Sam, and before that another guy…

The truth was, I wasn't very good at being single. I liked having someone to go places with, who could make new experiences less awkward, who gave me a little confidence boost thanks to the knowledge I had someone familiar at my side. Andy had fit the bill perfectly.

I blamed growing up in a small town in Nebraska with five brothers and sisters. I'd never done *anything* alone as a kid, had never had a second of time to myself. I'd done whatever I could to get some space from my family, but now I lived a paradox: being surrounded by people drained me and yet I hated being by myself, too.

Maybe that's why I spent so much of my free time talking to Hector online. He'd always made me feel less alone.

It was ridiculous. I was an adult, I should be able to do things by myself and not feel uncomfortable—but I did. Definitely something to work on in the future.

I'd have to get used to being alone soon, too. Other than Hector, all my friends were back in Boston. After graduating last month most of us were moving on, and I wasn't sure how many I'd keep in touch with in the future. We'd all promised to continue to be friends, but would we be anything more than social media acquaintances in a few months?

Once I moved to New York I'd have to make new friends, I supposed. I'd dreamed of working in publishing my entire life, so when I'd been hired to be part of the new comics division of Ostrich Books, one of the biggest publishers in the world, it had sounded like the ideal job. Yet, despite how perfect it seemed, I was hit with a massive wave of anxiety every time I thought about it. Probably because I didn't know anyone there or have a place to live yet.

Brazen finished and the audience cheered while the singer bounced off stage, holding the hand of her mentor from *The Sound*. As soon as they were gone, a girl with fiery red curls dropped into the seat beside me and smiled. "Tara, right?"

"Yeah…" I studied her face. She looked familiar, with very pale skin, a hint of freckles across her nose, and pretty green eyes. She wore a leather jacket and had a fancy camera around her neck. "You're Alexis! Kyle's girlfriend!"

She laughed. "That's me."

"I saw you in the audience at the panel. And Hector's told me all about you."

"Did he? Interesting. He's been very secretive about you."

"Oh…well, I guess there's not that much to tell." I tried not to sound disappointed, but it stung that he didn't talk about me with his friends. Then again, why would he? I was just some girl he knew online, after all.

"That's definitely not true," Alexis said. "Hector's extremely private, even with his closest friends. The fact that he hasn't told us anything means you must be *very* important to him."

"I don't know about that…"

"I do." She leaned close, like she was whispering a secret. "In fact, Kyle said Hector's going crazy because he's worried you wouldn't come tonight."

"He is?" Did he think I was upset about the drawing? Even if I was (which I wasn't), how could he believe I wouldn't come tonight? I wouldn't miss this for anything. "Maybe I should text him…"

"They're already on their way to the stage. But don't worry, I told them you're here."

"Oh. Thanks." I tried to relax in my seat but excitement bubbled under my skin, making me almost jumpy. "I can't wait. I've never seen them play before. Except on TV, of course."

She checked her camera lens and adjusted something. "They're pretty impressive. Even before they were famous they were good, but being on the show made them even better. Maddie helped a lot, too. She brought the band together and made everything click."

"So you've known them a long time?" I vaguely remembered Hector saying something about Alexis and Kyle getting back together at the Battle of the Bands they'd competed in, but I didn't know much more than that.

"Since high school. Give or take a few years when I went away for college."

"Do you know when Hector last had a girlfriend?" I slapped a hand over my mouth, cheeks flaring hot. "Sorry, I don't know where that came from."

She hesitated, not meeting my eyes. "You'll have to ask him about that. But as far as I can tell, it's been a long time."

I nodded. It's not like it really mattered or was any of my business. But the not knowing still drove me crazy.

The lights dimmed and the entire crowd seemed to jump to its feet at once, including me. Fog crept across the stage and a red glow slowly illuminated the darkness. The stadium was silent except for the buzz of excitement, the anticipation for the band about to come out. My chest was tight, my breathing difficult, my heart a speeding train that threatened to derail at any moment.

Just when I thought I couldn't take any more of it, the room burst into sound with the opening of "Uprising" by Muse. The lights brightened, gradually revealing the band already on stage. Maddie on the right, her fingers flying across her guitar, the fake wind blowing her hair like in a music video. Kyle on the left, rocking out behind his keyboard, his black hair hanging in his eyes. And Jared in the middle, playing bass.

A spotlight flashed on him when he started singing. In person he was even more drop dead gorgeous than on screen, with his tattooed arms, sinful blue eyes, and naughty smile. His voice had a way of creeping into your very soul, and he had this crazy magnetism that made it nearly impossible to take your eyes off him. Especially when he wasn't playing and could grip the microphone like a lover and croon into it. No wonder so many ladies threw themselves at him.

But while everyone drooled over Jared, my eyes sought out Hector, who had gone shirtless tonight. It was harder to see him in the back, but I could still glimpse his muscular arms and shoulders while his drumsticks danced through the air. He was an animal, pounding against the drums like he was possessed by something, yet somehow never completely losing control.

The big screens beside the stage flashed between the different band members and showed Hector from behind, giving a shot of his smooth back, all those coiled muscles flexing and rippling while he played. Sweat slicked his arms as he poured himself into the music, his drumsticks moving fast yet never missing a beat. He was glorious. Strong. Powerful. And ridiculously sexy. I wanted to lick the sweat off him, which was sort of gross, but I didn't care. I'd do it to taste him, to explore that hard, muscular body with my tongue. And my hands. And every other part of me.

I couldn't deny it any longer. Meeting Hector in person had awakened something in me. I'd always found him hot, of course. And sure, I'd fantasized about him a few times, but I'd never seriously thought of him as anything more than a friend. He'd always been too far away, too off limits, too impossible to even consider. But now he was more than a daydream I tried desperately to ignore—he was a very tempting reality.

Once we'd come face to face a flick had been switched, and I felt something…more.

And seeing him play tonight? That made me *want* him.

For the rest of Villain Complex's set, Alexis and I bounced along to the songs, arms in the air, throwing ourselves into the music with everyone else in the crowd. The band played through all the covers they'd done on the show, plus their own song, "Behind the Mask." Their former mentor, Dan, even came out to do a cover of one of his band's songs with them. They finished with their sensual cover of "Bad Romance," making the audience go wild.

When the lights went up, I felt like I'd just had the greatest sex of my life. All that anticipation, the buildup of excitement, the rush of the music, and finally the climax at the end. I was exhausted yet almost giddy with exhilaration. I wanted to see them play again immediately.

"How is it possible they didn't win the show?" I asked Alexis.

"Tell me about it," she said. "Ready to go backstage, or do you want to watch the country princess and her band perform?"

She was referring to the band that had won *The Sound*, Fairy Lights, but even if I'd been a fan I couldn't wait a second longer to see Hector again. "I definitely want to go backstage."

Alexis led me out of the aisles to a security guard along the side who checked our passes and let us through. I followed on her heels through the dizzying maze of backstage areas, packed with roadies, equipment, and more security guards. She seemed to know where she was going, taking us down long brightly lit hallways and past doors labeled only with letters. Finally she knocked on a door that said C, and then opened it without waiting for a response.

Music hit me—the sound of an acoustic guitar being played and Jared's voice raised in song, followed by a chorus of laughter. We stepped into a large room with a giant TV on one wall, a mini-kitchen in the back, and two large brown leather couches that the band was sprawled across.

"Hey!" Kyle looked up from the beer he was sipping. He patted the seat next to him and Alexis slid into his arms, curling against his side like she belonged there.

Jared and Maddie were tangled together on the other couch. She sat on his lap and they held the guitar together, playing it at the same time, completely in their own world. When Jared starting singing again I recognized the song as "Howlin' For You" by the Black Keys.

Hector sat on his own, apart from the other two couples, his well-developed arms draped across the back of the couch. I was disappointed to see he'd put on a shirt after their set had ended.

He jumped to his feet as soon as he saw me. "Tara. You're here."

Maybe it was the way he smiled at me, like I was the best thing he'd seen all day. Maybe it was an echo of desire left over from seeing him perform. Maybe it was all the other love in the room. But suddenly I had the strongest urge to kiss him.

SIX

Hector

Tara hugged me, fitting against my chest like it was the most natural place for her to be. I circled my arms around her, relieved that she wasn't upset with me. And instantly hard, thanks to the lush, feminine curves of her body pressed against mine. Damn, I could get used to that.

Except I couldn't, because no matter what happened at Comic-Con, she was still going to live thousands of miles away from me. I had to keep that in mind at all times.

"You were incredible," she said, looking up at me from behind her long lashes. "Thanks for inviting me, and for the backstage pass."

"No problem," I said, forcing myself to pull away. "Hey everyone, this is Tara."

There wasn't much space on the couch so she had to sit close to me, setting me on alert for the chance we might accidentally touch. The others were all grinning madly, looking back and forth between the two of us. Shit, they'd better not embarrass me in front of her. Or say anything to tip her off about how I felt about her. Maybe bringing her backstage to meet them was a mistake. It had been so much easier when no one knew about her and that part of my life was completely separate from this one.

"I'm so happy to meet you," Maddie said to Tara, with a big smile. "I wanted to come to your signing but Hector was being a total grump about it. Do you think you could sign my copy of *Misfit Squad* now?"

Tara looked startled for a second, but then laughed. "Of course! I didn't know you were a fan."

"Maddie's a *huge* fan," Jared said. "I am, too. But then again, I'm a fan of everything Hector does." He winked at me and I rolled my eyes.

Maddie brought out her copy of *Misfit Squad*, which I'd given her while we were on *The Sound*. She'd read it over the past week between rehearsals and had gushed over it constantly, asking me a million questions about what was going to happen next. She'd already made me sign it and now she handed it to Tara, who pulled out one of her metallic pens.

"I feel so weird signing this," Tara said as she opened the book up. "Like I should be asking for your autograph instead. I watched you all on TV every week and it's kind of intimidating to actually meet you in person."

Alexis groaned. "Don't tell them that. You'll make their egos even bigger."

"My ego is the perfect size, thank you very much," Jared said, grinning like a lazy cat. "Just like every other part of me."

I threw a pillow at Jared's head. "Dude, no one needs to know that. Except Maddie."

"Oh, she knows." He waggled his eyebrows and Maddie actually blushed. That made Tara laugh, and I relaxed a little at the sound.

"Thanks so much," Maddie said, when Tara handed the book back to her. "I keep trying to bribe Hector into giving me an early copy of the second one or give me some hints or *something*, but he refuses."

"I don't have any copies yet," I said. "And you know I don't give out spoilers."

"Hector *is* crazy about the no-spoilers-thing," Kyle said.

"They just really annoy me, that's all," I muttered.

"Forget him," Tara said to Maddie, in a low voice like they were conspiring together. "I'll hook you up. As long as you answer a few burning questions I have about the show."

Maddie grinned. "Deal. What do you want to know?"

"First, did it hurt when you fell off the stage?"

"It was more shocking than painful, though I did twist my ankle pretty bad." Maddie and Jared shared a small smile, as though they were both in on a secret. "But it led to Jared kissing me for the first time, so it was worth it."

"*That's* when you two got together?" I asked.

"Yep. In the elevator." Jared kissed Maddie on the neck. "And back in her hotel room. And…"

Kyle raised a tattooed hand to stop him. "We get the idea."

Tara asked a few more questions about the show, and then my friends asked her about writing *Misfit Squad* and going to college in Boston. I'd worried she'd feel out of place as the new person in the group, but it wasn't awkward at all. In fact, she seemed to fit right in.

We all discussed our plans for the next few days at Comic-Con and Jared handed Tara a flyer for our party on Saturday night. I'd designed it myself and it read "Villain Afterparty," with silhouettes of famous villains like Loki, Catwoman, and Magneto on a red background. The party was taking place in a club inside our hotel and promised drinks, costume contests, karaoke, and more. Across the bottom it said, "Wear your most villainous costume!"

"Sounds fun," Tara said. "Are you dressing up, Hector?"

Jared grinned. "Hell yeah he is."

I scowled at him. "I don't want to, but Jared and Maddie love this shit."

Tara nudged me with her shoulder. "Let me guess, Red Power Ranger?"

"What? That doesn't even fit the villain theme." I couldn't believe she would even bring that up.

"No, but it'd be hilarious."

"Hey, just 'cause I loved that show as a kid doesn't mean I'd dress up as one of them."

"We're all going as Batman villains," Maddie said, saving me from further embarrassment. "My roommate Julie designs the most amazing costumes and she made them for us. We're entering the Masquerade, too."

The Masquerade was the annual costume contest at Comic-Con. Julie planned to enter us as a group in the hopes of winning one of the many prizes and to show off her creations in front of thousands of people.

Cosplay was not my thing at all and I'd only agreed to be part of it to make Maddie and Jared happy. Not that I *really* minded dressing up, but hey, I had to keep up my tough guy act.

"Cool theme." Tara turned toward me. "So what's your costume?"

"They're making me go as Bane."

"Ooh. I want to see you all dressed up. I'll try to make it."

Maddie's eyes widened behind her black-rimmed glasses. "You should totally dress up with us. I bet Julie could whip up something quickly for you."

I gave Maddie a *back off* look. "She doesn't need to dress up if she doesn't want to."

"No, of course not. Sorry, I wasn't trying to pressure you, Tara."

"It's okay," she said, smiling. "I'd love to join you guys. I have a costume for tomorrow's Black Hat party I could use, but going as a group sounds a lot more fun."

"Oh, yay!" Maddie clapped her hands together. "Hmm, which Batman villain could you be?"

Jared tilted his head and considered. "Talia Al Ghul is the other big female villain in Batman."

"True, but she doesn't have a distinct, recognizable costume."

"Good point. Ah, I have an idea!" He whispered something into Maddie's ear and her face lit up.

"Yes! I'll text Julie now so she can start preparing! This is going to be good."

"What's happening?" Tara asked me, resting a hand on my bicep as she leaned closer.

I shook my head. "It's best to just let them do their thing when they get like this. No one can stop them."

She laughed and Maddie eyed us closely. She tugged on Jared's shirt. "We should go back to the hotel and let Hector and Tara catch up."

He nuzzled against her neck. "I like the sound of that."

Jared and I were sharing my room, which had been provided by Black Hat Comics, while Maddie was staying with her two roommates in a different hotel down the street. Unfortunately that meant they kept trying to get me out of the room so they could fool around. It sounded like I'd be locked out of the room for a while tonight. Lucky me.

Jared stood up, and he and Kyle shared one of those looks where they seemed to communicate telepathically. They'd always done that and it could be annoying as hell sometimes. Like now, when I wondered what they were up to—at least, until

Jared patted me on the shoulder, discreetly slipping me a handful of condoms with a wink. Fucking typical of him.

Kyle nodded and hopped up from the couch, pulling Alexis with him. They had their own hotel room, since Alexis was working as a photographer while at Comic-Con. "We're going to head out too," he said. "We'll see you guys tomorrow."

They all rushed out of the room like it was on fire, leaving me and Tara alone on the couch, still sitting close from when there had been too many people on it.

Neither of us moved apart. Our eyes locked and it struck me again how pretty she was. Her soft lips twitched up into the slightest hint of a smile before she looked away, almost like she was shy or nervous.

I was hit by the overwhelming urge to draw her. I just hoped she wouldn't take it the wrong way. Or read too much into it.

"Stay like that." I grabbed my sketchbook off the other table and sat beside her again, just as close. She still didn't inch away.

She tilted her head. "Like what?"

"Don't move. I want to draw you."

She laughed and tucked a piece of golden hair behind her ear, folding her legs beneath her. "I'm all sweaty and tired and gross after a long day at Comic-Con."

"You look beautiful." The words slipped out by accident, but her warm smile made me not regret them. "I want to capture you just like this, on the day we finally met in person."

"What do I do?"

I took my pencil from the corner of the sketchbook and opened to a blank page. "Just act normal. Tell me what you most want to see at Comic-Con."

"Um, I don't know. The usual stuff. The Marvel and DC panels, but I've heard those are hard to get into." She shifted awkwardly, like she was trying to get comfortable but was too self-conscious now that she knew I was drawing her.

"We're camping out all night in the Hall H line tomorrow so we can get into them." I started my sketch, focusing on her cobalt blue eyes first. I couldn't capture them properly with just a black pencil, but I would do my best.

"Oh yeah?" She put her hands on the couch for a second, then moved them to her lap, like she couldn't decide what to do with them.

"We've got sleeping bags and food and beer. It'll be one big party. You should join us."

"That sounds fun. I might have to take you up on that."

She slowly relaxed as she told me about the things she'd heard would be revealed at the DC and Marvel panels about the upcoming movies. I kept her talking as I sketched her smile, her bright eyes, the feminine curves of her face, the trail of blond hair down her shoulder, the delicate slope of her neck.

"I want to go to a couple different book panels tomorrow," she continued. "There's one with a bunch of bestselling fantasy and sci-fi authors that sounds amazing. Then in the afternoon there's a panel about writing and drawing diverse characters that I can't miss."

"I saw that in the schedule. It looked good."

"We should go together!"

I grinned, pleased that she wanted to spend so much time with me this week. "We will. Although we should have been *on* that panel."

She laughed. "True. You can complain to Miguel that he didn't hook us up."

"Nah. The less I have to talk in front of people, the better."

"I thought that stuff didn't make you nervous?"

"It doesn't. But I still hate it."

I stopped to examine my work. For the first time I felt like I was able to capture her, the *real* her, now that I'd finally met her in person.

"Are you done?" she asked, trying to sneak a peek.

"Mostly."

I could tweak the thing forever, but it was good enough to show her. Still, I hesitated, taking a moment to add a little more shading to her hair. She'd seen hundreds of my sketches before, along with that other drawing of her, but this one felt more important than anything else I'd done.

"Can I see?" She inched closer to me, her hip nudging against my side.

I relented, unable to deny her anything when she was this close. She gasped as soon as she saw the drawing. "Hector, this…this is beautiful."

"You like it?"

"I *love* it. I want to hug it to my chest, that's how much I love it, but I'm worried I'll smear it." She smiled down at my drawing before setting it beside her on the couch. "I'll just hug you instead."

Then she was in my arms again, soft, warm, and curvy, and I wrapped myself tight around her. This time neither of us pulled away. Instead, she smoothed her hands along my chest and looked up at me, her rose-colored lips parting. As I stared at her mouth I was tempted to do the thing I'd dreamed about for so long.

I'd never seen a more beautiful girl than her. Never wanted a girl more. Other women had been easy to resist. Jared had lured many of them away, and the rest weren't difficult to turn down. But not her. She was my weakness.

When she didn't move back, even after the reasonable time had passed for a friendly hug, courage flared in me. I bowed my head and brushed my lips across hers, the softest, lightest touch in case she didn't want this kiss. I expected her to pull away, to ask, "What are you doing?"

But she didn't.

She let out a quiet sigh, barely audible against my mouth, and closed her eyes like she was waiting for more. I took that as my cue and gave her another kiss, a real kiss this time. I was still hesitant, half-convinced she would stop me at any moment. This was crossing the line beyond friendship. I wasn't sure I should be doing it, but I couldn't help myself either. I'd dreamed of kissing Tara for years and now it was finally happening.

And impossibly, amazingly, she kissed me back.

I'd kissed girls before, but it had never been like this. Kissing Tara was like being kissed for the first time. Her lips were so sweet I wanted to taste her all night. I eased her mouth open softly, sliding my tongue inside, still waiting for her to stop me. I did everything slowly, giving her the opportunity to end it. But she didn't.

I kissed her deeper. Harder. Demanding more from her.

And she let me.

Then she kissed *me*, shifting so she was on her knees on the couch and leaning against my chest, almost in my lap. She clutched my face and I drew her in closer, gripping her waist, her breasts rubbing against me through our clothes. My hands dipped down to cup her ass, to slide along her curves for the first time.

I'd suffered through years of lusting after her and now I finally had her in my arms. I couldn't stop myself. I wanted, *needed* to touch her everywhere. I had to explore her and see if she lived up to the fantasy in my head. Except after that kiss I knew she would be even better than anything I'd imagined.

When we finally broke apart she whispered my name and it had never sounded so good. "Are you sure those drawings mean nothing?" she asked.

I tensed up, completely caught off guard. "What?"

"I…forget it." She shook her head, pulling back. "God, what are we even doing?"

I drew in a ragged breath. "Do you want to stop?"

"Maybe…maybe we should."

It was hard to stop touching her, so fucking hard, but I lifted my hands off her. "Whatever you want."

She slowly climbed off the couch and yanked down her shirt, which had ridden up to show off her smooth, pale stomach. She looked dazed, like she wasn't sure what to do. "I…I should go. Before this goes any further."

I stood, but didn't say anything. I wasn't sure how to convince her to stay. Wasn't even sure I wanted her to stay.

No, that was a lie, as evidenced by my raging hard-on. I was dying for her to stay.

She walked to the door, but once there she paused and turned around. I took a step closer, unable to resist her magnetic pull. She stared at me and I was hypnotized by the way her breasts rose and fell with each of her quickened breaths. I moved even closer, until I was only an inch in front of her. Still, she didn't leave. It was almost like she *wanted* me to stop her.

Did she?

"The drawings do mean something," I confessed.

Her eyes widened. "What do they mean?"

I reached up to cup her face with my hands. My fingers were too big and unwieldy, too rough for her perfect, soft skin, yet I wanted to touch her everywhere.

"That I've been dying to kiss you for years."

I captured her mouth with mine again, showing her exactly how much the drawings meant.

And she kissed me back even harder.

SEVEN

Tara

────────

Hector's kisses nearly undid me. I knew I should go, that this could only lead to trouble, but I couldn't. My body simply refused.

I couldn't resist him.

I didn't *want* to resist him.

He nipped at my lips and moved to kiss my neck, just below my ear. "Jesus, you have no idea how long I've thought about doing this."

I closed my eyes as his mouth continued down to my shoulder. "How long?"

"For as long as I've known you."

His confession shook me to my core. All this time, he'd desired me and I'd never known. If I had, would it have changed anything over the past three years? Would I have stayed with Andy for so long? Would I have taken the job in New York? I wasn't sure of anything anymore.

All I knew was that once I felt his lips on mine I needed more.

"What else have you wanted to do?" I asked.

"Tara…" He broke away and studied me with those smoldering brown eyes.

I dug my fingers into his shirt and pulled him closer, pressing myself against his hard chest. "Tell me."

"I want to see you naked. I want to taste every inch of you. I want to bury myself inside you." His voice was rough, like his words were strained. Like it was hard for him to speak. "I want you. *All* of you."

I felt drunk and out of control, all my inhibitions flying out the door. But I wasn't drunk, or not on alcohol at least. I was drunk on Hector, on hearing him speak to me like that. It was a powerful thing, knowing someone had desired you for years in secret.

And, if I was honest with myself, deep down I'd always desired him, too.

"Do it," I whispered. "Do everything you've thought about all this time."

His eyes blazed with lust and he pushed me against the door I'd been about to leave through, pressing my back against it. His hands gripped my face, directing me, tilting my head exactly the way he wanted as he kissed me. His mouth was demanding, his grip strong, his desire rock hard against my waist. And I loved every second of it.

He raised his arms and pulled his shirt over his head, giving me a glorious view of his chest and abs. His body was all muscle and I wanted to trace every contour. I pressed a hand on his broad chest and slowly slid down, feeling each groove of his abs under my fingers, trailing along the dark hair from his waist into his jeans. They hung low on his defined hips, and the top of his briefs teased me with the promise of what was underneath. I wanted to explore that area so bad, but not yet. I moved my hands back up, to touch the rest of his strong body, to circle his dark nipples, to wrap my fingers around those firm biceps I'd been dying to touch. They felt as good as they looked, so firm and powerful and masculine.

He watched me explore him with an expression that looked almost… concerned. Like he was worried about something. With a body like that he had nothing to worry about. How was he still single? I know most girls fell all over Jared, but were they *blind*?

"You're gorgeous," I said.

He grunted. "That word doesn't apply to me. To you, hell yes. But not to me."

"Don't argue with me," I teased.

I slid my hands around his neck and pulled him down to my mouth, kissing him roughly. His fingers slipped under the lower hem of my shirt, sneaking across my bare skin, sliding up, up, up. We broke apart long enough for him to yank off my shirt and toss it on the floor, and then we were kissing again, like we couldn't stand to not be connected for even a second.

He pulled back and spun me around before I knew what was happening. My palms lay flat on the door, my breasts pressed against it, my head forced to the side. He unhooked my bra and let it drop, then ran his fingers across my naked back, making me shiver. As I whimpered, he shifted my hair to the side and kissed along the curve of my neck and down my spine. His hands pinned mine to the door, and all I could do was stand there and let him explore me with his mouth. He was so gentle it made me tremble, even as he roughly held my wrists in place. I'd never had a guy do this before, be both so tender yet so firm and demanding all at once. The combination turned me on more than I'd ever thought possible.

I arched against him, feeling how hard he was even through our clothes. "Hector, please."

He released one of my hands and I heard the scrape of fabric and the sound of his jeans hitting the floor behind me. A second later I felt him from behind, without those layers of clothes between us. Only my own clothes stopped our bodies from rubbing against each other.

He was naked behind me and I couldn't see him. I wanted to turn around so bad, but he still held me in place. "Please," I begged again. "I need to see you."

He relented and turned me around, but before I got a chance to look at him he kissed down my chest and popped one of my breasts into his mouth. I moaned and clutched his broad shoulders for support as he sucked on my nipples, one and then the other. I still had a hard time believing this was happening, a part of me convinced that at any moment I'd wake up from this impossible dream and find myself alone in bed. There was a niggling voice in the back of my head that said this could never work and I should stop it before one—or both—of us got hurt, but it was easy to ignore as Hector's tongue swirled around my nipple.

Only when he'd completely worshipped both breasts did he pull away. Finally I was able to take him in, and naked Hector did not disappoint. His entire body was an ode to masculinity, like he was one of those Greek God sculptures, all nude and glorious. Every inch of his body was big and hard and powerful.

Oh yes. *Every* inch.

I wrapped my fingers around his length, needing to feel him in my hand. He groaned and tossed his head back, and I loved seeing what I did to him with the slightest touch. I wasn't normally this bold with a guy I'd just met, but then again, we weren't exactly strangers, were we? I'd known him for years, even if I'd only thought of him as a friend until now. Tonight he'd brought out something reckless and wild in me between his performance on stage, his demanding kisses, and his confession of desire, and I wanted more, more, more.

I let him go to undo my own jeans and lower them to the floor while he watched. I slowly stripped off all my clothes, until we both stood naked in front of each other. I hoped he liked what he saw.

He sucked in a breath. "Damn girl, you're even sexier in person than in my naughtiest fantasies about you."

His words made me warm and wet all over. I gripped his hips and dragged him toward me, and he took the hint. As he backed me against the door I raised one of my legs, trying to give him access, practically begging him to slip inside.

"Not yet," he said. "I have one more thing on my list first."

He slid down my body, his hands and mouth working me over together, moving lower, to my breasts, to my stomach, and even lower, to my hips, and *still* lower, spreading my legs apart. Of course—he'd listed three things he wanted to do to me. He'd seen me naked and now he was moving on to number two: tasting me all over.

I trembled when he sank to his knees and pressed his lips to my upper thigh, realizing he was about to go down on me right there where I was standing. He hooked one of my legs over his shoulder and his hands cupped my butt to support me. He teased me at first, kissing everywhere but where I wanted, building up the desire until I thought I would explode just from the anticipation alone. He ran his tongue along me slowly and I felt every inch of what he did like fire lapping along my body. I closed my eyes and leaned back against the door, weaving my fingers into his thick, curly hair, using my grip to steady myself as he continued his delicious torment.

He flicked his tongue against me, rubbing back and forth, sucking and licking. I spiraled higher and higher until I thought my legs would give out, but he held me up with his strong arms and I knew he wouldn't let me fall. I let go of any lingering fear about what we were doing and gave in to his adoration. My fingers tightened in his hair, my legs trembled uncontrollably, and my every nerve burst with pleasure that never seemed to end.

When it did, an eternity later, Hector unhooked my leg from around him and set it down. He stood slowly, his naked body rubbing along mine, and when he kissed me I tasted myself in his mouth.

"That's two out of three," he said. "One more to go."

While I recovered, he ripped open a condom and eased it along himself. He was going to take me right there, right against the door where he'd just gone down on me, and I was relieved because I didn't want to wait even the short amount of time it would take to get to the couch. And because having sex with a rock star against his dressing room door was hotter than anything I'd ever experienced before.

He grabbed my thighs and hefted me up with one quick, powerful movement, spreading my legs around him, bringing his body against mine at exactly the right height. I held onto his strong arms as he positioned us, lining up our bodies, and felt him nudging against me.

"This is the last chance to back out," he said. "To go back to the way things were before."

I tightened my legs around his hips to show I was just as eager as he was. "I'm not going anywhere."

With those words he thrust inside me, pinning me hard against the door. I cried out as he filled me, stretching my body in the most amazing way. I tightened my fingers around his biceps as he held me up, his large hands gripping my butt as he moved in and out of me with strong, powerful strokes.

I opened for him, accepting everything he gave me, letting myself become his completely. He was an animal as he pounded into me, straddling the line between creating a steady tempo and losing all control, just like when he played the drums. I couldn't get enough of this rough, demanding Hector, and my already sensitive body responded eagerly to him.

His smooth chest rubbed against my breasts as he hammered into me, making the door bang with each thrust. I let the passion he stirred take over as he created a relentless beat with our bodies. I slid up and down on him, taking him deeper, my knees gripping his waist while I grinded myself along to his movements. The friction built between my legs and Hector's grunts made me even more excited. I cried out so hard my throat became raspy, my body clenching around him as I came for a second time that night. He rammed his desire home inside me and moments later released himself with a long groan.

He stilled against me, but didn't put me down yet. We kissed each other softly, our bodies joined and twitching with the last echoes of pleasure. The rest of the room came back in focus: the hard wood of the door at my back, the cool air from the vents above us, the muffled sound of music in the distance.

As our heartbeats slowed, he pressed his forehead against mine. "I'm sorry. I couldn't hold back. Not after wanting you for so long."

"Don't apologize. I wanted you just as bad."

"It's been a while since I've been with anyone. Next time it will be better." He looked away, his eyebrows pinching together. "I mean, if there is a next time."

I gripped his chin and forced him to look at me. "Hector, that was the best sex I've ever had."

"It was?"

"God, yes. I wish you'd told me you wanted me sooner."

"You were with Andy. Now you're not."

He gave me one last lingering kiss before carrying me to the couch. My head spun as I lay there, my body tingling and pulsing all over. I'd never had sex standing up before. Andy had been great in bed, but he would never have been able to do it.

Hector was strong enough to hold me up throughout all of it. I didn't know how he could still stand after what we'd just done. He barely even seemed tired. His muscles were gleaming with sweat, but otherwise he didn't seem anywhere near as wiped out as I was. I couldn't take my eyes off his body. I'd never been with anyone so…big before. So hard and strong, all six foot whatever of rippling masculinity and dark, smooth muscle. God, I was a lucky girl.

He brought us a blanket and curled up behind me on the couch, his warm, naked body tucking around mine. It was a tight fit, but neither of us seemed to mind. He ran a finger along the chain at my neck, down to the amethyst at the end. My birthstone.

"You're wearing the necklace I got you." He sounded surprised.

"I never take it off."

Hector had mailed it to me for my twenty-first birthday. I was allergic to gold, so he'd had to special order one in sterling silver. It had meant a lot to me that he'd remembered.

I relaxed against him as he kissed my shoulder and draped an arm across my waist. My fingers idly traced the dark hair on his forearm. "How come you don't have any tattoos, like Jared and Kyle do?"

I felt him shrug behind me. "I've thought about it, but never came up with anything I'd want on my body for the rest of my life. I designed some of the guys' tattoos though, like the dragon and phoenix ones on Kyle's arms."

"Those are so cool. I should get you to design something for me."

"You? I can't see you with a tattoo."

I laughed. "No, I guess not. But if you designed it, maybe…"

His lips brushed the side of my neck. "I'll draw you anything you want."

"Maybe something to celebrate the publication of *Misfit Squad*? I always swore I'd get a tattoo when my first book came out."

"For that I might be tempted to get one with you. Although my *abuelita* would kill me if she found out."

"You'd have to get it somewhere your grandmother couldn't see it."

He chuckled, low and deep against my back, and we discussed what kind of tattoos we could get together. The more we talked about it, the more I wanted one.

"If we had time this week I'd take you to the place the guys got all their tattoos from." He traced lazy circles along my shoulder with his thumb. "You'll have to visit me in LA sometime. Although I'm sure there are plenty of good tattoo parlors in New York, too."

His words were like an electric jolt, clearing my head. Oh god, what had we done?

We'd definitely crossed over the "just friends" line but…into what? No matter how mind-blowing the sex had been, we still lived thousands of miles apart. Would he want a long-distance relationship? Or did he just see this as a quick fling during Comic-Con?

I didn't know if I was even ready for something more than that. I'd just graduated college, gotten out of a long-term relationship, and wasn't sure where I'd be living in a month. My entire life was in flux. I couldn't handle yet another complication right now.

But how could it ever be the same between us after what we'd done?

Did I even *want* it to be the same?

I wasn't sure.

All I knew was that we had to figure it out before things went any further.

Except my eyes were so heavy and he felt so good around me, behind me, against me. I couldn't bear to bring it up yet. We would have to discuss this soon… but for now I just wanted to enjoy this moment a tiny bit longer.

EIGHT

Hector

I'd thought nothing could be better than being inside Tara, but having her fall asleep in my arms? That was pretty fucking fantastic, too.

I wasn't sure how long we stayed curled up together on the couch under a shared blanket, drifting in and out of sleep. At some point she turned to face me, nuzzling against my neck and melting further into my arms. I wrapped myself around her and let myself slip away.

Until the door opened with a loud click, jolting us both awake.

We sat up, confused, and Tara scrambled to cover herself with the blanket. I shifted in front of her, blocking her from view of whoever had barged in on us.

A woman stood at the door in a uniform, with a cart of cleaning supplies. She took one look at our naked, entwined bodies and flushed. "So sorry," she said. "I thought the room was empty. I'll come back later."

The door shut behind her and Tara put a hand to her head. "What time is it?"

I grabbed my phone from my jeans, which were in a pile on the floor. "Fuck. It's five in the morning."

"Oh god. Last night...." She blinked sleep from her eyes. "I mean, it was amazing, but..."

Yeah.

But.

Jesus, I'd let things get way out of control. Tara was never supposed to know how I felt about her. I'd resolved to never let her get that close, to never let *anyone* in like that again. But I'd been so overwhelmed by her sheer presence I hadn't been able to help myself.

We sat face forward on the couch, neither of us looking at each other. It was like we'd forgotten how to talk now that we'd had sex. One thing was obvious: we couldn't go back to the ways things were before Comic-Con.

"What are we going to do?" she finally asked.

"I don't know."

"Do you want...." She chewed on one of her fingernails, like she often did when she was nervous. "Do you want to—"

I cut her off. "To get some breakfast? Yeah, I'm starving."

"That's...not what I was going to ask."

She looked so serious, but I couldn't have this discussion right now. Or ever. "Tara—"

"Do you want to talk about last night?" she blurted out.

"No. I really don't."

"Why not?"

"Isn't that talking about it?" I tugged on my jeans, feeling way too exposed sitting there buck naked beside her. I should tell her...something. Not that I loved her, hell no, but that she looked beautiful this morning or that last night was amazing, or something, *anything*. But there was a tightness in my throat that I couldn't seem to get words around. I didn't know what to say. I had no fucking clue what we should do next.

"I know this whole thing is kind of crazy," she said, slowly. "Andy and I just broke up, and you and I have been friends forever and we don't want to mess that up, especially since we still have to work together, and then there's the distance problem..."

It sounded like she thought the whole thing was a mistake. Maybe it was. I lived in LA and she was moving to New York and there was no future for us. When Comic-Con ended she'd be leaving me behind. Like my parents. Like Amanda. I wasn't going through that shit again.

"I can't do long distance," I said.

"Oh. I just thought, maybe..." She drew in a long breath and stood, clutching the blanket to her chest. "So what are we going to do? Go back to being friends? Try to forget last night ever happened?"

Like I could ever forget last night. I'd always remember the way she'd moaned and gripped my arms. The feel of being sheathed inside her. The taste of her on my tongue. I wished I didn't know those things, but I did and I would never be the same.

I grabbed my shirt from the corner. "Whatever you want."

"But what do *you* want?"

"I don't know!"

"God, Hector, just talk to me! Tell me what you want from me!"

"I don't want anything from you!"

She flinched, like I'd hit her, and I instantly regretted my words. That had been way harsh. I hadn't meant it the way it had sounded, but I didn't know how to smooth things over either.

She gathered her clothes off the floor while covering her breasts with one arm. She tried to put her bra on but had a hard time, like her hands were trembling. I started to move forward to help her but stopped myself. I got the feeling she didn't want me to get any closer.

"Tara..."

"No, I understand perfectly now. It was just sex, right?" She finished dressing and snatched her shoes. "Fine. It doesn't have to be anything more than that."

At the door she hesitated like she was waiting for me to say something. But I'd stopped her from leaving last night, and in the end it had backfired on me. I should never have drawn her or kissed her, should never have revealed how much I wanted her.

I turned away. "Yeah. It was just sex."

The door opened and closed with a click. She was gone.

I slumped down on the couch and my head dropped into my hands. I waited there for an hour in case she came back. Wishing I could rewind time and go back to before I had fucked everything up.

But she didn't return.

———

I got back to my hotel room and hopped in the shower without a word to Jared, who was still in bed, alone. Maddie must have returned to her room already. Good, one less person to deal with.

The hot water washed away all physical traces of last night but couldn't erase the memories. My mind was stuck on a loop, replaying this morning and trying to figure out how I could've handled things better. I came up with a thousand better responses to Tara's questions now that it was hours later, but that only made me even more miserable.

Because it hadn't just been sex. It had been so much more.

When I got out of the shower, Jared was making a cup of tea using hot water from the room's tiny coffee maker. He wore a t-shirt with Freddy Krueger on it and gave me an appraising look. "Long night?"

"Leave me alone," I muttered, rubbing my hair with a towel.

His eyebrows shot up. "Good morning to you, too. I'll make you some coffee."

I plopped onto the bed. "Don't bother. I'm going back to sleep."

He ripped open a packet of honey and poured the entire thing into his tea. For his voice, he always said. "You can't go back to sleep. People are already lining up outside the convention center to get in."

"I don't care."

"It's Comic-Con. You can't spend your entire day in the hotel room."

"Fuck off. I can do whatever I want." I was being a total asshole but I couldn't help it. Everyone wanted to talk, talk, talk, and I just wanted to be left the fuck alone.

"What the hell is going on with you?"

"I don't want to fucking talk about it!"

He threw up his hands. "Okay, chill."

He dropped into the chair behind the desk, playing on his phone while drinking his tea. For a few minutes I lay there with my eyes closed, but my mind wouldn't shut up. Regret and anxiety created a sick feeling in my gut that I couldn't get rid of. I rubbed my face, then dug out my phone to check if Tara had texted me. Yeah, right.

"Last night's show went pretty well," Jared suddenly said, almost as if to himself. He leaned back and propped his booted feet up on the desk. "Although I think we should add some lights behind the Villain Complex logo so it stands out more."

He continued on about how we could improve our performance for our next shows on the tour, but I knew he didn't expect me to reply. It was his way of letting me wallow for a while and showing he wasn't pissed at me for snapping at him. And something about his steady voice droning on about the band made me feel a little better.

"Though I never expected Becca to show up in our dressing room," he said, with a short laugh.

I'd missed whatever had led to that comment, but now I sat up, head spinning. My situation with Tara was not that different from Jared and Becca's. They'd been friends with a working relationship who'd had one night of sex they'd regretted the next morning. After that, things fell apart between them until Becca left the band, and then they never spoke again. Until last night, anyway.

Would something like that happen with me and Tara? We were better friends than Jared and Becca had ever been and we'd known each other a lot longer, but that didn't mean we weren't heading for the same fate.

"If you'd known Becca was going to leave the band, would you still have hooked up with her?" I asked.

Jared frowned, but didn't look up from his phone. "I wasn't really thinking straight when it happened. But what does it matter? It worked out in the end, and we got Maddie instead."

"That's not what I meant."

Jared put down his phone and studied me. "What are you really asking?"

"I don't know." I gave up on going back to sleep and started making myself some coffee. "Do you think you and Becca could ever be friends again?"

"I'm not sure. Before yesterday I would have said no chance in hell. Even now, I don't think we'll ever be friends, but as least there won't be any bad blood between us. Which is why I invited her to the party tomorrow."

I stared off into space while the coffee maker gurgled. They'd patched things up, but they were both moving on with their lives and would probably never speak again. Would that happen to us, too? Would Tara and I both drift apart to separate lives? It seemed likely, with the band gaining popularity and her new job.

I didn't want our friendship to be over. Or to stop collaborating with her on *Misfit Squad* and future books. But I didn't know if I could repair the damage to our relationship after what had gone down.

I didn't notice the coffee maker had finished until Jared moved to my side. He added two sugars the way I liked before handing the paper cup to me. "Becca and I were never as close as you and Tara. I don't think you need to worry." He coughed. "You know, *if* something like that ever happened to you."

I wasn't sure I liked this new, perceptive Jared. He seemed to have figured out the whole story without me even telling him. Damn best friends. I scowled but took the coffee from him. "Thanks."

He grabbed his wallet and slipped it in his jeans. "I'm meeting Maddie and Kyle for breakfast, then we're going to some panel on movie scores. You can come if you want. Or stay here. But you shouldn't waste a day of Comic-Con moping in your room."

As much as I hated to admit it, he was right. I'd never be able to sleep and would just make myself crazy lying in bed thinking about Tara. I could hit the gym and try to work some energy off, but then what? Sit around, driving myself insane until the party tonight? Get drunk and try to forget?

"Fine. I'm in." Hanging out with my friends would distract me from obsessing over Tara, if nothing else. I'd force myself to put her out of my mind completely.

Until the party tonight, when I'd have to face her again.

NINE

Tara

I should have been having fun. It was Friday at Comic-Con and there were a million things to do and see and each one was better than the last.

But all I could think about was Hector.

As I wandered the exhibit hall alone (yes, I was trying to get better about that) everything reminded me of him. A woman dressed as Cruella de Vil brought to mind his friends and their villain-themed party. An artist doing a live sketch awakened memories of Hector's drawings of me. A poster for a sci-fi TV show made me recall the times we'd watched it "together." I'd had to record each episode and wait to watch it since I was three hours ahead of him, but it was worth it to hear his snarky live commentary, which always made me laugh.

I couldn't even *look* at the Black Hat Comics booth, where our book was prominently on display. Especially since going near it ran the risk of me running into him. It was bad enough I'd have to see him at the Black Hat party tonight. Maybe it would be crowded enough I could avoid him or something. But that was stupid, because I couldn't avoid Hector forever, and I didn't want to either.

I paused beside a Pokémon display and pulled out my phone to text him, but couldn't find the right words. Nothing seemed appropriate for the situation. I wanted to ask if we were okay, but I was so worried the answer would be no. Or that he'd shut me down again like this morning.

God, I wished he had just told me what he wanted. One second he'd said the drawings meant something and that he'd wanted to kiss me for years, but then he'd said it was just sex and he didn't want anything from me. But if he didn't want to try a long distance relationship where did that leave us?

The problem was, I didn't know what I wanted either. Twenty-four hours ago I'd only seen Hector as a friend, but now my feelings for him were all jumbled and confused. There was no denying that our sexual chemistry was off the charts. Or that last night had been incredible. Or that I felt more comfortable with him than with anyone else in the world. But even if we didn't have the distance problem, I'd just gotten out of a serious relationship with Andy a week ago. I didn't want Hector to be a rebound, or to use him to make me feel better about my breakup or less alone. In the past, I'd jumped straight from one boyfriend to the next because I hated being single, but I was trying to change. Hector deserved better than that.

Of course, that was assuming he saw this as more than a one night stand. He'd never had a girlfriend in all the time I'd known him, but every now and then he had some brief hook-ups. Was that all he wanted—a short fling over the next few days? But then what?

Last night threatened to ruin everything between us, but I couldn't lose my friendship with him. He was not just the artist of my graphic novel, but the person I looked forward to talking to every day, the person I texted first with news, the person whose opinion I trusted the most about both my writing and my life. But it seemed the two of us were not meant to be anything more than friends.

And I wasn't sure if we could even be that now.

I gave up on texting Hector and went to that panel on writing and drawing diverse characters, even though I knew he might be there. Or because I *hoped* he would be there. But I scanned the room and didn't see him, and then spent the entire panel wishing he *was* there because I wanted to talk to him about it. I missed him so much already.

After the panel ended, I walked a couple blocks away to an area of the Gaslamp Quarter that wasn't quite as busy as around the convention center. I ducked into a bright, modern café and found the person I was looking for, already seated at a table.

Giselle Roberts.

I made my way over to her, completely star struck, still clueless as to why she wanted to talk to me. She was a curvy black woman in her forties with dark, wavy hair and confident eyes. She always looked stylish, and today she didn't disappoint in a form-fitting blue dress that was both sophisticated and sexy. Next to her I felt underdressed and sloppy in my ripped jeans and *Legend of Korra* t-shirt.

"Tara, right?" she asked, standing. She held out her hand. "I'm Giselle."

"So nice to meet you." I shook her hand and sat down, trying not to openly stare at her. The woman was a legend. Not only had she created some of my favorite TV shows, but she'd broken down barriers for women and people of color in entertainment and media, too. She was the closest thing I had to a role model.

"Thanks for having lunch with me," she said. "I know it's hard to find a spare moment during Comic-Con."

"No, thank *you*. I'm flattered you wanted to meet with me. And I'm sure you're even busier than I am."

She laughed, a sound that seemed to bubble out of her like champagne. "Luckily, I have assistants to do all the things I don't want to do."

"Oh. Of course." I wondered where her blond hipster assistant was. Off running an errand probably.

"I've been wanting to talk to you for a while." She leaned forward, pressing her hands flat on the table. "I love *Misfit Squad*. I've read it three times. I'm confident it's going to win a ton of awards next year."

My fingers tightened on the menu, the edges digging into my skin. I wasn't sure how to handle all this praise from someone I held in such high regard. "That's… wow. I'm honored. Thank you."

She waved a hand like it was nothing. "Just speaking the truth."

I let out a nervous laugh. "I'll have to make sure my editor gets you an early copy of the next book."

"Already taken care of." She leaned back in her chair and studied me. "I'm sure you're wondering why I asked you to meet me today. Part of the reason is that I wanted to sit down with you so I could fangirl over your book in person. And the other reason…" She took a long sip of water and I thought the suspense might kill me. "I'm starting my own superhero show and I want you to be a part of it."

"You…what?" Suddenly it seemed a lot harder to breathe in the café. Giselle Roberts doing a superhero show was the best news I'd heard all day at Comic-Con, and that was before it hit me that she wanted *me* to be a part of it.

"It's already getting a ton of interest from the networks. Think *Arrow* or *Heroes* but with a female lead. *Hunger Games* meets *Batman Begins*. It's going to be huge."

"I would watch that in an instant."

"Good. Because I want you to be one of the writers."

"Shut the front door." The words slipped out before I could stop them, but at least I'd used the censored version my mother would say. I couldn't imagine swearing in front of a classy woman like Giselle Roberts.

Luckily, she laughed, like she found my reaction amusing. "I already have the pilot done but I need good writers for the rest of the season. Based on your work on *Misfit Squad,* I know you'll be perfect."

"Wow." I sat back and let her words sink in. I couldn't believe she wanted me. I was just a small-time comic book writer whose graphic novel happened to get popular thanks to Hector's newfound fame. Working on a big TV show was way out of my league. Though I supposed writing for TV wouldn't be *that* different from writing comic books—I'd write the dialogue and action, then someone else would take it from there.

"I'm stunned. And flattered. And I think it sounds amazing. But I've never written for TV before."

"I'm sure you'll pick it up quickly. You'd have to move to Los Angeles immediately of course, but we'd cover all of your moving expenses."

I sucked in a breath, my head spinning with possibilities. Hector lived in Los Angeles. If I moved there maybe, just maybe, we could have a future together.

If he wanted that.

If *I* wanted that.

Or it would only make things more uncomfortable between us if our one night of passionate sex had been nothing more than that.

Or if it ruined our friendship forever.

Hang on, what was I thinking? I already had a job lined up. My *dream* job. The job I'd been working my ass off for years to get. They were also paying for my moving expenses to New York, and I'd already agreed on a start date in a few weeks. I couldn't back out now. But somehow this unbelievable job had practically fallen into my lap like some kind of *deus ex machina,* and how could I possibly say no to Giselle Freaking Roberts?

"Is something wrong?" she asked.

"No." I realized I'd been chewing on my fingernail and forced my hand down. "It's just that I've already accepted a job in New York at Ostrich Books in their comics division."

"How much are they offering?" she asked. "I'm sure I can beat it."

I swallowed hard. The job didn't pay much and New York was crazy expensive, but…I still wasn't sure. "Thank you, but it's not about the money, it's about the direction I want for my future career. Can I have some time to think it over? I'd love to work for you, but I have to be sure I'm making the best decision for me."

"I completely understand. I can give you a few days to think it over, but after that I'll have to look for someone else."

"I'll get back to you by the end of Comic-Con." It was Friday and Comic-Con ended on Sunday. That didn't give me much time, but I preferred it that way. It forced me to make a decision instead of waffling on it forever. And I had a feeling that once I talked to Hector he would help make the decision easier, one way or the other.

"That would be perfect. Let me give you my direct number." She handed me her card. "When you're ready to accept my offer, give me a call."

The food arrived, and as we ate she told me more about her show and asked me questions about *Misfit Squad.* It was hard to give coherent answers, because the entire time I kept thinking about how I had a job offer in Los Angeles, and what that could mean for me and Hector.

TEN

Hector

I've never been good at parties. Give me a beer and somewhere to sneak off to with my sketchbook and I was happy. But that wouldn't work at the Black Hat Comics party, not when Tara and I were the guests of honor.

The party was on an actual pirate ship docked in the marina and had a pirates vs. ninjas theme. The invite had said to pick a side and dress in costume, and upon arrival guests were handed either a pirate hat or a ninja hood. The Black Hat staff all had on wizard hats so they were neutral in the battle, while hired actors hung from ropes and engaged in sword fights in the shadows.

The most I could bother with was wearing all black—which I would have done anyway—so they'd given me a ninja hood. Miguel had insisted I wear it, and I'd only agreed because I thought it would give me some anonymity in the crowd. But, no. Everyone wanted to talk to me—about the book, about the band, about *The Sound*. About Tara.

Where the hell was she? I was already on my third beer and there was no sign of her. I kept chugging them, hoping talking to people would get easier, but it never did. How did Jared do this shit? To think I'd actually gotten mad at him for hogging the interviews on *The Sound*. Now I'd give anything for him to be here to take some of the attention off me. But he was with Maddie and I was in the middle of a crowd of people who wanted to talk to me when all I could think about was Tara.

"When's the next book coming out?" someone asked, a question I'd heard about three hundred times already. I wanted to make a sign with the answer and hang it around my neck so I could point to it and grunt. Shit, I could do a whole FAQ, including other winners such as:

"Is there going to be a *Misfit Squad* movie?"

"When's your band's next album coming out?"

"What was it like being on *The Sound*?"

Over and over, the same annoying questions, nonstop. Even when I got a moment to myself the crowd of ninjas and pirates pressed around me, yapping away with their incessant small talk, making the warm summer air heavy and thick. I was sweaty and tired and just wanted to get the fuck out of there.

If I could escape before Tara arrived, even better.

Was she ditching the party on purpose to avoid me? If so, I didn't blame her. I'd been dreading the party for hours, knowing we'd have to face each other. Hell, I'd been a total asshole all day. Jared, Maddie, and Kyle had dragged me to a couple panels, but I barely remembered any of it. At least they'd known better than to ask me any questions. And I'd made sure to steer us clear of the diversity panel, knowing Tara would be there.

But I couldn't avoid her forever.

She walked onto the ship, her golden hair trailing from under a black pirate hat, and my chest tightened like a fist at the sight. Especially once the crowd parted enough for me to see her entire costume: a frilly, white, shoulder-less dress with a tight black corset over it that gave me an amazing view of her large breasts. It was so short it only just covered her curvy ass and left her shapely legs bare except for knee-high black boots. She looked so fucking hot I couldn't help but imagine bending her over the rail of the ship, pushing that skirt up, and taking her from behind.

Great, now I was hard as a rock and even more miserable.

She looked around like she wasn't sure she was in the right place, and then was swarmed by people. Somehow through the crowd she spotted me across the ship and our eyes met for a fraction of a second. I looked away quickly, unable to take any more of her gaze. If I had to actually talk to her I'd be really fucked.

I dove into the crowd in the opposite direction, debating whether I could avoid her for the rest of the night. How soon could I leave before it was rude? Maybe if I slipped out without Miguel noticing…

I was dragged into another conversation with two pirates about *The Sound* and suffered my way through it. Ten long minutes later, I saw Tara's pirate hat heading toward me, and I had to dart away again.

Hiding worked for another twenty minutes, until she found me at the front of the ship. She emerged from the crowd and backed me into the railing, with nothing but the ocean behind me. "There you are."

She looked determined, like a sexy pirate captain about to make me walk the plank. That corset was killing me with its tempting view of her chest. She had no idea how much I wanted to bury my face in her breasts. I chugged the last of my beer, my jeans growing uncomfortably tight again.

"Are you avoiding me?" she asked.

"No."

She frowned at me with those rosy lips. "Yes, you are."

I crushed the red cup in my hand and tossed it into the nearby trash can, turning away from her. But she wouldn't have any of that and grabbed my arm, pulling me back.

"Hector, please. Talk to me."

"What's there to say? Look, I'm sorry for this morning. I was a jerk. Let's just forget it, okay?"

Her fingers tightened around my bicep. She hadn't let go. "I don't want to forget it. I want to talk about it."

"There's nothing to talk about." The words were forced out through gritted teeth. "We live across the country from each other. After Comic-Con, things have to go back to the way they were before."

"What if they didn't?" She glanced around and lowered her voice. "I had my meeting with Giselle. She offered me a job as a writer on a new superhero TV show with a female lead. And the position is in LA."

"No shit?" I struggled to keep my face a blank canvas, but it was tough. That sounded like a pretty sweet gig, and she deserved it. And I didn't want to get too excited, but damn, the idea of her moving to LA was almost too good to be true. New paths opened up in my head like a sunrise dawning over a dark sky, and I was tempted to pull her into my arms and cover her face with kisses. For the first time ever I had real hope for a future with her.

But then reality crashed back in. She already had a job lined up. A job she'd been really excited about, that she'd worked her ass off to get, that she'd spent hours telling me about. She'd dreamed about working in publishing her entire life. How could she give that up?

She watched my reaction closely. "You don't seem as excited about this as I hoped you'd be."

"What about the job in New York?"

She turned to face the ocean, where the setting sun painted the sky in pink and purple. "I'm so torn. Both jobs are great opportunities. My heart was set on moving to New York and working in the comics division at Ostrich Books, but…"

I held my breath. "But what?"

"But this other job sounds like something I'd be stupid to turn down." She turned back to me, her eyes sparkling. "And you're in LA."

The words hit me so hard I stepped back. "Me?"

She closed the distance between us and placed a hand on my chest. "This morning you said you couldn't do long distance, and I get that, I do. But if I move to LA, you and I could try to be more than friends. That is, if you wanted to…"

Fuck yes I wanted to. Hearing that she wanted to try made something inside me ache in the best possible way. The selfish part of me wanted to get down on my knees and beg her to take the LA job so we could be together. I could already picture it: working with her on *Misfit Squad* in person instead of through email or chat; watching a movie with my arm around her, no longer thousand miles apart; being able to spend hours talking to her with no screen between us. And of course, all the hours I'd get to spend with her in bed. And against the wall. And in the shower…

But I'd be the biggest asshole in the world if I made her give up her dream for me. How could I live with myself if she chose the LA job to be near me and then hated it? Or what if things didn't work out between us? I didn't want her to resent me for the rest of her life because she'd followed me instead of her dream. Above all, I wanted her to be happy. Even if that meant it was without me.

"Please, Hector, say *something*," she said. "What do you think about all this?"

"I think…" I didn't know what to say, or how to express the thousands of conflicting feelings racing through me. Her hand was still on my chest and I pressed it against my heart, which I'm sure she could feel hammering away. "I don't want you to move to LA for me."

Her face crumpled. "Oh."

Shit, that wasn't the reaction I wanted. I was so bad at this. "Wait. Let me explain." With my free hand I cupped her chin and made her look up at me. "I want you to move to LA. More than anything. But I don't want to be the reason you pick one job or the other. I think you should choose the one you want the most, no matter where it is."

"I don't know which one I want the most."

"Take some time to think about it. When do you have to decide?"

"I have until Sunday. I hoped that talking to you would help me…"

"Sorry. You need to make this decision on your own."

She nodded, but still didn't look happy. I pulled her into my arms, wrapping her in a hug, burying my face in her silky hair. She relaxed into my body with a long sigh, and I knew she needed this as much as I did, if not more.

"If you decide to move to New York, we'll still be friends," I said. "Everything will go back to the way it was before." That was such a lie. Nothing could ever be the same between us. But I wanted her to believe it anyway. "Whatever happens we'll be okay."

She peered up at me, her lips dangerously close to mine. "I don't want to lose you, Hector."

"You won't. I promise."

She lifted on her toes and kissed me, a soft, quick one, right on the border between friendly and more. I wasn't sure whether to return her kiss or not. I voted for not, only because if I kissed her I wouldn't be able to stop.

"What are we going to do for the rest of Comic-Con?" she asked, her hands still on my chest. "Today was horrible. I missed you so much."

"I missed you, too." Another repeat of today would kill me. I couldn't spend the next few days avoiding her, even if there was no hope for us beyond Sunday. If this was my one time to be with her in person I wanted to enjoy every second of it. "We have two more days together. We should have some fun, try to enjoy them."

"I like that idea. Just living in the moment. No worrying about the future or what will happen with us. And then when it's over…I guess we'll figure that out later."

"Exactly. What happens at Comic-Con stays at Comic-Con."

She laughed, and it was all worth it just to hear that sound. "I thought that only applied to Vegas."

We were interrupted by two artists in ninja costumes who wanted to introduce themselves. For a few minutes we talked shop, and I let Tara do most of the speaking while I admired the way she handled them. She was much better with people than I was.

Once they moved on, she said, "We should probably mingle."

"I don't want to mingle. I don't want to talk to anyone but you."

"Me either. We should leave before more people corner us."

"Miguel will be pissed."

"True. We'll have to sneak out."

"Good thing I have a ninja hood," I said, pulling it lower on my face with a grin.

She giggled. "Please, you're built like a tank. You'd be the worst ninja ever."

"Hey, I'm super stealthy! Besides, you're way too pretty to be a pirate."

She flashed me a coy smile. "You think I'm pretty?"

I took a piece of her golden hair in my fingers. "Girl, you know I think you're smoking hot. You're the sexiest pirate on this whole ship."

She gave a little shiver, even though it wasn't cold. "Let's get out of here."

ELEVEN

Tara

It took longer to sneak out of the party than we'd hoped, thanks to all the people who stopped us on our way off the ship. Thirty minutes later we were finally free, and together we headed back to the hotel we were both staying at courtesy of Black Hat Comics. Not a single person we passed gave me an odd look for walking around downtown San Diego in a skimpy pirate costume. One of the perks of Comic-Con.

Hector had taken off his ninja hood and donned his Villain Complex hat again. I was relieved things were back to normal between us (or as normal as they could be), although I wished he'd made my decision easier. I couldn't tell if he was truly happy about my job offer or not. I'd wanted him be thrilled that I might be moving near him, but he seemed especially closed off tonight. He was right though, I had to make that decision on my own, independent of my feelings for him.

But…how?

Even if I ignored my feelings for him the fact remained that in New York I wouldn't know anyone, whereas in LA I'd know Hector and his friends. If everything else was equal then having friends in a new city definitely edged one out over the other. But if this thing with Hector ended badly, I'd wind up alone in LA, too.

I had to make my decision without factoring him in…somehow.

"Tell me about LA," I said, as we walked along the brightly lit streets packed with people in cosplay and pedicabs decorated with advertising. "I've never been. What's it like?"

"Um, I've lived there my whole life, so I'm not sure how to compare it to anywhere else. It's crazy expensive to live there. It's big and spread out. There's a shitload of traffic and public transportation sucks. The weather is great year-round, but you'll probably miss having a real winter with snow and stuff."

So far he wasn't making it sound too appealing, almost like he *wanted* me to choose New York. "Cold weather is fun for the first month or two, then it gets old pretty fast. What else?"

"There's a million things to do there. Shopping, clubs, beaches, hiking, restaurants of every type of cuisine you can think of.…" He rubbed the back of his neck. "Shit, I don't know. I'm starting to sound like a tour guide or something."

"Okay, then tell me something *you* love about LA."

"Hmm. I like the music scene, obviously. Love the art museums. I've spent many hours wandering through LACMA and the Getty."

I smiled at the image of big, brooding Hector spending all day in an art museum. It was one of my favorite things about him—he was this perfect image of hulking masculinity, yet completely owned the fact that he was an artist, too.

We turned onto a quieter street before he spoke again. "But I guess my favorite thing is the diversity. Anyone can find a place to belong there. Queer, straight, brown, white, vegan, goth, hipster, whatever—it's all good. No one bats an eyelash at me being in a band with two white boys. Or when my cousin Carlos married another guy, no one freaked out. Well, except my *abuelita*, but she's old fashioned to the extreme. And even she got over it pretty fast."

A place to belong. The one thing I'd been searching for my entire life. "That sounds nice. And so different from where I grew up."

"Your parents would probably freak out if you brought home a Mexican guy, eh?"

Was he implying that he wanted to meet my parents? I tried to study his face, but it was hard to read his expression in the dark. "Maybe, but I'm used to their disapproval."

I'd grown up in a huge, conservative Midwestern family complete with stay-at-home mom, white picket fence, and Golden Retriever. It sounded idyllic, but as I'd mentioned at the *Misfit Squad* panel, I'd always been an outcast. My small town in Nebraska had been suffocating and I'd escaped the first chance I could.

It was only once I started college in Boston that my eyes opened to a bigger world with all sorts of different people in it. I discovered just how sheltered I'd been my entire life, and that I wasn't fundamentally flawed or inherently strange for being different. Now I felt like a stranger every time I returned home.

My family loved me, of course, but they'd always thought I was crazy for reading books instead of watching football, for staying in to write stories instead of going to parties, or for wanting more from my life than following in my mother's footsteps and popping out babies as soon as I could. I didn't think a single one of them had read *Misfit Squad* yet, though they'd all said how proud they were of me. And it was true, they wouldn't love the idea of me dating a Mexican guy either.

Good thing I didn't care what they thought.

"What about your grandmother?" I asked. "Would she be upset if you brought home a white girl?"

"Nah. I'm sure she'd love it if I married some super traditional Mexican girl who spoke perfect Spanish and could make tortillas from scratch, but that's not going to happen. In the end, she just wants me to be happy."

I tried not to read too much into his words, but I so wanted to be the girl who made him happy. How had that happened? Yesterday, I'd only seen him as a friend, and now I wanted him to take me home to meet his family. It scared me a little, how quickly my feelings had changed for him and how fast this was progressing. We were almost, but not quite, talking about a future together. Feeling things out without making any actual plans or firm commitments to each other. Skirting the line into dangerous territory but not yet crossing over it.

Time to bring the conversation back to safer waters. "Will she and your sisters be okay with you gone for the next month?"

"They'll be fine. Rosalia just turned sixteen so she's old enough to help look after Yasmine and Ana now. I hate to leave them for that long but this tour is important, and we're getting some good money for it. Enough that I'll be able to send a bunch home to my parents, too."

"Have you spoken to your parents recently?" I asked softly, knowing it was a difficult subject for him.

"Last week, after the show ended. They were able to watch it while it was on TV, which was cool." He sighed. "I wanted to visit them this summer but the timing didn't work out. Maybe after the tour. I haven't seen them in forever."

Hector's parents had been deported to Mexico when he was thirteen. He and his three little sisters had all moved in with his grandmother, and he still lived with them so he could help out with the bills and taking care of them. He rarely talked about it—or about anything involving his past—but I knew it was a heavy burden on him sometimes. And that he missed his parents like crazy.

"I wish I could help them out more," he continued. "Find a way to get them back here."

I took his hand in mine, wishing I could help *him* in some way. "You do everything you can, and more."

"I hate that they haven't been around for most of my sisters' lives. Rosalia's driving now, Yasmine just got her first boyfriend, and Ana started wearing makeup. Shit, they're all growing up way too fast if you ask me, and our parents are *missing* it."

He sounded so pained, it made my heart ache for him. "Maybe with the money from your new recording deal you'll be able to visit them more."

"Yeah, maybe."

I squeezed his hand and made my voice light, trying to brighten the mood. "I've heard so much about your sisters. I'd love to meet them sometime."

His shoulders relaxed and he returned the squeeze. "They wanted to come to Comic-Con so bad. Especially Yasmine. She's obsessed with that *Arrow* show and told me to get the guy's autograph."

"That guy *is* pretty hot. He's always running around half-naked on the show, like they have some shirtless quota to fill every episode. Not that I'm complaining. I mean, those abs, my god."

"You trying to make me jealous? Maybe I should take my shirt off so you won't think about that other guy."

I laughed, relieved he was joking around again. "I wouldn't complain if you did. You have incredible abs, too."

"Oh yeah?" He quickly tugged his black shirt over his head. "Done."

He shouldn't be allowed to remove his shirt like that without some kind of warning first. I shoved him lightly in the side, mainly so I could touch him. "Show off."

He grinned and flexed his arms in an exaggerated way, and it was hard not to stare at his rippling muscles. "Sorry, should I put my shirt back on?"

"No, definitely not. In fact, you should never wear a shirt again. You'd be doing the world a favor."

He let out a deep, hearty laugh that rumbled down my spine, and it made my day knowing I'd caused it. I made a resolution to try to make him laugh more often.

Ahead of us, a girl yelled, "Oh my god!" She dragged her friend down the sidewalk, and they were both dressed in identical Slave Leia costumes from *Return Of The Jedi*. "You're Hector, from Villain Complex!"

Hector didn't move to put his shirt back on, but he shifted on his feet, like he wanted to bolt. "Hey…"

"Your band is so freaking hot," Slave Leia No. 2 said, leaning forward and drawing attention to her barely there gold top and impressive cleavage. "I watched every episode of *The Sound*."

"Me, too," the first one said. She played with her long braid, her eyes glued to Hector's naked chest. "I love you guys."

"Um, thanks," he said.

"Aren't you two cold in those costumes?" I asked, eyeing their exposed legs. I wasn't wearing much more than them, but I wanted to make it clear that I was with Hector.

They cast me a confused glance, like they wondered what I was doing there. The first Slave Leia took a step closer to Hector, invading his personal space. "Hey, you want to come party with us?"

The second girl moved in too, licking her lips. "It'll be fun, we promise."

I didn't have a violent bone in my body, yet I had the sudden, primal urge to growl and shove them back, to make sure they knew he was mine. My god, what had gotten into me?

"Sorry, I'm busy tonight." Hector placed a hand on the small of my back, an intimate gesture not lost on them…or on me.

"She can come along, if you want," Slave Leia No. 2 said, with another brief glance my way.

I laughed. "Yeah, that's going to happen, oh…how about *never*."

Hector tried to suppress a grin. "Thanks for the offer, but we're good."

We walked away, his hand a steady, almost possessive presence on my lower back. I leaned against his side and the heat rising off his skin enveloped me.

Sorry ladies, Hector was all mine. At least for the next few days.

I nudged him with my hip. "You better put your shirt back on. I don't want any other girls getting ideas."

"That was unusual. They always go for Jared, or sometimes Kyle. Never me." He removed his Villain Complex hat and shoved it into his jeans, shaking his hair out. "Not sure I like the attention."

"No? I thought every guy dreamed of scantily clad women inviting him for a threesome."

He pinned me with his smoldering dark eyes. "Not this guy."

The intensity of his gaze took my breath away. The chemistry between us was thick, the desire so strong I could practically smell it in the air. He was still shirtless, a large, handsome, solid mountain of a man. A mountain I wanted to climb and conquer.

We entered the hotel and his hand slipped lower, to the top of my butt, pressing into the thin fabric of my dress. As we stepped into the elevator my eyes trailed from his hips up his defined chest to his strong jaw shadowed by dark stubble. I had the strongest urge to press my lips to it, to feel that roughness against my mouth. He had to know what he was doing to me standing there in nothing but his jeans.

He didn't hit the button for his floor, and I didn't comment on it. My breath quickened at the thought of him coming to my room. I wasn't sure what we were doing, but didn't want to stop. Inviting him inside would only complicate things further between us. The more time I spent with him, the more I never wanted to let him go, and the harder my decision got.

Once at my room, he leaned against the door, the sexual masculinity practically rolling off him. "Are you camping with us tonight in the Hall H line?"

I reached up to wrap my finger around one of his short curls, unable to help myself. "I don't know…"

"Come on, it'll be fun. We have food, alcohol, and Cards Against Humanity. What more could you want?"

I laughed. "A warm bed?"

"I'll keep you warm. Although I have to warn you, I only have one sleeping bag…"

Well, that settled it. The thought of sleeping against Hector under the stars was too good to pass up. "Okay. Just give me a minute to change my clothes."

"Are you sure?" His eyes roved up and down my body in a way that sent a rush of warmth between my thighs. "Cause I could look at you in that costume all night long."

The chemistry between us threatened to combust at any moment. Screw it, we'd both agreed to have fun for the rest of Comic-Con—and I had a great idea how to start.

"I could keep it on a little longer." I slipped my fingers into the belt loops of his jeans and pulled him closer. "Do you want to come inside?"

TWELVE

Hector

As soon as the door shut, we were on each other. My discarded shirt hit the floor while our bodies and mouths joined in a desperate, hungry crush. Tara's hands were instantly on my chest, stroking me all over like she couldn't get enough of my skin. I knew exactly how she felt.

I pressed rough kisses down her delicate neck to her bare shoulder to the top of her lush, soft breasts. They'd been shoved up and forced together thanks to her tight corset, nearly exposing her nipples. I sucked on them through the fabric, scraping at them with my teeth, making her whimper.

She tangled her fingers in my hair and yanked me back to her lips. Any worries about what we were doing vanished as she slipped her tongue into my mouth. Our future together was uncertain, but none of that mattered when she kissed me like that.

"Ever since you took your shirt off, I've been dying to do this," she said, licking across my jaw and down my neck, sending hot sparks throughout my entire body.

"Your costume has been driving me crazy all night," I said, though it came out more like a growl. "That corset. That short dress. Those boots. I've been walking around hard for the past hour."

"Have you?" She slipped a hand between us to check the front of my jeans and I groaned as she rubbed me there.

"Damn, girl. I wanted to go slower this time, but you're making that difficult."

"I don't want slow. Or gentle. Not tonight."

"Thank god."

I gripped her ass and yanked her against me, grinding her hips against mine. She kissed me with the same ferocity while I slid a hand down her thigh, forcing up the bottom of her dress, finding the edge of her panties. I tore at them, pushing them aside, and she moaned against my mouth as I made contact. Fuck, she was already so warm and slick and ready for me, and I had barely even touched her.

I fondled her breast with one hand, teasing her nipple through the corset, while my other hand continued exploring between her thighs. I shoved her legs apart with my knee, making her open wider for me. She clutched my arms and made the most delicious sounds as I slipped my fingers into her, one by one. Her nails scraped against my skin while I stroked her both inside and out and the slight pain made me even harder. Soon she was holding on to me for dear life, eyes closed, her face even more beautiful as she came undone. It gave me so much satisfaction knowing I had the power to do that.

Before she could recover, I turned her around, pushing her toward the edge of the bed. "All night I've thought about taking you from behind in that costume. And now I'm going to do exactly that."

"Oh god, yes," she said, arching against me.

I nudged her forward and she crawled onto the bed on her hands and knees, still wearing those knee-high black boots that made her legs look sexy as hell. I shoved her dress up around her hips, taking in her perfect, round ass and every other inch of exposed skin.

"God, you are so hot." I bent my head to taste between her thighs, giving her one long, lazy lick to let her know how much I meant it. She rewarded me with another of those sexy moans, and I couldn't wait to be inside her. I quickly undid my jeans, too eager to take them off completely, though I managed to grab a condom from my pocket and get that on.

Still standing, I palmed her smooth legs, so pale against my own skin, and spread her wider. She completely opened for me and glanced over her shoulder with raw lust in her eyes, turning me on even more.

I found her entrance and pushed just the tip inside to tease her, but she moaned and pressed back against me, trying to take me deeper. Fuck, that was hot. She really didn't want gentle or slow, my sexy little wench. But I was in control here, not her. I grasped her hips, holding her in place, and rubbed up and down, in and out, just enough to make her beg.

And oh, did she beg.

"Please, Hector. *Please.*"

I'd never heard anything sweeter in my life. How could I refuse when she asked like that?

With my hands on her hips, I plunged inside her in one smooth motion, all the way to the hilt. She gasped and threw her head back, her golden hair falling around her bare shoulders. Her pirate hat must have fallen off at some point in our frenzy.

At this angle I filled her completely and oh god it felt so good, so fucking tight. I wanted to take my time, but each thrust nearly sent me over the edge. Especially when she pressed back against my body with the same urgency. There was no holding back or going slow, and there was definitely no way I could be gentle. There was just this primal need for each other, like we were animals. Tonight she was mine, and I was hers, no matter what happened after this weekend.

My fingers dug into her skin as I pumped in and out with wild abandon, unable to control myself. She worked with me, rocking back and forth in time with my movements, forcing me deeper and deeper. Her hands clawed at the sheets, fisting them as she cried out. It was too much, and I was already so close, but I needed to take her along with me.

With one hand curled around her waist, I reached between her legs, rubbing her in exactly the right spot to make her shudder. It wasn't long before the orgasm hit her hard and she pushed back against me, clenching around me, shouting my name into the air. I rode through it, never letting up my pace, not wanting this moment to ever end. But I couldn't hold on and soon gave myself completely to her, the pleasure so intense I thought I might black out.

I slipped out of her and collapsed onto the bed, pulling her on top of me. She draped her arms around my neck and kissed me softly, her body relaxing into mine. We were both still partly dressed, our clothes a messy tangle around us, but neither of us moved to fix them. Soon our breath and heartbeats slowed together in sync.

"Last night was incredible," she said. "But that? That might have topped it."

I chuckled and tightened my arms around her. "You're good for my ego."

"I'm only speaking the truth."

One of her hands smoothed up and down my chest, tracing every ridge and curve with her fingers like she was fascinated by them. "I could touch you for hours."

"I wouldn't complain." I closed my eyes as she continued her investigation of my body. All my hours at the gym were definitely paying off. I didn't work out to impress women, but to keep my stamina up for shows and because it helped me stay calm and grounded. Tara's appreciation was just a huge bonus.

She propped herself up on one arm to look at me. "What does *te quiero* mean?"

I tensed and nearly jumped off the bed. "What?"

"You said it at the end, over and over."

Jesus, I'd said that out loud? I'd never done that before. I only spoke Spanish with my *abuelita*, since my sisters and I grew up speaking English to each other. But that moment at the end with Tara had been so intense it must have slipped out.

"It means, 'I want you.'" I gave her the literal translation instead of the one I'd really meant: I love you. At least I hadn't said *te amo*. She'd probably be able to guess the meaning of that one.

She smiled, idly running her fingers through my hair. "I like it when you speak Spanish. Even if I have no idea what you're saying."

"Oh yeah?" I switched to Spanish, whispering in her ear. "Tara, you are my sunshine, my moonlight, the light of my life. I love you, no matter what happens this weekend." Even though it was cheesy as hell it felt good to confess that, and no one would ever know what I'd said except me.

"Mmm." She nuzzled her face into my neck. "What did you say?"

"That you look so damn sexy I want to take you all over again." I'd never before been so happy that she'd taken French as her language elective in college. I kissed her forehead. "But we need to get going."

"Too bad."

"Later. We still have another night before Comic-Con ends." And after that…

I forced myself not to think about it. All that mattered was right now, this moment together, and it was enough. We'd work the rest out later.

THIRTEEN

Tara

Hector's band was already in the lobby by the time we got down there, along with Alexis and two of Maddie's friends—Carla, a tall, stunningly beautiful black girl with wild curls and a *MythBusters* t-shirt, and Julie, an Asian girl dressed in a steampunk Wonder Woman costume. Maddie and Jared were cosplaying as Princess Leia and Han Solo, and they were insanely cute together. Maybe I should have worn my pirate costume after all—but it needed a good wash after what had just been done in it.

Jared explained that we had to hit the store to get food and drinks before joining the Hall H line. We all stepped outside the hotel as one big cluster, carrying backpacks with clothes, sleeping bags, and games. It felt good to be surrounded by friends again, even if I didn't know them very well. If I moved to LA I'd be hanging out with these people a lot, I hoped. Tonight would be a tiny glimpse of what my life might be like if I chose the LA job…and Hector.

"Where's your Villain Complex hat?" Jared asked.

Hector ran a hand through his short curls and scowled. "I stopped wearing it because people kept recognizing me from the show. It got annoying."

"What? No one's recognized me so far. Maybe I should wear the hat from now on."

"It wouldn't go with your costume," I said.

"True." Jared grinned, looking back and forth between me and Hector. "Glad to see you two patched it up. I thought I'd have to hug it out of him."

"Keep your arms to yourself," Hector growled.

"You know you want some of this." Jared grabbed him in a big hug and tried to kiss him, while Hector squirmed away.

"Knock it off," Hector said, but I could tell he secretly loved it. The two of them started wrestling and then Jared darted down the street with Hector chasing after him, both of them laughing. They reminded me of my brothers, who were constantly beating each other up with smiles on their faces.

"Are they always like this?" I asked Maddie, moving to walk at her side.

"Pretty much. Sometimes Kyle joins in, too." She watched them with obvious affection. "I'm so glad you could make it tonight. Camping out for Hall H is a Comic-Con tradition everyone has to do at least once."

"How could I resist the lure of sleeping in front of a convention center with thousands of other sweaty, tired nerds?"

"Exactly! And now we can discuss your costume for the Masquerade. Julie's already putting it together."

"Oh, cool. What Batman villain am I going to be?"

Julie explained her plans for my costume, and I got even more excited. She eyed me up and down. "We have some clothes that might work, but it would help if I knew what you brought to Comic-Con."

"I don't have much. Just a couple t-shirts, some jeans, and a pirate costume." I described the costume for her and her face lit up.

"Yes! I think I can make that work for what I have in mind. We'll have to get a bowtie and a top hat, but I'm sure someone is selling those here."

"If it's too much trouble don't worry about it. I don't need a costume."

"No way. Challenge accepted!"

"Trust me, she lives for this stuff," Maddie said.

"I love your costume," I said, gesturing at Julie's steampunk Wonder Woman outfit. "It's so badass and clever at the same time. Did you make it, too?"

"I did! Thanks!" She donned her goggles and tossed her long, black hair over her shoulder, exuding major confidence and sexuality. I liked her instantly.

Carla shook her head, smiling. "Don't encourage her."

Julie struck another pose, hands on her hips. "You're just upset that guys are looking at me instead of you for once."

"That must be it."

As we walked, we discussed my costume in more detail and made arrangements for us to get together a few hours before the Masquerade. Alexis joined us and added her own thoughts, and I felt this overwhelming sense of belonging and happiness bubble up inside me. Hector's friends had immediately accepted me as one of their group and involved me in all their plans. They really felt like *my* people.

Hector moved to my side, sliding a hand around my waist. "Are these pretty ladies bothering you, Tara?"

"We totally are," Julie said, grinning at me. "You should rescue her."

Hector rolled his eyes, but the other girls giggled and gave us some space.

"Everything okay?" he asked.

I couldn't contain the smile bursting out of me. "Everything is great. I really like your friends."

He chuckled and kissed me on the forehead. "Yeah, they're not so bad."

We entered the supermarket, and Hector and the others stopped inside the entrance next to a row of cupcakes with tiny superheroes on them. Jared rubbed his hands together. "Time to play a little game."

"Ooh, I've been dying to play this ever since Maddie told me about it," Julie said.

Alexis groaned. "Don't tell me you guys still play Supermarket Treasure Hunt."

"What's that?" I asked.

"A game they invented when we were teenagers," she said. "I assumed they'd outgrow it but I guess not."

Kyle draped an arm around her. "If I recall, *you* were the one who invented the game."

She laughed and gave him a quick kiss. "That is *so* not how I remember it."

We all crowded around Jared, who seemed to be the unspoken leader of the group. "Since there are so many of us we're going to do a team version of Super-market Treasure Hunt. Grab a partner and a shopping cart and find the three craziest, weirdest, and, most importantly, the funniest items you can find. Make sure they all follow a theme for bonus points. Since this is Comic-Con, I expect some seriously messed up shit. Meet at the banana stand in ten minutes and we'll vote on the winner. Now...go!"

The others ran off, grabbing carts while hooting and cheering. Hector grasped my hand and tugged me toward the alcohol aisle. "Come on. I saw some weird shit in this section when I picked up beer yesterday."

I laughed and followed him, snagging a cart along the way. I'd never done anything like this before, but I could already imagine what my life would be like if I moved to LA...and I liked the image. Especially if it included more of Hector holding my hand.

In the alcohol aisle, we scanned the options quickly and pointed out a few things that might work. Then I spotted cans of alcoholic whip cream. In multiple flavors. "Look at this!"

"Perfect."

"We need one of each." I grabbed them off the shelf and dumped them into our cart.

"You're a natural at this game." He pulled me against his chest and kissed me deeply, like I was the only thing in his entire world. And for a minute, he was the only thing in mine.

Once we finally broke apart I checked the time. "We need to hurry. I'll look through the other aisle, you keep working on this one."

He nodded and I took off. I scoured the wine section in the next aisle, trying to move fast with the clock ticking away. I was about to grab a bottle that said Dry Sack Wine (ha!) when a familiar voice behind me said, "Tara?"

Oh no.

Andy.

"Hey." I spun around, feeling guilty even though I had no reason to be. Thank god he hadn't caught me a minute ago when I'd had my tongue inside Hector's mouth. Not that I'd done anything wrong by kissing Hector, but it would have made this moment that much more uncomfortable. "What are you doing here?"

He wore a black polo shirt with a tiny Rubik's Cube for the logo, and his dark blond hair was messier than normal, hanging nearly into his hazel eyes. He was ridiculously handsome, and my stomach tightened at the sight—a reminder that I still cared about him.

"Grabbing some beer." He walked over to me, frowning. "I texted you like five times. I thought we were going to have dinner tonight."

"You did?" Shit, shit, shit. I'd completely forgotten I'd told Andy I would text him when the party was over. "I'm so sorry! My phone was on silent and the party ran late and..."

I cringed inwardly at the white lie, but I couldn't exactly say I'd forgotten to call him because Hector had been banging my brains out. I fumbled through my bag for my phone and yep, there they were: five texts from Andy, plus a voicemail. I hadn't checked it while Hector had been distracting me so thoroughly, but now I felt like a total bitch.

"That's okay. We can go get something to eat now." It was such an Andy response. He was always polite, always kind, always forgiving.

"Oh, um...I can't." Ugh, I really was the worst.

Hector turned onto the aisle with our cart, but froze mid-stride when he saw Andy. The two of them stared at each other for the longest minute of my life. My perfect night instantly turned into my worst nightmare.

Andy slowly looked back and forth between me and Hector. "Ah. I didn't realize the two of you were hanging out tonight." He held out his hand. "I'm Andy. Tara's told me so much about you."

Hector shook his hand, though he looked like he'd rather touch a dead fish, despite being allergic to them. "Hey, man. Nice to meet you."

I caught myself biting my nails again and forced myself to stop. "We, uh, ran into each other at the Black Hat party, and um…"

"Cool, cool," Andy said, shoving his hands in his pockets.

An awkward silence settled over us and I had no idea how to end it. Finally, Hector cleared his throat. "I'm going to find the others. See you later, Andy."

After he left the tension eased by a small percent and I stepped closer to Andy. "I'm really sorry about dinner. Maybe we can do something tomorrow? I'm busy in the morning, and I have a signing in the afternoon, and then I'll be at the Masquerade that night, but…"

"I'll definitely be at your signing. Maybe we can grab a coffee after?"

"That'd be great."

Another uncomfortable silence. My ten minutes for the game were probably up by now. I glanced behind me, trying to figure out a polite way of ending this conversation. "Well, I better go…"

"Oh. Yeah. Me, too."

Andy looked so lost and alone I almost invited him to join us tonight, but that wasn't my place. Instead, I hugged him and was surprised by how comforting his familiar, easy presence was. "It was good to see you."

"You too." His hands tangled in my hair as he squeezed me back. "I missed you."

"I missed you, too."

It was true…except now that I'd been with Hector my time with Andy seemed shallow and lacking in comparison. If I was completely honest with myself, one of the reasons it had never worked with Andy (or any of the previous guys) was because Hector had always been there. He'd been unattainable, but even so there had been an ever-present feeling of wrongness with anyone else. I'd felt guilty, almost like I'd been cheating on both guys. I'd done nothing wrong, but it had always *felt* wrong.

I still cared for Andy a lot. How could I not, when we'd been together a year? He'd been a good boyfriend that entire time. There had never been anything *wrong* with him. He was a great guy, but it was clear now—I'd never been able to love Andy the way he deserved because there had always been the shadow of another man in my thoughts.

I left him in the wine aisle and found the others waiting for me by the bananas. They gave me curious looks as I approached, but didn't ask where I'd been. Hector searched my eyes and I gave him a weak smile.

"Sorry," I said to the group. "I ran into a friend."

"No problem," Jared said. "Now that you're here, we can present our goods. Maddie is our defending champion, so our team will go first."

"Our theme is, 'who thought this was a good idea?'" Maddie reached into a basket and pulled out her finds. "We have cappuccino potato chips. Watermelon Oreos. And…bacon mac and cheese ice cream! All of which somehow got past many committees to arrive on our shelves."

"I can't decide if I'm intrigued or horrified," Kyle said.

"Same," Julie said. "We should buy each of them and try them tonight."

"Good idea," Jared said. "Okay, Kyle and Alexis, you're next."

"The theme for tonight is 'naughty food.'" Alexis said, while Kyle displayed the items one by one. "We start with some delicious Perky Jerky, then move on to Breast Munchies. And for a happy ending, some creamy white finishing sauce."

"Gross," Carla said, wrinkling her nose.

"We could not even make this stuff up," Kyle said, shaking his head.

"Yeah, not super tempted by any of those," Jared said. "Okay, who's next?"

"We'll go," Julie said. She gestured to Carla, who looked embarrassed as she pulled out the items in their cart. "Behold, three items we call, 'so wrong, it's right.' First up, condoms with superheroes on them. I think some of you might need to buy these." That got a few grins from the group. "But for those of us flying solo this weekend, we can still have some fun with a *Harry Potter* vibrating wand."

"What the actual fuck," Hector said.

Alexis covered her eyes. "No! My childhood!"

"Okay, then maybe I can tempt you with this perfectly shaped frosting decorator?" Julie waved at the item in Carla's hand that looked suspiciously like a clear plastic dildo.

Maddie shook her head. "That is definitely wrong, but I'm not sure it ever goes all the way into right."

Julie grinned. "True, it's a bit small for my tastes."

Everyone laughed and some of my apprehension over seeing Andy faded away. This felt good and right, and I couldn't spend my entire time at Comic-Con worrying about him. I had to find my own happiness, and he had to find his.

"Very nice," Jared said, once the laughter died out. "And now, our final team…"

Hector raises his eyebrows at me, and I nodded for him to continue. He grabbed a six pack that he must have picked up while I was talking to Andy. "We call this theme, 'you sure you want to drink that?' First, we have sticky toffee pudding ale." He triumphantly held up another six pack. "Along with…spicy chipotle beer."

The group all groaned or made faces, and Julie said, "I'm going to throw up."

"It's either going to be amazing or disgusting," Maddie said.

"I'm voting for disgusting," Kyle said.

"Let's buy it and find out," Jared said. "What's your third item?"

Hector grinned and pulled out two cans of the item I'd picked out. "For the grand finale: alcoholic whip cream in a wide variety of flavors."

"Okay, we definitely have to get those," Julie said. "All the flavors. Multiple cans."

"Don't worry, we're buying some," I said.

"Thank you, Hector and Tara," Jared said. "All right. Time to pick a winner. Keep in mind you're not allowed to vote for your own team."

He went through all the teams and we each voted for our favorite, but it was clear that Carla and Julie were the winners. For their prize they got bragging rights for the rest of the night, which Julie seemed much more excited about than Carla.

We all split up again to put the items back and get food and drinks for our little evening picnic. I didn't see Andy again, luckily.

Now if only I could scrub the lingering guilt and sadness from my mind, I could get back to having a good time.

FOURTEEN

Hector

The line for Hall H was already long by the time we got there. It wove back and forth on the grass outside the convention center, where a cold breeze came in off the nearby marina. Our group got a spot in line and spread out our sleeping bags, settling in for the night.

I popped open one of the sticky toffee pudding ales and took a whiff. "Well, it smells good." I held it out for Tara, who took it and nodded. "Anyone else brave enough to try?"

A few of the others agreed, and I passed the bottles around. I grabbed one for myself, popping the lid off with my bottle opener keychain.

"Okay, we down it on the count of three. One…two…three!" We all took sips, and I nearly gagged. "Fuck, that is repulsive."

Jared made a choking sound. "It's like if a cat pissed on an ice cream cone."

"If someone made a cake, waited 'til it got moldy and then ate it, that's what this would taste like," Tara said.

"It can't be *that* bad," Maddie said.

"Oh no, it really is. Try it." Tara handed the beer to her.

She took a sip and made a face. "Okay, you were right. It is that bad."

The spicy chipotle beer wasn't quite as terrible, but not something I'd ever buy again either. We tore open the rest of our food and snacks, trying out the items we'd found in the store and testing the different flavors of alcoholic whip cream on each one.

"I have a great idea for what to use these for," Jared said, spraying some of the whip cream in his mouth. He pulled Maddie in for a kiss and she licked it off his mouth.

"Later," she said.

I threw a bag of chips at them. "Knock it off, you two."

Jared grinned. "Don't tell me you didn't have the exact same idea."

He'd got me there. My eyes darted to Tara, who smiled at me but then looked down at the grass. She'd seemed quiet and reserved ever since we'd run into Andy.

That moment had been pretty fucking weird for me, too. I'd spent the last year resenting Andy for being with the girl I loved, even though he seemed like a decent enough guy and he'd always treated Tara well. If I had to pick some other guy to date her I doubt I'd find anyone better than him. In a different situation, he and I might even be friends. But from the way he'd looked at Tara in the supermarket I'd known he wasn't over her, and something had definitely changed in her after seeing him, too.

Did she still have feelings for him? The two of them had just broken up, and I sure as hell didn't want to be a rebound. I knew how Tara worked—she immediately moved from one boyfriend to the next, and I was the newest link in her chain. But I didn't want to be a temporary boyfriend. If we did this I wanted to be the last guy she was with. The one she stayed with forever.

We spent the next few hours eating, drinking, and playing Cards Against Humanity, and Tara relaxed with each round. It was past midnight by the time we climbed into our sleeping bags to get a few hours of rest before they let us inside Hall H early in the morning.

Like I'd warned Tara earlier, I only had one sleeping bag, but it was a two-person bag because I could barely fit in a normal-sized one on my own. Tara and I both slipped inside, but she didn't snuggle up against me as I'd hoped. Instead we lay on our sides, facing each other but not touching.

"You okay?" I asked, keeping my voice low since the others were trying to sleep.

"Yeah." She sighed. "Running into Andy just threw off my night, I guess."

"Trust me, it wasn't my favorite thing either."

"No, I suppose not." She rolled onto her back, staring up at the stars.

"You two were pretty serious. Makes sense you'd be upset after running into him."

"It's extra hard because we broke up only a few days ago." She let out a sad little laugh. "And yeah, we were pretty serious. My parents loved him, too. Wanted us to get married and have babies the second we graduated college."

The thought of her marrying Andy and having blond babies with him made me want to punch something. Or someone. Or myself. I wasn't sure.

And of course her parents loved him. From what she'd told me, they'd rather have their daughter end up as Tara Smith—or whatever Andy's last name was—than Tara Fernandez.

"Is that what you wanted?" I asked.

"No. I'm not ready for any of that. I think Andy was, though. And sometimes the fantasy did sound pretty good…." She covered her face with her hands. "God, I'm such a mess. I'm sorry."

I didn't need to punch myself after all, 'cause her words hit me right in the gut. There was a whole future she'd imagined with Andy that had never included me. She obviously still had feelings for him, even if she didn't want to admit it. We were having fun this weekend but it didn't even come close to what they'd had. And how could it? They'd been together a year. We'd been friends for three, but she'd never thought about me as anything more than that until what? Yesterday?

"Enough about me." She propped herself up on an elbow to face me. "Tell me something about you I don't know."

"Um, there's not much you don't know after all this time."

"No? You never talk about your past. I want to know everything!"

I hated talking about my past. Or thinking about it at all, if I could help it. But her enthusiasm made me grin, and for once I didn't mind. "Like what?"

She played with the chain around her neck. "Like…how did you become friends with Jared and Kyle? I know you met in high school, but I want the whole story of how the band got started."

"Not that exciting of a story, but okay. I was always pretty good at drawing and shit, and my *abuelita* got me a scholarship at this fancy high school for visual and performing arts. Freshman year, Jared and I got teamed up for a project in English class where we had to write a poem and create a corresponding art piece to go with it. He wrote the words, I drew something, and after that we started hanging out."

"Sounds kind of like what we do for *Misfit Squad*." She rested her hand on my chest, tracing idle patterns in my shirt. "Did you like going to school there?"

"For the most part. It was a good school, but there were some guys who liked to give me shit for being the poor scholarship kid. First time Jared punched one of them, I knew he would always have my back."

Her eyebrows shot up. "The *first* time?"

"Uh." I coughed. "We used to get in a lot of fights, but that was years ago. We're both done with that shit now."

"Good." Her hand moved up to my neck, her fingers warm against my skin. The more I talked the more she touched me. I'd have to remember that. "Then what?"

"I used to hang out at Jared and Kyle's house all the time. One day I tried out their drum kit and was hooked. Jared said we should start a band and it took off from there." I shrugged. "Like I said, not that exciting of a story. Though it's kind of crazy how fast it all went down. Seems like only yesterday we were playing frat parties and parking lot shows, not huge stadiums."

"It wasn't *that* fast. You worked hard for years to get the band to where it is now. You practiced every night for hours and hours. I remember, even if you don't."

"That's true." I brushed a strand of golden hair away from her face. "Any more questions?"

She searched my eyes, opening and closing her mouth like she wanted to ask something but was hesitant. How bad could it be? I draped an arm around her waist. "You can ask me anything."

"Why have you been single all these years, Hector?"

I released her, my whole body tensing up. Shit, not that question. Anything but that.

"You don't have to tell me," she said, playing with a string on the edge of the sleeping bag.

"No. It's okay." I couldn't just flat out say that I never dated anyone because I'd been in love with her for three years. Or explain that I'd tried to go out with other girls, but always broke it off after a night together because it had never been fair to them.

Though if I was honest, Tara wasn't the only reason I was single.

I sucked in a breath and spoke slowly, considering each word before I said it. "You know my parents were sent back to Mexico when I was thirteen. Worst day of my life. I got home from school and they were just…gone. No note or anything. No one knew what happened to them. My sisters wouldn't stop crying…" I closed my eyes against the flood of memories I usually kept buried deep. This was why I never talked about my past: it was too fucking hard. "We moved in with our *abuelita* and I had to become the man of the house overnight. We got through it, but taking care of my sisters, on top of school, the band, my job at the art supply store…it never left much time for dating."

"That makes sense." She slid her arms around my neck and pressed a soft kiss on my lips. I knew I could leave it at that, but I wanted to come clean with her. About this, at least.

"There's another reason." Shit, this was tough. I'd never told anyone this. The guys knew, but we never talked about it. "I did have one serious girlfriend in high school. Amanda. Pretty blond girl, like you. An aspiring actress. Parents were rich." I gritted my teeth and forced the last words out. "She got pregnant."

"Oh my god."

"We were so stupid. Mostly me. But I loved her, or thought I did anyway. I was going to do whatever it took to be there for her, to be a good father to our kid. I was saving up to buy her an engagement ring and everything. And then, like my parents, one day she was just gone."

Tara's arms tightened around me. "No."

"Her parents hated me. They tried to have me arrested when they heard I'd knocked her up. Didn't work, so they took her away, moved across the country so we couldn't be together. When I finally tracked her down she told me she'd lost the baby. She never talked to me again after that. It fucking killed me."

I could still remember the exact moment I'd learned I wasn't going to be a father after all. I'd expected to be relieved to not have the burden of a baby on top of everything else I was dealing with, but instead I'd been heartbroken. And it only got worse when Amanda had shut me out completely. After that, I'd resolved to never let anyone hurt me like that again.

I'd done a good job, until the other night with Tara, when I'd let my guard down. Somehow she'd managed to worm her way inside my heart—and all I could do was brace myself for when she broke it, too.

"I'm so sorry, Hector." She held me closer, gently stroking my hair. "No one should have to go through something like that."

I shrugged. "After that I stopped getting close to people. I don't let anyone in. It's just easier that way."

"You let me in."

"You were different. I didn't have to worry about you leaving because I never had you."

She kissed me on the corner of my mouth. "You have me now."

For another day, yeah. But after that? I was afraid to ask.

"Thank you for trusting me with that," she said.

She snuggled closer against me, but I held back from touching her. I'd let her see too much of me, opened myself up too far, and I had to shut it down somehow. Too many emotions were digging their way out and I had to bury them again. I needed to end the moment, to lighten things up and get the focus off of my past.

"Hey, I couldn't let you think there was anything wrong with me, with not having a girlfriend all these years. Believe me, there have been plenty of women here and there, but nothing serious."

Jesus, what a douchey line. I had to stop myself from cringing as I said it.

"Nothing serious," she said slowly. "Like this weekend?"

"Exactly."

Her face fell, and I wondered if she'd been hoping to hear something else. What did she want from me? A declaration of love? I couldn't do it. Not when I didn't know what would happen beyond tomorrow. Our future together was a black hole and I couldn't see what it held for us—and that terrified me.

I slid a hand around the curve of her ass, pulling her closer, fitting her against my body. "Hey, we're having fun, remember?"

She gave me a faint smile, but it didn't reach her eyes. "I remember. What happens at Comic-Con stays at Comic-Con."

I wished I'd never said that, but it was too late now to take it back. I pressed kisses to her neck and whispered, "No worries. No regrets. No complications."

She slipped her fingers under my shirt, along my abs. "In that case, we need to be having a *lot* more fun."

"Now?" I let out a sharp laugh. "We're surrounded by hundreds of people."

"Everyone is asleep." Her hand moved to the front of my jeans and popped open the button.

"Damn, you are one naughty girl." I looked around, but the others did seem to be sleeping. "Maybe we could have a *little* fun…"

She drew me in for a kiss and it was easy to lose myself in her, in the way she nibbled on my lip while unzipping my jeans, in the feel of her hand sliding into my pants.

"I just want to touch you," she said, between kisses. "No one will notice."

"Only if I'm allowed to touch you, too."

She didn't protest as I raised her shirt to seek out her breasts. She wasn't wearing a bra—she'd discreetly removed it before getting in the sleeping bag—and it gave me easy access to her already hard nipples. I loved the way her breasts felt in my hands, so full and soft, and the little sighs she made as I teased them were even better.

She helped me push her jeans down, kicking them off in the bottom of the sleeping bag. I grabbed her leg and draped it across my hip, opening her up to me. Her breathing sped up as I dipped a finger inside her panties, just along the edge. I inched closer. And closer. I traced every inch of her until she pressed against me and moaned, like she wanted more.

"Shhh," I said. "Don't want everyone to hear you."

"I can't help it," she whispered.

"Then I'll have to keep you quiet."

I crushed my mouth against hers, taking her little cries into my mouth as I slowly slid a finger inside her. She tightened her grip around my length and clutched at my neck, keeping my lips locked to hers. She stroked me up and down and sucked on my tongue with the same rhythm, driving me absolutely fucking insane. The girl knew how to use her hands. And her mouth. I couldn't help but imagine what it would be like if she used both of them together…. Maybe next time.

We touched each other without the desperation or ferocity from before. This time we were slow and gentle, taking time to learn each other. I found the spot that I'd already discovered made her lose control and she practically howled.

Someone moved in a nearby sleeping bag and we froze. We stared into each other's eyes in the darkness, hearts pounding in sync, worried we'd been caught. Our greedy fingers were still on each other, but had paused in the middle of the action. We waited a minute, then two, but there was only silence. Until she giggled.

"Thought I told you to be quiet," I whispered.

I covered her mouth with my hand, which seemed to excite her even more. Her teeth dug into my skin while I began to rub her again and her fingers continued to work their magic on me.

We kept up a steady give and take, back and forth, with a slow build toward heaven. I wanted it to go on forever. Once we stopped we'd have to go back to reality, to our uncertain future. But here, like this, I could show her how much I loved her without having to admit it out loud.

When I knew I couldn't hold on much longer I increased my speed and pressure, making her arch her back. She clenched up around my fingers, making muffled sounds against my hand over her mouth, her entire body shuddering with pleasure. She kept pumping me as she lost control and I let her take me along with her, releasing myself into her hand.

We stroked each other until we were both completely sated, until exhaustion settled over us. I melted into her, my entire body warm and fluid as I cradled her against me. I never wanted to move again.

"Thank god you guys are done," Julie said, from the next sleeping bag. "I thought that would last all night. Nice job Hector, and good for you Tara, but some of us are trying to sleep."

Tara laughed and covered her face with her hand.

"Eh, you're just jealous," I said to Julie.

"No kidding. I wish I had some of that right now. Hey, if you're up for sharing…"

"Definitely not," Tara said, tightening her arms around me. "He's all mine."

"Oh well, I tried," Julie said. "Get some sleep, love birds."

"Yours?" I asked Tara, kissing her neck. "I like the sound of that."

"Me, too." She snuggled against me, and I played with her hair while she settled in to sleep.

FIFTEEN

Tara

I woke in Hector's arms, blissfully warm against his hard body, while the sun rose over the convention center. Soon we'd go inside to watch all the big movie panels until it was time for our book signing. After that, we had the Masquerade and the afterparty and then one final night together before Comic-Con ended.

I had one more day to make my decision.

One more day with Hector.

I watched him sleep, admiring his long, dark lashes and his full, pouty lips. Careful not to wake him, I traced a finger over his face, along his eyebrows, his nose, his jaw. I drank in the sight of his broad shoulders, the way his dark hair curled over his forehead, the swell of his bicep around my waist. I wanted to memorize every inch of him before the day was over.

Last night he'd opened up to me for the first time ever, telling me things about his past I suspected he never revealed to anyone. My heart had broken when he'd told me about his high school girlfriend and the baby they'd lost. No wonder he had a hard time letting people in. Yet he'd let me in—for a few minutes, anyway. I'd felt closer to him than ever…and then he'd shut me out again. I'd only been able to bring him back to me by making things "fun" again.

From what he'd said, he didn't want anything serious—with me or any other girl. Yet those few moments when he did manage to let his guard down made me think he cared for me. He pushed me away and said we were just having fun, but then he said he wanted to be mine.

So which was it?

He opened his eyes and gave me a sleepy smile. "Hey, beautiful."

I pressed a soft kiss to his lips and he drew me closer against his body. Desire flickered inside me, like a red hot flame. I wanted to climb on top of him and ride him, despite being surrounded by people. Hector just brought out that side of me.

I brushed my mouth across his jaw. "*Te quiero*," I whispered, repeating his words from yesterday back to him. The ones that he'd said meant, "I want you."

He tensed up and swore under his breath, pulling away from me. "Jesus, Tara. Don't say that."

His reaction doused my lust like a bucket of ice water. I sat up, pulling my shirt down, feeling hurt and exposed. "Sorry."

"It's okay, just…." He took a deep breath and raked a hand through his already messy hair. After a second his body relaxed, and he flashed me a grin. "I want you, too. But when you speak like that it turns me on way too much, and we don't have time to do anything about that right now."

I nodded. He was right, of course. The rising sun cast a warm glow across the grass, where people were standing up and getting ready to go inside the convention center. Still, his reaction had been so extreme, it made me wonder if there was something else that was bothering him.

We spent the entire day together, sitting through the panels in Hall H with his friends, laughing and joking about the things we saw, gorging ourselves on bad convention food while checking out the cosplay. I was never eating another pretzel dog ever again after this weekend, that was for sure.

In between panels, Maddie told me about how she and Kyle became friends as freshmen in college, and how that led to her joining the band even though she'd been more of a classical musician before that. She had me cracking up with her story about how Jared had walked in on her playing his guitar at a party, and then showed up at her class to beg her to go on *The Sound* with his band.

Next, Alexis told me about how she and Kyle had gotten back together at a Battle of the Bands competition, and I discovered she was a photographer who was taking photos at Comic-Con for an entertainment news website. I also learned that Julie was a pre-med major but spent most of her free time designing clothes, and that Carla did modeling while getting a theater degree, loved fixing cars, and had a vintage Mustang.

Hector sat beside me the entire time, staying quiet while his friends did most of the talking. He was a steady presence, his arm resting on the chair behind me, his muscular thigh pressed against mine. It was a struggle to not touch him constantly, or grab him for a kiss in front of his friends, but I managed to restrain myself. Barely.

Our signing was scheduled near the end of the day in the same large, bright room as before. After a quick pit-stop in our hotel rooms to shower and change clothes, Hector and I made our way there together, chatting the entire time about how DC had better TV shows while Marvel had better movies. We pushed our way through the huge crowd and got to our section right on time—and it was packed. The line snaked back and forth in contained rows before bursting out and taking over the nearby wall, too.

"Oh, wow," I said, as we sat at our table behind our name tags. "I did not expect this."

"Same," Hector said. "I assumed everyone who wanted the book signed would have gotten it the other day."

Miguel joined us and set a box of Sharpies on the table, next to a huge stack of our books. "Big crowd, eh? All ready to start?"

I pulled out my own sparkly pens. "Ready."

We signed books quickly, with Miguel managing the line so it didn't become overwhelming but also moved at a brisk pace. It wasn't as stressful this time since we knew what to expect, and I was able to enjoy talking with the fans. Even Hector seemed more relaxed and chatty than normal, and he doodled silly sketches inside the books of people who asked him a good question—usually anything that didn't involve his band or *The Sound*.

I looked up to see who was next and saw Andy's smiling face. I glanced at Hector, but he was talking to Miguel and didn't notice my ex-boyfriend approach.

"Hey, Andy," I said, trying to keep my voice light. *Please don't let this be awkward*, I prayed.

"Hey!" He slid a copy of *Misfit Squad* in front of me to sign. "I'm so glad I could catch you at this signing. Look how many people there are!"

"I know, isn't it nuts?" I signed his book and added a personal thank-you note. "You didn't have to come though, you already have a copy of this."

"I had to see you signing books like a real author." He grinned. "Besides, I wanted a copy signed by both of you."

I slid the book to Hector. He kept his face neutral, but he gripped his Sharpie so hard I thought it might snap in half.

"Hey man, good to see you again," Andy said.

"You, too." He signed Andy's book with deep, sharp strokes, the pen squeaking as he wrote.

"Again, I'm really sorry I bailed on our dinner last night," I said. "I've just been so busy…"

"That's okay. Look how popular you are. I knew you would be."

Hector doodled a little cartoon devil inside Andy's book, but eyed us both with a surly look on his face as we spoke. The guy next in line cleared his throat.

"I'd love to talk to you for a minute," Andy said. "Maybe after your signing? We can grab that coffee."

"Sure, that would be fun."

"Great. I'll wait for you." He moved away and the next guy immediately replaced him with another copy of *Misfit Squad*.

I scribbled my name in more books than I could count. Miguel had to cap the line off, but even then we went well beyond our appointed time limit.

When the area finally cleared out, I shoved my sparkly pens in my bag and smiled at Hector. "That was even more fun than the first signing."

"Not as scary this time?"

"Nope. I knew what to expect. But now my hand hurts again."

"Let me help you." He took my hand in his and brought it to his lips, then started to massage it with slow, sensual strokes, never taking his eyes off mine.

I relaxed into his touch. "Mmm, you're so good with your hands."

"Come back to my room and I'll show you just how good."

"I approve of this plan." I wanted those hands all over me. And every other part of his body.

"Hey, Tara," Andy said, walking up to us. He frowned when he took in how close Hector and I were standing, how he held my hand against his chest. "Er, did I interrupt something?"

I jerked my hand away and took a step back, flexing my wrist. "No, he was just showing me a hand exercise. It got sore after signing so many books."

"Oh. Good."

The two guys gave each other long, silent looks. God, this moment was awkward. I stepped forward and hugged Andy, not knowing what else to do. "I'm so glad you're here."

"Me, too." He took his time to pull out of the hug, his hands lingering on my lower back. "Ready to get that coffee now?"

I checked the time and sighed. "I'm so sorry, Andy, but I can't. Please don't hate me, but the signing ran long, and now I have to get ready for the Masquerade. But, um, you should come to the Masquerade with us and hang out. Or if you can't make that, you can come to Hector's party after!"

I fished through my bag and handed him the flyer Hector had given me for the afterparty. Inviting Andy to either of these things wasn't very cool of me, since they'd been organized by Hector and his friends, but I had to do *something* after ditching the poor guy over and over. I shot Hector a *please-forgive-me* look, but he was glaring across the room and I couldn't catch his eye. Shit. Was he mad?

"Okay," Andy said, examining the flyer. "Just as long as we get to hang out *some* time before Comic-Con is over."

"Of course! We will. For sure." I smiled at him, but caught Miguel waving me over. "Be right back."

I moved around the table, to where Miguel was stacking the empty boxes that had once held copies of our books. We'd sold out of them again. Go us.

"What's up?" I asked.

"I got a call from that producer Giselle Roberts. Well, her assistant actually. He said she was meeting with you and wanted early copies of the next two *Misfit Squad* books. What was that about?"

"I met with her yesterday. She loves the book and asked me to work for her as a writer on her new TV show."

"No way! That's great!" He rubbed his goatee. "I don't suppose she'd want to buy the film or TV rights to *Misfit Squad*, too?"

"She didn't mention it, but who knows? Maybe someday."

He nodded slowly. "We've been trying to get in with her for years, but she's so selective. This could be big for us. Really big. When do you start?"

"Um. I haven't accepted. I already have a job in the comics division of Ostrich Books. I really want to work for Giselle, but…I don't know."

"Ah, yes. I forgot about that. Well, Black Hat supports you no matter what you choose, of course. But…I mean, it's *Giselle Roberts*."

His phone rang and he said, "Excuse me a second." He started speaking in Spanish to whoever was on the other line, and ended it with, "*Te quiero*." I jerked at the words, remembering what had happened this morning.

He shoved the phone back in his jeans. "Sorry about that. My wife wanted to know what time I was done here. She wants us to go to some Godzilla experience in the Gaslamp."

"That's okay." I chewed on my pinky nail. "This probably sounds like a weird question, but what does *te quiero* mean?"

"It means either 'I like you' or 'I love you' depending on who you're saying it to."

The world seemed to tip around me. *Love?* "It doesn't mean 'I want you?'"

"Nope. That's the literal translation, but it's not used that way. Why?"

"Oh, just…something I heard."

That must be why Hector freaked out this morning. He'd thought for a second I'd said that I loved him, and it had scared him before he realized what I'd meant. After what he'd told me last night it made sense—he was scared of getting close to anyone and getting hurt again.

But why had Hector lied about the translation? And which way had he meant it when he'd said it last night? Could he…? No. He must have been saying that he liked me.

My gaze traveled back to the other side of the table where Hector and Andy were chatting, their voices drowned out by the low buzz of the crowd. I couldn't see Hector's face but Andy was smiling, so it must not have been too going too terribly. The sight made me happy because it meant Hector was trying—for me.

All day long, I'd had an overwhelming sense that I belonged with Hector and his friends. I didn't want that feeling to disappear after Comic-Con. I would be crazy not to take the LA job. To be able to wake up next to Hector whenever I wanted—how could I say no to that? Or to Giselle Roberts and the opportunity of a lifetime?

It was terrifying, giving up the job I'd dreamed about for years. But in my gut this felt right.

I made my decision.

SIXTEEN

Hector

Tara ran off with Miguel, while Andy and I stood together in uneasy silence in the corner of the room. I crossed my arms and tried to look at anything but him.

Shit, the guy was wearing a polo shirt. It had a Batman symbol for the logo, but still—who wore a fucking *polo shirt* to Comic-Con?

And what the hell was he still doing here? She'd already said she couldn't get coffee with him. Of course, then she'd gone and invited him to the Masquerade and the afterparty. Bad enough I'd had to see them hug in front of me, now I'd be stuck watching them together all fucking night.

"So, uh." He gestured in Tara's direction. "Are you and her…you know…"

"No."

He exhaled in a rush. "Good, because I have something to tell her. And to ask her." He patted his pocket. "I just hope she says yes."

I grunted. "What, are you proposing?"

I'd meant it as a bad joke, but he smiled wider. "Yeah, I am. Do you think she'll say yes?"

"I…" Fuck. I could barely get the words out. He'd knocked all the air out of me without even hitting me. "I don't know."

"I think she will…the only reason we broke up is because we were moving to different cities, but I found a job in New York so we can stay together. I can't wait to tell her."

I stared at him. "You got a job in New York?"

"I did. I'm going to ask her to marry me so she'll see that I'm serious about us. That I want to make this work, whatever it takes."

I should have just handed him a knife to stab me with. It would have hurt a lot less. My fists clenched, my first reaction to punch his face in, to tell him to back off from my girl. But she wasn't mine, and I wasn't that kind of guy anymore.

Jesus, this guy was going to propose to Tara and I'd been inside her only hours ago. I was the other man, stealing Tara from Andy without even knowing it. Yeah, they'd been broken up at the time, but clearly it wasn't over. I'd seen the way she'd jerked away from me the second he'd arrived, and the way they hugged each other. She'd even admitted last night that she'd thought about marrying him.

I needed to end this thing with her immediately. I couldn't be the reason she said no to Andy or had any doubts about taking the New York job. I refused to get in the way of her happiness.

I'd been an idiot to hope for even a second that we could be anything more than friends. We'd had some "fun" moments together, but that was it. And I wanted her to be happy even if she wasn't with me, even if it killed me to see her with someone else. Hell, I'd done it for years and I'd survived. I could do it again. Maybe if she was engaged I could finally get over her.

Something burned at my eyes, like I was about to cry. But that was crazy. I *never* cried. Not since I was thirteen, anyway. I'd shed my last tears the day my parents were sent away, when I realized I had to toughen up and become a man for my sisters so they could cry as much as they needed. And now I had to suck it up and do what had to be done, for Tara.

"You should ask her tonight." Better to get the whole thing over with so we could all move on with our lives. She had to make her decision by tomorrow, so Andy didn't have any time to mess around.

"I will. Thanks, Hector." He shook my hand again. "You've always been a good friend to her."

"Yeah." A good friend. And that's all I would ever be.

"I have to admit, I've always been jealous of you, even though she told me over and over that there was nothing going on between you two. But I'm really glad you're in her life."

My throat closed up, as though his hands had tightened around it. No, there had never been anything going on between us. Our few days together at Comic-Con were the perfect reminder of why I kept people at arm's length and barricaded my heart. I'd made the mistake of letting Tara in and all it had done was get me hurt again. No more. I was done with that shit.

"Good luck tonight," I said.

"Thanks! Tell her I'll catch up with her later. I'm going to make some plans."

He vanished into the crowd and I rubbed my face, scrubbing off any lingering emotions. Wondering what the hell I'd just done. Dreading what I was about to do.

I wanted her to be happy even if she wasn't with me, even if it killed me to see her with someone else. Hell, I'd done it for years and I'd survived. I could do it again. Maybe if she was engaged I could finally get over her.

Tara bounced back to me with a bright smile. "Where'd Andy go?"

"He had to run, but he said he'll see you tonight."

Her smile wavered as she studied me. "What's wrong, Hector?"

I must not have hardened my face as much as I'd hoped. Hell, it was a miracle I'd kept it together this long. "Look, Tara. I've been thinking. We had fun over the past few days, but I don't want you to get the wrong idea."

She took a step back, confusion painted across her beautiful face. "The wrong idea?"

"This thing between us, it can't go any further. We're just friends. For Comic-Con we were friends with benefits. That's it." I shrugged as if it was nothing, as if forcing those words out wasn't the hardest thing I'd ever done.

She clutched the amethyst pendant around her neck, the one I'd given her. "So our nights together, everything you said…none of that meant anything?"

"Nope. It was just sex. Nothing more." I forced myself to maintain eye contact, even as her blue eyes filled with tears.

She blinked them back. "I don't believe you."

Jesus, why was she being so difficult? I'd told her before I couldn't do long distance, that I didn't want anything serious. If she wouldn't listen, I'd have to pull a card from Jared's player days, though I was about to be way more of an asshole than he'd ever been.

"Last night you asked me why I haven't had a girlfriend in years. You want to know the real reason? It's 'cause I sleep with girls a few times and then get bored. And it's time for me to move on."

A tear trickled down her face. "Hector, stop. I know you're not like that."

"Hell, yeah, I am. I never mentioned it 'cause why would I tell you about all the girls I've fucked? And trust me, there were a lot of them. With Jared taken, I'm in demand more than ever, and with the tour…well, let's just say I plan to fuck a *lot* more girls."

Everything I said was a lie and I hated myself a little more with each word, but it had to be done. I'd probably ruined my friendship with her too, but that was for the best. It'd be easier to forget her if she hated me. Easier to move on if she was out of my life completely. Even if it left my heart a barren wasteland.

She stared at me with tears dripping down her cheeks, and the sight made me want to take back everything I'd said. I was this close to confessing my real feelings for her and begging her to move to LA when she nodded slowly, wiping at her eyes. "If that's what you want."

"It is. I don't want anything serious, with you or anyone else."

"So what happens now? With us?"

"You take the New York job and we go back to being online friends. We keep working on *Misfit Squad* as we've always done. If you move to LA it will just be weird now, you know?"

"But…." She sucked in a breath, her voice faltering. "Please, Hector. Just tell me the truth. All this time, have you felt *anything* for me as more than a friend?"

I hesitated. This was my chance to be honest with her. To end the lies and try to win her back. But I shook my head.

"No. Never."

SEVENTEEN

Tara

I turned on my heel and slipped into the crowd without responding. I couldn't look at Hector for another second longer. I couldn't let him see me fall apart completely.

By the time I made it out of the convention center, I was running, the tears falling freely down my face. I blinked them back, trying not to let them escape, quickly wiping away the ones that did. It was stupid to cry over what he'd said. Over our two nights together. Over the future we would never have.

I didn't know what to do or where to go. Everything inside me hurt, like Hector had taken a scalpel to my heart and sliced out every piece that belonged to him. I'd made my decision, had been all ready to commit to a future with him, and then he'd crushed that dream into dust only seconds later. My entire life had been thrown into a tailspin and I wasn't sure how I could ever recover.

He'd said it meant nothing to him, but I didn't believe it. He'd said we could go back to being friends, but we both knew that wasn't going to happen. He'd said he wanted to sleep around, but that didn't sound like the Hector I knew. He wasn't that type of guy at all. In fact, he'd often complained about Jared doing exactly that. Had he changed his mind because of all the girls throwing themselves at him over the past few days? No. That didn't make any sense. There had to be something else going on.

I made it to the Gaslamp Quarter but stumbled into something out of a horror movie. Hundreds of people covered in fake blood and ripped clothes moaned and shambled slowly down the road. Great, a zombie walk. As if this moment couldn't get any worse.

I had to push my way through people calling for brains, but finally made it back to my hotel room. Once inside, my stomach clenched at the sight of my pirate costume. Earlier I'd rinsed it out and hung it up in the shower so it would be ready for tonight. But how could I go to the Masquerade now? I wasn't ready to face Hector so soon. Or maybe ever.

I texted Maddie: *Can't make it tonight. I'm so sorry.*

She immediately called me. I was tempted to ignore it, but that would be rude. She'd never been anything but nice to me. I sighed and answered the phone.

"What's going on?" she asked.

"Hector..." I paused, trying to figure out how to explain what had happened. He hadn't dumped me per se, since we hadn't exactly been together. "I don't know what happened. One minute everything was great, and the next..."

"Come to our hotel room. We'll drink wine and eat ice cream and you can tell us the whole story."

"I don't know..." I wasn't sure I should talk to Maddie or the other girls about this. They were Hector's friends, after all. Our involvement should probably end here.

"Would you rather be alone? If so, I completely understand."

The tears threatened to return with a vengeance. Of course I didn't want to be alone. I wanted to spend my evening at the Masquerade with Hector and his friends, but now I couldn't do that. My other options were to sit in my hotel room and weep, or hang out with Andy. I didn't want to do either of those.

"Are you sure? It won't be weird since you're in the band with him?"

"Not at all. Trust me, if anyone knows how difficult Hector can be, it's me. When I joined the band, I was convinced he hated me, but I've gotten to know him a lot better since then. I'll help you figure out what's going on with him."

"Thanks, Maddie. I'll be there in a few minutes."

"Good. Oh, and Julie says to bring your pirate costume."

———

Fifteen minutes later I found myself in the hotel room Maddie was sharing with Carla and Julie. I'd collapsed onto one of their queen-sized beds, watching while they got ready for the Masquerade.

"We don't actually have any ice cream, but hopefully this will help." Maddie brought me a glass of red wine and sat on the other bed, eyebrows pinched together. She had on a nearly white blond wig that was done into pigtails. "Tell me exactly what Hector said."

I repeated the conversation as best I could, cringing when I remembered some of his harsher words, and was biting back tears by the end. It hurt just as much the second time and made even less sense.

The other night he'd said it had been a long time since he'd slept with anyone. Now he was trying to tell me he was a player? Something didn't add up. Was it because of the *te quiero* thing this morning? He hadn't brought it up again, but something had bothered him then. Or had Andy said something while I was talking to Miguel?

Carla leaned out of the bathroom, where she was doing her makeup. "I'm shocked. I didn't think Hector was that kind of guy."

"He's not," Maddie said. "Not even close. I've never even seen him flirt with a girl."

"So what's his deal?" Julie asked, from where she sat at the desk. She was in the middle of hand-sewing the hem of the red and black skirt Maddie was going to wear for her Harley Quinn costume.

"I wish I knew." I took a long sip of my wine and sighed. At least I had Maddie and her friends to talk to about the whole mess. I'd worried they would take Hector's side, or shut me out as soon as they heard he was done with me, but they were acting like they were *my* friends, too.

"Hang on." Maddie grabbed her phone.

"What are you doing?"

"Texting Jared. If anyone can find out what's going on with Hector, it's him."

EIGHTEEN

Hector

I returned to our hotel room and found Jared and Kyle getting ready for the Masquerade, their costumes already laid out across one of the beds.

"What's up?" Jared asked from the bathroom. His hands were in little plastic gloves and were slicking half of Kyle's head with hair dye.

"Nothing." I flopped on the bed, facing away from the bathroom door. I didn't want to talk to them. Maybe if I ignored them they'd leave me alone. Ha, fat chance.

"All done," Jared said to Kyle a few minutes later. "Have to wait twenty minutes now."

"I'll set a timer on my phone."

They both walked out of the bathroom and Jared sat on the edge of the other bed, eyeing me. "What's with you? Did your signing not go well?"

"It went fine."

"Did something happen with Tara?" Kyle asked, sitting next to his brother. One side of his head was covered in white hair dye, making it stick up all crazy. The other side was still black, but pinned back so it wouldn't get any color on it.

I turned away from them. "I don't want to talk about it."

Jared kicked my bed, making it shake. "Spit it out. What'd you do?"

Fuck, he was annoying. "I ended it, okay?"

"What?" Kyle asked. "Why?"

I let out a long groan and rolled onto my back, covering my face with my arm. "Her ex-boyfriend showed up with a wedding ring. He's moving to New York to be with her. I couldn't stand in the way of that."

"Oh, shit," Jared said.

"Does she *want* to get back together with him?" Kyle asked.

"I think so. She still has feelings for him. And she's been dreaming about that publishing job in New York her entire life. Ending it with her was the right thing to do."

The brothers were quiet, frowning at each other. Doing that near-telepathy thing they did. It was even more freaky because, if you ignored Kyle's wild hair, they looked so much alike.

"Does she know how you feel about her?" Kyle asked.

I grunted and rolled onto my side to face the wall again.

"I'll take that as a no."

"It doesn't matter. I was a total asshole. I told her I wanted to fuck a lot of girls now that we're popular and going on tour."

"Wow," Jared said. "Even I would never say that to a girl."

"No? Cause I was trying to channel you in that moment."

"Hey, despite what you think of me, I tried not to be an asshole to the girls I was with. I was up front with them that I wasn't after a relationship."

"Yeah? What about Becca?"

"I can't believe you're bringing that up again! First of all, that was a mistake I've apologized for a *hundred* times. You know I would go back and fix that if I could. Second, Becca knew what she was getting into. She just didn't want to accept it. And third, I'm not like that anymore. Give me a fucking break here."

"Knock it off," Kyle said. "Hector's just trying to piss you off so we'll stop asking him questions about Tara."

Jared drew in a long breath but said nothing. I felt bad for being a dick to him, but it was so nice to lash out about something, at *someone*, instead of sitting here wallowing in my own misery.

"Sorry, man," I muttered. I sat up and faced them, scrubbing at my eyes with my palms.

"Whatever." Jared checked something on his phone. "But you have to tell Tara how you feel. Otherwise you'll regret it."

Kyle nodded. "Jared's right. It's up to her to decide her future, but she needs to know you love her."

"I don't love her."

They both laughed. The exact same laugh at the same time, like they'd synchronized it. Damn, they were irritating. How had I put up with them for so many years?

I scowled at them. "You guys think you know everything about relationships now that you're both in love and on your way to two-point-five kids and a dog, but I don't need your advice."

"Sure you don't." Jared said, typing on his phone before looking up at me. "Now get your shit together so we can head out in approximately…fifteen minutes."

"I'm not going. Tara will be there."

"Maddie just texted me. Tara isn't going."

"Oh." Of course she wasn't going. Not after what I'd done. I'd probably never see her in person again.

Good. It was better when we'd only known each other online. Meeting in person had just fucked everything up. Andy would be proposing tonight, and then she'd be busy with him and her engagement ring and her new life. They'd get married and have babies like her parents wanted and everyone would be happy.

Everyone except me.

Whatever, I had other things that made me happy. My family. My band. My art. I didn't need anyone else.

I didn't need *her*.

NINETEEN

Tara

Alexis arrived with her costume in a bag under her arm while Carla and Julie did their makeup in the bathroom and Maddie and Jared texted back and forth. I had to explain the whole painful story all over again, and watched her green eyes get wider and wider with each word.

"I don't get it," she said. "That doesn't sound like Hector at all."

"Nope, not even close," Maddie said.

Alexis chewed on her lower lip as she considered. "Hector *is* pretty bad about expressing his emotions and stuff. Maybe he just…freaked out or something."

I sighed. "But why would he say all that stuff about sleeping around?"

"I don't know. He hasn't had a serious girlfriend in years. Probably not since we were in high school when…well, never mind that. But maybe he panicked because things between you two were moving so fast."

Maddie frowned at something she read on her phone. "Jared won't tell me what's going on. Bro code or something. But he says Hector is just as miserable as you are."

"I doubt Kyle will be any help either," Alexis said.

Maddie refilled my wine glass. "One thing I do know: Hector cares about you. A lot. If he's pushing you away it's probably for a reason."

"A reason…" I closed my eyes, replaying the memory again. "My ex-boyfriend Andy was talking to Hector right before it happened. Maybe he said something to set him off?"

"Could be," Alexis said.

I grabbed my phone and dashed off a text to Andy, asking what he'd said to Hector. But he just replied that he'd talk to me soon. "No help there. Ugh."

"Was there anything else that happened today?" Maddie asked. "Anything else Hector said?"

"He did tell me to take the New York job at the end…" I sat up straighter, sloshing a drop of wine on their comforter. "He must think that's what I really want! And that I was going to turn that job down because of him."

"Were you?" Julie asked, peeking out of the bathroom.

"Yes. Maybe. I don't know." I set my glass down and flopped back on the bed. "Oh, god, I'm so confused! I thought I knew which job to take, but now I'm not sure. Yes, a big part of the reason I chose the LA job was because Hector lives there, but now that seems so dumb. After today it will be weird for us to be in the same city. But if I pick the New York one I'll never have another chance with him."

Alexis sat next to me on the bed. "Why don't you tell us about the two jobs? But this time, forget Hector. Leave him out of it."

"Okay." I sucked in a breath and gave them a quick run-down about both positions and the kind of work I'd be doing at each one. I played with my necklace the entire time, and they listened patiently as I laid it all out for them.

"They're both great, but totally different," I added. "The LA job is scary because I feel so unqualified for it, but it's such an amazing opportunity. To work for Giselle Roberts, writing for a TV show like that…it would be incredible. But I've heard that TV writing jobs are high stress and not very stable." I was just pondering out loud now, but they let me talk it out without interrupting. "Whereas in the New York job I'd be more of an editor or producer, choosing and directing other people's projects and putting them together, shaping the future of the comics division at Ostrich Books. It would probably be just as high stress as the other job actually, and I wouldn't be writing anything myself either."

"Hmm. A tough decision," Maddie said. "Being an artist of any kind is a strange thing. Music for me is almost a…compulsion. An addiction. A form of madness. I can't imagine not doing it. It's always there, in the back of my mind, demanding my attention. Even on the days it's hard, even when I want to give up, I do it anyway, because I can't imagine *not* doing it. It's like breathing for me.

"And I think to make it in any kind of creative industry you have to feel like that or it's not worth it. It's just too damn hard otherwise. So my question for you is, are you *compelled* to write? Does it eat at your brain until you do it? Do you feel like you're missing something from your very soul when you don't? Or would you rather direct other writers, to guide them on their path and help them make their own stories even better? Both are equally important, it just comes down to what's right for *you*, and what you want to do with your life."

"I never thought about it that way." I chewed on one of my fingernails and considered what she said.

"Don't think about Hector," Alexis said. "Or whether you know people in a city or not. You'll meet people no matter where you live. Pick the job *you* want and everything else will work out the way it should."

Just like that, I knew what my decision had to be, and why I'd been so anxious about the New York job this entire time. It had nothing to do with the city, or with the people in it.

I was a writer. An artist. A *creator*.

I had to take the LA job. Even if Hector didn't want me. Even if his friends never talked to me again after today. Even if I was alone in the city forever.

Because I wasn't doing it for him or for anyone else. I was doing it for *me*. This was what *I* wanted.

And, thanks to Maddie and Alexis, I had an idea that would make the job even better—assuming Giselle liked it, too.

I gave the girls each a hug. "Thank you so much. I know what to do now. I'm going to take the LA job."

"Glad we could help," Maddie said.

Alexis smiled. "Hey, if you need a place to stay in LA, let me know. My roommate just graduated and moved out."

Her offer was so tempting, but I shook my head. "Thanks, but I think I need to live on my own for a while. I've always relied so much on other people. It's time for me to be independent for a while. But I hope we can all stay friends, even if this thing with Hector doesn't work out."

"Of course!" Maddie said. "You're one of us now. One of Gotham's most wanted."

"Um, I never said I was going to the Masquerade."

Julie sank down on the other side of me, now wearing a long red wig. "Of course you are. You're not going to let a stupid man ruin your weekend, are you?"

"Julie's right," Carla said, dropping onto the bed beside Maddie. "You *have* to join us for the Masquerade. She's got your costume all ready and everything."

"I don't know. Hector will be there…" I looked around at the four girls surrounding me. They barely knew me, yet they were all on my side, completely supportive of my decisions and trying to make me feel better—like real friends should be. I didn't want to let them down. But I was scared to see Hector again so soon, too.

Julie wrapped an arm around me and squeezed. "Girl, when Hector sees you in the costume I've put together he'll *beg* you to come back to him."

TWENTY

Hector

After Kyle's hair was done and they rinsed out the white dye in the sink, we walked to the convention center to meet the girls. Comic-Con had a rule that you couldn't wear your costumes for the Masquerade before the competition, so we all had to finish getting dressed backstage. But when we arrived I wanted to turn around and run out—because Tara was there. She was talking with Carla and had her back to me, but I would recognize that blond hair and perfect ass anywhere.

"Thought you said she wasn't coming," I growled.

"Oops." Jared shrugged, flashing a devious grin. "She must have changed her mind."

"You planned this, didn't you, you son of a…"

I shut up when Maddie ran over to us with a big smile on her face. She ruffled Kyle's black and white hair. "Nice job."

"Why thank you," Jared said, giving her a quick kiss.

"Hector…" She gave me a disappointed look from behind her glasses that made me feel like an even bigger asshole than I already did. Tara must have told her everything. "Don't even think about leaving. And be nice."

What did that mean? I wasn't going to start anything. Hell, if it were up to me I'd be back at the hotel already. The absolute last thing I wanted to do was be around Tara knowing I couldn't have her.

She turned toward me and, even with the crowd rushing around us, all I saw was the cobalt blue of her eyes. She paled and quickly looked down, tucking a strand of golden hair behind her ear. Her face looked puffy, like she'd been crying, yet was still the most beautiful thing I'd seen all day.

Julie immediately whisked our group to the backstage area where we had to get ready. I didn't get a second to talk to Tara or even catch her eye. And who was I kidding—there was no way in hell she'd want to talk to me anyway. I was shocked she'd come at all, after what I'd done. She must not have spoken to Andy yet or they would be together, celebrating their perfect future. I hated that I'd hurt her and was unable to apologize, at the very least. Maybe the guys were right, and I should tell her how I feel. But that would only complicate things more.

Backstage was pure chaos, with everyone in the competition scrambling to get their costumes on. We pulled our clothes out of wardrobe bags and it became a mad rush to get them on as fast as possible.

Julie darted back and forth between us, making sure our outfits were okay, fixing any last minute emergencies, and making any tweaks to the fitting. She was cosplaying as Poison Ivy with a bright red wig, a leather choker with ivy leaves, and a green plaid dress with metal buckles that was so tiny I'm not sure it actually qualified as a dress. Carla helped her with hair and makeup, dressed as Catwoman in a black leather jacket with spikes all over it, pants with jagged slices cut through them, and cats-eye sunglasses perched on her head.

We were Gotham's finest villains with a punk twist. If all of Batman's enemies had formed one giant rock band, that would be us. Julie had put the entire thing together, designing and sewing many of the clothes herself, taking inspiration from the traditional comic book costumes for each character but giving them a tough, modern edge. I had to admit we all looked pretty fucking awesome.

The others had made me go as Bane, in a black military-style vest, black cargo pants covered in zippers and straps, and combat boots. Not too different from what I wore on stage, though I missed my Villain Complex hat.

"Looking good," Julie said, inspecting my costume. "But where's your mask?"

I crossed my arms. "I'm not wearing the mask."

"You have to wear it. Without it you just look like a muscular guy in black."

"Fine with me."

She gave me a look that didn't leave any room for argument. I groaned and grabbed the stupid bandana. It was black and white and went over my mouth and nose, a more everyday version of Bane's mask. "Fine."

"Mmm, you are the sexiest villain ever," Jared said to Maddie, yanking her close and kissing her. They were dressed as Gotham's most notorious couple, with Jared as the Joker in dark purple pants covered in patches and chains, a black t-shirt that said "Ha ha ha" in green letters, and a studded leather jacket. Maddie was Harley Quinn with a short, sexy dress that alternated between red and black under a jacket like Jared's, plus matching knee-high tights and boots. Her look was complete with a light blond wig done in pigtails, a leather collar around her neck, and her signature black-rimmed glasses.

"No kissing!" Julie snapped at them. "You'll ruin your makeup."

Kyle had his arms around Alexis and looked like he was about to break that rule, too. He was going as Two-Face with his wild hair and a costume that had one side in black leather with spikes and chains, the other side smooth, simple, and white. Beside him, Alexis looked super hot as a genderbent version of the Riddler, wearing a tight green top with question marks all over it, black cut off shorts, purple sunglasses and boots, and a tiny bowler hat over her long red hair.

I enjoyed checking out all the girls in their costumes, but the only one that made me absolutely speechless—and instantly hard—was Tara. Julie had somehow pulled off an amazing last minute costume, transforming Tara into a female version of the Penguin. She was in all black and white with a leather mini-skirt, thigh-high fishnets, and those killer leather boots that showed off her shapely legs. She had on that corset from her pirate costume that brought back all sorts of erotic memories, along with a bowtie at her neck, fingerless biker gloves, and a top hat.

She looked so hot I wanted to bend her over and take her from behind like I'd done last night. Or pin her against the nearest wall and wrap her legs around me like I'd done the other night. But neither of those was going to happen ever again. I had to accept that we were over.

As we got ready, she stayed as far away from me as she could. The other girls hovered around her, keeping her busy at all times, like they were protecting her from me. I was glad they'd become friends and that she with us tonight, even if it meant I had to spend hours in her presence, trying not to go crazy knowing Andy could show up and propose at any minute.

Once Julie approved all of our costumes, we were taken to another room with a panel of judges. They had us pose for pictures and inspected our costumes. I reluctantly wore my Bane bandana the entire time even though it was uncomfortable as shit. I hoped Maddie and Jared appreciated it. I liked Julie too, but for my best friend and the girl who'd turned his life around? I'd dress up in whatever the hell they wanted.

After the judging and photos we were sent backstage again and told to wait until it was time to go on. Inside Ballroom 20 the show was starting, but we could only make out muffled microphone voices and music. There were no chairs backstage, so we leaned against a wall and surveyed the other costumes around us.

I couldn't stop looking at Tara. Every second I was near her was pure torture. I had to say something. I had to apologize to her. I couldn't leave things the way they were, even if all I did was try to repair our friendship. The thought of not having her in my life at all was just too unbearable.

But right as I was about to summon the courage to talk to her, she jumped up and walked away, clutching her phone in her hand.

TWENTY-ONE

Tara

Andy texted me that he was inside the convention center, so I told him to meet me at the room we were all stuck in. He couldn't get inside since he wasn't part of the Masquerade, and I had to get a bathroom pass from one of the volunteers to slip out for a few minutes. How annoying.

I'd been dying to speak with Andy ever since Hector had flipped out on me, hoping he could shed some light on what had happened. All night I'd been tempted to say something to Hector, but wasn't sure what. I wanted to tell him about my decision, but I was still too upset with him. If he wasn't ready to apologize for being a jerk then I had nothing to say to *him* either.

The convention center had thinned out a lot now that everyone at Comic-Con was off to either grab dinner, crash in their hotel rooms, or head to other events and parties. I found Andy leaning against the second floor railing, staring down at the lobby. He'd changed clothes from when I'd last seen him, wearing a black button-up shirt over dark blue jeans, his blond hair slicked back. He looked handsome but out of place, especially next to me.

He eyed me up and down, obviously surprised by my costume. "Wow. You look…striking."

Was that a compliment? I couldn't tell. Hector would have just said I looked "smoking hot" or something. God, I missed him. I missed what we'd almost had.

"Thanks," I said, adjusting my top hat, which kept threatening to fall off despite the bobby pins Carla had stuck in it. "What did you want to talk about?"

He gestured for me to follow him and we moved down the hall and around a corner, to where it was a little more quiet. There wasn't really any privacy in a place like Comic-Con though. I hoped he would be fast; I wasn't sure how long I had before we would be sent on stage.

"I don't have much time," I said. "What's going on? Did you say something to Hector earlier?"

"I wanted to do this over dinner, but you've been so busy. But it doesn't matter. I have some great news." He took both my gloved hands in his, and I let him. "I'm moving to New York."

I blinked at him, the words not registering for a second. "What happened to the job in Dallas?"

"I changed my mind and found a job in New York so I can be with you." He gave me a huge smile and took a step closer, so we were only inches away. "Isn't it great? We can even get an apartment together. I know you were worried about moving there on your own, and now you don't have to."

I stared into his warm, hazel eyes, and for a second I was tempted. Maybe it was my destiny to take the New York job and get back together with Andy. Things with him had always been good. Our relationship had been easy, comfortable, and practical. We'd been together a year and had never fought. We'd always had fun together. He was great in bed. Not Hector great, but pretty close.

And working in publishing in New York was my dream job. It was more stable than the LA one, and didn't have the complication of being in the same city as Hector.

Being with Andy would be easier than being alone, right?

I could see my future stretch out before me...and it wasn't bad at all. Andy didn't set me on fire from the inside out like Hector did, but maybe that was better. In the end, Hector had only burned me.

Hector didn't want me. Andy did.

I didn't know how to respond. My head said one thing and my heart said another. "I'm just...I'm shocked."

"I know it's a lot to take in. But the last few days without you have been miserable. I'll do anything to win you back." He got down on one knee in the middle of the hallway and held out a small jewelry box. "I love you, Tara. Now that we're both going to be in the same city, I know we can make it work. Will you marry me?"

TWENTY-TWO

Hector

"What are you doing? Go after her, you idiot," Jared said.

I crossed my arms. "Why? What's the point?"

Kyle rolled his eyes. "The point is that you love her, dumbass. And you need to make this right, before it's too late."

"It's better off this way."

Jared draped an arm across my shoulders. "Hector, we've been friends a long time, and I know what a stubborn ass you can be. I also know that you're one of the most sensitive guys in the world, even though you'll never admit it. Now get over yourself and tell her how you feel before she gets engaged to some other guy. If she turns you down, at least you tried. But if you don't do it, you'll spend the rest of your life wondering what could have happened."

"Shut up," I growled.

"Face it, you're a big, grumpy teddy bear," Kyle said, grinning. "And for some crazy reason Tara seems to think that's hot."

"She's going to marry Andy. I don't want to get in their way."

Maddie lightly placed a hand on my arm. "But Hector, she doesn't want to be with Andy. She loves *you*."

Impossible. Someone as perfect as Tara loving me? No fucking way. She was sunlight on warm summer days and I was a starless night with cold, stiff rain. She could have any guy she wanted. Why in hell would she choose me?

"She doesn't love me."

"She does. Trust me on this one." Maddie sounded so confident I almost believed her.

Almost.

But if Tara really did love me that changed everything.

My whole life was heavy and there were only three things that made it lighter: drawing, drumming, and her. I was good at building walls, not tearing them down.

But for her? I'd try my hardest. For her, I'd give this long distance thing a shot. No matter what job she took, no matter what city she lived in, I'd move mountains to be with her.

Unless I was too late already.

Jesus, what had I done? I'd told her I didn't feel anything for her as more than a friend. I'd told her to take the New York job. Hell, I'd practically shoved her into Andy's arms. I had to find her and tell her how I felt before I lost her forever.

"Where did she go?" I asked.

Maddie gestured to one of the doors. "I saw her get a bathroom pass, so she must be right outside."

Jared thumped me on the back. "Good luck."

I rushed past them and to the volunteer at the door, snatching the bathroom pass from her hand without a word. Tara wasn't right outside, but she had to be around here somewhere. I headed in the direction of the closest bathroom to look for her, preparing a speech inside my head. Trying to come up with something that would convince her she belonged with me and not Andy.

But when I turned the corner, I saw them. Tara's back was to me so I couldn't see her face, but in front of her Andy was on bended knee, holding out a ring. The sight tore through me like a grenade going off at my feet, flaying every inch of my heart with shrapnel. I could only watch in stunned silence for a beat, before turning on my heel and walking away, choking on the words I'd never be able to say to her.

I was too late.

TWENTY-THREE

Tara

A ndy flicked open the jewelry box, revealing an engagement ring. I gasped and covered my mouth with my gloved hand, too stunned to speak. He stared up at me with a hopeful expression on his face, and a few people stopped outside the bathroom to watch the scene unfold.

He waited for an answer, but I didn't have one. My eyes were locked on the box with the ring I'd wear for the rest of my life if I said yes. Inside was a small diamond solitaire on a gold band.

A *gold* band.

I clutched at the amethyst pendant around my neck, with its sterling silver chain. I was allergic to gold. Hector knew that.

After a year, how could Andy not?

I'd told him before that I wasn't ready for marriage. We'd broken up and I'd never hinted I wanted to get back together with him—and now he was *proposing?* Why in the world would he think that was a good idea? Especially at Comic-Con, of all places.

No, I couldn't do this. I couldn't accept a life that wasn't *bad*. I wanted a life I woke up every day feeling grateful for and excited about—even if the path to get there was difficult. And I didn't want a love that was easy, comfortable, or practical. I wanted a love that set my every nerve on fire, that made me forget what day it was, that breathed life back into me.

That life was in LA.

That love was Hector.

"I'm sorry Andy, but I'm not moving to New York."

"You're not?" His hand faltered, dropping to his side, but didn't put the ring away.

"No. I'm taking a job in LA."

"I see." He nodded slowly. "Okay. That's not ideal, but we can make it work. I'll find a job there instead."

"No!" I blurted out. "Andy…even if we live in the same city, it's over."

He stood up and shoved the jewelry box in his pocket. "I don't understand. We broke up because we were moving to different cities, but that isn't a problem anymore. We can still be together."

I sighed. "That wasn't the only reason we broke up."

"But…I love you. You said you loved me. We've been together for a year. I don't get it. What did I do wrong?"

"You didn't do anything wrong. You were a great boyfriend. It just…wasn't enough. I'm sorry."

"It's him, isn't it?" Andy asked, his eyes narrowing. "All this time, you've been in love with Hector. I tried not to be jealous of your relationship with him. I tried to give you space because you said you were just friends. But you've been cheating on me with him, haven't you?"

"No! It was never like that between us."

Except now I realized it kind of was.

Hector was the one I dreamed about when I went to bed and the one I woke up thinking about. He was the first person I rushed to share both good and bad news with. The person I trusted more than anyone else in the world. The person I missed when I didn't talk to him for even a few hours. The person who made me smile even on my darkest days.

We'd never had anything romantic until this week—but in my heart it had *always* been him.

I realized now I'd been in love with Hector for years, I'd just never allowed myself to admit it because we couldn't be together. I'd tried to deny it, tried as hard as I could to fall in love with Andy, but the person I wanted to spend all my waking hours with had always been Hector. Andy and the guys before him had just been substitutes, at least subconsciously. Once I'd finally met Hector in person, it made me realize just how much I'd been missing with everyone else.

"Just give me another shot," Andy said. "Please. I'll do whatever you want."

My eyes watered because I knew this was going to hurt Andy and because this hurt me, too. It was hard to say goodbye to someone who had once been so important in my life, but I was confident in my decision. There had been nothing wrong with Andy or with our relationship—but there hadn't been anything special about it either. We were together because we'd been together for months and got along great and because change was hard. That's why graduation and moving to new cities had been the perfect excuse to break it off.

But even if I didn't end up with Hector, I couldn't be with Andy. I'd rather be alone than with a guy who wasn't right for me, and it wouldn't be fair to him to keep leading him on. As difficult as it was, this had to end now—for good.

"I'm sorry, Andy, but I can't. You need a girl who will love you the way you deserve and I am just not that girl. I'm so sorry."

He bowed his head and looked so dejected I wanted to hug him. "I guess I knew it was over but I thought…I don't know. I wanted to put everything out there and see if I could make it work between us. I even asked Hector and he told me to do it. Guess we were both wrong…"

My heart stopped, like the entire world had fallen out from under my feet. "Hector knew you were going to propose?"

"Yeah, I told him about it at your signing. Why?"

"Oh my god. It all makes sense now." All the pieces connected in my head, making me dizzy. Hector's sudden reversal. His lies about how he wanted to sleep around. His insistence on me taking the New York job. He must have thought I still had feelings for Andy, and believed he was doing the right thing by pushing me away.

"I need to get back," I said to Andy, giving him a quick hug. "Take care of yourself, okay? You're a great guy, and I know you'll find the right girl for you soon."

"Yeah. Thanks." He muttered the words and I hated that it had to end this way between us. I hoped he could forgive me and move on, and that maybe one day we could be friends again.

But right now, I had to find Hector.

TWENTY-FOUR

Hector

It was done. Tara was engaged.

And somehow I had to get over her.

I drew in a ragged breath. I knew I should return to my friends and get ready to go on stage, but I needed to be alone for a few minutes first. The patio outside Ballroom 20 had fit the bill perfectly since it was cool, dark, and, most importantly, empty.

I leaned against the balcony and stared across the marina at the twinkling lights on the water. The sun had set, but I could make out the pirate ship we'd been on the other night, a large cruise ship, and even a huge Navy battleship. On the grass below me, people were already camping out for tomorrow's Hall H panels, like we'd done last night.

Comic-Con was almost over. Tomorrow, Tara would fly back to Boston to prepare for her future in New York. I would get on a tour bus and start working with the band on songs for our album. Everything would return to the way it was supposed to. I just wished it didn't feel so fucking *wrong*.

"Hector!"

Tara's voice was breathless, like she'd been running. I turned, taking in her flushed cheeks and disheveled hair. She looked as beautiful as ever, and it made my heart clench. What was she doing here? Why wasn't she with Andy?

This was it. My last chance to tell her how I felt. Jared and the others were right—I would regret it forever if I didn't try to fight for her. I was done pretending, done making excuses, done lying and keeping secrets. I'd just throw everything out there and if she turned me down, well, things couldn't be any worse than they were now.

"Tara, I—"

"Hector, why—"

We both spoke at once and then shut up. I held up a hand to stop her. "Please, I need to tell you something before you marry Andy."

She opened her mouth like she wanted to interrupt, but I kept going. I had to, otherwise I'd never get the words out.

"Tara, I love you." Damn, it felt good to say that out loud after keeping it a secret for so long. "I've loved you for years. From the very beginning, it's always been you."

Her eyes widened, sparkling with starlight. "Hector—"

"You asked me why I haven't had a girlfriend in a long time, and I lied to you twice. The real reason is because my heart belongs to you. I haven't been able to even look at another girl for years." I took a step toward her, more nervous than I'd been in ages, yet unable to stop the confession now that I'd started. "I know it's too late, but I had to tell you how I really feel about you. If you still want to marry Andy, I'll accept that and we never have to talk about this again. We can go back to being friends, if that's what you want. But if you do feel something for me, then I'm willing to do the long distance thing. I'll do whatever it takes so I don't lose you. These past few days with you have been the best in my life, and I can't let you go home without—"

"Hector, stop!" She yelled the words but she was smiling, her face radiant. "I told Andy no."

"You…you said no?"

"I turned him down." She wrinkled her pretty nose. "He got me a gold ring."

"But you're allergic to gold."

"I know!" She smiled wider, gripping the necklace I'd given her. "But that's not the only reason I said no."

I couldn't breathe, couldn't think, couldn't dare to hope. "It's not?"

"No. I don't love him." She closed the distance between us, sliding her arms around my neck, looking up at me with shining eyes. "I love *you*, Hector."

For a long beat all I could do was stare at her, too shocked to respond. Then I hauled her against me and captured her mouth with mine. She responded eagerly, locking her fingers in my hair, fitting her body against me. It was a kiss full of love and hope, a kiss that promised happy endings, a kiss that sucked all the darkness out of me and replaced it with light. Her light.

I rested my head against her forehead. "I never thought I would hear you say those words."

"I didn't realize it until this week, but I've been in love with you for a long time. I should have figured it out sooner."

"No, *I* should have told you how I felt sooner."

"It doesn't matter. We're together now." Between each word she pressed small kisses all over my mouth, my cheek, my jaw. "Oh, and I'm taking the LA job."

"You are?"

"Yep. Not because of you, though, but because I want it more than the other job."

I laughed and picked her up, spinning her around once before setting her on the ground and kissing her again. My heart was so full it nearly hurt. She loved me and she was moving to LA. I didn't know how it was possible, but I wasn't going to argue it. If she wanted to be with me I was never letting her go.

"There you are," Julie said, behind us. "I hate to ruin your happily ever after, but it's time for us to go on stage. And you better not have messed up your makeup or, god forbid, your costumes."

Oh right. The Masquerade. I'd forgotten about that.

"Sorry," Tara said, blushing. "We'll be right there."

We followed Julie backstage, holding hands the entire time, and the group whooped and cheered when they saw us enter together. I scowled at them, or tried to, at least. It was hard to don my usual grumpy face at the moment.

Julie checked our costumes and makeup, clucking at Tara for messing up her hair and lipstick. They fixed it, I wrapped the bandana around my face, and then it was time to go on stage.

Ballroom 20 wasn't as big as the massive Hall H but had a grander feel to it. Aisles and aisles of red chairs had been set up across the scrolling carpet in front of the stage, and screens hung from the ceiling at regular intervals so everyone could see what was happening, even in the back.

Our song "Behind the Mask" started playing through the speakers, and the Comic-Con volunteers waved us on. We went out in pairs, with Alexis and Kyle first, in their Riddler and Two-Face costumes. They strolled onto the stage and posed while the music played behind them. Tara and I were next, as the Penguin and Bane, and I lifted my bandana to give her a quick kiss before we joined them out there. Next up were Carla and Julie cosplaying as Catwoman and Poison Ivy, walking onto the stage like they owned it. Finally, Jared and Maddie emerged as the Joker and Harley Quinn. When they got to the middle he took her in his arms and dipped her on the stage, pulling her in for a kiss while the audience cheered and clapped.

For a few beats we posed while the announcers read out our names, and then our time was up and we walked backstage again. It all happened so fast, but I was used to that kind of chaos from our concerts and from being on *The Sound*. Still, it was always a rush to be in front of an audience, whether it was playing drums or doing something like this. And this time it was even better because I had Tara at my side.

TWENTY-FIVE

Tara

After we exited the stage we were directed to the press area to pose for photos as a group in front of a white background with the Comic-Con logo all over it. We stood there for a good fifteen minutes or so before they brought the next group up, who were all dressed in extremely detailed *Bioshock* costumes.

A Comic-Con volunteer ran up to us. "Which one of you is Julie Hong?"

Her eyebrows shot up. "That's me."

"Your group won an award." The man checked his paperwork. "The, ah…*Behind The Seams* Award?"

"What?" Julie shrieked.

"*Behind The Seams*, like the reality TV show?" Alexis asked.

"That's the one," the guy said. "You did enter to win that, yes? It was an optional category…"

"Yes, I definitely entered." Julie fanned herself with her hand. "I won? Seriously?"

"You did. You have to come on stage and accept during the awards ceremony at the end of the show, but the sponsor wants to talk to you first."

"No freaking way!" Julie turned to us, her eyes like saucers. "You guys, can you believe it?"

Maddie hugged her. "I believe it. Your costumes were amazing!"

We all crowded around Julie and offered congratulations. I gave her a hug too, and she squeezed me back as hard as she did the others.

"Thanks, everyone," she said. "I couldn't have done it without you. It was originally just going to be me, Maddie, and Carla, but it became so much better after the rest of you joined us."

"You did all the hard work," Kyle said. "We just had to stand there and look pretty."

"Easier for some of us than others," Jared said, winking.

Julie laughed and wiped at her eyes. "But seriously. I wouldn't have won without your help."

"We'll have to celebrate at the afterparty," Hector said, wrapping an arm around me.

"Definitely," I said. I was so happy to be part of this group and so excited for my future with them. My new friends. My new love. My new life.

Giselle Roberts appeared next to our group, with her blond hipster assistant at her side. "Sorry, am I interrupting?"

Julie's eyes flared as she recognized who had joined us. "Oh wow, *you're* the sponsor? I mean, of course you are! You created *Behind The Seams*. I just…I didn't expect…"

Giselle gave one of her bubbly little laughs. "I am the creator and producer, yes, and I'm delighted to offer you a spot in our upcoming season as part of the award, if you're interested. The only thing is it starts filming next week and lasts a few weeks, culminating in New York Fashion Week in early September, so I'll understand if you can't make it. But I was impressed with your villain-themed punk rock collection tonight, and I think you would do really well on the show. I'd love to have you on it."

"This is the most exciting thing that's ever happened to me!" Julie said. "Um, yes! I would love to be on the show. I'm on summer break until the middle of September, so I can definitely make it."

"Perfect. My assistant here will take down all your information and contact you after Comic-Con with all the details."

Julie threw her arms around the woman. "Thank you, thank you, thank you. I won't let you down, I promise!"

"I'm sure you won't." She pulled back and caught my eye with a smile. "Hello, Tara. I didn't realize you were part of this group. I swear, I didn't pick Julie as the winner for that reason."

"I would never think that," I said. "But could we talk alone for a minute?"

"Of course."

We moved away from the group and into a quieter corner of the backstage area. Her assistant stayed behind, jotting down Julie's contact information.

"Have you come to a decision?" Giselle asked.

"I have. And I want to take the job."

"Great! I never doubted you would."

"There's just one thing I want to run past you." I resisted the urge to bite my fingernails and instead gripped my amethyst pendant. It had always given me strength, and I realized it was because it made me feel like Hector was with me even when he wasn't. "I think you should do a comic book tie-in for the show. You could have one come out each week online and use it to give origin stories for different superheroes and villains, or show superheroes in different parts of the world and what they're up to. It would make the world of your TV show feel so much bigger, and be a fun thing for your fans. Plus it might bring in more of the hardcore comic book readers."

She tapped a finger against her lips as she listened to my spiel. "I like this idea. A lot. So you'd write this for me?"

"I would, if you're open to it."

"Hmm. I think that could work. I want you to help with the individual episodes, too, though. I want you to be a vital part of the team, shaping the direction of the show for as long as it's on. But you could split your time between the two projects." She nodded, her eyes far away as the gears in her head turned. "Yes, I love this idea. You'll be even more involved this way. Now we just need an artist or two…"

I smiled. "I know the perfect guy."

TWENTY-SIX

Hector

After Julie got her award and the show ended we headed back to our hotel for the villain afterparty Jared had set up. I just wanted to sneak up to Tara's hotel room, but everyone insisted we stay and celebrate for a while.

The club was small and had a goth look to it, with chandeliers dripping with red lights, black velvet walls, and leather booths. The bar was lit in an eerie blue and the drinks all came in glowing skull glasses. Jared had talked extensively with the DJ earlier to make sure the music met his approval, and he must have done a good job because the club was packed with people dancing, wearing costumes ranging from Maleficent to Loki to Green Goblin. We were all still in our costumes too, the eight of us crammed into the largest booth in the corner.

Jared raised his glowing glass in a toast. "Julie, let's hope your reality TV show experience goes much smoother than ours did."

"Hey, it didn't turn out so badly," Maddie said, giving him a playful shove.

"Very true." He raised his glass higher. "To Julie!"

We all toasted as a group and took a sip of whatever we were drinking. I chugged my beer, feeling content for the first time in as long as I could remember. Good friends, good drinks, and good music. Not to mention a beautiful girl at my side who loved me. What more could I want?

"So you're really going on that show?" Alexis asked.

"I think so," Julie said, laughing. "My parents won't like it, but…yeah, I'm going to do it. Why not?"

"You should get Carla to be your model," Kyle said.

"Hey, that's a good idea. What do you say, Carla?"

She tilted her head and considered. "I'll have to think about it."

A blonde walked into the club wearing a tank top that read, "This *is* my slutty costume." I straightened up. "Oh, shit. Becca is here."

"Your former bassist?" Tara asked.

Jared shrugged. "Well, I *did* invite her."

I kept my eye on her as she perched at the bar. "Just as long as she doesn't cause any trouble."

"Nah, I think she really has changed," Kyle said.

"We'll see."

"Come on, let's dance," Alexis said, dragging Kyle out of the booth.

Julie downed the rest of her glowing drink. "Time for me to find a guy I can bring back to our hotel room."

"Hey, that's my hotel room, too," Carla muttered.

"And mine," Maddie said.

"Nah, you'll be in my room all night," Jared said, nuzzling her ear. "I have all sorts of naughty things planned for you in that costume. And I still have some of that whip cream…"

Tara leaned against me and whispered, "Sounds like you'll be spending the night in my room."

"Can't complain about that." I slid an arm around her back and pulled her in for a kiss.

"Check out that guy in the Rocket Raccoon costume," Julie said, nodding toward the bar.

"Does that even count as a costume?" Maddie asked. "He's wearing an orange shirt with raccoon ears and a tail. That's not trying very hard."

Julie stood up and smoothed out her dress. "When he looks like that, who cares?"

"It's just…not right," Carla said. "He's hot, but then he has ears. And a tail."

"I know. That just makes it hotter." She grinned and slipped off to flirt with him. Carla trailed behind her, shaking her head.

The group split up, with each of us going our separate ways inside the club. Tara and I stayed in the booth while she told me about her idea for a comic book related to Giselle's show. She'd suggested that I do the art, but I wasn't sure how I'd juggle the band, *Misfit Squad,* and another project on top of that. I told her I'd consider it. At least I was finally making enough money from my music and my art that I wouldn't have to go back to my job at the art supply store after the tour.

On stage, Maddie and Jared started belting out "Don't Stop Believin'" by Journey, beginning the karaoke portion of the night. They both had amazing voices and alternated the verses but harmonized on the chorus, sending little chills down my spine. From the way they sang together, working the stage with their eyes locked on each other, it was obvious how much they loved each other.

As they sang, Alexis and Kyle danced close, lightly brushing their lips together like they were in their own world and nothing existed around them.

And this time, I wasn't jealous.

"Never thought I'd see the Joker and Harley Quinn singing *that* song," I said.

Tara smiled as she watched them. "They're so cute together."

"I know. Hard to believe that a few months ago Jared would sleep with anything with boobs and Maddie was too shy to even play guitar on stage."

Tara laughed. "I remember you telling me you were worried they would sleep together. But it worked out."

I glanced between Jared and Kyle and the women they loved before turning back to mine. "I guess it did…for all of us."

I was about to drag her in for another long kiss, when I spotted Andy moving through the crowd, wearing the same clothes as when he'd proposed to Tara. I nudged her. "Look who's here."

"Oh, god." She shrank down in the booth, but Andy had already seen us. I was surprised he would show up tonight after what had gone down, but he didn't look mad or anything. Still, I moved away from Tara, since there was no need to rub it in his face or anything. I felt bad for the poor guy.

"Hey," he said, with a weak smile. "Just wanted to say that I'm sorry about everything. And I do want to be friends."

"You don't need to be sorry for anything," Tara said, but from her rigid posture I could tell this whole encounter made her uneasy.

"Thanks." He shoved his hands in his pockets. "I decided to take the Dallas job after all. Don't suppose you know anyone there?"

"I do, actually. A friend of mine is moving there soon." I stood and slapped a hand on his back. "Come on, I'll buy you a drink and introduce you to that hot blonde over there." I directed him toward the bar, and Tara gave me a grateful smile as we walked away.

I led him over to Becca and practically shoved the guy at her. I noticed she was drinking a soda—no alcohol for her anymore. "Hey, Becca. Glad you could make it. This is Andy. Andy, Becca used to be the bassist in my band."

"Nice to meet you," Andy said, shaking her hand. "I like your shirt."

She looked him up and down with a flirty smile. "Thanks. I don't do the whole costume thing."

"No, me either." He sat on the stool next to her. "So Hector said you're moving to Dallas?"

I waved for the bartender to get them whatever they wanted and put it on our tab, and left the two of them alone to talk. Maybe nothing would come of it, but at least I'd tried. They might even be good together—Becca needed a nice guy, and Andy could probably use a little bit of trouble.

I returned to Tara with another round of drinks, and Maddie and Jared joined us after their song was over.

"You two were amazing up there," Tara said.

Maddie smiled, leaning against Jared. "Thanks. I wasn't sure I could hit some of those notes but it wasn't too bad in the end."

He kissed her cheek. "You were incredible, just as I predicted. We should ask Dan if we can add that song to our set."

I kicked him under the table. "Dude, no. The last thing we need right now is another song to learn."

"But I already know the guitar for it," Maddie confessed, with a smile.

"Of course you do."

Julie was up next at karaoke, taking on Beyoncé's "Single Ladies." Rocket Raccoon was nowhere to be seen, but Carla joined her on stage and the two of them got tons of whistles in their Poison Ivy and Catwoman costumes as they did the famous dance together. They gestured for Maddie and Tara to join them, but they shook their heads. Instead, Alexis hopped on stage and started doing the dance with the other girls while Kyle cheered them on.

"That'd be a fun song to try to cover, too," Jared said.

"No more songs," I growled. "Unless they're our own."

He laughed. "Okay, fine. But maybe once the tour is over and the album is done…"

"Pretty sure we'll have enough to practice as is."

"When I'm in LA, can I come watch you practice sometime?" Tara asked.

A thrill ran through me at the reminder she'd be living there in a few weeks. "Any time you want."

"And I want to go to that tattoo parlor you mentioned, too."

Jared arched an eyebrow. "You want to get a tattoo?"

"Thinking about it. Hector's going to design something for me in honor of *Misfit Squad* coming out."

Maddie bounced a little in the booth. "Ooh, I want to get one, too! We can all go together."

"What will you get?" I asked her.

"I'm going to get a heart made out of a treble clef and a bass clef. Maybe on my wrist. Or my shoulder. I haven't decided."

"I still don't know what to get," Tara said.

I wrapped an arm around her. "I'll sketch out a few things while we're on the road and email them to you."

"Okay, I—" Tara suddenly pointed at the bar. "Oh my god, look!"

Becca was in Andy's lap, her tongue down his throat, his hands on her ass. The first couple buttons of his shirt were undone, and the drink next to him was empty. Damn, he'd moved on fast. I grinned, pleased with myself for introducing them. Even if it never went further than tonight, at least they were having some fun.

"Good for her," Maddie said. "He's cute."

"That's my ex," Tara said, laughing. "I'm so glad he's okay."

"Not jealous?" I asked.

"Not even close." She slid her hand along my thigh, higher and higher. "You're the one I want to be with."

I buried my face in her silky, gold strands. "I can't wait to get you alone so I can do dirty things to you in that costume."

"We could go up to my room if you want…"

"Oh, I very much want."

TWENTY-SEVEN

Tara

Once in my hotel room, we couldn't keep our hands off each other. He grabbed my top hat and flung it across the room before his mouth descended on my bare shoulders. "I can't decide if I want to rip those clothes off you or take you in them."

I closed my eyes as he pressed kisses across my neck and nipped at my bowtie. "Julie will be mad if you rip them."

"Option two it is." He trailed a finger from my collarbone down to the gap between my breasts.

"Not yet," I said, pushing him away with a smile. "It's my turn to touch you."

His dark eyes flashed with lust, his pouty lips curling in a grin. I moved behind him to remove his military vest, sliding it off his broad shoulders and admiring his powerful back. I ran my hands across his beautiful skin, feeling the strength coiled under those muscles. He turned around, and my gaze lingered on the masculine contours of his chest, drinking in the sight of him.

I took my time, thoroughly exploring every inch of his bare skin, from the definition of his stomach to the swell of his biceps to the darker skin of his nipples. He was so insanely touchable and I couldn't get enough. I opened his pants and took his length in my hand, loving the soft yet hard feel of him. I was still wearing my fingerless biker gloves from my costume, but, if anything, that only excited him more.

"Fuck, Tara, you turn me on so much."

"I do?" I asked, even though I held the evidence of it in my hand. But I wanted to hear him say it.

"You always have," he said, his voice husky. "You don't know how many times I had to jerk off or take a cold shower after talking with you."

"God, the thought of you touching yourself while thinking about me…it makes me want you even more." My lips brushed against his jaw and he caught my mouth with his. He ran his tongue against mine in the most erotic way, making me completely weak in the knees.

"I thought about you too, all the time," I said, while I undid his belt buckle and eased his pants off. I removed every other stitch of his clothing so he stood before me naked, while I remained dressed.

He groaned. "Tara..."

Before he could say another word I dropped to my knees. He cried out something in Spanish as I slid my lips over his length, flicking my tongue along the tip of him. I stroked his shaft as I licked up and down in one long motion, before taking him deeper in my mouth.

His hands locked in my hair as I glided him in and out, licking and sucking and worshiping him with both my mouth and my fingers. I looked up his long body and saw his head thrown back, his throat exposed, his eyes clenched tight. I had never seen anything more arousing than that image, and knowing I had done that to him made it even hotter.

I dug my nails into his perfect, hard butt, bringing him closer, deeper, working him over completely with my lips and tongue. His hips jerked, his hands tightened, and he muttered that he was close, but I didn't want to stop. I wanted to do something just for him, to feel the power of making him fall apart for me. And seconds later, he did. I watched it all, memorizing the sounds he made, the way his face tensed up, the way he lost control.

It took a minute for him to recover, but then he reached down and picked me up in his arms in one easy movement. "You are one naughty girl," he said, giving me a long, thorough kiss before gently tossing me on the bed. "But how is this fair? I haven't had a chance to play with you yet."

He slid up my body to brush his lips along the top of my breasts, which were pushed up from the corset. He loosened the laces on the front, just enough to make my breasts burst out of them. The cooler air hit and I gasped, but then his mouth descended on my nipples, warming me instantly. His tongue did amazing things to each one, making me arch up against him.

He dragged off my panties but left everything else on. He definitely liked when I wore costumes. I'd have to remember that...

He gripped my boots and forced my legs apart, placing a tender kiss on each inside thigh right where my fishnets ended. He worked his way up, my mini-skirt inching higher and higher as I opened wider for him. I moaned as his head dropped between my thighs, his tongue flicking along my sensitive skin. He dipped a finger inside me as he sucked and licked, and it nearly sent me over the edge right there.

I spread for him, letting him worship me with his mouth and his fingers, taking everything he wanted to give me. Hector made me feel desirable and powerful and adored in a way that no other man ever had. Like he loved me, but also desperately wanted me.

But soon it was too much and I thought I would burst from the intense sensations moving through me. He had me writhing on the bed, gripping his hair so hard I knew it had to hurt, making me practically scream his name. I fell apart, and he put me back together again.

I wiped sweaty hair off my forehead, trying to catch my breath, while he sat up and moved beside me. I noticed he was already at attention again. "Ready so soon?" I asked.

"Hey, I've been holding this in for years." He played with my bowtie, slowly undoing it and pulling it off my neck. "And going down on you turns me on."

I pushed against his chest, forcing him to lie back on the bed. I found a condom and got it on him, both of us laughing when I had a hard time getting it over his impressive size. We were giddy, wrapped up in love for each other, in the knowledge we didn't have to rush because we could do this for many nights to come.

He grinned up at me as I moved over him, straddling his waist. I slid onto him slowly, closing my eyes and savoring the exquisite way he filled me. My skirt was pushed up around my hips, my boots resting on either side of his thighs, my breasts hanging free from my corset. He seemed to love the view, and with my gloved hands pressed flat on his well-defined chest I certainly wasn't complaining either.

I started to ride him, slowly at first but building into a frenzy. He gripped my butt, helping me along and matching my pace with his hips, and we moved together in a rhythm that soon spiraled out of control. My back arched as the sensations grew stronger, as my body took him deeper inside. Our eyes stayed locked the entire time, and there were no secrets between us, no more pretending, just raw honesty and intimacy. Pleasure swept through me like a tidal wave, threatening to drown me. I let it take me away, and Hector joined me a second later.

I lay against his chest and he circled his arms around me, his body rising and falling with each heavy breath. "*Te quiero*," I said, and this time he didn't flinch away. "I know what it really means."

"*Te quiero, te amo, te adoro*," he whispered, pressing a kiss to my forehead. "Three ways of saying I love you."

I closed my eyes, relaxing into his warmth. "Mmm, you can speak Spanish to me all night long."

"Only if I get to do other things to you, too."

And that's exactly what he did.

TWENTY-EIGHT

Hector

Tara and I spent the last day of Comic-Con wandering the exhibit hall together, where many of the vendors were having sales so they didn't have to drag home all their stuff. She bought me a Red Power Ranger keychain, which she found way more amusing than I did. I got her a mug that said, "Writing Is My Superpower" with a silhouette of a girl with a cape holding a book. I also picked up a few things for my sisters, including an autographed picture of that *Arrow* guy for Yasmine. We signed a few extra copies of our book for Black Hat Comics to sell, and said goodbye to Miguel and the rest of the crew working there.

The day went by way too fast, and was over before I knew it.

Our giant tour bus waited in front of our hotel, with *The Sound* logo and a picture of Dan and the other mentors plastered on the side of it. The band's home for the next month while we were on tour. All our stuff had already been loaded into it, and we had to hit the road if we wanted to make Phoenix in time for our show tomorrow night.

For the first time, I no longer wanted to go.

I wrapped my arms around Tara, holding her against my chest. "I can't believe I finally have you, but now I won't see you for a month."

She smiled up at me. "We've done the online thing for years. One more month is nothing."

"Yeah, but now I know what I've been missing all that time."

She lifted up to kiss me on the nose. "You're such a grump. But as strange as it sounds, I think this time apart will be good for me. I need to move to LA on my own and be alone for a while, at least until I'm settled in. The girls will help me if I need anything, but I'm looking forward to being independent, too."

I nodded. If she was happy, then I was happy. "And then you'll be in LA and we'll see each other all the time. I'm already dreaming about the things I want do to you when I get back."

"God, I can't wait. Being able to see you whenever I want…what a delicacy."

I chuckled. "A delicacy? Hey, I'm not a piece of meat."

"You were definitely good enough to eat last night."

"Damn girl, if I didn't already have a million reasons for loving you, you just added another to my list."

"Aw, I love you too," she said, drawing me in for a kiss.

"Sorry to break up the party, but we need to get going," Jared said, wearing a t-shirt that said, "Life's More Fun With Villains."

I gave Tara one long kiss, while Kyle did the same with Alexis. Maddie hugged Carla and Julie, then gave Alexis and Tara each a hug, too. We each said our final goodbyes, the girls all teary-eyed, and me pretty damn close to losing it myself. Not that I'd ever admit it.

Jared and Maddie boarded the bus first, holding hands, followed by Kyle. I was the last one to step on, not wanting to be away from Tara for even a second longer than I had to. But as the doors shut she flashed me one of her dazzling smiles, and I knew it was only a temporary parting. She was moving to LA to start her new job, and when I returned we would finally be together.

As the bus drove away, Kyle and I watched the women we loved disappear behind us through the window.

"Damn, I already miss her," I said.

"I know what you mean. But I lived without Alexis for three years and we managed to find our way back together. After that, I know we can handle one month apart. That time is a drop in the bucket when we have the rest of our lives to be together. And the same is true for you and Tara."

"There you go, being cheesy again."

"You know you love it." He grinned at me before moving further inside the bus.

I lingered at the window, until Jared came up behind me and draped an arm across my shoulder. "You okay?"

"Yeah. It's just…weird. Tara is moving to LA. Our tour is starting. We have an album to record. Everything is changing."

"No, everything is happening exactly the way it's supposed to."

"Damn, you're even cheesier than Kyle. And when did you become the smart one in the band?"

"Please, I was always the brains of this operation. Maddie's the heart, Kyle's the soul, and you're the body. Obviously."

I laughed and he slapped me on the back with a grin. We joined Maddie and Kyle on the couch, who were trying to throw popcorn in each other's mouths. We crashed beside them and started discussing songs for our upcoming album. I was surrounded by laughter and music, and even though I missed Tara, I knew I would see her again soon. Until then, I had my band.

A few months ago, the four of us had each been lost in our own way. Things had been tough at times, but we'd stuck together and found love, started down new paths, and fought our way through the darkness. Now we faced an uncertain future, but no matter what happened we would always have each other.

We were more than a band. We were a family.

Bonus Epilogue

I hope you enjoyed More Than Comics! Read on for a bonus epilogue - exclusively in this box set!

———

This scene takes place a month after the end of More Than Comics.

TARA

I spread the pages across my dining room table. Maybe if I saw each part of the script as a whole I could figure out how to fix the gaping plot hole in the story. I stared at the mess, chewing on my lower lip, clicking my red pen in and out. Two weeks at my new job and I was already working my butt off, but I loved every minute of it.

Someone knocked on my front door. Odd, I wasn't expecting anyone today. It was Saturday, but the only visitors I'd had in my new apartment so far had been Julie, Carla, and Alexis. Last weekend they'd taken me shopping for all the stuff I'd needed to settle in, and afterward we'd ordered pizza, marathoned Parks and Recreation on Netflix, and drank enough wine to give me an epic hangover the next day.

I peered through the peephole and saw a baseball cap that said, "Villain Complex."

Hector! He was here!

I threw open the door and took him in, my eyes greedy after being away from him for a month. He towered over me, looking as handsome as ever in a black t-shirt that couldn't hide the hard, muscular body underneath. A dark curl peeked out from under his hat, trailing down his forehead, and a smile tugged at his pouty lips.

"Tara," he said, and then he took me in his strong arms and kissed me without another word. My lips parted for him eagerly and I gripped the thin fabric of his shirt, pulling him even closer. He took the strap of my dress and eased it off my shoulder, pressing a kiss to the exposed skin. My hands slid down his chest and under his shirt, along his abs, desperate to touch his skin, to be as close to him as possible. It was all I could do not to beg him to take me right there in the doorway. Wouldn't the neighbors just love that?

"I missed you so much, Hector." I pulled him inside and shut the door behind us. "But I didn't know you were back from your tour already."

"We got back early this morning. I'm tired as hell, but I couldn't wait another second longer to see you." He wrapped an arm around my waist, but instead of kissing me he traced a finger slowly down my face, across my cheek and along my jaw, his brown eyes staring into mine. "I can't believe you're really here, living in LA."

"I'm here and I'm not going anywhere." I leaned my head into his palm, smiling. "Do you want a tour of the apartment?"

"Later," he growled. "All I want right now is you."

He picked me up in his arms in one easy movement, like I weighed nothing. I laughed and directed him to the bedroom, not that it was hard to find in my tiny apartment. Once inside, he took a moment to kiss me thoroughly as I clung to his neck. I grabbed his baseball cap and dropped it on the floor, then ran my fingers through his beautiful, dark curls. God, I'd missed his gorgeous hair. It was longer than when I'd last seen him and sexier than ever. I couldn't wait to tangle my fingers in it as I screamed his name.

Hector set me down on the bed and stood over me, his gaze raking over my body. The morning sun streamed in through the sheer curtains on my windows, making his bronze skin practically glow in the light.

I smiled up at him and tugged on the bottom of his shirt. He got the hint and lifted it over his head, and the sight of his bare chest and muscular abs sent a flash of heat between my legs. He was so sexy he didn't look real. And he was *mine*.

"Wait," he said. "I brought you something."

He sat beside me on the bed and opened up a brown paper bag I had somehow failed to notice before. From inside, he pulled out one of the alcoholic whip cream cans we'd bought at Comic-Con.

I laughed. "I didn't know you kept that."

"I stole it from Maddie and Jared. Don't worry, they didn't use it first." He flipped off the cap. "Want a taste?"

"Yes." I grabbed the can from his hand before he could stop me. I pressed the top, intending to spray a tiny bit on his neck, but it was stronger than I expected and went all over his face. He jerked back and some even got in his eyes.

He laughed and wiped his face. "What was that for?"

"You moved!"

"How am I supposed to get this off me?"

My hands clutched his jaw, just under the whip cream. "Hold still."

He closed his eyes as the tip of my tongue touched his neck. I licked the whip cream off in one long stroke up his jaw and he groaned. It tasted surprisingly good, like spicy vanilla cream with a touch of rum. And Hector tasted even better.

I continued kissing all over his face, sucking the whip cream from his cheekbones, his nose, his chin, his forehead. It gave me an excuse to explore him, to really show him how much I'd missed him.

"How's that?" I asked, as I kissed the other side of his jaw.

"Pretty good…but you missed a spot."

"Did I? Where?" I kissed the very corner of his mouth. I wasn't sure there was any whip cream left but it didn't really matter. "Here?"

"Closer."

"Here?" I traced my tongue along his lower lip and he opened for me, his breathing heavy.

"Closer."

"Here?" I pressed my lips flush to his, flicking my tongue inside.

"Yes, exactly there."

His mouth captured mine in a deep kiss, while his hands pushed down the straps on my dress. He slid the fabric lower and lower until my breasts were bared, then lightly traced the sensitive skin with his fingertips until he found my nipples. He circled them slowly, sending tingles throughout my entire body. I threw my head back, the whip cream momentarily forgotten.

I tugged at the front of his jeans. "Take your clothes off."

He stood and removed the rest of his clothes, each new glimpse of skin turning me on even more. And there was no doubt he was just as excited as I was.

He was so big and hard, and I remembered how good he felt and couldn't wait to have him inside me again. But first, I wanted to have some fun.

I shook the whip cream and then sprayed it all over his shaft, completely covering him. He yelped a little, so I guessed it was cold, but he didn't move away. I grinned up at him and grabbed his butt, pulling him closer.

He groaned as I flicked my tongue along his tip, then sucked in the cream there. As he watched, I licked down his length, lapping up every drop.

"Holy shit that's hot," he said, his voice strained.

His fingers darted into my hair, gripping it hard, but I didn't stop, moving up and down, eating the cream off every inch of him. My lips dipped lower, along his balls, sucking them inside my mouth. I'd never done that before, but his hips twitched and jerked forward, so he seemed to like it.

I licked my way along him again, then swirled my tongue along his tip. All the whip cream was gone, so I took him all the way into my mouth, lips closing around his skin.

"Jesus, Tara," he said. "You're going to kill me."

He pushed me back. I licked a tiny bit off cream off the edge of my lips and smiled up at him.

He grabbed the can from me. "My turn."

———

HECTOR

I tugged her dress down to her hips, taking in the sight of her kissable shoulders and golden blonde hair trailing down her back. Her full breasts and pink nipples were stunning, both of them taut and straining for me to touch them again.

I eased her back against the bed until she lay flat, then dragged her dress all the way off. She wore only a tiny strip of lace underneath, like she'd been hoping I'd show up today, even though I wasn't supposed to be back 'til tomorrow.

Her cobalt blue eyes watched as I hooked a finger in her panties and slid them down her legs, placing a kiss on her thighs, her knees, her shins, her ankles. She giggled and pulled away, like her feet were ticklish. I'd have to remember that. I knew so much about her, but all of this was new. I wanted to discover even more of what she liked, and how her body responded. And now that we lived in the same city I had plenty of time to do that.

First, payback time.

I sprayed the whip cream onto her breasts, completely covering them, and she gasped and arched up from the shock of cold. With her full, round breasts and her pink, hard nipples on top she looked like some kind of delicious desert, just waiting for me to taste her.

I licked along the outer rim of her breast, swirling around and around, moving in closer and closer. Finally, I moved to her nipple, flicking my tongue across her, making her cry out. Damn, she tasted good. I took that nipple into my mouth, sucking and getting every last bit of cream off her. She moaned and raked her fingers through my hair as I moved to the other breast and repeated my attentions until she was clean there, too.

I sprayed the cream again, making a line down her stomach, to her hips, and between her legs. When she was completely covered I followed the trail down her soft skin with my mouth, lapping at the cream. It was a perfect way to explore her body, moving down her smooth stomach, her curvy hips, the triangle of short hair between her thighs.

She spread them wide, letting me in, and I couldn't get between them fast enough. I was hard as a rock, but I didn't want to rush this. I licked slowly, teasing along the edges, cleaning her up. She whimpered and tried to lift her hips, wanting me to taste other places, but I held her down and made her wait.

"Patience," I said, grinning up at her. "There's a lot of whip cream I have to clean up."

I dove back in, licking along her folds, lapping up both her juices and the whip cream. She moaned as I continued my exploration and licked her from the inside out. I sucked at her core, mouth pressed against her, literally eating her out, devouring her yet hungry for more. She rubbed against me, gasping, pushing my tongue deeper inside.

I flicked my tongue up, making her cry out and dig her nails into me. I couldn't decide what was more delicious: the taste of her, or the sweet sounds she made. No whip cream was left, it was just my mouth and her body, my lips and her skin, my tongue and her pleasure. I increased the pressure until she jerked under me, her thighs twitching, her hands clutching my upper arms as she came against my mouth.

While he was still trembling I slid up her body and pushed inside her to the hilt, making her cry out. I was still hard, so turned on from what she'd already done to me, and she was so wet and slippery that I pushed inside easily, filling her completely. We'd already had the birth control/STD chat a week ago on the phone, and fuck, it was amazing to be skin to skin with her for the first time.

"Every day I was on tour I thought about you," I said, staring into her eyes as I began to move. "I'd imagine you naked, the way you tasted, the feel of being inside you. But now I realize my memory never even came close to the real thing."

Her fingers tightened in my hair as she looked up at me. "Every day you were gone I listened to Villain Complex non-stop. No matter where I went or what I did, you were always with me."

Her words hit me right in the gut and I kissed her, so full of love I thought I might burst. Our eyes stayed locked together as I thrust in and out of her, slowly at first to really feel every inch of her. The tempo increased, a steady beat in time with our hearts, both growing faster and faster. She wrapped her legs around my hips, taking me deeper, lips parting as her eyes remained glued to mine. I loved the way she felt around me, how hot and tight she was, how amazing she looked below me.

"Hector, please," she cried. Damn, I loved hearing her say my name too, especially like that.

I wanted to hear it again, so I moved my hand between her thighs, seeking her out, rubbing her as I pounded into her. The bed creaked as our bodies moved together in sync, but we never looked away from each other.

Her eyes finally fluttered shut and she cried my name over and over, and I knew she was there. When she clenched up around me it sent me over the edge too, yet I kept thrusting until we were both completely spent.

I relaxed against her and she slid her arms around me, holding me close, burying her face in my neck. I breathed her in, still in disbelief that we were together again.

"*Te quiero,*" I whispered. "*Te amo. Te adoro.*" While I was gone it had become a ritual to say those three things to her every time we hung up on the phone.

"I love you too, Hector." She toyed with my hair idly, pressing light kisses to my neck.

"I'm definitely a fan of that alcoholic whip cream."

"We need to get one in every flavor."

"Good idea. I want to see which one tastes best with your skin."

"Hmm, that might require a lot of experimentation…"

"Exactly. Many, many nights of it."

And the best part was, now that we lived in the same city we could do it. We were finally going to be together. Offline. In person. In a real relationship.

She smiled up at me, her blue eyes sparkling in the morning light. "What do you want to do today?"

I'd thought about this a lot while I was gone, and it exploded out of me in a rush. "I want you to meet my sisters and my *abuelita*. I want you to hear the new songs the band wrote and watch us practice. I want to take you to all my favorite places in the city. I want to make you come a hundred more times. I want to—"

She laughed and put her hand over my mouth, stopping me. "I'm dying to do all of those things, and soon. But what's the rush?" She slid her arms around my neck. "We have plenty of time."

I returned her warm smile, and for the first time in years I felt like the darkness around me had lifted. "You're right. We have our entire lives ahead of us."

More Than Fashion

CHASING THE DREAM #3

Chapter One

S leep would be impossible tonight, even after a couple drinks. I had that jumpy kind of feeling I always got right before a big event. Christmas Eve. The first day of college. Leaving on vacation.

Or the night before going on a reality TV show that could change my life forever.

I tipped back my head, swallowed the last of my pink martini, and slammed the glass down. Staying up all night with a mix of anxiety and excitement swirling in my gut wouldn't do me any good. If I wanted to forget what was coming, for a few hours at least, I had to find a guy to take my mind off things.

I surveyed the hotel bar. Everything in it was shiny and slick, from the countertops to the lights to the barstools we sat on. The place was dark enough to give everyone a little anonymity and privacy, but not so dark it looked seedy. Most people sat alone or in pairs, travelers searching for a quick drink before bed or for someone to make their stay a little less lonely. Places like this always had guys interested in a casual, no-strings-attached hookup. Which is exactly what I wanted, too.

"Julie, are you really going to pick up a guy tonight?" Carla asked from the barstool beside me.

"You already know I am."

"Are you sure that's a good idea?" Her voice had that annoying tone it always got when she didn't agree with something I did. Which was pretty often.

"Hey, don't get all judgy on me."

"I'm not. I'm just…suggesting you might want to go to bed early. You have a big day tomorrow."

"Which is exactly why we need to celebrate *tonight*." I waved a hand at the bartender and ordered another strawberry martini. My third. Fourth? Eh, who was counting?

Carla still looked dubious, swirling the ice cubes in her drink, which had been empty for fifteen minutes now. She was probably right about heading to bed early, but hello, we were in New York, in a free hotel, and tomorrow I would embark on the most incredible and terrifying thing that had ever happened to me.

I'd won a spot on the fashion design reality TV show *Behind The Seams* through a costume contest at San Diego Comic-Con. For the next few weeks, I'd be trapped in a building and competing against other designers to impress the judges with our clothes. And if I won the entire show? I'd get $200,000 to launch a business, plus a complete sewing studio, a year's worth of hair and makeup products, and a fashion spread in *Charmed* magazine for me and my model. It was the kind of prize that could launch a career in fashion.

I had to win it.

"We're going on *Behind The Seams*," I said. "Maybe that's not a big deal to you, but it is to me."

Carla gave me a warm smile. "It *is* a big deal. And you're going to be amazing."

"Hell yeah, I am."

I chugged my martini. I *had* to be amazing. I'd already seriously pissed off my parents by agreeing to go on the show in the first place. My senior year at UCLA started in a month, but they didn't approve of me spending the rest of my summer break on a reality TV show. Nope, they wanted me to do something productive that could go on applications and resumes, even if it was only for a few weeks.

I could still hear my mom's shrill, nagging voice through the phone when I'd told her my plans. "But why couldn't you volunteer at a local hospital?" she'd asked.

"Mom, this is a big deal for me. I was invited on the show by Giselle Roberts, the woman who created it. I didn't even have to audition! And don't worry, I'll be back in LA in time for classes to start again."

"You should have done an internship this summer. Your sister could have gotten you one at her hospital. Or found you a job at a local practice. It would look much better on your medical school applications. Have you even started on them yet? And don't forget you have to study for the MCAT…"

I'd rubbed the bridge of my nose, a sharp headache coming on as it always did during these discussions. "I didn't get a job or an internship because we had the Seoul trip already planned. Should I have stayed here instead?"

My grandmother was ill, and the entire family had gone to visit her in Korea for two weeks. And I didn't even want to think about my med school applications, which were due way too soon. Or the MCAT exam, which I had been trying very hard to pretend didn't exist.

"No, don't be silly. But your sister could have asked someone for a favor…"

That was when I'd tuned her out. On and on it went until she'd finished with her endless speech about how I wasn't living up to my older sister's shining example. Helen had become a doctor like they'd wanted, and I was expected to follow her path. They would never see fashion design as a valid career choice.

Which meant I *had* to win the show to prove them wrong.

Which meant tonight was about getting drunk and finding a man to make me forget all of that.

I gazed across the bar, looking for the perfect guy. Most of them were too old or too married—men on business trips trying to hook up for one night without their wives knowing. No thank you. I wanted no-strings-attached sex, but I wasn't ruining any marriages. Alas, tonight I didn't see even one fuckable guy in the entire bar.

Screw it, maybe it *was* time to head back to my hotel room and get some sleep.

Just as I was about to give up, a guy sat down at the other end of the bar who instantly caught my eye. His silky chestnut hair was short on the sides, but long enough on top to tangle my fingers in. I couldn't tell what color his eyes were in the dim light, but he had the perfect amount of dark stubble dusting his strong jaw and framing his very kissable lips. A stylish charcoal button-up shirt clung to his broad shoulders and fit like it had been made just for him. The sleeves were rolled up to his elbows, revealing colorful tattoos running down both arms. Something about the contrast made him even sexier—that balance between classy and edgy, hard and soft, good and bad.

I nudged Carla. "I think we have a winner."

He looked at us then, hit by that sixth sense hot guys had when you were talking about them. Carla immediately dropped her eyes, but I let a sultry smile curl across my lips. My gaze lingered on him long enough to let him know I was interested, before I turned back to Carla.

"Yep, definitely him."

"He's hot." She yawned and set her empty drink on the bar. "And I'm heading to bed."

"Already?" I pouted, although I wasn't *too* sad. Being on my own tonight would give me a better chance at picking up a guy. Ideally Mr. Gorgeous Hair over there.

She stood up and grabbed her purse. "You found your guy, and I need my beauty sleep."

"Oh, please. You'd make everyone in here look like trolls even if you stayed up all night and didn't shower for a week."

Carla laughed and gave me a warm hug. "Not true, but I love you for saying that."

It *was* true, though. Carla was ridiculously, impossibly beautiful, no exaggeration. She towered over me, with boobs I would kill for, rich dark skin you couldn't help but want to touch, and a head full of bouncing, natural curls. Without even trying, she put every other girl in the room to shame. And even though her pouty lips and mysterious eyes could be seen on billboards, ads, and runways across the world, it never went to her head. She was the sweetest, most loyal friend a girl could have. She'd even come to New York to go on *Behind The Seams* with me.

Normally designers didn't have any say over which model they worked with on the show, but she'd pulled some strings so we could be together. I suspected her famous supermodel mother had something to do with it, but Carla told me not to stress over it. It meant a lot to me that she was taking time out of her summer break to come with me. Sure, if we won, she'd get a sweet prize herself—$10,000 plus the photo shoot in *Charmed* magazine—but she didn't need it. She'd been in Paris last week doing a photo shoot and had cancelled others to go on the show. She was here for *me*, and I loved her for it.

She kissed me on the cheek and said goodnight. From across the counter, the guy's intense gaze lingered on me. He took a sip of his drink, and I spotted a tattoo of a rose on the back of his right hand. I gave him another flirty smile, leaning forward on the bar to show off my cleavage in my low-cut red dress. The hint of a grin touched his full lips.

He was hooked. Time to reel him in.

Another guy plopped next to me in Carla's vacant seat, ruining my seduction moment. He looked ridiculously all-American with a wide chest, strong jaw, and short blond hair, like he should be playing college football or working as an Abercrombie model. Not really my type, but not bad looking either.

He grinned at me, flashing bright white teeth. "Hey, Hello Kitty. Can I get you a drink?"

Did he just…? I blinked at him. Tilted my head. Waited a beat to make sure I'd heard him correctly. "I'm sorry?"

"Drink?" he repeated, then made a drinking movement with his hand, like he thought I might not understand English.

"No, what was the other thing you said? What did you call me?"

"Hello Kitty. It was a joke." He grinned even wider, like I was supposed to laugh at this.

"How is that funny?"

His grin faltered a little, but then rallied. "Um…just 'cause, you know, you're…um…"

I clenched my fists at my sides, resisting the urge to punch his stupid face in. "What, because I'm Asian?"

He tugged on the collar of his shirt and glanced away. "Yeah."

"Okay, for one thing, I'm *Korean*, not Japanese. Second, I don't look anything like Hello Kitty, who is a fucking *cat*. I'm not even wearing a bow on my head. So unless you were trying to make some sort of 'pussy' pun, which is just gross, that joke doesn't even make sense."

He held up his hands. "Whoa, chill. You don't need to get upset. It was a joke. Calm down."

"Oh, I got that it was a joke. A racist, sexist, stupid joke." I grabbed my martini and turned my back to him, hoping he'd take the hint and leave.

He didn't budge.

I waved my hand dismissively. "You can go now."

"So…you don't want a drink?" He sounded confused.

"Nope. Got one."

He leaned in closer, his breath hot on my cheek. "C'mon, let me get you something. One drink."

"I told you no."

This guy could *not* take a hint. Or a flat-out rejection. Time to listen to Carla's advice and head to bed. I finished my martini in one long chug, ready to get the hell out of this bar, even if it meant not getting laid tonight.

But before I could get up, the guy put a large, rough hand on my back, pressing hard against my skin, physically preventing me from leaving. "How about we go up to my room, then?"

Oh, hell to the no. "How about you get lost?"

He didn't listen, just moved even closer, completely invading my personal space. "It'll be fun. You and me, my bed, and a lot less clothes."

I was about to go off on him, to yell at him to take his hand off me before I karate-chopped it off—not that I knew karate, but his type always assumed every Asian person was a martial arts master—when the tattooed guy from across the bar showed up at my side.

"Are you bothering my girlfriend?" he asked in a cool, direct voice. Good god, he had an English accent. As if he wasn't hot enough already.

Wait, did he just say *girlfriend?* I raised my eyebrows at him, but he kept his gaze focused on the other guy.

The douchebag looked confused again, but he removed his hand from me at least. "Girlfriend?"

My "boyfriend" moved a little closer, draping an arm across the back of my chair, yet not actually touching me. He was tall, though smaller in build than the jerk beside me. Even so, he had more of an edge to him. A dark, imposing presence, like he tended to get what he wanted.

"I believe she told you to leave." He said it in a polite way, but his voice had an underlying menace to it.

"Whatever, man." The douchebag got up and walked off, muttering to himself. He left the bar, probably heading back to his hotel room or to a different bar to pick up another girl. I hoped, for his sake, he didn't try that Hello Kitty line again.

"Thanks, but I didn't need you to rescue me," I said to my fake boyfriend with a flirty smile.

"No, I'm quite sure you could handle it on your own." He sat beside me and gestured at the bartender to refill our drinks. "But it's a gentleman's duty to help a lady in distress."

"A gentleman? I thought those didn't exist anymore."

"Clearly you've been hanging out with the wrong men."

"You just saw proof of that."

He laughed, and it practically set my panties on fire. His voice was like butter, and I wanted it spread all over me. That didn't even make sense, but it was true. Wow, maybe I was drunker than I thought. But the bartender slid another martini in front of me and I took a sip without a second thought. When in New York, right? Or was that Las Vegas? Rome? Whatever.

"Besides, I wasn't in distress," I said. "I was already getting rid of him when you showed up on your white horse and just had to save the day."

"Maybe I wanted an excuse to talk to you. Forgive me?"

Up close, he was even better looking, with steel gray eyes that seemed to dance under the bar lights. Damn, he was almost *too* pretty. Guys that hot always knew it, and they were usually trouble. But for tonight, I'd suffer it. And with those lips and that body…well, there wouldn't be much suffering.

I dragged a lazy finger around the edge of my glass and smiled. "I suppose."

He held out his tattooed hand. "I'm Gavin—"

God, even his name was sexy. I pressed a finger to his soft lips. "No names."

"No?" he asked, arching his dark eyebrows. "Not exactly fair, since you know mine now."

"I tried to stop you." I preferred not to use names when I hooked up with a guy. Names made everything far too personal and that didn't work for me. Especially not tonight. Not when I only had a few hours and then would be on my way, never to see Gavin again. I was already trying to forget his name.

"What shall I call you, then?" he asked.

"Whatever you want, as long as it's not Hello Kitty."

"Why in the world would I call you that?"

"That's what the other guy called me."

"Not a very good pickup line."

"Obviously not."

"Worked out for me, though." A sly smile spread across his lips. I couldn't stop staring at his mouth. Couldn't stop imagining what it would be like to taste him.

"Yes, it did." I was dying to get him up to my room already. I placed my hand on his knee, hoping he'd get the hint. But he seemed to want to talk.

"What are you doing in New York, mystery girl?"

"I'm here for business." *And I don't want to talk about it,* I hoped my tone conveyed. I inched my hand up his leg, along his smooth black jeans. I bet they fit as well as his shirt did and wondered how his ass looked in them. I'd have to sneak a peek before I dragged them off him. And another peek once they were in a pile on the floor.

"What do you do?" he asked.

Enough already. When could we skip to the making out part? Maybe if I told him something he would shut up and kiss me. "I'm a pre-med student."

It slipped out without a thought. Technically that *was* my "job" at the moment. But that wasn't why I was in New York. Not that he of the gorgeous hair, enticing lips, and oh-so-sexy accent needed to know that.

"I'm here on business, too. I'm…an artist." There was a touch of hesitation to his words, like he was worried I'd be turned off by that. "Where are you visiting from?"

"You ask a lot of questions."

An eyebrow shot up. "Is it so terrible I want to get to know you?"

Yes, because I had no intention of seeing him again after tonight. And no, because when a guy as sexy as him wanted to get to know you, it wasn't terrible at all. Especially when he brushed hair away from my face with the softest touch and lowered his head to my ear. "Tell me where you're from," he whispered, his breath tickling my neck.

"Los Angeles," I confessed, silently begging him to kiss me. But he didn't.

"Los Angeles? Sounds glamorous."

I had to laugh at that. "Not really."

"I'm from London. Well, Mum's from Wales and Dad's from the States, but that's where I grew up."

"I can tell from the accent. But you talk too much." Enough chit-chat. It was obvious he wanted me, and I wasn't exactly being coy either.

He gave a sharp laugh. "No one's told me that before. I thought Americans loved the accent."

"Oh, we do." I played with his shirt, inching up his chest with my fingers. "But what I want to do? Doesn't involve talking."

"Is that so?" He rested the hand with the rose tattoo on my thigh, his fingers dipping under the hem of my skirt. "What is it you want to do, then?"

I gripped his shirt's collar, pulling him down to my mouth. Our lips touched with a fierce heat that sent warmth through my entire body. A little moan escaped me as his tongue met mine and stroked it slowly. He tasted of rum and coke, bitter and sweet, spicy and smooth.

"That," I said, "is what I want to do. And a lot more."

Chapter Two

His gray eyes stared into mine, as though trying to search out all my secrets. "Tell me your name."

"No names," I repeated.

He claimed me in a deep kiss, hands gripping my hips and possessing my body right there in the middle of the bar. That familiar numbness washed over me, blocking out every worry, every thought other than this moment with him. Yes, this was exactly what I'd been aching for all night. Or, at least, this was a good start.

"Let's go to my room," I begged, breathing faster, heart pounding, my entire body warm from the alcohol and his touch. I wanted him now. Without all those clothes on. Or maybe with those clothes on. That would be hot, too. I could just unzip his pants, yank up my skirt, and let him have his way with me…

He gave me a slow smile, like he knew exactly what I was thinking. He paid the bartender for both our drinks, and while we waited, I ran a dark red nail up and down his neck until he shivered. He grabbed my hand and slipped my finger into his mouth, sucking on it with sinful eyes that promised me more to come. I sighed, desire burning through me, wishing we could hurry it up and get to my room already.

We left the bar and stumbled across the hotel lobby to the elevator. Or at least, I stumbled, from a combination of all those martinis and my tall heels. But every time I swayed, he held me with those tattooed arms and firm hands, and I didn't mind one bit.

The elevator doors shut, and we were alone. He pinned me back against the mirrored wall, hands pressed to the glass on either side of my head, caging me with his body and his intense gaze.

"Tell me your name," he demanded again in that sexy accent.

"No names." I began unbuttoning his shirt.

"I've already told you mine."

"I've already forgotten," I lied.

I buried my mouth in the spot of skin I uncovered below his collarbone, tasting him there. He groaned and pressed his firm body against me, and I wanted, wanted, wanted. One of my legs went up around him, and he caressed my thigh, dipping under my skirt, inching closer and closer along my bare skin.

"I have to call you something," he said into my neck, nipping and kissing in a way that made my head spin. And made the room spin. Had he said something? I couldn't focus. All I could think about was the feel of his lips on my neck and his fingers on my thigh and the aching between my legs.

We tumbled out of the elevator and onto my floor. I tripped on the carpet as we walked to my room and lost one of my heels, which made me giggle. He picked the lost shoe up and dangled it in front of me with a grin. I kicked off the other shoe, and he snatched that one up, too.

Barefoot and laughing, I scampered down the hall to find my room. What was the number again? I soon found the right door, but then I couldn't locate the keycard in my purse. He came up behind me, holding my heels in one hand, looking impossibly sexy with his shirt half-unbuttoned. His fitted black jeans hung low on his hips, hugging his long, lean legs, and his hair was messy from me running my fingers through it.

Forget the room. I pushed him against my door and kissed him there in the hotel hallway. Hard. Intense. Sliding my body against his. He wanted me. I could feel the evidence of it pressed against my stomach. My hand fumbled at his waist, seeking the front of his jeans. No one would notice if we did a little something right here…

He took my hand, stopping me. "Let's go inside first."

Oh, fine. I redoubled my search for the key and then remembered—aha! I'd shoved it in my bra. Totally his fault. If he'd been going to town on that area, we would have found it already. I pulled the card out of my breasts triumphantly and shoved it into the slot. Or tried, anyway. It took me three attempts before I finally got it open. Okay, maaaaybe I'd had a little too much to drink tonight.

He followed me into the room, dropping my shoes on a side table. I tried to reach for him, but he walked all the way in to stand in front of the floor-to-ceiling window. Maybe he was suddenly nervous or something. I'd seen that before. I'd pick up a guy in a bar, and they'd seem all gung-ho to get in my pants, then panic as soon as they got to my room. I'd have to give him a little help.

I shimmied out of my panties. Or tried. Those suckers were tight, and why was it so much harder to get them off than I'd remembered? Finally I succeeded in sliding them down my legs, while he watched with inscrutable eyes.

"Come here," I said, throwing them at him. They missed, landing on a lamp-shade, the red lace casting dark shadows across the room. He laughed, and some of the tension in his shoulders seemed to ease. Yet still he didn't move.

"It's late…" he said, glancing at the clock on the nightstand, which read 1:26 AM in neon blue letters.

I crossed the room and slid a hand up his chest. Yes, it was late and I had to be up early, but if he left now, I'd lie awake all night, tormented by all those doubts and worries that kept trying to creep back into my brain. But more than that, I didn't want him to leave. Sure, I could go back to the bar and try to find someone else, but I didn't *want* anyone else. I needed *him*. Bad.

"Don't go," I whispered. Our eyes locked, and the air between us crackled. I licked my lips, and his gaze fixed on them.

Then he was on me, hands in my hair, tilting my head so he could devour my mouth. I surrendered to it, clutching at his shirt, his back, his shoulders. Anything to bring him closer. He tasted like sin, and I couldn't get enough. I'd kissed a lot of guys before, more than I could count, but this one blew them all away. This was a kiss I'd remember long after his name was forgotten.

Gavin.

He spun me around and my back pressed against the floor-to-ceiling window, the thick glass cool through my clothes. He dropped his mouth to my neck, to my collar, to my chest. With each touch of his lips, all my anxiety was swept away.

His fingers skimmed up and down my sides slowly while he kissed me all over, sending little shivers across my skin. My head fell back against the window, and my entire focus narrowed to the man in front of me, just like I'd wanted. When his mouth covered my breast through the fabric of my dress, I gasped. And when his teeth lightly scraped over my hard nipple, I had to grab onto the curtains beside me for support.

I was ready for him to rip my clothes off, but instead he kneeled in front of me and pressed his lips to my knees. He pushed my dress up to my hips as he left burning kisses along the inside of one leg, then repeated with the other. My panties were long gone and he was so close. All I could do was hold my breath and pray for more. Closer…closer…

He nudged my legs apart even wider and gazed up my body, fixing me with those smoky gray eyes. "Is this what you want?"

"Yes." My butt was pressed against the glass, but we were high enough up that I doubted anyone would see us through the tinted windows. Not that I cared if all of New York saw us at this very moment. "Yes, this is what I want. *Please*, Gavin."

At the sound of his name, he dropped his head between my thighs, finally kissing me *there*. Right where I wanted him. My breath escaped me in a rush as the feel of his mouth took over. His tongue—flicking, darting, setting me on fire. His lips—those beautiful, perfect lips, pressing against me. His teeth—grazing and nipping at my tender skin. I couldn't stop myself from grinding against him, wanting more, more, more. I spiraled higher and higher, so close…

"Gavin," I begged over and over. "Oh god, don't stop."

One of his hands moved up my legs to dip between my thighs. He ran a finger along me slowly as he gave me one long lick, then slipped that finger inside. I gasped and dug one hand into his silky hair, pressing his head harder against me, while clinging to the curtain with the other hand.

Another finger dipped inside, curling, darting, touching me deep. He slid them in and out while his tongue flicked me back and forth, fucking me with both his fingers and his mouth. I lost all control of my voice and my limbs, twitching and trembling and moaning until I exploded, stars everywhere, spinning, gasping, crying. He kept going through it all, and I thought I'd surely die if it continued. But god, what a way to go.

Finally the spasms subsided and his tongue slowed, like he was lapping me up. I fell back against the window, my entire body a warm gooey mess of pleasure and satisfaction. I'd had guys go down on me before, plenty of guys, but never on their knees like that and never so…intense.

I wanted to return the favor. Wanted the rest of his body against mine. Wanted him inside me. He was so fucking hot and obviously talented. It could only get better from here. But first, I needed a second to recover. I closed my eyes, breathing heavily, feeling drowsy and satisfied all at once. I never wanted to move again. I wasn't sure I could.

"Ready to tell me your name yet?" he asked, sliding up my legs, standing in front of me.

"Not a chance." I was pressed against the window with my dress pushed up around my hips, totally vulnerable and exposed, just waiting for him to fuck me. Silently begging him to take me hard and fast and rough. One second away from asking him out loud.

"I'll get it out of you eventually," he said with another sly grin.

"Do that again and I *might* tell you."

One eyebrow arched up. "Is that so?"

"Guess you'll have to find out."

I dragged him toward the bed, but suddenly my head throbbed and the room rolled around me, making me dizzy. The world seemed to tilt, spin, dance in my stomach. Next thing I knew, my knees had buckled and I was in his arms.

"All right there?" he asked.

I nodded, pressing a hand to my temple. "Head rush."

He steadied me, and I shook it off. I reached for his black leather belt, but my fingers were clumsy as I undid the buckle and I giggled. It took me way longer than it should, but finally I got it off him and dropped it on the floor.

But he didn't get on the bed, didn't start taking off his clothes, and didn't kiss me again. He studied me, his brow furrowed. Even his eyebrows were sexy. That was crazy, but they were. I'd never noticed a guy's eyebrows before, but his were dark and framed his gray eyes perfectly. I wanted to run a finger over each of them. I wondered if he plucked them and giggled at the image.

"You're swaying," he said.

I giggled harder. His accent was funny. "What?"

"Lie down."

"Mmm, yes, sir."

I liked a man who took charge in bed. I loved taking charge myself, too, but if that's what he was into, I could go for that tonight. I laid back, trying to look hot, giving him my best sex-kitten stare. He grabbed a bottle of water from the mini-bar and handed it to me. "Drink this."

Not a bad idea. I took the water and tried to drink it in a sexy way, licking my lips, but managed to spill it over my chest, water dripping down the front of my dress. Well, if he wanted me wet…

"You want some?" I asked in a seductive voice.

"Thank you, no."

I shrugged and left the water on the side table. He still didn't move, just stared at me from beside the bed. I crooked a finger at him with a smile. "Get over here."

"Trust me, love, I want to."

"Love?" I wasn't a fan of silly nicknames, but the way he said it sounded like "luv" and that was pretty hot. God, that accent. I wanted to listen to him whisper all sorts of dirty things in my ear. Preferably while doing them to me. Why wasn't that happening already?

"Give me your name and I'll call you something else," he said.

"No, I like that." I raised an arm over my head, draping it across the pillow, trying to look sexy. "Come to bed."

"I don't think that's a good idea."

I sat up, dropping my arm. "Why not?"

"You're pissed."

"No, I'm not," I said, confused. "I mean, I'm a little annoyed that you're not already naked…"

"Not that kind of pissed." He gestured like he was trying to find the word. "Drunk."

I rolled my eyes. "I'm not that either."

"No, love, you really are."

"I don't care. I want this. I want you. Right. Now." I slid down the bed to him, running my hand across the front of his pants. Judging by the hard—and very large—bulge there, he definitely wanted me, too.

He took my hand off him. "That's not a good idea."

I didn't understand what the problem was. He was in my room, he'd gone down on me, and he was obviously interested in more. Why stop now? "Why are you here if you don't want this?"

"I didn't realize how drunk you are until now." He nodded at the water. "Drink that and get some sleep."

He turned away, like he was about to leave. Oh, hell no. Guys did not walk out on me. *I* walked out on them.

"Stop being a gentleman. I don't want sleep. I want to get laid. And if you won't help me out…" I stood up, flipped my long hair, and gave a little shrug. It took all my energy not to topple over again. "Well, maybe some other guy at the bar will."

He turned back to me, crossing his arms. "Don't be a twat. You can barely stand on your own."

"A *what?*"

"And you're definitely not going back down there to find some other guy."

"What, now you think you have some claim over me?" I huffed. "Just 'cause you called yourself my boyfriend doesn't make it true."

He closed his eyes, taking a long breath. "No, of course not."

"Then get out of my way."

"You're far too drunk. I'm not letting you leave the room like this. Even if I have to stay here all night."

Rage swept through me, fixed on this arrogant, obnoxious, annoyingly handsome guy. "You…" I pressed my hand against his chest, a feeble attempt to get him to move, but couldn't help but enjoy the feel of his body underneath my palm. Instead of pushing him away, I pulled him closer. "You can't keep me here. Or tell me what to do. This is *my* room."

"No, I suppose I can't."

With a soft groan, his mouth covered mine in a hungry, fierce kiss, showing me how much he wanted this, too. I finished unbuttoning his shirt, the job I'd abandoned earlier in the elevator, while his hands circled my waist. He nudged me backward, toward the bed. Yes! Now we were getting somewhere.

But when the back of my knees bumped against the bed, he stopped and removed his hands. "No, I'm sorry. I can't. It's not right."

I groaned. "Forget right and take off your clothes already."

"Love, believe me when I say that all I want to do is pin you against this bed and bury myself in you until you scream my name. But I'm not going to take advantage of you while you're drunk."

"It's not taking advantage if I'm asking you to do it. And really, I'm not *that* drunk. Watch." I walked in a straight line up and down the room, not even wavering once. "See?"

He ignored my plea and began buttoning his shirt again. I hadn't even gotten a good look at his chest, and now it was gone. Dammit.

I sat on the bed, hard. My head spun, my stomach twisted, but worst of all, those creeping doubts and worries crept back in. "Stay with me," I begged, digging my fingers into his shirt, pleading up at him. I sounded vulnerable and pathetic, but I didn't care at this point. "Just for tonight. Don't leave me alone. Please, Gavin."

He considered me for a long moment and then sighed. "I'll stay, but we're not doing anything more until you've sobered up." He grabbed the water bottle off the table and handed it to me again. "Drink this. I'll be back in a moment."

I fell back on the bed with a groan as he disappeared into the bathroom. God, he was infuriating. I wasn't even that drunk. Fine, I'd drink this water, and when he came back, I'd make sure we continued where we'd left off.

But now that I was lying down, I was suddenly so, so tired. My head hurt, my body was so relaxed I could barely move, and this bed was so comfortable I melted right into it. Maybe I could just close my eyes and rest while I waited for him to come back…

Chapter Three

S omething buzzed by my head, and I swatted at it. A fly? A bee? I met only air. I peeked an eye open, and bright light sent painful stabs through my skull. Ow, ow, ow.

More buzzing near my head. Sunlight spilled in through nearby windows, along with the sound of cars honking outside. The bed felt wrong, and the pillow was too soft. Where was I?

I sat up fast. All the blood rushed to my brain, and with it came a new wave of pain. I pressed a palm to my throbbing forehead, remembering everything. New York, a hotel room, and way too much alcohol.

Oh, and a gorgeous guy who'd gone down on me.

I was alone now and still wearing my dress from last night—sans underwear, of course. At some point, Gavin must have helped me under the covers, and he'd left another water bottle on the bedside table. I popped off the cap and chugged it, but it did little to relieve the sandpaper feel of my mouth or the pounding in my head.

The buzzing continued behind me. I groped around the bed and found the source of the incessant noise: my phone. Carla, calling me. Shit. She hated talking on the phone even more than I did. If she was calling and not texting, this had to be bad. Really bad.

I hit answer and braced myself. "Yeah?"

"Where are you? Are you in your room? Are you ready to go?"

Shit, shit, shit. I glanced around the room and found the clock. 8:15 AM. A car was picking us up at 8:30 to take us to the show.

I had a raging hangover, I probably looked like ass, and I was going to be late for *Behind The Seams*. FML for sure.

"I'll meet you in the lobby in ten minutes," I said and hung up.

I dashed into the bathroom and washed my face. No time for a shower, though I desperately needed one, so I used a washcloth to do a quick once-over. After a hasty brush of my hair and my fastest makeup routine *ever*, I ran out to get dressed. Thank god I'd taken Carla's advice and planned each outfit to wear on the show in advance.

As I got dressed, I spotted my red lace panties hanging off the lampshade and flashed back to last night. How I'd picked up a tattooed guy with a sexy accent and a very talented tongue. How I'd practically begged him to screw me and he'd refused. And then he'd left. Without a word.

Okay, to be fair, I'd passed out, but he could have left a note or something. Whatever. His loss. It wasn't like I'd planned to see him again anyway. There was a reason for the no-names policy, after all. Especially since I'd be on *Behind The Seams* and unable to contact anyone for the next few weeks. There was no point wondering about what might have been. Or why he hadn't stuck around. Nope, none of that mattered. I'd gotten what I'd wanted out of him—an amazing orgasm—and now I was moving on.

I put on a cute green-and-black A-line dress I'd made and inspected myself in the mirror. My long black hair looked frizzy and my brown eyes had some bags under them, but considering a hammer was pounding my skull in, I called it good.

Before I left, I threw everything into my luggage, downed a couple pain pills, and scanned the room. Oops. Almost forgot those panties. I shoved them in the front pocket of my luggage and wheeled myself out.

Carla was already in the lobby, looking flawless (of course) in a pair of blue jeans and a black V-neck shirt. She had her arms crossed and tapped one perfectly manicured finger against her arm.

"Cutting it close," she said, when I approached.

"Shh," I said. "Not so loud. I have a major hangover."

"No sympathy. You brought this on yourself."

"Trust me, I know. I'll tell you all about it in the car."

We rushed outside, and the warm, humid air instantly wrapped around me in a suffocating embrace. I had to fight off the urge to vomit until we slipped into the large black car the show had sent for us.

I gave Carla the lowdown of my evening once we were in the backseat and driving through the crowded streets of New York. I tried to keep my voice down, but I was sure our driver heard all the sordid details anyway. Whatever, he'd probably heard a lot worse in his line of work.

"The guy just…left?" Carla asked when I was done.

I shrugged. "Yeah, but it's not like anything would come of it anyway. All I wanted was a quick hookup with a hot guy, and that's what I got. Even better, I got it without the awkward morning-after chat. If only all my one-night stands could go so well…"

The driver cleared his throat, and I smirked. Yep, definitely listening.

"So it doesn't bother you that you won't see him again?"

"Not at all." I mean, maybe it bothered me a tiny bit that he hadn't even *tried* to keep in touch with me. Not that I would do it, but damn, he *was* ridiculously hot. And good with his mouth. I was curious if he was good with his other body parts, too. But he lived in London, and I was going on the show, and it didn't matter what I wanted because it was over. Just a memory and nothing more.

Besides, I'd made a total fool of myself last night. I cringed at the memory of how I'd begged him to stay with me. God, how embarrassing. It was better that we never see each other again. No one needed to know just how pathetic I'd become to get some action from a hot guy. Better to leave the entire night behind and forget it ever happened.

"Are you nervous?" Carla asked. I wanted to kiss her for changing the subject.

"A little." I yawned and started to rub my eyes, but stopped because it would mess up my makeup. "Mostly I wish I had some coffee. And some greasy food." I leaned back against the seat and groaned. "I'd murder someone for a cheeseburger right now."

Carla pulled some sort of organic vegan gluten-free low-fat blah blah blah energy bar out of her purse. "Here, eat this."

"I'd rather sit here and suffer."

She shrugged. "If that's your choice."

She unwrapped the bar and took a bite and chewed...and chewed...and chewed. My god, was she ever going to stop chewing? And it was so freaking loud, with all that crunching. Who knew chewing could be so damn noisy? It made the pain in my head crank up to max.

"Please, for the love of all that is good in the world, stop that."

"Stop what? Eating?" She took another bite. *Crunch crunch crunch.*

"I hate you a little right now."

She pointed at me with the offensive thing. "Hey, I didn't make you stay up all night drinking and sexing it up."

"It was worth it. No one looks back and remembers the nights they went to bed early."

To distract myself from her noisy eating, I gazed outside my window at the city scrolling past us. I'd never been to New York before, although I'd always secretly dreamed of moving here, and I wanted to soak it all in. Sidewalks overrun with people in suits and black clothes rushing to work. Tourist shops with *I <3 NY* T-shirts and snow globes with the Statue of Liberty. Pizza places that all claimed to be the best in New York. Skyscrapers towering over us, gleaming in the sunlight.

A grin broke out on my face as I craned my neck up to glimpse the Empire State Building. I was really here. In New York. Going on *Behind The Seams.*

Forget last night. Today was the beginning of my new life. I knew exactly where I was going, and I was never looking back.

The car pulled up outside a brick building with no signs or other identifiers on it. Our driver got out our luggage, while a brunette with chunky blonde highlights bounced out to meet us, exuding perkiness.

"Hi! You must be Julie Hong! And Carla Jackson! I'm Kelsey—with a K—and I'll be your handler!" She spoke in a high-pitched voice at a mile a minute and seemed to use an exclamation point after every sentence. Or every word.

"Shoot me," I muttered to Carla.

"That's us," Carla said to Kelsey, nudging me in the ribs.

"Great! It's so wonderful to meet you both! Please follow me!"

I gave Carla a *please make her stop* look, but she rolled her eyes at me.

"You know, it's unheard of for designers to have met their models before the show starts," Kelsey-with-a-K continued. "We usually pair them up randomly, but in your case, we made an exception! How great is that?" She beamed at us, like this was the most amazing thing she'd heard all day. I wanted to tell her to lower her voice and calm the fuck down. Excitable people and hangovers did not mesh.

"We're very grateful we can work together," Carla said.

"There's just one teensy little thing we need to discuss first," Kelsey said, still sporting her giant smile. "We would prefer it if you didn't tell the other designers that you two knew each other in advance. It's not a big deal if they do find out, but we don't want the other contestants to think Julie has an unfair advantage."

Honestly? It *was* an unfair advantage. Knowing Carla was going to be my model gave me a huge confidence boost. After all, I'd designed or modified clothes for her plenty of times. But it made me uneasy knowing it was a secret we had to keep for the next few weeks. If it got out, it might turn the other designers against me. Then again, I wasn't going on the show to make friends. I was there to win.

Whatever it took.

"Not a problem," I said, and Carla nodded.

"Great! I knew you'd understand!" Kelsey said, as she led us inside the building. "We're going to have so much fun this season!"

I didn't trust myself not to say something bitchy, so I stayed silent as I took in the lobby of the building they used for *Behind The Seams*. It was super modern, all tarnished metal, sharp angles, cement walls, and exposed ceilings. Like the people who designed it had been screaming, *"Look how cool and edgy we are!"*

Despite my pounding head, excitement surged through me, mixed with the prickling of nerves. Further inside, I would meet the other designers and see where I'd be living for the next few weeks. And then we'd get our first challenge. How soon would it be? Right when we got in? I hoped not because I could really use something to eat and drink. And a shower. And a nap.

Kelsey had us sign some paperwork at the front desk, then clapped her hands and flashed that giant smile at us. "Great, we're all set! Carla, please wait here and someone will take you for photos and to get your measurements. Julie, come with me and we'll get you set up for the show!"

An assistant took my luggage, and I felt a sudden rush of panic. This was really happening now. No turning back.

Carla gave me a hug, and even though she was about a foot taller than me and I got a face full of boobs, I appreciated it. And, to be fair, they were damn nice boobs.

"Good luck," she said.

"You too."

"You're going to be amazing."

"I know." I gave her a confident smile. Fake it 'til you make it, right? "And you already are."

Kelsey and I headed down a hallway. To my dismay, she continued her perky chirping. "First up, I'm taking you for photos and a quick interview! Then you'll join the other designers for a quick reception!"

I wanted to throw up. And not just from my hangover. "Are the other designers already here?"

"Some of them. We're staggering the arrivals so we don't get overwhelmed, since there are fourteen of you to start. Oh, and you're the youngest designer this season! Isn't that cool?"

"Um, sure." That definitely fueled my already-large ego, but it also meant everyone else would have more experience than me. All those doubts crept back in, that nagging voice that said I didn't belong here, but I forced them to the back of my brain.

Fuck that noise. I was meant to do this.

Kelsey pushed open a frosted glass door and led me into a room with a backdrop with the *Behind The Seams* logo. Bright lights were fixed on a metal stool in the middle, with a camera crew set up in front of it.

Kelsey directed me to sit and then stood back so she wasn't in view of the camera. A guy came over and added more makeup, slapping powder on my shiny forehead, while a girl ran a brush through my hair. I was tempted to apologize to them for looking like such a hot mess, but just gave them each a weak smile. Anything more was too much effort at the moment.

Once they decided I looked decent, the cameras began to roll and Kelsey rattled off questions. They were all pretty basic and expected—about my childhood, how I started designing clothes, why I wanted to win the show, and what my design aesthetic was. I somehow made it through them all without throwing up, but when it was over, I had no idea what I'd actually said. I prayed they could work some editing magic to make me sound halfway coherent.

Kelsey led me into another room, where I smiled and posed for promotional photographs, while mentally kicking myself again for drinking so much last night. After that, Kelsey slapped a name tag on my chest, and a cute sound guy fitted me with a portable microphone. He showed me how to turn it off and on, stressing that I should turn it off during downtime so the battery lasted longer. Then he attached the battery pack to my ankle before hiding the tiny mic inside the bust of my dress. On any other day, I'd be all over a hot guy with his hands inside my clothes, but today all I could do was concentrate on not throwing up on him.

"You were so great in your interview!" Kelsey said as she led me to an elevator. "I wish I had time to give you a full tour of the building, but the reception has already started. As you saw, this floor has the lobby, along with the theater for the runway shows and the production offices. The third floor is what we call the Loft, where you'll be staying with the other designers for the next few weeks. There's also a lounge area on the roof. And right now we're going to the second floor, where you'll find the design room, the fabric room, and the hair and makeup rooms. Most of the other designers should be waiting there already!"

Acid rose up in my throat. The show was starting *now*. From here on out, just about every moment of my life would be filmed. Eating. Sleeping. Working. And even worse, I was about to meet my competition for the next few weeks while looking like a total wreck.

I tried to use my phone's camera to do one last quick check of my hair and makeup, but Kelsey held out her hand with an apologetic smile. "Sorry, but I'm going to have to take your phone. You're not allowed to have them while you're on the show."

I already knew this, but a shot of terror hit me at the thought of not having my phone for weeks. Contestants were completely cut off from the rest of the world, banned from leaving the building or having any outside contact—including Internet or TV.

I checked my email and texts and everything else real fast for that one last fix, then reluctantly handed my phone over to her. Immediately I considered grabbing it and making a run for it, but no—I was doing this. Even if giving up my phone felt like losing a chunk of my brain.

Once on the second floor, Kelsey led me past the closed doors of the design room to an adjacent breakroom. From the open doorway came the low buzz of conversation, but before I could get a glimpse of my future, Kelsey gave me a hug and wished me luck. I hadn't realized we'd progressed that quickly in our friendship already, but hey, I could use all the luck I could get.

I peered inside the room, which was done in the same modern style as the lobby. It had a lounge area with charcoal gray couches on one side and a dining area with three groups of four-person tables on the other. Along the wall, a table had been set up with an assortment of appetizers and champagne. Normally I'd be down for champagne at 10:00 AM, but alcohol was just about the last thing I needed right now.

The other designers stood around the room, chatting with each other, while cameras and crew filmed everything, our hidden microphones recording it all. I scanned the crowd, a diverse group of both men and women. Most seemed to be in their late twenties or early thirties, but there were a few who were older. The variety of clothes they wore ranged from preppy to goth to hippie chic.

Head high, I walked through the doorway. Everyone in the room turned to face me, probably as anxious as I was to size up the competition. I offered the best smile I could with my head pounding and my pulse shooting through the roof.

And then I froze.

My smile fell.

I was pretty sure my heart stopped, too.

Because in the middle of the group stood my one-night stand with the glorious hair, sexy tattoos, and English accent—looking just as shocked as I was.

Gavin.

Chapter Four

This could not be happening to me. Nope. Not possible. No way in hell.

How could Gavin be *here?* On the show. Standing in the middle of the designers. Drinking champagne.

Wait, wait, wait. Hold the fuck up. Was he a designer, too?

No. Freaking. Way.

His HELLO MY NAME IS read *Gavin Bennett,* so yes, it was really him. Today he wore a black-and-gray plaid shirt with the sleeves rolled up, showing off his tattoos, and jeans that hugged his body in all the right ways. His dark hair still had that sexy tousled look. I wasn't sure how it was possible, but he was even hotter now than he'd been last night.

Memories flashed in my head. The way he'd looked between my legs. The way he'd *felt* between my legs. How I'd made a fool of myself in front of him. And how he'd disappeared in the middle of the night without a word.

Now I had to spend the next few weeks with him. In close quarters. On camera.

Fuuuuuuuuuck.

I never in a million years would have pegged him as a fashion designer. Sure, his clothes had been well made and he'd said he was an artist, but I just couldn't wrap my head around him being *here,* of all places. When you hooked up with a guy from a different country, you weren't supposed to ever seen him again, after all.

He stared back at me, and his mouth twisted, like he wasn't all that thrilled to see me either. Well, he could go straight to hell because I wasn't leaving.

Maybe he'd get kicked off the show early. I could only pray he wasn't very good.

A woman I guessed to be in her sixties with big hair, a pink pantsuit, and a kind smile approached me. "You look a bit overwhelmed."

You have no idea, I almost said. I tore my gaze off Gavin and turned to her. "A little, yeah."

"Don't worry, we all are. I'm Molly, by the way."

I shook her hand. "Julie."

She introduced me to a couple other people standing near us, who I barely registered meeting and whose names I instantly forgot. As we made polite small talk, all I could see was Gavin, talking to a girl with dark purple hair and the sides of her head shaved. He laughed, but then his eyes slid back to me, like he knew I was watching him. Heat rushed through me, and I quickly looked away.

Out of all the guys I had to pick up in a bar, *of course* it ended up being a guy on the show. Yes, I probably should have considered the possibility since we were staying at the same hotel and all…but to be fair, I'd been pretty drunk last night. And if it weren't for this fucking hangover, maybe I'd be able to figure out how to handle this whole mess.

I snatched a glass of champagne off the table and took a sip, hoping that hair-of-the-dog thing would work. But as the cool, bubbly liquid slid down my throat, I nearly gagged. Food—that was the solution. I grabbed a cheese puff and took a small bite, but my stomach twisted as soon as it hit my tongue. Ugh. Maybe food wasn't such a good idea either.

"Aren't the appetizers yummy?" Molly asked, smiling at me.

"I love the mini-quiches," added a pretty girl in a loose floral dress. Her name was something fitting like Summer or Sunny, but her long, golden hair hid her name tag.

I gave a noncommittal grunt and silently swore I was never drinking again. Yes, I said that every time I had a bad hangover. But seriously, I meant it this time.

Then *he* was at my side. I didn't turn, but I still saw him out of my peripheral vision. A flash of his tattooed hand. The familiar whiff of his cologne. More than that, I sensed his tall, imposing presence towering over me. Brooding—that was the word for him.

I wished he'd go brood somewhere else.

"Hello, everyone," he said to our little group. "I'm Gavin."

"Oh, I just *love* your accent," Molly said, smiling and touching his arm. She quickly doled out all of our names, including the pretty blonde—Dawn. "And this is Julie," she said, gesturing to me as I crammed the rest of the cheese puff into my mouth. Crap.

Gavin's steely eyes focused on me, and I swallowed hard. I could tell he was about to say something, probably something about last night. Something I desperately didn't want him to say.

"Nice to meet you," I blurted out, thrusting my hand toward him.

His dark eyebrows shot up, and for a second, I worried he wouldn't go along with it. But then he smiled and took my hand in his own, slowly raising my fingers to his mouth. A little shiver went through me at the brush of his lips on my knuckles. "Julie, is it?"

My eyes narrowed, and I jerked my hand away. Of course he would make a big deal about my name. "That's right."

His grin widened at my reaction. "Lovely to meet you."

I held my breath, waiting for more, expecting him to say something damning. But he turned back to Molly, who'd asked him about living in England.

I exhaled in a rush. He was going to keep our secret. For now, anyway. He could always try to use it against me later, at a more strategic time. After all, he *was* my competition. I'd have to watch out for him. What did I even know about him, really?

Absolutely nothing.

As the others talked, the room began to blur and sway around me. I was barely keeping it together, my head still pounding, my stomach still churning. All I wanted was to lie down somewhere dark and quiet for a few hours. And Gavin's presence beside me definitely wasn't helping matters. The last thing I needed was for him to see how hungover I was. No way was I giving him the satisfaction of knowing he was right about how drunk I'd been last night.

With everyone in our circle focused on Gavin, I slipped away unnoticed. The champagne wasn't helping, so I swapped it for a soda, hoping the caffeine would wake me up. The purple-haired girl stood by herself next to the drink table, and she watched as I rubbed the bridge of my nose.

"Rough morning?" she asked.

"Very."

"Been there plenty of times." She had a shiny stud in her nose and wore tight black ankle pants and suspenders, with a white shirt and red bow tie. Her name tag said, *Trina Rodriguez.*

I leaned against the wall beside her, sipping my soda. "Have you met everyone already?"

"Nah. I'm not exactly a people person. And half of these designers will be gone in a few days anyway."

"Exactly my thought."

"You made that, didn't you?" she asked, her dark eyes scanning my green-and-black dress. "It's cute. I can tell you'll stick around for a while."

"I did, and thanks. I love your outfit, too. Great mix of masculine and feminine."

"Thanks. That's my design aesthetic. I just hope the judges like it, too."

"Who do you think is going to be the biggest competition?"

She crossed her arms and surveyed the crowd. "Hard to tell. But I have my eye on the blonde over there."

"Her name is Dawn, and yeah, her dress is really well made."

"Oh, I just think she's hot," she said with a grin. "But her dress isn't bad either. Maybe I'll go introduce myself."

"Go for it." I raised my soda to her. "Good luck."

Trina strolled across the room and said something to Dawn, who looked up and smiled. I wanted to watch what happened next, but as soon as I was alone, Gavin found his way back to my side. Jesus, I could not get away from this guy.

"So your name's Julie?" he asked, his voice low enough that no one else could hear us. Except for the mic recording everything, of course.

I gestured to my name tag. "That's what it says."

"Sorry, it's just a bit…anticlimactic."

I rolled my eyes. "What did you expect, something more *exotic*?"

"No, but after all that build-up, I expected something a little more… I don't know. Dramatic. Mysterious." His gaze skimmed down my body. "Naughty."

"Sorry to disappoint you."

One side of his mouth curled up. "I suppose I'll have to keep calling you 'love.'"

"That really won't be necessary. Julie is fine."

"Oh no, I can't do that. You said no names, after all."

I quickly switched off my mic. Did Gavin not understand this was all being recorded? That the sound guys were probably listening to our every word? Or did he just not care?

I moved closer, reaching for his shirt as though I was flirting with him. He didn't pull away, and I heard his sharp intake of breath as my fingers slipped inside his collar. I turned off his mic and kept my voice low.

"That was last night. Things have changed. Obviously." I dropped my hand and stepped back. "And you need to be careful what you say while the mics are on."

"Speaking of last night, how are you feeling today, love?"

"I'm fine, *Gavin*," I snapped. "How are you? Get lots of sleep after you took off without a word?"

"I did, actually." He gave me a devious grin that only annoyed me more. "I admit, I never expected to see you again. I'm quite surprised you're here."

"*You're* surprised? You told me you were an artist visiting from London!"

"I *am* an artist visiting from London. *You* said you were a pre-med student."

"I *am* a pre-med student!"

"Then what are you doing on the show?"

"Same as you, I imagine. Trying to win."

"That's too bad, love. Because *I'm* going to win."

I snorted. "I'd tell you to kiss my ass, but you'd probably fall in love with me and then I'd never get rid of you."

He gave a sharp laugh. "Trust me, there is zero chance of that happening."

"Good. Because I don't have time for complications like you."

"Oh, now I'm a complication? You didn't seem to think that last night when I was between your legs."

His words sent a rush of unwanted desire through me. "Last night never happened," I whispered, stabbing a finger into his chest. "And we're never going to speak of it again."

He looked like he was about to argue, but then a tall, dark-haired woman swept into the room and stole everyone's attention. She was in her early fifties and had a delicate, aloof beauty that was only enhanced by her little black sheath dress and long, thin limbs.

Lola Baudin had once been one of the top supermodels in the world, but for the last four years, she'd been the host of *Behind The Seams* and in the last two seasons had also become one of its judges. I'd watched her on TV, seen her in magazines and on fashion websites, and now she was in front of me, sweeping her eyes over all of us. She clapped her hands sharply, and the entire room dropped into silence. I quickly switched my mic back on and saw Gavin do the same.

"Welcome to season six of *Behind The Seams*," she said, with a faint French accent. "Your first challenge begins now."

Chapter Five

Some of the other designers groaned or gasped, but I stood up straighter at Lola's words. I'd expected our first challenge to come quickly, even if I'd been hoping for a little more time to recover first. Judging by his calm expression, Gavin wasn't surprised either.

Lola led us through a door and into the adjacent design room. Even with my raging hangover, I couldn't help but speed up as we walked inside. Long white tables had been set up around a large room, and the mint green walls were decorated with portraits of famous fashion designers like Coco Chanel, Yves Saint Laurent, and my personal favorite, Alexander McQueen. Cameras were discreetly stationed around the edges of the room, and a few crew members stood along the sidelines, watching us. It was strange to get this behind-the-scenes look at one of my favorite TV shows, but otherwise, the room looked exactly as I'd seen it on previous seasons.

Each workstation had a dress form next to it labelled with our names. I found mine and sighed when I saw Gavin's name at the table next to me. I'd never be rid of the guy.

It didn't matter. I wouldn't allow myself to be distracted by him. I'd dreamed of standing inside the design room of *Behind The Seams* for years, and now it was my reality. I wasn't going to screw this up. And definitely not because of some stupid guy.

Even a ridiculously hot stupid guy.

Lola stood at the edge of the room, with a camera focused on her. "Good, you've all found your workstations. The room is crowded now, but not for long. There are fourteen of you here—but three of you will be going home today."

Holy shit. Three eliminations in the first challenge? They were not fucking around.

"Your challenge is to make a little black dress," Lola said, gesturing at her own elegant sheath. "That may sound simple, but you need to find a way to make a dress that is unique and shows us who you are as a designer. And…you only have six hours." Her voice turned cold, and her eyes narrowed. "Impress us, or you'll be going home today."

Hmm. Six hours wasn't much time, although little black dresses were pretty basic and something all designers should have made before. The trick would be to design something that stood out from all the rest in that amount of time.

"There's a box under your workstation with fabric and trim for this challenge," she continued. "You're not allowed to use anything that wasn't from inside a box, but you *can* trade with other designers."

Crap, I should have socialized with the other designers more. Some of them had already formed connections, which might put them at an advantage in this challenge. The only connection I had was with Gavin, and I was pretty sure that wouldn't help me one bit.

"The winner of each challenge gets one thousand dollars and a night in the private winner's suite," Lola said. "The losers will be sent home. You have six hours, starting now."

She swooped out the door, leaving the fourteen designers, plus the camera crews filming everything. While others gasped about the room, complained about only having six hours, or laughed about how surreal it all was, I grabbed the black box under my workstation and popped it open without hesitation. Next to me, Gavin did the same. He must have also realized that the clock was ticking and standing around chatting would only cut into our working time.

Inside I found two types of black fabric: a simple cotton-polyester blend that had a nice weight to it and a heavy brocade with an embossed swirly pattern. The brocade was out; it reminded me too much of old lady curtains. Damn, I'd have to find someone to trade it with. The box also had buttons and zippers, along with other supplies like needles and thread, scissors, pins, measuring tape, and a sketch pad and pencils.

Around the room, there were a few murmurs and quiet conversations, but most of the designers were silent, sketching and checking out their fabrics. A few had already left their workstations to start trading with others. If I wanted new fabric, I'd have to act fast.

I caught a glimpse of Gavin's box and noticed he had some lace and a thick mesh that looked almost like netting. Well, shit, I wanted one of those fabrics. Nothing to do but swallow my pride and ask him for help.

I leaned across my table. "Psst!"

Gavin glanced up from his sketch pad, where he was drawing something with quick flicks of his wrist. "Yes, love?"

"Don't call me that," I snapped, keeping my voice low. "Want to trade one of your fabrics for one of mine?"

He went back to his sketching. "Sorry, no."

Jerk. He hadn't even *looked* at my fabric. He just didn't want to trade with *me*.

I huffed and headed over to Trina's workstation, but she'd already traded with Dawn. I rushed over to the next familiar face, worried that everything good was already getting snatched up.

"Hey, Molly. I want to trade this brocade for something. Interested in a swap? I'll take anything at this point."

"Hmm." She inspected it, then checked inside her black box. "I'll give you this tulle for it."

"Deal! Thank you!" The tulle was thick and fluffy, but I could work with that. We switched fabrics, and I ran back to my station, an idea already forming in my head.

At Gavin's table stood a girl with wavy black hair and so much makeup she'd probably have to chisel it off. Her name tag said *Nika Kazakova*, and she wore a dress with a low V that flaunted the goods. A minute later, she walked off with his lace after giving him a cotton fabric identical to the one I had. He caught me glaring at him and smirked.

Asshole.

Ignore him, I told myself as I pulled the sketch pad from my box. I grabbed my pencil and mentally flipped through all the things I'd sketched at home while preparing for the show. Originally I was going to just wing it all, but Carla had insisted I do some prep work first. That was more her style than mine—Carla was always prepared for everything. She was a plotter, a worrier, an obsessive list-maker. She had an unhealthy obsession with spreadsheets, and don't even get me started on her extensive, color-coded daily planner. I was pretty sure she spent half her modeling paychecks on stickers and fancy pens.

Not me. I tended to jump into things headfirst, confident I'd figure things out as I went along. But now, with a massive hangover and only six hours to come up with a dress, I was happy I'd listened to my friend for a change. Designers weren't allowed to bring anything that could help them on the show, but there was no rule against studying previous episodes and preplanning some of your designs. It wouldn't always help, since there was no way to know the challenges in advance, but I'd come up with a bunch of ideas that could work and stored them away in my mind for future use.

I sketched out a basic idea I hoped would both show off my geek chic aesthetic and stand out among the others, while still fitting the challenge. It wasn't as easy as it sounded, especially since we were limited by our fabrics, but I thought I'd have a pretty good shot at winning the challenge if I could pull off the design I had in mind. Assuming I could finish it in time.

Once my sketch was done, I cut the fabric using Carla's measurements, which I'd also found in my box. I went faster than normal, silently praying I didn't screw up, but for this challenge, there was no time to waste. I still felt like total shit, which wasn't helping matters either. I'd just about murder someone for some more pain meds for my headache. And, in related news, I was somehow both starving *and* nauseous. Basically the worst combo ever.

I shoved all of that deep inside while I worked and managed to block out everything around me, including the other designers' conversations. The few that were going on anyway—most of us were quiet and focused. We didn't have any time to mess around.

I pinned the cotton fabric to the dress form, trying to get it into the correct shape, making adjustments as I went along. Satisfied, I took my tacked-together dress into an adjacent room with sky blue walls and top-of-the-line sewing machines. With fourteen designers, there were nowhere near enough sewing machines and the room was crowded, but I spotted a free one near the back. I rushed to grab it before someone else did.

At the sewing machine next to me, a black guy with a shaved head and muscular arms was telling that Nika girl a story. I'd missed the beginning, but as I sat down, he said, "The producers told me I needed more experience! Can you believe that? After I'd worked on shows at Paris Fashion Week two years in a row, *still* they turned me down! But I came back again and again until I finally got picked."

"They told me the same thing," Nika said, with an accent that sounded Russian. "I auditioned three times before they finally let me on the show. Three times!"

"It took me three auditions as well," a man behind us said in a soft-spoken voice. He was older, maybe late thirties, and had short black hair and brown skin. His name tag read *Tom Nguyen*, and he had a cool geometric tattoo on his upper arm.

"It's just so unfair! What about you?" the other guy asked me. *Derrick Jones*. "How many times did you have to audition for *Behind The Seams*?"

"Um…" Crap. I totally blanked, trying to figure out what to say. I should probably tell them the truth—that I hadn't auditioned at all, but instead had won a spot on the show at Comic-Con. But somehow I didn't think they'd want to hear that, not when they were commiserating and bonding about how hard it had been to get on the show.

Nika gave me a long once-over, sizing me up. "Don't tell me you're one of those lucky bitches who got picked on the first audition."

"No!" Great, yet another thing to lie about. Another secret to keep that would probably come back to bite me in the ass.

Derrick snorted. "Yeah, right. I mean, look at you, you can't be older than what, eighteen? Nineteen?"

"I'm twenty-one," I said. "And I've been working my ass off to get on the show for years." That was true, even if I'd never auditioned. But I'd wanted to for as long as *Behind The Seams* had been on TV.

"Aw, such a baby," Nika said in a sing-song voice, although she couldn't be much older than I was. Thirty, at most. "So tiny, too. Like a little Asian doll. I want to put her in my pocket and carry her around."

Derrick snort-laughed, and the harsh sound made me break one of my needles. Dammit! I swore under my breath, but that only made them laugh more.

"She's so cute when she's mad!" Derrick said.

That was it. I wasn't going to let two jerks who were barely older than me treat me like I didn't belong here. "You two sound jealous. Sorry, I can't help it if I'm the youngest designer this season."

Their laughter died. Derrick sat up a little straighter. "Youngest just means least experienced."

The words stung because I secretly worried he was right, but I gave a little shrug. "Remember those words when you're at home, watching me on the finale."

"You'll be lucky if you make it past this challenge," Nika snapped.

I was firing up another comeback when a commotion in the design room distracted me. The models had arrived and were pairing up with the designers they'd been assigned to. Shit, how much time had passed? This challenge was going by *way* too fast.

I quickly finished my seam and rushed out. Carla was already standing at my workstation, and I was relieved to see her smiling face, even though it had only been a few hours since we'd parted. That is, until I saw the other designers introducing themselves to their models and remembered I had to pretend I didn't know her.

"Hi, I'm Julie," I said loudly, extending my hand.

"Carla," she said, her lips pursed. I could tell she wasn't a fan of this deception either.

"I'm really excited to work with you." I tried to sound enthusiastic, but I was sure it seemed forced. "Let's see if this dress fits."

She took off her top and jeans, leaving her in just a bra and underwear, with zero hesitation about undressing in a room full of people. All around us, the other women did the same. Such was the life of a model, I supposed. It would all be blurred or cut out when the show was edited later, so the viewers at home wouldn't get to see the full, half-naked glory in front of me.

I helped her get the dress on and stood back to check it out. It fit great, but I did know Carla's body pretty well by now. I could pull it in a little on the waist, but otherwise it looked good on her. I switched off my mic and grabbed some pins to make a few adjustments, a good excuse to get close enough that no one could hear our conversation.

"Thank god you're here," I whispered as I brought in the waist. "Today has been a disaster."

"How's your head?"

"Fucking miserable. Feels like someone is pounding nails into my eyes. And my stomach feels like someone has set it on spin cycle." I quickly glanced at Gavin's workstation, but he wasn't there. "But that's not even the worst thing. That guy from last night? He's here."

"What do you mean, here?" She looked around the room. "Are you sure?"

"Of course I'm sure! He's one of the other designers and he's stationed at the next table and oh god don't look, but he's coming back now."

Too late. She tried to be subtle about checking him out, but failed horribly. Not that I blamed her; he did stand out as the hottest guy in the room. Half the other models stopped whatever they were doing to eye him up, too.

"Could you be any more obvious?" I lightly smacked Carla on the arm, and she turned back to me.

"Sorry. I just can't believe he's on the show. Although now we know why he was at the hotel last night…"

"If you're about to tell me I'm an idiot and I should have been more careful, trust me I've already yelled at myself a hundred times in my head."

"I would *never* call you an idiot, Julie."

Gavin returned to his workstation and began speaking with his model, a tall, golden blonde who looked like a warrior princess. Give her a sword and she could be Thor's sister. Even she seemed dazzled by Gavin, launching right into the "I love your accent" spiel I'd heard from so many other girls already today.

His eyes locked on Carla for a long moment, then slid to me with a frown. He gave a faint shake of his head before turning away. Shit, he must have recognized Carla from last night. Another thing he could use against me.

I dropped a pin, and when I bent over to grab it, my head throbbed even harder. Like it just wanted to remind me how much today sucked, in case I'd forgotten. I rubbed my forehead with a soft moan as I stood back up.

Carla looked around, then sneaked something into my palm. "Here, take these."

"What are they?"

"Heavy-duty pain pills. I had them in my emergency travel kit."

"You are an angel sent from heaven." Thank god for Carla's over-the-top planning. I downed the pills and chased them with a big gulp of water. Hopefully they'd kick in fast.

"I've got to head to hair and makeup. Take care of yourself, okay?" She gently rested a hand on my shoulder, her dark eyes worried.

"I will."

She looked like she was about to hug me, but then stopped herself and left with a little wave. Behind me, someone chuckled. Gavin.

I kept my back to him, but I could *feel* his eyes on me. Judging me. Distracting me. Making me fucking crazy. I slammed my scissors down, ripped off a corner of my sketch pad paper, and scribbled, *What's so damn funny?*

I crumpled up the note and threw the tiny paper ball on his table. I refused to look at him, but I heard him chuckle again. A minute later, he discreetly slipped me the wrinkled piece of paper as he walked to the sewing room. He'd written underneath my message, his handwriting neat and precise, with sharp, bold strokes.

Just that I'm not the only one you're pretending you didn't know before the show.

I scratched off another message with my pencil and dropped it at his feet after he returned. *I don't know what you're talking about.*

Anyone else? he wrote back. *Is Lola secretly an old family friend?*

I blew out a long breath and closed my eyes, too tired to deal with his bullshit. *Could you please just not mention this to anyone?*

Don't worry, love. Your secrets are safe with me.

Maybe. Maybe not.

I continued working on my dress, but right when I was in the zone, Kelsey popped into the room and told us we had to take thirty-minute breaks in shifts. My name was called for the first shift, naturally. With the clock ticking and so much work to do, I didn't want to spend a second away from my workstation. Even if lunch would probably be good for me.

Back to the breakroom from earlier, but this time it had more substantial food than just champagne and tiny appetizers. I forced myself to eat a turkey sandwich and chug some soda, ignoring the other designers in the room as best I could. I didn't have the energy to socialize with people I might not know after today.

I finished eating in five minutes and felt about a thousand times better for it, but Kelsey refused to let me get back to work. "Labor laws, sorry!"

I scowled at her, but crashed on a sofa in the corner. Maybe if I closed my eyes for a minute my head would stop spinning.

Ah, blissful darkness, with only the sounds of the low buzz of conversation and the familiar hum of sewing machines. Perfect. One fifteen-minute cat nap and I'd be back to work and better than ever.

———

A hand on my shoulder jolted me awake. I blinked, dazed and blinded by the bright light above me. Gavin stood over me, his dark eyebrows drawn together, a frown on his pretty mouth.

"Wake up, love," he said, nudging me again.

Trina stood beside him, her arms crossed. "C'mon, Julie, you need to get up."

I groaned and sat up, the darkness in my mind slowly receding. A quick survey of the breakroom showed that all the designers during my lunch shift were gone. A sick, dizzy feeling settled in my stomach, but this time it wasn't from my hangover.

"How long?" I asked.

Gavin and Trina exchanged a look. "We're not sure," Trina said. "We came in for our break and found you like this."

"No, how long left in the challenge?"

"One hour," Gavin said.

Shit.

Chapter Six

I rushed into the design room in a panic, my brain stuck on a loop of *fuck shit fuck shit* before taking a detour to *oh god what have I done* and *I'm so fucking screwed*.

I'd lost almost an hour while passed out on the couch. Not a single person from my shift nor the shift after that had woken me. Those jerks. And where was Kelsey? If Gavin and Trina hadn't taken pity on me, I'd probably still be asleep.

Once at my workstation, I weighed my options, trying not to freak out even more. I had so much to do on my dress and very little time left. My original design wouldn't work; I'd never get it finished for the runway show. I'd have to do something a little less complicated, something I could get done in less than an hour. But what?

My little nap might have ruined my chances of staying on the show, but I had to admit I did feel a lot better now. My headache and nausea were gone, replaced only by a grim determination to get this dress done in time, however I could.

Before I knew it, Carla was back with her hair and makeup done, her skin practically glowing. The dress was still nowhere near what I wanted it to be, but we got it on her and it didn't look too bad. I made a few adjustments, snipping strings off the hem, and found her some black knee-high boots in the nearby accessory room, which had more necklaces, purses, bracelets, and hats than I'd ever seen in one place before. I even spotted some bronze goggles, of all things. I made a mental note to use those for a future challenge.

Once Carla was dressed, I stepped back to survey my work while she walked back and forth in front of me—and I wanted to cry. The dress looked rushed and sloppy and, even worse, uninspired. I slouched against the table, rubbing my face.

"It fits great," Carla said, twirling a little and making the skirt flare out. "I'm sure the judges will love it."

"It's a disaster. They're going to send me home for sure."

"They won't. Not a chance."

"I'll be happy to just get to the next challenge. Today's been rough."

She moved to give me a hug, but then paused, glancing around. Instead, she gave me a warm smile. "You will. I'm sure of it."

Lola appeared in the doorway, clapping her hands sharply and calling out, "Designers! Time for the runway show!"

Carla and I rushed out of the room behind Gavin and his Valkyrie model, the other designers and models right on our heels. It was a mob of little black dresses as we went down to the first floor in groups on the elevator, then followed Kelsey into the backstage area behind the runway.

She had a list of what order our models would walk in, and we had five minutes to do any last minute touch-ups before the show began. I did one final check of my dress, but there was nothing more to do. The dress was done. As much as I wanted to rewind the day and go back to last night, to stop myself from ever having a drink or taking Gavin back to my room, time travel didn't exist. I had to live with my bad mistakes and accept the consequences of them.

For the first time, I allowed myself a second to look around the room and take in what the other designers had created. Molly had made a high-necked babydoll dress using the brocade I'd given her. It looked a little dated or stuffy, but it was well-made and flattering on her model. Trina's model wore a short velvet dress designed to look like a man's suit jacket, but with a plunging neckline and high hemline. It was a bit stiff, but very sexy. I didn't think either of them would win, but they definitely wouldn't be going home either.

Gavin's dress stood out from the others, even off the runway. He'd made a structured V-neck dress, but he'd used the mesh to overlay different areas on the bodice and skirt, creating his own geometric pattern that only enhanced her shape. It was subtle and deceptively simple, but when she walked, the mesh caught the light and showed how intricate the work was.

I hated to admit it, but he was good. No, really good. Which meant he was going to be on the show for a while. Dammit.

Before I could check out the rest, the designers were sent to wait in the back-stage lounge while the models did test runs, which consisted of walking up and down the runway while the crew checked the cameras and lighting. I crashed on the couch next to Trina.

"Thanks for waking me. If you hadn't…" I shook my head, the thought too much to even consider.

"No problem. Sucks that you lost so much time."

"I can't believe everyone else just let me sleep."

"I can. We have to look out for ourselves first." She shrugged. "Or maybe they thought you didn't want to be disturbed."

"Still a jerk thing to do," I muttered. I understood her point though. If the tables were turned, if another designer had been passed out while I was awake, would I have woken them? Or would I have thought it was their loss and considered it not my problem? And maybe been a little happy because their lack of time might get them kicked off instead of me?

I honestly didn't know the answer.

"You should really thank that English guy," Trina said. "He was the one who noticed you'd been gone a while."

"I will." Ugh, thanking Gavin was just about the last thing I wanted to do.

I must have made a face because Trina laughed. "I get the feeling you don't like him."

My eyes found him easily. He stood across the room talking to Tom, leaning against the wall and looking effortlessly sexy. Damn him.

"No. I don't know. He…bugs me."

"Oh yeah?" She turned and glanced at him in a super obvious way.

"Don't look at him!"

She did a snort-laugh and turned back to me. "Eh, he seems decent enough. And not bad looking. For a guy, anyway."

I gestured, trying to find the right words without giving away our secret history. "He seems kind of…full of himself."

"Pretty boys usually are."

When Kelsey returned and took us to the runway room, all the designers oohed and aahed. It looked like a theater and was dark except for a long, raised runway that ran down the middle of the space, with lights shining on it. Chairs had been set up on either side of it—fourteen on one, four on the other—and around them, more cameras.

Kelsey directed us to take our seats. I was in the front row, with Gavin directly behind me. My stomach twisted, nerves jumping under my skin, both excited and terrified to see my dress walk down the runway. It was my dream, especially after watching the show for so many years, but now that I was here—and even worse, maybe going home for my stupid dress—I just wanted to throw up. Or maybe that was a lingering effect of my hangover.

Once we were all in place, Kelsey disappeared. We waited for many long minutes with only the sound of people fidgeting in their seats, all too aware we were being filmed. Finally, the judges walked in and took their seats on the other side of the runway. It was tough not to fangirl a little over them—I'd watched them on TV before so many times and now they were about to watch *my* look walk down the runway.

First was Italian designer Ricardo Romano, with his thinning salt-and-pepper hair, wearing one of his own fashionable gray suits with a sky blue shirt. He was one of the original judges on the show and taught a few classes at Parsons on the side. He tended to give constructive feedback, but was a bit more conservative than the other designers. His label had been dying a slow death until he joined the show, and now his clothes were popular with the older viewers.

Ricardo was followed by Beverly Payton, the editor-in-chief at *Charmed*, one of the premier fashion magazines in the world. She had wispy blonde hair done up in a bun and always wore bright red lipstick. She was widely respected as a fashion trend maker and had been on the show since the second season. During her critiques, she could be sort of overbearing but had a great eye.

The next judge was new this season, and they'd kept her identity a tight secret so far: Kiara Jones, a black actress who was only twenty-two but had already started her own fashion line about a year ago that targeted young, trendy women.

She had long, beautiful dark hair and wore a stylish dress I guessed was from her own brand. I was surprised they'd picked her as one of the judges and wondered what kind of critique she would give.

After they were seated, Lola walked out onto the runway in her own little black dress, clearly loving the spotlight. She tossed her hair back and stopped to face us.

"Welcome to your first runway show, designers. Your challenge was to create a little black dress in only six hours. We'll decide now if you showed us anything fab…or if it's all drab. One person will win a thousand dollars and a stay in the private suite tonight, while three of you will be going home. Let's begin."

She walked off the stage and took her seat next to the other judges. The lights dimmed around us and brightened over the runway. Low techno music began to thump in the background. The other designers seemed to freeze, like we'd all taken a big, collective breath we would hold for the duration of the show.

The first model walked out, wearing a tight black dress with cutouts along her sides. I didn't know who the designer was—with fourteen of us it was hard to keep track of whose dress was whose. The judges took notes as the model walked, and when she got backstage, the next model stepped out immediately.

Over the next few minutes I saw more little black dresses than I'd ever seen in one place before. A few stood out from the rest as clear frontrunners, but overall most of them were forgettable. And a few were downright hideous.

When Carla came out, I cringed. My dress wasn't horrible, but it wasn't even close to what I'd originally envisioned. I'd made a cute skater dress that was tight at the top with a low-cut neckline, then flared at the waist thanks to the tulle under the skirt. To make it a little more unique, I'd added a hood, which was pulled up over Carla's head, giving her a mysterious look as she sauntered down the runway.

Carla rocked it as best she could, her hands in the pockets and twirling at the end to show off the skirt's movement, but to me the dress just seemed sloppy. I could have done so much better if only I'd had more time. If only I hadn't gotten drunk or stayed up so late or hooked up with Gavin or or or…

No, thinking like that would only drive me crazy. If I got kicked off, I deserved it for my poor judgement last night. But I would do just about anything to not go home in the first week. I couldn't even imagine it: to finally be on the show and then sent home immediately, like it was a mistake I'd gotten on in the first place. I was sure Nika and Derrick would think so if I was kicked off. I could practically hear their snotty laughter already. I couldn't let that happen. I had to prove to them, to my family, to everyone else that I deserved to be here.

Please, I prayed, *just let me make it to the next round.*

They raised the lights around us, and the four judges walked past the runway and into the back, where the models waited. I knew from watching the show on TV that they got closer looks at the dresses and also discussed their results with each other. Once they were done, they would come out to talk to the designers and decide who was going home—and who was the winner of the challenge.

After they were gone for a few minutes, quiet conversations started up amongst the designers, like we were all a little unsure if we were supposed to talk or not, but couldn't keep it in any longer.

"Your dress was charming," Molly said to me.

"Thanks. I loved yours. You seriously owned that brocade."

"That was all thanks to you. I'm glad we could work out a trade."

"Me too."

"I made a dress like that for my granddaughter on her birthday. That's why I started designing—to make clothes for all nine of my grandkids. Buying them got too darn expensive!" She continued on and on about her family, but I was too worried about my place on the show to do anything but smile and nod.

An eternity later, the judges walked back out, and all the conversations died instantly. The judges took their seats across the runway, except for Lola, who faced us.

"If I call your name, please come up to the runway so we may speak with you. If I don't call your name, you're moving forward and can leave the room." She checked an index card and began reading off names. Some were names of designers I didn't know. She also called out Gavin, Dawn, Tom, and Nika. Nine names in total.

Including mine.

Chapter Seven

As I stood up, Molly whispered, "Good luck." I gave her a hesitant smile and shuffled behind the others toward the steps leading up to the stage. The designers who were safe this week left the room to wait in the backstage lounge for the judging to be over.

Once we were on the runway, Kelsey came out and made sure we stood equal distance apart, before flitting off again out of sight. Our models came out and stood in the gaps between us. Carla gave me a warm smile, and I wanted to grab her hand but knew that would be too obvious. The fact that the judges had called my name could be either good or very, very bad. And I had a sinking suspicion it wasn't good.

Lola surveyed the nine of us before speaking. "We're going to go down the line and talk to each of you. Remember: three of you will be going home today."

They spoke with Dawn first. She'd made a soft, feminine dress that was backless, with two panels of sheer lace running down her model's shoulder blades. The effect was elegant and classy, yet very sexy. They continued down the line, talking with the other designers with the best and worst dresses. Nika's dress barely covered her model's ass and had darts that made her boobs look like cones. Another girl had a dress that looked like it was barely hanging together by a thread and might slide right off if the model moved too much. Both of them were on the bottom. The judges loved Gavin's dress, to no one's surprise.

I was next.

Lola started off the critique. "Your dress looks like something I could pick up in a costume store. On the clearance rack."

Ouch. My body seemed to deflate, like someone had popped me with a pin and all the air was sucked out of me. I was so going home.

Ricardo nodded. "I agree. It looks like she's Red Riding Hood or something."

Kiara looked down at her notes and then back up at me. "Julie, I actually really liked your dress. It stood out on the runway."

I wanted to hug her. If only one judge liked me, it might edge me out over the others.

Beverly cocked her head. "I think you have an interesting idea here, but I don't know if it really fit the challenge. It doesn't *feel* like a little black dress."

"Exactly," Ricardo said. "And I don't know if anyone could really wear it out."

I would totally wear it out, but I just nodded, too tongue-tied to speak without falling apart.

"But it looks fun," Beverly argued. "I could see a young girl wearing it."

Lola rolled her eyes. "To a Halloween party maybe."

"I'd wear it," Kiara said. My new favorite person. "On a cold night? Totally. That hood is fierce, and I love the cut of the dress." She shrugged. "I like it."

I gave her a thankful smile, but it was quickly ruined by Lola's harsh voice. "Of course you'd like it. It looks like something a kid would wear."

Kiara's eyes widened at the nasty comment, but Beverly held up a hand. "I do have to say, it would photo nicely in a magazine. And it fits the model perfectly."

"True," Ricardo said. "But does it fit the challenge?"

I cleared my throat, finally finding my voice. "It's black. And it's a little dress. It just…has a hood, too. And pockets." Carla demonstrated, twirling around and making the skirt flare with her hands in the pockets. If anyone could work this dress, it was her.

Lola sniffed. "It's sloppy."

"They only had six hours, to be fair," Beverly said.

"The other designers managed in that time."

I bowed my head, fighting back tears, ready for the next verbal lash, but they moved on to the next designer. This was my worst nightmare come to life. I was on the bottom and Gavin was on top—and not in a sexual way.

I couldn't go home today. I couldn't.

They made comments to the last designers that I barely heard, then dismissed us to sit down while they went into the back to make the final decision. Carla gave me a sympathetic arm squeeze before she left, but I couldn't even look at her. If I was sent home, she'd be out of the competition, too.

"I'm shocked you're on the bottom," Gavin said, after we returned to our seats.

"Really?" My head snapped up. I'd already convinced myself that my dress was the worst thing ever designed, that I had no idea what I was doing, and that it had been a terrible mistake when they'd invited me on the show.

"Your dress was one of the better ones up there. What a load of rubbish."

"Thanks. And…thanks for waking me up earlier. If you hadn't…"

"You would have done the same for me, love."

I wasn't so sure. Shit, did that mean Gavin was a better person than me?

Another thirty minutes passed. One thing I was learning: we did a *lot* of waiting around on this show while the behind-the-scenes stuff happened. It was a strange contrast to our time during the challenge when we had to rush. Hurry and wait—that seemed to be the way things went around here.

The judges returned and we got back up on the runway to hear the verdict.

"We've made our decision." Lola's gaze swept back and forth across the designers. "And Dawn is the winner of this week's challenge."

"Thank you so much." Dawn's voice was quiet, soft, and feminine, like everything else about her. She was like some sort of forest nymph who had gotten lost and wound up in New York.

"Congratulations, Dawn," Lola said. "You've won one thousand dollars and use of the private suite tonight. We can't wait to see what else you do this season. Gavin, we also loved your dress and expect great things from you, too." She paused, her eyes lingering on him before turning back to us. "And now…as you know, we are sending three designers home this week. It was a difficult decision, but we're going to say goodbye to Jessie, Rilah, and Kathy."

I replayed the names in my head one, two, three times.

None of them was mine.

My breath rushed out of me in a *whoosh*. I was safe for another week.

The eliminated designers muttered insincere and disappointed thanks, although one of the girls flat-out burst into tears. The judges left the room, and Kelsey whisked us into the backstage lounge. The three designers going home said their goodbyes, but it all went pretty fast since no one had gotten a chance to know them very well yet. It sucked for them to be the first ones off the show, but if I was honest, I was just relieved it wasn't me.

The remaining eleven designers were all directed to the third floor, to the space where we'd be living as long as we were on the show: the Loft. Like the lobby, it had that same modern and hip feel to it, with tall exposed ceilings, bamboo floors, and brushed metal everywhere.

The elevator opened directly into a large living room area with a bunch of boxy charcoal couches, and beyond that was a kitchen with granite countertops and stainless steel appliances. There was a hallway that led to four full bathrooms, plus two large shared bedrooms—one for the women and another for the men.

A camera crew followed us inside as we checked the place out, and I knew from watching the show that there were other hidden cameras around the Loft. The only rooms that weren't filmed were the bathrooms and the special private suite that the challenge winners got to use for a night. On previous seasons, the suite had had its own bathroom, eating area, and even a TV and music player. The door to it was in the middle of one of the living room walls, like it was lording over everyone else. Tonight, Dawn would be sleeping in there. Lucky girl.

Kelsey beamed at us once we were all squeezed into the living room. "You have the rest of the night free and dinner will be served soon. Make yourself at home and relax because tomorrow morning, bright and early, you'll have another challenge! Isn't that just the best? See you then!"

Her perkiness seriously grated on me. If I made it through the rest of the show without stabbing her, it would be a freaking miracle.

Our luggage was lined up along the wall. I grabbed the handle of mine and turned to follow the other women into the bedroom—and crashed right into Gavin, who must have been standing behind me. My bag toppled over and I might have gone with it, but he steadied me with a touch on my elbow. Even that slight connection caused a rush of warmth to shoot between my legs.

"Watch it." I yanked my arm away, hoping he couldn't tell how flustered he made me.

"My apologies." He reached down to pick up my bag, but I bent to grab the handle first and jerked it away, the wheels clattering on the hardwood floor. I didn't need or want his help. But as he straightened up, his eyes caught on something on the floor.

A sly grin spread across his lips, and he bent to grab it. He held the offending item up: my red lace panties from the other night. "Lost something, love?"

"I don't know what you're talking about." I snatched the panties out of his hand and wadded them into a ball in my fist, glancing around. Everyone else was too busy with their own luggage to pay attention to us, thank god.

"No? You seem to have a hard time keeping track of those. Maybe I can help…"

"You are the last person I would ever go to for help."

I spun on my heel and walked away before he could reply, but heard him laugh softly behind me. I came close to turning around and giving him another piece of my mind, but I forced myself to keep going. With another challenge early in the morning, I needed sleep.

The bedroom had six twin beds with small nightstands in between. I took one in the corner, and Trina and Molly took the beds near me, which saved me from being stuck next to Nika. Not that it really mattered where you slept because there was no privacy, no space, no escape. We were all going to be *very* familiar with each other over the next few weeks.

Or days, for some of us.

From here on out, one designer would go home every day or two. That didn't leave much time to really get to know people. There were ten challenges per season, narrowing it down to three designers at the end. The finale was always at New York Fashion Week in September, one of the biggest fashion events of the year. It was every up-and-coming designer's dream to show a collection there, and the three finalists at the end of *Behind The Seams* had the chance.

One challenge down. Nine more to go.

Chapter Eight

Day two. We were all up early—way too early for my jetlagged, exhausted self, but at least I didn't have a hangover this time—and once we'd made ourselves pretty, we shuffled down to the design room to start the next challenge.

Lola waited as we spread out around her, her arms crossed like she was already annoyed at us for making her wait even that short amount of time. Today she wore a red dress that showed off her killer legs. She might not have been a runway model anymore, but she was still pretty damn hot.

"About time. I was beginning to wonder if not all of you would make it." She glanced at me as she said it, even though I'd been one of the first in the room. The hell was *her* problem? "But before we start the next challenge, we have a surprise for you."

I cringed, and some of the others gasped or groaned. A surprise on this show was *never* good for the designers.

The door behind Lola opened, and a man walked in with slicked-back hair bleached almost to white, a chiseled jaw, and icy blue eyes. Not to mention toned abs that could be seen clearly through his too-tight, black V-neck shirt. He was hot, no doubt about it, and he knew it, too. He was also a total arrogant jerk, if I remembered correctly.

"This is Jeff Jayson," Lola said with a smile, clearly delighting in our displeasure. "You may recognize him as a contestant on the last season of *Behind The Seams*. We thought he deserved a second chance, so we've brought him back to join you."

He moved to stand beside Lola and flashed the room a smile that was more predatory than friendly. "It's great to be back in the design room. It looks exactly the same as last time I was here."

Shit, this was bad. Jeff had an advantage from being on the show before, giving him extra insight into how it worked and the best way to stay in the game. But more than that, he was a really good designer who was willing to play dirty if needed. He'd come in fourth last season, barely missing out on showing a collection at New York Fashion Week, and I had a feeling he wouldn't let the opportunity pass him by this time. He would do whatever it took to make sure he got to the end.

Jeff found his new workstation, which had been someone else's yesterday, while Lola went on. "For today's challenge, we want you to make an unconventional wedding dress. Something bold, something unique, something we haven't seen before. It doesn't have to be white, but it does need to look like something a bride would wear. You will have two days and two hundred dollars to spend on fabric."

Ooh, this would be a fun challenge. I could already think of a couple unique things I could do. And with two days and a decent budget, I'd have time to make something that would impress the judges. After the last challenge, there was no way I was going to be stuck in the bottom again.

Once Lola left, the crew opened the fabric room for the first time. Some of the designers started sketching, but I rushed right for the fabric. Once I had an idea of what I'd be working with, I could figure out my design.

Inside was like a designer's paradise. Row after row of gorgeous fabrics of all different colors and types, plus all the buttons, zippers, and trim we could ever hope for. I wanted to run my hands along every single one of them, but that would take too much of my precious time. Besides, I would be back for future challenges.

For this challenge, I wanted to use color, but I also wanted to make sure my dress felt bridal. Hmm…what if I got white fabric but dyed it, creating an ombré effect? If I screwed it up, it would go horribly wrong, but an idea was starting to form in my mind that I thought would work.

I spotted a lovely white silk fabric that would be perfect, but it was up high and with my barely five-foot height, I couldn't reach it. And the only other person in this aisle? Gavin.

He was checking out an off-white satin I'd also considered. I debated waiting for someone else to come by or finding someone from the show to help me, but that would take too long. I tried to reach up and grab the bolt myself, but the tips of my fingers only managed to push it back even farther on the shelf. Dammit.

Gavin watched the entire thing with an amused expression that I wanted to smack off his face. I finally sighed and gave in to defeat.

"Would you mind getting that down for me?" I asked. "Please?"

"Funny, I thought I was the last person you would ever ask for help."

"I don't see anyone else around, do you?"

He tapped a finger on his lips, considering. "And if I help you, what will you do for me?"

"Absolutely nothing."

"That doesn't seem fair."

"Fine. What do you want?" I asked, glaring up at him. He was so much taller than me, probably a full foot at least, and being so close to him triggered a rush of unwanted lust. His head was tilted down to mine, his dark hair falling just above his gray eyes, his lips parted. If he wanted a kiss, all I had to do was lift up on my toes and press my mouth against his. Our previous kisses had been so amazing, so unforgettable, that the urge to kiss him again was so strong it was almost painful to resist it.

"Tell me something personal about yourself," he said.

I blinked at him. *That's* what he wanted? "Like what?"

"I don't know… Where do you go to school? Who's your favorite designer? Do you often pick up strangers in hotel bars?"

"UCLA. Alexander McQueen. And it's happened more than once." I held out my hand. "Fabric, please?"

He got it down easily, but didn't give it to me. "McQueen is my favorite, too."

"McQueen is everyone's favorite." I snatched the roll from his arms and stomped out of the aisle. Yes, he was hot enough to melt my panties off, and yes, his accent was doable all by itself, but every time he opened his mouth, I wanted to wrap my hands around his throat. And not in a sexual way.

Okay, maybe also in a sexual way.

Damn him.

In the next aisle, I grabbed four boxes of dye, then had one of the "employees" cut me enough fabric and ring me up. We didn't actually have money to spend, but we were given a budget for each challenge, and all the fabric and trim had prices, which set limits on us. That way, no one could buy ten different fabrics to play with or go back over and over if their fabric choices didn't work out as expected. We had to be strategic with our purchases.

I rushed back to the design room to get to work. A few people talked now and then—sometimes to themselves, sometimes to others nearby—but overall the room was so quiet you could *actually* hear it when someone dropped a pin. From watching the show, I'd never realized how much time the designers spent working in silence. Now I was starting to suspect most of the hours in the design room would be that way. It made sense; the show had to cut down a day or two's worth of recordings into only an hour. They picked out the juicy bits, then edited them all together to make it seem like the designers were surrounded by drama and chaos all the time. But the reality was much different.

In fact, it was almost…soothing. Being surrounded by others hard at work, who loved fashion and designing clothes as much as I did. Even though they were my competition, I felt a kinship with them. We were creators chasing after a shared dream. We all wanted the same thing: to win.

———

The first day of the challenge went by in a blur of dying and sewing, and by the time we were sent back to the Loft, I was exhausted. Most of the designers, including me, crashed immediately, knowing we'd have to get up early to finish our dresses before the runway show.

The next morning, the models arrived only an hour after we'd started working, but luckily my dress was almost done. I'd dyed the silk fabric the day before and let it dry overnight, giving it a beautiful ombré effect: snow white at the top, flowing into a soft blue and pink below the waist, swirling into lavender at the knee, then darkening until the bottom hem was completely black. The dress was lush and magical, and there was no way I'd be in the bottom this time. I might even make it into the top three.

"Are you feeling any better?" Carla asked me while she undressed. I hadn't seen her since the runway show. She was staying back at our original hotel with all the other models who didn't live in New York, so I didn't have any chance to chat with her outside of these moments.

I switched off my mic so we could talk freely. "Much. Although sleeping in a room with a bunch of other women sucks. Some of them snore like you wouldn't believe. But hey, at least I'm not hungover anymore."

"That's good. I was worried about you." Her eyes cut to Gavin, who was hunched over his table as he worked. As usual, he was impeccably dressed in a fitted black shirt with the sleeves rolled up to his elbows and those jeans that fit his ass perfectly. "How are things with you-know-who?" she whispered.

"I'm trying to avoid him as much as possible and pretend he doesn't exist."

"How's that working so far?"

"Not great," I admitted with a sigh.

I helped her into the dress and stood back to inspect it. It was stunning, with the sweetheart neckline showing off her lovely chest and the colors contrasting nicely with her dark skin. The silk hugged her curves as it gradually flared into a trumpet silhouette, then pooled into darkness around her feet.

"Julie, it's so beautiful." Carla looked at herself in the mirror as I stuck a pin in the side of the dress. I'd made the strapless bodice a little too big and needed to bring it in near her underarms so her boobs wouldn't pop out mid-runway show. "I want a dress like this when I get married someday."

"As long as it's not to Daryl," I muttered under my breath. She'd been with her boyfriend for six months, but he was the absolute worst. He'd be possessive and controlling one minute, then act like they weren't even together the next, yet Carla let him get away with it. Maddie—our other roommate back in LA—and I had told Carla to dump him a hundred times, but she never listened to us.

"I know you don't like him, but he's really not that bad," she said, keeping her voice low so no one could hear us.

"No? How does he feel about you coming on the show?"

Her gaze dropped to the floor. "Well, he's not thrilled about it, but…"

Before I could answer, Lola swept into the room and we all froze. "Designers! I have another surprise for you!"

Uh oh. I gripped Carla's hand. We only had a few hours to go; this could *not* be good.

"You have a dress for your bride…but what about her friends?" An evil smile danced on her red lips. "We want you to make a bridesmaid dress that goes with your wedding dress. We'll give you an extra hour and one hundred dollars for fabric. Your additional models will be in shortly."

She walked out, and the entire room seemed to groan at once, me along with them. The bridesmaid dress would have to be pretty simple if we only had an extra hour to do it.

"How am I supposed to make a second dress when I barely have time to finish this one?" I asked Carla, as I helped her take the wedding gown off.

"You'll figure something out. You always do. Like that time when I ripped my dress at—" Her eyes widened when Nika and Derrick walked by, and she coughed. "Um...I better get to hair and makeup."

"Good idea." I didn't think anyone had heard her, but she needed to be more careful. With competition as fierce as it was, I didn't want any of the other designers to know our secret and try to use it against me somehow.

"Sorry," she whispered as she walked away.

Once she was gone, I returned to the fabric room to buy more of the silk I'd used on the wedding dress. I had an idea for what to do, but I'd have to dye the fabric fast and pray it would be dry in time for the runway show. Maybe there was a hair dryer I could borrow somewhere.

When I got back, I found a note on my table, written in Gavin's precise handwriting.

You two should be more careful. Wouldn't want anyone to find out your secret. One of them, anyway.

Is that a threat? I wrote back, nearly ripping the paper with the rough, jagged strokes of my pencil.

Of course not, love. Just an observation.

My head snapped up, and I caught him watching me. Good. I ripped up his note in an exaggerated way, walked over to the trash, and tossed it inside. His eyes followed me the entire time, and I gave him a pointed look before returning to my table. Hopefully he got the hint that this conversation was *over*.

———

I managed to finish both my looks in time, and my bridesmaid dress paired perfectly with my wedding gown. It was knee-length, with the ombré effect done in reverse—the bodice all black, fading to lavender at the waist, then blue and pink, and finally snow white along the hem. Together, the two dresses were stunning, and I thought for sure the judges would love it.

But I ended up in the middle.

I tried to be happy about that. Being in the middle was better than being in the bottom three and possibly going home, after all. But I'd really thought I would be in the top this time.

Those of us in the middle returned to the backstage lounge to wait for judging to finish. I took some pleasure in seeing Gavin among us, even though—and I would never admit this to *anyone* out loud—I'd loved his wedding dress and thought he should have been the winner. He'd made a very structured, high-collared ball gown with long sleeves and a low neckline, all in black satin except for white tulle underneath that peeked out. It was incredibly beautiful, straddling the line between elegant and sexy, modern and classic, goth and bridal.

Trina had made my second favorite look, a cream-colored pantsuit with a plunging neckline and a cape. Her bridesmaid dress was actually a cobalt blue romper done in a similar style, and both looks had a unique blend of masculine and feminine, while still being very sexy. It was a bold and risky take on the challenge, and she'd known the judges would either love it or hate it. She was out on stage now, but I didn't know if she was in the top three or the bottom three.

I picked a seat across from Gavin to avoid any moments like the one we'd had in the fabric room. Unfortunately, that meant I was stuck on the couch with Jeff. Derrick sat on the other side of him, and he stared at Jeff so hard I could practically feel the fanboy waves coming off him.

"Your look should have been the winner," Derrick said.

"The judges just didn't want to give me a win on my first challenge back on the show," Jeff said. "Not to mention, my model is far too busty. It's really unfair for me to have to design around that. Everyone else has a normal-sized model."

Give me a fucking break. He had a gorgeous redheaded model with an amazing body, and now he wanted to blame her for not winning? When he should have been the one designing for her proportions? What an asshat.

"Totally unfair," Derrick agreed. "You were my *favorite* designer on last season's show. I was shocked you didn't win! It should have been you."

Jeff shrugged, smoothing his bleached hair. "It's my fault, really. My work last season was too conceptual for the judges. Too avant-garde, too fashion-forward. They didn't get it."

I rolled my eyes so hard I gave myself a headache. Too avant-garde, my ass. His problem was he refused to take constructive criticism from anyone. And I doubted he'd gotten any better since then.

"Is it tough being back on the show?" Derrick asked.

"Not really. The hardest part is leaving my boyfriend for such a long time again. He misses me so much when I travel all over the world for work. He's totally lost without me."

Wow. It wasn't that *he* missed his boyfriend. It was that his boyfriend couldn't handle it without Jeff for a month or so. I wondered if they would still be together once this footage was aired on TV.

They carried on, but I draped myself over the armchair of the couch and tried to tune them out. Across from me, Nika scooted *very* close to Gavin, and I couldn't help but notice how short her skirt was and how her bare thigh pressed against his and how she leaned toward him to show off her low-cut top and huge breasts.

Not that I cared. She could have him. Really.

"It must feel good to be the only straight guy on the show this season," she said to him, and it was tough not to gag.

He looked taken aback by her question. "I'm not sure what that has to do with anything."

"It means you can have your choice of just about any girl here."

He gave a short laugh. "I didn't come on the show to meet women."

She rested a hand on his knee. "Nothing says you can't have some fun while you're here. I bet every girl here would be happy to help."

It was pretty clear she wanted to be the one he picked for that fun, but I couldn't stop myself from muttering, "Not this girl."

His eyes met mine, and an amused smile lit up his face. Dammit, I should have pretended I wasn't listening.

"You sure about that?" he asked, his gaze traveling down my body in a way that made my face flush. Not from embarrassment, but because I remembered the way he felt between my legs and couldn't help but want him again. And, from the smug look on his face, I could tell he knew exactly what I was thinking.

Cocky asshole.

"True. Some girls here don't like dicks." Nika flashed me a pointed look as she said it. Like I gave a single fuck if people thought I was gay.

"Somehow I don't think that applies to Julie," Gavin said, giving me a devious grin.

Nika laughed in an exaggerated way, throwing back her head and exposing her neck. She squeezed Gavin's leg at the same time, clearly trying to get the attention back on her. But he ignored her, keeping his eyes locked with mine.

We stared each other down while the rest of the room looked on, neither one of us willing to back down from the challenge…or able to deny the heat flickering between us. If we'd been alone, the urge to kiss him would have been impossible to resist, not with the fire in his eyes that matched the one inside me. It was only the space between us and the other designers walking back in—with Trina as the winner, luckily—that saved me from the temptation.

But a girl could only resist for so long.

Chapter Nine

I managed to avoid Gavin for the next two days, which was the only way I got through the third challenge without being tempted to kiss him…or kill him. My urges flipped back and forth every fifteen minutes, usually triggered by him looking hot and then saying something arrogant. One second he'd stretch and show off his sexy tattooed arms, and then he'd open his mouth and ruin it all.

For the third challenge, we had to design an outfit for a "real" woman, not a model—and her dog. I made a short, princess-cut dress out of a gorgeous print with stark gray vines, then layered it with a long black vest. The dog got a matching vest with a strip of the print running along the sides.

The judges put me in the middle again, but I was just glad to get through it without my finger getting chomped off. I loved dogs, but I'd gotten a pampered Chihuahua that liked to nip, and his owner hadn't seen a problem with that at all. Not that I was surprised, since she'd decked him out in a collar studded with diamonds and named him Prince. She was even more difficult to work with than her dog.

But the worst part about the challenge? Gavin won.

———

Back in the Loft, I grabbed some dinner from the buffet they'd set up in the kitchen and sat with Trina and Dawn at one of the tables. I hoped Molly would grab the last seat, but instead Gavin took it. Since he'd won the challenge, he could have spent dinner in his private suite, but no. And now Molly was forced to sit at another table. Thanks a lot, asshole.

"Congratulations," Dawn said to Gavin, giving him a friendly smile. "Both your looks were great. I was so impressed with everything you did in such a short time."

Gavin had created an awesome chainmail jacket for his dog, a short-haired dachshund, along with an off-the-shoulder top and cropped pants with chainmail trim for the owner. He'd made the chainmail himself, painstakingly crafting it by connecting different aluminum rings with a pair of pliers. I had no clue how he'd managed to get it done in time.

"Thanks, although I think they should have given it to Julie."

"No, you deserved it," I said, stabbing my salad with my fork. I kept waiting for the guy to screw up, to not make something amazing, but he kept letting me down. "How did you learn to make chainmail?"

"I watched some YouTube videos and taught myself. It was a great way to pass the time while my sister made me watch TV with her hour after hour."

Wow, I'd learned something personal about him. "Is she back in England?"

He paused, fork halfway to his mouth, and his brow creased. "She's…home, yes."

Okay, that was awkward. There was obviously more to the story there, but for once, the guy looked uncomfortable. I was torn between reveling in his discomfort and wanting to make him feel better somehow. Stupid emotions, always causing me trouble.

"Gavin deserved the win, but I'm sure going to miss the private suite tonight," Trina said, in an obvious attempt at changing the subject. Today she wore a purple bow tie that was the same color as her hair. "I'm not looking forward to sleeping in the women's room again."

"Why's that?" Gavin asked. He'd finished eating and now stacked mini cups of coffee creamer into a pyramid, higher and higher.

She leaned forward and lowered her voice. "Let's just say one of the women snores like a donkey being strangled."

Dawn lightly smacked her hand. "Trina, that's not polite!"

"Sorry, but it's true." Trina laughed, and I noticed their hands lingered on each other. Was something going on between them? I knew Trina was into Dawn, but this was the first hint I'd seen that Dawn might return the feelings.

"She's right," I said. Trina was talking about Molly, and the description was spot on. "I think I need to invest in some earplugs if I'm going to get through the next few weeks."

"I'd be happy to share the private suite tonight," Gavin said, giving me a sly smile.

"You wish."

"Thanks, but I don't sleep with dicks," Trina said, and we all chuckled at her double entendre.

"Touché," Gavin said. "I would have taken the couch anyway."

"Wow, such a gentleman," I said. "But I'll still pass." I flicked a finger at his coffee creamer pyramid and knocked it over. Bitchy? Maybe. But the guy got under my skin like no one else ever had.

"Pity." He grinned and grabbed the cups rolling across the table and began stacking them again. The urge to mess up his pyramid a second time was hard to resist, but I restrained myself. Barely.

"I'm sure you'll win a challenge soon," Dawn said, smiling at me.

"The next one, for sure," Trina added.

I waved my hand dismissively. "Whatever. I'm just happy I wasn't in the bottom again. The middle is good enough."

"No, you deserved to be in the top on the last two challenges," Gavin said. "Your wedding gown was unique, with that ombré effect. And both your looks today were brilliant."

His praise was almost enough to make me feel better, but not quite. "Thanks, but you guys don't need to cheer me up. I was just lucky to get through this challenge without any bite marks. Mostly from the woman, not her dog."

The others laughed and launched into stories about the dogs they'd worked with. I laughed with them, but all throughout dinner, I couldn't ignore the fact that I was sitting at a table with three winners, while I felt like the biggest loser ever.

I'd been confident when I'd come on the show. Maybe too confident. When I'd learned I was the youngest designer this season, I hadn't let it phase me. I'd taken it as a sign that I deserved to be here. Even when Derrick and Nika called me inexperienced, I'd brushed it off.

But now I keenly felt my lack of experience and schooling. Yes, I was a pretty good designer, but the other contestants had gone to college for fashion design, had worked for other designers, and had spent years in the field already. Me? I'd spent the last few years preparing to be a doctor while tinkering with clothes in my bedroom in my spare time. And that wasn't enough.

I was out of my league here. If I didn't step up my game soon, I would be out.

Problem was, I didn't have the first clue how.

———

I couldn't sleep. I stared at the ceiling for hours, my poor, exhausted body begging my mind to shut off already, but nothing worked. That damn anxiety was back, giving me insomnia again. And Molly's foghorn snoring definitely wasn't helping.

After another hour, I couldn't take it any longer. I got up and tiptoed past the other sleeping girls and into one of the bathrooms. I stayed in there for a few minutes, enjoying the beautiful sound of silence, until I thought I could brave the bedroom again. But as I walked down the hall, I heard Gavin's voice.

"Julie," he said, calling me by my real name for a change. "You're still awake."

"Just using the bathroom." I was suddenly all too aware of what I was wearing: a thin tank top and tiny shorts—nothing else. Not that he hadn't already seen plenty of me before. But this seemed more intimate somehow.

He leaned against the doorway of the winner's suite, one tattooed arm arched over his head. He was still dressed in his usual button-up shirt with the sleeves rolled up and dark jeans. Neither one of us was wearing our mics. "Do you want to talk?"

"Not really." I should walk away. Say goodnight. Yet I didn't move.

"The offer to stay tonight is still on the table. And I'm happy to take the couch." He lowered his voice. "Unless you don't want me to."

Heat flickered through me from his gaze and at the offer in his words. "Ask Nika. I'm sure she'd love to join you."

"I don't want Nika." He took a step forward and brushed the hair away from my face. "Come inside. We can discuss whatever's bothering you."

"Nothing's bothering me," I said, although I didn't move away.

"That other night you begged me to stay with you. You said you didn't want to be alone." His voice was quiet, too low to be picked up by the cameras recording us. He placed his hands on my bare arms, rubbing my cool skin as though to keep me warm. "Perhaps I can help you sleep tonight, too."

I stiffened at his words. Yes, I often had trouble sleeping, but I hated the reminder of how pathetic I'd been that night. "What, you think because we hooked up one time that you know me? You're wrong. You don't know anything about me."

"No? I know you're smart and passionate and not afraid to speak your mind. I know you're creative and talented and hard-working." His words were too much, making me feel things I didn't want to feel. I looked away, but he bowed his head to whisper into my ear. "I know how you taste between your legs. I know the way it sounds when you moan my name. I know the look on your face when you come."

How dare he bring that up, and how dare my treacherous body respond so easily, practically melting right into his arms. The smell of him, the sound of his voice, the feel of his hands on me—all combined to fill me with an overwhelming rush of desire. It was all I could do not to crush my mouth against his.

And yet, at the same time, I wanted to tell him to go to hell.

He shrugged and took a step back, completely unaffected, and returned to the suite's door. "Have a lovely evening."

Oh, hell no. He thought he had all the power in this relationship, and I had none. But I was going to find a way to tip the scales. I planted my hand on the door, stopping him from closing it. "Wait."

A smile spread across his face. "Change your mind?"

"No. We…we need to talk."

He stepped back and let me in. The door shut behind me.

We stood in a large room with a king-sized bed covered in a luxurious, fluffy duvet that looked a thousand times more soft and comfortable than the one on my twin bed in the other room. It practically begged me to lie down on it. Across from it was a huge flat-screen TV, the only one in the Loft. On the other side was a seating area, plus a table and chairs and a mini-fridge. A bottle of wine and two glasses sat on top.

Shit, what was I doing? I didn't want to talk. I wanted to throw him on that fancy bed and ride him like I'd stolen him. But that was a bad idea. A really, really seductive bad idea.

"So talk, love." He started unbuttoning his shirt. In front of me. Slowly. Like he wanted me to watch. And at that first flash of skin, all the words I was going to say slipped from my mind.

"Hmm?" he asked.

I forced myself to look away as another button popped open. "Stop that."

"Stop what?"

I gestured at him, eyes averted. "Undressing."

"Just getting comfortable." He draped his shirt over the back of a chair, and I pointedly did *not* look at his naked chest. "You're welcome to stay. We could finish what we started the other night."

"You mean, before you disappeared?"

"If I remember correctly, *you* fell asleep."

I gave a little shrug. "You didn't seem very into it anyway."

"I was *very* into it." He crossed the room to me, and now I couldn't help but take in his toned, lean chest, dusted with a touch of dark hair trailing down into his black jeans. "But I don't have sex with drunk women."

"No, you just go down on them and then leave."

He moved closer, almost touching me, only an inch apart. He lowered his head to speak into my ear, and his breath was soft against my skin. "I don't remember you complaining. Or should I remind you?"

His accent made every word sound like sex, and I had a hard time thinking straight. I shook my head, trying to clear it. "Why did you leave then?"

"You were passed out. I waited for a bit, but then I went back to my room. Staying any longer would've only complicated things." He didn't touch me, and yet we stood so close that I felt him everywhere. Every word was like a physical caress, every breath a promise.

"You could have left a note."

"You made it clear you didn't want anything to do with me after that night."

"I didn't. I *don't.*"

"And yet you're in a bedroom with me in the middle of the night."

He'd got me there. I scrambled for an excuse. "I'm here to talk about…Carla."

"Ah. Don't worry. I won't reveal your secret."

I should move away from him—standing this close to someone for so long was far too intimate—yet I couldn't pull away. The sexual tension was so strong it practically crackled between us, and it was everything I could do to hold myself back. But he hadn't touched me either, like he was waiting for me to make the first move. "Why should I trust you?"

He gave a casual shrug. "I didn't tell anyone about us, did I?"

"There is no *us.*"

"No, of course not."

Our lips crashed together, our bodies closing the slight gap between us. I kissed him hard, forcing his mouth open, flicking my tongue inside. He gave as good as he got, his hands gripping my waist and pulling my body against his. My chest rose and fell against his, my breasts brushing his bare skin through my thin top. I couldn't stop myself from touching his shoulders, sliding my hands down every ridge of his toned abs to his hips…and even lower. He was already hard; I could feel it through his jeans and my clothes. Proof that I affected him as much as he affected me.

"This means nothing," I said when we broke apart.

"Keep telling yourself that, love."

His lips trailed down my neck, and his hands glided down my lower back. I closed my eyes and leaned into his body, into his warm kisses and the desire that swept through me every time he touched me. He made everything else in my head vanish except this moment with him, and that scared me. I couldn't afford to forget that, outside this room, he was my competition—and I had a feeling that if I let him in, if I let him get too close, he could really hurt me. He knew too many of my secrets already.

Besides, I wasn't looking for anything serious. I didn't want to like him or get involved with him. I just wanted to fuck him. What we had was purely physical, that was it. And I was tired of this power imbalance between us. He knew me in an intimate way, and he seemed to think that gave him the upper hand. No more.

I pushed him back, palms flat against his chest. He watched me as I focused on his jeans. Popping the button open. Sliding the zipper down. Gripping the fabric and easing them off. He didn't stop me, and soon he was in nothing but black boxer briefs, straining at the front.

Those had to go, too.

Every new inch of skin revealed only made him hotter, and by the time he stood naked before me, I was dying for a taste of him. I wanted to devour him, to lick every inch before filling my body with him. He watched me silently, letting me take control, but even without words, it was obvious how much he wanted me. I loved having that power over him. And now I'd seen him completely naked, while he'd seen only part of me. The balance was beginning to shift back into my favor.

He reached for my shorts, but I pushed his hand away. There was something I had to do to even the scales. Something I'd been dying to do since that first night we'd met in the bar.

I kneeled in front of him, like he'd done to me the other night, and pulled his hips to me. I slid my hands along his thighs, along the coiled muscles in his legs that must come from some sort of exercise or sport. I knew so little about him. But, I reminded myself, that was the way I wanted it.

My fingers explored him, cupping, stroking, and squeezing. He watched me, growing harder with each touch, his entire body straining for more. I moistened my lips, sliding my tongue across them, and his hungry eyes followed my every move. But I wanted him to suffer a little.

He groaned. "Julie…"

"Stop talking."

He opened his mouth like he was going to protest, until I flicked my tongue along his tip. That shut him up real fast.

I gave him one long, slow lick down his length, and he shuddered. I took my time, teasing him, exploring him with tiny, quick kisses and tastes. Giving blowjobs was a specialty of mine, honed and refined over many years and many guys. Maybe that made me a slut in some people's eyes, but fuck that. I liked men, I liked sex, and I liked myself, and I didn't give a damn what other people thought. And as Gavin threw his head back and moaned while I took him in my mouth, my experience was paying off.

"Julie, love," he managed to get out as my lips closed around him.

I drew him in, taking him deeper into my mouth, working him over with my tongue. His hands dug into my hair, gripping it hard, pulling until it almost hurt. The slight pain turned me on even more and I wanted him inside me, but that wasn't going to happen. Tonight was about making him suffer like I had, about knowing him in a way only a lover could, about settling the score between us.

I cupped his balls in one hand and grabbed his ass with the other, digging my nails into his tight skin. His hips jerked, sliding my lips along his length as he moved in and out. I yanked him closer, deeper, pulling him in. His hands fisted tighter in my hair, and even though he tried to direct me, I had all the power in this position. My hand slid up and down his length in time with my mouth, while my tongue swirled around the head. He bucked against me, groaning, but I didn't let go.

"Love, if you keep that up, I—"

I let him slip from my mouth and glared up at him. "Stop. Talking."

I took him deep again before he could say another word, and between my lips, tongue, and fingers, he soon lost the ability to speak. Only grunts and groans came from him, along with a few murmurs of my name. I increased my pace, flicking my tongue along him harder, faster, deeper. My eyes trailed up his long, lean body, and I watched as his face twisted, his hands gripped my hair tighter, and every inch of his body seemed to clench up for an instant before he let go, releasing himself into my mouth. I kept going until he was completely done, until he was practically falling over in front of me. Only then, when he was completely spent, did I release him.

His hands slowly extracted themselves from my hair. I stood up, fingers trailing along his bare hips and up his chest. He lowered his head to kiss me, but I turned away, despite the overwhelming urge to meet his mouth with mine. He reached for the hem of my tank top, pushing it up, and his touch sent flurries of lust across my skin.

"Stay with me tonight," he said.

I moved to the door, even as my body hummed for his touch, aching to feel him inside me. But no matter how much I wanted to turn around, to push him down onto the bed and climb on top of him, I resisted.

"Now we're even," I said and walked out.

Chapter Ten

There was no phrase that elicited more groans and sighs on *Behind The Seams* than "team challenge."

Even as an adult, I had terrible memories of being picked last on teams, and it wasn't like I'd done very well on the show so far. I didn't expect anyone to want me as their first or even second choice.

"Gavin, since you won the last challenge, you get to choose your partner first," Lola said.

He tapped his lips, and I couldn't help but remember how they tasted. I waited for him to call out Dawn or Trina or even Tom, since the two of them seemed to get along well. I'd overheard them discussing their tattoos during lunch breaks.

"I'll pick Julie."

His words didn't register at first until Trina nudged me forward. I moved to stand beside him, frowning. Why had he picked me? No, how *dare* he pick me? I had finally evened the score between us, finally taken back some power from him, and now he'd done *this*. He'd chosen me out of all the other designers, even though he could have picked whomever he wanted.

Yet, as annoying as it was, it was also a relief to be chosen.

Dammit, now I owed him again.

He didn't look at me as I took my place at his side, but I was already dreading this challenge after what I'd done last night. How awkward would it be, working with him after I'd given him a blowjob and then taken off? Would he bring it up? Or pretend it hadn't happened?

Lola pursed her lips as I joined Gavin. "Trina, you're the next team leader."

"Dawn."

No surprise there. Dawn gave a little squee and moved to Trina's side, her flowing dress trailing behind her. I was happy they got to work together, even if I was a little jealous. I'd give my left boob to work with either of them instead of Gavin.

The rest of the designers paired up one by one until finally Derrick chose Nika, who looked particularly sullen at being picked last. Once the teams were settled, Kiara Jones walked into the design room, wearing a short pink dress that hugged her curves. She smiled and waved at all of us. "Hi, everyone!"

We all muttered a "hi" in response. It was strange to see her outside of the runway show, but not uncommon for the judges to sponsor certain challenges.

"My next movie *Fear the Reaper* comes out October 10, just in time for Halloween. It's about a reaper who goes on a killing spree at a high school prom. For this challenge, we want you to make a look fit for the movies and perfect for Halloween."

Ah, the Halloween challenge. Always one of my favorites to watch because the dresses tended to be more fantastical. It was a little weird to be designing something for Halloween when it was the middle of August, but I guess that was how TV worked. They'd film the episode now, but air it in a few months.

Kiara held up one of those black plastic witch cauldrons used to hold Halloween candy. "We have five different movie genres in here. Your team will randomly pick one, and you'll have to make a costume for the heroine in that kind of movie. Feel free to go big for this one! Make it dramatic, make it fun, or make it scary! As long as it fits your genre and looks good, the judges will be happy. You have two days and two hundred dollars."

She had each of the team leaders come up one by one and pick a piece of paper from the cauldrons. Derrick and Nika got horror, Molly and Paige got fantasy, Dawn and Trina got fairytale, and Jeff and Tom got sci-fi.

I held my breath as Gavin reached his hand inside, but completely deflated when he read off, "Historical."

Well, shit. That was the worst one he could have chosen. I'd have killed for sci-fi or even horror. I'd have even taken fairytale. Gavin and I were so not the designers for historical. We both had more modern styles—his more structured and edgy, and mine more geek chic. How could we possibly translate that into a historical look?

They sent us to our workstations to brainstorm ideas. Gavin pulled up a stool and sat, which put him at about eye level with me for once. He grabbed the sketch pad and a pencil. "All right, we're doing historical. Any ideas?"

"None. You?"

"Not a single one."

"We are so fucked."

"I suppose we should pick a historical period first." He propped his elbow on the table and idly played with his hair as he thought, flashing his tattooed hand.

"Why a rose?" I blurted out.

"Pardon?"

I touched the back of his hand where the red rose had been inked into his skin. "Your tattoo."

"Rose is my sister's name." He pulled his hand away, resting it on the sketch pad like he didn't want me touching him. Probably upset about last night. Fine, we'd stick to business. I shouldn't have asked him anything personal in the first place.

"1920s? 1940s?" I suggested.

"Both too expected."

I blew out a long breath. "You have any better ideas?"

"Not really." He sighed. "Why couldn't we have gotten sci-fi?"

"I know. That would have been perfect for us."

I looked over at Tom and Jeff on the other side of the room, who were quietly discussing something on their sketch pad. Tom had an elegant, minimalistic aesthetic, while Jeff had an experimental, modern style, so sci-fi was a good fit for them. They'd probably win.

But I wasn't giving up that easily. I tried to think of what Gavin and I could bring to a historical look. Maybe I could draw upon my cosplay skills here. "Um, I can make a mean corset."

"That could work. But if we do medieval or Renaissance, it might look too much like what the others are making for the fantasy or fairytale looks."

True. Gah, if only we'd been given fantasy, I had a ton of ideas for—oh!

"I have an idea!" I grabbed Gavin's arm before I realized what I was doing. "We could make a steampunk dress!"

"Steampunk?" He didn't seem nearly as excited as my genius idea warranted.

"It's like Victorian-era sci-fi, with corsets and clockwork and gritty colors and…"

"I know what it is. But I don't think that really counts as historical."

"Why not? They said to do a movie costume. They said it could be over-the-top and dramatic. I even saw some bronze goggles back in the accessory room. And like you said, if we do a generic period piece, it will be too predictable, too expected, too boring. This will make us stand out."

"We'll definitely stand out…but I'm not sure if they'll love it or hate it. They could fault us for not sticking exactly to our genre."

I threw up my hands. "Then by all means, come up with your own idea. I haven't heard you offer anything better."

"No, I like this idea, but I think it's risky. It could very well get us in the bottom."

"Well, I'm used to being there. But I'd rather get there making something fun than something that bores me to tears."

He shook his head. "Fun. Bah. I hate that word. Americans are always using it. You're all so damn excitable. Why does everything have to be *fun*?"

I rolled my eyes. "Fine, it won't be fun at all. It will be very serious because we're serious artists who make serious clothes. No fun on this team, no sir."

"All right, love. We'll have a *little* fun. Not too much though. Let's not get carried away here."

We figured out our design, bouncing ideas off each other, compromising so that the design represented both of us. We decided to give our steampunk look more of a Wild West feel so we could do something sexier and give it more of a movie vibe. Eventually we nailed down a sketch we were both excited about and divided up tasks so we would contribute equally over the next two days.

And for a few minutes, I completely forgot what a total pain in the ass he was.

Once inside the fabric room, we spent far too long arguing over which fabrics to get, then split up once it was finally settled so I could get the boning and buckles. I would be making the corset, which would probably take me both days, so Gavin would make the shirt underneath and the skirt. Tomorrow we would combine the pieces and work on the details and finishing touches.

Back at our workstations, we laid out all our materials and began measuring the fabric. Since Gavin was the team leader, we'd be using his Valkyrie model, which sadly meant another two days without Carla. I needed to talk to her about all of this Gavin mess, but I didn't have any way to contact her. I was on my own.

I missed my phone so bad. And the Internet, gah. I was going through serious withdrawals. I missed checking up on all my friends on social media, playing silly quizzes, and browsing the latest gossip and news headlines. I had no clue what was going on in the world, with my friends, or with my family.

But at the same time it was kind of…nice. I could focus on the present, on the people around me, and on my own headspace without all the drama of the rest of the world interfering. Maybe it was good to unplug sometimes.

"You know," Gavin said, as he cut into the brown fabric we'd bought. "If we win, one of us gets to use the private suite again."

I should have known he would bring up last night eventually. "Uh-huh…"

"Shall we continue what we started the other nights?"

I sighed and gave up on trying to hide our previous encounter from the cameras, since he couldn't seem to let it go. "There's nothing to continue. The first night I was drunk and horny, and you happened to be in the right place at the right time to get me off. Last night I was just returning the favor. Now we're even, and we're done."

"Ouch," he said, placing a hand over his heart. "You crush me. I was starting to think you might actually like me."

I snorted. "Don't get your hopes up."

He pointed his scissors at me. "You can't deny you enjoyed yourself."

I ignored that comment and instead asked, "Is that why you picked me for your team? Because of last night?"

"No. I picked you because you're a great designer and our design aesthetics could work well together. And because, believe it or not, I like you."

"You *like* me?"

"Sure. You're like a baby T-rex."

"Full of hate, but in a cute way?"

"No, small yet fierce. And you have a mean bite."

I couldn't help but laugh. "And short arms?"

"I didn't say it, but I did have to help you get that fabric down…"

"Hey, it's not my fault they put everything good up so high only giants like you can reach it."

"Aha, so you're just using me for my body."

"You know it."

"I can live with that." His grin sent a flush through my entire body, and I grabbed the measuring tape from around my neck and turned to my corset.

No more flirting. Back to work.

A loud giggle caught my attention at the next workstation—Dawn, covering her mouth as she laughed at something Trina had said. Trina looked especially dashing today in black suspenders and a pinstripe bow tie, a nice contrast to Dawn's vintage floral dress and golden hair. Trina winked at me and grinned. I gave her a thumbs-up.

Gavin and I worked for hours side by side, sometimes in silence, sometimes asking for the other's advice or offering an opinion. My corset was beginning to come together nicely. I couldn't do a true Victorian-style corset in such a short amount of time, but I was going to do my best to make a simpler one with the same look. It wouldn't cinch the model's waist as much as a real corset and wouldn't be as durable, but whatever, it only had to last one runway show.

Meanwhile, Gavin was working hard on the skirt, which would be a real show-stopper if he could pull it off. The keyword here being *if*. He'd promised me an adjustable length skirt and his sketch looked like a blueprint for some complicated feat of engineering, but I wasn't confident it would work. Still, he was a great designer, so I was willing to let him try.

"Lunchtime is in five minutes!" Kelsey called out, breaking me out of my working trance. "You'll send one of your team members for the first shift, then you'll switch off for the next one."

"I'll go," I said. "I'm at a good stopping point."

Gavin kneeled by our dress form with a pin in his hand, trying to get the location of the ruffles on the back perfect. "Bring back some good intel."

"Like what?"

"Anything we can use to win. Someone must have a dark secret we can exploit. Other than you, of course."

"You're ruthless. What house did the Sorting Hat put you in? Slytherin?"

"Which one is that again?"

"Oh my god, how do you not know this?"

He shrugged. "I never read the books. I saw the first *Harry Potter* movie, but that's it."

"But you're English. Aren't those books required reading over there?"

"That's exactly why I never read them. Too much hype."

"You have no idea what you're missing. As soon as the show ends, we're getting you a box set of all the books."

"We?" He grinned. "See, you do like me."

"You," I corrected, shaking my head. "I'm going to lunch."

He laughed and stuck his head under the dress, bringing back memories of our first night together. That man was always getting under my skirts.

Molly, Trina, Jeff, and Derrick were also taking this lunch shift. While I grabbed my food from the buffet, I overheard Jeff telling Derrick, "It's hard to interact with your fans when you have so many. Once you hit ten thousand followers on Twitter, it just feels so *impersonal*. Not like the small, intimate feel of five thousand."

It took all of my self-discipline to not upend my entire plate on Jeff's head. Like any one of us wouldn't *kill* to have even five thousand Twitter followers. He was such a freaking humblebragger. How could Derrick stand it?

The guys took one table, while Trina, Molly, and I took the other. "I saw you and Dawn getting cozy," I said.

"Mmhmm," Trina said with a slight grin.

"Good for you two," Molly said with a warm smile. Her hair was so big today it practically needed its own zip code. "And Julie, how are things going with Gavin?"

"You mean, when we're not trying to claw each other's eyes out?" *Or tear each other's clothes off*, I silently added.

"Aw, what a shame. I thought the two of you might have something there. You're cute together."

"Please. I'm cute with everyone."

Trina laughed. "He's not so bad. And even I can tell he's damn nice to look at."

Molly patted my hand. "Since you're paired up for this challenge, it wouldn't kill you to be nicer to him."

"It might!"

Molly sneezed into her arm, then blew her nose with a napkin. "Lordy, I hope I'm not getting sick. I'm so sorry, girls."

"Are you getting enough sleep?" Trina asked.

"As much as I can. But all these long hours on my feet are rough on me. I'm too old for this."

"Stop that," I said. "We're having just as hard a time as you are."

"You're sweet, dear." She sneezed again. "Oh no. Stay far away from me so you don't catch it."

"Are you going to be able to make it through the challenge?" I asked.

"I should be okay. I just hope I don't make everyone else sick. Probably a lingering illness from my grandkids. I swear, they bring back every single illness in the schoolyard."

After we finished eating, I washed my hands for a good three minutes under scalding hot water with a ridiculous amount of soap. I was *not* getting sick, dammit.

<h1 style="text-align:center">Chapter Eleven</h1>

The next morning we dove right back into work, all too aware we had a lot to get done and only a few hours to do it before the runway show. But we'd only been in the design room for thirty minutes when Kelsey rushed toward us. "I need to talk to you two."

For once she wasn't smiling or speaking in exclamation marks. Gavin and I shared an *oh shit* look and waited for her to drop the bomb.

"Gavin, your model is sick and can't make it," she said.

"What?" I blurted out. We'd already made the look to fit her measurements. What were we going to do now?

"Is she all right?" Gavin asked. Always a gentleman, at least in public. In private, well…

"She's fine. Just caught that bad cold that seems to be going around. She'll be back for the next challenge I'm sure. In the meantime, we're having Carla come in to take her place for the runway show. Unfortunately, we can't give you any extra time. Sorry!" She rushed off, like she was worried we would yell at her for being the bearer of such bad news.

"Bloody hell," Gavin said, leaning against our work table. "How are we going to finish in time?"

"We just will. We have to."

He slowly exhaled. "I need more coffee."

"Same. But aren't the English all supposed to drink tea?"

"I can't stand tea, much to my grandmother's dismay. But if we're going to use ridiculous cultural stereotypes, shouldn't you be drinking green tea?"

I laughed. "Okay, you may have a point there. Although I do like green tea."

"Score one for me."

"Since when are we keeping score?"

"When have we not been keeping score? By my count, I'm up to four. One for that first night, one for the other night, one for picking you for my team, and one now." He ticked them off on his long fingers. "You're only at two, love. Better step up your game."

"Two?" I poked him in the chest. "I have way more than that. And you don't get a point for the other night since I did all the work."

"Fine, we'll take that one off. But I'm still ahead."

"I have at least three!"

He flashed me a cocky smile and walked over to the dress form, leaving me hanging. Infuriating man! I spun around and stomped back to my workstation to get Carla's measurements from my supplies.

When I got back, Gavin had written me a note and left it tucked into my fabric.

Your score:
One point for bringing me to your hotel room.
One point for doing lovely things with your mouth.
Care to earn another?

I flipped the page over and scribbled: *Keep dreaming.* I crumpled the note up and threw it at his head before turning back to the table. Out of the corner of my eye I saw him open the note and laugh, and I couldn't help but smile.

Over the next few hours, we adjusted our dress to fit Carla. She was a little wider in the bust, hips, and butt, but a few inches shorter than Gavin's model. It wasn't too difficult to make the changes; it just took time. Time that was quickly running out.

As soon as Carla arrived, we had her try the dress on. The corset was too tight and wouldn't close properly, the ruffles were in the wrong place on her butt, the skirt's length didn't adjust properly, and basically the whole thing was a disaster. We got the dress off and sent her to hair and makeup while we tried to figure out what to do.

Nika and Derrick walked past on their way to the breakroom, smirking and giggling as they eyed our dress form. Gavin ignored them, but I couldn't stop myself from asking, "Got a problem?"

"Just admiring your look," Derrick said.

"It's so…*different* from everything else in the room," Nika added with a snicker.

They kept walking, but I overheard Derrick say in a fake-whisper, "She is so going home today."

To hell with that. I turned to Gavin and pointed to a spot on the skirt. "Can you raise the back of the skirt here, so the ruffles are higher?"

"If I do that, then the front will be too long. Maybe if I…" He tried to undo the stitching holding the ruffles on. "No, that won't work." He changed tactics, but a second later I heard a ripping sound and he yelled, "Bollocks!"

"What happened?" I bent down to check and saw a gaping hole in the back of the skirt, where the ruffles had once been attached. They'd come off, but had ripped the fabric in the process. "Oh my god."

"It's this goddamn fabric," he said, throwing the ruffle on the table. "I told you we should have chosen the thicker one."

"That one was way more expensive! We wouldn't have had any money left to buy fabric for the shirt." I put my hands on my hips, staring him down. "And don't you *dare* try to pin this on me. You should have been more careful removing the ruffles instead of yanking them off."

He scowled and inspected the damage. "I think I can patch this up. I'll try to attach the ruffles in a way that covers the seam. It won't be perfect, but we don't have time for anything else."

"No, you still need to fix the adjustable length of the skirt." I grabbed the ruffles and searched for the correct thread. "Here, let me help—"

He snatched the ruffles out of my hand. "I don't need your help!"

"Um, hello, we're on the same team." God, what was his problem? It wasn't like I was trying to change his design or anything. I just wanted to get this done in time.

"You worry about your part of the dress, and I'll worry about mine," he said, his voice sharp. "That was the deal."

I turned away from him, fuming. "Fine. Whatever. Just don't screw this up."

"Me? You were supposed to get the corset fitted to Carla. You had one job, and you properly buggered that up. One job!"

I spun back around, glaring at him. "Oh, I'm sorry! Maybe your stupidity is contagious!"

With that, he burst out laughing. A second later I had to join in because what else could I do? It was all so ridiculous, and we were fighting over nothing. But when you're held captive in a stressful environment, running on very little sleep and stuck with your competitors 24/7, it was no wonder silly little things blew up into giant dramas.

He placed his tattooed hand on my arm. "I'm sorry, Julie."

"Me too." I took a deep breath. "God, could anything else possibly go wrong?"

"Don't tempt the fates, love." He placed his fingertips on the table. "Touch wood."

"You mean knock on wood," I said, rapping my knuckles three times on the same spot.

"Why would you knock? Do you expect it to answer? It's not a door."

"I don't know. But at least I'm not feeling it up like some creepy wood-lover."

"If I remember correctly, you're the wood-lover."

A laugh escaped me. "Okay, I'll give you credit for that one."

He grinned. "Score another point for me."

"That totally doesn't count!"

The teams were seated together to watch the runway show, but I could barely hold still while we waited. Gavin and I had worked so hard on this dress, but it was such a risky gamble and I wasn't sure if it would pay off or not. It was hard to tell what the judges would like.

And if we were on the bottom, I would be the one sent home, not Gavin.

The lights went up and the music started. Trina and Dawn's model was first, wearing a sheer, floor-length dress covered in tiny flowers and butterflies they'd created with fabric that cleverly hid all of her naughty bits. It was a beautiful dress and definitely had a whimsical fairytale feel, but I could already hear the judges saying it was "too crafty."

Tom and Jeff's model was next, wearing a long silvery dress that fell straight down her body and had pointed shoulders, giving it a slight sci-fi feel while still looking modern and sexy.

Carla came out third, and I held my breath the entire time she walked down the long strip of runway. Every step she took felt like a mile, and I was torn between watching her move (and damn, did she work it) and watching the judges on the other side of the stage to gauge their reactions. But with the bright lights, it was tough to see their faces.

Our steampunk saloon girl look definitely stood out from the others. The over-bust corset was made of a beautiful dark-brown-and-gold brocade, with matching laces in the back and black leather piping and trim. We'd also added buckles along the front and thin chains that hung across her ribs, along with a pocket watch Gavin had found somewhere.

Underneath the corset, Carla wore the white, long-sleeved shirt Gavin had created, which dipped low to show off her cleavage and had big shoulders to give it more of an authentic period look. Below it, Gavin had created a bustle skirt in a nearly identical shade of brown as the corset. It was tiered in the back with three layers of ruffles, each one edged in black lace, which hid the rip he'd made earlier. The skirt fell to the ankle, but the front could be raised to Carla's thigh while remaining long in the back. The raised front would then clip on to metal rings at her hip, giving her a Wild West saloon girl feel with a distinct steampunk edge. Assuming it worked, that is.

The entire thing fit Carla perfectly, even with all the problems we'd had redoing it for her. We'd also given her knee-high brown leather boots and those awesome goggles I'd found in the accessory room, which were perched on top of her head.

When Carla reached the end of the runway, she posed for a split second, then raised the front of the skirt up to mid-thigh, showing off her beautiful dark legs. It worked! I let out a little squee, unable to help myself, and Gavin laughed beside me, sounding relieved. Carla posed another instant longer, then turned around and walked back down the runway.

Once she was gone, I could finally breathe again. Gavin leaned over and whispered, "Great job, love."

"You too." I reached over and gave his hand a quick squeeze.

When the show was over, Lola announced that Dawn and Trina were safe and could go into the lounge to wait. The rest of us stood on stage, and our models joined us.

They talked to Tom and Jeff first and said they loved the dress, but thought it might not be sci-fi enough for the challenge. They called it "gorgeous but safe," although Lola said she would wear the dress herself.

Next, the judges critiqued Paige and Molly's look, which I had rightly guessed would be in the bottom. They'd picked fantasy and had gone for a pretty generic

Renaissance princess gown in burgundy velvet with gold trim. It wasn't bad, but I couldn't argue with Ricardo when he said it was too frumpy and not sexy. Paige tried to throw Molly under the bus, saying she wasn't pulling her weight because she was sick. But the judges had the biggest problem with Paige's part of the dress, so I wasn't sure who would be going home if they lost.

We were next, and I had no idea if we would be on the top or bottom.

"Gavin and Julie, your genre was historical," Lola said. "Please tell us about your look."

Since Gavin was team leader, he did the talking. "We didn't want to make something boring or predictable, so we decided to go with a Wild West steampunk look. Julie did the corset and a lot of the detail work, and I did the skirt and shirt."

"I absolutely love this look," Kiara said. "I would wear it to a Hollywood costume party in a second."

We were in the top three! For once I wasn't in the middle or the bottom! Oh my god, I might even win this challenge! I grabbed Gavin's hand, and he smiled at me, his eyes sparkling under the bright lights.

"I love it too," Ricardo said. "She looks fierce and tough, yet also feminine and sexy. It's a fun blend of historical and fantasy, perfect for the movies."

Lola tapped her notecard against her hand. "I like that you took a risk with the challenge and made something unexpected, even knowing we might kick you off for it. But I am not entirely sold on this look."

"I am," Kiara said. "I want to see a movie with this character in it. Maybe I need to find myself a steampunk role next!"

Beverly pursed her bright red lips. "I can definitely see this in a movie, although it might be even too costumey for the challenge. Whose idea was it to do a steampunk look?"

"It was Julie's," Gavin said. He sounded almost…proud.

They moved on to Derrick and Nika's dress next, but I already knew we weren't being eliminated, so I could relax during the critique. For horror, the two of them had made a black backless dress with long sleeves and high slits on both legs. They'd kept it fairly simple, but had red fabric trailing along the sleeves and down the back of the dress to the floor. They called it a sexy vampire queen dress and said the red represented dripping blood, but I didn't quite see it. The judges had mixed feelings on it, but overall thought it was a bit too trashy. I hoped one of them would be going home instead of Molly, but it was hard to tell what the judges would do.

The deliberations seemed to take an eternity, but in the end, Paige and Molly were the losing team and Paige was sent home. Molly was still safe, for another challenge at least.

Then it was time. Gavin and I stood beside Tom and Jeff, waiting to hear who would get the $1,000 and a night in the private suite. Even though we'd worked in pairs, only one person would be given the prize.

"The winner of this challenge is…Julie," Lola said.

I shrieked and hugged Gavin. He wrapped me in his warm arms and the spicy scent of him. I was so happy I could kiss him. I looked up and saw his lips part, and when he lowered his head, I thought for sure he was going to do it—kiss me right there on the runway in front of the judges and the designers and the cameras. And I stood there, eagerly waiting for it.

But all he did was kiss me on the cheek. "Congratulations."

———

Kelsey led me to the interview room, the same one I'd been to before the show had started. After each challenge ended, the winner and loser had to do bonus interviews. All I wanted was to crash on that king-sized fluffy duvet in the winner's suite, but that would have to wait.

Kelsey had me briefly talk about how great it was to finally win a challenge after being in the bottom so many times and about how we'd come up with the idea for the look. Then she asked, "What was it like working with Gavin? Please remember to phrase your answer with the question in it, if you can!"

"Working with Gavin was surprisingly good," I admitted. "I was worried we would clash, but even though we had a few rough moments, we worked really well together overall."

"So what do you think of Gavin?" she asked and winked.

"I…I think Gavin's a good designer." I wasn't sure what she was getting at, but I had to be careful what I said on camera.

"That's all? C'mon, there must be more there!"

"Um…" I let out a small laugh. "He's not bad to look at. And that accent is pretty hot. Oh god, don't air that please. I don't want him to hear me say that."

Kelsey laughed. "He *is* very hot. We're all really enjoying the chemistry between you two!"

"I'm not sure if 'chemistry' is the right word…"

"I don't know, it definitely seems like there's a mutual attraction there! Don't you think?"

I coughed, shifting in my seat. "I don't know. Maybe? I can't speak for him, of course. But even if there was, it doesn't matter. As long as we're on the show, nothing can happen, since we're competitors. And only one of us can win."

"That's too bad."

The interview ended and we left the room. But she stopped me outside the elevator, glancing around like she was imparting a secret. "Just so you know, the producers would *love* to see something happen with you and Gavin."

"What do you mean?"

"We think it could provide some good drama, that's all. Viewers would probably love it, too." She giggled. "I know I definitely ship it!"

"Sorry. I don't think it's going to happen."

"Bummer." She gave me a quick hug. "Congrats again on winning! You'll receive the bonus thousand dollar prize after the show is over, and you're free to use the private suite in the Loft until the next challenge starts."

I'd forgotten about the bonus prize, but I could definitely use that extra cash. My parents were paying for me to go to college, but they could only do so much. Just another reason why winning *Behind The Seams* would be amazing. The

$200,000 cash prize would get my new career started, and for once I wouldn't have to rely on my parents to help me.

But what was I going to do about the private suite? I wasn't sure I could make it through the whole night in there without inviting Gavin inside. He was just too damn tempting.

"Can I give the suite to someone else?" I asked Kelsey.

"Sure! It's yours to do whatever you want with. You can also invite someone to join you." Kelsey gave me another exaggerated wink. Yeah, it was pretty clear what she wanted me to do.

In the end, I offered Molly the winner's suite. Doing so both saved me from temptation and gave Molly a chance to recover and get over her cold. Not to mention, it let the rest of us ladies get a better night's sleep without her snoring. She thanked me profusely, giving me a tight hug, and I knew I'd done the right thing.

Even if I was a tiny bit sad I wasn't getting any action that night.

Chapter Twelve

Now that I'd won a challenge, my confidence returned in full force. We were on our fifth challenge, almost halfway through the show, and my new plan was: Wake up. Kick ass. Repeat.

But all that went to hell when I got up the next morning with a sore throat.

Molly's cold. Perfect. Just what I needed.

Kelsey gave me some cold medicine, but there wasn't much she, or anyone else, could do to help me. My one consolation was that most of the other designers seemed to be hit with the same illness. Not Gavin though. He looked as perfect and handsome as always. That jerk.

We were asked to design a dress for Lola to wear to a red carpet event, which made me especially nervous because I had a feeling she hated me. No clue what that was about, but I worked my ass off on my dress or as best as I could with a waterfall of snot running out of my nose every couple minutes. I went through an entire box of tissues. It wasn't pretty.

The second day was even worse. The design room had become a hellish place, full of coughing, sneezing, and people who stumbled around like zombies. Only Jeff and Gavin seemed to be immune to the plague sweeping through our ranks. Some of the models didn't even show up. But by some miracle, all nine designers finished a dress and made it to the runway show.

And once again, I ended up in the bottom.

I stood before the four judges with Carla at my side. She wasn't sick, but then, she never got sick. It was her superpower, and one I would kill for right now.

They started with Nika and Tom, ripping apart their dresses while we all sniffled and coughed on the runway. The judges seemed especially nasty tonight. Tom's dress wasn't even that bad, just kind of boring and simple. When they got to my dress, I could only brace myself for what was coming.

I'd made a black vintage-looking strapless gown with tiny silver stars all over it.

Along the top of the bodice, I'd cut the fabric to look like crescent moons and covered them with rhinestones that trailed down and vanished into the body of the dress, giving the impression of a twinkling night sky. There were a few places where the dress was a little sloppy, due to lack of time and my cold, but I couldn't believe I was on the bottom. Not for this dress.

Lola's mouth twisted as she eyed Carla. "Julie, you won the Comic-Con Masquerade contest, yes? That's how you were invited on the show?"

"Yes." I sighed. I knew it would come out sometime. The other designers on stage all looked at me with varying levels of surprise written across their faces. Except Gavin, who stared straight ahead, his expression neutral.

"It shows," Lola snapped. "Every challenge you make us another costume."

I heard Nika do her mean giggle and wanted to die right there on the stage. But instead I stood up straighter. I wasn't ashamed of how I'd gotten on the show. I hadn't even applied—they'd *asked* me to be on it. And I was proud of the clothes I'd made so far. My dress was a thousand times better than Nika's. It was obvious she would be the one going home today. Not me.

"I love this dress," Kiara said, and Lola's eyes rolled. "It's feminine and magical. A little rough at the bottom with the hem, but I can see what you were going for."

"I like it also," Ricardo said. "It's beautiful and unique. But I'm not sure I can picture Lola wearing it on the red carpet."

"I could see someone *younger* wearing it," Kiara said, with a pointed look at Lola. Their rivalry had gotten intense over the last few challenges, and I seemed to be caught in the middle of it. Maybe that's why Lola hated me? Either way, I was grateful to have at least one judge on my side.

"*No* one would wear that," Lola snapped.

"I would!" Kiara argued. "In fact, if you make me a dress just like this, Julie, I will totally wear it to a big event next year. Proudly."

"I would love to make you one," I said, smiling at her.

Beverly chimed in before Lola could reply. "This dress would photograph really well, but I agree, it's a bit too…theatrical. In the future, try to tone down the costumey elements."

I nodded, hoping that meant I still had a future on the show. But who knew what the judges would decide in the end?

They moved on to Gavin next, who'd made a long dress composed of geometric pieces of leather arranged over his model's body. He'd figured out the exact layout using complicated math and an intricate blueprint, like some sort of engineer, then spent hours cutting and laying out each piece. There was a tiny slit between each triangle, giving just a glimpse of skin. The effect was stunning, and if they didn't give him the win, they were fools.

"Gavin, we all really liked this dress," Lola said. "The pattern, the silhouette, the way it moves…"

"Did you cut out every triangle yourself?" Kiara asked.

"I did."

"It's so clever," Beverly said.

"And very well made, too," Ricardo added.

He bowed his head, hands clasped behind his back. "Thank you."

"Gavin, you have a great understanding of the female body," Lola said.

I couldn't help it—I let out a sharp laugh. I quickly covered my mouth, but Lola narrowed her eyes at me. It was just so ridiculous. The judges loved him. The other contestants loved him. I was the only one he seemed to drive absolutely insane. Even if he *did* know his way around a woman's body.

They praised him for at least another five minutes and then moved on to Tom. He'd made a sleek, elegant off-white dress that fit his model perfectly. It was beautiful in its minimalistic simplicity, but Lola wasn't a fan.

"There's nothing here I haven't seen before," she said. "Where is the drama? Where is the flair?"

Tom cleared his throat. "I was planning on adding this trim to the edges, but ran out of time…"

"No. You need to think bigger. You need to wow us. This? This does not wow me. This makes me fall asleep."

Harsh. But it was good to know I wasn't the only one Lola loved to rip apart. I figured he would be safe anyway because Nika had made a leopard print dress that was so short I could see the model's butt cheeks as she walked.

Jeff won the challenge with a rose-colored gown with a high cowl neck and a two-tiered skirt with feathers. Lola was going to wear it (or a slightly modified version, more likely) to a red carpet event in a few months. It was a great opportunity for Jeff to get his work out there, and I so wished it had been me instead.

In the end, they sent Tom home. Tom, whose dress's only flaw was that it was a little boring. I couldn't believe it. Nika had basically made a 1980s hooker dress, and they'd kept her over him. It made no sense.

There was a good chance I was going to be next, too. Even though Lola didn't like my dress, I had not deserved to be in the bottom three. Jeff's dress had been just as costumey as mine. I could try to work on that, but I didn't want to lose who I was either. I had to stick to my aesthetic, and that included being a little dramatic and quirky sometimes. But not all the judges were a fan of that.

I'd been certain I would make it to the end of the show and be one of the final three contestants. Now, I wasn't sure I'd even make it another week.

But I wasn't going to give up. Not when I'd been given this chance. When Giselle Roberts had invited me on the show, I'd taken it as a sign I needed to break out of the rut I'd been in. A sign that I had to do what I needed to do, instead of what my perfect sister did or what my demanding parents wanted. Fashion design was where my soul was. It was what I wanted to do with my life. And that meant I'd have to work my ass off to make sure I made it to the end and won this thing.

"I think Lola hates me," I said to Trina and Dawn that night at dinner. We were sitting at our usual table, the two of them holding hands throughout their meal. I kept cracking up because they were having a hard time eating like that, yet didn't want to let go. Too cute.

"I'm starting to think you're right," Trina said, wearing a plaid bow tie tonight.

Dawn blew her nose, but she still looked as lovely as ever. Or maybe that was just the way she seemed to glow when she was around Trina. "Why would she hate you?"

"I don't know, but she's always glaring at me. And even if the other judges love my dress, she always hates it. Her loathing is like a wave of heat that follows me around. I can't see it, but it makes me all hot and sweaty."

Gavin set his plate down and joined us. "What makes you all hot and sweaty? And can I be a part of it?"

"Don't get too excited. We're discussing how I was in the bottom, yet again."

"You shouldn't have been there," he said. "Your dress was beautiful."

"Lola didn't think so."

"The judging tonight was all fucked up," Trina said. "I still can't believe Tom was sent home."

"Me either," Gavin said. "He was the only halfway decent guy here. Now I'm stuck sharing a room with Jeff and his fanboy."

He scowled as he glanced across the room at the other table, where Nika and Derrick were conducting another session of the Jeff Jayson Fan Club. Jeff was in the middle of a story that made me want to choke him.

"After last season, the show made me fly *coach* when they sent me across Europe to tour all the big fashion capitals. Paris. London. Milan. *And* it wasn't even Fashion Week in any of them."

"Ridiculous," Nika said, while Derrick nodded eagerly. I wanted to scream at Jeff that he should feel lucky to even be sent on such an amazing trip, especially one he didn't have to pay for, but they just ate it up.

"Nika should have been kicked off," I said to my table. "It all feels so…rigged."

"I always did suspect the producers influenced the judging," Trina said. "Every year the people who cause the most drama stay on longer, while the boring ones go home early. And Tom was definitely boring. He barely said a word to anyone. Nika, on the other hand…"

Trina's words brought back what my roommate Maddie had said about her time on a different reality TV show, *The Sound*, where bands competed to win a record deal with a major label. The producers had manipulated the results of that show, too, to make sure a certain band won. Could the producers be doing the same thing here? Kicking off the more boring designers while keeping the ones who created good TV?

Kelsey's comments rushed back to me, about how the producers would love it if Gavin and I got together. And with a sinking feeling, I knew what I had to do to stay on the show.

———

I took a long, hot shower and felt a thousand times better. My cold was pretty much gone, thank god. I couldn't afford to spend another challenge sick.

When I finished up and left the bathroom, the living room was a ghost town. The communal areas always cleared out quickly after dinner. Some people took showers before bed, but most just crashed, hoping to get as much sleep as possible before the next challenge in the morning. Especially tonight, when so many people were still sick.

Gavin emerged from one of the other bathroom doors a moment after I did, and I spotted my chance to get him alone. Before he could say anything, I grabbed his arm and yanked him back inside his bathroom. I shut the door behind us, checking to make sure no one had seen us go in together. The cameras would catch the entire thing, but that would only help my plan.

The bathroom was small, and when I turned back to Gavin, he was close, nearly touching me. If he was surprised I'd pulled him in here, he didn't show it. The room was steamy and his hair was damp, so he must have just gotten out of the shower himself.

His hands slid around my waist. "You know, you could have gotten me alone the other night if you hadn't given your room to Molly. Though I have to admit, that was a pretty nice thing you did for her."

His voice was right at my neck, sending goosebumps across my skin. God, I loved his accent. And he smelled so good, like soap and heat and the promise of sex. I put a hand on his chest but couldn't summon the effort to push him away. Instead, my fingers dug into his shirt, tugging him closer. "Don't get any ideas. That's not why I dragged you in here."

"No?"

He didn't wait for me to answer. He lowered his head and caught my mouth with his, claiming my lips in a passionate, demanding kiss. I groaned as his tongue found mine, sliding, stroking, making my every nerve dance. His hands tightened around my waist, pulling my hips against him, closing that slight distance between us. I gripped the collar of his shirt, kissing him back even as my mind yelled at me to stop, that this wasn't why I'd wanted to meet with him. But my body didn't want to listen.

Finally my brain reclaimed control, and I pulled away. "Stop that."

His eyebrows shot up. "Stop what?"

"Kissing me."

"You're the one who kissed me."

"I did not!"

"At the very least, you kissed me back."

He had me there. I stared at the blue tile in the shower behind Gavin, hoping if I kept my eyes averted I'd be able to get through this conversation without jumping him. Good thing I'd given away my room the other night. Being alone with Gavin made my body lose control of itself. I couldn't trust myself around him, and for once, I was trying my best *not* to sleep with a hot guy.

"This is the only safe place to talk without being recorded," I said. "And I have a proposal for you."

He leaned against the counter, an arrogant smile on his lips. "A proposal? Maybe we should go on a date first, love."

"Not that kind of proposal." Aaaaaaaand there went the desire. Now I just wanted to smack his sarcastic, smug face. His really handsome, sarcastic, smug face.

Never mind. I still wanted to jump him.

"It's related to what we discussed at dinner. How the judges are keeping people who cause drama over people who are better designers. And I don't want to go home."

"I'm not sure I follow."

"Kelsey told me the producers want us to get together because they think it would make for good TV. I bet if we pretended to hook up, it would increase our chances of sticking around 'til the finale."

"You want to pretend to be what…a couple?"

"Yes. A fake relationship for the cameras, just until the end of the show."

He crossed his arms, flashing his tattoos. "What's in it for me?"

"Um…" I hadn't thought that far ahead. The idea had seemed good at the time, and I'd confidently rushed forward without thinking it through. "Wouldn't you rather I make it to the finale than Nika?"

He gave a lazy shrug. "Sure. But it doesn't really matter who else is at the finale, since I'm going to win either way."

God, he was arrogant. I stood taller, looking him in the eye, hands on my hips. "You're cocky now because you've been in the middle or on top every week, but we only have five episodes left, and Dawn, Trina, and Jeff have all won challenges, too. What happens when it's down to the wire, you against them, and someone has to go home? Dawn and Trina are together, so they'll be safe. Jeff? He's a good designer, he was on last season, *and* he's an asshole. He's not going anywhere. I wouldn't be surprised if the judges are grooming him to win. Are you really that confident you'll make it into the final three and get to New York Fashion Week?"

It was a big speech, but I needed him more than he needed me. I had to convince him, or I would probably be out next week. And definitely before the finale. As much as I liked Molly, Dawn, and Trina, I wanted to win. Whatever it took.

Gavin stared at the wall for a long minute, and I couldn't read the expression on his face. I held my breath, waiting to see if he would go for it. If he said no, I didn't know what I'd do. Find another way to cause drama somehow? I could try to get into a big fight with Nika…

Finally, he uncrossed his arms and met my eyes. "All right, love. I'll play along with your game. But what happens when we make it to the end and are competing against each other in the final three?"

"Then…I guess we break up."

He nodded, his mouth set in a grim line. "How do you want to do this?"

"Tomorrow, during the challenge, we should make it obvious we're interested in each other. Then we can get caught kissing."

"I'll make sure to take the same lunch shift as you."

"Perfect."

I was tempted to say more, struck with a sudden urge to tell him I wasn't just using him to stay on the show. Except I was. And why should I feel guilty? I didn't want to date him. I didn't even *like* him. I wanted his body, and that was it. In fact, I should probably set some boundaries so he didn't get any ideas about this turning real.

"Remember, this is all just pretend," I said. "I'm not interested in you. At all."

His eyes narrowed. "Good, because I'm not interested in you either."

"Good! Because you are the *last* person I would ever actually date."

"The feeling is mutual, love."

Then we were kissing again, a kiss that was as much a battle as it was a caress. Our tongues fought for domination, our hands clawed at each other's clothes, our bodies strained to touch. My back hit the wall, pressing against some half-wet towels. I barely noticed. His hand was under my shirt, sliding up my skin, and he groaned when he found my bare breasts, my nipples already hard. He circled each one with his fingertips, and I moaned, tugging at his hair.

I was doing a real shitty job of setting boundaries here.

"Just don't go falling in love with me," I got out between kisses. "This is strictly a business arrangement."

"Not a problem, love."

"And stop calling me that!"

"Whatever you want, Julie."

But my name on his lips, with his accent, felt far too intimate. I changed my mind—it was better when he called me anything but that. I pushed him away before this could go any further.

"Tomorrow," I said and left the room.

Chapter Thirteen

The sixth challenge was perfect for me. We were taken up onto the roof of the building, where we had a 360-degree view of New York. The rooftop patio had a few potted plants and some comfy couches and chairs, creating a relaxing outdoor lounge. I'd been out there a few times before to sunbathe and get some fresh air on the rare occasions we had a few spare minutes that weren't spent sleeping or eating or designing.

Once there, Lola gave us our challenge: to make a functional, real-life superhero costume. The catch? We only had eight hours to do it. Yep, another speed challenge. That wouldn't be a problem for me though. I'd already designed a ton of superhero clothes—that's how I'd won my spot on the show, after all. It made me wonder if they'd chosen this challenge just for me because they'd told me to tone down the costumey elements. Were they were trying to set me up to fail?

Either way, it was time to put my new plan into action. In the fabric room, I made sure to ask Gavin to help me get a bolt down in front of Derrick and Nika, since they were big gossips.

"Please, Gavin," I said, batting my lashes and putting my hand on his tattooed forearm. "Help a girl out?"

"Anything for you, love," he said. "I know it's tough to get things down with those baby T-rex arms."

He stretched up to get the bolt, and his shirt rode up, exposing a patch of skin along his stomach. His jeans were low, showing off his hips, the very tops of his boxer briefs teasing me. Thoughts of him without those jeans on flooded my mind, but I pushed them away. I had to stay on task.

I tried to look sexy-cute and formed my hands into claws. "Rawr."

He grinned as he handed me the bolt. "You think you're ferocious, but when you do that, I just want to hug you."

"Is that all you want to do?"

"Not even close."

We were being ridiculous, but Nika and Derrick were staring, so it must have been working. Derrick rolled his eyes and walked out of the aisle, but Nika looked like she might stab me in the back with her scissors. Perfect.

I grabbed some zippers in the next aisle, but when I went to pay, I saw Nika blowing a kiss to Gavin—and carrying the same fabric as me. Oh, hell no. She was not getting *my* fabric and using *my* methods on *my* guy.

Wait, when had he become *my* guy?

Okay, scratch that last one. But the fabric was mine first, if nothing else.

"Seriously?" I said to her, as she got in line behind me. "You're getting that one, too? I know you saw me grab it first."

She shrugged. "Nothing says we can't use the same fabric."

I nearly growled I was so annoyed. I was even tempted to get different fabric, worried the judges would think I was copying her and not the other way around, or that they'd complain about two similar looks on the runway. But fuck it. That was the fabric I wanted, the one I'd picked out first, and I was going to hold my ground and get it even if Nika was going to be a pain in my ass. But if she copied my outfit, there'd be hell to pay.

Back in the design room, I scratched a note and left it on Gavin's table. *Helping Nika steal my fabric was* not *part of the plan.*

He scowled when he saw it and quickly replied, dropping it in my lap as he walked past. *She asked me for help. What was I supposed to do?*

Stop being a gentleman for five minutes?

Never. And do I detect a hint of jealousy?

Ugh. He was impossible. I crumpled up his note, refusing to answer him.

The show was down to eight designers, which meant it was a lot easier for us all to talk to each other. Unfortunately, that also meant I could overhear other conversations in the design room. And the only gossip Jeff and his fan club wanted to talk about? How I got on the show.

"I can't believe she never had to audition," Derrick said, while he was draping something on his dress form.

"No wonder her looks are so costumey," Nika added.

"This challenge should be perfect for her, then," Jeff said. "How nice of the judges to go easy on her this time. Meanwhile, it will be a miracle if I can get this top on my model with her cleavage."

"So unfair," Derrick went on. "First Julie gets invited on the show, and now the judges practically guarantee she'll win this one."

I was tempted to pretend I didn't hear them, to sulk silently and whine to Trina and Dawn in private later. But no, I was done with their bullshit. I stomped over to the other side of the workroom and waved my scissors at them. "You know, I can hear all of you."

They each gave me innocent looks, and Nika said, "We weren't—"

But I was just getting started. "No, I didn't audition for the show, and I'm not going to apologize for being invited on it. But hey, I'm flattered you talk about me and my clothes so much, especially since I barely think about you three at all. And if you have something else to say? Next time say it to my face."

Behind me, Trina started clapping, and soon the other designers joined in, including Gavin. Nika muttered, "Whatever," while Derrick and Jeff busied themselves with their dress forms.

After I returned to my table, Gavin walked past and slipped me a note. *Looks like you don't need my help to get the producers' attention. Still want to do this?*

I looked up at him and nodded. I may have caused some drama, but I doubted it was enough to secure my spot on the show to the end.

When it was lunchtime, Gavin and I both volunteered for the first shift. I wasn't sure how we would get to the kissing part, but that never seemed to be a problem for us. It was when we talked that he drove me crazy.

This shift also had Jeff and Derrick, but they took the table across the room. Gavin and I got our food from the buffet and sat down, but while Jeff loudly complained yet again about how large his model's breasts were, we sat in silence. Jeff had to be the only guy who would complain about a girl's boobs being *too* big.

Now that Gavin and I were supposed to kiss, I couldn't think of anything to talk about, couldn't stop thinking about him actually kissing me, and the fact that I was eating salad and probably had kale stuck in my teeth or tasted like garlic and oh god this whole thing suddenly seemed like a terrible idea.

"I want to hear about this Comic-Con contest," he said, and I was grateful to him for breaking the awkward silence between us.

"This year I made costumes for me and my two roommates so we could enter the Masquerade." I was about to say their names, but didn't want to admit in front of Jeff and Derrick that Carla was one of them. "We decided to go with a Batman villain theme, but I wanted to do something different so I made punk rock outfits inspired by each character's costume. My friend Maddie, the one I told you was on *The Sound*, was Harley Quinn, and…my other roommate was Catwoman. I was Poison Ivy."

"I think I'm going to need to see photos of that." He was stacking the mini coffee creamers into a pyramid again, but this time I wasn't tempted to knock them over. Okay, maybe a tiny bit.

"Once the show is over, I'll find some. Maddie's band members and their girlfriends joined in, too, so by the time we were on stage, I'd made eight costumes. A whole rogues gallery of Batman villains, all with a modern, punk rock look. The Masquerade has a lot of prizes, but Giselle Roberts herself awarded me the *Behind The Seams* prize and asked me to come on the show."

"That's brilliant." He leaned closer, lowering his voice. "I auditioned twice, by the way."

"You mean your good looks and sexy accent didn't win them over the first time?" I asked with my flirtiest smile. "I'm shocked."

"Some people take longer to win over, I've discovered." He gazed at me with smoldering eyes, and my heart sped up. I knew it was all for the cameras, but when he looked at me like that, it was hard to tell my body it wasn't real.

"But no, my first audition was a complete disaster," he said, adding another mini creamer to top off his tall pyramid. "It was my first time in New York, and I was jetlagged and overwhelmed and didn't have the slightest idea what I was doing. I presented my clothes to the panel, which was Lola, Ricardo, and two of the producers. They asked me questions about my aesthetic, and I stammered through them. When they asked me to pull a dress out to show them, I couldn't get the hanger off and tugged too hard and ended up knocking the entire rack over. Then, to top it off, I called Ricardo 'Roberto.'"

I laughed. "It's hard to imagine you like that."

"It's a miracle they let me audition a second time."

He went on to tell me about his second audition, which had gone much better. Before I knew it, our lunch break was over and we'd forgotten to kiss, so wrapped up in our conversation. It was the first time we'd just sat and talked and the first time being around him hadn't made me want to strangle him at any point.

I had to be careful. I was in serious danger of actually liking the guy.

———

Carla soon arrived to try on my superhero look—a kick-ass pair of black pants that were tight, yet easy to move in, under a fitted coat that was sexy, yet kept the ladies safe and secure. It had a hood and a bit of extra fabric around the neck that could be pulled up like a mask to cover the mouth and chin. Throw in a utility belt and boots she could run in, and it was a perfect modern, functional crime-fighting costume.

While she got dressed, I switched off my mic and explained my agreement with Gavin in whispers. Her eyebrows got closer and closer together with every word.

"It's good you have a strategy," she said once I'd finished. "But are you sure this is a smart idea?"

"I don't know if it's smart, but I think it will work."

She nodded, biting her lower lip. "I want you to stay on the show as long as you can, but I don't want you to do anything that makes you uncomfortable either."

"Don't worry about that. Since when have I ever had a problem hooking up with a guy?" I handed her the coat, and she slid it on.

"True, but…"

"But what?"

"The way you interact with Gavin is different."

I snorted. "Only because I'm forced to see him day in and day out. Any other guy would have been kicked to the curb a long time ago."

"Maybe that's all it is," she said, but she sounded doubtful.

We walked to the mirror to check her out, and I could see the worry etched across her face. I turned her toward me and stared into her big brown eyes. "Seriously, it will be fine."

"I trust your judgement. I just don't want you to get hurt."

"Me? Never."

She gave me a hug, and at first I stiffened, but then hugged her back. She'd been my model on the show long enough that it was fine. No one would suspect anything.

After she left, I heard Gavin muttering under his breath, his voice growing increasingly upset. His look—a crop top with a geometric pattern, plus a cape and a tight pair of leather pants—still needed a lot of work. Since I was in a good mood from our lunch and was pretending to be all doe-eyed for him for the cameras, I figured I'd offer him a hand.

I finished up the final touches on my coat, then moved to lean against his table. "You need some help? I'm already done."

"No, thank you."

"You sure? I could finish sewing those pants for you in no time while you work on that cape."

"I can manage on my own," he snapped.

I stared at him, trying to figure out why he was being so stubborn. "But you have less than an hour. You won't be able to finish all this in time. I just want to help."

"I don't need your help!"

I blinked and threw up my hands. "Fine. Never mind, then."

Stunned, I went back to my workstation and checked over my look again. What was his problem? One second we'd been bonding over lunch, and the next he'd bitten my head off. He was supposed to act like he was into me, not like a total dick.

I should have known this wouldn't work out.

Sexual chemistry? Not a problem.

Getting along for more than five minutes? Nearly impossible.

The runway show was a fun one. Carla rocked her costume, looking fierce and sexy and amazing. I wanted to snap a photo of her and send it to my friends Tara and Hector, who'd created a graphic novel together called *Misfit Squad*. How cool would it be to have a half-black, half-Portuguese superhero with natural hair as the lead in a comic book? Or in a TV show or movie? I wished I had my phone so I could send them the idea immediately.

When the challenge ended, I was in the top three, and it was so obvious my look should win—yet they gave the prize to Jeff. *Jeff*. Even though all of the judges loved my look the most—except Lola, who inexplicably hated it, of course. Gavin was in the bottom for the first time ever, since his look was sloppy and barely finished, but he was safe. The only good news was that Derrick was out. The Jeff Jayson Fan Club was starting to break apart.

I trudged back into the backstage lounge, where the designers in the middle waited, and then kept on walking out into the hallway. That superhero challenge should have been *mine*, dammit. I'd worked so hard on it, and I knew with every fiber of my being that my look was better than Jeff's. Seriously, what superhero would run around in a skimpy miniskirt that would only ride up her ass while she was fighting? I was so mad I wanted to punch something.

I leaned against the wall, burying my face in my hands, enjoying a second of solitude. I was nearly in tears, which was silly because I'd been in the top. The pressure of the show must have been getting to me. The long hours, the lack of alone time, being completely cut off from the world, plus all the design room drama...it was too much. I was starting to crack.

The door to the lounge opened. Gavin. He must have followed me out. "Are you all right, love?"

After his attitude today, I had zero desire to talk to him. "Go away."

"I want to apologize for earlier." He moved close, taking my hands in his. "I'm sorry for being so rude to you."

"It's fine, whatever," I said, keeping my eyes fixed on the floor. I wished he would leave me alone to sulk by myself.

"No, it's not fine. My behavior was unforgivable." He drew in a long breath. "I have a hard time accepting help from others. I suppose I…prefer to do things on my own. With my own hands. But that is no excuse for the way I treated you."

He sounded sincere, and when I looked in his eyes, I believed he was genuinely sorry. I tightened my hands around his. "It's okay. I think we're all having a rough day. I'm sorry you were in the bottom."

"I deserved to be there." He traced patterns on my skin with his thumbs. "Are you upset about something other than my very ungentlemanly behavior?"

That got a little smile out of me. "It's…it's stupid."

"I doubt that."

"I came in second, but I should have won. If it weren't for Lola and her vendetta against me…but no, I shouldn't complain. I was still in the top. Just ignore me."

"Lola does seem to have it out for you. Maybe you should talk to someone?"

"Who?"

"I don't know. Kelsey? One of the producers? Maybe even Giselle Roberts?"

"Why would they listen to me over her?" I sighed. "No, I'm going to be sent home soon. I can feel it."

He wrapped his arms around me, pulling me into his chest and his warm embrace. "We're not going to let that happen."

I buried my face in his shoulder, breathing in the scent of him, digging my fingers in his black shirt. "How?"

"By making sure they won't dare send you home."

A small laugh escaped me, and I raised my eyes to his. "What's in it for you?" I asked, repeating his question from last night.

"This," he said and pressed his mouth to mine. Unlike last night's fervent kisses, this one was slower, softer, a gentle teasing at my lips, a light flick of his tongue. He eased me into it, slowly bringing me out of the darkness, making me forget why I was upset at all. I clung to him, gradually opening up and kissing him back with more and more passion. It was the first time I'd kissed him without wanting anything from him other than his comfort and the sheer pleasure of being close to him.

"But what about this exactly?" I asked, my voice breathy.

"The longer you stay, the more I get to kiss you," he said against my lips.

"The longer I stay, the higher the chance of you going home."

"I'm willing to risk it."

Then we were kissing again, and I moved my hands up to weave my fingers in his beautiful hair. God, I loved his hair—short on the side, long on top, and soft all over. I loved the way it felt like silk against my skin and that I could grab a good chunk of it and tug. I loved that he put an effort into making it look good, like he did with every aspect of his appearance.

Someone whooped, and we pulled apart. "It's about time you two finally hooked up," Trina said behind us.

She stood there with all the other designers, each of them openly ogling us. Molly clapped her hands together, like she was delighted with this turn of events. Dawn wore a big smile, while Nika glared at me so hard I thought she might burn holes into my clothes. Jeff just looked bored by it all.

I snapped back into reality, where Gavin and I were competitors, on camera, and only pretending to be together. Of course he hadn't meant what he'd said. It had all been an act for the camera recording everything.

I'd let myself forget, as I always did with him. When he kissed me, it was far too easy to lose myself, to give in to his soft lips and hard body. To forget that, no matter how good a kisser he was, this was still pretend.

The others went back inside the lounge, leaving us alone to make out some more, I presumed. But the moment was over.

I switched off my mic and stepped back from him with a deep breath, trying to regain control of my runaway heart. "It worked. Thanks for playing your part."

He frowned and turned off his own mic. "You don't need to thank me, love."

"It must have looked convincing. Now they'll all be talking about the two of us being together."

"Yes, you got exactly what you wanted." His voice sounded almost…bitter. What was his problem? Last night he'd said he wasn't interested in me and had agreed to this plan. Crap, he better not be having second thoughts.

"What *we* wanted." I smoothed my dress, making sure I looked presentable. "We should go back inside."

"You go ahead. I need a moment." He adjusted his jeans in that way guys did when they were trying to be subtle about having a hard-on, but it only made it even more obvious.

I grinned as I joined the others. I almost felt bad for the poor guy.

Almost.

Chapter Fourteen

I was pretty sure I'd never heard sweeter words than: "For today's challenge, we're letting you leave the building."

We stood in the lobby, the door to the outside world only a few feet away. All of us had been cooped up in this place for almost two weeks, our only moments outside being quick breaks on the roof or sticking our heads out of the Loft windows like dogs in a car. But now they were letting us leave, thank god.

"This challenge is all about New York," Lola said, today wearing a black-and-white, color-blocked dress. "You're going to have a few hours to wander the city and breathe it in like inspiration."

Yes! I did a quick fist-pump. This was my first trip to New York, and so far I'd seen a hotel, a short car ride, and the inside of this building. My only real glimpse of the city was from the windows or from a five-story rooftop. Now I would actually get to explore it.

"But don't get too excited," Lola said, crushing all my hopes under her pointy heels. "For this challenge, you don't have a budget. Instead, you're limited to anything you can find around the city for free."

"Like, dumpster diving?" Nika asked, sounding disgusted. For once, I was in agreement with her.

"It's up to you how you get the materials. There are no restrictions, as long as you don't pay for them with money. And don't do anything illegal, obviously. But I will say this: we are hoping to see some unconventional materials. If your dress is made entirely of fabric, we won't be impressed."

Exploring New York seemed a lot less fun now that I knew I'd have to be scouring the city for free stuff to make an outfit with. I'd known a challenge like this was coming, since they always did one where the designers had to use unconventional materials, but that didn't mean I was prepared for it.

"You have four hours to explore," Lola said. "And one day to design your New York-inspired looks with the materials you find."

Kelsey handed us each an oversized tote bag to put our materials in, plus a map of the city. Then they released us into the wild. Gavin was at the door first and held it open for the rest of us, being a gentleman again. I waited until everyone else had dashed out into the city, then slipped through the door. Once on the other side, I took a moment to close my eyes, feel the morning sun bathing my skin, and listen to the vibrant pulse of the city before I turned back to Gavin.

"I've never been to New York before. I can't wait to check it out. Do you have any ideas on where to go?"

"Not really. My two visits before were brief. I auditioned and didn't have time for much else."

We studied our maps for a moment. We only had four hours, and I was torn between hunting down materials and wanting to experience as much of New York as possible. But if our time ran out and we hadn't collected enough materials we could use to make a look, we'd be screwed.

I gave up and tried to close my map, but couldn't figure out how to get it folded correctly, finally crumpling it up and shoving it in my bag. "I think we should just pick a direction and start walking."

"Spontaneous. I like it." He folded his map precisely, not a single crease out of place. "Central Park isn't far. I suggest we wander in that direction."

"That sounds perfect."

He slipped his hand into mine, and I was so startled I almost pulled away. But of course, he was doing it for the cameras. I smiled at Gavin in my best impression of a lovesick girl, and together we started down the street in the direction he said would take us to Central Park. My idea of wandering the city and seeing where it led us would have made Carla crazy, but Gavin seemed willing to go with it, as long as he could provide some sort of direction or goal. The cameraman followed, recording everything.

The city flowed around us, people hustling to work, grabbing coffee and hot dogs, honking and walking and living their daily lives. We passed small neighborhood markets and hole-in-the-wall restaurants packed with people and used bookstores that looked like they'd been there forever. The skyscrapers towered over all, and the street was flooded with a sea of yellow cabs.

The city was so different from Los Angeles. LA was more relaxed, more spread out, with a few clusters of tall buildings scattered around the city. New York was more frantic, more rushed, more crammed together. But I loved its energy.

The air was especially cool for the last week of August, and clouds blotted out the sky, casting everything in a fierce gray tone. Fall seemed to be coming early this year. Yet I was outside and had a handsome man at my side in a city I'd never explored before. It couldn't get much better than that.

"How did you become a designer?" Gavin asked me as we walked down the street together, scouring the sidewalk for anything we could pick up and use for the challenge.

"My parents came here from Korea before my sister and I were born. They opened up a dry cleaner in northern California, and for most of childhood we were pretty poor. I got all of my older sister Helen's hand-me-downs. Her clothes. Her Barbies. I hated it. I wanted my own stuff. All my friends wanted to be just like their older brothers or sisters, but even back then, I didn't want to be anything like her."

I picked up an empty Dr. Pepper can on the side of the road and tried to imagine how I'd make a dress with it, but ended up throwing it in a nearby trash bin. "We didn't have money to buy new things, so I started making clothes for my Barbies. Then I switched to making clothes for myself. I used to even steal clothes from my mom or from our house for fabric. My parents hated it. They told me to stop wasting my time on stuff like that. And they weren't super happy about me ruining their curtains or seat cushions either."

"Why does it not surprise me that you were something of a handful?" Gavin asked with a laugh.

"I really was. Still am, I guess. My poor parents." I laughed with him. "As I got older, my parents were able to expand their dry cleaners into a chain, and things got a lot better for us. But by then, I was hooked and loved making my own clothes. As much as my parents hoped I would grow out of that phase, I never did."

We passed a street vendor making something that smelled amazing and both of us stared at it with longing, but unfortunately neither of us had money on us. Once we'd pulled ourselves away, Gavin asked, "So why are you in a pre-med program and not in fashion school?"

"I don't know. I guess… I guess my parents convinced me I'd never make it as a fashion designer. They said it was a waste of time and effort to try something that had no guaranteed payoff or to pursue a career that was so uncertain and unstable. And when my sister became a doctor, they pushed me to follow in her footsteps. Being a doctor was a much safer path, even if it bored me to tears, so I went for it."

We checked the steps leading down to a subway station that reeked of urine, but didn't find anything we could use. We briefly considered taking a lone traffic cone, but a cop on a horse trotted by and we decided against it.

"Why didn't you say no to becoming a doctor?" Gavin asked.

I shrugged. "I was raised to respect my parents. I figured they were probably right, and it was too risky for me to go into fashion. And I guess I worried I wasn't good enough to make it as a designer."

He stopped in the middle of the busy sidewalk and turned to me, taking my face in his hands as he stared into my eyes. "Never doubt for a second that you deserve to be on this show."

He rendered me speechless, my heart racing under his touch and his gaze and his words. Even with the city rushing around us, all I saw were his eyes, the same color as the sky above. I smiled at him and took his hands, kissing each one, including the one with the rose. I wanted to know the story behind why he had his sister's name tattooed on his hand, but I suspected it wasn't something he shared easily, judging by how he'd shut down when I'd mentioned it.

"Now it's your turn," I said as we continued walking. "How did you become a designer? You don't really seem the type."

"Why? Because I'm not gay?" He said the words sarcastically. "What a load of rubbish. I don't know why everyone keeps dwelling on that. Apparently in the States, if a man is clean, well-dressed, and interested in art and culture, he must be gay."

"No! That's silly. Straight guys can like clothes and sewing and design, too. You just seem… I don't know." I remembered the way he'd designed our steampunk skirt like a blueprint and how he built pyramids out of coffee creamers when we ate. "You seem like you enjoy the structure and design of it more than the fashion aspect. If that makes sense."

He lifted a dark eyebrow. "I'm surprised you noticed that."

"You also introduced yourself as an artist to me. Not a designer."

"I've learned many women lose interest if I tell them I'm a fashion designer. And I very much wanted your interest."

"Those women are dumb," I said. "But you haven't answered the question."

"My little sister, Rose, was the one who grew up interested in fashion. We both loved art and design and creating things, but as you guessed, I was more interested in architecture and structural engineering. That's what I planned to do with my life. But when my sister…" His voice trailed off, and he cleared his throat. "When my sister got leukemia, things changed."

I took his hand again, and this time it wasn't for show. "How old was she?"

"Fifteen. I was seventeen."

"I'm sorry." I squeezed his hand, both dreading this story and desperately wanting him to go on. I'd never heard Gavin speak so openly about his past or his life outside the show.

"It got harder for her to work on her clothes with the chemo, but it made her happy, so I started helping her more and more. We created beautiful looks together, but as she got weaker, I ended up taking over completely. She would guide me and supervise, and once the clothes were done, I'd convince her to wear them. Even once she was in the hospital. Even after she lost all her hair. Even when she was so weak she couldn't sit up without help. I still wanted her to feel beautiful."

My heart clenched, and something shifted in me. "Gavin, that's…" My throat felt tight. His story had brought out all sorts of emotions in me that I usually tried very hard not to feel. "That's a really wonderful thing you did for her."

We walked together in silence for a minute before he spoke again. "She passed away when I was twenty, just shy of her eighteenth birthday. By then, I'd already switched my focus from architecture to fashion design so I could carry on her dream and her memory. I got the tattoo on my hand the day after her funeral. As long as I'm designing clothes, I feel like she's still with me, guiding my hand."

God, this guy was nearly bringing me to tears. I'd had no idea this incredibly sweet, thoughtful, dedicated man was under his cocky, sarcastic exterior.

No, that was a lie. I'd always known it was there. I just didn't want to see it. Because if I did? I'd have to admit that he wasn't a jerk. That he wasn't an asshole. That he was a good guy.

And that I liked him a lot.

Dammit, when had that happened?

We passed a homeless guy with a giant cart full of stuff we'd be able to use, but I didn't have the heart to ask him for anything.

"Is being a designer what you really want to do with your life?" I asked Gavin.

"Of course it is. Why?"

"You originally wanted to be an architect. Do you ever miss it?"

"Sometimes. Like when I look at buildings like that," he said, gesturing to the Empire State Building in the distance. "I wish I could make something as permanent and lasting as that. But many of the same things I love about architecture, I love about making clothes, too. The design aspect. The creation of something that is both useable and beautiful. The merging of function and art." He shrugged. "I started doing it to be closer to my sister, but I grew to enjoy it. So don't worry, I'm very happy with my direction in life. The question is, are you?"

"No," I admitted. "I don't want to become a doctor. I don't want to follow in my sister's footsteps. That's why I came on the show. I thought if I won, I could prove to my parents that I can succeed at this."

His fingers tightened around mine, his face serious. "Julie, the only person you need to prove that to is yourself."

I slid my arms around his neck and gave him a fierce kiss, showing him how much his encouragement meant to me. I didn't know how much of what he said was for the camera, but I appreciated it either way. And after today's conversation, I could guarantee the producers wouldn't be sending us home any time soon.

As we broke apart, something caught his eye. He moved around me to a bus stop and grabbed a newspaper off the bench. He held it up to me, before shoving it into his bag. "My first material."

"Nice one." I'd completely forgotten about the challenge and all of that. Dammit. He was always doing that to me, distracting me from the goal. I needed to get my head back in the game. Gavin was still focused on the challenge. He hadn't forgotten, not even for a second.

It's not real, I reminded myself. *He's your competition. And this is all a game.*

Chapter Fifteen

We reached Central Park and started exploring, looking for materials we could use. Gavin collected more newspaper, even grabbing some out of the trash and recycling bins. As we carried on, I couldn't stop admiring the leaves, which had just started to blanket the grass and walkways with a hint of autumn color. I began collecting them, grabbing the best ones, ranging from green to yellow to red to brown. I gathered some branches and sticks that had fallen, too. Even a few stray flower petals.

I had an idea for what to do with my look, but I needed *some* sort of fabric to arrange my materials on. How was I supposed to get fabric for free? While Gavin spoke with two men playing chess, I wandered off on my own, the cameraman right at my heels. I looked on park benches, under trees, beside fountains, and even inside trash cans. I was going to need a good long shower after this. Yet I couldn't find any useable fabric. The stuff I did find was either too small, too gross, or completely wrong.

Overhead, the sky was growing darker and more ominous, threatening to open up and unleash on us at any moment. The air had that crisp, misty feel that always preceded rain, but they hadn't given us umbrellas or anything. Hopefully the weather would hold out for another hour until the end of the challenge. I wondered how the other designers were doing and where they'd gone.

I had almost given up on finding any useable fabric when I came to an area with vendors selling different wares or handing out pamphlets and flyers. I spotted a pretty redheaded girl about my age setting up a table with candles and soap on a thin, flowy, white fabric almost like gauze. Exactly what I needed.

"Hey," I said to her. She looked up at me and then at the camera guy behind me. "I'm a designer on *Behind The Seams*. Have you heard of it?"

"Sure," she said. "I love that show."

"Great!" I gave her a big, friendly smile. "For our current challenge, we have to wander around New York and find materials and fabric for free. I was wondering if, by any chance, I could use your tablecloth?"

She looked down at it with a frown. "It's the only one I have with me. Sorry."

"Are you sure? Because I'm desperate here. I'll do anything."

Gavin strolled up to me at that moment, flashing one of his charming smiles. "How's it going?"

The girl's eyes widened, and she clutched the candle she'd been holding to her chest. "I *love* your accent. Where are you from?"

Oh my god. If I heard one more girl ask him that question, I would scream.

"London," he said.

"Wow, I've never been there, but I've always wanted to go." She batted her eyelashes at Gavin. "Are you a designer on the show, too?"

"I am."

It took some serious effort not to roll my eyes at the way the girl fawned all over him and the way he lapped it up. I turned back to Gavin. "I was hoping to use her tablecloth, but she says she needs it. Guess I'll ask some of these other vendors."

Gavin rested a hand—the one without the rose tattoo—on the girl's table. "That's too bad. Are you sure there isn't anything we can do to convince you?"

Her cheeks flushed bright pink. "Oh, um… Gah. I don't know."

"Whatever you want," I said. "I'll sing you a song. Do a little dance. Hell, I'll even get Gavin to take off his shirt for you."

That earned me a raised eyebrow from him, but he flashed the girl another smile. "If that's what it will take."

The girl laughed. "Seriously? It's freezing out here."

"I'm from England. This feels like a warm summer day." He slipped off his coat and handed it to me, then reached for the buttons on the front of his checkered black-and-white shirt.

I'd meant the taking-off-his-shirt thing as a joke. I never thought he would go for it. But the girl laughed and said, "Okay, I'll give you the tablecloth if he takes off his shirt. *And* gives me his number."

"Deal," he said. Off came the first button, revealing a flash of his chest. He unbuttoned slowly, never taking his eyes off the girl, like he was stripping for her. A wave of jealousy rushed through me. I wanted to be the girl he took his clothes off for.

No, I couldn't think like that. Gavin and I weren't really together. He could get naked with whomever he wanted.

I'd just…prefer it if he wanted to get naked with me. And only me.

Once his shirt was unbuttoned, he slowly eased it off his broad shoulders, then folded it in half and handed it to me with a wink. His toned chest teased me with its trickle of hair trailing into his jeans. His nipples were dark against his skin and hard, standing out in the cool air.

"How's that?" he asked the girl.

By now we had something of an audience, and a couple women hooted and cheered. The *Behind The Seams* camera caught it all. Tiny flecks of water began to fall from the sky—not truly raining yet, but enough to tease us with the promise of it.

"Perfect," the girl said, her voice breathy. "Here's one of my cards." She handed him a business card with her contact information.

"Lovely to meet you, Cindy." He took a pen off her table, grabbed another business card, and wrote his name and a long string of numbers on the back. "I'm looking forward to chatting with you in a few weeks once I'm done with the show."

She nodded, biting her lip, and clutched the card with his number in her hand. I couldn't believe he'd actually given her his number—and in front of me, too. But why should I even care or expect anything different? We weren't dating. I had no claim over him. I just had to ignore how I wanted to grab the card and rip it into a million little pieces. And resist the desire to knee him hard in the balls, too.

"The tablecloth?" I asked. The girl blinked and removed her candles and soap from it, then folded it up and handed it to me. I snatched it out of her hands, muttered a thanks, and stomped off.

Gavin caught up to me quickly. "Could I get my shirt back, or should I keep flashing everyone in the park?"

Oh, right, I was holding it. I shoved it at his chest without a word, then kept walking. But he caught my arm, tugging me back to him.

"Don't tell me you're mad," he said.

"I'm not mad."

"Liar." His tattooed hand found my cheek, and he caressed it softly. "Do you think I go around taking my shirt off in public and giving fake numbers to strangers on a regular basis? No, Julie. I did all of that for you."

My breath caught. "You gave her a fake number?"

"Of course. I'm sure she's perfectly nice, but you're the only one I'm interested in." He pulled the business card from his pocket and ripped it in half. Then he walked to a nearby trashcan and threw it away. "See?"

I smiled, feeling silly for overreacting and for being so jealous when he'd been helping me. Not that I was willing to admit that. I gestured to his naked chest. "Put your shirt back on already. You're making me cold just looking at you."

Another lie. I was warm all over, thanks to him.

He grinned at me and slipped his shirt back on, his long fingers quickly buttoning it up. "Don't forget you're the one who suggested the whole thing."

"I didn't think you would actually do it!"

"For you, love? Anything."

Maybe his charming words and selfless actions were all for the camera, but I didn't care. I slid my arms around his neck, standing on my tiptoes to press my mouth against his. His arms circled my waist, and he kissed me with enough passion to almost make me believe it was all real.

As we kissed, the random, small splattering of drops shifted into a stronger downpour. The weather turned quickly, and it took us a moment to realize it, too wrapped up in each other to notice the outside world. We pulled apart and laughed, looking up at the water streaming down on us. We were quickly soaked from head to toe, but the cool rain on my face felt good, especially after being cooped up in that building for so long. I held out my hands, letting the drops trickle through my fingers, catching some in my mouth.

Gavin watched me with a smile, his chestnut hair dark and wet, his shirt clinging to his skin. It shouldn't be possible for him to get any sexier, yet seeing him standing there in the rain, water dripping down his face, made me ache for him more than ever. I wanted to grab hold of that wet, dark hair and yank his cool lips to mine. I wanted to rip off his soaked clothes and lick the droplets off his skin. I wanted to do naughty things to him until we were both warm again.

His eyes were the color of the storm around us and filled with the same longing and desire as mine must be. His gaze dropped from my face, slowly traveling down my body, then fixing on my breasts, which I'm sure he could clearly see through my thin, pale pink dress. My jacket hung open at my sides, and my nipples were taut, both from the cold and from desire. I could see his breath in the air, his chest rising and falling, his body poised like at any second he might spring forward and grab me in his arms to do all the things I wanted to do to him.

Gavin smoothed back his slick, wet hair. "Julie…"

Then I was in his arms again, holding his scruffy face in my hands as we kissed. Our wet bodies slid against each other, our skin burning up despite the cool rain trickling down our faces. I felt his arousal through our damp clothes, and I couldn't get enough of him. I felt dizzy, desperate, almost sick with the desire to be with him.

Our cameraman cleared his throat, reminding us we were not alone, but standing in the middle of Central Park in a rainstorm with a camera filming everything we did. "Your four hours are over."

We broke apart, sighing. Back to the show.

———

When we returned, they didn't give us much time to rest or recover, just fed us lunch and threw us right into the design room. We didn't stop working until late that night, then crawled back to the Loft to crash and do it all again in the morning.

Trina won the challenge, which was fitting since she was from New York. She'd gotten free maps, visitor brochures, and theater programs from around Times Square and other tourist spots, then turned them into a dress with a collar. She'd also found a broken umbrella someone had discarded and used it to create the skirt, giving it a nice flare at the hips.

Gavin and I were both in the middle, but by this point I wasn't surprised that I didn't win, even if I thought my dress was pretty awesome. I'd used the sheer fabric Gavin had gotten for me as a long, sleeveless dress, then attached the branches, leaves, and petals to it in a colorful, floral design I thought captured the beauty of Central Park.

Gavin, on the other hand, had taken his newspapers and created a complicated, highly structured dress. He'd folded and layered the paper to give it a full skirt and tight top, then used duct tape he'd found in a trash bin to give it a contrast hem. When he was done, it didn't even look like newspaper.

But I nearly burst into tears when they announced who was going home: Molly.

She'd made a dress using lots of different bits of fabric she'd collected or begged for around the city, creating a patchwork effect. It wasn't a bad dress, but the judges said it was too crafty, too frumpy, too uninspired. Plus, it didn't use any unconventional materials.

Backstage, I gave Molly a tight squeeze, my eyes watering. I wasn't all that surprised she was going home since she'd never been one of the judges' favorites either, but I still wished she didn't have to leave. Even though she was my competitor, I'd grown fond of her these past few weeks.

"It's fine," Molly said, patting my arm. "This isn't the end for me. It was a great experience and I learned a lot, but I miss my family. And you're all such talented designers I'm not upset that one of you will win. Now you take care of each other, okay?"

"We will." Gavin wrapped an arm around me, and it was so unexpected I nearly jumped. Jesus, when was the last time a guy had done that to me? It had been so long since I'd dated someone for any amount of time that I couldn't even remember. Most of my relationships were quick hookups and not much more.

I knew some people thought I was a slut or whatever and that I must have a reason for not getting serious with anyone, but I didn't have a tragic past. My parents were still happily married. No guy had ever broken my heart. I just liked sex and didn't want to be tied down to one guy. I was only twenty-one and still in college, after all. I had my whole life ahead of me and a career to focus on. What was the harm in having some fun while I was young, right?

But as Molly said her goodbyes, I leaned into Gavin and it felt…nice. He was a warm, solid presence beside me, supporting me, showing the world we were together. And that's when I realized—I wanted that. Me, who didn't have time for serious relationships. Who scoffed at the idea of settling down with one guy. Who'd never had a boyfriend that lasted longer than a month.

Yet in a few short weeks, I'd gone from lusting after Gavin's body and wanting him for one thing only to actually liking him—a lot. As a friend and as a person, but also as…something more. Maybe even enough to consider something long-term with him. A future, even.

And that scared me. Because I had a feeling when he and I finally got together? It would be good. Really good. Mind-blowing. It wouldn't just be a quick fuck. It'd be the kind of sex you remembered forever. The kind of sex that *meant* something.

I didn't want it to mean anything. I wanted to love him and leave him like I did with everyone else. If I let myself care about him, if I let him have a piece of my heart, I wouldn't be able to focus on what was important—winning this show so I could prove to my parents that I could do this. As long as we were on the show, he was a distraction, nothing more.

I was here to win. Not fall in love.

Chapter Sixteen

The runway show was earlier than normal that night, and we soon discovered why. The producers had arranged twenty-minute video chat sessions for all of us with our family members. Trina and Gavin went first, in separate offices on the first floor, while Dawn and I waited outside. After the first ten minutes, I spotted her biting her nails, ruining the French manicure she'd done the other night before bed.

"Nervous?" I asked.

Dawn dropped her hand and sighed. "I'm debating whether to tell my father I'm with Trina. He has no idea I'm bisexual and I don't want him to find out by watching the show when it airs…but I never imagined I'd tell him like *this* either. I'm not sure I'm ready. What do you think I should do?"

"Hmm. Is this thing with Trina serious? Do you think you'll keep dating after the show is over and we go back to our regular lives?"

"I think so." She gave me a shy smile. "I hope so."

I didn't know how either of them could be so sure. Life on the show wasn't like normal life. We were stuck together 24/7, with very little sleep and no contact with the rest of the world. Tensions were high, and we were competing against each other. Plus, they didn't live anywhere near each other—Trina lived in New York and Dawn lived in Oregon. But for some reason, I thought the two of them might actually make it work.

"Trina's crazy about you," I said.

Her smile brightened, lighting up her pretty face. "We've only known each other a few weeks, but it seems like much longer. I've never felt like this with anyone before."

"Then you need to tell your father. If not now, then as soon as you see him in person. Maybe at the finale show?"

She ran a hand through her golden hair. "If I make it that far…"

I wanted to reassure her, but there were six of us left—and only three of us could make it to the finale. Dawn, Trina, Gavin, and I had all become close while on the show, but at least one of us would be going home in the next few days. Maybe more than one.

"What about you and Gavin?" Dawn asked.

"I…I don't know. It's all still really new." I'd love to tell her the truth, that there was no me and Gavin really, but the cameras were recording everything.

The door to one of the offices opened, and Trina walked out, smiling. Today's bow tie was white and covered in tiny black moustaches.

"How'd it go?" I asked.

"Good. My parents can't wait to meet Dawn."

Dawn straightened up. "I'm going to tell my father."

"Are you sure?" Trina asked. "You don't have to do this now."

Dawn took Trina's hands in her own. "I want to tell him. If we both make it to the finale, I…I want to be able to introduce you to him as my girlfriend."

Trina's face lit up, and the two of them shared a kiss. "When you're done, come to the winner's suite," she said with a naughty grin. "We can celebrate."

"I can't wait," Dawn said, before slipping into the office for her call. I guessed it would be me and Nika alone in the women's bedroom tonight.

Gavin came out after his session ended, and I gave him a weak smile, then brushed past him into the office without a word. My throat was already closed up, my tongue tied in anticipation of speaking with my mom for the first time since I'd told her I was going on the show.

I sat at the desk, and soon my mom's round face and short black bob filled the computer screen. "Is this working?" she asked, moving closer to the camera. "Julie?"

"Hey, Mom," I said, forcing a smile.

"Oh, good. I can't believe you don't have a phone there. I have so much to tell you. Helen finished her first year of residency, and everyone at the hospital loves her…"

She launched right into a story praising my perfect sister, as usual. Why did this even surprise me anymore? And while I was happy for my sister, it'd be nice if my mom asked me how *I* was doing at some point.

Over the next few minutes, she told me all her news, including how my grandmother was doing (stable, thank god), how my parents were planning a cruise to Alaska, and how it had been in the 90s every day this week in northern California. Only when she'd finished with all her news (including how the neighbor's cat was peeing on her flowers again) did she ask, "How is New York? Are you having fun? Have you been to the Statue of Liberty yet?"

My mouth twisted. Did she think I was on some tourist vacation? "No, Mom. I'm on the show, so I don't have time to see much of the city. I'll try to go when the show's over."

She leaned closer, squinting at the screen. "You look tired. Are you sick?"

"I was sick a few days ago, but I'm better now."

"Hmm. You need to take better care of yourself. Are you drinking green tea?"

"I am. I'm just…exhausted. We don't get much sleep and we're working long hours every single day and there's so much pressure. It's *hard*."

Her lips pressed together in a thin line. "If it's too hard, you should leave. Come home. You need to prepare for school anyway. Don't waste any more time there."

"I'm not leaving. And this is *not* a waste of time." I barely got the words out through gritted teeth.

"No one would blame you if you quit. Your father and I are impressed you made it as far as you did."

I bit out a laugh. "Wow, thanks for the vote of confidence. I'm sure you'd love it if I gave up. Proof that you were right all along."

"Julie, we support you no matter what, but this is not a career. It's a TV show. A hobby, nothing more. So have your fun and when you're ready, come home and we'll discuss which schools you should apply to."

I slammed my palms down on the table. "It's not just a hobby, Mom!"

She looked startled by my loud voice, and I took a breath to try and control myself. That wasn't a respectful way to speak to her, and I was on camera, too. But how could she not understand that this wasn't just a silly summer break excursion? This was my life, my dream, my career. I wasn't going to walk away from this opportunity because it got tough.

"Are you saying you don't want to go to medical school now?" she asked.

"No, I…" I shook my head. Arguing with her was futile. She'd never get it and would never support me in doing what I wanted. And I wasn't sure *what* I wanted anyway. If I got kicked off the show in the next challenge, maybe it'd be better for me to go to medical school after all. "I have to go. My time's up."

"Julie—"

"Tell Dad and Helen I said hello. I'll call you when I'm done with the show."

I ended the session and sat back, fighting off tears. The worst part was I couldn't even have a second alone to compose myself because the cameraman was there with me, filming everything. I got up and bolted from the room, heading back to the Loft to hide in a bathroom for an hour or two, the one place I knew I could be by myself for a while.

But when I got to the Loft, Gavin was waiting for me. When he saw my expression, he asked, "Everything all right?"

We were the only ones there. Trina and Dawn were presumably in the private winner's suite getting naked, and Jeff and Nika were having their own video chat sessions. Of course, with the cameras filming and the eyes of the producers on us, we were never really alone.

"My mom…" My throat closed up and my eyes watered. "It didn't go well."

"I'm sorry, love." He wrapped his arms around me and kissed my forehead. "I have something that might cheer you up."

"What's that?" I asked, leaning into his embrace. "And you better not say it's in your pants."

He laughed. "No, it's not that kind of surprise. Grab some supper and come with me."

I made myself a plate from our dinner buffet and followed Gavin up the steps to the roof, one of the cameramen a few steps behind us. But when the door opened, I gasped.

Everything had been strung with white twinkling lights, giving the patio a magical feel. Gavin led me forward to a small table set up in the middle with a black tablecloth and candles, plus a bottle of red wine and two glasses. A romantic candlelit dinner for two on a rooftop under the bright lights of New York.

For a minute all I could do was stare, finding it hard to speak. "You did all this?" I finally asked, turning to face him.

"I confess I had a little help, but the idea was mine. I thought it would be nice to have a night alone for once." He gave a sharp look at the camera behind me. "Or as alone as we can be."

Something tugged inside me. Not desire, but something else. Something that made me both excited and terrified at once, that made my heart beat at a million miles an hour. I almost felt...nervous. Which was strange because I was never nervous around guys. Yet Gavin, with his spontaneous romantic gesture, had somehow disarmed me completely.

He watched my face closely, the wind whipping at his dark hair. "If it's too much—"

"No," I said, lifting on my toes to kiss him. "This is exactly what I needed tonight."

His shoulders relaxed and he smiled, almost like he was nervous, too. How odd. Gavin was usually overflowing with confidence. When had we become so awkward around each other?

He pulled out a chair for me, always the perfect gentleman, and poured us both a glass of wine. "Do you want to talk about your chat with your family?" he asked as he sat across from me.

I sighed. I'd nearly forgotten about my conversation with my mom, but he just had to bring it up again. "Not really. It's just the same old shit as usual. My mom thinks I'm wasting my time here and should come home and apply to medical school, blah blah blah."

"Have you told her you don't want to be a doctor?"

"Not...exactly. I wanted to win the show first, to prove to her that it wasn't just a hobby. But I don't know if even that will make her think fashion design is a valid career."

He nodded. "My father never supported my decision to change my major from architecture to fashion. He said it was 'gay' and that real men shouldn't be making clothes. I haven't talked to him in two years."

"I'm sorry."

"It's all right. Maybe he'll come around eventually, maybe not. I used to care, but then I realized I can't live my life worried about what he will think. I have to do what's right for me. This is my life, not his."

I knew what he was getting at, but things with my family were different. I'd been raised to respect my parents and honor their wishes and demands. And even though my mom was a pain, she only wanted the best for me. She might even be right—going into fashion design could be a terrible mistake. I'd spent years studying to be a doctor, preparing for that life, and I wasn't sure I was ready to give that up for something that could go up in flames at any moment.

"Let's talk about something else," I said.

"What did you think about the runway show today?" he asked.

"I loved your look. And Trina's. But I'm so sad about Molly. Nika should have been kicked off instead."

"Agreed. I'm surprised Nika's still on the show. Her looks are so…chavvy."

"What? They're pretty horrible, but not sure I'd call them chubby."

"Not chubby…chavvy." He tilted his head. "Not sure what the American equivalent is. Trashy, maybe? Either way, her clothes are an offense to fashion."

I giggled. "That's why I like you, because we hate the same things."

"Aha, so you admit that you *do* like me," he said with a grin.

Damn, he'd caught me there. "I…admit that I like kissing you."

"Is that all?"

"You're not too bad on the eyes or the ears either."

"Ah, I see how it is. All you want is my body." He said it in a teasing way, but there was a touch of vulnerability in his voice, too, like he was actually worried that might be true.

I took a sip of wine so I didn't have to answer right away, trying to decide on the perfect response. The cameraman was filming our entire dinner, and I had to keep up the act of us as this new couple falling for each other. But saying the words, even if they were for the camera, was tougher than I thought.

"No, I also…" I stared at the table as I spoke, rubbing a finger over the pattern in the tablecloth. *Just spit it out, Julie.* "I like spending time with you. You make me laugh. You're smart and creative and kind. You're… You're not who I originally thought you were."

His eyebrows shot up. "No?"

"Don't get me wrong, you're still a cocky asshole, but there's a lot more to you under that."

"Well, that makes two women who believe that: you and my mum."

"And your sister."

I regretted it the instant I said it. His smile dropped, and he seemed to withdraw into himself. "No, she thought I was an asshole most of the time, too."

"Sorry, I shouldn't have brought it up."

"It's all right." He idly traced the rose tattoo on the back of his hand. "It was years ago. I should be able to talk about it by now."

"It seems like the two of you were really close."

"We were." He shut his eyes, dragging in a ragged breath. "I keep waiting for it to not hurt as much, but it never does. I've just gotten better about living with the pain."

I reached across the table to take his hand, weaving our fingers together. "She would be proud of you for getting this far on the show."

He brought my hand to his lips. "She would be happy I'd found a nice girl for once."

I looked around us, eyebrows raised. "A nice girl? Where?"

"Don't worry. I won't tell anyone."

"You better not. I have a reputation to uphold, you know."

I grabbed my wine glass, something to distract me from the irresistible swell of feelings and emotions rising between us. We were still playing our roles, but it felt like something more, too. I couldn't tell where the line between pretend and reality was. Everything I'd said tonight was true, but I was afraid to admit it, even to myself. It was so much easier to pretend this was all fake. If I accepted it was real, I could get hurt. No, I *would* get hurt.

We switched to lighter topics as we finished eating, and the wine and conversation flowed easily under the soft, twinkling lights and the pale moon above us. It was almost like a real date, except for the camera trained on us the entire time. At some point Kelsey brought out another bottle of wine, and we didn't even pause to consider if drinking it would be a bad idea or not.

Gavin told me about how he had dual citizenship because his father was American and lived in Seattle, which is how Gavin was able to come on the show despite living in another country. He'd traveled frequently to the US when he was younger, especially after his parents got divorced. He'd gone to university—as he called it— at Central Saint Martins in London, one of the top design schools in the world, and after graduation he'd spent the last two years working for Gareth Pugh's clothing line.

In return, I told Gavin about growing up in a town in northern California with my best friend Maddie and how we'd both seen going to college at UCLA as a chance to finally break free from our families. We'd met Carla in my freshman year when I'd worked on the costumes for a theater production she'd starred in. Sophomore year, we'd moved out of the dorms and gotten a place together.

After that, the three of us were practically inseparable—until this summer, anyway. We were all so busy we'd barely had time to talk. But after New York Fashion Week was over, I'd be back at UCLA for my senior year, and I knew we'd be there for each other, no matter what happened. We always were.

By the time the second bottle was done, Gavin and I were both a little drunk.

"C'mon, you have to admit it's a little unfair," I said, waving my wine glass at him. "You get to see models stripping off their clothes all the time in the design room. We need some male models on this show!"

"Believe it or not, I hardly ever notice. I'm usually so focused on my clothes and getting them done in time."

"Oh, whatever. You know you love it, you player." I swatted him lightly on the arm. Sometime during the night we'd scooted our chairs close, and now we were practically sitting on top of each other.

He lifted a brow. "I am not a player. Far from it."

"No? It wasn't that hard to get you back to my room that night."

"That was the first time I'd ever done something like that. The only time."

That strange, fluttery feeling swirled in my stomach again. "Why that night? Why me?"

"I was feeling bold, I suppose. I was in a different city, going on a reality TV show, and you were so captivating I couldn't take my eyes off you." He took my empty wine glass from my hand and set it on the table. "I only planned to talk to you that night, but when you asked me to your room, I couldn't say no. I can never say no to you."

"Gavin…"

Before I could get another word out, he pulled me off my chair and onto his lap. My arms slipped around his neck, and I fell into his kiss. I turned so I was straddling him in the chair, and a reckless passion swept over us, fueled by pent-up desire and alcohol. I tugged at his clothes, sliding my hands under his shirt and along his chest. He found his way under my skirt, which was pushed up to my thighs, and his fingers gripped my ass. My lips touched his neck, and he groaned softly as I kissed him there. I'd noticed before that he liked his neck touched, and I hadn't forgotten. His head fell back, giving me better access to him, and my tongue flicked along his skin. I couldn't get enough of his taste, his touch, his voice.

All my earlier hesitation about sleeping with him vanished. I didn't care if it was a quick fuck or making love or what—I just needed *him*.

"Take me right here, right now," I whispered, finding the button on his jeans.

He laughed, low and deep, and it rumbled against my lips on his neck. "You're drunk again, love."

"I'm not drunk! Just tipsy. And you're as drunk as I am."

"There's also a camera filming us."

Oh right. I glanced behind us and saw the camera guy, who gave a little wave. How fucking awkward. And hilarious. I giggled, burying my face in Gavin's neck, and he laughed with me.

"Soon, I promise." His lips moved to my ear, and he whispered into them. "And when I'm finally inside you, you won't be drunk. You'll be completely sober. You'll feel every inch of me. And you'll remember it long after we're done."

I shivered in anticipation, half-tempted to say fuck the camera and unzip his pants anyway, but I knew he would stop me. With a sigh, I climbed off him.

One of us *had* to win the next challenge.

Chapter Seventeen

We all headed to the design room as usual to wait for Lola and our next challenge. And waited. And waited. No one knew what was going on, and no one would tell us.

Finally the doors opened, but another model walked in: Carla's mother, Eva Pereira.

She was in her fifties and still stunning, with mahogany hair that fell in waves down her shoulders and a killer body. She was Portuguese and had the same delicate, graceful features as her daughter, but lighter skin and hair that was more wavy than curly. In her day, she had been even more famous than Lola, and together they'd walked the runways for designers all over the world. But she gave most of that lifestyle up once she had Carla and her brother Daniel, instead focusing on raising her family and only doing a few modeling jobs here and there.

We'd met a few times before, but she didn't react at the sight of me. Good, she knew to pretend we were strangers.

"Hello, everyone. I'm Eva Pereira, and for this challenge, I'll be filling in for Lola as both your host and as one of the judges."

I wanted to drop to my knees and thank whoever or whatever it was that had made Lola miss this challenge. Now I might actually have a shot of winning it.

"Today you'll be working in pairs again," Eva said.

Some of the other designers groaned, but I locked eyes with Gavin. We *had* to be paired up. Not only for our fake romance, but because we worked well together. It was our best shot at winning or at least being in the top.

And we both desperately wanted to win that private suite.

"For today's challenge, you won't be working with your models," Eva continued. "Instead, you have three very special clients. And they've chosen the two designers they want to work with."

Shit. Being without Carla again for a challenge would be rough, and not being able to pick our partner meant I would probably be stuck with Nika or Jeff. Kill me now.

But when the door opened, three women walked in—and one of them was Maddie! I covered my mouth with my hands to keep from screaming in excitement and surprise. Her eyes found mine, and a big smile lit up her face. What was she doing here?

It slowly registered on me that the other two women were also from bands on *The Sound*. The blonde was Lacey, whose country band, Fairy Lights, had won the show. The other woman was in Brazen, the band that had come in third. They were all on tour together as part of their deal with *The Sound*, and I remembered Maddie had said one of their concerts was in New York. I just never thought I'd see her here, on *this* show.

The three women spread around Eva, who smiled at us. "You're going to design a rock goddess outfit for these three musicians that coincides with both their personal look and their band's music. The winning design will be worn on stage tomorrow night at their concert."

Oh god, I had to work with Maddie or I would die. I'd designed or modified more clothes for Maddie than I could remember, including many of the outfits she'd worn while on *The Sound*. Even the dress she'd worn during the audition for the show was one she'd borrowed from me. I knew how to make Maddie look good, I knew what she liked, and I knew her band's sound. Plus, I'd gotten to know the other members of her band, Villain Complex, over the last few months and when they'd cosplayed with us at Comic-Con. It was partly thanks to them I was even on this show, since I wasn't sure I'd have won the prize without their help.

Eva quickly introduced the three women and gave a brief bit of info about *The Sound* and how the bands had competed on different teams to try and win a record deal. Then she said, "Our musicians have looked through your portfolios and seen what you've done this season, and they've chosen your teams for this challenge."

Maddie, naturally, picked me. This time I let out a little squeal and did a fist-pump. She chose Gavin, too, and my first thought was: thank god. Then it struck me how odd it was that I was relieved to be paired with him again. A few challenges ago, I would have done anything to not be stuck with him.

Lacey chose Jeff and Dawn, while the Brazen singer chose Nika and Trina. All four of them looked like they might throw up as they moved to join their musicians at their workstations, but I was too busy running to Maddie and grabbing my best friend in a hug to care.

"I can't believe you're here!" I said.

"I know! Reunited at last!"

"It hasn't been that long since we were at Comic-Con, but it feels like forever." So much had changed in the few weeks I'd been on the show. I was sure Maddie felt the same—she'd been on tour the entire time, traveling around the country and performing.

"I know! I was so excited when they told us we were doing something with *Behind The Seams*!"

"So this is the roommate I've heard so much about," Gavin said behind us.

Maddie's eyes widened behind her black-rimmed glasses. She took him in with flushed cheeks, in that not-so-subtle way she'd always done when she met a hot guy. You'd think she'd be better at disguising it now that she was with Jared, the lead singer of her band, who was one of the hottest guys I'd ever seen in my entire life. I would have said *the* hottest, but then I'd met Gavin and that English accent edged him into the win.

No, she would always be slightly socially awkward Maddie, even though she was a rock star now. I was actually sort of relieved—it meant her newfound fame and her life on tour hadn't changed her at all. Actually, I took that back. Being on *The Sound* and joining Villain Complex *had* changed her; it had made her a lot more confident and much happier. Not only because she had fallen in love with Jared, but because she'd found her place in the world. Like she was finally the person she was always meant to be.

"It's great to meet you," she said to Gavin, then gave me an even bigger grin. I wondered what Carla had told her about him.

He leaned against our table, smiling at her. "I want to hear all sorts of embarrassing stories about Julie, but first we should discuss what we're going to make for you."

"Did you watch their season of *The Sound*?" I asked.

"No, I don't think they air it in the UK. We have our own version, with different mentors and all that."

For the next few minutes, Gavin asked Maddie what she liked to wear on stage, including colors, style, fabrics, and what worked and didn't work when she played guitar. He asked about the other members of the band, too, and what kind of music they played. Meanwhile, I sketched out some ideas I thought she might like. Maddie chose one and gave us her thoughts, and Gavin added his own twist to it, and by the end of our time, we had a pretty good idea of what we were going to do.

"I'll be back tomorrow," Maddie said, giving me another hug. "I can't wait to see what the two of you create together."

I was dying for Maddie to wear our look on stage in front of thousands of people. Gavin was going to make a chainmail tank top, while I was making some black pants and a leather jacket to go over it. I'd never made a leather jacket before, but I'd made other coats and had an idea of how it should work. Still, I didn't often work with leather, so I wasn't sure how tricky it would be. And I couldn't screw this up. We had to win this challenge—not just for ourselves, but for Maddie.

Not to mention, if we won, we'd get to use that private suite. I couldn't pretend I wasn't excited about the idea of that. Talk about some good motivation.

During lunch, Gavin took the first shift this time, while I took the second. When I walked in, Nika and Jeff were already eating together. Ugh, why had I picked this shift?

"Their season of *The Sound* was the best yet," Nika said. "So much drama. So much romance. So many hot rock stars."

Jeff popped a grape in his mouth. "You're lucky. I wish I had time to watch TV. But I'm too busy traveling around the world and designing clothes for all my clients."

I rolled my eyes as I got my own food. I was so tired of Jeff's elitist attitude. The guy needed a serious reality check.

Since I'd rather eat glass than sit with them, I sneaked out to the hallway, where I ran into Eva.

"Hello, Julie. It's so good to see you again. I think the last time was at our Fourth of July barbeque, wasn't it?"

"Yep. When Carla and Daniel got in a fight over the hamburgers."

"Yes, I remember. He refused to make vegan ones for her, and she pushed him into the pool." She laughed and shook her head. "But how are you doing? How has it been on the show?"

"It's been…rough," I admitted. "Exhausting and stressful. But good, too. Although I think Lola hates me and I can't figure out why."

I quickly told her what had been happening during the last few challenges. For some reason, it was easier to open up to Carla's mom than to my own. Maybe because she was so warm and kind, not at all what you'd expect from an internationally famous supermodel. Or maybe because she and Carla got along really well, almost like they were friends or sisters, which had always fascinated me. So different from my relationship with my mom, or Maddie's with her mother.

When I finished my story, Eva frowned. "Oh, dear. I'm afraid that's probably my fault."

"Your fault?"

"Lola and I have always had a friendly rivalry. Sometimes not so friendly. When we were younger, we competed over everything. Who was more popular, who got the better jobs, who dated the cuter guys—stupid things like that. But it turned into something more when the actor she was dating, whose name I won't mention, dumped her in public." She sighed. "A week later, he and I got together. It wasn't my finest moment, but I was young and swept away by how rich and famous and handsome he was. And maybe I wanted to make her a little mad, too.

"After that, things grew worse between us, even though that actor dumped me a few weeks later and moved on to the next model he could find. I hoped when I had children and quit modeling Lola would get over it, but it seems she still has a grudge, even twenty-something years later."

"But why take it out on me?"

"I assume because she knows Carla is my daughter and that I pulled strings with Giselle Roberts to make sure you were paired together. Lola doesn't really hate you, but you've been caught in this ridiculous, ancient feud between us. I'm sorry, Julie."

I blew out a long breath. "It's good to know she doesn't hate me for my clothes, I guess. But what am I supposed to do?"

"I'll try to talk to Giselle and see what I can do. I'm not sure it will help, but it isn't fair that my past should hurt you now."

"Thanks."

She gave me a hug, and when I pulled away, I spotted Jeff standing at the end of the hallway in front of the bathroom, watching us. Oh, shit. Had he heard that entire thing?

But all he did was shoot me a sharp glance before walking back into the breakroom. Maybe he'd been in the bathroom the entire time? Not much I could do about it, either way. If it got out that Carla was my friend, so be it. I was ready for whatever shit Jeff wanted to throw at me. And there were only two more challenges after this one anyway. What could he possibly do?

When I got back from lunch, Gavin was hunched over our workstation, using his pliers to construct the chainmail for the top, ring by ring. He was doing an alternating pattern of aluminum and rubber rings, which he'd found in the fabric room. The rubber rings were black and stretchy, giving the chainmail some extra movement so it wouldn't hang so tight and stiff on Maddie's body.

"How was lunch?" he asked.

"Fine. Jeff was doing his humblebrag thing again." I neglected to mention my talk with Eva. I'd tell Gavin about it later, when we weren't on camera and surrounded by other people.

"Of course he was." He straightened up. "I made something for you while you were gone."

"You…made me something?"

"It's nothing big." He took my hand and placed something cool and metallic inside, then closed my fingers over it. He brought my fist to his lips and kissed it. "I hope you like it."

I opened my hand, and inside was a bracelet, made from the same aluminum and rubber rings as the chainmail shirt. The way the rings had been woven together gave it a beautiful textured pattern, and the contrast between black and silver made it edgy and unique. I slipped it over my wrist and it fit perfectly.

"Gavin, I love it." I wanted to say more, but my throat had closed up and it was tough to get the words out. Instead, I pulled him toward me and kissed him, in full view of the other designers. "Thank you."

"I can make others to go with it later, when this is all over, in whatever colors you want. But I'm somewhat limited while we're on the show."

That sounded a lot like making plans for after the show ended, which I knew we should pretend to do for the camera. I'm sure the producers and Kelsey would eat all this romantic crap up. But even if the feelings between us were starting to become real, how could we ever have a future together? We were competitors. We lived in different countries. When this was over, I'd go back to UCLA, and he'd go back to his life in London. Soon, all we'd have were memories.

I ran my fingers over the bracelet, feeling the grooves and smooth curves, watching the way the metal caught the light above us. Even though this would all be over soon, I was glad to have this to remember him. A tiny piece of him that was all mine to keep.

Chapter Eighteen

When Maddie tried on our look the next day, we discovered the tank top was a little crooked and the pants didn't quite fit her in the butt. The jacket looked great, thank god, although the sleeves were a little long, which was an easy fix. But overall, the outfit was killer.

"I'm obsessed with it," I said as I helped her take the jacket off. "I love it so much I want to have sex with it."

"Should I be jealous?" Gavin asked.

"Probably."

"I'm going to get a new zipper for these trousers," he said.

I giggled. "Trousers."

His eyebrows shot up. "Pardon?"

"No one says 'trousers.'"

"But these *are* trousers. 'Pants' are underwear." He gave me an exasperated look that was really cute, then headed for the fabric room.

Maddie grinned at me. "Wow, not only is he crazy-hot, but he has an English accent. You hit the jackpot."

"I know. And he's a good kisser. And he's good at…other things, too."

"Now I want *all* the details."

"I'll tell you later. Too many cameras here." I held out my wrist. "But he made me this bracelet."

"Ooh, pretty." She checked it out and then studied my face. "So is this thing between you two serious?"

"I don't know." I busied myself pinning the sleeves on her jacket.

"I haven't seen you this interested in a guy since…" She cocked her head and considered. "Maybe never."

Gavin returned and dumped a bunch of metal rings on our table. "I got some more aluminium, too." Maddie and I immediately started giggling at his pronunciation. "Bloody hell, what is it now?" He was so hot when he was annoyed. It made me want to mess with him even more.

"Alumin-i-um is not a real word," I said. "You can't just add a random vowel whenever you feel like it."

"We invented the language, thank you very much. I think we get to decide what counts as a real word."

"I'm not sure you invented it. Isn't it derived from German or something?"

He rolled his eyes and grabbed his pliers for the chainmail. "I want my bracelet back," he muttered, but I just laughed.

"I'm surprised they even have materials like that in the fabric room," I said.

"I suspect they got them because of me. Yes, that sounds cocky, but during my audition, I showed them some chainmail pieces and they asked me if I would be able to do things like that on the show. I said I would, provided I had the right materials."

Huh. Even from the beginning Gavin was being set up as one of the favorites, given special treatment that would allow him to do well. Of course, was it any different from them allowing me to work with Carla? Or bringing Jeff back for a second season? Maybe we were all given different perks so we could do our best on the show. The producers wanted us to cause drama, but they also wanted us to make interesting and unique looks that viewers would talk about long after the show was over.

The door to the design room opened, and a steady stream of guys began walking in, heading for the other teams' tables. I stopped everything I was doing to stare. Had my wish for some male models finally been answered?

But then three guys I recognized walked in: Jared, Kyle, and Hector from Maddie's band, Villain Complex. All three of them were wearing black and looking as good as I remembered. Maddie jumped up off her stool and kissed Jared, then smiled at the rest of her band.

"Hey, Julie." Jared grabbed me in a hug. He wore faded black jeans and a black T-shirt with Voldemort on it that showed off his tattoos.

"Hey!" I hugged his brother Kyle next, whose dyed black hair hung in his eyes, giving him that sexy emo look, then gave Hector a smile. Hector wasn't a hugging type, although his strong-and-silent thing had always turned me on. Not to mention, he was both a drummer and an artist, which was pretty freaking sexy. I'd been planning to hook up with him at Comic-Con, but then he'd fallen for Tara, the writer of the graphic novel he'd illustrated, and the two of them were perfect together.

"What are you doing here?" I asked them.

Before Jared could answer, Eva walked in. "Hello, designers. I'm sure you've noticed that you have a few more people at your table today. We want you to make a corresponding outfit for one of your client's band members for their concert tonight. But here's the catch: you won't get any more money or time. You can, however, use one piece they're currently wearing and design around that. Good luck!" She gave us a sympathetic smile at our groans and then walked out of the room.

"Bollocks," Gavin muttered.

"So which one of you are we doing the look for?" I asked.

"Jared, definitely," Kyle said, and Hector nodded.

"Fine with me," Jared said, sliding a hand around Maddie's waist. "You always look gorgeous, but I'm really digging this chainmail top on you."

"All the credit for that to my partner, Gavin." I introduced him to the guys in the band, and they all shook hands.

"I've never done menswear before, have you?" I asked Gavin.

"I've made a few things for myself," he said. "I can take point on this one, if you'd like."

I nodded, and he grabbed his sketch pad and began asking Jared questions about what he preferred to wear on stage. While they talked, I turned to Maddie and the other guys. "How's it been going with the tour and all that?"

"It's been great," Maddie said, her eyes dreamy behind her glasses. "Every time I get on stage, I'm always amazed that so many people have come to watch us play."

Kyle brushed his hair back and grinned. "We even got an offer to tour with Gold Rush Standard next summer, but Jared said the lead singer is an asshole so we turned it down."

"Yeah, I heard from our manager he's a cokehead and sleeps with a million girls," Jared added.

Hector shot him a pointed look. "So, like you?"

"Hey, I'm not like that anymore! And I've never even tried that shit."

"How's Tara doing with her new job?" I asked Hector. Tara had gotten an offer to work as a writer for a new superhero TV show while at Comic-Con, which involved her moving to LA. Luckily that put her in the same city as Hector, so they could finally be together after being online friends for years.

"She's great," he said. "She really likes it. I can't wait 'til our tour is over so I can see her again."

"I'll have to take her shopping when I get back to LA."

He gave me a rare smile. "I'm sure she'd like that."

We decided to keep Jared's faded black jeans, since making a new pair of pants (or trousers, as Gavin said) for him would take too long. Instead, we'd create a shirt made from the black fabric we were making Maddie's pants out of, and Gavin would trim the edges with a touch of chainmail.

"Too bad we couldn't find a way to keep your Voldemort shirt," I said to Jared, while we took his measurements. "Can you believe Gavin has never read *Harry Potter*?"

Maddie looked horrified. "How is that possible?"

"Sorry, not sure we can be friends anymore," Jared said to Gavin. "Nothing personal, but…"

"Don't worry, mate. Julie already told me she's going to give me the books when the show is over. I promise to read them immediately."

His words instantly had an effect on the others. Jared raised one eyebrow, Hector studied me with an unreadable expression, and Kyle gave me a thumbs-up.

"Did she now?" Maddie asked with a smug grin.

Okay, they didn't need to make such a big deal about it. I wasn't actually going to do it. "Gavin doesn't even know which house he'd be in," I said, hoping to get the focus off me. "At first I thought he'd be a Slytherin, like me, but now I think he might be a Gryffindor."

Jared gave Gavin a high-five. "Welcome to the best house, my man."

"No way," Kyle said, grinning. "Hufflepuff is where it's at."

"I'm a Ravenclaw girl," Maddie said, then turned to Hector. "What about you?"

"I'm a Hufflepuff, too," he said.

"Somehow that doesn't surprise me," I said.

Later, after the band left and we were finishing up our two looks, Gavin folded a piece of paper and pushed it over to me. *Why Gryffindor now?*

I considered for a moment. I'd changed my mind because he wasn't as cunning or as arrogant as I'd originally thought. He wanted badly to win, but I didn't think he'd stab someone in the back to do it. Me, on the other hand…well, I was firmly a Slytherin, in both the best and worst ways.

But I didn't want to say that. So instead I wrote, *You're daring, determined, and annoyingly chivalrous. Like a true Gryffindor.*

He arched an eyebrow and scribbled back. *Is that supposed to be an insult or a compliment?*

Both. Neither. Simply an observation that you're one of the few gentleman left in the world.

Being a gentleman never goes out of fashion, he replied.

As long as you're not a complete gentleman in private.

Trust me, love, you'd never know it in the bedroom.

That a promise?

Better win the challenge so you can find out.

———

Maddie and Jared walked down the runway together, and I clutched Gavin's hand, holding my breath. Maddie looked freaking amazing, like a true rock goddess. The pants fit her perfectly, the black leather jacket was smoking hot, and the chainmail tank top hung nicely on her. This challenge meant so much to me— not just for the win, but because I wanted Maddie to look and feel great. That was the whole point of fashion. It was not only to make pretty clothes, but to make clothes that empowered the person who wore them. I wanted Maddie to wear this outfit on stage and feel confident and beautiful while she played guitar.

Jared looked hot, too, wearing his own jeans plus the new top we'd made for him with the chainmail trim. It was a perfect complement to Maddie's look, and I could totally picture them on stage together with the rest of the band in their black clothes.

Dawn and Jeff had made a bouncy, high-low dress in white, with a bright pink underside and accents. It was cute and perfect for their young country singer Lacey, who strutted down the runway and tossed her long blonde hair. Beside her, the band's drummer wore a big white jacket with pink fringe that didn't fit him right. It was clear neither Jeff nor Dawn had any experience in menswear.

Trina and Nika, on the other hand, hated each other so much it was a miracle the Brazen singer even had a finished outfit. Not to mention, Trina's androgynous aesthetic and Nika's trashy one didn't exactly fit well together. They'd created a bodysuit that was so revealing it bordered on the obscene, then covered it up with what looked like a man's suit jacket. The Brazen bassist wore a matching jacket over his jeans, which wasn't nearly as bad.

All three of our teams got a brief critique, and then the judges went backstage to make their decision. With only six designers left, no one was safe, and for this challenge they didn't tell us who was in the top or the bottom. We were all in danger of going home and we all had a chance of winning. Even though Gavin and I had nailed the challenge, I wasn't sure they'd pick one of us as the winner. It was hard to tell what the judges would do, even with Eva judging instead of Lola. I'd been burned too many times before.

I leaned over to Gavin. "Who do you think will be sent home?"

"I'm not sure."

"I'm worried it might be Trina."

He squeezed my hand. "Me too. At least Eva is judging instead of Lola today."

I nodded. Last night I'd told Gavin about my conversation with Eva, but neither of us knew what, if anything, we could do about Lola.

The judges returned only a few minutes later, making it the shortest deliberation so far. "Thank you for waiting," Eva said. "I'm sorry I have to do this, but the designer going home…is Nika."

I almost let out an excited squeal, but Gavin's calm presence beside me reminded me to keep it inside. I couldn't stop from grinning though. Nika's drama couldn't keep her on the show any longer, not with her questionable taste levels.

She cast daggers at the rest of us as she stomped off the runway. I gave her a little wave. Good riddance.

Eva watched her go and then turned back to us. "Gavin, you are the winner of this challenge. Congratulations!"

Gavin exhaled beside me, and I threw my arms around him. Sure, it would have been nice if I had won and gotten that $1,000, but it didn't matter. Maddie and Jared would wear our looks at their concert tonight, and the private suite was ours.

He squeezed me back and whispered, "Are you going to join me tonight?"

"Like you even have to ask."

Chapter Nineteen

I t was late by the time Gavin got back to the Loft after his winner's interview. The other designers were already in bed, and the place was quiet and dark. I'd been dozing on one of the sofas in the living room, but jumped up when I heard the elevator doors open. He stood inside, looking tired but so handsome it made my chest hurt.

Our eyes met in the dim light, and then he strode toward me without hesitation. His hands cupped my face, and he kissed me in a way that took my breath away and sent a rush of warmth between my thighs. I kissed him back, pressing myself against his body, clinging to his shirt.

"Shouldn't we go inside first?" I asked.

"I couldn't wait a second longer to taste you. To touch you." His breath tickled my ear as his voice dropped to a whisper. "This is our last chance to be seen on camera tonight. Have to make it good."

Oh, right. We had to make sure we were providing the producers with enough footage to keep us on the show for another challenge. But once we got inside, it would be only us. No cameras. No viewers. And this time, neither one of us was going to leave in the middle of the night.

As we kissed, he slipped a hand under the bottom of my dress, sliding up my bare thighs. Higher and higher along my skin, only to discover I had nothing on underneath. He sucked in a breath. "Seems you couldn't wait either."

I gave him a sly smile and slipped my red panties into his hand, closing his fingers over it. "I might have gotten a little impatient."

He made a *tsk tsk* noise. "Always losing these."

"I don't know what happened," I said with a dramatic sigh. "It's like they just take themselves off around you."

He laughed, and we fumbled and kissed our way into the private suite. We could have stopped once the door was closed and the cameras were gone.

But we didn't.

This wasn't for the cameras. It was about doing what we'd wanted to do since we'd first met, before we knew we'd both be on the show, before we'd become competitors. Back when we'd been two hot, horny, single strangers in a bar. Tonight, with the door shut and the show and everything else on the other side, we could go back to that and forget everything else.

Once inside, he hooked one finger under my spaghetti strap and slipped it off my shoulder. I wasn't wearing a bra, and the front of my dress dipped low enough to reveal one of my breasts. My nipple was already hard, and it tightened even more under his appreciative gaze.

"I've been dying for a glimpse of these ever since that first night," he said as he eased the second strap off. The silky fabric slipped down my body, releasing my other breast. His fingers lightly trailed down the sides of them, raising goosebumps across my sensitive skin. "They're even more beautiful than I imagined."

"I would have shown you that night. I would have done anything you wanted."

"You were drunk. I'd much rather you let me do whatever I want when you're sober."

With that, he lowered his head to my breast and clasped his lips to my nipple, making me gasp. His tongue flicked along my skin, and my knees weakened. I grabbed onto his shoulders, clinging to him as he worshipped one breast, then the other. He didn't stop with my nipples either, but rained a trail of kisses all over my breasts, covering the curves and dips, the area under them, the valley between them. No inch of my chest went unloved, and soon I was dizzy with pleasure.

His hands were under my dress again as he kissed his way up, along my shoulders and neck, then returned to my mouth. When he slipped his fingers between my legs, he groaned. "So hot and wet down here, just like I remember," he said. "I need to taste you again."

His words brought back drunken memories of his tongue lapping at me until I had one of the biggest orgasms of my life. Yes, I wouldn't mind him doing that again…especially now that I was sober and could enjoy it even more. But first, we had to get rid of some of these clothes.

I tore at the buttons on his shirt, although it was difficult to undo them with his fingers doing amazing things to me. He was way too good at distracting me, but I wouldn't stop until he had a lot less clothes on.

I pushed his shirt off his shoulders, letting it fall to the floor, and he pulled me against him for a deep, hungry kiss. My taut nipples rubbed against his bare chest, and I reached for the front of his jeans, quickly undoing them. Together, we pushed them off his long legs and tossed them aside, along with his boxer briefs. Between fervent kisses, he grabbed the bottom hem of my dress and yanked it up, over my head and off me. It joined the rest of our clothes in a heap on the floor, and then, finally, we were naked together for the first time.

He didn't kiss me, didn't touch me—just took me in, staring at me like he could tease every secret out of my soul. His eyes were the color of a rainstorm, and I wanted him to wash me away.

We fell into each other, onto the bed, our bodies sliding, touching, rubbing, getting as close to each other as possible. He rolled me onto my back, and his body was a nice, firm weight on top of me. His hard length rubbed between my legs, so hot, so tempting, and I wanted him inside me already, but he had other plans.

He kissed his way down my body, covering every inch with his lips and his tongue, until I was both so relaxed and turned on I thought I might dissolve into the bed at any moment. He licked at my waist, my hips, the curve of my thigh, not rushing like he'd done that first night when I'd begged him to get me off. Now he took his time, tasting me everywhere, making me nearly delirious with want.

When he finally kissed me down there, I was so aroused I nearly came just from the lightest brush of his lips. He licked me slowly, leisurely, like he had all the time in the world to eat me out. I was already moaning, and for a brief second, I wondered how thick the walls were between this room and the others. But then I was swept away again when his long fingers entered me.

He flicked his tongue, building up a tempo that had me lifting my hips to meet him. I had no control over my body. I was completely captive to the way his mouth worked me, the way his fingers fucked me. I came hard and loud, my hands gripping his hair, my legs trembling, my hips rocking along with his movement. It kept going and it was so intense I almost begged him to stop, but I couldn't speak, could only hold onto him and drown in the tidal waves of pleasure that kept sweeping over me.

My. God.

He finally pulled away, after my entire body had melted into the bed and even breathing seemed like a real challenge. I lay there, my muscles twitching, every inch of me warm and weak and happy. He slid up my body, his erection nudging against my thighs, and pressed a kiss to my neck.

"I love the way you taste," he said, nipping at my ear.

The L-word in any context usually scared me to death, but he must have made me lose my head because I whispered, "I love the way you make me feel."

His mouth descended on me, and with his skin against mine, sliding between my thighs, desire flickered inside me again. I wrapped my legs around him, nudging the tip of him inside me, silently begging him to slam the length all the way in. But he pulled back and turned to the side of the bed. The nightstand drawer opened, and he fished out a condom from inside. I didn't even know there were condoms in there. He must have done some exploring the last time he'd had the suite.

He slid the condom on, and I watched, enjoying the view of him sitting above me—of his toned chest, the V of his hips, his broad shoulders and tattooed arms. His dark hair fell in front of his eyes as he worked, and something other than desire made my heart tighten. I pushed it away, and before I could dwell on what that emotion was, the condom was on, and he was easing his body over me again.

When he entered me, it was like a shower after a long, tiring day. I'd been craving him, aching for him, longing for him, since the very first moment we'd met. And now that he was finally inside me? It was even better than I'd imagined.

He held himself up on his arms, staring into my eyes, not moving but just feeling us together, joined as one. Slowly, he began to slide in and out. My arms and legs went around him, holding on for dear life, clinging to him as he rocked into me.

"I've thought about this every night since we first met. Every. Damn. Night," he said, punctuating each word with a thrust.

"Me too."

"I know."

I laughed. "You know?"

"Oh yes. It kept me up every night. I couldn't sleep, knowing you were in the other room, thinking about me, too. Thinking about how it would feel when I was finally inside you."

"So cocky." I loved the way he talked dirty to me, especially with that accent of his. "Did you touch yourself?"

"Yes. Bloody hell, I had to or I would lose my mind. Even with the other guys only a few feet away, I would stroke myself and think of you." He pulled out of me, rubbing himself along my sensitive skin, making me nearly delirious. "Did you?"

"Yes. In the shower. I'd remember how good you tasted, how big you were, and imagine how good you'd feel inside me."

He entered me again with a hard, quick thrust, and I cried out at the sudden impact, at the feel of being filled so completely. My nails dug into his back, and I lifted my hips as he pounded into me, our bodies moving together as one. This wasn't just sex, not like it had been with the other guys I'd been with. This was something more.

I needed to take control of this, to grab hold of my ridiculous emotions. I pushed against his shoulders, making him pause, then rolled him over so I was on top. Oh yes. This was better. Like this, I could make sure this didn't get too emotional. That what we were doing stayed sex and not making love.

I sat up, taking him even deeper, and pulled my long hair back. He sucked in a breath, his eyes locked on me, taking me all in. In this position, he felt even bigger inside me, but I was in control now. I rocked my hips once, twice, three times, making him groan. His fingers gripped my hips, urging me on, but I wasn't ready for this to be over yet. I arched my back as I began to slowly ride him, moving in the exact way to build up that delicious ache all over again. Higher and higher I spiraled as we moved faster and faster, until every nerve ending in my body screamed for release.

He took my hands in his, locking our palms together, our fingers intertwined, pressing against each other for support. I leaned on him, and he held me up as the orgasm swept over me, making me tighten around him and cry out his name. His fingers squeezed mine and his hips rose up to meet me, his eyes slamming shut as he let go.

I rode him until we both had nothing left and then fell onto his chest. His arms went around me, his breath rising and falling, making my body move up and down with him. For a long minute, we simply held each other. I couldn't remember the last time I'd done that with a guy. Maybe never. But I was too relaxed to do my normal routine of fuck-and-run. And for once, I didn't want to leave.

I managed to smile at him as he brushed a piece of sweaty hair off my forehead. "That was worth the wait."

"You're so lovely," Gavin said, trailing a finger slowly down my cheek.

"Stop it," I said, but I smiled so he knew I didn't mean it. I could listen to him say things like that all night long.

He sighed. "I know. I'm just as upset about it as you are."

"Why are *you* upset?"

"Because I have to look at you all day and somehow restrain myself from kissing you senseless."

"You don't have to restrain yourself now."

He rolled us over so he was on top of me, staring into my eyes. "Good because it's damn near impossible to resist you."

"Then don't."

For the next few hours, he didn't. And he was very much *not* a gentleman.

———

When I woke, it was still early, the day only beginning to brighten, the sky a dark blue through the windows. Not quite time to get up yet.

But I was awake and there was a sexy, naked guy beside me. He lay on his side, eyes closed, one tattooed arm stretched above us under the pillow. The other arm was draped across my waist, his inked hand curled around my hip possessively. We must have grown hot sometime in the night because the covers were tangled down at our feet.

Lust flared within me at the sight of his naked body, at the way he reached for me even in his sleep, at the sight of the rose on the back of his hand. I didn't want to wake him when he looked so peaceful, but I didn't know if we'd ever get this chance together again.

I moved closer, fitting my body against his, skin to skin. He stirred and his hand slipped down to my ass to pull me even closer, but he didn't open his eyes. I lightly brushed my mouth across his jaw, his stubble rough against my lips. I wondered how fast I could turn him on. One kiss? One touch? One word?

"Gavin," I whispered in his ear.

He nuzzled against me, already growing hard. "Need something, love?"

There was so much power in knowing what I did to him. "You."

His eyes fluttered open. "I'm yours. Now. Tomorrow. As long as you want me."

His words made me tense up. There were no cameras in here. No microphones. No audience. Whatever he said was for me alone. And his expression was serious, as though he meant it in more than a sexual way. Like he wanted something real between us.

But the idea of being with Gavin outside of the show terrified me. I wasn't ready to face that possibility yet. I didn't want a serious relationship, with him or with any other guy. I was still in college and trying to figure out my life and my future. Settling down was not in the cards for a very long time.

Gavin was the first—the *only*—guy to ever make me consider something else. But it was too much, too soon. So I climbed on top of him, bringing us both to heaven again, because that's what I did when I needed to distract myself from my problems. He was just another guy, and this was just sex. Nothing more.

I just had to keep telling myself that until I believed it.

Chapter Twenty

Instead of sending us to the workroom for our next challenge, they directed us to the runway. Kelsey arranged us in the chairs we sat in during judging, and she put Gavin behind me. For once, she didn't smile at us, and I got the feeling something was wrong but I couldn't imagine what.

Lola was back and walked down the catwalk to face us in a slouchy charcoal dress. "Before we get to today's challenge, we're going to shake things up a bit."

Uh-oh. That couldn't be good.

Our models walked out, one by one. My stomach sank even further at the upset look on Carla's face.

"Today you have the opportunity to switch models," Lola said, and I swore she looked at me in particular as she said it.

Oh god. Was this my punishment for complaining to Eva about Lola? I wanted to take it all back. I would be completely lost without Carla. And with only two challenges to go before New York Fashion Week and the finale, I couldn't afford to be off my game. I just had to pray I got to choose my model early and no one else picked her first. Most of the designers would want to stick with the same model, since we'd been working with them for weeks now. It would be fine. It had to be.

"Gavin, you won the last challenge, so you get to pick a model first," Lola said.

I relaxed a little. Gavin loved working with his blonde Valkyrie model. Any second now he would say her name, and hopefully I'd be able to pick next.

But he didn't answer right away. We waited for his response, but he stayed silent. I twisted in my seat and saw he was staring at me. He slowly raised his eyes to the runway. "I choose Carla."

My jaw fell open so hard I was surprised it didn't snap off. I gaped at him, wondering if I'd heard him wrong. He met my gaze and whispered, "Sorry."

No. I hadn't heard him wrong. This was really happening.

Gavin had stolen my model.

The shock melted away to anger, and I gave him a nasty glare, then snapped back to face the front. I couldn't look at his stupid, pretty face for even a second longer without punching it. My hands were already in fists, my muscles tense, my pulse skyrocketing. That fucking asshole. How *dare* he take Carla? He knew we were friends. He knew I would be lost without her, especially so late in the competition.

But he also knew she was the best model on the show. And obviously he thought he had a better shot of winning with her as his model.

Nope, he was definitely a Slytherin.

Carla gave me a sad look as she left the runway, and betrayal cut through my rage like a sharp knife. This morning, when we'd been alone, I'd thought Gavin cared about me. That he wanted something more from our fake relationship. But all along he'd been playing me, winning over my trust and manipulating me into letting my guard down. Now he'd shown his true colors by stabbing me in the back.

I shouldn't be surprised. This was a competition, and we would both do anything win. Our relationship was completely made up for the show. Last night had been fun, but in the end, it had just been sex. And today, with only two challenges left, we were back to being rivals.

Fine. Enemies it was, then.

Jeff picked next, and it was no surprise he switched models after all his complaints about his first model's breasts. He picked Dawn's model, and she took Gavin's in return. I was next. My choice was either Jeff's model or Trina's. Trina loved her model, and I wasn't going to be a dick like Gavin and betray my friend. Plus I kind of wanted to show Jeff that his former model's breasts were assets, not hindrances. She just needed a designer who knew how to work with them.

After we all chose our models, Beverly walked out on the runway and joined Lola. Her red lipstick was especially bright today, exactly the same color as her shirt. "For today's challenge, you're going to make stylish snow wear. The winning look will be part of an upcoming photo shoot for *Charmed* magazine."

Dammit, I wanted to win that. Talk about some great exposure. But it was probably the worst challenge for me I could imagine, since I'd lived my entire life in California and could count on one hand the number of times I'd seen snow. I didn't even have a good winter coat.

The next few hours were…rough. My new model's name was Susan, and she had beautiful wavy red hair and freckle-kissed cheeks, plus a killer rack. She was great to work with, but it just wasn't the same. My entire game was thrown off. When you design for one model for so long, she becomes your muse, and without Carla, I didn't know what I was doing anymore. All I could do was shoot her sad puppy-dog eyes while she stood beside Gavin's table, trying on his clothes. Ugh.

My mood wasn't helped by the fact that Gavin kept leaving me notes all day long. I ripped up every single one unread. I didn't want his apologies or his explanations. When he tried to talk to me at lunch, I walked away. I didn't want to hear whatever lie he was going to spew because I knew the truth: he saw Carla as another chance to get to the finale, and he took it.

But once we went back to the Loft that night, I couldn't avoid him any longer.

He stopped me outside the bathroom, in full view of Jeff, Trina, and Dawn, who were eating dinner. "Julie, please. Can we speak alone?"

All that anger came back in full force. "Fine." I dragged him into the bathroom and slammed the door. Before he could get out a word, I yanked his bracelet off my wrist and threw it at his chest. It bounced off and hit the tiled floor. "You can have that back. We don't need to keep pretending anymore. We're done."

He bent and picked up the bracelet. "Let me explain."

"There's nothing to explain. You saw your chance to get ahead and you took it. I would have done the same thing."

"That's not how it happened at all." He reached for me, but I jerked away from his touch. He sighed. "Bloody hell, Julie, you can't really believe I'm that callous."

"I believe you'll do whatever it takes to win, same as me."

He shook his head. "No. I did it for you."

I bit out a sharp laugh. "For me? Give me a fucking break."

"It's true. Jeff has been saying for ages that he wanted the producers to switch up the models so he could get a new one. I've heard him say before how much he liked Carla, so I knew he would choose her. I picked her because she's your friend, to save her from having to work with him."

"You didn't know Jeff would go next! For all you knew, it would have been me, and I obviously would have picked Carla!"

"Yes, it was a gamble. The last thing I wanted to do was take Carla away from you. But I had a feeling they made us switch models because you complained to Eva about Lola. I guessed they would put you at the end, to make sure Carla would be picked by someone else. So I decided to choose her, even though I really liked working with Heidi, because I figured it was better than the alternative."

"But don't you see what you've done?" I asked, my voice breaking. "You've made Carla my enemy. She's my best friend, and now I have to compete against her. Now if I win, she loses, or vice versa. It was supposed to be the two of us in this together, all the way to the end, and now we're on opposite sides!" I was nearly in tears again. Jesus, I'd never cried so much in my life before this stupid show.

"I'm sorry. I really am. I don't like it either. But would you rather she ended up with Jeff?"

"No!"

We were silent for a minute, and then he finally spoke. "I know you're mad, but I hope you can believe I did it for you." He touched my cheek lightly. "Julie, I would never do anything to intentionally hurt you."

I didn't know what to believe. He seemed sincere, but I also knew he wanted to win as bad as I did. Even if he'd done it for me—and that was a big *if*—I couldn't forget how horrible I'd felt when I'd thought he'd betrayed me. I was in way over my head with Gavin, feeling things I couldn't afford to feel. I'd begun to think that the two of us might be able to have something more outside the show, but today had reminded me that getting involved with him would only lead to heartbreak.

"Fine, I'll accept that you *might* have done it for me. But I want to be clear: this thing between us is just sex. It's a good way to relieve stress while we're here. That's it. Once the show is over, we'll go our separate ways."

His lips pressed into a thin line. "If that's what you want."

"I do," I said, although my voice shook as I said it. "There's no future for us. Even if this wasn't all for the cameras, I'm not looking for anything serious. I don't want a relationship with anyone. I have lots of things to do before I can settle down, and my education and career come first. A boyfriend is not in the cards right now."

"Nice speech. You must have said that one a lot." He sounded annoyed, and that in turn made *me* more annoyed.

"A couple times, yeah."

"Sounds like you're trying to convince yourself more than me, love."

I grabbed the collar of his shirt, staring up at his stormy eyes. "There is no you and me. None of this is real."

"So this isn't real?" he asked, and he claimed my mouth in a rough, demanding kiss. I kissed him back even harder, desperate for his mouth and his tongue and his rough stubble against my face.

"Or this?" His hands cupped my breasts through my dress, rubbing his thumbs along my already taut, straining nipples. A small moan escaped me, and I hooked my fingers into the back of his jeans, tugging them down.

"It's just sex," I got out between frenzied kisses. "Lust. Desire. It doesn't mean anything. Now if you don't mind, I need to take a shower before bed."

"Is that so?" He rocked his hips into mine, rubbing against me through our clothes. My butt hit the counter, and he lifted me up onto it, spreading my legs around him. I sat at the edge, hanging over the sink, my dress pushed up to my thighs, only the fabric of our clothes separating us.

He stroked down my legs to the curve of my knees, then to the ridges of my ankles, and slipped my ballet flats off one by one. I wrapped my arms around his neck, breasts pressed against him, my mouth devouring his, unable to get enough of his taste and his touch and his scent.

Without warning, his hands went under my ass, and he picked me up, so that I straddled him. I tightened around his neck and hips, holding on as he carried me into the large, standing shower and shut the door behind us. He flipped it on with one hand, and a spray of hot water hit us. We were still both fully dressed, and our clothes got soaked, melding to our curves.

With my legs still wrapped around his hips, he pressed me against the back wall of the shower, and the cool tile against my skin made me gasp. Then we were kissing again, unable to stop, like the few seconds our mouths weren't connected was more than we could bear. I tore at his black-and-gray shirt, unbuttoning it with fervent hands while he grinded his hips against me in the most amazing way. His jeans scraped against my panties, the friction between us so hot I was surprised our clothes didn't catch fire.

I pushed his shirt off his broad shoulders and buried my face in his skin, licking the drops of water off his neck. When my mouth found his pulse, he groaned, head falling back, giving me better access. His fingers fisted in the back of my hair, holding me to him as I sucked the moisture off his skin.

As much as I enjoyed having my legs around him, I wanted his clothes off even more. "Put me down."

He did as I asked, and I tugged his shirt all the way off him, then tossed it out of the shower onto the tile floor. He moved under the water and dipped his head back, stretching his long neck, his tattooed arms lifting above his head as he ran his fingers through his hair. Water streamed down his chest and into his jeans, which hung low on his hips. I'd never seen anything sexier in my life.

He took a step toward me, the water hitting his back, and his eyes seemed to drink in the sight of me with my dress wet and clinging to me, revealing my every curve. His gaze had so much raw, primal desire in it, and my breath hitched with anticipation.

As he watched, I tucked my fingers into the edge of my panties and slowly slid them down my legs, then kicked them out of the shower. Then I took the bottom hem of my dress and dragged it up, making sure to torture him with each inch of skin revealed.

Our bodies came together, touching each other everywhere, wet skin and wet clothes sliding against each other. I undid the button on his jeans and slipped my fingers inside to circle his length and grip him, hard. He sucked in a breath.

"We have to stop," he said. "No condoms."

"I'm on the pill. I was tested earlier this summer and I'm clean."

He bent his head, and his lips tickled my ear. "Before you, there hasn't been anyone since my last girlfriend, over six months ago. I know I'm safe. But are you sure?"

"I'm sure." He hesitated, but I began stroking him with my thumb and he shut his eyes with a groan. "Gavin, I need you inside me."

Without warning, he spun me around, so my back was pressed against his naked chest. His hand went up around my neck, holding me in place, while his other dipped between my thighs. His fingers slid along my wet skin and into the even wetter spot, and I gasped as he slipped inside.

"Is this what you want?" he asked, his voice rough, the hard front of his jeans pressing against my ass.

"Yes," I gasped. It was difficult to speak with his fingers around my throat, although it didn't hurt at all. It only turned me on more.

"Say it."

"I want you to fuck me," I managed to get out. "Hard and fast."

He released my neck and pushed me against the wall, my hands bracing against the cold tile for support. He removed the rest of his clothes and threw them out of the shower, then nudged my legs wider, his hands on my ass. I was so eager for him I knew he'd slip inside easily. But he didn't. Not yet.

He rubbed against me from behind, sliding against my wet body until I was aching for him so bad I wanted to cry. "Gavin, please."

He leaned forward to speak in my ear. "If all you want from me is sex, then that's what you'll get. But don't pretend for a second there isn't something real between us."

With that, he entered me from behind. The angle was amazing, hitting me in all the right spots, filling me completely with his hard warmth. I hadn't had sex with anyone bareback in…well, ever. But with him it felt right and so fucking good, skin to skin.

For a second, he simply held me there, his head buried against the back of my neck, the two of us breathing in and out, joined together. Then he pulled back, almost out of me completely, and paused, letting me die in anticipation with each second he waited. When I thought I couldn't take it any longer, he slammed back into me again, making me gasp with the force.

Over and over, he pounded into me, so deep I knew I'd be sore later. His hands pinched my nipples roughly, and I loved it. I'd asked to be fucked hard, and he was giving it to me. This was not making love; this was sex, plain and simple. No emotions, just lust and passion and release. Last night had been too close to something more, but not this time.

His fingers moved down, rubbing me in exactly the right spot. The feelings he sent all throughout me made my body weak, my knees barely able to keep me upright. My hands grasped at the wall, trying to find something to grab, something to hold on to, but it was too slick.

He pushed me forward, my breasts crushed against the tile, the shock of the cold against my cheek and my nipples making me gasp. He forced my arms up, holding my wrists together with one of his hands, the other still buried between my thighs. And like that, with him completely controlling my body, I came.

He pulled out of me and spun me around, while I was still trembling, while pleasure still wracked my body. He hefted me up, wrapping my legs around his waist, then pushed into me again with one smooth thrust. He didn't even give me a second to catch my breath, to recover from my first orgasm, before be brought me all the way back to the edge.

Our wet bodies slid against each other, my breasts rubbing against his chest, the tile against my back. I clung to his shoulders, nails digging into his skin, as he thrust in and out of me. The friction between us was so good it set every nerve ending on fire.

He gaze locked with mine, his rainstorm eyes piercing deep inside me, watching what he was doing to me. It was too intense, and I tried to look away, to pretend this didn't matter, that this was just sex. But he grabbed my chin and forced my head back, making me look at him. My eyelids fluttered shut, but he nipped at my lips roughly, still holding my face as he moved inside me.

"Look at me, Julie. I want your eyes on me when you come."

I opened them, but it was hard to not squeeze them shut and block him out as the rush of emotions swept over me. This time, when the orgasm took me, it was too intense, too much, too strong. I tightened around him, crying out, my eyes still fixed on his. He watched me as I came and then he joined me, but he never once looked away. He released himself inside me, and it was so raw and real I was trembling, and not just from the amazing sex.

He slowly set me down and pressed his forehead against mine. Now his eyes were closed, and he breathed heavily, his hands clutching my shoulders. I held onto him, the only way I could remain standing, while the water sprayed against his back.

"Tell me that wasn't real," he said.

I couldn't. But I couldn't deal with what that meant either. Because if this *was* real? Then I was in big trouble.

We rinsed off under the hot water. Without a word, he took my hand and slid the bracelet around my wrist, the metal cool against my warm skin. I didn't stop him. But as soon as it was on, I pulled away from him and left the shower.

I wrapped myself in a towel, gathered up my clothes, and ran out of the bathroom. The bedroom was already dark, and Dawn and Trina were in bed. I got dressed in a long sleepshirt, trying to be as quiet as possible.

"You okay?" Trina whispered, her voice sleepy. "Are you and Gavin…?"

I climbed into my bed, pulling the covers up to my chin. "We're fine."

"Good. But in the morning, I'm going to give you some tips on discreet shower sex."

I groaned and covered my face with my hands. "Were we that loud?"

"I'd be surprised if anyone managed to sleep through it. Sounded hot though."

"Oh, it was."

I was still quaking from it, little spasms dancing along my legs and between them. I fingered the bracelet around my wrist and closed my eyes, taking deep breaths to try to calm my racing heart.

Even now, alone in the dark, I couldn't escape him.

Chapter Twenty-One

The next day, things went from bad to worse as we finished up our cold weather outfits. This was the second-to-last challenge, and there were only five designers left. The pressure was so high we all barely talked, and when we did, we snapped at each other. Dawn randomly broke down into tears a few hours in, and Trina had to stop and comfort her. Gavin and Jeff got in a shouting match because Jeff accused Gavin of stealing his sewing machine, even though there were plenty in the room and none of us had a claim over them anyway.

I wasn't in any better shape. I had to completely redo my look halfway through the challenge. I thought my snow bunny one-piece looked good until I saw it on Susan, and then it was all wrong. I was screwed. And so frustrated and upset and exhausted I was one inch away from falling apart.

It was no surprise when I was in the bottom again. But I wasn't sent home.

Trina was.

We only had a few minutes to say our goodbyes in the breakroom. Dawn was sobbing, covering her eyes, her slender shoulders shaking. It was even worse because not only was she losing Trina, but she'd won the challenge, too.

"Don't cry," Trina said, wrapping Dawn in a hug. "We knew not all of us would make it to the final three. And you deserved the win today."

"But...but..." She dissolved into a wordless cry, burying her face in Trina's neck.

My heart was already breaking knowing one of my favorite people on the show was leaving, but seeing this made it even harder. I thought it had been bad when Molly was kicked off, but this was so much worse. Tears trickled down my face, and when Dawn finally pulled back, I grabbed Trina for a hug.

"It's not going to be the same without you," I said, sniffing.

Gavin hugged her next, and even he had a little tear in his eye, although he tried to discreetly wipe it away.

"Take care," Jeff said, giving Trina a short nod. Then he walked out of the room. Jerk.

"Group hug," I said to clear the awkward moment in the room. I threw my arms around Trina, and Dawn and Gavin joined in, too.

"I love you guys," Trina said. "Promise me one of you will win. It has to be one of you. Not him."

"We promise," Dawn said, finally getting control over her crying.

"Good. And the four of us need to get together after the show is over."

We agreed to keep in touch and reluctantly let her go. She turned to Dawn, giving her one long, tender kiss before breaking away.

With one last wave, she was gone. The three of us stood around, wiping our tears and collecting ourselves before we had to return to the Loft. But Jeff walked back in with a sour expression, followed by Lola.

"It seems you're all having a rough day, but that's too bad," Lola said with an evil smile. "Because your final challenge starts now."

My head snapped up. Wait, she was kidding, right? She had to be. I couldn't do another challenge now, not when I was already emotionally and physically exhausted. No way in hell.

But no. She wasn't kidding.

We shuffled back to the design room, but everything was a blur. I wiped my eyes and tried to focus, but it was difficult. But my entire body jerked to attention when I saw what was waiting for us in the center of the room.

Lola stood beside four dress forms and gestured to them. "For your final challenge, we want you to redo one of your previous looks that landed you in the bottom. Find a way to transform your outfit from something we didn't like to something we love. You will only have fifty dollars to spend on extra fabric, and the runway show will be tomorrow. And remember: this is the final challenge. We expect to be wowed by your looks. There are four designers left, but only three of you will make it to New York Fashion Week. Good luck."

She left the room, and for a second we all stood there, stunned. Then we ran over to the dress form with our look on it because what else could we do? We had to get to work.

I'd been on the bottom for many challenges, but they'd chosen my vintage star-covered dress from Lola's red carpet challenge for me to redo. A dress I loved, that I already thought was perfect, and that Lola had hated for no good reason. I had no idea what to do with it.

Gavin had to redo his superhero look, the one he'd run out of time on because he wouldn't accept my help. Dawn was given her gown from the wedding challenge, which they'd called a pink Disney princess dress (which I couldn't really argue with). Jeff was stuck with his dress from the New York challenge, which he'd made from cardboard boxes he'd found on the side of the road and hung from his model's body in strange ways.

It was already well into the evening, but we were still in the design room, ripping apart our former outfits. On top of our other problems, we all had new models, which meant we had to redo our looks to fit them, too. The pressure felt like a razorblade dragging across my skin. I was already so overwhelmed and tired, and now we were expected to pull out another look—the most important one we'd ever done.

My mind raced, trying to figure out what I could do to my dress. I had some ideas, but nothing fully formed yet. God, if only I had more time, if only I could think about this for a little while…but no, that was the point of this show. You didn't have time to think. You just had to do.

I spread my dress across the table and studied it. They'd said my look was too costumey, so I'd start there. My plan was to remove some of those elements and make the dress shorter so it was more of a flirty cocktail dress and not a gown. Since I was taking things away from my dress and not adding, I wouldn't need to spend much, if anything, on fabric. I just prayed it would all be enough to keep me on the show.

I chopped off the bottom of the dress and ran into the sewing room to finish up the new hem. Jeff was already inside, busily sewing away, while a camera filmed him from the corner. I sat as far away from him as possible.

"How are you doing?" he asked.

"Why do you care?"

He shrugged. "I noticed you and Gavin have been fighting a lot lately."

I glared at him. "What's your point?"

"Nothing. Only that it's obvious you wouldn't have made it this far without your little romance drama." He smirked. "At least I got them to switch up the models. It wasn't fair that you got to work with your best friend this whole time."

"That was you?" I flashed back to when I'd spoken with Eva and had seen Jeff standing down the hall. He *had* heard me. And he'd gone to the producers and complained. The little shit. I'd blown up at Gavin, and he'd been right all along. I should have been thanking him for saving Carla from Jeff, not yelling at him.

"It must be hard for you without Carla. I was hoping to get her myself, but I'm happy with my new model. Anything is better than that plus-sized girl they originally stuck me with."

My hands tightened around my fabric. "Susan is not even close to plus-sized, you dick. And even if she was, it's your job to design around her body."

"I've worked with dozens of models. I think I know what the industry standard is."

"Good luck finding anyone who'll want to work with you after this show airs," I muttered.

"Don't worry about me. I'm going to win." He removed his dress from the sewing machine and stood up. "But I doubt you'll make it past this challenge. We all know the only reason you've made it to the end is because of Gavin and Carla. But now you're on your own—and you don't have the skills to get you to New York Fashion Week." He gave me a smug little shrug and then walked out.

All I could do was sit there, staring at my half-finished dress, fighting back tears. My hands shook too much for me to finish sewing it. I'd started out angry, but his last words had hit me hard. Because I knew he was right.

I'd only gotten to the final challenge because I'd been paired with Carla from the beginning and because of my fake romance with Gavin. Even before the show started, I'd had special treatment by being invited instead of having to audition like the others. The producers had given me a ton of help, and all I'd done was try to blame Lola when, in fact, I'd deserved to be on the bottom all along.

Carla came in the sewing room a few minutes later, wearing a T-shirt and jeans. "There you are!" She rushed over and put her arms around me. But when she pulled back, she searched my face. "Oh, Julie, what's wrong?"

"I have a question, and I need you to answer me honestly. Do you think I only made it this far because of you and Gavin?"

"What? Never! Why would you think that?" She dragged a chair over and sat beside me.

"It's…just something Jeff said."

"No, you one hundred percent deserve to be on the show. You made it this far because of your talent and all your hard work—not because of anything else."

"I don't know. I was invited on the show. I was paired with you. I even got to work with Maddie. And then this thing with Gavin…" I dropped my head on my arms, so tired I could barely keep my eyes open. "Maybe I deserve to go home."

"Stop that. Jeff is a terrible person. You should hear the horror stories the models tell about him. He's just trying to mess with your head. Don't listen to a single thing he says, okay?"

I nodded slowly and sat up a little straighter, taking a deep breath. "You're right. Fuck that guy. I'm making it to the finale."

"Good." She smiled at me. "How are you doing otherwise?"

I threaded my sewing machine and got my dress in position to fix the hem. "I'm a mess. I've never worked so hard in my entire life. I might literally die of exhaustion."

"You seem pretty calm."

"It's either that or run around screaming."

She gave me a long hug, tucking her head on my shoulder. "Hang in there. And don't forget, I believe in you. I'll be there at New York Fashion Week rooting for you to win."

"But if I win the show, you'll lose."

"I don't care about that. I want you to be happy." She stood up, her curls bouncing a little. "Now finish that dress."

———

The Loft felt so empty that night with only four of us. Dawn retreated to the private suite since she'd won the last challenge, and through the door, I heard the faint sounds of crying. I didn't know if she was crying because Trina was gone or from exhaustion from everything we'd been through that day. I was tempted to knock on the door and comfort her, but I had a feeling it would only make things worse. She clearly wanted to be alone, and maybe it was better if we all kept our distance from each other.

I was exhausted, yet once again I couldn't sleep. I was the only one in the women's bedroom and I should have been happy to finally have a minute to myself, but I only felt more alone than ever. I missed the company of the other girls, even the annoying ones like Nika. I missed Trina whispering to me from the bed next to mine long into the night. I even missed Molly's snoring. Sure, they'd been my competition, but they'd become my friends, too.

I went to the bathroom to get away from all the silent, empty beds. When I emerged, Gavin was in the kitchen, leaning against the counter. A glass of water sat beside him on the granite, but he stared off into space. He wasn't wearing a shirt, and the lights from the city cast shadows across his smooth, bare back.

"Couldn't sleep?" I asked.

He tensed at my voice, but then turned to face me. "No. You either?"

I shook my head and moved toward him. I wasn't sure how things stood between us after last night, but he opened his arms, and I fell into his comforting, warm embrace.

"Thank you for taking Carla. I know you did it to save her from Jeff, and I'm sorry I got mad."

He kissed my forehead. "You're welcome. I only wish it didn't have to come to this."

"I hate this competition. I hate that another one of us is going home in the next challenge. And I hate that only one of us can win at the end."

"I do, too. But whatever happens tomorrow, it won't change how I feel about you."

His words sent a pang through me, and I tilted my head up to him, whispering his name. He gave me a long, slow kiss, gently teasing at my lips, and I couldn't stand the thought of going back to my bed without him.

"Sleep with me tonight," I said.

"I don't think that's allowed."

"I'm the only one there." I dug my fingers into his shirt. "Please. I don't want to be alone."

"Anything you want, love."

We returned to the women's bedroom and climbed in bed together. I rolled on my side, and he spooned me from behind, his arm draped over my waist. His tattooed hand skimmed my hips, across the thin shorts I'd worn to bed. I leaned back against him, enjoying his warmth and support behind me. He swept my long hair to the side and kissed my neck and shoulder. I closed my eyes and relaxed, letting his presence envelop me, and for a second I was able to forget all the sadness, all the stress, all the worry over what was to come.

I'd been tired, but now that he was pressed up against me, my every nerve ending woke up. And judging by the hard bulge pressed against my ass, he was rising to attention, too. Just being this close, our bodies fitted together, our skin touching, sparked the desire between us. I'd meant for us to sleep, honestly, but as he kissed my neck, I wanted more.

I turned my head to kiss him, moving my hand behind me to stroke his hip. His touch became more insistent, our kiss deepening, our heartbeats quickening. His fingers slipped under my T-shirt and found my breasts, cupping them, stroking them, kneading them. I rubbed my butt against his hardness, gripping his hip, clutching his clothes.

His flannel sleep pants had that slit in the front, although it was buttoned up. He helped me undo it, and then I wrapped my fingers around him with a sigh. He felt so good, so smooth, so hard and big in my hand. He let out a soft moan as I stroked him and dipped his own fingers inside my shorts, searching me out. He found me already wet for him, and his touch sent bursts of pleasure shooting through me. He worked me with his thumb while his fingers slipped inside, rubbing me while he fingered me, slowly moving in and out. I stroked him with the same tempo, and my hips jerked to meet his fingers, my butt rubbing against him.

His hand left me so he could finish tugging his pants off, then do the same to my shorts. My T-shirt was still on, but whatever, we were too desperate to care. He moved behind me again, and I hooked a leg back over him, spreading myself wide. He positioned himself and easily slipped inside from behind. At this angle he couldn't go too deep, but even with just the head inside, it felt so good. Almost like he was teasing me, making me beg for more.

My butt pressed back against him as I took him deeper, and it felt amazing without a condom. His arm wrapped around me, holding me against his chest, his hand moving between my legs again. He started a slow, deliberate pressure, circling and rubbing me, while our hips rocked back and forth together. I wanted him to move faster, deeper, harder, but I got the sense he wanted to take this one slow and sensual. And I couldn't argue with that, not when it felt so good like this.

We didn't say anything. The room around us was completely dark. The covers were pulled over us. Yet a part of me knew the cameras and microphones were probably getting a little of it. Just a hint of what was happening in my bed. I didn't care. Especially not when he increased the speed and pressure, nipping at my ear with his teeth, kissing the spot just below it.

But then he stopped and pulled out of me. I was so close, and I ached with the loss of him. I let out a little whimper, but he rolled me onto my back and moved over me. There was enough ambient light coming from the windows and the bright city outside that I could just make out the shape of his face in the dark. Enough that I could see his look of pleasure when he entered me again and knew he could see mine.

I wrapped myself around his body, getting us as close as possible. Arms around his neck, legs around his hips, moving as one body instead of two. His fingers moved down, rubbing in just the right way as he thrust in and out. Warm tingles spread all over me, and he swept me away with him, our eyes locked on each other the entire time.

I loosened my tight hold on him, but he didn't move off me or leave my body. He kissed me softly, tenderly, making me feel like I was the most loved girl in the world. Like nothing could ever hurt me, not when he kissed me like that.

He stroked my face, brushing back my hair, staring into my eyes. He looked so serious, so impossibly handsome, it made my chest ache.

And then it hit me: tomorrow might be the last time I ever saw him. Our fake relationship was no longer necessary. After this challenge, it would all come down to who was the best designer, and no amount of drama would change that. And the thought of not seeing Gavin again, of not being with him, terrified me more than anything.

I pushed on his shoulder, squirming out from underneath him. I sat at the edge of the bed, legs dangling off it, and took deep breaths to try to calm my racing heart. I was feeling so much I worried my heart might burst, and I didn't know what to do with all of that emotion.

He sat up and trailed his fingers down my back, making me shiver. "Are you all right?"

I groped around on the floor until I found our clothes, then tossed his back to him. I couldn't look at him, even in the darkness. "You should go."

He got dressed in silence, and I was grateful he didn't ask me any more questions. If he did, I might confess things I had never confessed to a guy before.

He moved to the door, the city lights framing his dark silhouette, his hand lingering on the doorframe like he hoped I would ask him to come back to bed. But I said nothing.

Finally, he left.

Chapter Twenty-Two

I woke with the heavy realization that Trina was still gone and that this was the end. Not all of us would make it to Fashion Week. It had to be me, Gavin, and Dawn at the end. It had to be.

But then what? Only one of us would win. Maybe it would have been better if we'd never become friends. My heart was so conflicted I thought it might tear in two. I wanted them to succeed, but for *me* to succeed, they had to fail. I wanted to win, but I wanted *them* to win, too. And if they won, it would mean I had lost.

I never should have let myself get close to anyone. My plan had been to not make friends, to stay focused on the show. But I'd bonded with Trina and Dawn. And Gavin… I didn't know what I felt for Gavin, but I felt too much.

No matter what, I was not going home.

We had a few hours to finish our revamped garments before the runway show, and we spent most of those in a silent frenzy. The design room had never been so quiet before. All I heard was the brush of fabric, the hum of the sewing machines, and the occasional sighing from someone around the room. I had no idea if my new dress was any good or not. At this point, I just wanted to get it done in time.

Dawn and Jeff went on the first lunch shift together, and I heard Gavin muttering under his breath. He leaned against his table, elbows resting on it, his head in his hands. "Bollocks," he said.

"What's wrong?" I asked, placing a hand on his back.

"I'm out of fabric and money, and my dress doesn't fit Carla. I'm properly fucked."

His dress form did look a bit bare. I could help him, but if I did, that might lower my chance of making it to the finale. I should want him to fail, but I cared too much about him to do that. Stupid emotions.

"I have money left over that I'm not going to use. You can have it to buy more fabric."

"No," he said, turning away from me.

"No?"

"I don't want your help. I'll figure it out on my own."

"Is this because of last night?" I asked, dropping my voice. "Because I'm sorry. I shouldn't have sent you away like that."

"It has nothing to do with last night. I have to do this on my own, without your help or anyone else's. If I win, it will be because of my own talent and skill. And if I lose, then it will be my fault and mine alone."

"But—"

"I don't want your help! How many times do I have to say it?"

"Fine!"

I stomped back to my table. He was so stubborn he would turn down free money to buy fabric, possibly costing him a spot in the finale, and for what? His stupid pride?

His words reminded me of what Jeff had said yesterday, about how I'd had help getting where I was and how I wouldn't have made it to the end without Carla and Gavin. I had to prove to everyone that I deserved to be at the finale. I didn't need or want help anymore. And obviously, neither did Gavin.

We were on our own, as it should be. This was the end, and there was no reason to keep pretending there was anything real between us.

During our lunch shift, Gavin moved behind me and slid his hands around my waist. "I'm sorry, Julie. The pressure got to me. I didn't mean to snap at you."

I spun around, twisting out of his arms. "No. You were right. It's better if we do our own thing from now on." I dragged my bracelet off my wrist and handed it to him. "Here. Take this back. I don't need it any longer."

He stared at the bracelet in the palm of his hand. "I don't understand. You don't want it?"

"You only made it for me so it seemed like we were together. We don't need to do that anymore." Everything we said and did was being recorded, but I didn't care. If this was over, we might as well go out with a bang.

"Is that what you think?"

"We both know this was just a game. And now it's over."

His fingers tightened around the bracelet. "No, it's not. Not for me. And I don't think it is for you either."

"We made it to the end of the show. We don't need to keep pretending." It was hard to get the words out, but this had to be done. For me and for him.

"Julie, I'm not pretending. This is all real for me. It has been from the very beginning."

"Don't say that!"

"It's true," he said. "All I want is you."

"That's not true. You want to win, too."

He sighed. "Can you forget about the show for one minute?"

"No, I can't. And neither can you. Because only one of us can be the winner."

"You don't know that. We might both lose."

"Oh god, don't say that. Knock on wood," I said, rapping on the table.

He brushed his fingers next to mine. "Touch wood."

I jerked my hand back. We were silent for a minute, staring at each other. He looked more vulnerable than I had ever seen him before, and it was hard to not try to comfort him.

"It's better this way," I finally said. "Neither one of us can afford any distractions."

"You're not a distraction! I care about you, Julie. Why can't you see that?"

"Gavin, stop, please." I didn't want to hear it. I couldn't. Not now, not when we were so close to the end. If one of us was kicked off during this challenge, things between us would be over anyway. We'd return to our lives halfway across the world from each other. But even worse, if we both made it to the finale, we'd have to compete against each other.

Whatever happened, this thing between us had to end today.

He took a step closer. "No, I need to tell you. I need to get it out, even if you don't want to hear it."

I turned my head away, unable to look at him any longer, but he cupped my chin and turned my face back to him.

"Julie, I love you."

Oh god. Why would he say that? Especially now, of all times. I squeezed my eyes shut. "Please don't."

He released me and sighed. "Not the response I was hoping for."

"What did you expect me to say? We're in the middle of the final challenge. You didn't think this could have waited 'til a better time?"

"No, because there might not *be* another time. One of us might be gone today, and I didn't know if I'd get another chance."

I shook my head, trying to clear it. "I can't do this. I have a dress to finish."

He gave a sad little laugh. "I confess I'm in love with you and you don't even care."

"I care. I just…"

"You just care more about winning."

"No!"

"Tell me the truth. Do you feel anything for me? Or is this really just sex to you?"

I sucked in a ragged breath, my shoulders shaking. "It's just sex. Like I said, I don't want a relationship."

"Of course." He dragged a hand through his hair. "I don't know why I thought you might actually care for me."

"Gavin…" My heart was breaking into a million pieces. I didn't know what to do.

"No, I should have listened to you from the beginning. All you want is to win, and you'll do anything to get there."

He left the breakroom without another word, and I slumped down into a chair, fighting back tears. Gavin said he loved me, but he had to know this was best for both of us. We were at the end of the show, and it was every man—or woman— for his or herself. Better to cut off the relationship now than be distracted for the finale or have to go through another loss like Trina's.

No, it was better that I'd ended it with Gavin now. Even if he hated me for it.

Life was a bitch, and so was I. But fuck it. Bitches got stuff done. And my dress wasn't finishing itself.

———

With only four of us left, there was no top or bottom three. They critiqued every single one of us, and they seemed to hate everything. But what did they expect when they'd sprung this challenge right after the other, giving us little money or time to do it? Using looks they'd already hated?

They called my new dress "uninspired," Dawn's dress "boring," Gavin's top, jacket, and pants "predictable," and Jeff's dress with the cardboard boxes "weird." I had no idea who would be going home. It was truly anyone's game at this point.

None of us spoke while we waited on the runway for the judges to make their decision. Dawn reached across the stage and grabbed my hand, and I hesitated a second before taking it. I sneaked a glance at Gavin, but he wouldn't even look at me. His jaw was clenched, and his lips were tight. Fine, I deserved that.

The judges returned and sat down. Lola stared at the four of us, and I wanted to yell at her to hurry up already.

"The winner of this challenge is Jeff," Lola said. "Congratulations, you're going to New York Fashion Week."

Oh god no. My fingers tightened around Dawn's, and I glanced over at Gavin again. This time he met my eyes with an inscrutable expression. But I knew what he was thinking. One of us would be going home.

No matter who it was, I would be heartbroken.

"This was a very hard decision," Lola said. "And we had some differences of opinion. But unfortunately, only three of you can make it to the finale." She glanced at the other judges and then back at us. The silence seemed to stretch on forever.

"The designer going home tonight is…Julie."

My heart seized up. I couldn't breathe. No. Nonononono. This couldn't be happening. There had to be a mistake. I couldn't have come all this way to go home now. I refused to believe it.

But Gavin was staring at me with pain in his eyes and Dawn had started to cry again and Jeff was looking smug and it hit me: I'd lost. I was going home. My time on the show was over.

"I'm sorry," Lola said, except she smiled when she said it, so I knew she wasn't sorry at all.

Beverly gave me a sad smile. "This was a really tough decision. You've made some beautiful pieces, but you're still finding who you are and what your aesthetic is."

"I agree," Ricardo said. "You are a talented designer, but you need more experience. We are confident you will go on to great things, in time."

Kiara jumped up and ran to the runway. She gestured for me to bend down and then gave me a hug. "You were one of my favorites," she said. "I want you to make me some clothes when this is all over, okay?"

I nodded, blinking fast so the tears wouldn't escape—not when I was on camera, not with the judges and other designers watching. Later, I could have a meltdown. But not now.

"Julie, it's time for you to pack up your things," Lola said.

My throat felt like it had been sewn shut. I walked off the runway, head down, not making eye contact with anyone. Someone tried to hug me—Dawn, I think—but I avoided her pale arms and kept going. Gavin said my name under his breath, his voice a plea of some sort, but I ignored him. What could he do? What could he say?

I'd come all this way and gotten so close to the finale, and now I was going home. I wasn't going to design a collection or show at Fashion Week. I wouldn't be in the final three. I wouldn't be winning this thing, with or without Carla.

This was the end.

I was done.

I'd failed.

I packed up my things in record time, trying to finish before the others got back to the Loft. I moved quickly, efficiently, but it felt like I was outside my body, running on autopilot and watching it all happen to someone else. It wasn't real yet.

When I'd finished, I cast one final glance around the Loft, my home for the last few weeks, with its bamboo and metal and hard edges. I'd truly this miss place.

And then I left it behind.

In the lobby, Kelsey told me they wanted me to stay in New York until after the finale, and made me do a quick exit interview. I kept it as short as possible, giving clipped answers, not showing much emotion at all. I could tell they wanted more, that they hoped I would break down, especially when they asked me about Gavin, but I shut myself off completely. I didn't give them anything, and they finally let me go.

A car brought me back to the same hotel I'd stayed at before the show had started. Only once I'd collapsed onto the bed did I finally break down and cry. By then I had been holding it in so long it came out in a torrent, and I couldn't stop.

I fell asleep with tears in my eyes and an ache in my heart that I didn't think would ever go away.

Chapter Twenty-Three

I slept for most of the next day. I hadn't realized how exhausted and rundown my body was until I was able to sleep alone in a room for as long as I wanted. I'd been going at full-steam, both physically and emotionally, for weeks. Working long hours every day, dealing with an overwhelming amount of stress and pressure, all on not nearly enough sleep. It had been way too much. No wonder my emotions were a complete mess.

When I finally woke, the afternoon sun slanted through the thin gaps between the hotel room's blackout curtains. I immediately wanted to go back to sleep because the second my eyes were open, reality came crashing back in, and it hit me again that I'd lost everything.

I'd lost the show. I hadn't even made it to New York Fashion Week. Like my parents had predicted, I wasn't cut out to be a fashion designer. I could already hear my mom chiding me for not listening to her, reminding me that she'd been right all along.

And I'd lost Gavin. He'd wanted something more, something real, and I'd refused. He'd said he loved me, and I'd pushed him away. I'd destroyed whatever future together we might have had.

It was probably for the best. He had a whole other life in London and a real future in fashion design. He would go back to that and whatever came next for him, and I would finish up my senior year at UCLA and then go on to medical school to become a doctor like my sister. With any luck, Gavin and I would never see each other again.

I should be happy. This was what I'd wanted at the beginning, to move on with my life and forget him. It was over. Done. Finished. I was a single girl again.

So why did the thought bring me to tears?

Gavin had dug his claws into me, finding his way under my skin like no other guy ever had. I had to shake him off somehow. Get him out of my system.

And I only knew one way to do that.

―――――

I sat at the hotel bar, in the same seat I'd occupied when I'd first met Gavin, and asked the bartender for a martini. As he got it ready, I crossed my legs, hiking my skirt up my thigh, and scanned the crowd. It was a Tuesday and the pickings were slim, but there was a guy in a suit and tie sitting alone who showed promise. He had short blond hair, brown eyes, and a sharp jaw. His skin was smooth and clean-shaven. He was hot, and he wasn't wearing a wedding ring.

Better yet, he looked nothing like Gavin.

I grabbed my drink and made my way over. He looked up at me when I approached and gave me a warm smile.

"May I join you?" I asked.

He stood up and pulled the other chair at the table out. "Be my guest."

Oh god, he was a gentleman like Gavin. I wondered if, like Gavin, he would be the opposite in the bedroom. The thought made my stomach clench painfully, and I pushed it away. This guy looked like he enjoyed vanilla sex, which was perfect for tonight.

He held out his hand. "I'm—"

"No names," I said.

"Oh." He blinked a little and then shrugged. "Okay."

Jesus, he gave up on that easily. I flashed back to how Gavin had tried to get my name out of me over and over. And when that failed, how he'd given me a nickname instead. *Stop thinking about him,* I mentally yelled at myself.

We sat in silence, staring at our drinks, and I tried to think of what to say next. My mind was a complete blank. What the hell was wrong with me? My game was totally off tonight. It was like I'd forgotten how to flirt or something.

I gave him a sultry smile. "So what brings you here?"

"I'm a financial advisor. I have some meetings with some mutual fund money managers." He kept going, talking about stocks and investments, but I had already tuned him out. I wasn't picking up the guy for his job, after all.

"Let's cut to the chase," I said, interrupting him mid-sentence. "Do you want to go back to my room?"

He looked shocked by my bold proposition, but then his throat bobbed and he nodded. "Yes. Definitely."

I leaned forward, giving him a view of my cleavage. "This is what I'm offering. One night. No names. No strings attached. And no contact when it's over. Can you handle that?"

He nodded faster. "I can handle that."

"Good." I downed the rest of my drink and stood up. "Let's go."

He jumped to his feet, grinning. "Wow, this never happens to me."

Yeah, yeah, must be your lucky night. I wanted to roll my eyes, but I forced myself to smile. He signed the bill, then stood up and walked around the table to join me.

I moved stiffly and quickly to the elevator, making him match my pace, impatient to get this over with. Ugh, when had sleeping with a hot guy become a chore? Further proof that Gavin had seriously messed with my head.

As we waited for the elevator, the guy slid his arm around my waist, his fingers resting against the bare skin on my lower back. The second he touched me, my entire body screamed in protest. It was almost like physical pain, the revulsion and utter wrongness hitting me so strong I nearly gagged.

He pulled me closer and leaned in for a kiss, and all I could think was, *NO, NO, NO.* I jerked back, turning my head so his lips grazed off my cheek. Even that slight kiss was too much. I wanted to vomit.

I had never, ever felt this way before. Even ugly guys I could usually make out with, no problem, especially after a few drinks. And this guy was *hot.* He wasn't a creeper or a perv. He was exactly the kind of guy I would normally love to take upstairs for a quick night of fun and then conveniently forget to ever call again. He seemed on board with the plan, too. He was perfect in every way for a one-night stand.

But he wasn't Gavin.

"I'm sorry," I said, pulling away from him. "I can't do this."

"Are you okay?" he asked.

I clutched my stomach. "I don't feel well all of a sudden. Must be something I ate. I need to go."

I dashed across the lobby and into the women's bathroom without another word. It wasn't a lie. I did feel sick. But it wasn't something I ate.

The guy didn't follow me, and I didn't check to see if he looked stunned or disappointed or relieved. I waited a few minutes until I was sure he'd be gone and then headed back out.

I got into the elevator—the same elevator where Gavin and I had first made out—and leaned against the mirrored wall. I tried to get my breathing under control, but being in here only made it worse. Thinking of the way he'd kissed me against the mirrors buried me in an avalanche of emotions. Longing. Sadness. And something else, too.

I felt guilty for even *considering* fucking another guy, when the only one I wanted to be with was Gavin. That was a new feeling for me. And then a final wave of misery hit me because I couldn't be with him. I'd ruined everything between us. That hurt more than anything else—even more than losing the show.

Oh god, was I…in love?

Was that was this feeling was?

Shit. I didn't like it one bit.

I returned to my room and kicked off my shoes, then collapsed on the bed. It wasn't the same room as the one I'd shared with Gavin, but it might as well have been. They looked identical, down to the abstract painting hanging above the bed and the view of the city from the window.

I didn't even have Gavin's phone number. Once the show ended, I could try to find a way to contact him, but by then would it be too late? Would he be over me, able to brush off our time on the show as a fleeting thing born from being stuck together in a closed space for weeks under stressful circumstances? Would he have realized I wasn't worth all the pain I'd put him through?

I had to find a way to talk to him now, before the show was over.

I dragged myself off the bed and reached for my phone. They'd given it back to me when I'd been kicked off, but I'd been too tired and depressed to even look at it. Now I had so many emails, texts, missed calls, and social media notifications I wanted to throw it against the wall and never look at it again. I thought I'd be so happy to have the Internet back, to return to the real world, but now it felt too overwhelming to try and catch up on everything I'd missed over the past few weeks. All I wanted to do was crawl back into bed and disappear forever.

That wasn't an option. I ordered room service—the show was paying for it, so why the hell not—and once I'd eaten something, I felt like I could finally tackle the rest of the world. I told myself I didn't have to respond to anything today—only a few people knew I'd been kicked off, after all. I would go through the easy stuff for now and mark the things I needed to respond to later, when my head was clearer.

Kelsey had left me two voicemails while I'd been sleeping, urging me to call her back because the producers wanted me to come in and talk to them. More interviews probably. I didn't know if I could go back there and face all of that again, but it might be the only way to reach Gavin.

Carla had texted me and called me, too. She was worried about me and sad I was no longer on the show. No mention of Gavin, though, which only made me wonder even more how he was doing. Maybe I could send him a message through her, to let him know that I did care, if nothing else. But I couldn't figure out what to say.

I fell asleep with my phone in my hand. I woke in the morning when it started buzzing near my head, just like the morning of my first day on the show. Except this time, I wasn't hungover—just heartbroken.

The number was unfamiliar. "Hello?" I asked.

"Julie? This is Giselle Roberts. Is this a good time to talk?"

I sat up so fast it made my head spin. "Yes. Giselle. Hi."

"I spoke with Eva Pereira the other day, and she told me about your…problems with Lola Baudin. I went through the footage from all of the runway shows yesterday, and I have to agree with her. It does seem like Lola might have manipulated the results against you. We'd like to offer you a second chance on the show."

I was so stunned I couldn't speak. I just held the phone to my ear with my mouth open.

"Julie?" Giselle asked. "Are you still there?"

"Yes, I'm here. Sorry." I swallowed hard. "What do you mean by a second chance?"

"You'll be competing in the finale with the other designers. At New York Fashion Week. How does that sound?"

I covered the phone and screamed, doing a quick dance in my underwear on the bed. A second chance on the show *and* with Gavin. It was almost too good to be true. After a second, I composed myself and said, "That sounds amazing. Thank you so much."

"Good. Can you come in today? Say, in an hour?"

I scrambled off the bed and began yanking clothes out of my suitcase. "I'll be there."

———

Giselle walked with me through the lobby of the *Behind The Seams* building. She was a beautiful older black woman who still knew how to rock her curves. Today she wore a sharp pantsuit in red and black, radiating confidence and power with every step.

"I'm glad you decided to come back," she said. "Once I heard about what Lola had done and how she'd been biased against you from the beginning, I knew I had to make it right somehow."

"Thanks for giving me a second chance."

"Lola will still be one of the judges for the finale though. There's nothing I can do about that."

"I understand."

"I confess there's another reason we brought you back, too. The other producers and I all felt the show was missing a certain spark without you. In particular, without your relationship with Gavin. It's going to be one of the main focuses of this season once it's aired, and we think the viewers would like to see it come to more of a conclusion."

I took a deep breath, trying to figure out what I would say to Gavin when I saw him. We were competitors again, but maybe we could find a way to get past that somehow. "I'd like that, too."

She nodded and led me into the elevator. "For the finale, you have to design a collection of eight looks with the theme of the four elements: earth, air, fire, and water. Two looks per element. You have three thousand dollars and five days to do it. Unfortunately, you'll have one less day than the other designers, but we're willing to let you work late into the night so you can catch up. Also, all the finalists have the option to use one of the previous contestants as an assistant. You have a choice of Molly or Derrick. Let me know which one you would prefer to work with, and we'll get them here in a few hours."

"I'll go with Molly." Easy choice. "I assume Dawn chose Trina, and Jeff must have picked Nika. Who did Gavin choose? Tom?"

"Gavin declined an assistant."

"He *declined*?"

"He asked for you originally, but we couldn't get a hold of you yesterday morning. Then he changed his mind and said he didn't need any help, that he could do it on his own." She shook her head. "It's a pity, too, because many of us thought he had a strong chance of winning. But now I doubt he'll be able to finish his collection in time. Or if he does, I'd be surprised if it was up to the quality of the others. I suppose that's good for you though. It increases your chances of winning."

That idiot. With Giselle at my side, I walked down the hallway to the design room, completely furious with Gavin. He was going to let his stupid, stubborn pride get in the way of him winning. I told myself I shouldn't care, that it wasn't my problem, and that he was my competition. I reminded myself I had a chance to win and if he was going to shoot himself in the foot, so be it.

But then I spotted him through the doorway. Around him, the other designers worked in pairs, yet he stood alone. He was bent over his workstation, his chestnut hair falling into his eyes, and a light sheen of sweat dotted his forehead. He was using the scissors, but he finished cutting and threw them down on the table, then brushed his hair back with a quick, angry swipe. He was still as handsome as ever, but he also looked…lost. Tired. Like he had already given up.

Something flared up in me, and it wasn't only anger. I couldn't let him give up. I wouldn't let him throw this away. He'd supported me, believed in me, and taught me so much in the short time I'd known him.

I turned to Giselle and told her my idea. I didn't want to compete with Gavin anymore. Not when I knew what he was capable of. Not when I knew he could win.

It was my turn to help him, even if he didn't want to accept it.

Chapter Twenty-Four

I stepped into the design room and moved to Gavin's side. He straightened and turned to face me, but his expression was guarded. "I heard a rumor they invited you back."

"They did."

He gave a short nod. "That's good. You deserve to be in the finale."

I gave a noncommittal, "Hmm," and inspected his dress form. He had draped some gray fabric across it, but I couldn't make out any real shape to it.

"Checking out your competition?" he asked, crossing his arms. "There's not much to see yet."

"No, there really isn't. You're way behind the other designers. Why did you turn down an assistant?"

"Because I don't need one. I can do this on my own. Other people would just get in my way." He brushed past me, heading toward the sewing room. "But you should worry more about your own collection than mine."

Oh, hell no, he was not walking away from me, not now. I stomped after him, the other designers staring at us with wide eyes as we left the room.

I stopped in front of Gavin and planted my hands on my hips. "You stupid, cocky, stubborn man. Why can't you for once accept that you can't do everything on your own? That you do sometimes need help?"

"I don't need anyone's help. And you were right. Getting close to other people only distracted me. I won't let that happen—not now, not at the end."

"That's a bullshit excuse and you know it. I'm not moving until you explain why you're so set on doing this on your own."

He rubbed the back of his hand, the one with his rose tattoo. "Julie, I have to do this by myself. If I don't win this on my own, it won't be the same."

"What are you talking about?"

"I started doing all this for my sister, to honor her memory. She has to be the one guiding my hand, not anyone else. I have to win this for her."

I rolled my eyes. "As you would say, what a load of rubbish."

"Forget it. I don't expect you to understand." He tried to brush past me, but I wouldn't budge.

"Oh, I understand you're being a complete idiot. Gavin, your sister would want you to win, but not for her. She'd want you to win because you *deserve* to win. And if that means accepting help from someone, I'm sure she would be okay with that."

He turned his head away and wouldn't look at me. Fine. I'd have to convince him some other way.

"Last night I went to the hotel bar and picked up another guy," I blurted out. Harsh, but I knew it would make him listen.

There was a flash of pain in his eyes, and then it was gone. His jaw clenched. "Why are you telling me this?"

"I thought I could get you out of my system, that I could go back to my old ways of love 'em and leave 'em, but it didn't work. I couldn't do it." I had to steady myself before I could go on. The confession was too big, yet bursting out of me. "I don't want to take any other guys back to my room. I don't want to be with anyone else. I only want you."

"Julie…" He sighed and dragged a hand through his hair. "This really isn't the time. After the show we can talk, but at the moment we're still competitors. You were right about that all along. I can't let anything get in my way, and neither can you. You should get started on your collection."

"I'm not doing a collection."

"Then…what are you doing here?"

"I asked them if I could be your assistant instead."

He stared at me for an eternity. "They offered you a chance to make a collection, to compete in the finale, to show at New York Fashion Week…and you said *no?*"

I swallowed hard. When he said it like that—holy shit. But…no. I stood by my decision. "The judges were right when they eliminated me. This is what I want to do with my life, but I need more experience. I need to figure out who I am as a designer. I'm not there yet, but I will be someday."

He shook his head. "The judges were wrong. You're just as talented as any of us in the final three. And Giselle must agree with me or she wouldn't have invited you back."

I smiled up at him. "You've always believed in me, even when I didn't believe in myself. But I don't want to compete against you anymore. I want you to win."

"No, I can't let you do this. I can't let you give up your chance at winning for me."

"I'm not giving anything up. I'm *choosing* to help you. This is what I want. Please, let me do this."

He looked like he would argue some more, but I took his hands and moved closer. I took a deep breath and said the words I'd never, ever said to a guy before.

"Gavin, I love you."

His eyes searched mine, like he couldn't believe it. I stared back at him, letting him see the truth in my face. Then he swept me into his arms and kissed me until I was dizzy, until I forgot my own name and everything else in the world except him.

"Say it again," he whispered against my lips.

"I love you."

He kissed me again, taking my breath away a second time. "I love you, too."

"I know. Now are you going to let me be your assistant? 'Cause we really need to get to work."

He gave a dramatic sigh. "Yes, you can be my assistant."

"See? That wasn't so hard."

"I can never say no to you."

"And that's the way I like it."

"Now tell me about this other guy you picked up in that hotel. How far did it go? Do I need to hunt him down and stab him with some of these pins?"

"No violence required. I didn't even kiss him. He was hot, too. I mean, not as hot as you, but I totally would have done him before you came along and ruined me for other guys. You asshole."

"It's tough to feel sorry for that." He pulled me in for another kiss that made me weak in the knees and warm all over. I tangled my fingers in his hair, melting into his embrace, my heart nearly bursting with happiness. If this was what it was like to be in love, I could definitely get used to it.

We walked back into the design room, and I gave Dawn and Trina quick hugs, while Jeff and Nika shot me nasty looks. I rejoined Gavin on his side of the room, and he showed me what he'd made so far.

"Jeff and Dawn are doing the obvious thing by using the colors associated with the four elements, but I want to use the shape and texture and feel of the elements with only a hint of the colors. So for earth, I want to use metal. For water, I'm going to create a dress that looks like rain. For air, I'm making a dress inspired by a tornado, and for fire, one inspired by flames. I still have quite a lot to do, of course."

"Wow." I touched the chainmail dress he'd been working on. "This is going to be amazing. But it will be tough to finish all of this in time. This is…ambitious."

"True, but I don't want to be safe. This is the finale, after all."

"Good thing you have me now." I gave him a quick kiss, then picked up his sketch pad and flipped through it. "So what would you like me to do?"

He hesitated, glancing at his fabric, and I could tell it was tough for him to delegate something to me. "I started a corset for one of the earth looks, but turns out I have no idea how to make one."

"Perfect. I'll work on it while you finish the chainmail pieces."

He nodded and moved to one of the dress forms, but then turned back to me. "And…for the other fire look, perhaps you could do that ombré technique you did on your wedding gown?"

"Are you sure?" I asked.

He drew in a long breath. "You were right. I can't do everything on my own. And I want you to be represented in this collection, too." He touched the rose on the back of his hand and gave me a faint smile. "My sister would like that."

I stood up on my tiptoes to kiss him. "She would be so proud of you."

"I hope so."

While he got to work, I grabbed my sketch pad, ripped off a sheet of paper, and wrote I love you across it. I folded it up and slipped it in the back pocket of his pants as I walked by. I wanted him to know I meant it, both on and off camera.

When I got back, he had left me one final note, wrapped around the bracelet he'd made me. *I love you, too.* I slipped the bracelet around my wrist and smiled, running my fingers over the metal.

———

Eight looks in five days was almost impossible. Even with two of us. We worked our asses off. There was very little time for romance beyond a few stolen kisses and quick touches. The Loft was full of people again, and when we were in the design room, we were busy working on his collection. He guided me, explaining his vision, teaching me new techniques so I could help him create his collection exactly the way he wanted. I learned more about design in the few days working with him than I had in years. It almost felt like an apprenticeship. He'd gone to design school and had worked for some of the biggest designers in London, and now I was getting some of that knowledge and experience firsthand. It made me realize how much more I still had to learn.

The night before the runway show, we went up to the rooftop lounge and celebrated: me, Gavin, Trina, and Dawn, all back together again. Nika and Jeff declined to join us. Not that we cared.

Kelsey had found us some champagne, and Gavin popped it open. "A toast," he said, raising his glass. "To the four of us. We said we would make it to the end together, and we did. Cheers."

"Cheers!" We all clinked glasses and drank.

"Whatever happens at the end, I'm glad we all became friends," I said. "And when this is all over, we have to stay in touch."

We chatted about our collections, about the upcoming finale, and then we split into pairs. Trina and Dawn started making out on the nearby couch, while Gavin and I stared over the edge of the roof at the city skyline. He stood behind me, his arms wrapped around me, and he was tall enough he could rest his head on top of mine.

"What are you going to do when the show is over?" he asked.

"I don't know." It was something I'd been fervently trying to avoid thinking about. "I start my senior year at UCLA in a few weeks, but the idea of going back to all those pre-med classes I hate makes me want to throw up. I don't think I can do it anymore. Not when I've had a taste of what I want to do with my life. But…"

"But what?"

"My parents will flip if I drop out. I've already proved them right by losing the show. And I've put so many years into becoming a doctor."

"But think how many more you would still have to spend to get there. Medical school. Residencies. Better to get out now before you waste any more time doing something you hate." He turned me around, tilting my chin so I looked up at him.

"Julie, you're a designer. You live to create. You can't let anyone stop you from doing what you love."

"I know. I just… I need to think about it some more." He was right, but I was scared. What if I took this risk and it didn't pay off? What if I failed? It was such a huge life change, and I didn't know if I was ready yet. Being on the show had taught me I wanted to work in a fashion career, but also that I needed more experience and training. But was I willing to risk the disappointment and shame from my family if I let them down and went on my own path?

"What would you do if there were no limits?" Gavin asked. "If you didn't have to worry about money or your parents or the future? What would you do if you had no fear?"

The answer came easily. "I would transfer to a fashion design school—FIDM, Parsons, one of those. I've realized I still have a lot to learn to become the designer I want to be."

"Then that's what you should do."

"You make it sound so easy."

"Isn't it?" he asked.

"No, not even close. My parents would never approve. They're paying for school and would probably cut me off completely. Plus, it would take me even longer to graduate."

"You need to talk to them. See what they say. You might be surprised."

"You don't know my parents. It's doctor or lawyer or nothing with them."

"No, but I know you. You're a baby T-rex, small yet fierce. And you won't let anything stop you from getting what you want."

I wished it was as simple as he made it sound. But no matter how much I tried to explain it to him, he wouldn't get it. His mother supported him no matter what he did. Mine…not so much.

"What are *you* going to do after the show?" I asked.

He leaned against the railing and stared out at the bright city against the dark night. "I want to start my own company and my own line of clothing. If I win, I'll have the money to do that. If not…then it will be a lot harder."

A question burst out of me before I could stop it. "What about us? I live in LA, you live in London…"

"I've wanted to move out of London for some time now. It has too many memories of my sister." He looked across the city, then back at me. "I was thinking about moving to New York, actually."

"That makes sense." New York was still considered the fashion capital of the world. "I like LA, but I've always wanted to move here, too."

He took my hand, pressing it against his chest, against the pounding of his heart. "Then do it. Move here with me."

I laughed. "Yeah, right."

"I'm serious." He slid his arms around my waist and gazed down at me. "I don't want to lose you, Julie. New York seems like a good compromise, halfway between our two families. You can transfer to Parsons and finish school there. And being in the same city will make it a lot easier for you to go into business with me."

"What are you talking about?"

"I thought I had to do everything on my own, that my way was the only way, but I was wrong. I work better with you. I need you to balance me, to keep me in line when I become too stupid and stubborn, as you would say. We should start a clothing line together."

I sucked in a breath. "You want to go into business together? Isn't that a little…dangerous?"

"Maybe for others, but not us. We know what we want and we go after it. And right now, we both want the same things."

"I don't know…"

He kissed my forehead. "Just think about it. If we win, I'll split the prize with you. It's only fair, since you did so much of the work."

"No! It's your collection, not—"

He pressed a finger against my lips. "Stop talking, love," he said with a smile, recalling when I'd said that to him before. I scowled but kept silent. "We'll use the prize to start our own company. Together we can make a clothing line that will last, that combines both of our unique points of view and talents. We'll be the next Dolce & Gabbana or Marchesa. The next Stephan Weiss and Susan Karan."

Ideas churned in my head, possibilities making my stomach flutter with excitement. The thought of working with Gavin, of sharing a life and a career and a future with him, made me all tingly inside. But it was scary, too. It was an even bigger risk than leaving pre-med behind to become a fashion designer.

"What if we break up?" I asked. "What if none of this works out?"

"I don't know. I can't predict the future. All I know is that you inspire me to be a better man *and* a better designer. I want you at my side, as an equal partner, in all aspects of my life."

God, he really *did* love me. It was such a strange feeling and one I'd never experienced before. I liked it, but I worried it couldn't last. Would we still feel this way for each other outside of the show, when we were back to our regular, boring lives? Or what about five years from now?

"What happens if I say no?" I asked. "What if I become a doctor and stay in LA?"

"Then we'll find a way to make it work." He brushed my hair aside and pressed a soft kiss to my neck. "As I said, I'm yours, Julie. Now. Tomorrow. As long as you want me."

Chapter Twenty-Five

We woke before the sun rose, and there was a quiet buzz in the Loft as we all got ready. It was bittersweet, knowing we would all be going our separate ways after this. We'd be leaving the Loft forever, and only one of us would win the grand prize.

Cars shuttled us over to the Lincoln Center for the Performing Arts, and we were directed to the giant white tent where *Behind The Seams* would have their fashion show. The camera crew tracked us the entire time as we stepped inside, taking in the giant majestic runway with chairs on either side of it. The room was empty at the moment, but in a few hours, it would be full of hundreds of people.

We'd made it to New York Fashion Week.

Backstage was chaos, with a hundred and one things happening all at once. There was a frantic energy in the air that was both exhilarating and terrifying. We were all fueled by excitement and panic, by adrenaline and exhaustion, by hope and fear.

Crew members dashed around, camera people recorded everything, and Kelsey kept it all together, directing and organizing as best she could. Each designer had a separate space with curtains between them, their collections hanging from racks inside. We had a few short hours to do any last-minute touches, including ironing and steaming, snipping off any loose threads, and making any final tweaks.

When the models showed up, it truly became a whirlwind of activity. I dashed around, getting each model dressed, while Gavin barked out orders and inspected everything. He wore a fitted black suit, white button-up shirt, and black tie, looking both classy and incredibly sexy. His hair was styled to perfection, and only a hint of stubble brushed his jaw. Every time I looked at him, I felt a pang of both lust and love, to the point where it was hard to stay focused on whatever I was doing.

I'd worn a dark gray, strapless flare dress with a tiny owl print. I'd made it myself, and it was cute and quirky and so totally me. I'd saved it for the finale, imagining myself wearing this dress while I introduced my collection to a huge audience. Even though I'd pictured that moment a hundred times, I didn't feel any disappointment now, knowing I'd be backstage the entire time. Today my place was beside Gavin, supporting him, rooting for him to win.

"Where's the last model?" he asked, holding up his rain dress, the only one still on the racks.

I glanced around, doing a quick head count of all the models. Seven. How could there only be seven? "We're missing one. I'll find out what's going on."

I ran to Kelsey and asked her where our last model was, but she had no idea. She went to confer with someone, and they called someone else, and no one seemed to have a freaking clue what was happening. Meanwhile, the clock was ticking.

"She didn't show up," Kelsey finally reported to me and Gavin. "We're finding a replacement now."

"But the garment was already fitted to her," Gavin said.

"I'm sorry, but this is the best we can do."

I took a long, deep breath. Inside I was freaking out, but I had to keep it together for Gavin. "We'll figure it out. We can swap some of the clothes around if we have to."

I heard a commotion from Dawn's area and saw Trina running around in a panic, while one of the models stood around barefoot. "Where are her shoes?" Trina yelled. "Did someone steal them?"

I took a second to check on Jeff and found him hastily hand-sewing a dress that had ripped at some point. Nika was nowhere to be found. It seemed every designer had their own last-minute problems.

But even so, I loved the frantic energy. It was the one thing about being a doctor I thought I might enjoy because hectic, stressful situations actually spurred me on. But now that I'd been on *Behind The Seams*, I knew I never wanted to do anything else. This was my passion.

Fifteen minutes later, my former model Susan arrived. I threw my arms around her. "Thank god you're here."

I helped Gavin switch around the dresses to find one that fit Susan and her voluptuous figure. The whole process took way too long because we had to make the models walk for us, then make any changes we needed. But finally, *finally*, all eight models were dressed.

It was time. All three collections were ready to go down the runway, and we were shuffled to another section backstage where we could watch the show live on a screen. Hundreds of people were already seated in the audience, waiting.

And there, in the front row, were my parents.

Anxiety and dread shot through my stomach. I'd never invited them. How could they be here, in the audience? Oh god, did they know I wasn't in the final three? That I had failed? Or were they expecting me to walk out with a collection? I couldn't decide which was worse.

My head snapped to Gavin. "What the hell is my family doing here?"

"I asked Kelsey to invite them."

"You *what?*"

"Normally only the final three contestants' families are invited to the show, but my father isn't coming. You put so much effort into this collection and I wanted your family to be here to see how hard you've worked."

"How could you do this without telling me? Without *asking* me?"

He frowned, his brow furrowed. "I wanted to surprise you. I thought once they saw what you've accomplished in such a short time, they'd understand how much this means to you and that this is what you're meant to do." He reached for me, but I jumped back. He sighed and continued. "After the runway show, you can tell them you don't want to go to medical school and that this is what you want to do with your life. Before it's too late and you've wasted even more time doing something you hate instead of following your dream."

"But that isn't up to you! I should be the one to decide when and what to tell them!" Maybe I was being unreasonable, but I hated that he had done this without asking me or giving me some warning or *something*. He'd trapped me in a corner, and now I had to face my parents with no time to mentally prepare or consider what I would say to them.

"I'm sorry, Julie. I thought I was doing something to help you. I would do anything for my family—my *entire* family—to be here with me. I thought you would feel the same."

"Well, I don't. My family isn't like yours. And this wasn't your decision to make." I stabbed a finger into his chest. "I'll tell my parents if—or when—I'm ready to. But you don't have the right to tell me what to do or force me into this situation. You said you wanted to be equal partners in the future, but you wouldn't let me handle this on my own."

His shoulders slumped. "You're right. I shouldn't have gone behind your back. But I also knew this is one of the only times your family might be able to meet my mum, since she lives in Wales."

"Your…your mother is here?"

"Yes. She's sitting with your parents."

I checked the screen again. Right next to my mom, chatting with her and moving her hands quickly, was a woman with curly, chestnut brown hair. They were engaged in conversation, my mom nodding along with whatever Gavin's mother was saying while my dad smiled and watched the crowd. Beside him sat a handsome blond man who could only be Dawn's father. After their video chat, Dawn had told me her father was thrilled to meet Trina and completely accepting of the two of them together.

My parents were here. Dawn's father was here. But Gavin's father…was not. He didn't support Gavin's work, even though his son was showing a collection at New York Fashion Week. I understood now why Gavin was so adamant that he would have done anything to have his entire family here. He was not only missing his sister, but his father, too.

My parents had come to the show, even though I hadn't invited them. Did that mean they might actually support me a tiny bit? Maybe not as much as I wanted. Maybe they would never be completely on board with my dream to become a fashion designer. But the fact that they were here meant something.

I never in a million years would have invited them. Gavin knew that. But they would have missed out on seeing what I had done, what I had helped Gavin accomplish. And I'd have missed out on the chance for them to meet Gavin's mom —and him.

I was still upset he'd invited them behind my back, but I understood his reasoning. And maybe he was right to do it. I didn't know what I would say to them or how they would treat me when this was all over, but I couldn't keep lying to them or going after a career I had no interest in. I had to be honest with them about my dreams and about my plans for my future—even if they didn't support them.

"I'm sorry," I said, turning back to Gavin. "I never would have invited my parents on my own, but…I'm glad they're here."

"No, I'm sorry I didn't discuss it with you first. I only wanted what's best for you, but I shouldn't have made the decision for you."

I grabbed his tie and tugged him toward me. "I needed that little extra push to talk to them. But next time you think about doing something like that, run it by me first."

"I will." He brushed hair away from my face. "I love you."

"I love you, too." I pulled him down for a kiss, and some of the models made *ooh* noises. I wouldn't be surprised if some of them were jealous. Gavin was quite a catch. But he was all mine.

When we broke apart, I smiled up at him. "Our parents seem to be hitting it off already. I hope your mother likes me as much as she does my parents."

"She'll love you. She likes strong women."

"No wonder she and my mom are getting along. Maybe we should separate the two of them. They could be scary together."

He laughed and wrapped his arms around me, kissing my forehead. My face pressed into his chest, breathing in his warm, clean scent. It felt so good to be in his arms, to know that whatever happened, he supported me. It gave me the courage to make a decision about my parents and about my life after the runway show was over.

The audience erupted into applause, and then I heard the muffled voice of Lola on the microphone, introducing the show and briefly talking about *Behind The Scenes* and the different finalists. If my parents didn't know I wasn't in the finale, now they would for sure.

Dawn's collection was the first one out. They never found that model's correct shoes, so they used Kelsey's shoes, since they happened to be the same size. Dawn went out and introduced her collection, then came back to watch it on the screen with Trina at her side.

Her collection consisted of a bunch of flowy, pretty dresses, plus a few separates, using colors to differentiate between the elements: red and yellow for fire, yellow and green for earth, green and blue for water, and white and blue for air. The colors were all soft pastels and flowed nicely from one element to the next, giving the show a cohesive feel. The showstopper was a sea green dress that seemed to move like waves. I wasn't sure if her collection was unique enough to win, but it was all very pretty and feminine and I could see a lot of women wanting to wear her clothes.

Jeff's collection was next. He'd also used color to show the four elements, but his clothes were all done in bright, vibrant shades. Bright yellow for air. Fire engine red for fire. Electric blue for water. And finally, neon green for earth. He had a lot of separates but a few dresses in there, too, and the silhouettes had a hint of an eighties feel while still looking modern. It wasn't my style at all, yet I couldn't deny there was something about them that was interesting to look at.

Gavin's collection was last. I gave him a quick hug and said, "Go get 'em." Then I slapped him on the ass and shoved him toward the runway.

He walked out from behind the curtain, and I watched on the backstage screen as he introduced himself. "My name is Gavin Bennett, and my collection is called, 'Love Is the New Black.' I want to thank the three important women who made this day possible: my sister, Rose, who continues to guide me every day; my incredibly supportive mum, who came all the way from Wales to see this show; and Julie, the woman I love. I couldn't have done this without you." He gazed across the audience and gave them one of his charming smiles. "I hope you enjoy the show."

His voice was clear and confident as he said the words, and he looked so handsome in his suit I wanted to drag him off stage and jump him. Only when he turned on his heel and walked backstage did I see him start to shake. Just a little—in his hands, a slight twitch of his shoulder—to show me how nervous and overwhelmed he was.

"That was perfect." I gave him a quick kiss, my heart swelling three sizes thanks to his words, and we rushed to the screen to watch his show. He grabbed my hand, clutching it tightly as his collection came out.

He'd started with earth, and the first model wore a chainmail V-neck backless top paired with stone-gray ankle pants. I'd made the pants basic but stylish, so the focus would be on the intricate details of the top. Next was the black corset I'd made for him, with a chainmail skirt that swished as the model walked down the runway.

The third look was our ombré gown, done in red, yellow, orange, and blue, the colors moving like fire up and down the model's body. After that came a black sheath dress with geometric cutouts along the bodice that looked like flames licking up her chest.

For water, Gavin had made a gray gown with chainmail hanging from it in strategic places, making it look like rain when it moved. He'd also done a red raincoat, and under it was a black leather jumpsuit with a top shaped to look like waves. The final element was air, which started with a short white dress with a flared skirt, all of it trimmed with a touch of chainmail for cohesion.

Carla was last, wearing Gavin's most impressive piece: a storm-gray gown that looked like a tornado flowing around her body. I'd worried the dress might go too costumey, but Gavin had pulled it off. It was stunning the way the dress shifted and swirled around Carla when she walked, like a storm in motion. I was so happy Gavin had stolen her from me. If she'd been with me, she would have been eliminated, but now she was here at the end, all of us on the same team.

Gavin and I watched in silence, holding our breath the entire time. Seeing it on the runway was different than seeing it on the dress form or even on the models backstage. Each piece took on new life as it moved down the catwalk, and it was like seeing it for the first time.

When it was over, Gavin was supposed to walk with all of the models down the runway. I directed him to the curtain and gave him a kiss. "I'm so proud of you."

But he didn't let go of my hand. Instead he dragged me out with him. "Come with me."

"What are you doing?" I asked.

"You deserve to be out here as much as I do."

"No, I—"

But it was too late because we were already walking out into the spotlight. We trailed behind Carla and the other models, while Gavin smiled at the audience, still holding my hand. I smiled, too, though I still couldn't believe he had dragged me out in front of hundreds of people and all of the cameras. Down below, my parents clapped and smiled up at me, and Gavin's mother beamed at us. My eyes teared up a little at the sight.

At the end of the runway, Gavin took Carla's hand, too, and the three of us stood there looking out at the audience. He raised our joined hands up, kissed Carla's cheek, then kissed me on the lips. A rush of warm happiness spread throughout me as I stared out into the crowd while they applauded and cheered, and then we turned and walked back down the runway after the models.

I laughed once we were backstage. "I can't believe you did that!"

Gavin kissed me, trailing his fingers through my hair and down my back. "I couldn't go out there without you. It wouldn't be right. Not after everything you did for me."

"It was all worth it to see you out there with your beautiful collection. I want you to win so bad it hurts. I love you."

"I love you, too." He closed his eyes, holding me, resting his forehead against mine as he breathed and regained his composure.

"How do you feel?" I asked.

"Nervous. Relieved. But mostly happy. For the first time in my life, I can say I wouldn't change a thing."

"Your sister would be so proud of you."

"Your family *is* proud of you."

"I hope so." I glanced toward the nearest screen. The audience was getting up and heading to the post-show cocktail party next door, while the judges were coming backstage to inspect the models' clothes more closely. We had a few hours to mingle before the final verdict would be in.

Gavin and I quickly checked the models again, to make sure nothing had come loose or gotten messed up during the walk. We each gave Carla a quick hug and wished her luck, then headed for the door.

"Ready to face your parents?" Gavin asked.

I swallowed the lump in my throat and nodded. "Ready."

Chapter Twenty-Six

I'd never been in a room with so many stylish, wealthy people before—and all of them wanted to talk to Gavin.

We spent a few minutes working the room, saying hello to previous designers who had been kicked off and meeting winners from previous seasons of the show. We stopped to chat with Trina and Dawn and her father, and I couldn't tell if he was more excited that his daughter was in the finale or that she'd found someone who obviously made her so happy.

We were approached by a number of fashion bloggers and magazines, who wanted to interview one or both of us, and even a few representatives from different fashion labels, inquiring if Gavin or I wanted to work for them. We took everyone's business cards, but didn't offer any other commitments. It would all depend on if Gavin won or not.

"I think that woman works for *Vogue*," I said, pointing to a dark-haired woman across the room. "We should go talk to her."

"No more stalling," Gavin said, dragging me away. "Our parents are waiting for us."

I sighed. "Fine."

"Don't be nervous. You'll do great."

All I could do was nod as he led me through the crowd to where his mother stood at a table with her drink. She instantly brightened when she saw us, bursting into a big smile and moving forward to grab her son in a tight hug. I stood awkwardly to the side while she said something quietly to him, something I couldn't hear over the loud chatter and music in the room. Then they pulled back and turned to me.

"Mum, this is Julie."

She threw her arms around me next, giving me a warm hug. "Julie, it is lovely to meet you," she said, her voice sounding almost musical with her accent.

"So nice to meet you," I said. "Gavin has told me a lot about you."

"Has he? That's so kind of him. I can't wait to learn more about you. He and I were only able to talk that one time while he was on the show, but he did speak highly of you then."

"Did he?" I asked, giving him a smile.

"Oh, yes," his mother said, nodding. "I could already tell he was quite smitten with you." She took my arm and leaned close. "And trust me, that is rare. I knew then you must be special."

I flushed, but then my parents walked over to us and my stomach clenched. I couldn't remember the last time I had seen them dressed up like this—my dad in a charcoal suit, my mom in a knee-length skirt and a jacket I was pretty sure was Chanel, her favorite designer. Yet she wondered where I'd gotten my love of fashion from.

They were less enthusiastic at seeing me, but it also wasn't their nature to make a big scene. My dad hugged me first, with a little grunt. He never said much, but I knew that meant he approved. My mom hugged me next, but she wore her usual unreadable expression and I couldn't tell what she was thinking.

"Mom, Dad, this is Gavin." I hesitated, unsure how much more to say. But then again, he had made it pretty clear out on the runway that we were together. "My…boyfriend."

He shook my parents' hands with a warm smile. I'd never introduced a guy to my parents before, and they eyed him like he was in the zoo or something.

"How far did you get on the show?" my mom asked me once all the introductions were done.

Here it came. I stood a little taller, bracing myself. "I was kicked off in the last challenge, the one before the finale."

Gavin's mother gasped. "Oh no! You were so close to the end, you poor dear."

"You did well," my mom admitted, patting me lightly on the arm. "But the show is over. Don't worry about it anymore. Next week your final year at UCLA starts. You can get back to focusing on that and on your applications and studying for the MCAT."

My mouth fell open. Did she not get how important this was to me? That I couldn't just go back to my life the way it was before? That I couldn't forget everything that had happened over the last few weeks?

"Julie was invited back to the finale because she was unjustly eliminated," Gavin said, resting his hand on my lower back. "But she turned it down. Instead, she helped me finish my collection in time for the finale. I couldn't have done it without her, and she created many of the best pieces. You should be proud of her."

My mom blinked at him. "Of course we are proud of her."

"Very proud," my dad chimed in. "We never expected her to get so far."

"Gee, thanks," I said.

My mom's mouth twisted. "Julie, we didn't know how good you were. You used to make clothes when you were a little girl, but we've barely seen you the last few years. Until you announced you were coming on this show, we thought you had given all of that up to focus on your studies."

"No, I never gave it up. And there's something I need to talk to you about." I turned to Gavin, drawing strength from his solid presence at my side. But I had to do this alone. "Could you give us a minute?"

He nodded. "Good luck. I'll be right over there if you need me." He wrapped an arm around his mother's shoulder and led her over to the buffet table with a smile.

Once he was gone, I sucked in a deep breath. "Mom. Dad. I don't want to be a doctor."

"You don't?" my dad asked. My mom just narrowed her eyes, her lips pressed in a thin line.

"No. Not at all. Not even a tiny bit."

"But what about all your schooling?" my mom asked.

"I only chose pre-med because Helen did it and because you told me to…and because I didn't know what else to do. You made me think I only had two options: lawyer or doctor. But I don't want to be either of those. I want to be a fashion designer. It's what I've *always* wanted."

My dad frowned. "Why didn't you ever say anything?"

"Because you never approved! You wanted me to be like Helen. To follow in her footsteps. But I'm not like her. I'm not the perfect daughter, and I'll never be the perfect doctor. This is what I have to do."

"We never wanted you to become your sister," my mom said. "We wanted you to find your own path and to feel the same enthusiasm for it that Helen does. We never realized that fashion design was anything more than a hobby for you until now."

"Because you told me over and over how it wasn't a real career! How I needed a stable job with a steady income to rely on, not some artsy career where I would starve."

My mom looked a little uncomfortable. "While it's true that we would…prefer it…if you had a more traditional career, we want you to be happy, too."

"We don't want you to go into a career you don't feel passionate about," my dad said.

My shoulders relaxed a little, but there was still more I had to tell them. "Good. Because I'm going to apply for a transfer to Parsons, here in New York. Even though I did well on the show, I still have a lot to learn. It will probably take me an extra year or two to graduate, and I'll likely have to take out all kinds of student loans that I'll have to pay back for the rest of my life, but it will be worth it. Even if I become a starving artist, at least I'll be doing what I love."

"Are you sure about this?" my mom asked, placing her hand on my arm. "You only have one year left at UCLA. You could always graduate and then decide. At least then you would have a degree you could use for other things."

I hesitated. For a second, I doubted my decision and wondered if I was making the wrong choice. What was a year, anyway? I had already put three into my degree, after all. I might as well finish it up. And my mom was right—that degree could come in handy if I failed as a fashion designer.

But then I glanced at Gavin, speaking with his mother and Dawn and Trina. He gave me an encouraging smile, and I knew this was the right path. I didn't want to waste even a single second longer pursuing a career I hated. From now on, I wanted to follow my dream, even if it was harder, riskier, scarier.

"I'm sure," I said.

My parents exchanged a glance. Something passed between them, the kind of silent communication only couples who have been married for thirty years can share. My mom turned back to me. "If that's your decision, then we'll support you in it."

"Really?" I asked, my voice breaking a little. Tears welled up in my eyes.

"Of course. You are our daughter. We love you and only want you to be happy."

"And obviously you are very talented," my dad added. "Or you wouldn't have gotten this far in the show."

I laughed and hugged each of them. "Thank you."

"I wish you had told us earlier you wanted to be a designer," my mom said, after she'd hugged me back. "If we'd known, we wouldn't have pushed you so hard to become a doctor."

"I guess I didn't believe I could do it. But now I do. Now I *know* I can do it."

———

I fixed Gavin's tie, staring up into his stormy gray eyes. "Whatever happens, you are an amazing designer and are going to go on to great things. I believe in you and I love you."

"I love you," he repeated back to me. But he seemed in a daze, like he wasn't really hearing himself speak.

I gave him a long, lingering kiss, trying to infuse him with strength and love through the press of my lips, through my hands gripping his shoulders. He clung to me tightly before finally breaking away and heading out the door and onto the runway.

This was it. In a few minutes, the judges would decide who was going to be the winner of *Behind The Seams*. And there was nothing I could do but wait in the back-stage lounge with Trina and Nika for the verdict.

I slumped on the couch next to Trina, and we leaned against each other, not saying a word. We both loved someone out there, but only one of them could win. Nika picked at her nails across from us, looking bored. I decided then and there that if Dawn won, I would still be happy. She was a great designer and a good friend—and anything would be better than Jeff winning.

Kelsey stuck her head in the door. "Psst," she said. "Want to watch the judging?"

Trina and I both jumped to our feet. "Yes!" I said. "Where?"

"We can watch the live feed from the cameras in the other room."

She gestured for us to follow her, but Nika remained behind. I guessed she didn't care that much if Jeff won or not.

The three of us rushed into the next room, which was dark except for a number of screens, each showing a different camera angle, with one guy operating them all. Kelsey held a finger over her lips as we went inside, then quietly shut the door behind her. The guy gave us a brief, curious look, but then went back to monitoring the camera feeds.

On stage, the three designers stood on the runway with their models from the show. The four judges sat in front of them in their usual chairs, and it didn't look any different from a normal challenge except for the invisible, unspoken heaviness in the room. I'd watched this moment plenty of times on TV before, but it had never felt as real as it did now. This decision would decide the fate of one of the three designers.

Trina and I laced our arms together and watched it all go down. The judges were in the middle of critiquing Dawn's collection. They praised her feminine clothes and her use of color, but questioned whether it was unique enough. Ricardo liked it the most, arguing that women all over the world, of all ages and sizes, would find her clothes flattering. Kiara argued that it didn't feel fresh enough, while Lola thought the collection had too many similar pieces overall.

Jeff's collection was next. They liked his bold colors and his blend of modern and eighties style, but said that none of his looks really felt like the elements. Ricardo thought his clothes were ready to sell in a store, but Beverly questioned whether any woman would actually want to wear them. Lola loved it, calling it edgy and dramatic, but Kiara argued that some of the looks felt too outdated and mature.

Gavin's collection was critiqued last. I leaned closer to the screens, wishing I could be out there with him, holding his hand.

Lola looked up from her notes and smiled at him. "Gavin, your collection was definitely the most innovative. Many of the pieces felt new and avant-garde."

"I agree," Ricardo said. "You were the only one who didn't use color to show the elements, but instead tried to reflect them in the design itself."

"The only problem is that some of the pieces aren't as obvious as to which element they should belong to," Beverly said.

Ricardo rubbed his chin. "That's true. But the detail work was truly amazing, especially since the collection was done in only a few days. I'm assuming you did the chainmail pieces yourself again?"

Gavin cleared his throat. "Yes. I originally planned for the shirt to be a full dress but didn't have enough time. I turned it into a top, and Julie made the trousers to go with it."

"I actually like that it's only a top," Kiara said. "A dress could be a bit too much. This has a nice contrast between hard and soft."

Beverly checked her notes again, pursing her bright red lips. "I also loved your ombré dress. The cut of it was beautiful, and the way it was dyed was exquisite."

"Julie dyed that dress," Gavin said. "All the credit belongs to her, not me."

"But it's your design, yes?" Ricardo asked.

"Correct."

Ricardo nodded. "A good designer knows how to use the talents of their assistants to their benefit."

Gavin looked like he might argue, and I wanted to reach through the screen and shake him, to tell him to shut up. Yes, I'd done that dress, but it had been his design. It was still completely *his* collection. Maybe he felt my silent scream because he closed his mouth and nodded.

"Each of your pieces was beautifully made," Lola said. She gestured at Carla. "The real showstopper, though, was this tornado dress. It's stunning and so unique."

Kiara leaned forward in her chair. "It's gorgeous. I've never seen anything like it."

"There's no doubt it's amazing," Beverly said. "My only concern is that it's not really wearable. I'm not sure how some of these looks could be translated into clothes that a woman could buy."

"He has some ready-to-wear looks, though," Robert argued, showing her his notes. "This raincoat here or this corset outfit could both be very commercial."

Beverly cocked her head. "Maybe. I do think this tornado dress and some of the others would photograph well. They'd make for a really fun magazine spread."

They continued on for another few minutes, and Gavin somehow remained stoic and calm as they took apart each look like he wasn't even there. Meanwhile, I was clinging so hard to Trina I was surprised she didn't tell me I was hurting her. It was tough to tell who the judges would pick. They seemed to like all three collections, but also have some reservations about each one, too. It could really go any way.

The judges went backstage to discuss the three collections, and I paced back and forth while we waited. If I was this nervous, I couldn't even imagine how anxious Gavin must feel. But finally, they returned.

"Thank you, designers, for all of your hard work," Lola said, after they sat down. "This season had some of the most talented designers we have ever seen on the show. It was an incredibly difficult decision because all of your collections were truly impressive, but in the end, there can only be one winner. After much discussion, we have chosen who that will be."

On stage, Gavin and Carla grabbed each other's hands. I imagined myself out there, completing the chain. I was trembling, holding my breath, waiting for Lola to say the next words.

"The winner of this season of *Behind The Seams* is…"

There was a long pause. The longest ever in the history of the world.

"Gavin Bennett."

Confetti burst on stage, and I screamed in delight. The guy behind the desk gave me a look of pure horror, but I didn't care. Trina gave me a fierce hug, and I cried happy tears all over her shoulder. I whispered that I was sorry about Dawn, but she just smiled and shook her head and said how happy she was for Gavin.

When she let me go, I grabbed Kelsey in a hug next, and she laughed as I squeezed her. I was so happy I could barely breathe. After all our hard work, it was somehow even better than if I had won because I knew how well-deserved it was— and I felt like it was my victory, too, even though I wouldn't be getting the prize myself.

I ran out of the room, bursting onto the runway where Gavin and Carla were hugging. They broke apart, and Dawn hugged him next, smiling with tears in her eyes. Carla was crying, too, dabbing at her eyes so as to not ruin her makeup. I gave her a fierce hug and congratulated her—she would receive $10,000 and would wear Gavin's tornado dress in an upcoming photo shoot for *Charmed* magazine.

Finally, I threw myself at Gavin. He had confetti in his hair, and he laughed as I slammed into his chest, wrapping my arms around him.

"Congratulations," I said. "You did it!"

"*We* did it." He held me close, kissing my forehead. His gray eyes were watery, his smile bigger than I had ever seen. "This couldn't have happened without you."

"We do make a good team," I said, smiling up at him.

"Yes, we do…" He searched my face, asking me a silent question.

I gave him a sly grin. "You know, maybe we should continue being partners… both in and out of the bedroom."

His hands tightened around my waist. "Does that mean you'll start a company with me?"

"I will. I already told my parents I'm applying to Parsons and moving to New York. Even if you didn't win, I would have gone with you. We're in this together, after all. But I'm not going to lie—it's going to be a lot easier with that prize money."

"Yes, it will." He kissed me in the middle of the runway, in front of the cameras and the judges and everyone else, while confetti fell like snow upon us.

And I knew, without a doubt, that I was making the right decision.

Chapter Twenty-Seven

"It's perfect," Gavin said, his gaze sweeping across the large, empty room.

I squinted, trying to figure out what he saw in this dump. "Yeah?"

"The bones are all here." He moved across the hardwood floor and swept dust off a windowsill. Outside, snow dotted the buildings, and the sun struggled to peek through the clouds. "Look at the arches and the crown molding. And the lighting is lovely. The place just needs some cleaning, a fresh coat of paint, and it will be a perfect studio."

"You make it sound so easy, but all of that costs money and time."

"We have both of those."

"We do, but only a limited supply of each. We need to start making some money soon, or it will run out fast."

He moved behind me, his arms sliding around my waist, and we stared at the place we might soon call home. "Just imagine it. We'll each have our own workstations set up over there. Racks of clothing along the wall. Dress forms around the room. Sewing machines in the corner. Inspiration boards above our head. The sound of the city filtering through the windows. Our brand will come to life in here."

I couldn't help but be swept away by his vision of our future together. I leaned back against him and closed my eyes, letting his words take flight in my imagination, allowing myself a moment to dream.

Gavin had temporarily relocated to Los Angeles after *Behind The Seams* ended, and we'd spent the last three months dating like a normal couple. I was relieved that nothing had changed between us now that the show was over. If anything, our relationship had only grown stronger without all that extra stress and drama and worry. We didn't have to compete against each other anymore. From now on, we were on the same team.

I'd always worried about settling down, scared that if I got serious with one guy

I'd be giving something up. But Gavin made me realize that I could both be in love and do what I loved at the same time. I didn't have to choose between a career or a relationship—I could have both.

After Gavin won, I'd spoken with Ricardo, and he had pulled some strings to get me into Parsons. They'd used a combination of my credits from UCLA and my portfolio of work on and off the show and agreed to let me start in January as a senior. I'd take advanced classes and would graduate only a few months later than I was originally supposed to. I couldn't wait to start.

Over the last three months, Gavin and I had also begun the process of starting our own company. I'd somehow ended up handling a lot of the finances, and all those math classes I'd struggled through in college came in handy for once. Especially since I'd discovered Gavin sucked at anything involving money. We both had big dreams, but it was my job to keep us grounded in reality, too.

But first, we had to find a place to live and work in New York.

"Let me show you the best part," Gavin said. He took my hand and led me up the stairs, to a large, dusty loft with an attached bathroom. "We can live up here. That way we only have one rent check instead of two."

"Are you asking me to move in with you?"

"It seems I am," he said, raising his eyebrows. "What do you think?"

Everything was moving so fast, and yet, in my gut, this felt right. I moved across the room to the window, looking out at the snow-covered city that was my new home. I was going to need to buy a winter coat.

I turned back to him with a smile. "I think we should take the place."

"Brilliant. We can move in on Friday."

"Good. Now we just have…oh, about a million other things to do. And hundreds of things to buy. And we don't even have a name for our clothing line."

"We'll think of one." He swept me into his arms and smiled at me. "All that matters is that we're doing this together. Everything else will work itself out."

"I know." I grabbed his collar and pulled him down for our first kiss in our new apartment.

For the first time in my life, I was on the right path. I couldn't deny that going forward would be scary sometimes. Everything we did would be a huge risk, and there was no guarantee of success. But I wanted, more than anything, to create a future in fashion with Gavin at my side. And I knew we would make it.

Together, with love guiding us, we would be unstoppable.

Bonus Content

Chapter One

Sometimes the rose on the back of my hand felt more like a brand than a tattoo. Tonight was one of those times.

I couldn't shake the thought that it should have been my sister going on *Behind The Seams*, not me. But no matter how much I tried, I couldn't change the past. The only thing I could do was honor her memory by winning the show.

First, I needed a stiff drink to get me through the night.

I headed to the hotel bar, found an empty seat at the counter, and nodded to the bartender. While he fixed my drink, I spotted an Asian girl on the other side of the bar who watched me with intense eyes. She was gorgeous, radiating confidence and sensuality, with long black hair, smooth skin, and a cute nose. Her lips parted into a sultry smile when she saw she had my attention.

The girl beside her was beautiful too, tall and dark-skinned, with a head full of curls—but she quickly looked down, avoiding my gaze. The first girl though, her eyes were locked on mine and had a fire in them that called to me. I couldn't look away and something passed between us—some connection, some spark, something instant and indescribable that made my heart beat faster.

She turned to her friend to say something, and our connection was broken. I shook my head, trying to clear it. What was I thinking? No matter how hot the girl was, I was going on a reality TV show tomorrow that would last for weeks. When it was over, I'd return home to London. There was no reason to speak with the girl, no matter how much I wanted to.

While I sipped my drink, the two girls hugged. A moment later, the second girl left and the first girl smiled at me again. She leaned forward on the counter, giving me a tantalizing glimpse down her red dress, and I couldn't stop myself from grinning back at her. Perhaps I should go talk to her after all. Even if nothing came of it, she would distract me for a few minutes. Talking to a beautiful woman was hardly a burden, after all.

Before I could move, another guy sat next to her. He was built like a rugby player and looked like a right tosser. He said something to the girl that made her shoulders straighten up and her face twist. The shared some more words, yet with each second that passed her eyebrows drew closer and closer together. I couldn't hear their words over the ambient sound in the bar, but it was obvious she grew more and more angry, yet the guy didn't seem to care. Or perhaps he was too stupid to notice.

She turned her back to him and waved her hand, clearly not interested, but the guy wouldn't leave her alone. When she tried to get up, he boxed her in, his meaty hand pressed against her back. The sight made me sick. Men like him made all of us look bad. And if that was my sister he was harassing? I'd have murdered him on the spot.

My hand tightened around my drink and I moved across the bar to intervene. Up close, the girl's voice rang out loud and clear. "How about you get lost?" she said to the wanker.

"It'll be fun," he replied. "You and me, my bed, and a lot less clothes."

I couldn't believe he would speak to a lady like that when she was obviously rejecting him. It made my blood boil, but I managed to keep my face calm and my voice steady. "Are you bothering my girlfriend?"

The man removed his hand and blinked at me. "Girlfriend?"

He wasn't touching her any longer, but he wasn't far enough away from her either. I rested my arm across the back of the girl's chair and stared the guy down. "I believe she told you to leave."

"Whatever, man." The wanker muttered something under his breath, but he got up and left the bar. A smart move.

"Thanks, but I didn't need you to rescue me," the girl said, with a smile that told me she wasn't really upset.

"No, I'm quite sure you could handle it on your own." I sat beside her and waved for the bartender to refill our drinks. "But it's a gentleman's duty to help a lady in distress."

"A gentleman? I thought those didn't exist anymore."

"Clearly you've been hanging out with the wrong men."

"You just saw proof of that," she said, and I couldn't help but laugh. "Besides, I wasn't in distress. I was already getting rid of him when you showed up on your white horse and just had to save the day."

"Maybe I wanted an excuse to talk to you. Forgive me?"

She slowly circled the rim of her glass with her index finger, her eyes never leaving mine. "I suppose."

I offered her my hand. "I'm Gavin—"

She cut me off by placing that finger against my lips. "No names."

"No? Not exactly fair, since you know mine now."

"I tried to stop you."

Interesting. I wondered if she did this kind of thing often, or if this was a rule she came up with on the spot. "What shall I call you, then?"

"Whatever you want, as long as it's not Hello Kitty."

"Why in the world would I call you that?" I asked.

"That's what the other guy called me."

"Not a very good pickup line."

"Obviously not."

"Worked out for me, though."

"Yes, it did." She stared at my mouth and set her hand on my knee, leaning forward enough for me to peer down her dress at her glorious tits, but I forced myself to keep my eyes on her face. Something about her intrigued me, like a flickering flame you couldn't help but watch, even though you knew it could burn you.

"What are you doing in New York, mystery girl?" I asked.

"I'm here for business." Her hand slid up my jeans along my thigh and I sucked in a breath. Bloody hell, she was bold.

"What do you do?" I asked, hoping to distract myself from my growing erection.

"I'm a pre-med student." She sounded bored, like the answer was routine and she wasn't really interested in talking. Instead, her eyes were fixed on my mouth, as though she might pounce on me at any second. A large part of me hoped she would.

"I'm here on business, too. I'm…an artist." Not entirely true, but close enough. Not that she cared. She didn't even want to know my name, after all. "Where are you visiting from?"

"You ask a lot of questions."

"Is it so terrible I want to get to know you?" I brushed her hair away from her face and moved to whisper in her ear. "Tell me where you're from."

Her eyes fluttered shut, her voice becoming breathy. "Los Angeles."

She looked so beautiful and eager it took everything in my power to not kiss her right then. I focused on what she said instead. "Los Angeles? Sounds glamorous."

She laughed. "Not really."

"I'm from London. Well, Mum's from Wales and Dad's from the States, but that's where I grew up."

"I can tell from the accent. But you talk too much."

Now it was my turn to laugh. "No one's told me that before. I thought Americans loved the accent."

"Oh, we do." She slid her fingers up my shirt, tugging me toward her, and my jeans grew even tighter. "But what I want to do? Doesn't involve talking."

"Is that so?" I set my hand on her bare thigh, slipping just under the hem of her skirt. "What is it you want to do, then?"

Her eyes flashed and she grabbed the collar of my shirt, pulling me to her mouth. She kissed me hard, her lips demanding, her tongue flicking against mine.

She tasted so sweet, like strawberries and vodka, and I was instantly lost. With one kiss, I was hers.

"That," she said, "is what I want to do. And a lot more."

———

Chapter Two

"Tell me your name," I said, staring into her eyes. They were the most amazing color, like liquid amber, and I couldn't look away.

"No names."

God, this woman was difficult. For some reason, it only made me want her more.

This time I kissed *her*, my hands clutching her hips, my mouth devouring hers, as if I could tease her name out of her lips and her tongue and her soft skin.

She pulled back and her eyes gazed up at me with the same hunger I felt for her. "Let's go to my room."

How could I argue with that? I quickly paid the bartender while she skimmed her fingernail slowly up and down my neck, driving me completely mad. I took her hand and slipped that finger in my mouth, doing to it all the things I wanted to do to her, and she let out a pretty, breathless moan.

We rushed across the lobby and she tripped on her tall heels, but I was more than happy to catch her and kiss her again. But when we stepped inside the elevator I pressed her back against the mirrored wall and stared into her eyes, my hands flat on either side of her.

"Tell me your name," I said.

"No names." Her eyes were fierce, looking up at me with a challenge.

"I've already told you mine," I said, while she unbuttoned the top of my shirt.

"I've already forgotten."

Liar, I wanted to say, but her mouth touched my neck and the words slipped away. One of her legs hooked around my waist, bringing me flush against her soft curves. I stroked her thigh, teasing under her skirt, sliding higher and higher.

I kissed along her neck and whispered, "I have to call you something."

She didn't answer, just leaned her head back against the mirror as I pressed my lips against her skin. It drove me mad that she wouldn't tell me her name, but I sort of loved it too. Even so, I would never give up trying to get it out of her. I wasn't the type to back down from a challenge either.

As we walked to her hotel room, those silly heels made her trip again. She lost one on the carpet and I snatched it off the floor, dangling it in front of her and making her giggle. She flung the other shoe off her small foot, and I grabbed that one too.

She dashed down the hall to her room, laughing. I followed behind, admiring the view from behind. This girl was so fun, so fresh, so exactly what I needed right now. It had been many months since my last girlfriend, and things between us had been bad for a long time before that. This girl though, she made me smile in a way I hadn't done since Rose was alive.

She searched around for the keycard to her door, but when I approached, she stopped to push me against the door and kiss me hard. Damn, this girl could kiss. I had a feeling I could kiss her forever and never get enough. And the way her body moved against mine made me harder than I'd been in years.

But when she reached for the button of my jeans, I stopped her. "Let's go inside first."

She sighed and continued her search for the key, then pulled it out of her bra and used it to unlock the door. It took her a few tries, but we were both a bit excited. I could barely stand still myself.

But when she opened the door and walked inside, the sight of the bed made me question what I was doing. I didn't sleep with strangers while on holiday in another country. Especially ones who didn't even want to know my name.

I moved to the window to glance outside at the lights of New York, still bright even at this hour, hoping the sight would clear my head. She moved behind me and I turned around, to see her sliding a pair of red lace panties down her slim legs. Good lord.

"Come here." She threw the panties at me but they fell short, catching on a lampshade and bathing the room in shadows. I couldn't help but laugh at her terrible throw, but then I spotted the clock by the bed. 1:26 AM. Bollocks. A car was picking me up at 7:30 AM to take me to the *Behind The Seams* set. If I was smart, I would return to my room and go to sleep immediately.

But when the mysterious girl moved in front of me and rested her hand on my chest, looking up at my with those lovely amber eyes, I knew leaving would be damn near impossible.

"Don't go." She licked her lips, drawing my eyes down to them, and all I could think about was kissing her again.

Fuck it. Who needed sleep anyway?

I dug my fingers into her silky black hair, claiming her mouth in a demanding, passionate kiss. She clung to me, kissing me back with just as much force, and I couldn't get enough of her. She made my head spin in the best way and made every inch of my body ache to be inside her. But there was more than lust between us too, a connection I didn't understand, yet wanted to explore.

I had to taste more of her.

I pushed her back against the floor-to-ceiling window behind us, and then my mouth was on her neck, her chest, the swell of her breasts, enjoying the soft whimpers she made while I discovered her body. While my hands slid up and down her curves I closed my mouth over one of her breasts. Her red dress blocked me from tasting her skin and I tore at the fabric with my teeth, flicking at her hard nipple. She gasped and grabbed onto the curtains beside her, and the sound only made me want to taste the rest of her.

I dropped to my knees, kissing along the inside of her legs, sliding her dress up as I went. I moved higher and higher, nudging her legs wider, and she was so eager, so responsive, so beautiful. She leaned back against the glass, completely open to me and without any hint of hesitation. God, she was sexy.

"Is this what you want?" I asked, gazing up at her.

"Yes." Her voice grew stronger as she spoke. "Yes, this is what I want. *Please*, Gavin."

She *did* remember my name. I knew it.

I dipped my head between her thighs, pressing my mouth to her sweet skin. She tasted even better than I imagined, so wet and soft, and I couldn't get enough. She grinded herself against me as I ate her out, making the most beautiful sounds while I worked her over with my tongue, my mouth, and even my teeth. I soon realized she was saying my name, over and over again.

"Oh god, don't stop," she begged, her fingers tugging on my hair.

No way in hell was I stopping now. My hand found its way between her legs and I slipped my fingers inside her warmth. She was so wet and ready for me, and she gasped while I slid my fingers in and out of her. My tongue and my fingers worked together to bring her to pleasure, and soon she was moaning so loud I thought for sure someone would bang on the door at any moment. Her legs twitched, her fingers tightened in my hair, and I held her steady with my free hand while she let herself go for me.

She continued to tremble and I licked her until her body relaxed against the window, her eyes shut, her breathing fast. Only when I was sure she was satisfied did I slide up her body. "Ready to tell me your name yet?"

Her eyes snapped open, but they were unfocused, still recovering from what I'd done to her. "Not a chance."

"I'll get it out of you eventually."

"Do that again and I *might* tell you."

"Is that so?" I asked.

"Guess you'll have to find out."

She pulled me toward the bed, but her knees suddenly seemed to give out on her. I rushed forward to catch her in my arms and steadied her.

"All right there?" I asked, studying her face.

She nodded, touching her forehead. "Head rush."

But her words were slurred, and something about the way she was acting seemed…off. I helped her stand and she immediately reached for my belt, trying to take it off, but had a hard time with the buckle. She giggled and I watched with a growing unease as she fumbled around, before finally managing to get the belt off me after a few attempts.

"You're swaying," I said.

She giggled again. "What?"

Bollocks. The girl was pissed. I should have seen the signs all along. And now I felt like a complete tosser for going down on her. Yes, I hadn't known at the time, but I *should* have known.

I ran a hand through my hair, trying to get my thoughts in order, and gestured to the bed. "Lie down."

"Mmm, yes, sir."

She slid onto the bed, posing in a sensual way, but I couldn't look at her. She was far too tempting, especially with her dress pushed up around her hips like that, giving me a hint of what I'd just tasted. A teaser of what I could have if I wasn't such a fucking gentleman. Sometimes, I really hated myself.

I grabbed a bottle of water off the mini-bar and offered it to her. "Drink this."

She took a sip, but some of the water spilled onto her breasts. Yeah, she was definitely pissed.

"You want some?" she asked.

"Thank you, no." I watched while she drank some more water. I was hard as a fucking rock, but nothing was going to happen tonight. The sooner my dick accepted that, the better.

But she didn't seem to agree with that plan. She crooked a finger at me with a smile that nearly slayed me. "Get over here."

I closed my eyes, taking another long breath. "Trust me, love, I want to."

"Love?"

"Give me your name and I'll call you something else."

"No, I like that." She draped her arm over her head, looking incredibly sexy. "Come to bed."

"I don't think that's a good idea."

She sat up with a frown. "Why not?"

"You're pissed."

"No, I'm not. I mean, I'm a little annoyed that you're not already naked…"

"Not that kind of pissed. Drunk."

She rolled her eyes. "I'm not that either."

"No, love, you really are."

"I don't care. I want this. I want you. Right. Now." She moved down the bed and ran her hands across the front of my jeans, making me suck in my breath, but I grabbed her hand before she could continue.

"That's not a good idea," I said.

She gave an annoyed huff. "Why are you here if you don't want this?"

How could she actually think I didn't want this? It was killing me to resist her, but all I did was nod at the water bottle beside the bed. "I didn't realize how drunk you are until now. Drink that and get some sleep."

I turned away, unable to look at her a second longer. My control was stretched thin enough as it was. It took all the strength I had to not kiss her again.

"Stop being a gentleman," she said, jumping to her feet. "I don't want sleep. I want to get laid. And if you won't help me out… Well, maybe some other guy at the bar will."

The idea made me more upset than it should have, considering I'd just met the girl. I turned back, my arms crossed. "Don't be a twat. You can barely stand on your own."

"A *what?*"

"And you're definitely not going back down there to find some other guy."

She moved even closer, and the challenge in her eyes made it impossible for me to look away. "What, now you think you have some claim over me? Just 'cause you called yourself my boyfriend doesn't make it true."

"No, of course not."

"Then get out of my way."

"You're far too drunk. I'm not letting you leave the room like this. Even if I have to stay here all night."

"You…" She pressed a hand against my chest, but instead of pushing me away, her fingers dug into my shirt and pulled me closer. Our eyes locked again and that irresistible attraction flared to life between us. I could still taste her on my tongue, could still hear the sounds she made when she came, and I forgot every reason why I was resisting her.

"You can't keep me here," she said. "Or tell me what to do. This is *my* room."

"No, I suppose I can't." My control snapped and I lowered my head to kiss her, my hands sliding around her waist. I wanted her so bad I thought I would go mad if I didn't have her. She did something to me, something that made me feel reckless and wild, and I needed more.

She tore at the buttons on my shirt, yanking it open, and I pushed her back toward the bed. But then I realized what I was doing and jerked my hands off her. "No, I'm sorry. I can't. It's not right."

She groaned. "Forget right and take off your clothes already."

"Love, believe me when I say that all I want to do is pin you against this bed and bury myself in you until you scream my name. But I'm not going to take advantage of you while you're drunk."

"It's not taking advantage if I'm asking you to do it. And really, I'm not *that* drunk. Watch." She walked in a straight line up and down the room, but it wasn't very convincing. "See?"

I ignored her and buttoned up my shirt quickly, giving my hands something to do that didn't involve touching her.

She dropped onto the bed and her fingers tugged on my clothes, her eyes pleading up at me. "Stay with me," she whispered. "Just for tonight. Don't leave me alone. Please, Gavin."

My hands froze and I gazed down at her. I wanted to stay so fucking bad. But if I did, I'd have to resist her, no matter how much she tried to get me in bed with her. I knew I could do it, but it would be torture of the most exquisite kind. Yet I didn't want to leave, either.

"I'll stay, but we're not doing anything more until you've sobered up." I pressed the water bottle into her hands for a second time. "Drink this. I'll be back in a moment."

She groaned and fell back onto the bed, while I slipped into the bathroom. I washed my face off, the cold water clearing my head and distracting me from the half-naked, incredibly sexy girl out there who was begging me to sleep with her. Still, it took a while for my brain to regain control over my body.

When I finally left the room, the girl was passed out on top of the bed, snoring softly. In her sleep, her face was softer. The fierceness in her eyes and that bold, confident attitude had faded away, revealing another side of her. A vulnerable side that I suspected she didn't show to many people.

She was so lovely, but I felt like some sort of pervert for staring at her while she slept. I quickly moved to pull the blankets over her body, covering her body up, and adjusted the pillow under her head. Once done, I sat on the edge of the bed, my back to her, the clock taunting me with its early hour.

Now what?

She'd asked me to stay, but I didn't feel right lying in bed beside her all night. Not to mention, I desperately needed to get some sleep myself.

I debated back and forth for a few minutes, before finally deciding I would stay for a short while to make sure she was all right and then return to my room.

I waited until my eyes were so heavy it was nearly impossible to keep them open. She was still asleep and showed no signs of waking up. I stood and set another water bottle beside the bed for her.

Perhaps I should leave her a note or something. I didn't want this to be the end between us. I knew so little about this girl, but something about her called to me. I wanted to know her name. I wanted to know more about her. I wanted to see her again. But she didn't seem to want any of that from me.

I found a pen and started to scratch out a note, but I was stumped on what to say. How could I explain to a near-stranger that I was going on a fashion design reality TV show for a few weeks and wouldn't be able to contact her? It sounded like a made-up excuse to get out of speaking with her after what happened between us. I doubted she would even believe it.

And even if she did, I lived in London and she lived in Los Angeles. It was unlikely our paths would ever cross again. I shouldn't even have come up to her room in the first place.

I wasn't the kind of guy to hook up with a girl and never talk to her again. But in this case, what other option was there?

I crumpled up the note and threw it in the trash.

After one last look at her lovely face, I silently said goodbye and walked out the door.

More Than Once

CHASING THE DREAM #4

ONE

Becca

I'd discovered hell on Earth, and it was working in a department store on Christmas Eve.

I wasn't sure I could take even one more minute of it without losing my damn mind. Customers rushing around. Babies crying and children screaming. Clothes strewn about in every place but the racks they belonged on. Cash registers slamming open and closed. Not to mention the music. Good lord, the music. If I heard that sugary sweet, pop rendition of "Baby It's Cold Outside" one more time, I was seriously going to murder someone.

The second it slowed down and my line emptied out, I made my escape. I ditched my register, grabbed my leather jacket from the employee lounge, and rushed to the store's exit. But on my way out, my manager's voice stopped me in my tracks.

"Becca! What do you think you're doing, missy?" Marcie asked me, hands on her wide hips. She was probably in her mid-fifties and, as far as I could tell, had been working retail her entire life, which probably explained why she was always so damn cranky.

"It's time for my break." Way past time, actually. But I was trying to be a good employee and all that, so I'd kept working even though my head had begun pounding something fierce about an hour ago.

She gestured back at the chaos. "Look at the lines. You can't leave right now!"

I pinched the bridge of my nose, trying to ease the pain. "Give me ten minutes at least. This is the slowest it's been in hours. Otherwise I'm wringing the neck of the next person who asks me a stupid question, and I sure as shit won't be any help to you in jail."

Her lips pursed and her eyes narrowed. "Fine, take ten, but then get your butt back at your register. We still have two more hours before we close and we need everyone available."

I turned to the door but paused when she said, "Oh and, Becca? Cut the attitude. Don't think I can't hire another washed-up college dropout to fill your spot in a second. Y'all are a dime a dozen these days."

I took a deep breath and closed my eyes. *Don't,* I told myself. *You need this job, just for a little longer.*

It took all my energy to hold back a sharp response, but I managed to get through the sliding glass doors without a word. Little white puffs danced through the gloomy afternoon sky and onto the cars in the parking lot, which I wasn't prepared for—it didn't often snow this early in Dallas. I shivered and reached instinctively for a cigarette in my jacket pocket, but found only empty gum wrappers. I'd quit a few months ago, but working retail during the holidays was enough to drive anyone to reach for a fix.

I made my way across the lot to my beat-up old Buick, a hand-me-down from my grandmother, and climbed inside. The heater chugged on with a groan, and once it warmed up enough, I pulled out my phone. Brett had texted me earlier and said to call him when I got a chance.

"Hey," I said when he answered. "What's up?"

"Hey, doll," he said, his Texan accent strong. "Listen, about tonight…"

I tensed up, my head pounding again. "Oh, no, don't you dare bail on me."

Silence on the other end. That son of a bitch. He was supposed to come to my sister's house to meet my family for our Christmas Eve dinner. I was counting on him to impress them with his good looks, great job, and wealthy family. He had all the perfect credentials for the "nice guy" they kept telling me I needed to settle down with.

We'd met a few weeks ago in the store—I'd rung up a gift for his sister, and he'd asked me out with that sexy drawl of his. His father was one of those millionaire oil tycoons, and Brett worked for his company doing finances or something. He was blond, blue-eyed, and he'd even sported a cowboy hat when I'd first seen him. He wasn't my usual type of guy, but I figured that was probably a good thing since I was trying to change and all. Too bad he was boring as hell, and kissing him practically put me to sleep. But whatever. On paper, he was the perfect boyfriend, which was exactly what I needed right now.

"Doll, I don't think this is going to work out between us," he said. "You and I… We don't exactly run in the same crowds."

My hands tightened around the steering wheel. "What the hell is that supposed to mean?"

"Let's be honest. We had a fun couple of weeks, but now it's time to move on. You're not really long-term material. My family expects me to date someone a little more…"

"A little more *what?*"

"A little more…sophisticated."

I was speechless for a second, and then I exploded. "*I'm* the one who's not sophisticated? *You're* the one breaking up with me on Christmas Eve! You are a bona fide, prime grade asshole, Brett McKinley!"

I hung up before he could answer and slammed my hands against the steering wheel. Dammit! Now what was I going to do?

In the past six months, I'd done everything I could to get my life straightened out. I'd sold my motorcycle and moved back to Dallas to live with my sister and her family. I'd washed all the dye out of my hair, letting it return to a natural blonde, and removed all my piercings. I'd gotten a job and started helping out with the bills as much as I could. I'd even stored my bass guitars out in the garage, where they were collecting dust.

Now I had to convince my parents that I was no longer a complete screw-up—because if I didn't, they wouldn't give me the money I needed to go back to college next year. Introducing Brett, my perfect boyfriend, to the rest of my family had been the final part of the equation.

But now he was out of the picture, and I was doomed.

As if on cue, my phone rang. My mother.

"Hey, Mom," I said, trying to sound cheerful.

"Rebecca, dear, just wanted to check if you were still bringing the wine tonight?"

"I am." The one thing I could be counted on for: stocking up on alcohol.

"Oh, good. Your father and I are so excited to meet this mystery boyfriend of yours. He sounds so amazing. We can't wait!"

"Um…"

Before I could break the bad news to her, she continued on, as bubbly as ever. "We're just so happy for you, dear. You've really proven to us that you're becoming a smart, mature young woman. I'm proud of you, and I know your father is, too."

My eyes watered and my chest tightened up. My parents were *never* proud of me. I'd been a disappointment to them my entire life, and for the first time ever, things were getting better between us. I definitely couldn't tell my mom that my so-called perfect boyfriend had just broken up with me—not now. "Thanks, Mom."

"I'll see you in a few hours. Bye, dear!"

The call ended and I slammed my head back against the headrest, but that only made my headache worse. I'd have to figure out a way to break the news about Brett tonight, but I'd worry about that later. I had two more hours of hell to get through first.

My ten minutes were up, but I wasn't ready to face the shopping frenzy already. I switched on the radio, but that was a mistake. They were playing that new Villain Complex song yet again. I could swear the stations played it every five minutes, as if to taunt me. Like I needed another reminder that I was a total loser who fucked up everything good in her life.

I turned the car off and trudged back through the snow toward the store. At least once I was inside, I wouldn't have to listen to the number one hit song by the band I'd quit. I'd take overplayed Christmas music over *that* any day, thank you very much.

"You're two minutes late," Marcie said, tapping her watch as I walked through the doors. I kept my mouth shut and continued past the long line to take photos with Santa. Hey, maybe if I asked Santa nicely, he would bring me the perfect boyfriend for Christmas.

Yeah, and maybe reindeer would fly out of my manager's ass, too.

I took my spot at the cash register again, preparing to settle in for the longest two hours of my life. Why did so many people wait until Christmas Eve to shop? It's not like they didn't know it was coming. The holiday was on the same damn day every year, after all.

I rang up so many people I stopped seeing them anymore. They became a never-ending stream of blank faces buying generic, overpriced clothes. Next. Next. Next.

I shoved a red sweater in a bag with the receipt and handed it to a woman, then automatically reached for the next person's item on the counter: a green scarf. I scanned it without even looking up—until I heard a man's familiar voice.

"Becca?"

My head jerked up. There, at my register, was a guy I never thought I'd see again. He was yet another of my royal screw-ups, and now he stood in front of me, his broad shoulders filling out a black coat over a suit and a white button-up shirt, his gray tie slightly askew. His dark blond hair was slicked back, his bright hazel eyes stared into mine, and his lips were exactly as kissable as I remembered. He looked so damn good I wanted to climb over the counter and jump him, even with the massive line of people behind him.

Andy.

I didn't know his last name. Didn't know much about him at all, really. We'd hooked up during the summer in San Diego after being introduced at a party by Hector, the drummer in my former band. We'd shared one incredible, wild night and promised to keep in touch.

Neither of us had.

TWO

Andrew

I couldn't believe it. The girl I hadn't been able to get out of my mind was here, ringing up the scarf I'd picked out for my boss.

We'd only spent a single night together, but I'd recognize her anywhere. Those brown eyes that were a little wild, a little guarded, and a whole lot intriguing. Those soft, sensual lips that tasted like cherries and bad decisions and nights I'd never forget. That smooth, pale skin and those perfect, round breasts and that ass that had fit so nicely in my hands... Jesus, I was getting hard in the middle of the store remembering it.

I'd never, in a million years, expected to run into her and definitely not on Christmas Eve. Shit, what did you say to someone you hooked up with once and then never spoke to again?

She must have felt the same way because she stared back at me, the shock clear on her face. "Andy?"

Thank god. I'd been worried she wouldn't remember my name. "Actually, I go by Andrew now."

Her eyes widened. She'd been the first one to call me that, during our few hours together, and she knew exactly what it meant. "What are you doing here?"

"Buying a Christmas present for my boss. I work just down the road. Crazy, right?"

"Wow." She tilted her head and studied me. I wished she would smile or something, but she didn't. What did I expect after the way it had ended between us? "Last-minute shopper, eh?"

I rubbed the back of my neck and gave her a sheepish smile. "I didn't realize I was supposed to buy her something until the guy in the cubicle next to me asked me what I'd gotten. I know, I'm an idiot. But cut me some slack, it's my first office job."

The woman behind me cleared her throat and inched her stuff forward on the counter. The line was growing longer and longer and I felt bad about holding it up, but I wanted to talk to this girl who had magically appeared back in my life like some kind of holiday miracle.

She looked damn good, too. Her hair was different—still short, but more of a light gold instead of platinum blonde—and I remembered tangling my fingers in it to yank her head back and devour her neck. All the piercings that had run up and down her ears were gone, too, which was a shame. Not that it made her any less sexy.

She rang up the scarf, examining it, letting the silk slide through her fingers. "This is a nice scarf. She'll like it."

"Glad you approve." I took my time pulling out my wallet and flipping through it for some cash. "It's amazing to see you again. Listen, I'm sorry I didn't call you or anything—"

"It's fine," Becca said, although her voice suggested otherwise. "I didn't call you either, after all."

"I was planning on calling you, I swear. I've just been really busy and—"

She stared at the register, biting her lower lip. "That'll be $26.52."

"Oh. Of course." I counted out the bills slowly, trying to delay the moment as long as I could. The people behind me were really getting anxious now, sighing, shuffling, and making other annoyed noises. I handed Becca the cash, and my fingers brushed against her slim wrist. Her breath hitched and her eyes met mine again.

A memory flashed: My hands circling her wrists, holding her arms down above her head. Her legs wrapped tight around my ass while I slammed into her. Her voice at my ear, begging for it harder, faster, rougher.

That day had been one of the worst in my life, but that night had been one of the best—all because of her. But when it was over, we'd both walked away without another word. I should have contacted her, but I'd been too broken up after what had happened with Tara. I hadn't been ready to get involved with another girl back then—and still wasn't, really.

The longer I'd waited to call Becca, the harder it was to get in touch. I wasn't sure she really *wanted* me to contact her either. I'd even convinced myself she wouldn't remember my name.

But she did.

She gave me the slightest hint of a smile. Finally. "It's good to see you, Andy— er, Andrew."

"It is. You look…" My gaze ran up and down her body, and the heat between us flared to life, still as intense as it had been five months ago. "You look incredible."

"No, I don't, but thanks."

"You do." I was itching to touch her again, even for only a second. A piece of her hair was out of place, which seemed like the perfect excuse. I reached forward and smoothed it back slowly while I kept my eyes locked on hers. "Hey, since we ran into each other, would you like to—"

An older woman with big hair pushed her way over to us. "Taking another break, Becca?"

"Shit," Becca muttered. She turned to face the woman. "Not a break, Marcie. I'm just saying hello to a friend quickly."

Marcie crossed her arms. "Looks like a lot more than that."

"Oh, yeah? What does it look like?"

She gave me a sideways glance. "Looks like you're hitting on one of our customers here."

Hang on. If anything, I'd been hitting on Becca, not the other way around. "No, I—"

Becca shoved my scarf in a bag and thrust it at me, giving me a fake, sweet smile. "Here you go, sir. Have a nice day." She turned back to Marcie. "Got a problem with that?"

"You're damn right I have a problem. You're holding up the line with your shameless flirting."

Becca rolled her eyes. "I'm sorry. Next time I'll throw his bag at him and tell him to get the fuck out of here. That what you want?"

Marcie gasped and glanced behind me at the line, which had gone silent. "Missy, I'm tired of your attitude. Get your stuff and get out of here. Your paycheck will be in the mail."

Whoa, that escalated quickly. I flashed the woman a friendly smile. "Hey, it's my fault, really. I was the one talking to her and holding up the line. Don't take it out on Becca. I'll leave right now."

Becca tore her nametag off her shirt and slammed it on the counter. "No, this is good. I was ready to quit this shithole anyway."

Marcie huffed, while everyone else in the store watched it all go down and another Christmas song started playing in the background. "We don't need girls like you working in our store," she said. "You're just like the last one we fired. Your type is always trouble."

"My *type*?" Becca asked, standing up straighter. "What type is that?"

"Trashy," Marcie said under her breath, her eyes narrowing.

"What did you call me?" Becca's face turned bright red, and she strode toward Marcie with her hands clenched in fists. I didn't know what she would do next, but it couldn't be good. Even if the woman deserved it for calling her that.

I blocked Becca's path and looped my arm through hers. "C'mon. Let's get out of here."

Becca growled, but she let me direct her away while Marcie apologized to the people in line behind me. A security guard followed us while we took a detour into the employee lounge for Becca to grab her leather jacket, then headed for the exit through an aisle in the women's department. With all the clothes strewn about the floor, it looked like it had been hit by a tornado. No wonder she was ready to quit.

Once we got to the parking lot, Becca kept going without a word, through the falling snow that had picked up since I'd gone inside. She stopped in front of an older Buick and let out a frustrated yell that echoed through the cold air.

I shoved my hands in my pockets, feeling like a complete asshole. "I'm so sorry I got you fired."

"It's not your fault. My manager's had it out for me from the beginning. Trust me, it's not the first time I've been fired. And knowing me, it won't be the last either." She reached around in her jacket like she was looking for something. She stopped and kicked the car's tire with one of her beat-up combat boots. "God dammit!"

I flinched at the sharpness in her voice, guilt tearing me up inside. We hadn't spoken in months because I'd been too stupid to call her, and now I'd gotten her fired. On Christmas Eve. "No, this isn't right. I'm going back in there to talk to your boss. Once I explain that I was holding up the line, not you, she'll have to give you your job back."

"Thanks, but don't bother. I hated that job and it didn't pay for shit anyway. The real problem is now I have to tell my parents I got fired *and* dumped by my boyfriend on Christmas Eve. Not that they'll be surprised. They're used to me being a total screw-up all the time."

She leaned against the car and closed her eyes. For a second, her tough-girl mask slipped and her face showed only vulnerability and pain. She was having a terrible day and a huge part of that was my fault. I felt horrible about it but, at the same time, I was hit with some perverse pleasure hearing she was single. I immediately crushed it down.

"Sorry about your boyfriend, but any guy who would break up with a girl on Christmas Eve isn't worth your time," I said. "And you're not a screw-up. You've just had a rough day. Happens to all of us."

She snorted at that. "Somehow I doubt my parents will see it that way. We're having a family dinner tonight at my sister's place and I was hoping I could show them I was finally turning my life around, but guess that's not going to happen."

"They're your family. They'll understand that sometimes things don't work out the way you want." I knew that all too well after what had happened with Tara. One second I'd thought my future was all planned out. The next, I was snapping a ring box shut and walking away with my heart ripped to shreds.

"Yeah, sure."

She had to be cold, wearing only a black leather jacket over her clothes, but she didn't show it. I shrugged out of my coat and stepped close, draping it over her shoulders, even though I'd be freezing in a few minutes in only my suit. Her eyes fluttered open, and she gave me a faint smile. "Thanks."

I nodded, my throat tightening at the sight of that smile. She wore the sexy, bright red lipstick I remembered from before, and I had the strongest urge to kiss it right off her. God, this girl was dangerous. I'd spent the last few months completely dead inside, yet somehow she'd jolted me back to life in a matter of minutes. Problem was, I wasn't sure I was ready to be resurrected yet.

She pulled the jacket tighter around herself and took a deep breath. "What about you? Any big plans for Christmas?"

"No plans." I looked away so she couldn't see what it cost me to admit that. "I just started at this job a few months ago and I'm trying to make a good impression, so I didn't want to ask for any vacation time to visit my parents back in Michigan."

"That's rough. What about friends here? A nice guy like you must have made some by now."

"Nope...it's just me this year." Friends? Ha. I shrugged it off, rubbing my hands together for warmth. "It's all right. I have a lot of work to do, and the office will be nice and quiet. I'll even get paid time-and-a-half if I come in on Christmas Day." The excuse sounded pathetic even to my ears.

"No shit?" She let out a short, harsh laugh. "That is the saddest thing I've ever heard. You can't be alone at Christmas!"

"It's not that big a deal, really…"

She suddenly straightened up, her eyes widening. "I have the perfect idea."

"You do?"

"It's the best solution to both our problems. You come with me to my family's holiday dinner tonight and pretend to be my boyfriend. You're definitely the kind of guy who will impress my parents, and that way you won't have to spend Christmas Eve alone."

"Pretend to be your boyfriend?" A wave of panic swept over me at the thought. I wasn't ready to be anyone's boyfriend—fake or otherwise. "I'm not sure that's such a great idea. Couldn't you just tell your parents what happened?"

"Ugh, of course you would say that. Fine, forget it. It was a stupid idea anyway." She pushed off the car and unlocked the door with her key.

"Hang on," I said, taking her arm and turning her back to face me. If she got in that car, I'd probably never see her again, and I couldn't let her go just yet. Not until I fixed things between us somehow. "What kind of food are we talking here?"

A slight grin touched her lips. "My mom always makes enough food to feed the entire neighborhood. Turkey and ham, stuffing, mashed potatoes, yams with marshmallows, green bean casserole, five kinds of pies… I could keep going, but you probably get the idea."

"Hmm, that *is* very tempting. But are you sure they'd be okay with me showing up unexpectedly?"

"They expect me to bring the perfect boyfriend I've been telling them about for weeks. You'll fit the bill." She tilted her head and considered. "That reminds me, you'll have to go by the name Brett, too."

"Brett?" She was kidding, right? One look at her face told me she wasn't. I had zero desire to pretend to be some other guy on Christmas Eve, but after getting her fired, how could I possibly say no? I owed her this favor at the very least. "Anything else I should know?"

"Nah, I never told them that much. Just that I was dating a nice, handsome guy."

I arched an eyebrow. "Hmm, not sure I fit that description."

"You know you do, pretty boy." She met my gaze head-on. "Look, after tonight you don't have to see me again. Once the holidays are over, I'll tell them we broke up, and we can pretend it never happened. So are you in or out?"

The smart thing to do was to say goodnight and high-tail it back to my car. I wasn't ready to get involved with any girl, let alone one who turned my insides out with a single look or the slightest touch. But there was something about her that I couldn't walk away from, not this time.

"All right, I'll pretend to be your boyfriend tonight…but only if you agree to go on a real date with me later."

THREE

Becca

"A date?" I asked, certain I'd heard him wrong.

"Yes, one date," Andrew said. "Just you and me and a nice, quiet restaurant with great food. If you don't enjoy yourself, you never have to go out with me again."

"Why the hell would you want that?"

Andrew lightly touched my cheek, making my breath catch. "Because since that night, I've never stopped thinking about you."

His touch sent a rush of primal heat through me, but I couldn't meet his eyes. "You have a funny way of showing it."

"I know, I know. I'm sorry. I wanted to call you, but after Tara… I just needed some time to get my head straight. And you could have called me, too."

He had me there. But I'd known from the beginning that Andrew and I weren't meant to be. Guys like him didn't go out with girls like me. And if they did, they always ended it soon after. Brett was the perfect example of that.

Andrew had been the same. He'd said he would call me after we hooked up, but he never had. As the months passed without a word, it became obvious I was a brief mistake he wanted to quickly move on from. Why would it be any different this time?

"Look Andrew, you're a ni—"

"Wait." He held up his other hand. "Just stop right there."

I blinked. "What?"

"You're about to say I'm a nice guy, but you think we should just be friends, right? Believe me, I've heard that line more times than I can count."

Shit, that was exactly what I was going to say. "Um…"

Without hesitation, he pressed me against the side of my car, his fingers sliding to the back of my neck and into my short hair. I gasped and heat flared between us, so hot I was sure it was melting every inch of snow in the entire parking lot.

"You didn't think I was 'nice' that night, did you?" he asked, his voice low, his eyes locked on mine.

"No," I whispered. Memories of that night still haunted me in the best way. I'd lie in bed when I couldn't sleep and slide my hand between my legs, remembering the way he'd pounded into me, the way he'd held me down, the way he'd been rough and demanding and completely in control. We'd given each other exactly what we'd both needed, but I never imagined he would want anything to do with me after that. Because in the morning, we'd both gone back to who we were: the good guy and the bad girl.

But now Andy, the vulnerable, broken-hearted nice guy I'd met before, had vanished, and in his place was Andrew, who was bold, assertive, and really fucking sexy.

"One date," he said, his mouth so close to mine I could feel the words against my lips. "One date and then you can tell me to get lost. But give me a chance first."

I was painfully aware of every inch of Andrew's hard body pressed against mine. He seemed…bigger than I remembered. More muscular. I could tell from the way his collared shirt hung from his frame, and I was tempted to rip it open and see exactly how much he'd changed underneath. Not that I'd had any problem with his body before—but now he had a confidence to him that was all new, and he wore it damn well.

The Becca of a few months ago would have grabbed him and kissed him senseless, then suggested they go back to his place. Actually, the Becca of a few months ago *had* done exactly that. But now I was trying to be good and that meant not making out with guys I barely knew in the middle of parking lots.

Ugh. Being good was no fun at all.

"One date," I said. "But don't expect anything more."

"I don't." His face hardened for a split second, and he added, "Don't worry. I'm not looking for anything serious."

"Ah, I see. You want *that* kind of date." I gave him a teasing smile, but I wasn't all that surprised he was after sex and nothing else, not after the night we'd had together. I couldn't decide if I was disappointed or relieved. Both?

He shook his head. "That's not what I meant. Nothing has to happen if you don't want it to. But moving to Dallas has been lonelier than I expected and it'd be nice to have someone to go out with. As a friend, if that's what you want." He slowly traced a line from my lips down to my chin and along my neck. "If it leads to nights like the last one we shared, well…I wouldn't complain."

I shivered at his touch, wishing he would continue lower. "I'm not looking for anything serious either. But I wouldn't mind a friend with possible benefits."

"Good." He released me and stepped back, and I instantly missed his warmth. "I have to get back to work, but text me the address and I'll be there tonight. Anything I should bring?"

"No. Just be yourself and they'll love you."

He chuckled. "Parents always do."

"I bet." I returned Andrew's coat and opened the car door, but lingered outside. I'd never expected to run into him again and hadn't been thrilled to see him at first, but now I found I didn't want to say goodbye. "I'll see you in a few hours."

"I look forward to it." He brushed his lips against my cheek, then flashed me a charming smile and trudged through the snow to a brand-new silver Audi. Damn, was that his car? I had no idea what he did, but it must be paying him well. He was exactly the kind of guy my parents would love for me to date. Too bad I already knew it would never turn into anything more. Neither of us wanted that.

But for one night? He was perfect.

My phone rang when I started the car. Probably Mom reminding me to pick up booze again because I couldn't be trusted with the most basic tasks without being reminded twenty times.

I glanced at the phone, but when I saw the caller ID, I yelped and tossed it on the seat next to me. I stared at it like it was a writhing snake as it flashed, vibrated, and sang Blink 182's "I Won't Be Home For Christmas"—the closest I came to holiday music. Finally it stopped and the screen went dark, but the name of the caller stuck with me.

Jared Cross. The singer of my former band, Villain Complex. The reason I'd quit.

Why would he call me after all this time?

FOUR

Becca

FIVE MONTH AGO

I shouldn't have come to this party. All around me, people dressed in costumes were celebrating Villain Complex and I couldn't even get wasted. I mean, I *could*, but I'd sworn to try and drink less and make better decisions with my life. Hence my boring Coke with nothing else in it.

Across the club, my former band members seemed to be having a good time. Hector, the drummer, sat in a booth with some blonde I'd never seen before, their heads close together and their faces all smiles. Kyle, the keyboardist, was dancing close to his girlfriend, Alexis, the two of them practically making out in the middle of the floor. And on stage, Jared and Maddie were belting out "Don't Stop Believin.'"

Jared was the lead singer, and he used to play guitar for the band, too. After I quit, he switched to bass and Maddie joined to take over on guitar. With her help, the band went on the reality TV show *The Sound* and came in second place, resulting in multiple record deal offers—and along the way, Maddie and Jared fell in love, too.

I stared into the bottom of my glass, feeling my gut twist. I wasn't jealous. I *wasn't*. Really. Maddie seemed like a cool girl, and I'd accepted that Jared and I weren't meant to be. We'd slept together one time, that was it. And I didn't even want to be in their stupid band anymore. I'd been the one who had quit, after all. It had been the right thing to do, for me and for them.

But sometimes it really fucking hurt to be around them. Seeing Maddie so easily take my place and fit in better than I ever had. Hearing Jared mangle the basslines I used to play on stage (okay, he wasn't *that* bad, but I was better). Watching them perform in front of thousands and knowing it could have been me up there with them.

So, no, I wasn't jealous of them exactly. I was jealous of what my life could have been if I wasn't so damn stupid.

No matter how hard I wished things had turned out differently, my attempt at being a rock star had failed. I was done with that life, and in a few days I'd be moving home to Dallas, where my family would help me get my shit together. Ugh, talk about admitting defeat. And you could be damn sure my parents wouldn't let me forget it either.

I spent a few minutes watching the crowd, admiring the geeky costumes. The party had a villain theme, of course, and I guessed most of the people were also attending San Diego Comic-Con at the convention center a few blocks away. Not me. When I'd heard my former band was playing a show as part of their tour for *The Sound*, I'd decided to come and make amends. I'd sneaked backstage the other night, and after we'd settled our differences, they'd invited me to this party. Now here I was, with my non-alcoholic drink, sitting alone at a bar.

If I stayed any longer, I was going to order a real drink and that would be a bad move. I wasn't an alcoholic, but I tended to lose control when I drank and usually made some pretty terrible decisions. Like sleeping with Jared. Or quitting the band.

New plan: I'd finish my Coke, say hi to the band quickly, and then take off. I'd made an appearance at their party, so that should be enough. I'd probably never see any of them again after I moved to Dallas anyway.

Besides, I could really go for a cigarette right now. I was supposed to be quitting, but maybe I could have one outside the club to help ease me off. One and done. Not a big deal.

Just as I was about to stand up, Hector appeared at my side with another guy in tow. "Hey, Becca. Glad you could make it." He pushed the guy forward a little. "This is Andy. Andy, Becca used to be the bassist in my band."

I looked Andy up and down and smiled. *Hello, handsome.* Sure, he was a bit more preppy than the guys I usually went for, with slicked-back blond hair and no trace of stubble, wearing a black button-up shirt and dark blue jeans. But he had a face like an old-school movie star, all chiseled jaw and perfect cheekbones, and I decided preppy was perfect for tonight.

Okay, maybe I could stay a *little* while longer.

"Nice to meet you," Andy said, shaking my hand. "I like your shirt." His eyes flicked to my chest, which was the point of this tiny little tank top that read, "This *is* my slutty costume." Good to know it was working.

"Thanks. I don't do the whole costume thing," I said.

"No, me neither." He perched on the barstool next to me, while Hector ordered us another round of drinks before slipping back into the crowd. "So Hector said you're moving to Dallas?"

"I am, yeah. In a few days."

"Me too."

"Is that so?" That must be why Hector had introduced us. Well, it couldn't hurt to have a new friend in Dallas. Most of my high school friends had moved or gotten married and popped out a baby or two (not necessarily in that order). None of us kept in touch much anymore.

"Yep," he said, running his fingers through his hair, messing it up a little. I decided he looked more like one of those sexy soccer players I'd drooled over during the World Cup than a movie star. Either way, it was hard to take my eyes off him. "I live in Boston now, but I'm starting a new job there in a few weeks. What about you?"

"I'm from there originally," I said.

"Ah, a local. You'll have to direct me to all the good restaurants."

"Sure, although everything has probably changed since I lived there. I spent the last couple years in LA, trying to be a rock star. That obviously didn't work out, so now I'm heading home with my tail between my legs."

"Hector said you used to play bass for Villain Complex?"

"I did, but it wasn't a good fit," I said, blowing off the question as best I could. But then I looked at Andy's face and wanted to tell him the truth. There was something about him—a sadness to his smile, a hint of vulnerability in his eyes, a tension in his shoulders—that made me think he might understand somehow. "Okay, that's an excuse. What really happened was that I fucked everything up by getting drunk and sleeping with the lead singer. It made things uncomfortable between us, so I quit the band. Then they went and got all famous. Figures, right?"

"Ah." He took a sip of his drink. Whiskey, from the smell of it. My mouth watered. "That sucks."

"I don't know why I'm even here. I guess I thought I'd try to patch things up with them, but it's clear they don't want anything to do with me." I shrugged. "Not that I can blame them."

"That's why I'm here, too." He tilted his head toward where the band was sitting. "That girl sitting with Hector? I asked her to marry me a few hours ago."

"No shit?" I turned and checked her out. Oh, yes, the blonde I'd seen earlier. Who was now practically in Hector's lap. "Guess she said no."

"Yep." Andy downed the last of his whiskey and slammed the glass down. "I thought I'd get some closure by coming to the party and telling Tara I wanted to be friends." He gave a cynical laugh and shook his head. "That was a mistake."

It was probably a sign of how fucked up a person I was, but seeing Andy hurting like that made me like him even more. His bitter sadness made him all that more sexy in my eyes, maybe because I could relate to it so well. The poor guy had just gotten his heart broken, and I decided right then that I wanted to ease his pain for the night—and ease mine at the same time. Maybe we could both make each other forget for at least a few hours.

I lightly trailed a finger down his forearm. "We should get out of here."

"What, right now?" He blinked at me. "Where would we go?"

"We could get something to eat or…" Shit, this was probably another bad decision, and I wasn't even drunk this time. But what the hell. I was so good at making bad decisions. "You have a hotel room?"

"I do, but…" He rubbed the back of his neck, not meeting my gaze. "Becca, you're incredibly sexy and going somewhere with you sounds…well, really damn tempting. But today I got dumped by my girlfriend, who seems to be screwing the guy I thought she was just friends with for the past year. I don't think I'm ready to take anyone back to my hotel room at the moment."

"Somewhere else, then. You pick." I glanced over at the band's booth again— 'cause I liked pain or something—and my throat clenched up seeing them all laughing together. "We can get something to eat or whatever. I don't care. If I stay here any longer, I'll lose my damn mind."

"I'm not sure…"

"She keeps looking at you."

His head jerked toward the blonde. "Probably checking to see if I'm over here sobbing into my drink and—" Andy stopped midsentence when his ex started kissing Hector. He frowned and looked away, and the misery on his face nearly broke my little black heart.

I leaned toward him and didn't miss the way his eyes dipped down to my cleavage. "We should show them we're both okay. No, that we're even *better* without them."

He lifted his gaze to meet mine, and in that look I knew that every bit of self-doubt, guilt and regret I felt—he felt it, too. "How?"

I hopped off my stool and moved closer, sliding my hands up his shirt. "Like this."

The kiss caught him by surprise. I teased at his mouth with my lips, and at first I worried he would pull away. But after a second of hesitation, he relaxed and opened for me with a soft groan. His tongue slowly slid against mine, sending a rush of warmth between my legs.

Damn, Andy was a good kisser. Maybe I should go for preppy guys more often.

I pulled back to study his face, to make sure he was okay with this. If he wasn't interested, I sure as hell wasn't going to take advantage of him. Though judging from the way he kissed and the way his fingers dug into my hips, that wasn't a problem.

"That was…unexpected," he said, his voice husky.

"In a bad way or a good way?"

"Good. Definitely good."

"Want to do it again?"

"God, yes."

With something like a growl, he yanked me toward him, pulling me onto his lap. His mouth was rough against mine, demanding more, making me moan. He took my bottom lip between his teeth, and I could taste the need on his tongue.

When he deepened the kiss, it was easy to pretend the rest of the club didn't exist, that there was nothing but this moment between us, and it was such a relief to not *think* anymore. I tugged at the buttons on his shirt, undoing the top ones, while his hands slid down my hips to my ass. He gave a little squeeze and I gasped, and then his mouth was covering mine again, greedy, desperate, hard.

Oh, yes. Definitely hard.

When we finally broke apart, I felt dazed, like I'd been suddenly woken from a really good dream. The rest of the world had completely disappeared when Andy's mouth was on mine, and now it rushed back in: loud karaoke music, the smell of cheap alcohol, the vibrations from hundreds of people dancing. And Andy, looking at me like he was just as surprised as I was by how *right* that felt.

I glanced over and saw Tara and Hector—and everyone else at the table—staring at us. "They're watching," I murmured in Andy's ear.

"Are they?" he asked, burying his face in my neck, leaving a trail of kisses along it that made me shudder with desire.

"I think everyone in this club is."

"Good." He tugged at my earlobe with his teeth. "Still want to get out of here?"

I didn't know what I'd done to unleash this nice guy's inner bad boy, but I liked it. I couldn't wait to see what he'd do when I got him alone. "Let's go."

Screw it, I could start being good tomorrow.

FIVE

Andy

FIVE MONTHS AGO

We took the Comic-Con shuttle back to my hotel room, lips locked the entire time, hands roaming across each other's skin. I'd never done anything like this before, but what better time to have your first one-night stand than right after your first failed marriage proposal, eh?

Becca's kiss had been the only thing that had make me forget the pain of losing Tara for even a second. Even now, the little black box with the diamond ring was like a hundred-pound weight in my pocket. First thing I did when I walked into my hotel room was pull it out and leave it in the bathroom, where I couldn't see it. Then I returned to the bedroom—and to Becca.

She wasn't the type of girl I usually went for, but I was feeling reckless tonight. And good god, she was hot. She radiated trouble with her dark-rimmed eyes, short platinum hair, and bright red lips. She wasn't wearing much, other than her amusing (and very tiny) tank top—just black combat boots and ripped-up shorts held together by safety pins. Silver piercings ran up and down each of her earlobes, and I had the strongest desire to tease each of them with my tongue. I wanted to find out if she had more piercings under her clothes.

She studied the mini-bar, but when she turned toward me, I was hit with a second of hesitation and doubt. Tara's face rushed back into my mind, and with it, the crushing blow of rejection. The sadness and heartbreak washed over me again, too.

But then came the anger.

It had only been *days* since we'd broken up and she'd already moved on to screwing Hector, like our year together had meant nothing to her. It made me suspect the two of them had been secretly together the whole time we'd been dating, even though she'd always claimed they were only friends. Had it been a lie every time she'd told me she loved me? Had she been thinking about Hector every time we'd had sex?

Screw it. If Tara could move on that fast, then so could I. And Becca was perfect—because she was absolutely nothing like my ex.

Becca must have seen my hesitation because a flicker of concern crossed her face. "We don't have to do this, Andy. We can go grab a bite to eat or…"

"No." I strode over to Becca and tangled my fingers in the back of her hair, sliding my other arm around her waist and yanking her against me. She let out a little gasp, but her dark eyes flashed with pleasure. She liked that. Good.

I kissed Becca hard, forcing her mouth open, holding her tight against me. Her hands slipped around my waist to my ass, cupping it, pulling me closer. Her body fitted against mine, molding to me like we'd been made as a perfect match. All thoughts of Tara and my broken heart were forgotten; all that existed was this girl, this kiss, this moment.

Tonight I was done being hesitant. Done with the sadness and the doubt and the pain. And above all else, I was done being the nice guy.

We devoured each other, our kisses hungry and desperate. My mouth and my hands were rough, exploring her body, but she gripped me just as tightly and moaned with each touch. I found her breasts, so soft and full, and rubbed them through her thin top. With each squeeze and pinch, she moaned even louder.

"I don't know if I can be gentle tonight," I said, nipping at her earlobe.

"Thank god. I don't want it gentle."

I paused. "No?"

"No." She was breathing heavily, her face flushed with desire. "Be rough with me. I can take it. I *want* it."

My hands tightened around her arms, fingers biting into her skin. Her words had unlocked something within me, something I'd kept buried deep inside, something I'd always craved. I'd never found the right girl—had either been too worried about what my girlfriends would think or knew they wouldn't be open to it. But this girl seemed to want it as much as I did.

I didn't know her. I'd probably never see her again. Maybe for tonight, for one night only, I could finally let my darker desires out to play.

"Take off your clothes," I ordered. "Slowly."

She gave me a sultry smile and slid her hands down her body, tracing the curves of her breasts and the swell of her hips. She teased me with a swipe of her tongue across her lips as she undid her shorts, inching them down her smooth legs. Underneath, she wore a tiny black thong, and damn if that wasn't the sexiest thing I'd ever seen.

She slowly raised the tank top off her body and threw it across the room, revealing a black bra that barely covered anything. She stripped it off and looped her finger through a strap, holding it there for a second before letting it drop to the floor. There wasn't a single hint of hesitation or shyness on her face.

I swallowed hard at the sight of her gorgeous, supple breasts and her smooth, pale stomach. No more piercings, but she had a tattooed phrase on her left side, across her ribs, although I couldn't read what it said from here. I'd never been with a girl with a tattoo before, and the idea made me harder than anything I could remember.

She hooked a finger in her thong, raising her eyebrows at me. But I shook my head. I liked her like that, in nothing but her thong and her boots, waiting for me to take control.

"Tell me what you want," she said. "I'll do anything."

Anything? I unbuckled my belt. "Get on your knees."

She kneeled before me and knew exactly what to do after that. While she slid my jeans down, she gazed up at me with sinful brown eyes and moistened her red lips. Jesus, I was so excited just from watching her undress me I worried one touch of those sultry lips might set me off.

We'd find out soon enough.

I slid my hand into her pale hair and gripped it hard, holding her head in place. "Now, take it. Take it all."

A brief, naughty smile crossed her face, and then she opened for me.

Flicking her tongue along my skin.

Taking me inside her mouth, deeper and deeper.

Sliding me in and out, between her pinup-girl lips.

"Fuck, Becca, you have the sexiest mouth I've ever seen," I said, yanking at her hair as I thrust toward her. She opened wider, sucking me in all the way to the hilt. When her fingers squeezed my balls, I nearly lost control. If she kept this up, I'd explode in her mouth, and I wasn't ready to come just yet.

I reached for the slim measure of control I still had and shoved her back, popping out of her mouth. "Enough."

She licked at her lips and pouted up at me. "But I want more."

"Oh, you'll get more. Don't worry." I hauled her to her feet, one hand still tangled in her short, thick hair. With the other, I reached between her legs, searching her out, and she moaned as I rubbed against her. Her thong was practically dripping wet, clinging tight to her skin. "You liked that, didn't you? Sucking me off?"

"Yes," she gasped, as I ran a finger up and down the slick fabric.

Jesus, she really did enjoy this. Me being rough with her. Controlling her. Dominating her. I'd never done this with Tara or any other girl I'd been with. With them, I'd gone slow. I'd been gentle. I'd focused on making them happy, while holding back what I really craved.

Not tonight. With Becca, I was going to take what I wanted—but I'd make damn sure she enjoyed herself, too.

I dragged her head back, burying myself in her neck and in the taste of her. The thong was pushed aside, and my fingers found her even wetter underneath. She clung to my shirt, tearing it open and ripping it off me. I was pretty sure some of the buttons popped off in the process, but fuck it. I could get a new shirt later.

With one quick movement, I threw her on the bed. She bounced on the thick duvet and looked up at me from behind her dark lashes. She still wore that tiny black thong with those combat boots and nothing else, and she spread her knees wide in invitation.

I stripped off the rest of my clothes faster than I'd ever undressed in my life, then climbed over her, on top of her. Pressing her down into the bed. Rubbing against her. Only the thin fabric of her panties blocked me. I was dying to be inside her, but I wanted her to beg for it first.

I made my way down her body, stopping to lick every single inch of her beautiful breasts, taking extra time to worship her nipples. She liked it when I tugged at them with my teeth, when I sucked hard, when I mixed a little pain with the pleasure. It turned me on even more seeing her respond like that, with her back arching and little whimpers escaping from her lips. Her fingers found my hair, tugging at it hard, and I found I liked the pain as much as she did.

Next I kissed along her soft, smooth stomach and read the dark script tattooed along her ribs: *Every saint has a past. Every sinner has a future.* A quote by Oscar Wilde, one of my favorites. God, now I liked her even more. But who was the saint and who was the sinner tonight?

Moving lower, I traced the beautiful swell of her hips with my tongue. Every time she got too relaxed, I used my teeth, and each tiny bite made her moan even louder. By the time I got to the edge of her thong, she was writhing beneath me, thrusting up, trying to direct my head between her legs.

I tugged the thong down and off her, then kissed my way back up the insides of her thighs. For a moment, I just admired how sexy she was as I traced one finger slowly along her soft skin.

"So ready for me," I murmured. "But not yet."

The second my mouth made contact, she bucked underneath me, driving my lips harder against her. I sought her out with my tongue, lazily exploring her at first, then licking her with quick, deep strokes. Her knees tightened on either side of my head, and I dove deeper, sucking faster, taking her right to the edge. But right when her body started to tremble and tense, I pulled back, rising to my knees.

"Oh my god, you can't stop now," she said. "I'm so close."

"I know," I said, moving up her body. "But you're not allowed to come yet. Not until I'm inside you."

"Hurry." She was so beautiful, lying naked before me, her platinum hair spread across the pillow. She barely knew me, yet she was completely trusting and eager for me to do whatever I wanted to her.

A new thought made me pause.

"Condoms," I said. "Shit. I don't have any. Tara and I stopped using them and…"

A flash of pain hit me at her name, at how I'd believed we'd be together forever. I hadn't slept with anyone else in so long. Now she was off somewhere fucking Hector, no doubt. The image made me want to punch a hole in the wall and break down in tears at the same time.

Becca's palms cupped my cheeks, turning my face back to hers, like she could tell I was getting sucked into painful memories again. She pulled me down for a sensual kiss, fitting our naked bodies together, and her comforting, tender embrace helped dissolve all the anger and sadness.

"I have some in my purse," she whispered.

Thank god. I climbed off of her and fetched her purse. She fished out a condom and ripped it open, then slowly eased it onto me.

I drew her into my arms and kissed her, letting her sexy mouth wipe away any other thought but her. We licked and sucked each other's lips, like we couldn't get enough of the taste of us on each other. Then I pushed her down onto the bed and she parted for me.

I moved between her thighs, rubbing against her slowly, up and down, until she was gasping and digging her nails into my arms.

"Andy," she said. "I can't take it any longer. Please."

That's what I'd wanted to hear. I drove inside her, filling her in one hard movement. She was so warm and tight; for a second all I could do was stop and enjoy her. Then I began to move. Pounding into her with long, deep thrusts. Pulling myself nearly all the way out, then burying myself to the hilt, over and over again.

Her legs wrapped around my ass, drawing me in even deeper. Her nails bit into my back, probably leaving angry red marks there. I grabbed her hands, forcing them down onto the bed, pinning her wrists above her head. She gasped, but her thighs tightened around me, like this was exactly what she'd been wanting all along. Me too, it turned out.

"Harder," she whispered in my ear. "Faster. Rougher."

I'd been holding back, worried I might hurt her, worried I'd go too far. But that didn't seem to be an issue with Becca. Had I finally found the perfect girl for me, who would respond to every dirty thing I wanted to do to her?

"You want more?" I asked, impaling her with a sharp thrust.

"Yes, yes, yes," she said, her eyes clenched shut. I moved faster, giving her what she wanted, slamming into her again and again. Her fingers dug into the sheets above her head, and little cries escaped her lips each time I sank deeper inside her. Our bodies slapped together and the bed creaked beneath us as I let go of all control, losing myself in the exquisite feel of her.

The climax seemed to rush through her, making her back arch up and her heels dig harder into my ass. My hands tightened around her wrists, keeping her pinned down as she cried out so loud I was sure everyone in the hotel heard. Her entire body gripped me tighter, and the look on her face of sweet surrender tipped me over the edge, too.

The orgasm was so strong it was almost painful. I started to pull back as it crashed through my body, but she locked her legs around me, bucking her hips in time with my movements. She kept me deep within her, and we both rode the waves of pleasure until we'd given ourselves up to each other completely.

I'd never come so hard in my life. Then again, I'd never had sex that incredible before. Sweat dripped off both of us, but I wrapped my arms around Becca and buried my face in her neck, relaxing on top of her and inside her. She slid her arms around my shoulders, holding me close, her legs still draped around my ass.

Neither one of us said anything. We simply held each other, breathing each other in, like we both knew what we'd done together had been special. I'd never been so uninhibited with a woman before. With Becca, for once in my life, I felt like I could completely be myself.

I just wished we'd met when we weren't both so broken.

SIX

Becca

When I stepped inside my sister's house, more annoyingly cheerful Christmas music was playing in the living room and the air smelled of delicious carb-filled food. I set my keys on the front entry table, and Hannah slammed into me at top speed, her red cape trailing behind her, her little arms wrapping around my legs. "Becca, Becca, Becca!"

I laughed and kneeled down to give my five-year-old niece a hug. "Hey, Supergirl."

"Mommy says you're bringing a *boy* over," she said in a singsong way.

"Your mom is right. Where is she?"

"In her room." A sad frown tugged at her tiny mouth. "She was crying. I brought her a tissue box."

Oh, shit. I wondered if Trish was having problems with Matt again. "That was good thinking. I bet she appreciated that."

My mom stepped out of the kitchen, wearing a red apron with a snowman on it. "Hi, dear. Food is almost ready. Did you bring the wine?"

Shit, shit, shit. I'd been so messed up over running into Andrew and then Jared's phone call that I'd completely forgotten. Turned out I did need all those reminders—and more, apparently.

"Crap, I'm sorry. I got busy at work and forgot. I'll run out and get some now."

My mother's face took on that look she always got when I disappointed her. A strained smile, a tightness in her eyes. "No, don't bother. It's too late now and the snow is coming down something fierce. We'll have to make do without."

My gut tightened. Once again I'd proved to be a failure. "I'll text An—Brett and see if he can bring some."

Her eyes lit up. "Oh, that would be wonderful, but only as long as it's no trouble. He sounds like such a nice boy. I can't wait to meet him."

"He'll be here soon enough. Try not to smother him to death, Mom."

"I make no promises." She glanced up the stairs. "Go get changed, and then check on Patricia, would you? Hannah, come help me with the rolls, dear."

They disappeared into the kitchen, and I sent Andrew a quick text asking him to pick up some booze. He replied that he'd be happy to, and I felt myself smiling as I read his text. Why was I smiling? *One night of pretending*, I reminded myself. *Followed by one date, and then we'll probably never see each other again.*

I stuck my head in the living room and said a quick hello to my dad, who was nursing the fire beside the Christmas tree. Then I headed up the stairs two at a time and into the guest room I'd been using for the last few months.

I changed quickly, donning a short, hunter-green dress my sister had picked out, but I kept my combat boots on. It might piss off my mother, but I had to keep a tiny bit of myself somewhere in my outfit. I quickly fixed up my hair and makeup, reapplying the red lipstick I knew Andrew liked so much, then went off in search of Trish.

Her bedroom door was closed, so I knocked on it using our code from when we were kids. "Come in," she called.

I eased open the door and found Trish sitting at the window seat, gazing out across the front yard. Through the window, the neighborhood could be seen all lit up with lights and dotted with snow. A beautiful white Christmas, and Trish fit the picture perfectly, with her pale gold hair, red lace dress, and sparkling jewelry. But as I got closer, I saw that my twin sister's eyes were wet and puffy and the perfect image crumbled.

We had identical features, but we couldn't be more different. Instead of combat boots, she wore glittery ballet flats, and the only piercings she had were tiny diamond studs. Our hair was the same color now that all the dye had faded out of mine, but hers was long and styled into glamorous waves. My favorite color was black, while hers was pink. I loved music, and she loved books. And while I'd spent the last few years partying all night and making bad decisions, she'd been at home, raising her daughter and being the perfect wife.

I sank beside her on the window seat. "Hannah told me you were crying."

"Did she?" She gave a long, drawn-out sigh. "I tried to hide it from her, but she's very perceptive."

"Is it Matt?" I asked. "Where is he?"

"He left to get more firewood, but I think that was just an excuse to get out of the house." Her voice cracked a little at the last words, and I worried she might start crying again. She shook it off with a smile. "Can you believe it's snowing this much? We might actually have a white Christmas this year."

"Are you two fighting about me being here?" I asked, ignoring her question. "Because I plan to get my own place as soon as I have enough money saved up, I swear." Which would take longer now that I was without a job again. Dammit.

"No, we love having you here. You're such a help with Hannah. Marriage is just tough sometimes."

Once, they'd been Patricia Collins and Matthew Nakamura, valedictorian and class president, prom queen and king, that one couple everyone admired and predicted great things for—until they'd gotten married at eighteen when Trish found out she was pregnant. All Trish's plans for college had vanished after that, and she'd become a stay-at-home mom while Matt worked nights as a security guard and went to college (and now, law school) during the day. They were only able to buy this house with the help of his parents—with plenty of bedrooms for more kids in the future—but lately, I had the feeling that wasn't what my sister wanted.

She turned to face me and flashed a big smile, wiping at her eyes. "Enough about that. It's Christmas Eve and I'm done being upset. How was your day?"

Even though she didn't want to talk about it, I could tell things with Matt were strained lately. From my bedroom I could often hear them fighting, but I wasn't sure what about if it wasn't me. But with our parents waiting and Christmas Eve dinner about to start, this wasn't the time to talk about it. Instead, I'd do my sisterly duty and distract her with how much worse my own life was—one of our favorite pastimes.

"My day was shit," I said. "Don't tell Mom and Dad, but I got fired."

"Oh, Becca. What happened?"

"The usual. I mouthed off to my manager 'cause I can't seem to stay out of trouble for five minutes."

"That's why I love you." She gave me a quick squeeze, and I hugged her back hard, trying to give her strength. Or maybe I needed some of *her* strength.

"That's not even the worst of it. Brett dumped me, too."

"What? No! I really thought this one might be a keeper."

"Turns out he didn't feel that way about me. He said I wasn't the type of girl his parents would want him to date or some bullshit."

"What a butthole," my sister said, the closest she ever came to swearing. She wrapped an arm around me. "I'm sorry."

"It's okay. He was boring anyway." I leaned against her, and we stared out the window, at the snow dancing through the air and all the shining, decorated houses. "But um… I sort of ran into that guy I told you about. Andy."

She squealed, making me jump. "The Comic-Con hook-up? Who you had the best sex of your life with? No freaking way!"

"That's him. And, uh, he's coming to dinner tonight."

"Oh my gosh, this is the best news I've heard all day." She clapped her hands together in a way that reminded me so much of our mom. "I always knew the two of you would find each other again. And on Christmas Eve? It's so romantic!"

I rolled my eyes. "Let's not get carried away here. Besides, he's just doing me a favor. He's going to pretend to be Brett."

"Um, why?"

"Because that's who Mom and Dad are expecting tonight—my perfect boyfriend. Then they'll see that I've changed and will help me go back to college."

She stared at me for a heartbeat, and then she dissolved into giggles. "You can't be serious."

I crossed my arms, giving her a stern look, but secretly I was glad to see her laughing, even if it was at my expense. "Completely. Why is this so funny?"

"What happens if you and Andy start dating for real? Are you going to call him Brett forever? Will your kids call him that, too?" She kept giggling, covering her mouth, but her entire body shook as she tried to hold it in.

"Not going to happen. Neither one of us wants anything serious. There will be no dating and definitely no kids." I paused, remembering our deal. "Actually, I did agree to go on a date with him." At that, she started giggling again and I quickly said, "But just *one* date and that's it!"

"Mmhmm. Keep telling yourself that."

"Look, can I count on you to go along with this or not? At least for tonight?"

"You can always count on me, Becca." She held out her pinky and I shook it with my own. "Sisters first and forever."

"Thanks. And when Christmas is over, I want you to tell me what's going on with you and Matt."

"I will. I promise."

My phone beeped, letting me know I had a text. I checked it and cringed, my stomach twisting painfully. Kyle.

First Jared, now his brother? My phone only showed the first part of the text in my notifications. *Becca, call us ASAP. We need...*

"What's that?" my sister asked. "Is it Andy?"

"No." I swiped the message away without reading the rest of it. Whatever it was, I couldn't get involved with them again. It hurt too much to think about my former band, and I'd spent the last few months trying to move past that life. "It's nothing."

The doorbell rang, and Trish jumped to her feet with another squeal. "He's here! Are you ready?"

Outside the window, I saw Andrew's silver Audi parked in front of the house. I sucked in a deep breath. "Ready."

SEVEN

Andrew

I watched the snow quickly covering up my windshield, wondering what I'd gotten myself into. Sure, being alone on Christmas Eve sucked, but pretending to be Becca's boyfriend could only lead to trouble.

What was I thinking asking her out on a date? I wasn't ready for a relationship, not in the slightest, but the question had just slipped out of my mouth, like I'd been possessed or something. Luckily, she seemed to feel the same about keeping things casual. We could go on a few dates and have a good time without it leading to anything serious, right? And if she only wanted to be friends in the end that would be fine, although I couldn't deny I was hoping for a repeat of our night together at some point. Now that I'd found Becca a second time, all I could think about was getting her alone and naked again.

The clock ticked over to 6:03 and I shoved those thoughts to the back of my head. If I waited any longer, I would be late, and that would leave a bad impression on her parents. Had to be the perfect boyfriend and all.

I got out of the car, grabbed everything I'd picked up at the store on my way over, and trudged along the icy path to Becca's sister's house. It was two stories, with most of the windows lit up, a porch decorated with twinkling white lights, and a fresh-smelling green wreath on the door. I caught a glimpse of a Christmas tree inside as I rang the bell.

An older man opened the door, and he had the same warm brown eyes as Becca. "Well, hello, young man. Are you Brett?"

Oh, right, I had to go by that name tonight. What a pain. I already knew I'd mess that one up at some point. "That's me."

"Come in, come in! Wow, it's really coming down out there, isn't it?" He stepped back and ushered me inside, taking the bag that held the wine. "Let me help you with that. I'm Becca's father, David."

As we shook hands, a short, plump woman with Becca's smile entered the hallway, along with a tiny black-haired girl wearing a cape. The woman rushed forward and gave me a warm hug before I could react. "I'm Evelyn, Becca's mother. It is so wonderful to meet you!"

I offered her the bouquet of red and white flowers I'd brought. "Thank you so much for inviting me to spend Christmas Eve with you. I know it's not much, but I thought these might look nice on the table."

"They're beautiful," she said, taking them from me and smelling them. "That was so thoughtful of you."

"It's nothing," I said, giving her my trademark nice-guy smile. Parents always loved me. Too bad their daughters always left me for guys with tattoos and piercings.

"This is Hannah, Becca's niece," Evelyn said, patting the head of the black-haired girl. Hannah peered up at me with dark eyes but didn't say anything.

"Hey there," I said to her. "Do you like sparkling cider?"

"Yes!"

"Okay, good. Because I brought some and I need someone to help me drink it tonight."

She bounced up and down. "I can help! I can help!"

"I'm not sure this one needs any more sugar," Evelyn said, laughing.

"Grandma, pleeeeeeeease," the girl whined. "He brought it for me!"

She patted the girl's hair with a smile. "Fine, one glass of cider. But only because it's Christmas Eve."

"Yes!" She zoomed off into the other room, her cape trailing behind her.

I smiled at Becca's parents. "I also brought some wine, since Becca mentioned you were out. She didn't say what kind you liked, so I picked out some whites and reds that I know are good."

David pulled one of the bottles out of the bag. "We've had this wine before. Nice choice."

"Here, let me take your coat," Evelyn said. "Then you can relax in the living room while we wait for dinner."

"Thank you, ma'am."

As I shrugged my coat off, I caught sight of Becca standing at the top of the stairs, watching the entire scene with amused eyes. She wore a dark green dress that showed off her curvy legs and dipped low enough to tease me with her perfect breasts. Below it, she wore her signature combat boots, which made me smile. I was glad she hadn't changed *too* much since I'd last seen her.

Another woman joined her and I did a double-take because she looked almost identical to Becca, but with longer hair and a red dress. I'd had no idea Becca's sister was an identical twin.

Becca descended the stairs and gave me a quick peck on the cheek. "Thanks for coming. You look great."

I'd worn my shirt and tie from earlier, but ditched the suit jacket and changed into dark jeans. She hadn't said what the dress code was for tonight, but it seemed I'd chosen well. "And you look incredibly beautiful."

"Thanks." She smiled and gestured to the girl in the red dress. "This is my sister, Trish."

"It is so nice to meet you, *Brett*." Trish seemed to stifle a giggle at that last word, and I wondered if Becca had told her the truth.

"It's my pleasure. You're just as stunning as your sister is."

"Oh, I like him," she said, grinning at Becca.

Becca rolled her eyes, but any response was cut off by the front door opening again. An Asian guy with short black hair walked in and set down an armful of firewood. He yanked off his beanie, stomping the snow off his boots. Trish gave him a sharp look and left the room without a word.

"Can't believe how much it's snowing out there," he muttered, as he brushed ice off his coat.

"Daddy, you're home!" Hannah called out, racing over to him.

"Sure am, sweetheart." He scooped her up, swinging her around.

"Ew, you're covered in snow."

"Sorry about that." He set her down and looked over at me. "Hey, I'm Matt, Trish's husband."

"I'm An—Brett." I shook his hand, inwardly cringing at my near mistake. I'd have to be more careful. "Becca's…boyfriend." She'd called Brett that in the parking lot, if I remembered correctly.

"Cool. You driving home tonight?" he asked, and I nodded. "Be careful. Storm's getting worse out there and I bet the roads will be slippery. I haven't seen it this bad in years."

"Oh, dear. Well, it's nice and warm in here," Evelyn said, clapping her hands together. "We have a fire going and everything. And now that Matt's back we can eat in a few minutes. Until then, why don't ya'll wait in the living room?"

Hannah dashed forward, leading the way for the rest of us. Becca and I waited until the rest had gone through, and she slid her arm through mine, whispering, "Thanks for this."

"You're welcome." I set my hand on top of hers, enjoying the feel of her at my side, and led her into the living room. The house looked like something from a magazine, all perfectly decorated and tidy, with professional pictures of the family hanging from the walls. On one side of the living room was the Christmas tree I'd glimpsed from the window earlier, and a warm fire was going beside it.

When we passed through the archway, Trish yelled, "Stop!"

We froze. Everyone's eyes were on us, and Hannah was giggling. That couldn't be good.

"You're under the mistletoe," Trish said, pointing to the little red and green plant hanging above our heads. "You know the rules. You have to kiss."

"You did that on purpose," Becca said, narrowing her eyes.

Trish grinned, wearing the same naughty look I'd seen on her sister before. "I don't know what you're talking about."

"Well, it *is* tradition," I said, giving Becca a smile. She was the one who wanted us to pretend, after all.

"Kiss him!" Becca's mother called from where she was watching in the hallway. The others joined in, too, making it a chant. "Kiss! Kiss! Kiss!"

"Fine," Becca said. "One kiss."

I slid my hands around Becca's waist, keeping the pressure light. She moved closer to me, fitting into my arms, and gave me a quick kiss. Even that slight touch of her lips drove me crazy, and I was tempted to steal another, longer kiss from her.

"That's it?" Evelyn asked.

"Yeah, not sure that even counts as a kiss," Trish said.

Becca groaned, but I could tell by the way she leaned into me that she was enjoying being in my arms. I took her chin and directed her gaze back at me. "Guess they want a show."

I cupped her cheek, and this time I kissed her nice and slow, teasing her lips apart. Her eyes fluttered shut and her hands clutched my arms as I slipped my tongue inside, just a tiny bit, just enough to make her want more. Because now that I'd tasted Becca again, I knew there *would* be more.

I could kiss her all night long, but not in front of her family. So when they hooted and whooped and whistled, I forced myself to pull away, smiling down at Becca.

Her breathing was faster, her eyes dazed, her lips still parted like an invitation. I brushed my mouth against the side of her head, whispering, "You can have more later if you'd like." From the way her fingers tightened on my arms, I had a feeling the answer was yes.

I turned to our audience and gave them my most charming smile. "How was that?"

"Much better," Trish said, grinning.

She'd been covering Hannah's eyes, who now peered out, wrinkling her nose. "That was gross."

"Such a beautiful couple," Becca's mother said. "You'll make such pretty babies."

"Mom!" Becca's face turned red, but I just laughed. It was fun seeing her so frazzled. She was normally so fierce and cool, and I enjoyed the glimpse at this other side of her. Even if the idea of having babies anytime soon made my balls want to shrivel up.

We were directed into the dining room and found our seats at the table, which had all been labelled with our names (or, in my case, Brett's name). The flowers I'd brought sat in the middle and complimented the rest of the decorations, from the gold napkins to the red and green candles.

As the food was passed around—and wow, Becca had been right, there was a ton of it—the family laughed and talked about their day. I found myself smiling; this was a hell of a lot better than spending Christmas Eve alone in my apartment. I missed my own family, of course, but I appreciated that I could spend the evening with this one. Becca was doing me as much a favor as I was doing for her.

"Tell me, Brett, what do you do exactly?" David asked, once we'd all started eating.

Must be time for the obligatory father interview. I knew it well. Becca hadn't given me any insight into what Brett did or how I should respond to these sorts of questions, so I decided to be honest. "I work in advertising and PR for Statewide Airlines."

"They have a hub here, don't they?"

I nodded, and he asked me a few other questions about my job. As we talked, I noticed Becca watching me closely. Was she waiting for me to slip up and reveal something that didn't mesh with her description of the oh-so-perfect Brett? Who I kind of wanted to both punch in the face for leaving her hanging on Christmas Eve and also thank profusely for giving me the opportunity to be here?

"But why aren't you with your family tonight?" Evelyn asked.

"They're back in Michigan, and I couldn't make the trip out there this year. That's why I'm so honored that you invited me tonight. Thank you again for that, by the way. This food is delicious."

Evelyn beamed at me across the table. "Oh, we're just thrilled to have you. Becca never tells us anything about the boys she dates. It's so nice to meet one that isn't covered in tattoos."

"And one who has a real job," her father added.

"They weren't *all* like that," Becca muttered.

"Yeah, they were," Trish said. I noticed her husband, Matt, hadn't said anything since we'd sat down to eat. There was definitely some tension between the two of them, but everyone seemed like they were trying to ignore it.

Evelyn dabbed at her mouth with her napkin. "All we're saying is Becca's lucky to have finally found a nice boy to settle down with."

"Mom, please."

"What? It would be nice to have more grandchildren soon. By the time I was your age, I was already married and pregnant with you two."

Wow, they were laying the marriage thing on thick. Becca and Brett hadn't even been together that long—less than five months, at least. No wonder Becca felt so much pressure to bring home the perfect guy to show off. Although I couldn't imagine Becca settling down anytime soon. Which was fine, 'cause after my failed marriage proposal with Tara, I was definitely not interested in that either.

But for tonight I had to keep up the act, so I set my hand on top of Becca's and smiled at her mother. "It's me who is the lucky one."

"How did you two meet?" Trish asked, a little too innocently. "I'm sure Becca's told me, but I must have forgotten."

"Yes, I love how-we-met stories!" Evelyn said, with a dreamy look in her eyes.

I glanced at Becca, unsure how to answer. Should I tell the truth, or did she have something planned for this?

"We met at a friend's party," Becca said. "It's not very exciting."

The truth, then. Although maybe we'd leave out the one-night stand part. Or how we didn't speak again until this afternoon.

"That's it?" Trish asked when Becca didn't elaborate.

"No, there's more to it than that," I said. "When I met Becca, I was in a bad place. I'd just proposed to the girl I loved, who said no and then ran off with another man." Okay, that was a bit of an exaggeration, but they wanted a story, I could tell. And from the looks on their faces, they were eating this one up. "That girl broke my heart and I didn't think I would ever recover. But then I found Becca and everything changed. She made me forget. She helped me heal. And she got me to believe in love again."

All of the women around the table were completely enraptured, including Becca. I might have overdone it, but I knew they would believe us completely in love after that speech. I leaned over and kissed Becca on the cheek, sealing the deal. "As I said, I'm the lucky one."

"That's so romantic," Trish said, her voice soft.

It was all true, too. Well, except the part about making me believe in love again. No one, not even Becca, could do that.

EIGHT

Andy

FIVE MONTHS AGO

Neither one of us got much sleep that night. We had sex like wild animals for hours, trying out different positions, doing things I'd never been brave enough to do before. And still, we both wanted more.

We also talked for hours. Becca opened up to me about how she'd spiraled out of control as she'd gotten sucked into the rock star lifestyle. She recounted stories of nights spent drinking, dancing topless in bars, and screwing everything that moved. It had all culminated in her dropping out of college, losing her job, and getting kicked out of her apartment. She'd hit rock bottom after sleeping with Jared and leaving the band, and seeing them become famous had been the final push she'd needed to realize she was only sabotaging herself. That's when she'd decided to move home and get her life straightened out.

Her confession left her vulnerable and sad, so I stroked and kissed her until we were both so frantic for each other we could barely get the condom on fast enough. I pulled her on top of me, and this time she held *my* wrists down and nipped at my shoulder and my neck. She rode me until we were both crying out in unison, and I discovered I loved when she was rough and controlling with me, too.

She relaxed into my arms when we were finished, and then she asked me about Tara. I wasn't sure I could talk about her, not so soon, but Becca listened patiently while I got the words out. Slowly at first, but then the story rushed out of me. For some reason it was easier to talk to Becca, a near stranger, than anyone else I had ever met. Like I knew she wouldn't judge me—or that she might even understand.

"We met in English class our junior year. We seemed like the perfect match—we were both into books and comics, loved the same movies and TV shows, and laughed at all the same things. Being with Tara felt natural and as easy as being with one of my closest friends." I snorted. "Maybe that was the problem."

"Go on," Becca said, stroking my hair.

"We were together for a year, but after graduation we got jobs in different cities—me in Dallas and her in New York. We broke up because it seemed we had no other option, but I didn't want to give up on us so easily, so I found a new job in New York to be with her. I flew out to San Diego Comic-Con to give her the good news that we didn't have to be apart. I stupidly thought I could win her back by proposing, even going so far as to get my grandmother's ring. But I was wrong—she'd already moved on to Hector."

"How do they know each other?"

"They were online friends for years before I met her, and they worked on a graphic novel together—her writing it, him doing the art. That's why they both came to Comic-Con, to sign copies of the book. I'd always suspected there was more to their nightly video chats and phone calls, but she'd always assured me I was wrong. Obviously not, since she and Hector are together now. I guess it's possible nothing happened between them until this week when they met in person…but I still feel like a fool."

"You're not a fool." She kissed my forehead. "And if it helps, Hector was single the entire time I was in the band as far as I know."

"I was too nice," I said with a sigh. "Girls always tell me we should just be friends. Then they run off with a guy on the football team. Or in a band."

Becca ran a lazy finger up and down my chest. "You definitely weren't too nice tonight."

"Exactly. And you loved it." I stroked her ribs, tracing her tattooed quote. "Girls only want the sinner, not the saint."

"Maybe you should stop thinking of yourself that way."

"How?"

She draped a leg over me, fitting herself against my side, and I pulled her in even closer. "Andy is short for Andrew?"

"Yep. But everyone's called me Andy for as long as I can remember."

She nodded, like that explained everything. "Tonight at the bar you were Andy, the nice guy who had his heart broken. But once we were alone, you became Andrew, the bad boy who wasn't afraid to take control and go after what he wanted." She brushed her lips against my ear, and I grew hard all over again, which was amazing considering how many times we'd had sex already. "You can be Andrew all the time, you know."

I slid my hand down her back and around the curve of her ass. "You're the only one I've ever been 'Andrew' with. And once we leave this hotel, I'll go back to being Andy again."

"You're starting over in a new city where you don't know anyone. You can reinvent yourself. You can be whoever you want." Her fingers traveled down to circle my growing hard-on. "But right now, I want *this* bad boy inside me again."

"Again? You're insatiable."

"I blame Andrew for that."

I gripped her ass, digging my fingers into the soft skin. "Andrew can't get enough of you either."

I rolled her onto her stomach and kissed along her spine, making her shiver.

She opened up for me, and I took her from behind, hard and rough, just like she wanted. Soon she was screaming my name, my new favorite sound.

But when it was over, her words kept repeating themselves in my head. Could I get really stop being the nice guy?

Could I be Andrew all the time?

Would I want to?

NINE

Becca

———————

FIVE MONTHS AGO

When I woke, every muscle in my body was sore in the best way. It was the kind of ache that only came after a brutal workout—or a long night of amazing sex.

And my god, Andy was incredible. I'd never been with someone who was both so tender and caring, yet so rough and demanding. Now he was nestled against my back, spooning me, and it felt so nice I didn't want to move, even though I really had to pee.

Last night, we'd both opened up to each other, completely baring our souls for hours. With Andy, I felt an intense connection, a closeness I'd never experienced with anyone before. Which was ridiculous 'cause we barely knew each other. But we were both moving to Dallas soon; maybe we could see each other again and continue what we'd started. As I dozed in and out, I daydreamed of what might happen when we were both living in the same city, visiting all the restaurants I'd promised to introduce him to and spending more nights together like we'd just had.

I finally climbed out of bed and headed for the bathroom, unable to hold it any longer. I took a minute to freshen up, washing my face and brushing my teeth with my finger to get rid of morning breath. Just in case he wanted another round when he woke up.

As I grabbed a towel to dry my hands, I noticed something on the counter—a tiny ring box.

I couldn't help myself. I had to open it.

Inside, I found a big, sparkling diamond on a golden ring. The ring he'd proposed to Tara with only hours ago.

"Becca?" Andy asked from the other side of the door. "You in there?"

I snapped the box shut.

"Of course." I eased the door open and smiled at him. "Were you worried I would sneak out without saying goodbye?"

But I wasn't sure Andy heard a single thing I said because his eyes had dropped to my bare breasts and then lower, to my hand. Which was still holding the box with the ring.

A pained expression crossed his face, and I quickly set the box down on the counter. "I'm sorry," I said. "I shouldn't have touched it."

"It's fine," he said, but his voice told me it was not. He didn't seem angry, though, just in pain.

I took a step toward him, but he brushed past me and into the bathroom, then shut the door behind him. Dammit. I'd really fucked that one up.

I returned to bed, hoping we could talk about what was upsetting him when he got out. And maybe do something about that major morning wood he was rocking. He'd been completely naked, and it was hard to not want that beautiful body of his.

But when Andy walked out a few minutes later, he wouldn't even look at me. He began gathering up all his clothes off the floor with movements that were frantic and jerky.

"Come back to bed," I said, patting the empty spot beside me.

"I can't. I have a flight to catch." He bent over and grabbed his jeans from the corner, giving me a nice view of his firm ass.

I stood up slowly, letting the sheet slide off my naked skin. He stopped what he was doing to stare at my body.

"Be bad with me one more time," I said, sliding a hand down my breast to my nipple. "We can make it quick."

He sucked in a breath, his eyes hungry again. I moved toward him, loving the way his gaze trailed my movements and how his face became more and more desperate the closer I got. I played with my breasts the entire time, making my nipples hard.

When I crossed the room to him, I didn't have to say another word. He slanted his mouth over mine, yanking me against his body, his hands on my ass. But before it could go any further, he pulled away.

"I can't," he said, his eyes not meeting mine. "I really have to go. I'm sorry."

I could tell he was holding something back. It was strange, since we'd been so open with each other before. Seeing me holding that box must have upset him more than I'd thought.

"Was it the ring?"

"No. Maybe." He yanked his jeans on, and I knew it was really over. He threw on a polo shirt with a stomping Godzilla for the logo, which was so Andy it made me smile. Once he was fully dressed, he turned back to me and brushed hair away from my face with gentle hands. "I'm sorry. I just… I need some time to get over Tara. It wouldn't be fair to you otherwise."

I nodded. He'd asked a girl to marry him yesterday and been turned down. I couldn't expect him to recover from that right away or to be completely over his ex after only a day. I liked Andy a lot, but I didn't want to be his rebound.

"I understand," I said. "I'm kind of a mess right now, too. But maybe once we're both settled in Dallas, we can get together again."

"That's a good idea."

We traded phones and entered our contact information in them. While Andy finished packing, I quickly got dressed and gathered my things. Neither one of us talked. Our magical night together was over, the mood ruined with the morning sunlight and thoughts of days to come.

And then it was time to go.

We stood at the door, neither one of us opening it, like we both didn't want to leave. He touched my cheek, rubbing his thumb over my lower lip. "Becca, last night was incredible. Thank you for everything."

"You don't need to thank me," I said, leaning into his touch. He had the most amazing hazel eyes. I could gaze into them for hours, picking out all the different colors and watching the way they changed in the light. Would I ever see them again?

"I do." He lowered his mouth to mine and gave me a long, lingering kiss. I clutched at his shoulders, not wanting him to let me go. But this kiss wasn't desperate or hard or rough—he was back to nice guy Andy this morning and something about this kiss felt final.

"I'll call you," he said as he grabbed his suitcase.

But we both knew he wouldn't.

Andrew

Christmas Eve dinner was just as excellent as Becca had said it would be, and then it was on to dessert. Trish and Evelyn had been baking all day, and now they brought out five different pies for us to choose from. I was already full, but I asked for a tiny slice from each, which made both ladies smile.

"These are all amazing," I said. "I can't decide which is my favorite." The ladies beamed even more.

"I want more cider," Hannah said, as we dug into our pies. "More, more, more!"

"Sorry, baby," Trish said. "Grandma said you only get one glass. You can have milk now instead."

"But I want more! Mommy, pleaaaaaaaaaase. It was a present for me. Mr. Brett said so."

"Just let her have it," Matt said. "It's Christmas Eve after all."

Trish glared at him. "And what about when she's up all night bouncing around the house? Are you going to get her to sleep?"

"She'll be fine."

"Right, because you obviously know better than I do, even though I'm home with her *all day long*."

Matt's eyebrows furrowed. "Please let's not talk about that now."

"Patricia, is everything all right, dear?" Evelyn asked, looking back and forth between the two of them.

"Everything's peachy," Trish said, crossing her arms.

"I'm sorry," I said. "I didn't realize the cider would be a problem."

"It's not your fault," Trish said with a sigh.

Becca twisted in her seat to lean close to Hannah, then whispered something in her ear. The girl scrunched up her face as she listened, and then her eyes widened. She nodded at Becca and then loudly proclaimed, "I'm ready for bed now."

"Now?" Matt asked.

Hannah nodded quickly. "Becca says the sooner I go to sleep, the sooner Santa will come down the chimney with presents."

"That is true," Trish said with a faint smile.

"C'mon, let's go get Santa some milk and cookies," Matt said, standing up, his pie untouched.

"Okay!" Hannah said, and the two of them disappeared into the kitchen. The table seemed to collectively relax as soon as Matt was gone.

David cleared his throat. "What are you doing for Christmas tomorrow, Brett?"

"I don't have any plans, really."

"No plans?" Evelyn gasped. "It makes me sick thinking of you all alone on Christmas. You must come over again tomorrow. We're going to open presents in the morning, and then we'll have brunch together before heading to Austin to visit with my parents and my brother's family."

"Thank you for the offer, but I couldn't impose on your kindness again. Besides, I'm supposed to go in to work tomorrow."

"Work?" David asked. "That's just not right. Not right at all. It's Christmas!"

"It's no imposition at all, dear," Evelyn said, smiling at me. "We would love to have you."

I hesitated. It was tempting and it's not like I had any other real plans, but Becca had only invited me for one night. I glanced at her, silently asking her what I should do.

"Yes, you shouldn't be alone tomorrow," Becca said as her hand slipped under the table. A second later I felt it on my thigh, a warm pressure through my jeans. I gave her a sideways glance, but she smiled at me innocently while her hand crept higher and higher. "You should definitely come."

I didn't miss the hidden innuendo there, especially with her fingers inching up my thigh.

"Oh, I'm pretty sure he will," Trish said, giggling.

Neither had Trish, obviously. Luckily her parents seemed oblivious.

"Okay," I said. "I'll be here in the morning. Thanks."

Becca's fingers found the bulge in my jeans, which had sprung to life at her touch, and she slid her fingers along it through the fabric. I cleared my throat and shifted, hoping it wasn't obvious to anyone else at the table. Damn, she was naughty, doing this right under her parents' noses. I fucking loved it.

"This wine is really nice," David said. "You're not drinking any, Brett?"

It took me a second to realize he was talking to me, both because of the name and because his daughter's hand was in my lap. "No, sir. I have to drive home."

"You're so responsible," Evelyn said, flashing Becca a proud look. "But what about the storm, dear? I haven't seen it snow this much in December in years!"

"Not sure the roads will be safe to drive on," David said, nodding. "It's getting pretty bad out there."

Trish's eyes seemed to gleam, and she grinned. "You should stay with us tonight. You're coming back in the morning, after all, and we have a spare room you could sleep in. The bed is covered in gift wrap, but we can fix that right up." It might have been my imagination, but I'm pretty sure she winked at Becca when she said that.

I shook my head. "Please don't worry about it. I'll be fine driving home."

"No, that is a wonderful idea," Evelyn said. "Then you can have some wine with your pie, and you won't have to drive in this dreadful weather."

I was about to argue the point when Becca squeezed me in a way that made it hard to think. "You should definitely stay tonight," she said.

"Is that so?" I found myself sliding my hand over to her lap, inching up her dress. Her legs were bare under it, and I slowly smoothed my thumb across the inside of her soft thigh. I'd never done anything like this before, under a table with people only inches away, but she always brought out something wild in me. She parted her legs, giving me better access, and I rubbed against her panties, feeling how wet they were already.

"Yes," Becca said, her voice breathy. "Stay."

"It's settled, then," Evelyn said, beaming at us. "You'll sleep here tonight."

"Let me pour you some wine," David said, already reaching for the bottles. "White or red?"

"Red. Will you be staying, too?" I asked them. I wasn't sure I could do all the things I wanted to do to Becca if her parents were under the same roof.

David poured me a full glass of red and sat back. "No, we only live a block away. We'll be fine getting home."

"That's convenient." I took a sip while I teased Becca under the table. When my finger dipped under the elastic to seek her out, she let out a soft gasp and dropped her fork. I tried to hide my grin and failed. From the way Trish's eyebrows darted up, she had a pretty good idea what we were doing.

We finished our pies and everyone began to move into the living room to sit around the Christmas tree, but thanks to Becca, I needed a moment to calm down.

"If you'll excuse me," I said, standing up from the table. I tried to maneuver with my napkin so no one could see the tent in my jeans, then asked for directions to the restroom.

"I'll show you," Becca said, eyeing the front of my pants and licking her cherry red lips.

So much for calming down.

She led me down a hallway, and the Christmas music and conversation faded to a low hum. "Thanks for helping me tonight," she said in a quiet voice. "And I'm sorry about my parents. They mean well, but they're so desperate for me to get married and knocked up they don't know when they're crossing the line."

"It's fine. They're good people and they clearly want the best for you."

"You definitely impressed them. They'll be so upset when I tell them we've broken up."

"Hey, don't forget you owe me a date. And after that, maybe you'll want a second one. But we can figure that out later."

She stopped and grabbed my tie, sliding her hand down it and pulling me toward her. "I haven't forgotten. But I also haven't forgotten that you don't want anything serious."

I didn't. I really didn't. But god, being with Becca tonight and her family… For a second, I *had* wanted something serious with her.

No, I wasn't rushing into anything again. Not after Tara.

"You said you didn't, either," I reminded her.

"I *don't.*"

"Good," I said, although in truth, I was disappointed. Which was stupid. Jesus, what was wrong with me tonight? It must be all the holiday stuff getting to me. This time of year turned everyone sappy. "Glad we're on the same page."

We stared at each other for a long moment, like we were both defying the other to break first, to admit they wanted more out of this.

"I should get back," she said, tilting her head. "Are you going to kiss me or what?"

That was all the cue I needed. I took her face in my hands and claimed her mouth in a long, deep kiss, exploring slowly with my tongue and my lips. The kind of kiss I'd wanted to give her earlier, under the mistletoe. She moaned and slid her arms around my neck, kissing me back just as eagerly, like she needed me as much as I needed her.

I pressed her against the bathroom door, caging her in with my body. She tasted like pumpkin pie, and I couldn't get enough of her sweet lips. She was making me so hard I didn't know how I'd get through the rest of the evening without jumping her. We had to stop before I shoved her inside this bathroom and took her hard and fast against the wall.

"Go," I managed to get out. "Before your family suspects we're doing something."

"Maybe we shouldn't disappoint them…" She pressed her hips against mine, and a quickie in the bathroom was sounding better and better. All I had to do was lift up this dress, push her panties to the side, and I would slide so easily into her. She was the only woman I'd wanted in so long, and I knew how good it would be when we got together again.

No, I was going to take my time with her. I'd been dreaming about being inside her again for months, and I didn't want to rush it.

"Midnight," I said, pressing one last kiss on her lips before pulling away. "Come to my room and we'll see if you've been naughty or nice."

ELEVEN

Becca

Waiting until midnight was torture.

I crept down the stairs to the guest room where they'd put Andrew, moving slowly so I wouldn't make a sound or trip over anything in the dark. I'd stubbed my toes on Hannah's abandoned toys on the way to the bathroom more times than I could count.

My parents had left soon after dinner, promising to be over bright and early to open presents. Matt and Trish had tucked Hannah in after she'd laid out milk and cookies for Santa, and the light in their bedroom had gone out not long after that. Now the house was silent.

Andrew's room was at the end of the hall, and a sliver of light escaped from under the door. Good, he was still awake. I knocked softly, then opened the door— to one of the sexiest things I'd ever seen.

Andrew, lying on the bed, propped up on the pillows with a book in his hand. Wearing nothing but his dark jeans and a pair of black-rimmed glasses.

He looked up from his book and gave me a lazy smile. "About time."

One of his arms was draped behind his head while he read, showing off his muscled biceps and a six-pack he'd definitely not had before. There was something about the combination of his naked, toned chest and those geeky glasses that made my desire for him kick into overdrive. It was like he'd combined the best of both Andy and Andrew, and now he radiated pure sex appeal.

Preppy guys had never been my type at all, but since our night together, I'd been drawn to guys like Andrew. And I'd never found guys in glasses hot before, but he was definitely making me a convert. I couldn't get enough of this geeky-hot look he had going for him. Especially when I knew just how naughty he could be. It made me want to do whatever I could to unleash that part of him again.

"You said midnight." I shut the door behind me with a soft click. "What are you reading?"

"*The Count of Monte Cristo*." He set the book on the nightstand. "I grabbed it off the bookshelf. I hope that's okay."

"I'm sure Trish won't mind."

"It's a favorite of mine. Have you read it?"

"No. My sister's the bookworm. For me, it's always been music."

"She has an impressive library here."

I ran a hand along the packed bookshelves as I slowly moved toward him. I'd planned to come in here, rip off my clothes, and beg Andrew to bang my brains out. But something held me back. If we went down this path again, it would likely end the exact same way as before, with silence on his end and me spending months trying to forget our night together. I wasn't sure I could go through that a second time. It seemed my fate was always to be the girl that guys had a good time with but never wanted anything more from. And I was getting tired of it.

"Trish was always the smart one," I said. "The good girl. And me… I was always the bad one."

He grabbed me around the waist, dragging me sideways onto his lap. "I like you bad."

"I like you in these glasses," I said, touching the frames lightly, running a finger back to his ear and into his soft blond hair.

"Do you?" His hands splayed wide on my hips, holding me against his hard chest and in his strong arms.

"Mmhmm." I let my fingers continue down his cheek, his jaw, his neck. "You didn't wear them last time."

"I didn't think you'd be into a guy with glasses."

"You were wrong. You look cute in them."

"*Cute?*" He scrunched up his face, and I laughed.

"Cute in a 'I want you to fuck me senseless' kind of way."

His eyes flashed with hunger, and his fingers tightened on my dress. "That can be arranged."

I continued my exploration down his chest and his abs, along the hard ridges and smooth planes. "I don't remember *this* either."

"I spend a lot of time at the gym these days. Not much else to do when you're in a new city with no real friends or family."

"I'm definitely not complaining. Although I thought you were already hot as hell before. This is just an added bonus." I swirled my fingers around his hard nipples, making him suck in a breath.

"God, Becca. You have no idea how much I've thought about our night together. The second I saw you in that store, I knew I'd do anything to be inside of you again."

"Is that so?" I asked, arching an eyebrow.

He laughed, his voice low. "I had dinner with your family, didn't I? I even let them call me Brett."

"You did." I pressed a kiss to the curve of his jaw, which was dusted with a touch of blond stubble. "I definitely owe you for tonight."

His shoulders stiffened. "I don't want you to do this because you feel like you owe me."

"Trust me, that's not why I want to do this." The second he'd touched me, I'd thrown all my worries out the door and slammed it shut. Even if nothing happened between us after tonight, I wanted him too badly to walk away now. I'd done the just-sex thing plenty of times before. What was one more time?

I slid my arms around his neck and adjusted so I was straddling him, grinding against the hard bulge in his jeans. "I've thought about that night a lot, too. But now I'm wondering, who are you going to be tonight—Andy or Andrew?"

His hands cupped my ass, pulling me tighter against him. "Depends. Do you want the good guy? Or the bad boy?"

"Can't I have both?"

"Not tonight."

"Bad," I whispered.

"That's what I thought."

He set his glasses on the table, and then he grabbed my dress and tugged it over my head. I wasn't wearing anything underneath—I'd taken the rest off before coming to his room. He took me in with lust-filled eyes glinting gold in the light, and I felt his gaze move across my breasts and skim down, down, down.

"I love your body," he said. "Every inch of you is beautiful."

"Then kiss me." It had only been a few hours since our last kiss, but I was desperate to taste his lips again.

"Where?" he asked, arching an eyebrow. "On the mouth…or lower?"

A rush of heat flashed between my thighs. "Both."

With a groan, his mouth captured mine, kissing me hard and deep. He forced my lips apart, sweeping his tongue inside while he cupped my breasts with firm hands. I clung to his broad shoulders and lost myself in the taste of him. He found my sensitive nipples and rubbed his thumbs over them, rolling them between his fingers, tugging at them. I cried out at the slight pain, begging for more.

Andrew knew what I wanted. He remembered what I needed. And he was all too happy to give it to me.

When I thought I might come just from the way he was squeezing my nipples and sucking on my neck, he suddenly gave me a little shove, pushing me back on the bed, into the blankets. I was so surprised all I could do was lie there and look up at him.

"I'm dying to be inside you again," he said, his voice husky. "And I could play with your perfect breasts for hours. But it's been way too long since I tasted you here…"

His hands slid down my body, then he forced my legs wide apart. For a second he towered over me, pinning me with his intense gaze, taking in every inch of my nakedness. He looked as wild as I felt, and I held my breath, waiting for him to make his move.

When his head disappeared between my thighs and he pressed his warm mouth to me, I thought I might cry in relief. I'd been so desperate for him to ease the ache down there, so frantic for him to do something, *anything*, to relieve the pressure that had built up over the last five months without him that even the slightest touch from his tongue was like pure heaven.

He worshiped me thoroughly with his mouth, and I moaned as he burned me up with each lick. The warmth wrapped around me, sliding along my thighs, my stomach, my breasts. He slipped two fingers inside me, and I lost all sense of time and place. There was nothing but him and the incredible things he was doing to me.

He kept up a firm, steady pressure, and his fingers moved faster and faster in time with his tongue. Soon the heat reached a boiling point and the orgasm ignited inside me, making my entire body light up like a damn Christmas tree.

While my tremors subsided, he slid up my body slowly, kissing me along the way, pausing to lick the tattoo scrawled across my ribs. "God, you taste good."

He undid the front of his jeans, taking his sweet time on the zipper. I watched him intently as they hit the floor, and desire rushed through me when I finally saw him naked again. I'd pictured this moment for months, and it was even better than I'd remembered it.

He sat up on the bed, his back against the pillows, and patted his thigh. "Get on top of me."

I'd barely recovered from that smoldering orgasm, but I managed to sit up and straddle him, my knees on either side of his hips. He was big and hard as he settled between my legs, but he didn't enter me quite yet. Instead he clasped the back of my head and pulled me in for a kiss that I felt all the way down to my toes.

As we kissed, I slowly rubbed my hips against him, loving the way he felt against my slick, sensitive skin. The friction built up between us, and I grinded faster and faster, getting us both worked up and panting. I thought I could come again like this, just from the feel of him sliding against me, but he grabbed my hips and held me in place.

"Stop that, naughty girl."

I gave him my best innocent look. "Stop what?"

"You know what you're doing."

I licked my lips. "Maybe I should be punished."

His eyes flared. He liked the sound of that. "Yes, you should be. You've been very naughty."

"I have?"

"Sneaking around on Christmas Eve with the family asleep upstairs? Not sure Santa will bring you any presents."

"I don't know about that. He brought me you, after all."

"No, tonight you're a gift for me." He nipped at my neck with his teeth. "I'm going to tie you up like a present…and then I'm going to unwrap you. Would you like that? Being tied up?"

"Yes," I whispered, lust pulsing through me. I wanted to succumb to this man in every way, shape, or form. I was going to give him everything he wanted…and I knew he would give me everything I needed in return.

He grabbed a condom from the nightstand and rolled it over himself. He was prepared, unlike our first night together. Once it was on, he reached for a long golden ribbon from the pile of gift wrap beside the bed. My pulse spiked in antic-ipation.

"Arms behind your back."

I did what he said, clasping my hands together at my lower back. This position made my breasts pop out, making them look bigger, and he eyed them hungrily.

"That's better." He brought his mouth down to taste each of my breasts, sucking on my nipples, his teeth lightly scraping against them. I was soon lost in the feel of his mouth and his tongue, of the mix of pleasure and pain. But I couldn't stop myself from reaching for him, from grasping for his arms and his shoulders. I had to touch him.

Or maybe I just wanted him to tie me up already.

Andrew caught my wrists, gripping them tightly in his big, strong hands, and gave me a dark look. "I said, arms behind your back."

He yanked them behind me and then wrapped the ribbon around my wrists over and over, binding them completely. Not so tight that it hurt, but enough that I couldn't easily break free.

Once I was completely in his control and so turned on I thought I would explode at any second, he gripped my hips and lifted me up. With one smooth movement he brought me down on his hard length, impaling me deep inside. I cried out, and he muffled the sound with his mouth, giving me a long, thorough kiss, made even more sensual by the way we were locked together.

When the kiss ended, he looked me in the eye and squeezed my ass. "Now ride me."

I began to move, rocking my hips against him, keenly aware of how my hands were bound behind me and how his eyes stared into mine. My breasts were forced out, my nipples taut, and they rubbed against his chest with each movement. He looked and felt so good, it was pure torture not being able to touch him, but I loved it.

I threw my head back as I rode him, and his mouth found my neck. His fingers dug into my skin, and he urged me on, faster, harder, thrusting his hips up and then slamming me down against him. I strained against the ribbon at my wrists, feeling it bite into my skin. Tied up like this, all of my other senses became more heightened, and his every touch was electric. I gave up control to him, yet somehow I felt more powerful than ever.

Another orgasm rushed through me, like a tidal wave dragging me under, and I was helpless to stop it. Andrew's fingers gripped the ribbon, and he thrust up into me with a fast, relentless rhythm, making my back arch. I felt like I was going to break apart into a million pieces, but he held me together. Somehow I rode through it as wave after wave of pleasure washed over me, until he joined me, bucking his hips and groaning my name as he lost control.

I collapsed against his chest, unable to hold myself up any longer, and he cradled me against him, stroking my head. The moment had been so intense, both emotionally and physically, all we could do was breathe and recover.

He untied me and brought my wrists to his lips, kissing each one softly. "Becca, you're the best Christmas present I could have asked for."

"That was…" There were no words that could describe it. Amazing, incredible, fucking fantastic…all of those seemed to fall short. In the past few months, I'd often wondered if I'd imagined how good it had been with Andrew or if my memory had become exaggerated and blown out of proportion with time. But now I knew it was all true.

"I know," he said, drawing me into his arms again.

We relaxed into the bed together, wrapping around each other, pressing gentle, slow kisses to each other's lips and bodies. As euphoric exhaustion pulled us both under, I was left with one final thought.

Andrew was the nicest guy I'd ever met, but he sure fucked like a bad boy.

TWELVE

Andrew

Christmas morning. Snow falling outside the window as the sun rose. Becca, naked and nestled against me under a warm blanket. Could things get any more perfect?

Last night had been unforgettable. Seeing her hot little body all tied up and eager for me. Feeling her give herself over to me completely. Tasting her, sucking her, doing everything to her I'd dreamed about for the last five months…

I should have contacted her after I'd moved here. I'd started messages to her dozens of times, but had always deleted them. I'd just been so damn messed up after Tara turned down my proposal. Even being in a new city, being Andrew instead of Andy, hadn't been enough to get over her. It took me months before I could look at another blonde without my heart clenching up painfully. And every time that damn Villain Complex song came on the radio I wanted to punch something. Did the radio stations have to play it every five freaking minutes?

If I hadn't run into Becca at the department store yesterday, I might never have seen her again. Thank god for last-minute Christmas shopping.

She was so beautiful I could stare at her forever, with that smooth skin and those soft lips and dark eyelashes. I brushed hair away from her face, stroking the top of her golden head. She stirred, snuggling up against me like she belonged there. I closed my eyes and tightened an arm around her body.

As I dozed in and out of sleep, I found myself picturing other mornings spent like this, daydreaming of a life where I woke up with Becca at my side. My eyes snapped open when I realized where my thoughts were heading. Jesus, what was wrong with me? I couldn't think about anything like that. It was way too soon, and I wasn't ready for that kind of relationship yet. I might *never* be ready.

One date. That was what we'd agreed to. It didn't have to lead to anything more than that. We could have some fun together and then… Well, I'd worry about the rest later.

For now, I had another few hours to spend as Brett to impress the… Hmm, I really should know Becca's last name by now.

Her eyes fluttered open, and she nuzzled into my neck. She mumbled something and wrapped a leg around me, and I smoothed a hand up and down her thigh.

"Merry Christmas," I whispered in her ear.

"Mmm," she murmured, her voice sleepy.

"What's your last name?"

She tilted her head up, blinking at me. "What?"

"I just realized I don't know your last name."

"It's Collins."

"Nice to meet you, Becca Collins," I said with a smile. "I'm Andrew West."

"It's actually Rebecca, but only my parents call me that," she said, pulling the blanket up to her neck. "And I can't believe you woke me up for that."

"You were already awake."

"Maybe." She smiled and relaxed against my chest. "I'm very glad I ran into you yesterday, Andrew West."

"Me too. I wish I had called you sooner." I played with her hair, loving how soft it was against my fingertips. "I'm an idiot."

"Yes, you are."

"I'm sorry."

"So why didn't you call? Was it only because of Tara or…?"

"Partly, yeah. It took me a long time to get over her, and I'm still not ready for another relationship." I paused, debating whether to tell her the next part, but I wanted to be honest with her. It was one of the things I enjoyed most about being with her—how easy it was to talk to her. "But it was partly because after the way things ended between us, I didn't think you wanted me to call."

A throaty laugh escaped her. "That's why I didn't call you either."

"We're both idiots, then."

She traced lazy circles on my abs. "I didn't call you because I didn't want to be a rebound… And because I know I'm not good enough for you."

I grabbed her hand, stilling her. "Why would you ever think that?"

She gave a little shrug. "You wear suits to work, went to a fancy college, and drive an Audi. I wear beat-up combat boots, dropped out of college, and can't even hold down a shitty job. The two of us…we're complete opposites."

"I don't care about any of that. I like you the way you are."

"The way I am now? Or the way I was *before*?"

"Both. I like your new determination to make your life what you want it to be, and I love seeing you with your family. You're different with them. More relaxed. But I also like your bad-girl side." I touched her ear, running a finger along the lobe. "I miss all your piercings."

She brushed her lips across mine. "Tara didn't know what she had."

"And what's that?"

"A good guy who turns into a bad boy behind closed doors."

"Is that what you think of me?" I asked with a grin. "Maybe I am now because of you. I wasn't so 'bad,' as you say, with Tara. Or any other girl."

"Why was it different with me?"

"I don't know. Maybe because you were a stranger or because you told me you liked it rough or because I was just having a really shitty day and didn't want to hold back. Something about you made me feel like I could finally be myself."

She gave me a faint smile. "I like that I'm the only one who knows this side of you. But you must have dated someone since you moved to Dallas…"

I shook my head. "Some of the girls in my office seemed interested, but I avoided all of that. My head wasn't in the right place."

"Not at all? Not even quick hookups or casual sex?" She sounded surprised. She'd obviously moved on to other guys after moving back here and probably assumed I'd done the same.

"Nope. You were the last girl I was with."

For a minute she was silent, simply curled against me with her palm flat on my chest. "I haven't been with anyone either," she finally said.

"What? Since me?" I searched her face, unable to believe it. "What about perfect boyfriend Brett?"

"I never slept with him. We'd only been dating a few weeks, and I was taking it slow, trying to have a real relationship for once, with dates and meeting the parents and everything. You saw how well that worked out for me."

"Brett is a jerk. But I'm a selfish asshole 'cause I'm glad he broke up with you."

"I am too."

She slid her arms around my neck, pressing her breasts against me. I held her tight, and we fell into a slow kiss that started out tender and soft and then became more intense and demanding. She teased me with her tongue and I tugged at her lower lips with my teeth. When she spread her legs around my hips, I knew she could feel how hard she'd made me.

She drew back from the kiss and met my eyes. "Everything I just said about taking it slow with Brett was an excuse. I didn't want to sleep with him for one reason: he wasn't you."

"Becca…" The words fell away, my mouth suddenly dry. So many emotions rushed through me that it became hard to breathe. The desire was still there, of course, but it was pushed down by the overwhelming pleasure and relief from hearing that she hadn't been with anyone else since me and didn't want to be either.

And that was fucking terrifying.

I couldn't fall for her. I *couldn't*. There was too big of a chance she would rip my heart out, just like Tara had done. Becca made me feel more than I'd felt in months. Maybe ever. But falling for Becca would only give her the power to hurt me. If I felt this strongly about her after only a few days, what about in a few months? Or a year? When she walked away, as all my other girlfriends had done, how would I ever recover?

"Becca," I started again, my voice rough. "I know we're pretending to be together and all that, but like I said, I'm not looking for anything serious."

Her body tensed up and she pulled back. "I know. You've made that very clear." She laughed, but it sounded forced. "You're just my fake boyfriend. Don't worry. I wasn't starting to believe it was real."

Hearing the sharpness in her voice made my gut twist. God, I was being such a dick, but this had to be done now so neither of us got hurt later. I took her chin, drawing her eyes back to mine with a smile. "Hey, I still want us to go on that date. I just don't want you to get the wrong idea about where this is going."

"It's fine," she said, but I could tell it wasn't. "We can be fuck buddies and nothing else if that's what you want."

I wasn't sure what I wanted anymore, but "fuck buddies" sounded so harsh compared to what we had together. I didn't want her to think all I cared about was sex. "It will be a real date, I promise. No fucking has to happen, unless you want it to."

"Oh, I'm pretty sure I will," she said with the hint of a laugh.

I couldn't help but grin at that. "Are you free tomorrow night?"

"That works." She sighed and sat up, reaching for her clothes. "Now that I don't have a job, my schedule is pretty damn open."

"Again, I feel really bad about that. If there's anything I can do—"

"I'll figure something out, but thanks." She gave me a sly smile. "If all else fails, I can always go back to stripping."

Over my dead body, I wanted to say. Instead I coughed and said, "You were a stripper?"

"Sure. I told you I used to dance topless in bars. It paid well." She pulled her dress back on. "And since we're keeping it casual, I'm sure you won't mind if other guys get a look at the goods, right?"

I swallowed hard and didn't answer. She was teasing me, but her words had struck a nerve. I didn't want any other guy looking at her body, thinking about all the things he wanted to do to her. I wanted her to be mine, and mine alone.

Yeah, I was in serious trouble.

THIRTEEN

Becca

I managed to sneak back to my bedroom with no one spotting me, and I took a quick shower while the rest of the house stirred and my parents arrived.

As the hot water washed over me, I replayed Andrew's words while we were in bed, trying to get over the ache in my chest. I'd known from the beginning that he didn't want anything serious, and I thought I'd been okay with that. But Andrew pretending to be my boyfriend had been so nice that I couldn't help but wish, just a tiny bit, that it could be real.

He was the perfect package: smart, friendly, gorgeous, and amazing in bed. We'd only known each other a short time, but we had this intense connection that I'd never felt with anyone else. Even though we were complete opposites in every way, we *got* each other. Maybe because we both wanted to move on from our shitty pasts and start fresh. With Andrew, I thought maybe I could actually do it…if he ever wanted that, too. But from what he'd said this morning, that seemed unlikely.

Thirty minutes later, I met everyone downstairs wearing a red and black sweater over a pair of jeans. Andrew was stuck wearing his clothes from yesterday, although they were a bit rumpled and he'd skipped the tie today. He gave me a kiss on the cheek and a big smile, like everything was perfect between us. We were back to pretending.

We settled in the living room with some coffee and began to open presents. Hannah dashed around, grabbing gifts from under the tree and delivering them to their recipients, like some kind of Christmas pixie. She spent the rest of the time gleefully opening her own presents, throwing wrapping and ribbon around the room.

Andrew didn't get any presents, of course, but he seemed content sitting beside me on the couch with his arm around my shoulders like we were an old married couple. Mom and Trish promised to send tons of leftovers home with him, too.

"But why aren't you two exchanging presents?" my mom asked us.

I opened my mouth to answer, but didn't have a good excuse. If he was really my boyfriend, we should have presents for each other. I wracked my brain but couldn't think of a single thing to say.

Andrew tightened his arm around me and gave my mother a warm smile. "We have a date tomorrow night, and we're exchanging presents then."

"I bet we know what kind of presents those will be," my sister said with a teasing grin. I shot her a threatening look, but our parents wisely ignored her comment.

After the presents were opened and the gift wrap cleaned up, Mom and Trish went into the kitchen to fix brunch. I offered to help, but they kicked me out and told me to go enjoy my morning with "Brett" instead of getting in their way. I huffed at them, but was secretly relieved—I was a terrible cook.

My dad and Matt were sitting by the fire in the living room, so I went outside in search of Andrew. He stood on the back porch, gazing across the snow-covered backyard, while Hannah filled her new sled with her favorite superhero action figures. When he turned to face me, all my anxiety about the two of us faded away. It was hard to feel anything but warmth under the full force of his golden smile.

"Thanks for letting me spend Christmas with your family," he said as I moved to stand beside him. "They're a lot of fun."

I nodded and trailed a finger along the icy railing. "A white Christmas. I can't believe it. Haven't seen one of those in a while."

"No, I suppose not, especially not in LA." He turned toward me, leaning against the railing. "Do you ever miss it?"

"Every damn day," I whispered. I'd never admitted that to anyone. Not even Trish.

"Why don't you go back?"

"There's nothing for me there."

"You're happy here in Dallas?"

"I don't know. I have my family and…" I bit my lip to stop the next word. Because I didn't have Andrew, not in the slightest, and I had no idea why I'd almost just said that. "I've lived here since I was eleven and I love it—I really do. But LA…" I sighed, closing my eyes, remembering the feel of being on stage, of playing bass in front of a crowd. "LA is full of dreams."

"You miss playing music."

It was a statement, not a question. He already knew the answer from our long talk that one night, all those months ago. "Yes. I always will."

"Do you ever think you'll go back to it?"

"I don't know. Maybe someday." I tried to change the subject before my thoughts went down that dark path. "What about you? Do you like it here in Dallas?"

"Yeah, it's fine. I like my job, and the city is great. But I have no friends or family here, and sometimes I wonder if I belong somewhere else."

"Where? Back in Boston? Or with your family in Michigan?"

"No. Somewhere new, maybe." His thumb brushed across my lower lip. "Although now that I've found you again, Dallas is looking even better."

He lowered his mouth to mine for a kiss, his fingers sliding into the back of my hair. I loved the way he kissed, how he always cradled my head in his hand like I was precious to him. Like he didn't want to ever let me go.

But now I was more confused than ever. This morning he'd said he didn't want anything serious between us, and now he was making it sound like he *did* want something more. Which was it?

Dad called out that brunch was ready, and we reluctantly broke apart and headed inside. We all found our places around the table, taking the same seats as last night. Trish gave Matt a kiss as she sat, so I figured the two of them must have been having a better day today. Good. I hated seeing them upset with each other.

Trish and Mom had prepared a feast, with leftovers from last night, plus waffles, eggs, and bacon. While we ate and drank mimosas, my parents asked Andrew about his family back in Michigan, and I discovered he was the middle child—older brother, younger sister. He'd gone to college in Boston and had double majored in communications and English. Like my sister, he loved to read, especially mysteries. He used to play hockey and he liked to watch football, but wasn't into basketball or baseball. I filed away all these facts about him, greedy to know more. For once in my life, I found myself thankful for nosy parents.

As we finished up our huge meal, my parents shared a meaningful look and my father nodded. "There's one more thing, Rebecca," Mom said. She got up and retrieved a red envelope from the kitchen, then handed it to me. "Here. Your other present."

I wasn't sure what else they could be giving me, but I ripped through the envelope with my nail and pulled out a card with a snowman on it. Inside, my parents had written me a short note.

Rebecca,
We're so proud of the woman you've become and we know you have a bright future ahead of you. We can tell you've really changed and would be delighted to help you to go to college again.
Love,
Mom and Dad

My eyes teared up reading the note and my chest filled with warmth. I was so happy they'd realized how hard I'd worked to get my life back on track and that they were willing to help me take the next step.

"Thank you," I said, my voice catching.

Dad cleared his throat. "We were going to wait until you moved into your own apartment, but after seeing you with Brett, we changed our minds and decided to do it now."

Mom practically beamed at me and Andrew. "Ya'll are such a perfect couple. We want you to have a beautiful future together, and we know that going back to college will help with that."

My gut twisted, guilt and unease slamming into me like a freight train. They were giving this to me because of Andrew, because they thought the two of us were actually dating, because they believed we were going to settle down and get married—not because of anything *I'd* done.

For a second I was tempted to smile and go along with it. This was what I'd wanted all along—for my parents to be so impressed by "Brett" that they'd decide to help me out. But now it felt…wrong.

I flashed back to Andrew in the parking lot, telling me he thought I should be honest with my parents. He'd been right all along, and I couldn't keep up this act any longer. If I was trying to be a different person, a *better* person, then I had to be truthful with them. And if there was even the slightest chance of a future with Andrew, I didn't want it to be based around a lie.

I set the card on the table, taking a deep breath. "This is very generous and kind of you. I am so, so grateful, but…I can't accept this."

My parents exchanged a startled look. "Why not?" Dad asked.

"Because I haven't been entirely truthful with you." I met Andrew's eyes. He looked shocked, but he nodded like he wanted me to go on. "Brett isn't really my boyfriend. His name isn't even Brett. It's Andrew."

"I don't understand," Dad said, glancing at Andrew, who bowed his head.

"What do you mean, he's not your boyfriend?" Mom asked. "Not Brett?"

"I was dating a guy named Brett, but he dumped me yesterday. I knew you wanted me to have a perfect boyfriend like him, and I was scared to tell you that we'd broken up. Then I ran into Andrew and asked him to help me out at dinner by pretending to be Brett. The story about us meeting at a party was real. We just never started dating after that."

Trish and Matt watched with wide eyes, while Hannah focused on her new iPad. I was so thankful for whatever game she was playing that made her completely oblivious to all of this.

"Is this true?" my mother asked, turning to Andrew, like she believed him more than me. "Why would you pretend to be Brett?"

He rubbed the back of his neck, not meeting her eyes. "I'm really sorry about the deception. I didn't have anywhere to go on Christmas, and when Becca asked me to help her, I couldn't say no, especially since she'd just gotten fired because of me and—"

"You got *fired*, too? Oh, Rebecca," Mom said, in that disappointed voice I'd heard so many times before, her forehead pinching together. I wanted to shrink down and disappear into the gaps in the hardwood floor.

Andrew gave me an apologetic look, but it didn't matter at this point if they knew about my job. I'd already ruined everything with my parents, reminding them why they couldn't trust me, why I would never ever make them proud.

"We really thought you had changed," Dad said. "But you're still lying to us and can't seem to hold down a job."

"Was it *all* a lie?" my mom asked. "Everything you've told us over the last few months?"

"No, not all of it—" I started.

"So who are you, then?" Dad asked Andrew. "Do you really work for Statewide Airlines? What about everything else you told us?"

Andrew opened his mouth to respond, but my mom cut him off. "I thought for sure my baby had finally found a nice guy, but it was all a ruse," she said, taking a swig of her mimosa.

Dad shook his head. "Rebecca, this is really disappointing. We thought, with Brett, that you were changing your life and finally settling down. But now…I don't think we can help you with college after all."

I was almost in tears, but at the same time, I was kind of pissed off, too. I understood why they were turning me down and why they were upset, and I didn't blame them at all. Yes, I had seriously fucked up by lying to them, which is why I'd confessed and turned down the money. But it was like they cared more about the fact that "Brett" wasn't my boyfriend than anything else I'd done in the last few months to show them I had changed.

I slammed my napkin down on the table and stood up quickly, rattling the silverware. "I already said I was turning down the money. I know I messed up, and I don't deserve your help. But really, if the only measure of how I've changed is who I'm dating and whether I'm on my way to marriage and babies, then I'm not sure I want your help anyway."

I left the table and ran outside, slamming the front door behind me. The snow had stopped coming down but it was still frosty, although I was so upset I didn't care if I froze. I just needed to get away from them.

Ten seconds out on the front porch, I changed my mind. My sweater wasn't nearly thick enough for this weather. I really wished I had brought a jacket. Or a blanket. Or a space heater. But I wasn't going back in there, no way in hell.

I rubbed my hands on my arms, my breath misting the air as my parents' words replayed in my head. They didn't understand me, and it was becoming more and more clear that they never would. They wanted me to be Trish, to settle down and live a quiet, content life as a wife and mother. But that would never be me. Sure, I wanted to get married and have kids someday, but not anytime soon.

Maybe they were right and I hadn't really changed. Maybe I was still the exact same girl who had dropped out of college to become a rock star and then managed to fuck that up, too.

God, I really wanted a cigarette.

My phone beeped in my pocket, and I groaned and pulled it out. Shit, what now?

A text from Hector this time. *We need your help. Call me.*

No other words, but Hector was always succinct and to the point. One of my favorite things about him.

If they were contacting me this much, and on Christmas morning, it had to be important. I'd call them back later if only to get them to stop bugging me. But worrying about my former band members' problems was the last thing I cared about right now.

I had enough problems of my own to deal with.

FOURTEEN

Andrew

Becca rushed out of the room, leaving her parents staring after her with shocked expressions. I should probably leave, too, but I didn't want them to think I was a complete liar. Or that I cared nothing for Becca and was just using her for free food or something.

"Mr. and Mrs. Collins, please know that everything I told you about myself was true, other than my name. Well, that and the fact that I'm not actually dating your daughter." I paused and added, "Yet."

"So you *are* together?" Evelyn asked, sounding hopeful.

"No, but she's agreed to one date with me. After that…I'm not sure."

"She'd be a fool to only want one," Trish said, and I couldn't hide my smile.

"But why would you do this?" Matt asked. He was a quiet one, but he watched me now with suspicious eyes. "We let you spend Christmas with us. You even stayed in our house. Under the same roof as our daughter. Why?"

"I did it because I care about Becca and—"

"It's okay," Trish said, taking Matt's hand. "I knew who he was when I asked him to stay. He and Becca met back in California before she moved here. They have a…history."

"Patricia, you knew about this, too?" David asked as Evelyn drained her mimosa, her hand shaking.

Trish shifted in her seat. "I did, but cut Becca some slack. She's worked hard since moving to Dallas to show you that she's changed."

"But has she changed?" Evelyn asked, waving her empty glass. "She can't seem to keep a steady job *or* a steady boyfriend!"

"Her job was the worst," Trish said. "And why does it matter who she's dating? Her entire worth isn't wrapped up in the man she's with."

"Well, of course not," David said.

Trish's face took on the fierceness I'd glimpsed before in her sister. "Is it any wonder she lied when you've put so much pressure on her to find the perfect guy and settle down? She's completely changed herself to be exactly what you want, and yet she still can't get you to help her go after her dreams."

"Trish," Matt said, his voice uneasy.

She glanced at her husband and yanked her hand from his, and I got the feeling she was speaking about more than just Becca. "It doesn't matter who she's dating. You should help her because she's your daughter and she's trying to make her life better and she can't do it without your support."

Trish stood and walked out of the room, and Matt sighed and followed her a moment later. Hannah continued to play her game, completely lost in her own world. David and Evelyn just looked horrified and confused by both of their daughters' actions.

Probably time for me to get out of here as well. I scooted my chair back and stood. "I'm sorry that I lied to you both, and I'm very thankful for your gracious hospitality. For what it's worth, I think Becca is an amazing woman, and I know she just wants you to be proud of her. I'll see myself out, but I hope you have a merry Christmas." I gave them all a quick nod, then gathered up my things from the guest room before letting myself out.

Becca was outside, curled up on a bench on the front porch, shivering and staring off into space. With her knees drawn up to her chest, she didn't look like she wanted company, but I couldn't leave her like this. I ducked back inside and grabbed a white, fuzzy blanket off the guest bed we'd both slept in. When I returned to the front porch, I draped the blanket over her shoulders, tucking it around her. She barely seemed to notice.

As I sat beside her, I saw she was gripping her phone tightly. I rested my hand on her knee and gave her a slight, reassuring squeeze. "I'm sorry your parents are upset, but it was good that you told them the truth."

"Yeah." She sighed, finally registering that I was there. "You were right all along. I should have been honest with them from the beginning."

"Maybe, but you did the right thing in the end. I think they'll come around soon."

She nodded, but she seemed distracted. Her eyes kept flicking to the phone still clutched in her hand.

"Is there something else bothering you?" I asked.

She hesitated, but then shook her head and shoved the phone in her jeans. "No, nothing."

I waited a moment longer to see if she would reveal anything else, but for once, she didn't seem to want to talk to me. I missed the Becca who had shared so freely with me before, but I could tell she was hurting and I wasn't going to push her.

"You're cold," I said. "Come here."

She uncurled herself and moved into my welcoming arms, bringing the blanket with her. I wrapped it around us both and held her close, stroking her hair, tucking the flyaway pieces behind her ear. I hoped she would open up to me when she was ready, but until then I was happy enough to offer her some silent comfort, to be the guy she leaned against for support.

"Everything will be okay," I whispered into her ear.

She turned her head and found my lips with her own. It was a slow kiss, a soft brush of our mouths, the lightest touch of our tongues. Completely different from the fervent, rough kisses from last night and somehow even more intimate. She stroked her fingers across my jaw, gazing into my eyes, and we were both lost and then found in a single, shared breath.

I felt powerless against her, falling under her spell with each kiss, and it was too much, too dangerous, too close to something real. Something not at all casual and a whole lot serious. I couldn't stop it, wasn't even sure I wanted to stop it, but had to stop it somehow.

"I should get going," I said, extracting myself from our embrace. "I need to call my family back home and…"

She nodded, tugging at her lower lip with her teeth. "Yeah. We'll be heading to Austin soon. That'll be a fun three-hour car ride. But we still have our date tomorrow, right?"

"We do. I'll be here at seven to pick you up."

"We're not really exchanging presents, are we? Promise me you won't get me anything."

I tucked the blanket tighter around her. "I promise."

She gripped my shirt, looking up at me. "I'm serious, Andrew. No presents. I won't have time to get you anything and I can't afford to anyway, and if you get me something, I'll just feel bad."

"I swear, no presents. You don't need to worry." I bent down to give her one last kiss. "After all, I already got my present from you last night."

She gave me a faint smile. "If you're good, you might get another present like that tomorrow."

"I can't wait."

FIFTEEN

Becca

M y parents didn't discuss the college thing or mention Andrew even once during the long car ride to my uncle's house in Austin. There was a heavy tension in the air, and it wasn't just from me and my parents, but from Trish and Matt, too. I wondered what had gone down after I'd left the room.

Once we arrived at my uncle's house, all of that was forgotten in the spirit of holiday cheer. We opened more presents and had another huge, delicious meal with my uncle's family and my grandparents. I sneaked off once to text Andrew and wish him a merry Christmas, and he told me he'd gone to work after all. I scolded him, but hey, at least he was getting paid extra for it.

We stayed over after dinner, sprawled on couches and crammed into guest rooms, and then we all drove back in Trish's minivan in the morning. The storm had completely cleared up by then, and all the snow was melting away. Our magical, white Christmas was over.

Once we returned home, Trish and Matt took Hannah inside to make her some lunch. But as I moved to follow them, my parents cornered me on the front porch.

"Rebecca, can we speak with you for a moment?" Dad asked.

"Sure," I said, sliding my hands in my jacket pockets. Still no cigarettes in there, dammit. Quitting fucking sucked.

"We're sorry for how we reacted yesterday," Mom said. "We were just surprised and confused by everything you told us."

Dad nodded. "We've been putting too much pressure on you, but only because we want the best for you. At the end of the day, we don't care who you're dating."

"Well, we do," Mom said, nudging him. "But your dating life isn't as important to us as your happiness. We want to help you, with or without a man at your side. Obviously I would love it if you *did* find someone to settle down with, since I'm not getting any younger and would like another grandchild, but—"

"Evelyn," Dad warned.

"Sorry, sorry."

Dad turned back to me. "What we're trying to say is, we've decided we're still going to help you go to college."

Their words didn't register at first. I'd expected us to make up, because c'mon, they were my parents and it was Christmas and I knew they loved me no matter how many bad decisions I made. But I'd never expected them to change their minds about giving me the money so soon. I'd figured I would have to prove myself to them in some other way first.

"Are you sure?" I asked, my voice cracking with the words.

"Positive," my father said.

I gave him a quick hug and then brought my mom in for one, too. "Thank you for giving me another chance. I'm really sorry I lied to you."

"Just try not to do it again," Dad said. "You can always be honest with us. We love you no matter what, okay? And we've always been proud of you, even if we're not very good at showing it."

I nodded, my eyes filling with tears, my chest so tight with emotions it was hard to breathe. "Yes, Dad."

My mom patted my cheek. "Now, dear, you go get ready for your date with that handsome boy. I still have high hopes for the two of you."

"Evelyn…"

Mom shrugged. "What? You have to admit they'd make beautiful grand-children."

They each gave me another hug and then got in their car to drive the one block to their house with all the food, clothes, presents, and cooking supplies my mom had brought for Christmas.

I wanted to tell Andrew the good news, but I restrained myself. He hadn't texted me since last night, and I didn't want to seem too desperate. After all, I was seeing him in a few hours; I could tell him at dinner.

As soon as I entered my bedroom, I did get a text—but it was from Kyle. And he knew exactly what to say to get me to respond.

Jared's injured. Please call us.

A wave of pure panic hit me. Oh my god, was that why they'd been calling and texting me? Had something terrible happened to Jared? We hadn't talked in months, and our one night hook-up had only led to problems, but I still cared about the guy. As a former friend and fellow musician, if nothing else.

I shut myself in my room and debated which band member to call. I didn't know Maddie's number, so she was easy to eliminate. Kyle and I had always gotten along the best, but he also reminded me a lot of his brother. And no way was I calling Jared, even if he was hurt. Hector was the safest bet—and I knew he'd give it to me straight.

The phone rang only once before he picked up. "Becca. About damn time."

"What's going on?"

"Sorry for all the texts. I know it's Christmas and all, but we're in trouble. We had this holiday benefit concert the other day in Chicago, and Jared slipped on some ice and fell."

"Is he okay? How bad is he hurt?"

"Broken hand. He can't play bass or guitar until it heals. And…they say it may never be the same again."

My heart seized up. Jared lived and breathed music and could play just about every instrument, but guitar was his true passion. To not be able to play it the way he once had would kill him. I knew because it would kill me, too, even though I hadn't touched a bass in months. I couldn't think of a worse fate, and I ached for him.

"That's terrible," I said. "I hope his hand heals up soon. But what can I do to help?"

"We have a concert in Austin on New Year's Eve, and we need a bassist."

For a long moment I couldn't say anything. I simply clutched my stomach and stared at my wall, wondering if I'd heard him correctly.

"Just for the one show," he continued. "We don't have anything scheduled after that until Valentine's Day, and we're hoping he'll be able to play again by then."

"Why me?" I managed to get out.

"Couple reasons," Hector said. "One, we only have a few days before the concert and finding a bassist in that time is damn near impossible. Especially with our track record."

Villain Complex had always had terrible luck with bassists. Before me, they'd gone through half a dozen of them. Good ones were hard to find, especially since everyone wanted to play the guitar. Stupid, but that's how it was.

"Second, you already know our songs," Hector said. "At least, our older ones. Third, you live near Austin."

I felt shaky all over, my nerves on high alert, and my body was barely keeping it together. "I'm sure your manager could hire a local bassist who could learn your songs quickly."

"Maybe, but we want you."

After all the trouble I'd caused, I should be the last person they would ever invite to rejoin their band. First, Jared and I had gotten drunk and hooked up one night after a show. Big mistake. Especially since he hadn't returned my feelings for him. It had made everything uncomfortable for the band, and it had turned me into a jealous, lovesick fool. I'd wasted way too much time pining away for a guy who would never care for me that way.

Second, I'd gotten drunk and ditched them when they needed me to compete in the UCLA vs. USC Battle of the Bands. Kyle and his girlfriend Alexis had been forced to track me down and convince me to play that night—and to not quit the band then and there.

I'd tried to give the band another shot, but I'd been too bent out of shape over Jared and too stupid to see it would never work with him. Hell, I'd even gotten drunk at a party and thrown a beer bottle at his head. Then I'd quit and nearly ruined their chances of going on *The Sound*.

To top it off, I'd later gotten drunk (notice a theme here?) and whined to a guy in a bar about what a dick Jared was. The guy had turned out to be a reporter, and he'd used my words in an article about the band that had gotten them some bad publicity during *The Sound*. I'd apologized when they were at

Comic-Con and tried to make amends, but I knew it would never really be enough.

I'd done some stupid shit. I'd made some bad decisions. But I'd gotten away from that life. I'd put it behind me.

And I was never going back.

"I'm sorry, but I can't."

"Can't or won't?" Hector asked.

"Pick one."

"Would it change your mind if I told you that your cut would be about $3,000?"

My heart nearly stopped. Three. Thousand. Dollars. Shit, I could really use that money. My parents had agreed to help me with college, but I'd still have to get a job of some sort so I could get my own apartment. Even though Trish said she didn't mind me living with her and Matt, I didn't want to overstay my welcome. But…

"No," I said, forcing the word out. "It won't."

He was silent for a long time, so long I worried he'd hung up. "That's too bad."

"I can't get involved in that life again," I said. "Too many bad memories."

"Is it Jared? 'Cause I promise you, he won't be a dick. I'll make sure of it."

"No, it's me. It's all me. I don't even play bass anymore."

"The hell you don't."

"And how would you know?"

"I'd sooner believe you'd become a nun than quit music."

"Well, you're wrong." His words made me irrationally angry. He didn't know a damn thing about me or what I'd gone through the past few months. I hadn't spoken to him or any of the other members of the band since the night I'd met Andy. Not once had they contacted me or given any clue they gave a shit about what had happened to me. Now they wanted my help?

No. Not going to happen.

"How's Tara?" I asked, unable to hide the bitterness in my voice.

"She's…good. She started a new job here in LA and really likes it. Why?"

"You know, you two really did a number on Andy. I hope you're proud of yourselves."

"Andy? Is he there in Dallas? Are you two together?"

"Look, I have to go. Good luck at your show."

"Becca, hold up—"

I hit End before he could say anything else and collapsed onto my bed, feeling drained. I hadn't realized how exhausted talking to Hector would make me. It had brought up all those old feelings again, of guilt and regret and self-hatred.

If talking to him for five minutes made my stomach twist with anxiety, how could I possibly join their band even for one night? I couldn't touch a bass guitar without feeling that crippling sense of dread and unease. Returning to that life could only lead to more bad decisions and broken dreams, and I'd worked so hard to move away from all that.

No, I was done with that life. And I was never looking back.

SIXTEEN

Andrew

I opened the car door for Becca, and she stepped out, giving me a nice glimpse of her gorgeous legs. She wore a short black dress and heels, and it was impossible to look at her without getting hard. Her red lips and curled hair made her look like a classic beauty tonight, although I still thought she made one hell of a sexy bad girl, too. I'd meant what I said before—I liked both versions of her.

"Fancy," she said, gazing at the restaurant, my favorite steak place in Dallas. "Are you trying to impress me, Mr. West?"

"Definitely." I handed my key to the valet and took Becca's arm with a smile. She moved close, and I led her through the door, enjoying the way it felt to have her at my side, like we were an actual couple. The scary thing was, I found myself actually wishing we were.

We were done pretending. Our date tonight was real. And I was going to make sure she wanted another one.

The inside of the restaurant was all gold and black, with rich leather and dark wood. The faint sound of classical music could be heard in the background, and the room smelled of melted butter and red wine. A Christmas tree sat in the corner and twinkling white lights hung across the ceiling.

We were seated at a secluded table in the corner, and we each ordered a glass of wine. I already knew what I wanted, but Becca studied her menu with a frown.

"What are you having?" I asked.

"I don't know." She chewed on her bottom lip. "Everything is so expensive."

"Don't worry, I've got this. It's a date after all." I'd never let a woman pay for a first date. Surely she had to know that. Then again, she'd told me that she usually dated losers—when she dated at all—so maybe those guys didn't know how to treat a lady. It made me even more determined to give her a perfect night.

She still looked hesitant, so I said, "You told me no presents, but I wanted to take you somewhere nice to thank you for letting me spend Christmas with your family. If it weren't for you, I would have spent the entire time at work or eating microwaveable frozen meals, so please order anything you want."

She nodded slowly and set down her menu. "I don't usually go on dates this fancy. I feel a bit out of place in here."

"How about this—next time we go out, you can pick the place."

"That sounds good." She reached across the table to take my hand in her own, her dark eyes sparkling under the Christmas lights. "I've been dying to tell you my news. My parents changed their minds. They're going to help me go to college after all."

"Really? That's great, Becca. I knew they'd come around." I squeezed her hand, smiling at her.

"As soon as the holidays are over, I'll figure out when I can register for classes. I should probably look for a job, too. Something part-time maybe."

"No stripping then?"

"Not this time," she said with a teasing smile.

"Thank god. The idea of you getting naked in front of any other guy makes me livid."

She leaned forward, pinning me with sinful eyes. "The only one I want to strip for is you."

"Um, can we get the check now?" I asked with a grin, looking around for the waiter. She laughed, and the sound seemed to send sparks straight to my heart. I wanted to make her smile like that all the time.

Maybe, just maybe, I could give this relationship thing a real chance. For Becca, I would try.

"Later," she said. "I'm looking forward to this expensive steak."

"It'll be amazing, I promise. But I'm taking you up on that offer when we're done." The idea of Becca stripping off her clothes was making me practically burst out of my slacks. I couldn't wait to get her back to my apartment.

The waiter brought some rolls and then took our orders. Once he was gone, I asked Becca, "What are you planning to major in?"

"I don't know." She took a sip of her wine and considered. "I guess I haven't thought about it much."

"Well, you don't need to decide right away. Do you know what you want to do after you graduate?"

She shifted in her seat, not meeting my eyes. "No. Not really."

"What did you major in before you dropped out before?"

"What is this, twenty questions?" she asked with a nervous laugh.

"Just curious." I ripped apart one of the rolls while I studied her face. I knew I should probably drop it, but her answers seemed off. Like she was holding back. "There must be something you always wanted to do when you grew up."

She blew out a long breath. "Yeah. I always wanted to play bass in a rock band. Look where that got me."

"You could still do that..."

"No, I can't. I failed, big time. I'm not meant for that life."

"But—"

She held up a hand. "Don't. I'm not the same girl I was before. I've reinvented my life. You did the same thing when you moved here and became Andrew instead of Andy, so you of all people should understand."

I considered my answer while I buttered a roll and then handed it to her. She looked surprised, but took the roll with a quiet, "Thanks."

"Yes, I took your advice when I moved to Dallas," I said. "I started going by Andrew instead of Andy. I buried myself in work and went after what I wanted, not caring if I was a jerk along the way. Andy was weak and let people stomp all over him, and I was done being the nice guy. Now, no one at work ever treats me like a pushover, and girls sometimes hint that they want me to ask them out."

"I'm sure they do," Becca said. "Confidence is sexy."

"Maybe. But being Andrew gets pretty damn lonely. My life consists of work, the gym, and a whole lot of TV and video games. Running into you was the best thing that's happened to me in a long time."

"Do you want to go back to being Andy, then?"

"No, but I'm not sure I like who I've become either." I started buttering another roll, this time for me. "I don't want the same thing to happen to you."

"I know what you're getting at. But couldn't you find a way to balance both versions of yourself?"

"Perhaps." It sounded good in theory, but I knew girls always wanted the bad boy. Tara had ditched me for Hector, a ripped drummer who practically radiated masculinity. My previous girlfriend had left me for a college football player who seemed to spend most of his day chugging beers. And before she met me, Becca had gone after the lead singer in her band, even knowing he was a total player and had a new girl every night.

On Christmas Eve, Becca had asked me if she could have both Andy and Andrew. But when asked to choose, she didn't pick the nice guy. She didn't pick Andy.

If I stopped being the bad boy, would she run off with another guy, too?

Our food arrived and we soon lost ourselves in the rich, tender steaks. I steered the conversation back to safer topics. Even though I couldn't wait to get Becca alone and naked, I loved talking with her about everything from our families to movies we'd seen recently to music we both liked. Becca always called us opposites, but the more we talked, the more I discovered that wasn't true. Maybe on the surface we seemed different, but underneath all that, we shared a lot of common ground.

After I paid for dinner, Becca asked, "Do you still want that second date?"

"Yes," I said with no hesitation. "Definitely."

She arched an eyebrow. "I thought you didn't want anything serious?"

"I don't. But I also want you."

"You can have me anytime you want," she said with a wink and a naughty smile.

"That's not what I mean." I took her arm in mine as we walked out of the restaurant. "Yes, I want you in my bed. But I want you in other parts of my life, too."

She leaned against me, and her smile took my breath away. "Then I think you've earned a second date *and* a trip back to your place tonight."

I drew her in for a kiss, silently congratulating myself on giving her the perfect date and scoring a second one, too. I wasn't sure where this was going with Becca and I still wanted to take things slow, but for the first time ever I felt something like hope.

While we were waiting for the valet to bring my car around, my phone buzzed in my pocket. I pulled it out and checked the text—and nearly dropped the phone when I saw who it was from.

Tara.

SEVENTEEN

Becca

A ndrew stared at his phone with a stricken expression. The car arrived, but he didn't move. His entire body was tense. I thought he might have even stopped breathing.

"Is everything okay?" I asked, while he reread whatever was on his screen, his eyebrows drawing closer and closer together. Even upset, he looked especially handsome tonight, wearing one of his collared shirts and dark slacks with his blond hair slicked back. His face was clean-shaven, and he smelled of some sort of spicy aftershave. I'd been dying to undress him and bury myself in the scent and taste of his skin ever since he'd picked me up—but I had a feeling our perfect night was about to be over.

He lowered the phone. "I just got a text from Tara."

Oh, shit.

"Sir," the valet said, holding out the car keys. Andrew seemed to be in a daze, so I grabbed the keys myself and handed the valet guy a few dollars, then got inside the car. That finally snapped Andrew out of it. He settled into the driver's side and took the keys from me, then plucked a five-dollar bill from his wallet with shaking fingers.

I waved him away. "You got dinner. I can get the valet at least."

He nodded slowly, but I wasn't sure he'd actually heard me. He ran a hand through his hair, taking a long breath, but didn't start the car. In the space of a few seconds, he'd reverted back to Andy, that broken-hearted, miserable guy I'd met that night in the bar.

"Sorry. I didn't realize it would hit me so hard. We haven't spoken since the day I proposed."

Why in the world would she be texting him now? Just to torment him further? Surely she wouldn't be that cruel. "What did she say?"

He frowned and checked his phone again, like he still couldn't believe it.

Finally, he pulled himself together, turned the car on, and drove away from the restaurant. "She wants my help."

"With what?"

"With getting you to rejoin Villain Complex."

The words slammed into me, and for a second I was completely speechless. "Wow. That's low. They made her text you for *that*?"

"Is it true?" he asked. "They invited you back for a show and you said no?"

I stared out the window at the bright holiday decorations rushing past us. "Yes. It's true. But I can't believe they would get your ex to bug you about it."

"I don't think Hector knows she texted me. It sounded like she's doing this on her own." We stopped at a red light, and he glanced over at me. "They seem pretty desperate."

"They've been texting me non-stop since Christmas Eve. Jared's broken his hand and they need a bassist for a New Year's Eve show in Austin."

"And you said no?" He studied my face. "Why?"

"Like I said, I'm not that girl anymore. And if I did this, where would it lead? Nowhere. It would only remind me that I'm not meant to be a rock star."

"You don't know where it might lead. You could join another band or…"

I let out a harsh laugh. "I haven't even touched a bass guitar since I quit Villain Complex. There's no way I could get on stage and perform now. I'd have to spend every waking minute until the show practicing and learning their new songs. Impossible."

"But what if you did this and Villain Complex asked you to join them again? Permanently?"

"They wouldn't."

"But——"

"They *wouldn't*. And if they did, I would say no."

"Why?"

"Because that's not who I am anymore!"

"Just because you failed once at your dream doesn't mean you should give up on it forever. You've been given another chance. Why won't you take it?"

"Because I don't want to go down that path again! I've finally gotten my life straightened out. I've even convinced my parents to help me to go back to college. I can't screw that up by joining another band, even for one show. Especially not Villain Complex."

The light changed and we moved forward again. With his eyes on the road, Andrew asked, "Do you even want to go to college? Or are you just going because that's what you *think* you should do?"

I tensed up at his question. "What the hell does that mean?"

"I'm worried going to college isn't what you really want. If your dream is to be a musician, then you need to go after it, no matter what."

He set his hand on my knee, but I jerked away. "Oh my god. You've known me less than a week and you think you can plan my life better than I can?"

"No! I just think you're only turning them down because you're scared of failing a second time. But by not taking a chance, you might miss out on what you really want."

"You're one to talk! All of this bullshit about not wanting to get serious, but then you take me on a romantic date and talk about how you want me in your life and not just in a sexual way. Which is it? 'Cause I'm getting a shitload of mixed signals here."

He didn't answer, his eyes fixed on the dark road in front of us. That figured: he could ask me a dozen questions, but as soon as I turned them back on him, he shut up. I huffed and crossed my arms, trying to calm my racing heart.

"I don't know what I want," he finally said. "I'm still not sure I'm ready for a real relationship. Getting that text from Tara nearly broke me. I just… I can't go through that again, not anytime soon. But I don't want to lose you either."

"I don't know what that means. If you want us to be fuck buddies and nothing more, then we don't need to go on fancy dates. We can just go to your place and have sex and be done with it."

His jaw clenched. "That's not what I mean. I want to spend time with you without sex, too."

"But you want to keep it casual, right? So do you want to see other people?" I was pushing his buttons on purpose, but I was trying to make a point. Plus, he'd pissed me off with all of his questions—now it was my turn. "You'd be okay with me fucking other guys?"

"No!" He practically shouted that one, knuckles white on the steering wheel. "Definitely not. I just… I don't want to rush into anything and make the same mistakes again."

"That's exactly my point! So stop pressuring me to rejoin the band that ruined my life!"

He shot me a quick look. "That's…that's not the same thing."

"How? You're just as scared to try again as I am. Scared you're going to get hurt a second time."

"Yes, I'm scared!" he said. "I'm terrified you're going to break my heart like Tara did. And I'm *never* going through that again."

He drove into the parking lot of an apartment complex surrounded by tall, thin trees and parked the car. We'd lapsed into silence, me with my arms crossed, him with his lips pressed in a tight line. The tension in the car was so high, the slightest spark could set everything we had up in flames. But what *did* we have? A few nights of sex and one failed date. Nothing more. We'd had a fun escape in San Diego and we'd played pretend on Christmas Eve, but now it was back to reality—where the two of us didn't work.

Except between the sheets anyway. At least we had that. As pissed as I was, I couldn't deny the way my breath quickened at the thought of being in bed with him again. If this was our last night together, as I suspected it might be, I wanted him one more time before it was all over.

"Let's go inside and get to the fucking already," I said. "Since that's obviously what we're best at."

His head snapped toward me, but I couldn't read his expression in the dark. "What, just like that? From fighting to fucking in an instant?"

"That's what we both want, isn't it? Sex with no strings attached?" I rested my hand on his thigh and trailed it higher and higher, until I found the growing bulge in his slacks. "And we've always been so good at using each other to take out our frustrations on."

Andrew hesitated for an instant, his entire body tense, but then he said, "Fine."

He reached across the car and slid his hand behind the back of my head, pulling me into a hot, fierce kiss. I climbed across the seat to get on top of him, pressing frantic kisses along his jaw, his neck, anything. His hands were all over me and his mouth touched every inch of bare skin he could find, but when I started to unzip his slacks, he stopped me.

"Inside," he said. "Now."

He led me up the stairs and into his apartment. We were kissing again the second we got inside, before he could turn on the lights. We banged against the wall, lips locked, while he slammed the door shut behind us. Our movements were rushed, like we needed to burn off the anger from the fight as fast as we could. Or like we were trying to prove something to one another.

The moon peeking through the windows gave us just enough light to tear off our clothes. He dragged my panties off first. His shirt went next. Shoes were kicked away. His slacks dropped to the floor. Our bodies moved in tandem, and our tongues slid against each other as we kissed with an urgent hunger we both felt. I ran my hands across his deliciously male body, feeling the smooth, hard muscles in his chest. I didn't want to think about anything we'd said in the car or what it meant for us. I just wanted him inside me.

He urged me toward the bookshelf that covered an entire wall. My back pressed against it as he pushed my dress up to my hips, his fingers sliding along the bare skin of my thighs.

"Hands above your head," he growled.

I complied, crossing my wrists, gazing up at him as I waited, breathless, for the next command. I'd never felt this kind of feverish desire for anyone else. Only Andrew had ever made me feel this way, like I would fall apart if he stopped touching me for even a second.

He dragged the dress higher, caressing each new bit of skin revealed. His hands slipped under the fabric to fondle my breasts, while his mouth claimed mine in a fierce kiss. He was rough and demanding with his fingers and his tongue, and I arched against him, my body straining for more.

He released my wrists and picked me up by the waist, wrapping my legs around him, pinning me against the bookshelf. Then his mouth was on me again, his lips hungry, his teeth on my lower lip like he wanted to devour me. His erection was right at my entrance, so close all I needed was to adjust a little and he'd slip inside. I grabbed onto the shelf above my head for support as he nudged against me, sending a cascade of warmth throughout my body.

"God, you're so sexy," he said. "I could fuck you right here."

"Do it," I said, feeling reckless and wild, wanting him inside me with nothing between us. I was so desperate to be one with him again I couldn't think straight.

"Condom," he said, his voice rough.

"I'm on the pill and clean," I said. He hesitated, but I tightened my legs around him and felt the tip of him slide inside a little. "Please, Andrew. Be bad with me again tonight."

Something in my words made his face darken. He put me down and spun me around, pressing his hard body against my back. I was so turned on from his rough treatment I was sure I would come the second he was inside me.

"Is this what you want?" Andrew asked, nipping at my ear. He moved us toward a desk against the wall, and with one sweep of his arm, he shoved everything off of it onto the floor. He pushed me over the edge, my breasts pressed against the smooth wood, my palms flat on the surface. With my ass pointed up at him, he nudged my legs apart and bent over me from behind. "You want me to be bad?"

I started to reply, but then Andrew gripped my hair and tugged my head back and all those words were lost. I managed to get out a quick, "Yes, yes, yes," before he thrust inside me. No warning, but I was already so wet and ready for him, it didn't matter. I let out a sigh, so relieved to finally have him again, and this time with nothing between us.

Andrew was already big, but from behind he felt huge and I was completely at his mercy. My dress was pushed up against my waist, and he fisted it as he began to move with long, deep strokes that hit me in exactly the right spot. We were skin to skin, as close as we could get to each other, and he pounded into me faster and faster.

"Is this bad enough for you?" he asked.

I couldn't respond. I was so wrapped up in the way he rammed into me over and over and the waves of pleasure pulsing through me. But then he stopped and slapped my ass, hard. "Answer me."

"Yes!" I gasped, as the lingering pain seemed to make all my nerve endings tingle. "I love it when you're bad."

"That's what I thought."

He started moving again, and I grabbed onto the edge of the desk, pressing back against him, wanting him deeper, wanting every inch buried inside me. It felt so good it was almost too much, and I nearly begged him to stop. When he reached around to rub between my legs, I was completely lost. He already knew my body so well and he quickly brought me right to the edge.

"Andrew, please," I begged. "I'm so close."

"Not yet," he said.

I whimpered, but from this angle, all I could do was take what he gave me. He claimed me as his own with every touch, and I offered myself up completely to him. Under his skilled fingers, the tingling pressure built and built and built, until his teeth grazed my shoulder and he said, "Now, Becca. Come for me."

I exploded, the climax taking me hard and fast, just like he did. Little gasps escaped me as we became powerless to do anything except let our bodies take over. I tightened up around him as he pumped deep within me, and with one, last hard thrust, his body folded over mine.

He collapsed against my back and pressed a kiss to my neck as the tremors continued to shudder through us both. His hands reached up across the desk and found mine. Our fingers tangled together, gripping each other tightly.

For a while we remained that way, my chest against the desk, his face buried into my shoulder, our bodies still connected. Then he pulled himself out of me and tugged down my dress, covering me up again.

We stood in the dark in his living room, with nothing but moonlight and unsaid words. I straightened up, watching the way his chest rose and fell with each ragged breath. His naked body gleamed with sweat and sex, but he wouldn't look at me.

He went into the kitchen and a minute later returned with a glass of water, which he handed me. "I'm sorry."

I wasn't sure what he was apologizing for. The fight earlier? The amazing sex? Or the fact that what we had was nothing more than a few frenzied, delicious moments?

His phone buzzed from inside his slacks, which were in a puddle on the floor. Andrew visibly tensed, and even in the shadows I could tell his face was tortured. We both stared at the dark pool of fabric until it finally stopped vibrating. He didn't check the phone, but we both knew who was texting him again. It always came back to her, in the end.

I drew in a deep, shuddering breath. "You're not over her, are you?"

He scrubbed a hand over his face, his shoulders slumping. "I thought I was. I really did."

My chest felt like something was crushing it. I waited for him to say more, to change his mind or deny it, to tell me I was the one he wanted to be with now. When he never did, I wrapped my arms around myself, feeling naked and exposed, even though I was the only one dressed in the room.

"You should take me home."

"Becca, please—"

"Look, we tried the one date thing, and it obviously didn't work out," I snapped. "So if you wouldn't mind, I'd like to go home now."

He opened his mouth to reply, but then his jaw tightened and he nodded.

EIGHTEEN

Andrew

I'd screwed this date up so bad I didn't think it was possible to ever recover it. Things had been going so well, and then *she* had texted me and ruined everything.

When Becca asked me to take her home, I wanted to protest more, to somehow make everything right between us again, but after all that had happened tonight, I didn't blame her for wanting to leave.

The drive to her sister's place wasn't long, but it seemed to take an eternity. The silence felt like an invisible wall between us, and I couldn't figure out how to tear it down.

When I pulled up in front of the house, Becca hesitated with her hand on the car door. I didn't want her to get out, but I didn't know what else to say. I had to try, though. I couldn't let it end this way between us.

"Wait."

She turned toward me, her eyes gleaming like she was on the verge of tears. My heart clenched painfully at the sight.

"Becca, I *am* trying. That's why I invited you on this date. After that, I hoped we could take it one day at a time and see how it goes."

"I'm fine with going slow. And I'm not asking for a long-term commitment or anything, god no. But…" She bit her lip, not meeting my eyes.

"What is it?"

"I hooked up with Jared, and he didn't want anything more with me after that. I wasted months wishing it would turn into something real between us, and it never did. And you did the exact same thing when you never called. I seem to be the girl everyone wants to fuck, and no one wants to date." Her voice cracked, her bottom lip trembled, and I saw how much it cost her to admit that, to show me she was vulnerable and not the fierce, bad girl who looked like a pinup girl and screwed like a porn star. "I know I said I was fine with nothing serious, but I can't just be your quick fuck now and then. I need to know there's the possibility for more someday."

I reached across and took her hand, rubbing my thumb over her knuckles. "I'm not like Jared or any of those other guys you were with before. What you and I have…it's more than just a hook-up. It always has been."

"But if you're still in love with Tara, then what's the point?"

"I'm not. I swear it." I squeezed her hand, wishing she would look at me. "Becca, I need to do this at my own speed, but I'm not giving up completely. And…" I hesitated, but if this was our last conversation, I had to say the next few words. "I know you don't want to hear this, but you shouldn't give up on your dream either."

She snatched her hand back, and her eyes found mine in the darkness, fierce and angry. "I can't believe you're bringing that up again."

I was only shooting myself in the foot even more, but if I didn't try to convince her to do the show, I would hate myself. I cared about her too much to let her give up on what I knew she really wanted, deep down. "Tara says if you're going to join the band for the New Year's Eve show, they need to know by tomorrow. Otherwise, they're finding someone else. For what it's worth, I think you should do it."

"And I think you should follow my example and move on from the past for good. Until you're truly over Tara, don't even think about calling me again."

She got out of the car and slammed the door shut. A minute later, she was inside the house.

I let my head fall forward on the steering wheel and swore under my breath. *Nice job, Andy.* Now she'd probably never speak to me again.

I should have said yes when Becca asked me if I was over Tara, but the truth was, I wasn't sure. I wasn't in love with Tara, not anymore, but seeing her name on my phone had felt like a bullet slamming straight into my chest. I didn't want to get back together with her or anything, god no, but I'd once planned to spend my entire life with her and she'd said no. Could I ever truly recover from that?

If I wasn't ready to move on, then I had no business getting involved with Becca. It wouldn't be fair to her. She had big plans for her future, and she needed a boyfriend who would love her without the shadow of his past hanging over him. A guy who could give her everything she needed.

I wanted to be that guy, but I didn't know if I could be.

I watched the light go on in what I thought was her bedroom and tried to work up the courage to go to the door and beg her to give me another chance.

When the light went out, I drove away.

My phone buzzed as soon as I got home, and I eagerly reached for it, hoping it was Becca. But it was Tara. Again.

Any luck? she asked.

No. I tried. I'm sorry.

Thanks anyway.

I didn't respond and figured that would be the end of it. I had nothing more to say to her anyway. But after I stripped off my clothes and got ready for bed, another text came.

I hope you're doing okay. I miss having you as a friend.

My hands trembled as I tried to reply, but then I gave up and threw my phone across the room. It slammed against the wall and hit the floor with a clatter. Dammit!

I ran a hand over my face, forcing myself to breathe and calm down, and then I picked up the scattered pieces of my phone. Luckily it wasn't broken, just dented on one corner. The battery had popped out and I fixed it up, then read Tara's text again.

I miss having you as a friend.

I was tempted to write back, *Too fucking bad.*

Tara had ripped out my heart. She didn't get to be friends with me now, no matter what I'd said to her before. I just. Couldn't. Do it.

Instead of replying, I closed out the message and shut my eyes, gripping my phone tightly until my heartbeat slowed to normal again. Becca was right. I had to get over my past—because no matter how much it hurt to hear from Tara, the idea of never hearing from Becca again hurt even more.

I opened my closet and eyed the cardboard box tucked in the back corner. The one box I'd never unpacked after I moved to Dallas.

Five months later, it was time.

I dragged it out and sat on the bed, carefully setting it down in front of me like it contained a nuclear bomb. It was just a simple, brown box that had been taped shut, yet the thought of opening it filled me with dread.

I had to do this. I had to know if I was over her.

I grabbed the scissors and ripped through the tape, tearing it away from the cardboard. My heart was pounding and my hands shook as I slowly opened the box. Inside, I found my old hockey trophies and high school yearbooks, cards from my grandparents who had passed away, and squiggly drawings my brother's kids had made me when they were younger. All things I wanted to keep, but didn't necessarily want to look at every single day.

And there, in the bottom, was the small, black, velvety box.

I stared at it for a good five minutes, trying to work up the nerve to pull it out. Before moving to Dallas, I'd packed the ring and tried to put it out of my mind completely. I'd buried it deep, along with the memories and the pain. But now it was time to dig it up again, along with all those feelings I'd worked so hard to ignore.

I clutched the tiny box in my hand and took a deep, slow breath. Yes, I'd proposed to Tara. Yes, she had turned me down. Yes, it had almost killed me.

But it had also led me to Becca.

I opened the box and looked inside, and the sight didn't hurt me as much as I thought it would. The ring would never be on Tara's finger, but maybe on another girl, someday… The idea didn't seem as impossible now as it once had. I wasn't ready to propose, not even close—but Becca made me believe it might be possible.

I'd known her for—what, a handful of days when you put them all together? But somehow she'd done the impossible and brought me back to life again. She'd made me realize my past didn't have to determine my future. She'd made me want something *more*.

I wasn't the same guy who had proposed to Tara. Since moving here, I'd turned myself from Andy into Andrew. Maybe I would always be the good guy at heart, but I'd become a little bit of the bad boy, too. Becca had helped me uncover that dark part of me I'd been afraid to admit I had—and she'd embraced it. She'd taught me that I could change, that I could be whoever I wanted to be.

Right now, I wanted to be the guy who was dating Becca Collins.

I threw on some clothes, grabbed my keys and my glasses, and ran out the door. It was late and the road was empty, so I got to her house in record time. But when I ran up to the front door, I realized I couldn't just knock. Becca lived with her sister's family, and I didn't want to wake everyone in the house up.

I walked around the icy grass, looking up at the second story, picking out where Becca's window was. It was dark, like every other one in the house, but I had a feeling she was still awake. I thought about throwing rocks at her window like in the movies, but ultimately decided that was stupid. Why risk the chance of breaking the glass when we had technology?

With my dented phone, I sent her a text: *I'm outside. Can we talk?*

Go home, Andrew, she wrote back almost immediately. She was still awake, too.

I'm over Tara, and I can prove it.

Her face appeared in the window, gazing down at me. I gave her a small, hopeful smile, but she shook her head. With one last, lingering look, she closed the curtains.

Give me another chance, please. One more date.

She didn't respond.

I sent her one final text. *Please, Becca. I do want more with you.*

No response.

I waited for an hour in the cold, hoping she would change her mind and send me a text or walk outside.

But she never did.

NINETEEN

Becca

The next morning, the sun was shining and the air was warm enough for me to go outside with only short sleeves on. It felt like the kind of day when anything was possible.

A day for second chances.

Last night, Andrew had come to my window and said he was over Tara. I'd wanted to believe him, but how could he know for sure when only hours earlier he'd been a total wreck at the mere sight of her name on his phone?

I'd barely slept all night, unable to get his words out of my head. I'd reread his texts a hundred times and composed a thousand responses in my head. None of them were right. None of them got across what I really wanted to say: that I was scared of opening myself up to someone who might never love me back. That I was just as terrified to go after a possible future with the band. That I was worried I would never be good enough, never stop failing, and never get what I really wanted —in life or in love.

Andrew had asked me for another chance, but how could I give him one when I couldn't even give *myself* one?

I stood on the porch and let the wind blow through my hair as I sipped my coffee and stared at the garage. Andrew's words about the band had left a lingering feeling of unease in my gut. Sure, I was starting to turn my life around and get my shit together…but at what cost? What was I giving up by going down this path? And did I really want to become that person for good?

I couldn't let my past haunt me forever. If I wanted to move on with my life, I had to know for sure that I was ready to let go of that dream—and that I didn't want that life anymore. Maybe if I could do it, then I could believe that Andrew was ready to move on, too.

I opened the garage door and flipped on the light, scanning the dusty, cobweb-filled room. Pretty sure I saw a mouse scamper across the concrete floor. Gross. But there, in the back, underneath the summer yard toys and the kiddie pool, were my bass guitar cases.

I shoved the other stuff off and dragged them out to the middle of the garage, beside Trish's minivan. The first one was a long, slim box with a gleaming silver handle. The metal latches clicked open with a loud snap, and I lifted the lid slowly.

Inside, the electric bass shined in the sunlight, a Fender Precision with a candy-apple red body and a black pickguard. I clearly remembered the day my parents had given it to me, on Christmas morning when Trish and I were fifteen. She'd gotten a new laptop, and I'd gotten the instrument that would become my best friend over the next few years.

The strings looked like they needed to be replaced, but otherwise it was as perfect and shiny as when I'd put it away. It was practically begging for me to plug it into my amp and start playing again.

As soon as I touched the neck, memories of rehearsing with Villain Complex flickered through my head, so strong I could close my eyes and almost believe I was there with them again. Good memories at first: laughing with the guys, playing on stage with them, feeling the music flow through me, hearing the audience cheer.

But then came the bad memories—the drinking, the fighting, the ultimatums—and with them, a heart-wrenching slam of shame, guilt, and regret. If I did this, if I joined the band again even for one show, I'd be opening myself back up to that life and to the chance of returning to my old ways. I'd risk failing at my dream a second time.

I closed the case up and pushed it aside. I wasn't ready for that yet.

Underneath it was a curvy, thick black case covered in stickers for old punk and emo bands. I popped it open and gazed inside at my acoustic bass, made from the most beautiful pale wood I'd ever seen. The strings on this one didn't look as bad, but this case had always had excellent insulation with its thick, fuzzy walls. This bass was like an old friend, one I whispered all my dark secrets to in the middle of the night, even if we were rarely seen together in public. I'd learned to play on this baby, and it never let me down.

With a deep breath, I pulled it out and tossed the leather strap over my head. The familiar weight of the guitar settled on my shoulder and against my hip. I plucked one of the strings to check if they were still good and felt the low note hum throughout my body.

God, I loved that sound.

Most people wanted to play guitar. I'd started there myself, as most bassists did. But as soon as I'd picked up a bass guitar, I knew I'd found my match. There was something about the deep tones, the low frequencies, and the soulful pulse of each note that hit me in my core. Playing bass wasn't as flashy as playing guitar, but it was just as important to a band's sound. I didn't care about the spotlight or about being at the front of the band 'cause I knew I was the one getting the audience to bob their heads and tap their feet.

I tested each string, and they still sounded good, even if the bass needed to be tuned badly. I should really put it back—it wasn't like I was going to play it, after all—but before I could stop myself I began tuning it, plucking at the strings, twisting each knob until the note sounded right. I tested out a few melodies and was surprised how easily my fingers fell back into it. I was out of practice after six months without playing, but my subconscious seemed to know what to do—and it urged me to keep going.

Okay. *Okay*. I would play one Villain Complex song. Just one, to see if I still remembered how. If it was too hard or I got too emotional, I never had to do it again. I could put the bass back in the case, close it up, and shove it to the back of the garage, where it would collect cobwebs until I was ready again.

If I would ever be ready again.

One song. I could do this.

I set my hands on the strings and played the opening to Villain Complex's most popular song back when I was part of the band, "Behind the Mask." The chords came slowly at first, like I wasn't sure I could really do it. But as I kept going, note after note, the music began to rush out of me, bursting forth like champagne from a shaken-up bottle.

I remembered everything. All the basslines I used to play. All the words I used to sing backup on. *Everything*.

And it felt fucking amazing.

The music was still in me, even though I'd buried it deep inside and locked my bass guitars out here in the dark. Releasing it was so powerful, so intense, and so damn *right*, I found myself in tears as I finished the song.

My god, why had I ever given this up?

When I stopped playing, it was like coming out of a daze. The sun was shining. The wind was blowing. Birds were chirping. And my sister stood at the edge of the garage, watching me with a faint smile.

"It's nice to hear you play again," Trish said.

I nodded, quickly pulling the guitar off and wiping at my eyes, embarrassed that she had caught me in such an emotional, vulnerable moment.

"I'd forgotten how much I missed the sound," she said as she moved toward me. "It was such a constant in my life when we were younger. Remember? You would practice for hours, long into the night, while I'd be curled up with a book at your side. I used to pretend that whatever you were playing was the soundtrack to the book I was reading."

I couldn't help but laugh, and all the embarrassment faded away. "I remember. I was always practicing, and you were always reading. You used to go through a book a day."

"Still do." She smiled, but there was a touch of sadness in her eyes, probably undetectable to anyone but me.

"What's wrong?" I asked, setting the bass down in its case. "Is it Matt?" I'd heard the two of them fighting again last night when I'd gotten home from my date with Andrew. This morning, they'd barely said a word to each other.

Her face crumpled and she nodded. "I…I don't think we're going to make it."

"Oh, no." I wrapped my arms around her, letting her bury her head in my shoulder. "Why do you say that?"

"I just feel so…trapped. I love him, but he doesn't understand that I'm twenty-three and I feel like my entire life has already been decided for me. I'm a stay-at-home mom who never went to college, and I'll never be anything more than that."

"That's not true. You're the smartest girl I know. You were valedictorian in high school. You could do anything you want."

"I wish it was that easy. We just got married too young. I can't help but wonder —if I hadn't gotten pregnant with Hannah, would we even still be together? I don't regret having her, not for a second, but sometimes..." She ran a hand across my bass guitar case, wiping away the dust. "Sometimes I'm jealous of your life."

"My life?" I let out a bitter laugh. "Oh, god, don't be."

"Yes, your life. You've dated dozens of guys, lived in different cities, played in a rock band, and held all sorts of jobs. You've always done whatever you wanted, no matter what anyone thought. You went after your dream. I know it didn't work out, but at least you *tried*." A tear dripped down her cheek, but she kept going. "I've lived in the same city since I was eleven, and I haven't had a job since I worked in that ice cream parlor in twelfth grade. I married my high school sweetheart and had a kid at eighteen. I wouldn't give up Hannah for anything, but there are so many days when I wish I could be as free as you are."

"Trish, you have it all wrong. The reason I've done so much is 'cause I fail at everything. I dropped out of college. I've been fired from every job I've ever had. I quit my band and gave up on a career in music. I even got kicked out of my apartment and had to come crawling back home to beg you for a place to live. If anything, I've always wanted to be more like *you*—you always seemed to know what you were doing. You're an amazing mother, a loving wife, and you've never once let our parents down. You've always done the right thing."

"The right thing?" She let out a sad laugh and wiped at her eyes. "All these years I tried to be good and do what everyone else wanted or expected of me. I was the perfect wife and mom and daughter, but now I'm just so freaking *tired*. I had so many things I wanted to do with my life, and I don't think I'll ever do any of them."

I'd had no idea Trish was so miserable, and her confession was breaking my heart. How had I missed her unhappiness over the last few months? I'd always thought she was the bright light in the family, while I was the crushing darkness— but maybe we were more alike than I'd thought and she just hid it better. "What is it you want to do?"

She took a deep, shuddering breath. "I want... I want to go to college."

I took her hand and smiled at her. "I think that's a great idea. We could start at the same time and go to class together. We could even pretend to be each other in class, just like the old days. Wouldn't that be fun?" But she didn't seem as excited about this idea as I was, and I knew there was more. "What does Matt say about this?"

"He says he wants me to be happy, but he also says we can't afford it. He's barely making enough now to cover the bills, and he still has another year of law school. I could try to get a job, but without any experience or degree it wouldn't pay much, and then we'd have to pay for childcare, too..." She shook her head. "No, it's just not possible. Not right now."

"Mom and Dad would help you. Both with the money and with taking care of Hannah."

"I know they would if I asked, but they're already helping you and I can't do that to them."

"Then what will you do?"

"I don't know." She wrapped her arms around herself. "I just know I can't go on like this much longer. I need to do something more with my life or I'll go mad."

I couldn't stand to see my sister upset, especially knowing that this was causing problems in her marriage. Sure, maybe she'd sometimes wondered "what if," but I knew she and Matt loved each other and would be even more miserable apart. They were soul mates, and he was a great husband and a wonderful father.

I still remembered the day she'd told me she loved him, back when we were seventeen. A boy had accused me of cheating off his test because I wouldn't give him a blowjob—yeah, I'd had sort of a bad reputation in high school—and Matt and Trish had convinced the principal it was all a lie and that I shouldn't be disciplined. Instead, they'd gotten the guy written up for sexual harassment.

When it was over, Trish and I had stood outside the school office, pinkies locked together, while Matt had finished speaking to the principal in the other room.

"I'm going to marry him someday," she'd said, and her eyes had gleamed with love.

A year later, it was the truth. It might not have happened the way they'd planned, but I'd never had any doubts it was meant to be.

When I'd been at my lowest point, they'd let me come live with them. Both Matt and Trish had welcomed me with open arms, no questions asked, giving me a place to rest my head and the means to get my life back together. Never once had they implied I was overstaying my welcome or that I owed them in any way, even though I often felt bad for how much I abused their kindness.

Matt was like a brother to me after all these years. But my sister had always been my rock, the one who bailed me out of trouble every time, who soothed my worries and told me everything would be okay. I would do anything, *anything*, to help her in return.

"What if Mom and Dad gave you the money for college instead of me?" I asked slowly.

She grabbed my hands, staring into my face with a stern expression. "No. Don't even consider that. I would never take that away from you. Never."

"I don't want to go if it's at your expense."

"But it's your dream and you deserve it. Mom and Dad will help me out when they can. Until then, don't you worry your pretty head about me, okay? Matt and I will figure it out. We always manage somehow. Maybe there are online classes I can take or…"

"What would you major in?" I asked. "If you did go?"

"English," she said instantly. "I want to be an English teacher. Or a librarian." She let out a soft sigh, her expression dreamy. "I'd love to get a master's in library science. Can you imagine? Spending the entire day surrounded by books, helping people find their next great read? I can't think of anything better."

It was the perfect career for her. Books made her happy in the same way that music made me happy. Even though we didn't share the same passion, we had always understood that about each other.

I remembered Andrew's words from dinner and how I'd had no answer to his question about what I wanted to do with a college degree. The truth was, it had never even occurred to me. I had no burning desire to graduate and go on to become a lawyer or an engineer or work in an office or anything else I could think of. I'd set a goal of going to college because it's what I figured "good girls" were supposed to do. But did I really want that for myself? Was that really my dream?

Trish was so sure about what she wanted for her future. But me? I didn't know who I was if I wasn't a musician. I'd tried to give it up, but it was impossible. I was born to play bass, and I wanted it more than anything else. A few minutes alone with my bass guitars had reminded me of that fact.

I had to talk to my parents.

I had to find Andrew.

But before I did anything else, I had to call Hector.

TWENTY

Andrew

I spent all day pacing around my apartment, trying to figure out what to do about Becca. It was a Sunday, so I didn't even have work to distract me from her or from how much I'd screwed things up between us. For hours, I debated whether I should stand outside Becca's house until she agreed to talk to me again or whether I should give her space. I'd asked her to go slow with me, yet now I wanted to rush to win her back, no matter what it took. I was such a mess.

God, maybe it was better if it was over between us. I'd go back to work tomorrow as Andrew, who didn't take shit from anyone and didn't let anyone in. Andrew, who never let anyone get close enough to break his heart. Andrew, who was alone and completely miserable.

Before I could decide, I heard a sound outside my window—a low, deep hum that seemed to pulse through my bones.

A bass guitar.

I ran to the window and threw it open. The mid-afternoon air was crisp and clouds were gathering in the sky, but Becca stood on the grass outside my apartment building under the canopy of trees. She wore a tight black dress with her beat-up combat boots, and her pale hair blew freely in the wind while she played an acoustic bass.

As she plucked out the notes, she didn't seem to notice I was watching her. Then she started to sing, and her clear, beautiful voice stole my breath away. It took me a second to realize what the song was—that Mariah Carey song, "All I Want For Christmas Is You." I remembered it from that one English movie my mom always watched during the holidays. Somehow it totally worked on the bass guitar.

Her eyes lifted to my window, and her face burst into a hesitant smile when she saw I was watching. She kept singing and playing, staring up at me as words fell from her lips and music was born from her fingertips—and it hit me that she was doing this for *me*. She wanted *me* for Christmas.

I couldn't wait a second longer. I dashed out of my apartment, not even bothering to shut the door behind me, and ran down the stairs and out the front of the building.

By the time I reached her, she was near the end of the song, and people had stopped to gather nearby on the sidewalk, while others watched from their windows or balconies. She didn't seem to care one bit, and I loved her confidence. She inspired me to be confident, too.

I walked right up to Becca, took her face in my hands, and kissed the song right off her lips. Her hands slipped off the bass and slid into my hair, and she gave a soft moan as we clung to each other. The guitar was in the way and people around us clapped and whistled, but I barely noticed because Becca was in my arms and in my mouth and in my life and I never wanted to let her go.

"You have me," I said. "I'm yours, for Christmas and New Year's and Valentine's Day and… Crap, what holiday comes after that?"

She laughed, pulling the bass off her shoulder and returning to my arms. "You didn't let me finish the song."

I rested my forehead against hers. "I'm sorry. I couldn't wait any longer to kiss you, but you were amazing. You're really good, and your voice…it's incredible."

"Eh, I'm not *that* good."

"No, you are. I've never heard you play before today, but I can tell. You were definitely meant to do this."

"Okay, you're right," she said with a sly grin. "I am pretty damn good."

I rubbed my thumb across her lips, staring into her dark eyes. "I didn't think you wanted anything to do with me after last night."

"I just needed some time to cool off and to think about what you said." She traced a finger along the side of my glasses and down my rough, unshaven jaw. "I called Villain Complex. I'm going to do the New Year's Eve show."

"You are?"

She nodded. "You were right. The second I picked up my bass guitar again I knew I had to say yes. I won't be happy doing anything else with my life, and I can't give up on that dream so easily. I have to try again, at least once more. I'm driving to Austin tomorrow to start practicing with them for the next few days. And once the show is over, I'm going to find another band. Or who knows? Maybe I'll start my own."

I was so damn proud of her for coming to this decision and pleased that I'd helped in some way. I wanted Becca to be happy, and it was obvious music was the key. "That's a great idea. But what are you going to do about college?"

"I told my parents to give the money to my sister instead. She wants to be a librarian."

My mouth fell open, and I struggled for words. "Are you sure that's what you want?"

"She needs the money more than I do, and she'll put it to better use. I know in my gut that this is right. College isn't for me. I gave it a shot, but we weren't a good fit. But Trish? She'll love it."

"I imagine she will. That's really nice of you to do that for her."

"It's all because of you. You pushed me to ask myself what I wanted and to believe that maybe I deserved a second chance. That we *both* do."

She gripped the front of my shirt and pulled me in for another kiss. The first hint of snow began to softly fall on us, even though the sun was still peeking out overhead, but neither of us seemed to care. We were too wrapped up in each other.

But as the wind kicked up and the snow came down faster, I realized neither one of us had a jacket on. I rubbed her bare arms with my hands. "What are you doing out here in the snow with no coat on? You must be freezing."

She shrugged. "I was trying to be romantic or some shit."

"By freezing to death?"

"Hey, I've never done anything like this before. Besides, I have a pretty good idea how you can get me warmed up," she said as she ran her hand down my chest. Her eye caught on the logo on my shirt, and she cocked her head to the side. "You're not wearing a coat either, just a really geeky polo shirt. Is that the Imperial logo from *Star Wars*?"

"I'm so impressed you recognized that," I said, taking her hand and kissing her cold fingers. "Let's go inside and get you warmed up."

I led her up the stairs and into my apartment, much like I'd done last night. As soon as we were inside, she set her bass down and I drew her into my arms, giving her a long, deep kiss—but I pulled away before it could go further. I didn't want a repeat of last night's quick fuck in the dark, not today. And before we could have a future together, I wanted to prove to her that I had moved on, too.

"Wait here," I said. "I need to show you something."

I went into the bedroom while she studied my wall-to-wall bookshelf, which was crammed with so many books I was surprised it didn't topple over. Much like her sister's, actually.

When I returned, she saw the ring box in my hands and her eyes widened. "Andrew, I..."

"I'm not going to propose or anything, don't worry," I said quickly. "But for months, I couldn't even think about this ring without falling apart. Last night, when you asked me if I was over Tara, I didn't have an answer for you. I didn't want to lie to you, but I had to prove to myself that I was truly over her." I opened the box, and the diamond ring inside flashed under the fading sunlight. "I made myself look at the ring, and that's when I knew I had moved on—because instead of thinking about how it should have been Tara wearing it, I was able to imagine myself giving it to someone else eventually. Not now. Not anytime soon. But... someday." I closed the ring box and shoved it in my pocket. "What I'm trying to say is, I'm over her. And I want the possibility of more. With you."

The most beautiful smile lit up her face. "You do?"

I moved closer and took her hands in mine. "I still want to take things slow and see what happens, but I'm not going to pretend I can keep things casual with you. I want to take you on more dates, to fancy restaurants and movie theaters and little hole-in-the-wall places no one knows about. I want to take you back to my place at the end of each date and make love to you for hours. I want to be the guy you exchange presents with and take home to meet your parents."

She wrapped her arms around my neck. "Technically, I already took you home to meet my parents. Pretty sure you passed that test."

"Yeah, but this time I want them to call me by my real name." I slid a hand to the back of her head, my fingers weaving into her short hair. "What do you say, Becca? Will you give me one more date?"

"No," she said. "I'll give you as many as you want."

When we kissed, my heart seemed to grow a thousand times bigger. She was giving me another chance, giving *us* another chance. "In that case, how about we order some food—your choice this time—and have our second date right now?"

"That depends," she said, cocking her head to the side. Her hands roamed down my chest and to my jeans, tugging the button open. "Can we start with the making-love-for-hours part first?"

"Yes, although I have to warn you, you're going to be *very* hungry when I'm done with you." I brushed my lips across her earlobe as I spoke. "I'm going to go slow, worshipping every part of your body, making you come a dozen times, until there's no doubt that I'm yours and you're mine."

She shivered a little at my words. "We should get started on that right away then. But I have one request."

"Anything you want."

"Keep these on." She touched the edge of my glasses. "And be Andy with me tonight."

My breath hitched. "Are you sure?"

"I am. I want you to be the good guy sometimes." She smoothed her hand down my cheek, across the stubble on my jaw. "I love it when you're bad, too. Hard and rough, sweet and slow, I love it all from you. But the first time I wanted you, you were the nice guy I met in that club, who wore geeky polo shirts and turned out to have a secret dark side, and that's who I want again now."

That was it. I was a total goner. If she wanted me, I was hers. Completely.

"You've got him." I picked her up, wrapping her legs around my hips, and when I kissed her, I could taste the excitement on her lips. I walked us into the bedroom and set her on the edge of the queen-sized bed so I could remove her clothing slowly.

She looked up at me with eager eyes as I undressed her and pressed a kiss to every inch of skin I uncovered. First, her combat boots, with a kiss to her cute little toes with black nail polish on them. Then I worked my way along her legs, using my mouth on her ankles, her knees, the insides of her thigh. She relaxed with each touch, tangling her fingers in my hair.

Our eyes locked as I moved up her body, sliding the dress higher and higher, replacing the fabric with my mouth on her bare skin. The curve of her hips, the slope of her stomach, the tattoo on her ribs: I made it all mine.

The dress hit the floor, and I trailed light kisses across her shoulder and neck. She tilted her head to the side, and her eyes fluttered shut as I nipped at the soft skin below her ear, then tugged on the lobe with my teeth.

I reached behind her to unhook her bra and then worked my way down her arms, kissing her elbows and wrists, dragging the bra off them as I went. When her beautiful breasts were freed, hovering in front of me, I moved in for a taste. Her nipples were already taut, but they hardened even more as my tongue slid around them. First one breast, then the other, giving them both equal amounts of attention. No pinching, no teeth, not this time. Just long, slow licks, over and over, until she was writhing and moaning against me.

Once again, she wore nothing except a little black thong that looked very familiar. I hooked a finger under the elastic and raised my eyebrows. "Is this the one?"

She nodded, tugging at her bottom lip with her teeth. "You remember."

"I remember everything about that night. You were the first girl—no, you are the *only* girl—I've ever been completely myself with." I slid the thong down her legs and off them, trailing after the fabric with my mouth. She let out a beautiful sigh, and I eased her onto her back. "Becca, you set me free."

I replaced the thong with my mouth, licking at her wet warmth, tasting her sweet skin. I ate her out slowly, like we had all the time in the world, until she begged me to go faster, until she tore at my hair and tightened her thighs around my head and screamed my name.

One orgasm down. Many more to go.

She gripped my shirt and pulled me toward her, so my fully clothed body covered her naked one. Her fingers found my jaw, tracing the stubble there, wet with the taste of her.

"I need you," she whispered, her lips finding mine, her legs wrapping around me. "Inside me." As the kiss grew deeper, her fingers clutched my face, her eyes pleading. "Hurry, please."

"I still owe you many more orgasms," I said as my hand slipped between us to stroke her down there. "We don't need to rush."

She whimpered at my touch, her back arching, and I loved seeing how easily I made her come undone. As I rubbed her in slow, lazy circles, she pushed my shirt up my stomach and slid her hands under it, her palms against my chest, fingers digging into my skin. She was panting now, making soft little cries against my lips as we kissed, and I slipped a finger inside her warm depths.

"I love touching you," I said as I slowly moved my finger in and out. "So warm and wet."

"You do that to me," she said, and now she'd found the front of my jeans and unzipped them, sliding her fingers inside. "You always have."

Her hand wrapped around me and I groaned into her mouth, and that's when she came a second time, like my pleasure set her off. I felt it the second it hit her, the way her body clenched up, the way her fingers tightened around me, the way she bit at my lips and moaned my name. I watched her face the entire time, so beautiful in its surrender.

When she returned to me, she pushed at the top of my jeans, nudging them down my hips. "I want the next one with you."

We sat up and she removed my clothes, and now it was her turn to kiss me all over, until I was so desperate with need for her I thought I'd lose my mind. I gently pushed her back on the bed and covered her body with mine, and we fit together skin to skin, perfectly made for each other. Not opposites at all, but a complete, matching pair.

We didn't bother with the condoms. She'd said she was on the pill, and we'd had no one else since our first night together, all those months ago. I trusted her.

I entered her slowly, so that we both felt every inch as our bodies connected. Her red lips parted as I sank deep inside, our eyes locked the entire time, and she looked at me with an expression that was both intense and adoring.

Before, I'd been rough with her, desperate to forget everything else in the world. Our sex had been frenzied and frantic, hungry and wild, like we were using each other to lose ourselves. Together, we'd freed ourselves from our inhibitions and found ourselves in the process.

But now, being gentle, taking my time to savor every moment, it brought about a new kind of intimacy between us, one that was almost devastating in its intensity. This was what I'd been missing all these years and what I'd failed to find with any other girl, no matter how hard I tried.

We came together, and it felt like it lasted forever. I kissed her the entire time, her hands clutching my face, her quiet moans vibrating deep in my chest. As she tightened around me, I released myself inside her one with long, shuddering groan, and we both gave ourselves up to each other completely.

I took her into my arms, breathing in her scent, basking in her warmth and her taste and the way she made me feel. Sex with Tara had always been good, really good. But with Becca... I lost my mind with her. I lost *myself*. But in doing so, I found myself, too.

And that's when it hit me: I could fall in love with this girl.

Not could. Was.

I *was* falling. Hard. Even though I barely knew her.

But that wasn't true. I knew Becca inside and out and not just on a physical level. Maybe I didn't know all the details of her life yet, but I knew *her*. And she knew me, too, down to my very soul.

I'd sworn to myself I would never fall that hard a second time, not for Becca or anyone else. Tara had destroyed me, and I'd convinced myself that I'd never love someone again, not like that.

But Becca made me want to try.

TWENTY-ONE

Becca

I stared at the black door, but couldn't muster the courage to open it. *You can do this,* I told myself. *They invited you here. You, not anyone else.*

But I couldn't quiet the other voice in my head, the one that told me I was a complete fuck-up, that I would never be good enough, that I was doomed to repeat all of the same mistakes over and over.

That voice told me I should turn around, get back in my car, and drive home. I clutched my guitar case tighter, unwilling to run away, yet unable to take that last step.

"Is it locked?" a smooth voice said behind me.

Jared.

I turned around slowly, bracing myself for the impact of seeing him again. I remembered when that voice could turn me into a puddle at his feet with just one word. When a glimpse of his handsome face and piercing blue eyes would make my panties instantly wet. When one touch from those talented fingers made my entire body nearly sick with desire.

Now? I stood in front of him and didn't feel a damn thing.

Jared almost always wore a villain shirt when he wasn't on stage, and today's had Jack Nicholson's face from *The Shining* in black and white. With his tattooed arms, low black jeans, permanent five o'clock shadow, and dark, spiked hair, he looked as sexy as ever. But geeky guys with glasses were more my type now.

Okay, maybe just *one* geeky guy.

I ignored his question and asked, "How's the hand?"

"It sucks," he said, holding up his arm so I could see the cast. His words were casual, but I knew Jared well enough to know there was real pain behind them. And fear.

"I bet. But I know you're going to recover quickly."

"Hope so." He glanced over at the door, then back at me. "Hey, thanks for helping us out with the show. I know things have been…messy between us in the past. But I'm really glad you're here."

"Me too," I said and was surprised it was the truth. "Though I still don't know why you wanted me. You could have found someone else."

"You're a damn good bassist. The best we ever had."

I rolled my eyes. "True, but we both know that's not why."

He frowned and ducked his head, running a hand through his dark hair. "Okay, you got me there. The real reason is I felt bad about what happened between us and I wanted to try and make it right."

I snorted. "You? Felt bad? I don't believe it."

"Believe it or not, it's true. Losing you was a huge loss to the band, and it was completely my fault. I fucked things up between us, and I take all the blame for what went down. I was an asshole and I'm really sorry."

Wow, Jared really had changed. Gone was the cocky, arrogant player who did what he wanted and damn the consequences. Now he was actually *apologizing*? Maybe I needed to give Maddie a little more credit for taming that bad boy.

"It wasn't *all* your fault," I said, lowering my arms with a sigh. "In fact, most of it was my fault. I got us drunk and dragged you into bed. Then I got pissed when it made everything awkward. And I'm the one who quit the band in the end. But I've changed since then, and it seems like maybe you have, too."

"Do you think we can move forward and forget all the stupid shit we did in the past? A second chance for both of us—and for the entire band. What do you say?" He held out his hand, the one not in a cast.

"I say…" I took a deep breath and took his hand, shaking it. "I say yes. I'm excited to join you guys again for one show. But I'm warning you, I might be a bit rusty."

"That's why we're here in Austin a few days early. Though no one warned me it would be this fucking cold," he said with a grin, gazing at the cloudy sky that threatened rain at any second.

"It's unusually cold this year in Texas. But hey, you're not in California anymore. You can't walk around in T-shirts and flip-flops all the time."

He pressed a hand to his heart. "Becca, you wound me. When have you *ever* seen me wear flip-flops?"

I looked down at our feet, at our nearly matching black combat boots. "Good point. We'd both sooner be caught dead than wear anything other than our boots."

"Damn straight."

Our eyes lingered on each other for a minute, both of us smiling. We hadn't worked out as lovers—maybe because we were too similar or something—but there was an understanding between us. If we kept this up, Jared and I might be in danger of becoming friends.

He rubbed his arms. "Come on, let's head in before I freeze my ass off." He opened the door and gestured for me to go in first. "The rest of the band is already in the studio."

I took a deep breath, clutched my guitar case tighter, and walked through the door. That voice in my head that told me I wasn't good enough was still loud, but drowned out by the excitement I felt as Jared led me into the studio they'd rented for the next few days.

Inside, Maddie was laughing at something, while Kyle grinned and Hector shook his head. Their instruments were already set up around the room, but they lounged in chairs on one side, sipping coffee while they waited.

For a second I just took them in. Maddie, with her black-rimmed glasses, long brown hair, plaid shirt, and friendly smile. Kyle, covered in tattoos and piercings, wearing an old Sex Pistols T-shirt, with the same blue eyes as his brother. And Hector—big, dark, muscular Hector, wearing his signature Villain Complex baseball cap and twirling a drumstick in the air.

Damn, it was good to see them again.

They all jumped up when they saw us walk in. They stared at me for the longest moment ever, and my heart seized up, worried they didn't want me here after all or that it was going to be uncomfortable.

Then Kyle rushed over and gave me a hug. It took me by surprise at first, although it shouldn't have, since he'd always been a hugger. "It's been way too long, Becca. Thank you so much for coming."

Hector slapped me on the back, maybe a little harder than was necessary, but hey, at least he was enthusiastic. "I knew you'd change your mind."

Maddie was last, and to my surprise, she gave me a quick hug, too. I always figured she must hate me after everything I'd done or would feel weird about the fact that I'd slept with Jared before she met him, but from her warm smile that didn't seem to be the case. "I'm really glad you're here," she said, and it sounded like she actually meant it.

I felt myself tearing up a little, which was not okay. That totally did not go with my bad-girl image. I blinked quickly, hoping they wouldn't notice the myriad of emotions flowing through me. "Thanks, guys. And thanks for giving me a second chance. After all the shit I pulled, I never expected one, but I'm grateful for it."

"Becca, everyone deserves a second chance," Kyle said.

"Not to mention, you're a much better bassist than this guy," Hector said, nodding at Jared.

"Hey now," Jared said, but he was grinning.

"I've seen you play," I said. "You're not bad. But Hector's right, I'm better."

"Maybe you can teach Jared a few tricks," Maddie said.

"You mean, assuming I can ever play again?" he said, his mouth twisting.

"You will," she said. "I have no doubt."

Jared put his arm around her and kissed her forehead, and I could see that the two of them were perfect for each other. This time, I *really* wasn't jealous. I was just happy for them. Like me and Andrew, the two of them seemed to balance each other out. Maybe opposites really did attract.

It had been only hours since I'd last seen Andrew, after I'd reluctantly left his bed this morning so he could get to work and I could get ready for my trip to Austin, but I already missed him.

Last night something had changed between us. He'd kept his promise and had made love to me for hours, making me come more times than I could count, although we'd taken a short break to order Chinese food and recover our energy sometime in the middle. And somewhere along the way, I realized I cared more about him than I'd ever imagined possible when I'd picked him up that night in San Diego.

"All right," Jared said, bringing me back to the present. "We have a lot of work to do before the concert, and only four days to do it."

"In other words, our fearless leader says we need to get off our asses and start practicing already," Kyle said.

The others groaned and moved to grab their instruments, but they were all grinning, too. Hector was in the back on drums, while Kyle stood off to the side on keyboard. I pulled out my bass guitar and took my place among them, opposite Maddie and her guitar, with Jared in the middle on the mic.

Jared handed me a folder. "We've already prepared bass tabs for all the new songs we'll be performing, and included the old ones too in case you need a refresher."

"I don't." All I'd had to do was listen to their old album, the one I'd performed with them dozens of times, and it had come back to me immediately. I'd spent the entire car drive from Dallas to Austin with the songs on repeat, and now the basslines were still humming in the back of my head. But they had a new album that had just come out this month, and that's what I would be focusing on learning over the next few days. Including that song that was on the radio all the damn time.

"We're also doing a special cover song just for the concert," Kyle said. "'New Year's Day' by U2."

"Nice choice," I said as I flipped through the tabs. "It's going to be rough to learn all this before the show, but I can do it."

"We know you can," Jared said.

Hector nodded. "That's why we wanted you."

As we started to play, I could tell that they all worked together like a well-oiled machine now. There was a strong feeling of camaraderie in the air, like this wasn't just a band, but a family. A wave of longing hit me, knowing I wasn't a part of that. Sure, I was one of them for the next few days, but after that we'd all go our separate ways again. It was for the best, but I found myself wishing, just a tiny bit, that I could be in the band again—for good.

TWENTY-TWO

Andrew

"How did it go?" I asked as I kicked off my shoes and loosened my tie. After a long day at work filled with meetings and petty office politics, all I wanted was to plop down on my couch and talk to Becca for hours.

"It was…surprisingly good," Becca said over the phone. "We rehearsed all day, and now my hands hurt since I haven't played that much in months, but it felt…right."

"That's great. You made the right decision by doing the show."

"All thanks to you. I couldn't have done any of this if you hadn't believed in me and pushed me to give myself another chance. But…"

"What is it?"

She sighed. "It's stupid, but I'm going to be sad when the show is over and the band returns to LA."

"You could go with them. Back to LA."

"I doubt they would like that."

"You never know. If Jared's hand doesn't get better…"

"Don't say that! It's too awful to consider. But even if it didn't get better, I wouldn't move back to LA. My family is in Dallas. And so are you."

I leaned against the granite countertops in my kitchen, gazing across my apartment. It was a good space and I'd tried to make it home, but in the end it was mostly a bachelor pad filled with Ikea furniture and a whole lot of books. There wasn't much else—basically whatever I'd had in college and brought with me when I'd moved here for work. It was a temporary home, at best.

"What if I moved with you?" I asked.

I heard a sharp intake of breath over the phone. "Andrew, you can't be serious."

"There's nothing holding me here except my job…and you."

"I thought we were going slow. We've only been together a few days. Now you want to move to a new city with me? What's next? Marriage and a house and two kids?"

"No, god no. Of course not," I said quickly. Although if I was honest, the idea didn't sound as terrifying as I expected it would. "But I don't want to lose you again."

She was silent for a moment, and I gripped the phone tightly, worried I'd scared her off. Shit, there I went giving her mixed signals again. I didn't know what was wrong with me. Yes, I wanted to take it slow, to give ourselves time to ease into this relationship, but I also had a feeling Becca was it for me. Now that I'd found her again and proved to myself I was over Tara, I wasn't going to let her go.

"Well, I'm not moving, so it doesn't matter anyway," she said.

"Okay." I cleared my throat. "How was it seeing Jared again?"

"A little awkward at first, but not too bad. I didn't feel anything for him, so you don't need to worry about anything there."

"I wasn't worried."

"No?"

"Well, maybe a little," I admitted. "Exes always bring back some old feelings, one way or another. You saw how messed up I was after just texting with Tara."

"Oh, that reminds me. I asked Hector, and he said Tara won't be at the show. So you don't need to worry."

"Thank you." My throat tightened up, and it was hard to get the words out. I'd never mentioned to Becca that I was nervous about seeing Tara, but she must have known it was on my mind. It wouldn't have stopped me from attending the show, but now I could go to Becca's concert and enjoy myself without any anxiety. I wasn't sure how to tell Becca how much I appreciated that she was looking out for me like that, so all I said was, "I miss you."

"You just saw me last night," she said, but I could hear the smile in her voice.

"I know. Way too long. Not sure how I'll make it till the show."

"I miss you, too. Hey, let me call you back in a minute."

"Sure." I hung up the phone and crashed on my couch, trying to figure out how to spend my evening. Normally I'd be grabbing the remote and clicking through whatever my DVR had recorded. Now it seemed silly to watch anything unless I could do it with Becca at my side so I could talk to her about it. How odd that in only a few days she'd so completely turned my life around.

My phone buzzed with a text. I reached over and grabbed it, then sucked in a breath when I saw what she'd sent: a picture of herself in nothing but a red lace bra and matching panties, the same color as her lipstick. Her arms were over her head with her fingers in her blonde hair, and her dark eyes stared at the camera with a sensual, confident look.

"Are you trying to torture me?" I asked when she called me back.

She laughed softly. "Just wanted to give you something to think about until I saw you again."

"I've already spent my entire day thinking about you. Now I'm not going to be able to sleep until you're in my bed again."

"Perfect. Now it's your turn."

"Uh. What do you want, a dick pic? Trust me, it's nice and hard right now, thanks to you, but I'm not sure I will *ever* be the kind of guy who sends a woman a picture of my junk."

She laughed again. "No. Well, maybe… But what I really want is a picture of you the way you normally look. In your glasses. In your suit and tie. Or wearing one of your geeky shirts."

"That's what does it for you, eh?"

"Mmhmm. The nerdier, the better."

"I *did* just get a new polo shirt with a Companion Cube on it for the logo."

"I have no idea what that is."

"It's from the video game *Portal*."

"God, you're so hot. Keep talking nerdy to me."

"Only if you touch yourself at the same time."

"Oh, I already am."

I swallowed hard at the thought of her hand sliding into those red panties to rub herself. *Portal* wasn't a sexy game by any stretch, but if hearing me talk about this stuff turned her on, I'd do my best. "In the game, you run around with a gun."

"A big gun?" she asked, her voice sultry.

I opened up my slacks and took myself in hand, stroking up and down, imagining it was her fingers instead of mine. "Very big."

"What do you do with it?"

"You use it to open dark, round holes…and then you enter them. In and out. Over and over."

She moaned a little. "Oh, god, Andrew. I want you so bad."

"I know, Becca. I want you, too. Only a few more days and then I'll be inside you again."

"What will you do to me?" she asked in a breathless voice. I fisted myself tighter, jerking off faster as I imagined all the things she was doing to herself on the other side of the phone, wearing nothing but that tiny bit of red lace.

"As soon as you finish your show, I'm taking you somewhere where we can be alone, and then I'm going to fuck you. Hard and fast the first time 'cause we'll be so desperate for each other we won't be able to wait. And then again, nice and slow, until you come so many times you won't be able to walk straight the next day."

She whimpered a little at that. "I'm so close, just keep talking. I need your voice, please…"

"I'm close, too. Just thinking about you touching yourself gets me all worked up. I had to start stroking myself. Imagining your hands on me. Or your mouth. God, I love your sexy lips, especially in that lipstick you wear. Every time I look at your lips, I want to slide between them."

"Andrew," she cried, and I could tell she was coming from the sound of her voice. I recognized it well now—it always got more high-pitched when the orgasm took her. I pictured her coming undone at the sound of my voice and imagined the expression on her face I'd seen before when she came, her lips parted, her eyes closed, her back arching. It was too much, with her voice in my ear making those sweet sounds, and I pumped myself once, twice, and then I was exploding too, groaning her name into the phone.

When I came back down to reality, I heard her soft pants through the phone. Or maybe they were mine. "You still owe me a picture," she said and then hung up.

I chuckled, but then I stood up and cleaned myself off. I was wearing my contacts; I always did at the office. But now I went into the bathroom and removed them, then switched into my glasses. If she thought they were hot, I'd wear them all the damn time.

I changed shirts, putting on the *Portal* one, and left my slacks unbuttoned and hanging open, not enough to show anything, but enough to tease her. Then, feeling like a total idiot, I took a dozen bathroom mirror selfies until I deemed one of them decent and sent it to her. It was nowhere near as sexy as her photo, but she'd said she wanted one of me looking geeky, after all.

The phone rang a second later.

"I love it," she said with a dreamy sigh. "New Year's Eve can't come fast enough."

I couldn't agree more.

TWENTY-THREE

Becca

I faced myself in the dusty mirror, and it was like looking into the past: black-rimmed eyes, lashes heavy with mascara, bright red lips, and silver piercings running up and down my ears. The only thing that was different was my hair—I'd left it natural. No crazy dyes today. Not for one show only.

Shit, what was I doing?

Outside the bathroom door, Villain Complex and the other bands performing tonight were checking their instruments and getting ready to go on stage. The second I'd arrived backstage, the walls and the crowd and the music had all seemed to close in around me, and I'd felt like I was going to throw up. I'd made an excuse, rushed into this bathroom, and hadn't come out since.

The concert was a special New Year's Eve bash featuring previous bands from *The Sound,* the reality TV show Villain Complex had competed on. As the runner-up, they were performing second-to-last tonight—which gave me plenty of time to freak out.

Anxiety wrapped itself around my throat and choked me hard. A thousand worries ran through my head at a mile a minute. Other than the rushed practices over the last few days, I hadn't played bass in months. What if I messed up? What if I forgot the songs or where to stand or the lyrics I was supposed to sing?

I had no business walking out on that stage with the rest of the band. And not just any stage, but a bigger stage than I'd ever played before. The audience was already filling up the stadium, and soon there would be thousands of people watching Villain Complex and the other bands tonight. Thousands of people who could see me screw up, making a fool of myself and embarrassing the rest of the band. And as soon as I made a mistake, I'd only be proving to everyone that I wasn't cut out for this life. That I was a complete failure and a total loser who should never get on a stage again.

Even if I pulled it off—even if, by some miracle, the show went perfectly and I managed not to do anything stupid—the band would go back to LA tomorrow and I'd return to Dallas. In a few hours, this would all be over. No matter how much I wanted to stay with the band, it wasn't going to happen.

My phone buzzed—a message from Andrew saying he had arrived at the stadium. Thank god. I'd gotten him a backstage VIP pass, and the thought of seeing him again was the only thing that gave me the courage to leave the bathroom.

I reapplied my lipstick, smoothed my hair down, and checked my outfit—ripped-up fishnet tights, a short, silver dress trimmed with black leather, and of course, my combat boots—and walked out the door in search of Andrew.

"Becca!" Kyle called out.

I stopped in my tracks and turned toward him, my stomach twisting with anxiety. He stood with Maddie, Jared, and Hector while a couple of roadies and sound people tuned their instruments and got them ready. How far they'd come since the days I was in the band, when we had to do all of that ourselves, usually before we played in some tiny parking lot, at a seedy club, or for a drunken frat party. Now they had other people to do all the grunt work, and they were playing sold-out giant arenas with thousands of fans. They'd changed so much since I'd first met them and they'd left me in the dust.

"You okay?" Jared asked. "We haven't seen you in a while."

"We were a little worried you'd ditched us again," Kyle said with a grin. He was teasing, but his words held some truth. I'd abandoned them during the Battle of the Bands almost a year ago, and I couldn't deny I was tempted to do it again tonight.

"I'm fine," I said, brushing off his comment. I wasn't fine, not really, but I would be as soon as I saw Andrew. He'd make everything okay. I just needed a few minutes in his arms to remind myself of who I was and who I could be.

"It's okay if you're nervous," Maddie said. "I always get nervous before shows."

I found myself messing with my hair and made myself stop. "It's just…a lot bigger than I expected."

"That's what she said," Kyle muttered. Maddie elbowed him, while Jared and Hector snickered.

"I know what you mean," Maddie said to me. "But you look great. I love your dress."

"Thanks. I like yours, too."

Like me, Maddie had dressed up for the New Year's Eve theme of the night and wore a sparkling gold dress that shimmered whenever she moved. Kyle and Hector were wearing their usual all-black jeans and T-shirts, but Jared was wearing a dark silver collared shirt, unbuttoned at the neck to give the audience a peek, with his black leather jacket over it.

"Don't be nervous," Kyle said, patting my arm. "You're going to kick ass out there."

"We go on in twenty minutes," Jared said.

I thought I might start hyperventilating and looked around for somewhere to escape to. "I just have to say hi to Andrew quickly."

"He's here?" Hector asked, his dark eyes scanning the crowd.

"In the VIP room." I started forward and called over my shoulder. "I'll be back in a few."

The chaos sucked me up, so I had no idea if any of them responded or not. It didn't matter. I had to find Andrew before I had a full-out panic attack.

TWENTY-FOUR

Andrew

I'd first started listening to Villain Complex over a year ago thanks to Tara, who got all their songs from Hector long before they became famous. I'd always liked their music, but after the break-up, I'd avoided listening to them because it brought back too many bad feelings. It wasn't easy since their new album had just come out and was all over the place, but now that Becca had joined them—at least temporarily—maybe I'd be able to listen to their music again without wanting to set something on fire.

Traffic from Dallas to Austin was a disaster, and I got to the stadium much later than I'd originally intended. By the time I walked in, the first bands had already performed, but there were still a few minutes before Villain Complex would go on stage. Plenty of time to give Becca a kiss and wish her luck. Or maybe should I say break a leg? Was that only for actors?

I'd spoken with Becca every night since she'd gone to Austin to start practicing with the band, and I couldn't wait to see her again. It had only been a few days, but I'd stared at that sexy photo she'd sent me a hundred times already, and now I was dying to see the real thing. To touch the real thing.

Backstage was crowded, with hundreds of people with tattoos and piercings and black T-shirts rushing around, getting the equipment ready, and doing other things I couldn't even guess at. A security guard directed me to wear my badge at all times, then gestured for me to enter a VIP room set up with a bar, seating areas, and a door to an outside patio. The room was high up in the arena and overlooked the stage, which was currently empty as they set up for the next band to go on.

I texted Becca to let her know where I was and then ordered a beer while I waited for her to come find me. The room was packed, with some people standing around and checking their phones, others doing shots and passing around brightly colored pills, and a few couples making out in the corners.

I stood to the side with my beer and scanned the place, hoping to see Becca.

When I spotted a flash of golden hair enter the room, my heart sped up. There she was.

I moved forward through the mob of people, anxious to wrap Becca in my arms and kiss her senseless. But as the crowd parted, I realized it wasn't Becca walking toward me, with a nervous smile on her face.

It was Tara.

Before I could process what was happening, my ex-girlfriend rushed forward and gave me a warm hug. I stood frozen with her arms around me as my brain went into some kind of crazy loop, repeating "what the fuck" over and over in my head.

Becca had said Tara wouldn't be at the show tonight. What the hell was she doing here? Why was she hugging me? Shit, what was I going to do?

This wasn't supposed to happen. Not like this. I'd known, on some level, that if Becca got involved with the band I might run into Tara, since she was dating Hector and all. But I hadn't mentally prepared myself to see her again, not yet, and now I had no clue how to react or what to say or how to feel.

The next band started playing on stage, and loud music burst into the VIP room. It jolted me out of my zombie state, and I managed to jerk back from Tara. She said something to me, but I couldn't hear her.

"Let's go outside!" I shouted, and she nodded. I took her elbow to lead her through the crowd, to the outdoor area I'd glimpsed earlier. I didn't really want to talk to her and had no idea what I'd even say, but I needed closure if I was going to move on with Becca—for good.

TWENTY-FIVE

Becca

I slipped inside the VIP lounge and searched for Andrew—but when I saw him, he wasn't alone. He was with a blonde girl. And they were hugging.

I stared at them for an endless moment, waiting for him to notice me, to push the girl away, to run off or yell at her, to do *something*, anything. But as they pulled apart, they exchanged a few words, and then they walked away together, out the door to the patio.

I recognized her from the night of the party at Comic-Con. The girl who had been making out with Hector, who Andy had just proposed to, and who he'd spent the last months trying to forget. But why was Tara here tonight? Hector had said she wasn't coming—she was living in LA now and wasn't flying out here for the one show. I'd promised Andrew she wouldn't be here.

Not that he seemed that upset to see her, judging by the hug and the way they'd walked off together. Oh, god, maybe he wasn't over her after all. Maybe seeing her again had dragged up all those lingering emotions he'd tried so hard to repress or ignore. I remembered his words on the phone the other night: *"Exes always bring back some old feelings, in one way or another. You saw how messed up I was after just texting with Tara."*

He'd sworn to me he was over her, even showed me the ring to prove it, but I should have known better. He obviously still had feelings for her. That was clear after the night she'd texted him. And now that they were together in person... I couldn't even think about it.

Shit, shit, shit. I couldn't handle this, not now, not on top of all the panic I'd already been feeling about going on stage. I needed a drink or I would lose my fucking mind and have a meltdown right here in the middle of the VIP lounge.

I rushed to the bar and ordered a shot of whiskey, then tossed it back without hesitation.

And then another.

But when I reached for the third, I hesitated. My fingers slid around the shot, my palm sweaty, the glass cold, the alcohol strong. But I resisted the urge to drink it, no matter how much I wanted to.

Almost all of my screw-ups in the past had started with me getting drunk and making bad decisions, which I'd later regretted. I couldn't go down that path again, even if it felt like the only way to block out the pain. Drinking was easy; it was dealing with life that was difficult. But if there was one thing that was becoming clear to me tonight, it was that the past should remain in the past.

I had to move on for good.

And I had to get the hell out of this place before I made another huge mistake.

Andrew

The music died to a low throb as soon as the door shut behind us. We moved to the far end of the patio, away from the smokers, and for a long moment I just stared at Tara, speechless and overwhelmed by seeing her for the first time in five months. She looked almost exactly the same—long, straight golden hair and bright blue eyes, wearing a T-shirt for *Misfit Squad*, the graphic novel she and Hector created together. But there was something that was different, something under the skin maybe, like she practically glowed with happiness.

"Andy, it's so good to see you again," Tara said, gazing up at me.

I was tempted to correct her and tell her I went by Andrew now, but I let it go. To her, I would probably always be Andy, and that was okay. "What are you doing here?"

"I decided to surprise Hector and fly out for the show. I had no idea you'd be here, too!" She studied me closely, eyeing me up and down with a smile. "You're wearing your glasses."

I touched them self-consciously out of habit and then lowered my hand. "Becca likes them."

Her smile got even wider. "So the two of you *are* together."

"It's a new thing, but…yes. We are." It felt good to admit it out loud. And okay, maybe I also wanted to show Tara that I had moved on myself.

"Hector was right. He always said the two of you would be perfect together." She reached out and lightly touched my forearm. "I'm really happy for you."

"Thanks." I rubbed the back of my neck. "And you and Hector…?"

"We're good. Really good."

"What about your new job?"

"It's amazing. I'm so glad I moved to LA. How about you? How do you like Dallas?"

"I like it," I said, shoving my hands in my pockets. "I'm not sure how long I'll stay there, though. It kinda depends on Becca."

She nodded slowly, like she was taking it all in. By some miracle, it wasn't as hard to be in Tara's presence as I'd expected it to be. Uncomfortable, yes. Awkward, yes. But soul-crushingly painful? Not even close.

"Andy, I'm sorry about everything that happened between us. And I just want you to know that nothing went on between me and Hector until after you and I had broken up. We got together at Comic-Con, and I had no idea you were going to…" She let the words trail off and looked away, but we both knew what she was going to say.

"I know." I took a deep breath, and when I exhaled, I let go of the past. All that lingering resentment, doubt, sadness, and anger—gone. For good this time. "It's okay. You were right to turn down my proposal."

"It broke my heart to do it. You were my first love, Andy. But things with Hector are just…different."

"I know what you mean." Until this week I never would have understood that comment, but she was right—what I felt for Becca was completely different and much stronger. She made me complete in a way I'd never been with anyone else, in a way that made me wonder how I'd lived the previous twenty-three years without her. I'd been searching my entire life for Becca without even knowing it.

"Do you think you and I could ever be friends? For real this time?" Tara asked. "I miss you so much. You were my best friend, other than Hector."

At first, my knee-jerk reaction was "hell no." But seeing Tara in person had solidified it for me: I was truly, one hundred percent over her—and I'd missed her friendship, too. Not to mention, if Becca did end up moving to LA and hanging out with the band, I'd probably see a lot more of Tara and Hector.

"I'd like that," I said, and this time I was the one who initiated the hug.

A part of me would always love Tara. She'd showed me it was possible to dream of a future with someone and taught me how to be a better boyfriend and lover. But even though we'd had a great relationship, I'd always hidden a piece of myself with her.

With Becca, I was one hundred percent myself. From the moment we'd met, I'd never had any trouble opening up to her without fear of judgement or ridicule. After just a few days, we knew each other better than Tara and I had after dating for an entire year. Not only that, Becca made me want to be a better version of myself. Not Andy or Andrew, but the best parts of both of them.

I hadn't fallen in love with Tara so much as eased into it. We were together for a long time and we cared about each other a lot, so I'd assumed it was true love. But with Becca I had fallen hard and fast, like someone had shoved me off a rooftop. That's how I knew for sure she wasn't a rebound and never had been. She was so much more than that.

I was in love with Becca. I had to tell her. Not now. But soon. When we were both ready.

"There you are," Hector said behind us. He gave Tara a quick kiss, and my stomach didn't twist with jealousy for once. Then he offered me his hand. "Hey, Andy. Good to see you, man."

I shook his hand. "Likewise."

"Have you seen Becca by any chance?"

"No. She texted me that she was going to meet me in the VIP lounge, but…" I pulled out my phone. No new texts from her. Strange.

"Shit. We go on stage in a few minutes, and we can't find her anywhere. I bet she bailed on us again."

"No way," I said. "Becca would never do that."

Hector crossed his arms. "You have no idea what she was like before. She used to pull this shit all the time back in the day. We'd hoped she had changed but…I guess not."

"Something must have happened. I'll find her." I sent Becca a quick text: *Where are you?*

No response.

"What will you do if you can't find her?" Tara asked Hector.

"I don't know. Cancel the show? We have no other bassist. We're completely fucked."

"Give me a minute." I sent her another text. My skin prickled, and I knew something was wrong. She should have found me in the VIP lounge by now. *Please talk to me.*

Parking lot, she texted back.

"I know where she is," I said to Hector. "But let me talk to her alone first."

"You have ten minutes."

TWENTY-SEVEN

Becca

Andrew found me outside in front of the stadium, where I paced back and forth in front of my Buick.

"What are you doing out here?" he asked. "Are you leaving?"

"No. I couldn't leave. But I couldn't stay either."

He stared at me from a few feet away, his glasses inching down his nose, his hands shoved in the pockets of his dark jeans. He wore a white button-up shirt with a skinny black tie, and his blond hair was slicked back in that way I loved. I hadn't seen him in days, yet somehow he looked even more handsome than I remembered. Like he was more comfortable in his body than he'd ever been before, and it was drop-dead sexy.

"What happened?" he asked.

I sighed and wished for the hundredth time that I had a cigarette. "It all just hit me, hard. The show, the band, and then I saw you with Tara…"

"Ah," he said, like that explained everything. "You saw her hug me."

My throat tightened, and I looked away, rubbing my arms. It was way too cold to be standing out here in nothing but this skimpy little dress, but I hadn't planned on going outside when I'd put it on. At least it wasn't snowing.

"Tara and I were just trying to get some closure," he said. "It meant nothing, I promise you."

I bit my lower lip, but managed to nod. "I'm totally overreacting, I know that. But after all the stress of the night, I saw you together and something just… snapped. I started drinking to numb the pain, and I realized I had to get out of there before I did something stupid."

"I understand. But you don't need to worry. Tara and I are going to try being friends, but I don't have any feelings for her anymore, and she's happy with Hector." He stepped closer and fixed me with his intense gaze. "Becca, the only one I want is you."

Andrew had a way of looking at me that never failed to take my breath away. Like he was always studying me, always interested in everything I said, always memorizing every moment we spent together. He saw below the surface to the real me and somehow, surprisingly, liked what he saw.

I loved the way he looked at me—like I mattered.

"I knew you'd find me," I said.

"You didn't give me much to go on. This parking lot is huge. But I wasn't going to let you walk away from the show tonight or from me. Not without a fight."

"I don't know if I can do this. The arena is so damn big and there are so many people and the band is seriously famous now. What if I fuck up and ruin the show? What if I blow *everything*?"

He brushed his fingers softly across my face. "You won't. They asked you to join them for a reason, and you've spent the last few days practicing with them. It's okay for you to be nervous, but I have no doubt that you'll do great."

I closed my hand around his, pressing it to my cheek. "What if I go back to my old ways? What if I fail again? What if—"

"I won't let you do that. I'll keep you good…and you'll keep me bad." He pressed a soft kiss to my forehead, his hands cupping my face, eyes staring into mine. "Remember what you said to me? That I could be both Andy and Andrew? You showed me that I don't have to be bad or good. I can be some combination of both. You can be both versions of yourself, too—the rock star *and* the new you. They're not mutually exclusive. They're both you, good and bad, light and dark."

"I get what you're saying—that together we can be the best versions of ourselves. But how can we ever really move on from our pasts?"

"We can't, but maybe we don't need to. It was our pasts—my relationship with Tara, your involvement with the band—that brought the two of us together. I wouldn't change a single thing about my past, because everything that happened led me to you."

His lips found mine, and his hands slid to the back of my head, cradling it like he always did. I fell into his arms and melted into his kiss, while his touch infused me with strength and love. Andrew saw the best in me and made me want to try harder, to get back up every time I fell down, to go after the things that scared me. He believed in me, and in turn, he made me believe in myself.

I rested my forehead against his, clinging to him. "Everything is better now that you're here," I whispered. "But what happens after the show is over? What do I do then?"

"We'll figure that out tomorrow. For tonight, just focus on this show."

"Okay." I pulled myself together, gazing up at the arena. "I can do that."

Maybe Andrew was right, and the mistakes we'd made weren't really mistakes at all. Maybe we needed to fall down, so we could get back up again and resolve to keep standing. Maybe we needed to have our hearts broken, so when we fell in love again, we'd know it was real.

Our pasts had made us stronger. They'd made us better. And they'd brought us together.

Now it was time to go after the future.

TWENTY-EIGHT

Andrew

Becca rejoined the band backstage with only a minute to spare. I gave her a quick kiss and then found my seat out in the stands beside two people who were *very* happy to be in the audience—Becca's parents.

"Did you see her?" Evelyn asked, her face flushed with excitement.

"I did. She looked amazing."

Before I could say more, the lights went dark and the crowd started to cheer. Evelyn and David gripped each other's hands, staring up at the stage, and I smiled at the sight of them. When they'd told me they had never seen their daughter play with the band before, I knew I had to find a way to make it happen.

The band came out on stage together, and the audience went wild. Everyone in the arena seemed to jump to their feet at once, including me. Becca had a red and black electric bass, and she moved across the stage, taking her place beside Jared. She looked ridiculously sexy in that silver dress and those combat boots. But best of all, her piercings were back, running up and down her earlobes. I couldn't wait to tease them with my tongue later tonight.

When the entire band was in place, they started to play. Their first song was "Behind the Mask," their most popular one off their old album, the one Becca had performed before. At first, she looked like she might bolt off the stage at any second as she gazed across the audience. But then her fingers began to move deftly across the bass guitar, and the tension seemed to slide off her face. Her body relaxed into the music and swept her away. By the time the song ended, I could tell she was at home up there, with the rest of the band, performing for thousands of people.

She didn't screw up once. And when Jared introduced her as their bassist for the show and explained how she'd come to their rescue when he'd broken his hand, she actually looked pretty damn proud. The crowd cheered, and then they launched into their very cool, modern cover of U2's "New Year's Day."

She looked so hot up there, playing her bass guitar, moving across the stage like she owned it. My girlfriend was a freaking rock star. And in a few hours I was going to rip all her clothes off and make her mine again.

After the band left the stage, I texted Becca to come meet us in the parking lot, since her parents didn't have backstage passes. When she walked out, her face shifted into shock at the sight of them standing with me.

"Mom? Dad? What are you doing here?"

Evelyn grabbed her daughter in a hug. "We wanted to surprise you! Andrew was able to get us some tickets to the show with the help of a nice boy named Hector."

"What did you think?" Becca asked, her voice hesitant.

"You know, in all these years, we've never seen you perform on stage with a band," David said. "When you asked us to give Patricia the money for college instead of you and said that you planned to focus on music instead, we were…skeptical."

"What your father is trying to say is, we were very worried," Evelyn said.

David nodded. "We were concerned that you were going back to your old life-style in order to help your sister or because you worried it would be too hard to return to college. But after the show tonight, we understand—this is your dream, and you have to follow it. And we'll support you however we can. Both you and your sister."

Evelyn wiped at her eyes, a big smile on her face. "You were wonderful, dear. We're so proud of you."

Becca hugged her dad, and her eyes were wet, too. "Thank you. I never imagined you would come to one of my shows, but…" She turned to me and smiled. "Thank you. All of you."

"Now, I know it's New Year's Eve and not even midnight, but I'm exhausted," Evelyn said. "We're heading to your uncle's for the night. Will you be out late?"

She ruffled her hair, looking down at the ground. "I…um, I'll probably stay out with Andrew."

"I'll take good care of her," I said with a grin. "In fact, this is technically our third date."

"Oh my," Evelyn said, clapping her hands together. "We all know what that means. Your first time!"

"Mom!" Becca said, her cheeks going instantly red.

"What? I have the Internet. I know how these things work."

If only they knew. Becca and I had done everything backward, but it worked for us.

"We won't wait up," David said, taking Evelyn's arm.

"I hope you won't be a stranger, Andrew," she said.

"I don't intend to be, ma'am."

"Such a nice boy," Evelyn said to David, as they walked back to their car.

Ha, nice. They had no idea what I was planning to do to their daughter the second I got her alone. And she still owed me that strip tease…

"Thank you," Becca said, sliding her arms around my neck and drawing me in for a kiss. "That was really nice of you."

I grinned. "I'm just glad they're not calling me 'Brett' anymore."

We returned to Villain Complex's dressing room. The other members of the band, plus Tara, were all relaxing on couches. There was an air of exhaustion in the room, but also of celebration. On a TV in the corner, the ball dropped in New York and fireworks went off, one hour ahead of us here in Austin.

"Come join us," Jared said, patting a spot on the couch for us. "We just opened some champagne."

Becca introduced me to the band members I had never officially met, and they poured us a glass of champagne as we sat down. I slid my arm around Becca and she leaned against me. Across the room, Tara nudged Hector and smiled.

"I'd like to propose a toast," Jared said, raising his glass. "To Becca, for helping us tonight. The concert was a success—one of our best ones ever—all thanks to you."

She ducked her head, her cheeks flushed, but I could tell from the way her eyes danced that she was pleased. "Thanks for giving me the chance. It was amazing being able to perform with all of you again."

"We're really glad you said that because we've all been talking and…" Jared looked at Kyle, Maddie, and Hector in turn. They each nodded and he continued. "We'd like you to join our band again. Permanently."

Becca nearly spit out her champagne. She wiped at her lips, her eyes wide, and gripped my hand hard. "What?"

"Sorry, we know it's sudden," Kyle said. "But even if Jared's hand gets better—"

"Which it will," Maddie said.

"—we think it works better if we have a separate bassist so he can focus on singing and charming the crowd during the shows. The audience seemed to love that tonight."

"Also, it allows him to play rhythm guitar now and then," Maddie said. "Which I know he's missed."

Jared nodded. "Basically, having a bassist gives us a lot more freedom on stage, and we know you work well with us. We'd like you to be a permanent member of Villain Complex."

I gave Becca a reassuring squeeze. I'd had a feeling this would happen after she performed with them. She was so incredible—how could they not want her back now that she'd gotten her life straightened out? And I knew from our phone calls over the past few days that she wanted to join the band again, but she was scared, too. She just had to be willing to take that one, final leap and say yes.

"Are you sure?" Becca asked. "I know I haven't been the best band member in the past. Even tonight, I freaked out and thought about quitting on you guys."

"But you didn't," Hector said.

Maddie gave Becca a warm smile. "We've all screwed up in the past. We've all made mistakes. But what matters is that we move forward together as a band."

Jared leaned forward, pouring more champagne into Becca's glass. "The only thing is, you'd have to move to LA with us so you can start practicing and learning all our other new songs. And you'd have to agree to do all our shows and go on tour with us this summer, plus all the publicity crap that goes along with that. You'd be paid of course, but I know it's a lot to ask…"

Becca glanced at each member of the band, biting her lip. "Do you need an answer tonight?"

"No, but we'd love to get one sooner rather than later," Kyle said.

She turned toward me, gripping my hand so hard it hurt. "I have to talk to Andrew first. Just give us a minute, okay?"

Jared raised his eyebrows and studied me for a moment, but he nodded. "Of course."

We went into the hallway and shut the door behind us. As soon as it was closed, she let out a huge sigh and fell back against the wall. "Oh my god, I can't believe this is happening. What do you think I should do?"

I leaned against the wall, stroking her cheek softly. "Isn't it obvious? This is what you wanted, and I can see in your eyes that you're dying to do this. Say yes."

She grabbed my hand again, holding on like it was her lifeline. "It's everything I was hoping for, but at the same time, it means taking a huge risk and moving away from my family…and from you. I don't know if I can do it."

"It's a risk, but it's one you should take. And your family will always be there for you. You'll still be able to visit them all the time."

"But what about you?" she asked, her voice breathless. "Did you mean what you said about moving to LA?"

"I did. I may not be able to move right away, but I won't lose you again, Becca." I took her into my arms and kissed the top of her head. "Besides, I found you in the department store. I found you in the parking lot. I'll find you again in LA somehow."

She looked up at me with the happiest smile I'd ever seen on her face, and then we fell into another long kiss. Even if she moved away, I knew it wouldn't be the end of us. I wouldn't let it be.

When we returned to the dressing room, she took a deep breath and faced the band.

"I'll do it."

TWENTY-NINE

Becca

"Nervous?" Maddie asked.

"No," I said, smiling at her. "Excited."

It was my first live show with the band since New Year's Eve, and we were doing a special Valentine's Day concert at a club in Los Angeles. The venue was more like what I was used to playing with them, although bigger than any clubs we'd performed in before they'd gone on *The Sound*.

"Me too," she said, gazing across the organized frenzy happening backstage. "There's nothing like it, is there?"

I nodded. Maddie and I were pretty different, but we both loved music in the same way. I'd never thought she and I could be friends, not after what I'd done, but I was happy to be proven wrong.

I'd moved to LA about a month ago, into a vacant room in Maddie's apartment. One of her roommates had recently moved to New York, so she'd needed someone to sublet the place until their lease ran out in June. At first I'd been nervous about living with Maddie, worried it would be uncomfortable between us, but she'd given me lots of space and been nothing but kind to me.

Being back in LA just felt right. Like when I was with Andrew or on stage with the band...it was home. The only downside was that I missed Andrew and my family like crazy.

Maddie hopped off the stool she'd been sitting on. "I better make sure Jared's not getting into any trouble."

"Good luck with that," I said, grinning.

She disappeared into the blur of people who were frantically getting our instruments ready. A minute later, I caught a glimpse of her across the room, talking with Jared. He was checking the sound on his black Fender guitar, and he looked up at Maddie and smiled. He played a chord for her and then stretched out his fingers. The cast was gone, and although he still needed some physical therapy, the doctors said his hand would be completely recovered soon. Thank god.

Even though Jared could play again, they still hadn't changed their minds about wanting me in the band, too. In the past month, they'd made me feel like part of the family, like I truly belonged with them. I'd never expected that, but we'd been able to put all of our problems behind us and move forward. Now we had a huge tour lined up for the summer, and I couldn't wait for it to get started. For once in my life, I felt like I'd found my place in the world.

The only thing missing was Andrew.

He'd been searching for a job in LA for the past month with no luck. I knew he would find one soon, but until then, the long-distance thing was the absolute worst. I talked to him every day, but it wasn't the same as being with him.

We still had a few minutes before the show, so I tried calling him, but he didn't pick up. Maybe he was eating dinner or something. I called my sister instead, and she answered on the second ring.

"Becca! I'm so happy you called. We just got Hannah to bed, and Matt and I are about to have a little romantic evening together."

"How are things between the two of you?"

"They're perfect." Her voice was warm and happier than I'd heard her in months. "Thank you again for everything."

"Thank *you* for always being there for me."

"Always. Sisters first and forever."

She spent the next few minutes telling me about all her new classes. She was taking three at a local community college, which gave her enough time to take care of Hannah while still doing a full semester. Our parents were paying for it and were helping with Hannah, too. Even Matt's parents had chipped in a little, to make sure Trish and Matt could cover their bills and both go to school at the same time.

We switched to talking about me, and I told her about my days spent practicing with the band and doing publicity stuff with them. I'd also started looking into online classes I could take on the side, although I hadn't decided on anything yet. I had plenty of time to figure it out.

"So is he there yet?" Trish asked when we were both caught up.

"Who?" I asked.

As soon as I said the word, I saw him. Dark blond hair. Geeky glasses. And those hazel eyes that turned a million colors under the lights.

"Oh my god," I said, my hand trembling as I clutched the phone to my ear. I was so excited I could barely speak. "You knew he was coming tonight?"

She laughed. "Have a good Valentine's Day, Becca."

I hung up without another word and rushed forward, flinging myself into Andrew's arms. He swept me up and slanted his lips across mine, giving me a fierce, passionate kiss that trailed off into a dozen smaller, lighter ones. In between each kiss he whispered my name in something like a plea. Over and over, between each gentle press of his lips, like he couldn't believe we were together again either.

"Andrew," I said, breathless. "What are you doing here?"

"I came to see you," he said, smiling at me. "Happy Valentine's Day."

I kissed him again, unable to get enough after being separated for a month. "You're the best present I could have asked for."

"Oh, yeah?" he asked. "Maybe later you can tie *me* up this time."

"I'd like that," I said, desire rushing straight to my core. I slid my hand down his shirt, feeling his hard muscles underneath. "As soon as this show ends, we're getting naked."

He grinned and yanked me harder against him. "Trust me, that was the plan."

"How long are you in town for?"

"Only a few days. I have a couple of things to take care of…but then I'll be back."

My heart leaped, but I tried not to jump to any conclusions. "Back?"

"Back for good. I got a job here in LA."

"You did? How? Where?"

"Hector helped me, actually. Your manager Dan needs someone to take over PR for his clients now that his new management company is taking off, thanks to Villain Complex's success. Hector sent him my resume, and we had an interview the other day, and then I was hired. Now I just need to find a place to live."

"That's amazing. I can't believe you didn't tell me!" I gave him a dozen more kisses but then pulled back to study his face. "Wait. Are you sure this is what you want? I know you liked your old job, and I'd feel awful making you move here just for me."

"Of course I want this. I always knew Dallas wasn't going to be my permanent home, and this new job is perfect for me. But most importantly, I get to be with you. Wherever you are is where I'm meant to be." He ran his thumb across my lower lip in that way that always made me wild. "Becca, I love you."

My heart fluttered almost painfully. It was the first time he'd said that to me. I'd known for some time that I loved Andrew, ever since New Year's Eve really, and I'd had a feeling he loved me too, but I'd waited for him to say it first. I didn't want to pressure him since he'd wanted to take it slow—but in the end, he'd said it much sooner than I'd expected.

"I love you, too, Andrew," I said, giving him another kiss.

"I know." He grinned and lightly smacked my butt. "Now get out there on stage and make every guy in the audience want you. And then come back to me afterward."

I laughed. "I think most of the guys are more into Maddie than me. She has that sexy librarian thing going with her glasses and all."

He nipped at my ear and whispered, "I happen to know there are plenty of guys who prefer the bad girl."

THIRTY

Andrew

TEN MONTHS LATER

The taxi dropped us off in front of the house, and we wheeled our luggage up the icy walkway. It hadn't started snowing yet in Dallas this year, but it must have been raining recently because the air had a brisk, damp chill in it. The trees running up and down the street were bare, and all of the houses were lit up with sparkling, colorful lights and holiday decorations. I stopped for a second and breathed it in. I liked living in Los Angeles, but I definitely missed having real winters.

"Hang on," I said to Becca before she got to the door.

She stopped and turned toward me. "Hmm?"

"There's something I have to do before we go inside."

"Did you forget something in the taxi? Because we can—"

She stopped mid-sentence when I got down on one knee in front of her, right there in the middle of the walkway. The ice instantly soaked through my jeans and was almost painfully cold, but I didn't care. All that mattered was her face when I pulled out the tiny black box that had started all of this.

"Becca, when I met you I was lost. I was a broken man who never thought he could ever love again. But Hector introduced me to you, and you rocked my world in ways I'd never imagined. You were perfect for me in every way, but I was scared. I needed time to find myself again. And one year ago today, fate brought us back together."

She covered her hands with her mouth, her beautiful brown eyes wide. "Oh, Andrew."

I kept going, worried I'd lose my momentum. I'd practiced this speech a dozen times and I couldn't stop now. "Every second I was pretending to be your boyfriend, I wanted it to be real. I asked you for one date, but I knew it would never be enough. And when you moved away, I decided I would do whatever it took to follow you. I'm so glad I did because these last few months with you have been the best in my life."

I opened up the little black box, showing her the ring inside. A gold band, perfectly sized for her finger (thanks to Trish's help), with a big round diamond on top. It had once belonged to my grandmother, and one day I hoped Becca would pass it on to our one of our grandchildren, too.

"Becca, I never thought I would ever ask anyone to marry me again, but you made me believe in love—and in second chances. I know we may seem like opposites on the surface, but we're more like two interlocking puzzle pieces, two sides of the same coin, a salt-and-pepper set that can never be split up. We complete each other, and I can't imagine a life without you."

"Oh my god, get to the point already," she said, laughing, her eyes glittering with unshed tears.

I smiled up at her. "Becca, will you marry me?"

"Yes, yes, yes!"

I slid the ring onto her finger, and she pulled me to my feet and into a fierce kiss. I'd kissed her thousands of times in the past year, but it was never enough. I wanted to spend the rest of my life kissing her. And now that she'd said yes, I could do exactly that.

"I love you," she said against my lips, clinging to my sweater.

"I love you, too."

When we broke apart, Becca glanced at the front window and laughed. "We should probably go inside before my mother explodes with happiness."

Through the window, her family stood beside the Christmas tree, watching us with big smiles. Evelyn was clapping her hands together and beaming, while a much bigger Hannah jumped up and down. Trish wiped at her eyes with a big smile, leaning against Matt, who had his arm wrapped around her. David just gave me a proud nod. I'd asked him for his permission a week ago, and he'd gladly given it. Like I'd told Becca last year, parents always loved me.

Becca slipped her hand into mine and led me inside, to our second annual dinner with her family on Christmas Eve. This time, they greeted me by my real name.

In the past year, Becca and I had started over together. With each other's help, we'd gone after the things that had scared us the most. For her, life as a rock star in what was now one of the most famous bands in the world. For me, a second chance at love and marriage, with the right woman this time. I had no idea what the future held for the two of us, but I couldn't wait for it to start.

Bonus Content

I hope you enjoyed More Than Once! Read on for a bonus scene - exclusively in this box set!

———

This scene takes place after the concert on Valentine's Day (between Chapter 29 and 30).

BECCA

Music pumped from the speakers around the living room, which was packed so tight with people I could barely move. Last time I'd been here I'd thrown a beer bottle at Jared's head and quit the band in a drunken rage. Now people smiled at me as I passed by, or clasped me on the arm and shouted, "Great show!" One guy even said, "Glad you're back!"

It was hard to believe this was my life now. In less than a year, I'd managed to turn everything around with the help of my family, my friends, and the man at my side. Thanks to him, I was back on track and following my dream again.

We made it to the kitchen and fished out some drinks from a cooler. It was a lot less crowded and noisy in here, and I leaned against one of the dark granite countertops as I popped open my beer.

Andrew slid his arm around my waist, pulling me close, pressing a kiss to my forehead. "I missed you so damn much."

"Why are we here again?" I asked, only half-joking. The plan had been to get naked with him as soon as the show was over, but the band had insisted we attend their after-party at Jared and Kyle's place. After over a month apart, I was dying to get in Andrew's pants, plus I wanted to hear all about this new job he'd mentioned and catch up on everything else I'd missed. Unfortunately, all of that had to wait.

"Tonight was your first show now that you're a real member of the band again," Andrew said, his hazel eyes fixed on me from behind his glasses. "As much as I'd like to back you up against the wall and wrap your legs around me right this minute, you should be here, at least for a few hours. Plus, I'm going to be working with the band soon, and it'd be good for me to get to know everyone a little better."

I groaned, but I couldn't stop myself from smiling, too. "Fine, fine. As long as you back me up a wall later tonight."

"Oh, I plan to." He pulled me in for a kiss, resting his hand on the back of my head. I closed my eyes and melted into his touch, and the rest of the party faded away. My fingers dug into his shirt, not wanting to let him go anytime soon.

"I had a feeling we'd find you two making out somewhere," Jared said, behind us.

We reluctantly pulled apart, although Andrew kept his hand on my lower back, like a reminder to everyone around us that I was his. "We have a lot of catching up to do," he said, grinning.

"I'm sure you do," Jared said, with an equally naughty grin. "Thanks for coming tonight. I know it's Valentine's Day and all, but we like to have a party for our friends after our hometown shows."

I raised my beer to him. "And for once, I'm not drunk and angry at this one!"

"Hey, there's still time," he said, with a wink.

"There you are," Maddie said, as she walked into the kitchen and gave Jared a kiss on the cheek. Her roommate—and mine, as of a few weeks ago—Carla was at her side, towering over her. Carla was tall and gorgeous, with dark skin, a wild mass of curls, and amber eyes. In addition to all that, she was wealthy, smart, and as nice as could be, too. I'd wanted to hate her a tiny bit, just because she was so damn perfect, but she made it pretty much impossible.

"Andrew, this is my other roommate, Carla," I said.

They shook hands and Carla smiled at him. "I've heard a lot about you."

"Have you?" he asked, his eyebrows shooting up.

Carla laughed. "Well, no, actually. Becca isn't exactly a sharer on her best days. But I tried to get more out of her."

I rolled my eyes. "Hey, I told you all the important stuff."

"True." She grinned at me and fake-whispered, "You were so right about the glasses."

"Um, what?" Andrew asked.

I coughed. "Just, uh, girl talk. Where's Daryl?"

Carla sighed, and the light seemed to dim from her eyes. "We're not speaking at the moment. He said he needed space or something."

"That means he'll probably show up any minute now and glare at any guy who comes within five feet of her," Maddie mumbled.

I didn't know Carla well, but I had to agree with Maddie. From what little I'd seen of Daryl, he definitely went into the douchebag category. She could really do so much better. But the heart wanted what the heart wanted, I supposed.

Hector and Tara joined us next, holding hands. I tensed up, checking Andrew's reaction to seeing his ex with her new guy, but he didn't even blink.

"Good show tonight," Tara said. "Glad you could make it, Andy. I heard you're going to be around a lot more soon?"

"That's the plan. I'm moving to LA in a few weeks. All thanks to this guy." He turned to Hector and slapped him on the back. "Thanks again for helping me get that job."

Hector shrugged. "All I did was hand over your resume. Glad it worked out."

"I can't believe no one told me," I said, crossing my arms.

"Don't be upset," Andrew said. "I didn't want to get your hopes up in case it didn't happen."

Kyle and Alexis popped up out of the crowd and grabbed two beers. "Is there a band meeting going on that no one told me about?" Kyle asked.

"Yep," Jared said. "We all voted, and you're out. Sorry."

"Perfect. I'm ready for my solo career. See ya, suckers!" He pretended to walk off, but Alexis grabbed his arm and yanked him back.

"Not so fast," Alexis said. "You know the band would fall apart without you."

"Tell me about it," he muttered, but he was grinning.

"No one is leaving," Maddie said, with a fake stern expression. "The band finally feels complete now that Becca's joined us."

I ducked my head to hide my wide smile and the tears pricking my eyes. I had no desire to leave the band again, not this time. They'd given me a second chance, and I wasn't going to screw it up.

"I propose a toast," Jared said, raising his beer in front of us. "To Villain Complex…and to good friends, both old and new. We wouldn't be on this wild and crazy adventure without all of you. Happy Valentine's Day, everyone."

"Cheers," we all said, raising our drinks, and warmth spread through my stomach. I leaned against Andrew, smiling at my band and my friends, and truly felt like I was home.

———

ANDREW

"Finally," Becca said, while I unlocked my hotel room door and opened it for her. "I was tempted to rip off your clothes right there in the middle of the party. Or jump you in the car."

"We could have gone to your place," I said, following her into the dark suite. "It's a lot closer to Jared and Kyle's house, and I'd love to see it."

"True, but Maddie and Carla will be there. You can see it tomorrow." She gave me a naughty grin. "Besides, I love hotel sex."

"Oh, trust me. I remember."

I backed her against the wall, caging her in with the press of my body against hers, just like I'd promised. We fell into a long, desperate kiss, making up for all the weeks apart. Her hands dug into my hair and I was already hard, my entire body straining to touch hers again.

"What do you want tonight?" I asked, my lips at her neck, my hands circling her hips. "Fast and rough? Or slow and sweet?"

"Both," she said, arching her back to give me better access to her body. "Fast the first time, because I can't wait a second longer for you to fuck me." She unzipped my jeans and slipped her hand inside, gripping me tight. "And slow the second time, because we have all night together."

"My thoughts exactly." It was hard to speak with her fingers wrapped around me, stroking me. I buried myself in her skin and savored the taste of her on my lips. I kissed along her neck, her shoulders, then yanked the front of her dress down to free her luscious breasts. I'd dreamed about sucking on these hard nipples on the long nights without her, and it was heaven taking them into my mouth again. I wanted to lick every inch of her body before the night was over, but I couldn't wait that long to be inside her. Thank god she wanted fast and rough the first time.

I tore off my shirt and dropped it on the floor, but I couldn't be bothered to remove her dress. Instead, I tugged her panties off, sliding them down her bare thighs, finding her wet and warm underneath. The thought of going down on her was so very tempting, but she opened my jeans wider and pulled me toward her.

"Hurry," she said, dragging her dress up to her hips in invitation, revealing her naked skin underneath. From the wild desire in her eyes and the way she was breathing fast, I could tell she was as desperate for this as I was.

I slammed her back against the wall and lifted her up, wrapping her gorgeous legs around me. I slipped inside her so easily as our bodies came together, like we were a perfect fit, made as a matching pair. She was so tight and as I sank deep inside, all I could think was, *god I love this woman.*

"Andrew," she moaned, but all words after that were lost as I began to move. Hard strokes, slow at first, so I could close my eyes and really appreciate what I'd been missing after she'd moved to LA. And all those months before we'd run into each other at Christmas.

I rested my hands flat on the wall on either side of her head as I pressed her body back against the wall, using the leverage to angle my hips just right as I pounded faster. She held on to me, clutching my shoulders, her legs tightening around me. We were half-dressed and half-wild, our bodies rocking together as one, and I knew I would never get enough of her, not when it felt this good.

Her hands slid down to my ass and her nails dug in, pulling me deeper into her. The slight pain urged me on and I thrust harder, faster. I lost control, my body slamming into hers over and over, forcing her body to slide up and down against the wall. Little cries escaped her mouth and I could tell she was close. I was, too.

I nipped at her neck, dragging my teeth across her soft skin, and her moans grew louder. A look of pure pleasure took over her face and she clenched up around me as she came. I kept pumping into her, not wanting this to end, but it was too good, too much, and I couldn't stop. She dragged me along with her into heaven, and soon we were both completely sated. For now, anyway.

I carried her over to the bed and set her down, laying on top of her, still inside her. Neither of us wanted to let go, to be apart for even a second.

"Happy Valentine's Day," I whispered.

She gave a content sigh, her arms tightening around my neck. "I love you."

"I love you, too." A thrill passed through me hearing her say those words, and saying them back to her. I'd wanted to tell her how I felt ever since New Year's, but had been too afraid at first. What if she didn't feel the same? I'd been scared to rush things and blow it with her. But tonight, when I'd seen her at the concert, I knew I couldn't wait any longer to tell her.

She was it for me. And someday I would ask her to marry me—when we were both ready.

More Than Distance

CHASING THE DREAM #5

ONE

Carla

____

When I graduated from college I had my future completely mapped out: a five year plan for my life, with a more detailed plan for the next twelve months, and of course, a daily plan for each day of the week. Every Sunday I would plot out the next week in my color-coded organizer, using gel pens, stickers, and washi tape, while I drank my coffee and ate my cereal. Above all else, I was going to be prepared.

Nothing could have prepared me for every single one of my plans falling apart.

I parked my '67 Mustang outside of my parents' house. The car made a worrisome rattling sound in the engine before I shut it off. I'd have to check that out tomorrow and see what was causing it this time. Another thing to add to my extensive To Do List.

I got out of the car and sweat immediately started sliding down the back of my tank top. June in Los Angeles was usually pretty mild, but not this week. I grabbed my sweater anyway.

As I walked up the path to the house, my phone buzzed in my shorts pocket. A text that said: _Baby, I miss you. Can we talk?_ I swiped it away and knocked on the door. No way was I dealing with him right now.

The door opened and my mother smiled at me. The setting sun highlighted her bronze skin and the dark waves that cascaded down her shoulders over her little black dress. Even when she was cooking dinner for her family she looked every inch the supermodel she used to be.

"Hello, my angel," she said, kissing both my cheeks.

"Hi, Mom." I stepped inside the house and the warm aroma from her cooking wrapped around me. I closed my eyes and breathed it in, feeling my tense muscles unravel slightly. This was exactly what I needed after the horrible week I'd had.

The front hall was immaculate as always, with dark wood floors, patterned rugs, and pictures of our family on the walls. Mom set her hands on my arms and studied my face. "Are you feeling well? You look a bit sweaty." She reached to touch my forehead with the back of her hand, but I slipped away.

"It's ninety-five degrees outside." Although you wouldn't know it from inside my parents' house. The thermostat was always set at near-Arctic levels because my dad was perpetually hot. I'd need my sweater to make it through dinner without turning into an icicle.

"Yes, but you look a little tired. Your eyes are red. Are you sick? Any pain?"

My eyes *were* red, but not from what she thought. "I'm okay. Really. You don't need to worry."

"I'm your mother, it's my job to worry. I simply want to make sure you're not…" She waved her hands around. "You know."

"I'm not relapsing, I promise. I went to the doctor the other day and everything was fine." I didn't mention the doctor I'd seen was my gynecologist and that I'd been getting checked for STDs. Mom definitely didn't need to know *that*.

"Good girl." She patted my cheek. "My angel."

It took all my willpower to not roll my eyes. "Where's Dad?"

She shrugged. "I don't know. Probably in the garage, where else? Dinner will be ready in a few minutes."

Now it was my turn to study her more carefully. Her eyes looked sad, like her bright inner light was dimmer somehow. "Is everything okay?"

She hesitated, but then gave me a smile that looked forced. "Yes. We'll talk during dinner."

Anxiety twisted in my stomach. "Smells great. Can I help with anything?"

"No, no. Go relax. Food's almost done. Give me a few minutes."

She headed into the kitchen, but I lingered in the hall. Something was definitely wrong, although I couldn't imagine what it would be. I was tempted to follow her, but Mom ruled over her kitchen with an iron fist. None of us were welcome in there while she cooked. She said all we did was get in her way.

I found my older brother Daniel watching TV in the living room, with his dark, muscular arms folded behind his head and his long legs stretched out across the entire sofa. Since there was no room for me, I sank onto the smaller couch. Like the rest of the house, the living room was tidy and comfortable but also elegant.

"What's with mom?" I asked.

"What do you mean?"

"She didn't seem off to you?"

"Not really." He shrugged. "But I did hear her giving you the third degree when you walked in."

"Of course. It wouldn't be our Sunday family dinner without the constant fussing and worrying over my health."

"She's the queen of worrying, you know that." He gave me the side-eye. "Although you *do* look tired…"

"You're just as bad as she is!" I grabbed one of the couch's throw pillows and launched it at his head.

He caught it easily and laughed. "Sorry, sorry."

His eyes lingered on my face a minute longer, like he was checking that I really was okay. I scowled at him and reached for another pillow. He grinned and turned to the TV again, which was showing commercials.

"What are we watching?" I asked, relaxing deeper into the cushions.

"There's a *Road Trip Race* marathon on."

"Perfect."

Road Trip Race was a reality TV show where teams of two—usually couples, siblings, or friends—drove across the country and competed in scavenger hunts and other challenges to win a million-dollar prize. I'd always wanted to go on with Daniel, even if we'd probably try to kill each other by the end of it. The show was one of our favorites. We used to watch it with our dad in the evenings before we both went off to college, and now I watched it with my roommates.

The show came back on and I recognized it as an episode from three seasons ago. "Ooh, this is the one where the sisters get in a big fight and one drives off without the other and then gets disqualified for doing the challenge alone."

"You just missed the one where that surfer couple crashed into a tree because they were making out and not watching the road."

"Oh yeah! That was a good season. Much better than the recent one."

He flipped the remote over and over in his hand. "The show's getting kind of stale now. They need to mix it up somehow."

Dad walked into the living room and his warm presence immediately filled the space. He was a large man, both tall and broad, and I'd always thought of him as a big teddy bear. He sat beside me on the couch, draping his arm behind me. "Hey, sweetheart. How you feeling?"

"I'm fine, Dad." You'd think after seven years in remission they'd stop fretting over me, but no. I reminded myself that they only did it because they cared. "What's going on with you and Mom?"

He tensed beside me. "Nothing. How's the Mustang?"

It obviously wasn't nothing, but I let it go for now. "It's making that rattling noise again. I might bring it by the shop sometime this week."

Dad owned a chain of auto repair shops across Southern California called Jackson Automotive, which he'd started before we were born. Daniel and I had spent most of our childhood and teenage years hanging around the original location in Culver City, learning how to repair and fix up cars. Most of the time, Ryan Evans had been with us too.

Whoa, were had *that* thought come from? I squashed it down as fast as it popped up. I tried to avoid thinking about Ryan as much as possible. My brain must have slipped because of everything that happened last week. One heartbreak made me think of another.

"What are you going to do with the car when you go to New York?" Daniel asked me.

"Leave it here, probably. That okay, Dad?"

"Sure, sweetheart. When are you leaving?"

"Two weeks."

"So soon." There was a heavy sadness to Dad's voice, but he gave me a quick squeeze. "I'm proud of you. Doing what you love. It's great."

"Thanks, Dad." I learned against him and tried to lose myself in the show, except all I could think about was how in two weeks I'd be on a reality TV show too—as a judge this time.

I'd always loved reality TV shows, but never expected they would become such a big part of my life. It started a year ago when my roommate Maddie went on *The Sound*, a show where bands competed for a record deal, and a few months after that our friend Julie was invited on *Behind The Seams*, a fashion design competition. I worked as Julie's model on the show, thanks to some strings Mom had pulled, but I ended up being switched to her boyfriend, Gavin. When he won the show I earned ten thousand dollars, plus we got a photo shoot in *Charmed* magazine.

My modeling took off after that, although it was tough to juggle my busy schedule with my college classes. Now that I'd graduated from UCLA I could focus on my career, but I honestly wasn't sure if I wanted to keep modeling. I enjoyed the travel part of it and I loved the makeup and fashion, but I wanted something more stable. Something long-term.

The solution came when Giselle Roberts, the producer of *Road Trip Race* and *Behind The Seams*, offered me a once-in-a-lifetime opportunity as a judge on her other show, *American Supermodel*. It combined two of my favorite things—modeling and reality TV—and was my ticket into a new career. The only requirement was that I move to New York and leave behind my family and most of my friends. Sure, Julie and Gavin were there, but it was going to be hard to leave behind so many people I loved in Los Angeles.

Even so, I was looking forward to starting over somewhere new. A place where my parents and brother wouldn't be able to hover over me constantly, fussing over everything I did. A place where my ex-boyfriend couldn't show up at my apartment in the middle of the night, begging me to take him back. A place without memories of the other guy I could never quite banish from my thoughts.

Yes, I definitely needed a fresh start.

Mom called us in for dinner and we made our way to the dining table, which was covered in food along with candles and a vase full of daisies. She'd even used her best silverware and her fancy wedding china. Had I forgotten some sort of special occasion? No, of course not—it would have been in my planner, and the only thing on today's list had been *do laundry, start packing,* and *family dinner*.

"Looks good, Mom," Daniel said, as he pulled up a chair. "How'd you know I was craving this?"

She gave him a warm smile. "Mothers always know."

Tonight Mom had cooked some of her favorite Portuguese dishes, which only confirmed she was upset about something—her hand-me-down recipes from her grandma were always her go-to comfort foods. First up, some *caldo verde* soup, plus some *broa* cornbread for dipping. Once that was done, we'd move on to the *bacalhau com natas*, before finishing with a *tarte de amêndoa* for dessert.

I sat across from Daniel and he kicked me under the table, like he'd done every family dinner since he shot up to his current height of six-foot-five. Both of our parents were tall too—my mom liked to joke that she married my dad because he was the only guy she could find who was taller than her. We always laughed about it, but at six-foot or so myself, I could sort of relate.

As soon as our parents sat down, the doorbell rang. Everyone froze except Daniel, who shot to his feet. "I'll get it."

While my brother headed for the front door, Mom tilted her head and asked in a way-too-loud whisper, "Did he invite a girl?"

Dad's eyebrows jumped up. "He hasn't done that since Jennifer…"

We all strained to listen as my brother opened the front door and said hello to someone. Heavy boots stepped into the front hall, along with the sound of a deep, male voice. One I hadn't heard in years, but recognized instantly.

No, it couldn't be. Surely my brother would have mentioned *he* was coming?

I sank down into my chair, hoping I was wrong, wondering if I had time to escape. I was so not ready for this. I needed time to prepare first, to get my emotions under check, to figure out what I would say. I definitely wouldn't have worn this outfit, for one thing. This old tank top and these beige shorts were not doing me any favors. I wasn't even wearing any makeup.

Before I could plot my exit, Daniel walked in with a man who was nearly as tall as he was. My eyes locked on our guest and my breath caught in my throat as I took him in. Leather jacket over broad shoulders. Motorcycle helmet under one arm. Shiny black hair cut short, framing a chiseled face and strong jaw. And those eyes—the second they honed in on me with their dark gaze, I knew I was in trouble.

After six years, Ryan Evans, my brother's best friend and my first love, had returned.

And all I wanted to do was run away as fast as I could.

TWO

Carla

Daniel clasped Ryan on the shoulder and grinned at us. "Look who's here!"

My heart seemed to have stopped working properly, judging from its erratic behavior. I couldn't remember how to breathe either. What was Ryan *doing* here? He couldn't just…just show up like this! In the middle of family dinner night!

Mom jumped to her feet. "Ryan! Daniel didn't tell us you were in town!"

She swept him up in a big hug and he quietly laughed. That *laugh*. I remembered it so well. Deep and rich, like hot chocolate on a cold day. I wanted to drink it up. Or cover my ears to block it out.

Everyone was standing now, welcoming Ryan back to town, except me. I forced myself to my feet, but shuffled to the back of my chair and gripped it tightly, in case my knees gave out—and so I'd have a barrier between us. Getting too close to Ryan would be dangerous. Just being in the same room with him again was doing serious damage to my nervous system.

Dad gave Ryan a man-hug with a lot of back thumping. "Good to see you again, son."

"I apologize for crashing your dinner," Ryan said to my parents. "I wasn't sure what time I'd make it to LA, and Daniel told me to stop by if it wasn't too late."

Mom had a slight moment of hesitation that was completely unlike her—she *adored* Ryan—and she glanced at Dad for a split second. But then her beaming smile returned and she dragged Ryan over to the table. "Of course! You're part of the family too. Come, sit and tell us everything you've been doing. Here, let me take your helmet. Henry can get you a chair."

"Thank you." Ryan unzipped his black leather jacket and shrugged it off, while I tried not to notice how his muscular chest filled out his crisp white dress shirt all too well, or how the collar was open a little at his neck, like he'd hastily ripped off a tie. But I noticed. My entire *body* noticed.

His gaze returned to mine and a little shiver ran through me. "Carla."

His voice was low and he said my name like only the two of us were in the room. A rush of heat washed through me as my eyes devoured every inch of him, from his intelligent brow to his all-too-familiar mouth to his strong, tall frame. He was really there, really standing in front of me after all these years.

He didn't move to hug me and I didn't move to hug him. We stared at each other for far too long, neither one of us speaking, and the invisible sparks between us were so explosive I was surprised the dining room furniture didn't catch on fire.

Finally, Daniel broke the spell. "Ryan's going to be staying with me for a while."

I couldn't find my voice. Thank goodness I was moving to New York in two weeks. "That's great."

It wasn't great. After the way things had ended between us, I'd hoped to never see Ryan again. Ignoring his existence had been the only way I could forget what had happened and move on. Now he was here and all those feelings I'd spent the last six years burying were rushing to the surface again. The embarrassment and pang of rejection were still as sharp as ever, but so were the longing and desire. Unfortunately.

Dad pulled up a chair next to me for Ryan, which meant the man I'd once loved was only inches away when we sat down to eat. I tugged off my sweater, suddenly boiling up despite the frigid air conditioning. This was going to be the longest dinner *ever*.

Ryan surveyed the food spread across the table. "This looks incredible. My compliments to the chef."

Mom's smile got even bigger. "Please dig in. I don't want it to get cold."

We passed around dishes and I was careful not to touch Ryan as I handed him the food. Every inch of my body was aware of him though, and it took everything in my power not to look at his face. It was bad enough feeling his magnetic presence beside me. Looking at him would surely do me in.

As he reached for the soup, I couldn't help but catch sight of his masculine wrist, and then my eyes naturally traveled along his tan forearm, where his sleeves had been rolled up, and then to his broad shoulders, and finally to his jaw and his mouth. Damn. That *mouth*.

So much for my willpower.

He tasted the soup and closed his eyes for a moment, like he was savoring it. "I forgot how delicious this is. I haven't had this in probably…"

"Six years?" I asked, with a trace of bitterness I couldn't hide.

He focused on me again, his gaze so intense it made me want to squirm. One of his black eyebrows lifted. "Have you been counting?"

"No, of course not." I pictured stabbing him with my fork. I pictured knocking all the food off the table and dragging him onto it, tearing open his shirt, pressing my mouth against his neck. I took a sip of water instead, hoping it would cool me down.

"What are you in town for?" Dad asked Ryan.

"I'm visiting my father."

There was an awkward pause—we all knew Ryan and his father didn't get along, so there must be more to the story. When he didn't offer it, Mom shoved another piece of cornbread onto his plate. "I'm so glad you could join us tonight. It's been far too long. Have some more *broa*. I bet you never eat any homemade meals anymore."

"No, not very often."

Dad chuckled. "He doesn't need homemade meals. He probably goes to fancy five-star restaurants every night."

"Sometimes I do," Ryan said. "But none of them are as good as your cooking, Eva."

Mom playfully swatted his comment away. "Please, you know you can call me Mom after all these years."

"Of course. Mom." The way he said it sounded hollow, as if he'd forgotten how to pronounce the word after so long.

She'd told Ryan to call her Mom when he was ten, after he'd become a permanent fixture at our house. He'd met my brother in school, when they'd been paired up to do a project on ancestry and discovered their moms were both from another country. Like me and Daniel, Ryan was biracial. Our dad was black and our mom was from Portugal, while Ryan's dad was white and his mom was from China.

Ryan's mother had passed away when he was seven and his dad had always been working, so Ryan began to spend more time with us than at his own house. It wasn't long before my parents came to treat him like a second son. He even had his own bed in Daniel's room. But hearing him call my mother "Mom" always made me inwardly cringe. Thinking about Ryan like a brother was impossible for me.

"Would you like some wine?" Dad asked him.

"No, thank you," Ryan said. "I'm on my motorcycle tonight. Drove it down from Seattle."

"You're so responsible." Mom rested her chin in her hand, staring at Ryan like a proud mother.

"Is business going well?" Dad asked. "Everything's good with Meta Entertainment?"

Daniel leaned forward, like he was telling us a secret. "He got an offer from Slade Industries to buy out his company."

Dad whistled softly. "Slade? That's a big deal. You going to take it?"

"I haven't decided yet," Ryan said. "I like running my own business, but it's too good an offer to not consider."

Dad nodded like he approved. "Wise man."

It really wasn't fair. Not only was Ryan the sexiest man I had ever met, but also the smartest and most successful. He'd developed a video game app in his senior year of college called Outerworld that was sort of like Pokemon Go mixed with Harry Potter, where everyone played a wizard or a warrior and interacted in this virtual fantasy world that overlaid the real one through your phone's GPS and camera. It was genius, really—and a lot of fun. Yes, I played it sometimes, too.

Outerworld had turned into a huge viral success almost overnight and was still one of the most popular games around. Under Ryan's guidance, he'd formed Meta Entertainment by buying up a lot of other, smaller startups. Now at twenty-four he ran an entire multimedia company and was one of the youngest billionaires in the world. He spent his days in a boardroom and his nights dating actresses and pop stars. Not that I paid attention to that stuff, of course. I just happened to see it since we were still Facebook friends, plus the internet loved talking about his various high-profile flings. I didn't care who Ryan dated. I'd gotten over him long ago. Really.

"That's so exciting," Mom said. "And are you seeing someone? I heard you were dating that one country singer…"

"No one right now."

Daniel smirked. "Only 'cause he never keeps them around very long."

Ryan arched an eyebrow at him. "You're one to talk. When did you last have a girlfriend?"

"I've dated a few women," Daniel said. But we all knew my brother's last girlfriend was Jennifer. She'd broken his heart by turning down his marriage proposal because she didn't want to get tied down, then went and married a guy at her office a month later. That was a year ago and he hadn't dated anyone since.

Mom tried to shove more food at the guys. "You are both young. You have lots of time before you need to settle down. I tell Carla the same thing, but she doesn't listen. She's been with that boyfriend of hers for almost two years, yes?"

As of last week I wasn't with him anymore, but now was not the time to tell her about my break-up. I definitely wasn't going to mention it in front of Ryan either. I stared at my food as heat rose up the back of my neck, wishing this entire conversation could be over already. It was only made worse by the feeling that Ryan was staring at me intently, like he was waiting for my answer.

"Angel, are you okay?" Mom asked. "You look a bit flushed."

"I'm fine."

She studied me a moment longer and then turned back to Ryan with a smile. "I must confess, I always hoped you and Carla would fall in love and get married one day. Silly, I know! But then you would truly be part of the family."

I choked on my soup, while Ryan dropped his fork on the table with a loud clatter. Anger and embarrassment flared inside me, competing for dominance. Where had that comment even come from? What was my mom *thinking*?

Daniel made gagging sounds. "No way. That's disgusting. She's like his little sister! And no offense Ryan, you're like a brother to me and all, but I'd have to kill you if you even looked at my little sister like that. We all know what your track record is like, and Carla is way too good for you."

"Yes," Ryan said, his voice dry. "She definitely is."

"Besides, she's not his type, Mom," Daniel continued. "He likes them blond, pale, and tiny. Or redheads, like that one actress, what was her name?"

I wanted to suffocate my brother with the tablecloth. Thank you Daniel for reminding me that I was the absolute last girl Ryan would ever be interested in.

"Skylar," Ryan muttered.

"That's right. Damn, she was hot."

"Yes, but Carla's beautiful too," Mom said. "Don't you think so, Ryan?"

"Mom, please!" I cried.

"Sorry." She waved a hand dismissively. "I know you don't like being called beautiful, but it's true."

That wasn't why I was upset, but it was easier to stay quiet and let her think that. Tears pricked the back of my eyes and I stared at my food, wishing a black hole would open up and suck me into it. Suddenly I was an awkward sixteen year old girl with a secret crush again, instead of a twenty-two year old woman about to start a new career in another city.

I'd had a crush on Ryan for most of my life. I was eight when we first met, and I remembered thinking he was the prettiest boy I'd ever seen, with his raven's black hair and midnight eyes. I'd spent the next few years trying to join in on whatever he and Daniel were doing, whether it was swimming in the pool, playing video games, or working on cars. I was that annoying little sister who tagged along after her big brother and his best friend, but as I grew older, I realized I had real feelings for Ryan that went way beyond friendship. He was the first boy I ever thought of as a *boy*.

I hid my crush for most of my teenage years and watched him date other girls with a burning pit of jealousy in my gut. Until I was sixteen, when I finally got the courage to confess my feelings for him, and got my heart broken in return.

That was the last time I'd spoken to him. Until tonight.

"Carla's more than just beautiful, of course," Mom said, still trying to salvage this awkward conversation. "She recently graduated from UCLA and is moving to New York soon to be a judge on *American Supermodel*. Did Daniel tell you that?"

"No, he must have forgotten to mention it." Ryan's eyes shifted to my face again. I wished he would stop looking at me. "Congratulations."

Mom began serving dessert to each of us. "Normally I would be worried sick over my baby moving to a new city on her own, but... Well, it turns out she won't be the only one moving there."

"What?" I asked, my head snapping toward her.

Dad's wine glass slammed down on the table. "Eva..."

"We have to tell them. And Ryan is family too! He should hear this."

Dad shook his head, his lips pressed in a tight frown, and Daniel and I shared a nervous look.

"Mom, what's going on?" I asked. Were my parents moving to New York to watch over me? I knew they were overprotective, but surely they wouldn't go *that* far.

Mom donned a hesitant smile. "We have some news, which you might find a tiny bit...upsetting."

"What are you talking about?" Daniel asked.

"I got a job. Giselle Roberts offered me the host position on *Behind The Seams* now that Lola's gone, and I took it." There was a heavy pause as she let the words sink in, but then she beamed at us. "I'm moving to New York too! We'll both be on reality TV shows this fall! Isn't that great, Carla?"

"That's...that's... Wow." I was too stunned to say anything else. I should be happy for her, but I couldn't help but feel like she was taking something away from me. I'd wanted to get away and start over, yet that wouldn't be possible with my parents hovering over me the entire time. This was supposed to be *my* new career, *my* big move, and now she was following me? Going after the exact same dream?

"That's great, Mom," Daniel said, although he was frowning. "I'm happy for you, but what about the business, Dad? How will you run it from New York?"

"I'm not going to New York," Dad said, his voice low.

"You're not?" Panic rose up in me, but I refused to put together all the clues. "I don't understand."

Mom sighed. "Your father and I… Oh, there's no easy way to say this. We're separating."

"*What?*" Daniel asked.

I stared at her, too shocked to speak. No, this couldn't be happening. My parents had always been the perfect couple. They were the image I had in my head of what a strong marriage was, of what true love looked like. They were the goal I set for myself in all my relationships. If they were splitting up, then everything I knew about love and all my beliefs about marriage were wrong.

"I know this is difficult, but please try to be happy for me," Mom said. "I've been a stay-at-home mother for the past twenty-four years and I've loved every minute of it, but my babies are grown up now. I need to do something for myself again."

"But does it have to be *this* job, on a reality TV show in New York?" I blurted out. A pang of guilt hit me for being selfish, but come on! This was supposed to be my big moment, not a matching mommy-and-me career change. "Surely there are lots of other places that would hire you here in LA."

"Dad, couldn't you go with her?" Daniel asked. "Why do you have to split up?"

Dad shook his head. "I can't leave now. We're opening that new location in Marina Del Rey and it's going to be our biggest one yet."

Daniel sat up straighter, his mouth set in a hard line. "Let me handle it. Now that I'm done with business school I can take on a lot more responsibility at the shop."

"It's not just that," Mom said. "This has been coming for a long time. We both just…need our space. We still love each other very much, but twenty-five years of marriage is a long time and we need to be on our own for a while. I gave up so much of myself when I quit modeling to be a mother, and I need to find that part of me again. Alone."

"You can't be serious," I said. "Dad, you're not going to do anything?"

"All I want is for your mother to be happy." He sounded completely miserable.

Daniel slammed his palm on the table. "That's bullshit."

"Language!" Mom turned to Ryan with a sympathetic smile. "I'm so sorry to spring all this on your first night back."

Ryan's face was a tight mask, showing little to no emotion, but his hand gripped his fork with white knuckles. "No, I'm sorry. I should have checked first to see if tonight was a good night."

"Nonsense. You're always welcome here, and this will probably be our last Sunday family dinner for some time."

Or maybe ever. She didn't say it out loud, but she might as well have. We were all thinking it.

I felt like I might start hyperventilating at any moment. Everything was falling apart around me. My own breakup had been bad enough. I'd spent the entire week crying my heart out and trying to get past the pain of catching my boyfriend screwing another girl. Tonight was supposed to help me forget about that. I'd look at my parents and their perfect life and remind myself that relationships could last and that true love was real. But now Ryan was here—a reminder of my other biggest heartbreak—and my parents were splitting up and I just couldn't handle it. I *couldn't.*

Tears pricked my eyes. I had to get away fast before I broke apart completely.

I threw my napkin on the table and stood on shaky legs. "I'm sorry, I…I have to go."

"Carla?" Mom asked, her expression worried.

I heard them call after me, but I was already grabbing my keys and rushing out the door. Before I knew what I was doing, I'd slid into my old Mustang and switched it on. The engine rumbled to life and I fixed my eyes on the road. I did the only thing I could with my entire life crumbling to dust around me.

I drove.

THREE

Ryan

Well, that was a shit show.

I slammed my motorcycle helmet on and climbed onto my bike. What the fuck was I thinking coming back here tonight? The second I walked in and saw Carla's face I'd known it was a mistake. Then there was all that shit with her parents. I couldn't have picked a worse moment to show up out of the blue after six years.

I revved the engine on my Ducati and took off, zooming down the quiet street lined with nearly identical ranch houses and well-manicured lawns. Even though I hadn't been here in years, it still looked exactly the same as when I'd left for college. I'd expected Daniel's family to be exactly the same too. My mistake.

Instead of heading for my next destination, I turned onto a busy street and really took off, the motorcycle roaring to life under me. I needed a few minutes to clear my head, especially after what I'd just seen. The Jacksons had always been like my real family and their house had always felt like my true home. They were the perfect parents with the perfect marriage and the perfect kids. For some reason they'd let me be part of it, even though I wasn't perfect in the slightest.

Now I'd just watched it all implode right in front of me.

If my perfect family was falling apart, how could I expect to repair things with my total shit one?

And seeing Carla again…fuck. I hadn't expected it to hit me so hard after all this time. In the past six years, Carla had become a *woman*. No longer was she the lanky kid who'd always seemed too long-legged and clumsy for her own body, nor the flustered teen with long lashes and a shy smile whose cheeks darkened every time I'd said a word to her. No, she'd transformed into a stunning beauty with legs that went on for miles, dark skin that looked impossibly smooth and soft, and those wild brown curls I'd always loved.

I'd seen pictures of her, of course. It was tough not to, when her photos were all over the damn place these days. But those photos never seemed real, almost like there was an actress playing Carla in them. I could pretend the images of her were airbrushed to perfection, that it was all a trick of lighting and makeup. Once I saw her in person again I realized that none of it was fake. If anything, she was even more stunning in real life than in those photos.

Thinking about her now made my jeans tighten uncomfortably and I adjusted myself on the bike's seat. I knew better than to think about her that way. Carla was off-limits and it was obvious she hadn't been happy to see me at all. In fact, I was pretty sure she hated my guts. After the way I'd been a total dick to her last time, who could blame her?

No, I definitely shouldn't be thinking about those long legs, or remembering how soft and sweet her mouth had been, or picturing what it'd be like to have her naked and underneath me with her wild curls splayed out on a pillow. She had a boyfriend and it sounded pretty serious. Even if she was single, Daniel would beat the shit out of me for even imagining the things I wanted to do to her.

I turned my bike around and headed into another area of the city. Even with the wind rushing against me and the miles flying past, nothing was working to clear my head. I had to suck it up and confront my past already.

Twenty minutes later I stopped my motorcycle outside a small house I hadn't seen in years. A familiar dread rose up at the sight of the bar-covered windows, peeling paint, and dead grass. The sound of the freeway was almost deafening here, with the house tucked right under it. Not a prime location by any means, but hey, it had been cheap.

I yanked off my helmet and propped it under my arm, then slowly approached the front door. Felt like a damn death row walk, even if I wasn't the one dying. I stared at the doorbell for a good minute, trying to steel myself for what was coming, before I finally rang it.

My stepmother Dolores opened the door. Her graying hair was in a messy bun and she wore a green bathrobe with a small hole in the shoulder. I'd known her for much of my life as my father's secretary, but hadn't seen her since their wedding three years ago. Actually, I hadn't seen my father since then either, come to think of it.

"Hi, Ryan." She stepped back to let me in. "Thanks for coming. I know it was a burden with your company and all."

"It's no trouble." I swept my gaze across the small living room, noting the dark brown carpet I'd grown up with, the beige couch that still had the ketchup stain I'd gotten on it, and my mom's Chinese brush paintings on the wall. Nothing had changed in this place since I was a kid. "Where is he?"

Her face was tired and more wrinkled than I remembered. "In the back, watching TV."

"How is he doing?"

"He's grumpy as can be. He started chemo this week, so I had to hear his bitching non-stop, but otherwise he's hanging in there."

"How are *you* doing?"

She blew out a long breath. "Busy. Overwhelmed. Worried. But I'm hanging in there too." She gave me a weak smile. "It'll be better now that you're here."

I wasn't sure about that, but it sounded like she could use some help. I'd been shocked when she had called to tell me about my father's lung cancer, but immediately agreed to come down to LA to see him. I'd taken a month off work, even though it meant putting a hold on the Slade Industries offer. Slade's CEO was pissed, but my team insisted I go since I hadn't taken a single vacation day since starting the company three years ago. They promised me they would handle everything in my absence and I had complete faith in them.

A guy with ginger hair came out of the kitchen, eating a sandwich and walking around barefoot like he lived here or something. It took me a moment to place him as Jay, my stepmother's son from her previous marriage. I supposed that made him my stepbrother, although I'd met him only once, at the wedding. He was about the same age as me, but I doubted we had much in common besides our parents' marriage.

He looked me over slowly and stood up straighter, his chest puffed out like he was trying to be intimidating even though he was smaller and shorter than me. He wore a frown and I got the feeling he wasn't thrilled to see me. *Not my first choice either*, I wanted to tell him.

"The great Ryan Evans finally decided to grace us with his presence?" Jay asked. "So kind of you to slum it with us poor people."

What the fuck was his problem? I stepped right up in his face, my anger flaring. "Don't talk to me about being poor," I growled. "I'm the one who grew up in this house, not you."

He opened his mouth to reply, but I fixed him with the hard-eyed stare that made businessmen quake in their expensive leather shoes. After a moment, he looked down at his feet. *Yeah, that's what I thought.*

"Be nice," Dolores said, hands on her hips. I wasn't sure if she was talking to me or to him. I took off down the hall without another word, toward the family room and the sound of sports on TV.

My father sat in his usual brown recliner, but he looked so different from my mental image of him that I had to pause in the doorway to take him in. He was tall, like me, but his broad, hulking frame seemed small and frail now, like he'd been shrunk down to half his size. His brown hair had gone completely gray and a rough, scratchy beard covered his face. An empty ash tray sat next to him. At least he'd stopped smoking finally.

When his blue eyes snapped to mine they were as tough and alert as ever. "What are you doing here?"

So much for a nice family reunion. "Dolores called me."

My father scowled. "Damn meddling woman."

"She told me about the cancer. Why didn't you say anything?"

He sniffed and turned his attention back to the TV. "No one's problem but mine."

Shit, he was stubborn. I'd forgotten how infuriating he could be. "I'm your *son*. It's my problem, too."

"Yeah? And what do you think you can do about it?"

I ran a hand through my hair, forcing myself not to get pissed and rise to his challenge. "Whatever I can. I'm back in town for a while and I can help with anything you need."

"I don't want your damn money," he snapped.

"That's not—" I clenched my jaw and tried again. "Just tell me what I can do."

My father glared at me for a long moment before speaking. "You want to know what you can do? You can come work for me like I asked you to six years ago. Learn the ropes so you can take over the company when I'm gone."

Fuck. I should have known this was coming. "I can't do that."

"Figured you'd say that." He took the remote and turned the volume up on the TV so it became almost deafening.

"There must be something else I can do." When he didn't answer, I grabbed the remote from him and turned the TV down. "For Christ's sake, I'm talking to you here."

"What's there to talk about? You never gave a damn about the family business when you were younger and I see that hasn't changed. There's nothing else you can do, so we're done here."

My father owned a company—Evans Construction—that had been passed down to him from his father and his grandfather before that. He'd always expected me to grow up and join him in the family business, but I'd never been interested in that path. When he'd wanted me to build things with blocks, I'd wanted to play video games. By sixteen, I was designing the games. My brain had never worked the way he'd wanted, and it never would.

"Of course I care about the business, but I have my own company now. I can't just abandon it to go work for yours."

"That video game company?" He snorted. "You need to make something *real*. Something with your hands, that you can touch, that will last a hundred years. Not that computer shit."

He was right about one thing, nothing had changed. I was still getting the same shit I'd gotten when I was eighteen and went off to college instead of going to work for him. It wasn't good enough for him that I'd been the first of the Evans to go to college, no—I was a disgrace for not coming to work for the family business. When I graduated and still didn't go work for him, it was even worse. He was the reason I'd stayed in Seattle after I finished school. Him, and Carla.

"I won't come work for you, but I can still help in other ways." I gestured around the room. "Look at this place. It's a mess. Dolores can't do everything on her own. Let me get you some help. If nothing else, I'll get you to the best cancer specialist—"

"I already got a good doctor. And Dolores is fine. We're both fine. We don't need your help."

Damn my father and his pride. Why wouldn't he let me do anything for him? "Is the company in trouble? Because if you're worried about losing it, my company could buy it out, or I could loan you—"

"I don't want your damn charity!" he roared. "Take your money and get out of here!"

Gritting my teeth, I used two words I never said to him. "Dad. Please."

He struggled to his feet, his eyes hard. "I don't need anything from you and I don't want your help. I already told you once, if you won't continue the family business, then you're no son of mine. Now go. Get out of here. I don't want to see your face again."

Flashbacks of being eighteen and having this exact same conversation with the exact same outcome came back to me. I didn't even bother to argue this time. I already knew he wouldn't change his mind.

I grabbed my motorcycle helmet and stormed out of the house without another word. I jumped back on my bike, kicked it to life, and went to the same place I went when this happened before: to my real brother.

Wasn't there some saying about how you could never really go home again? Yeah, I was definitely finding that to be true tonight.

I parked outside Daniel's apartment complex and let myself in the front door. He'd slipped me a key before we'd left his parents' house, shortly after Carla had taken off. His place was a typical bachelor pad with only the bare essentials and not much in the way of decoration, but he had an extra room with a pull-out bed and that was good enough for me. Sure, I could easily afford to stay in a nice hotel, but I missed this—feeling like I was part of his family, pretending he was my real brother, not being alone for once. It was one of the reasons I debated moving back to LA all the time. Five minutes with my dad had killed that idea pretty fast.

Daniel was on his leather couch, watching that show he and Carla were obsessed with, *Road Trip Race*. Three empty bottles of beer stood in a row on the table, and he nursed another one in his hand.

"How'd it go?" he asked, as I shut the door.

"About the same as your family dinner."

He snorted and took a sip of beer. "That good? Sorry, man."

I dropped onto the couch beside him and he handed me an unopened beer. I snapped the top off. Even with how terrible this evening had been, sitting here with Daniel immediately made me feel a thousand times better. I was transported back to the old days, when I'd escape my house and crash at his as often as I could, when Eva would make us dinner, Henry would pull out an extra plate for me, and Carla would plop down beside me with a smile. Back then, I'd felt like I was part of something bigger. Like someone actually cared about me.

"My dad's an asshole. Nothing new there. I'm sorry about your parents too."

"I can't believe they're splitting up." Daniel's eyes were on the TV, but I could hear the pain in his voice. I doubted anyone else would be able to, but I knew Daniel like the back of my hand. He didn't show it, but he was taking this hard.

"It's not right," I agreed.

"Seriously. They were the one couple I could point to as having made it work and still being in love a million years later. And now…" He downed the rest of his beer. "Now it's all gone to hell. Proof that long-term relationships don't last."

"I'll drink to that." We clinked beer bottles.

"You're the smart one. You keep it casual. No promises, no strings attached, and no complications."

I shrugged. "It works."

There was a reason I never kept a woman around for more than a week or two, one that Daniel could never know. It was the same reason I never dated models, and why I stuck to shorter women, pale girls, and blondes and redheads.

The one woman I wanted was the one woman I couldn't have.

FOUR

Carla

I shouldn't have come here. This beach had too many memories and I'd managed to avoid it for the last six years without a problem. Until tonight anyway, when I'd gotten in my car and taken off.

I'd found myself heading north on Pacific Coast Highway, along the dark strip of road with the pitch black ocean on my left and the stars above me. Before I'd registered what I was doing, I'd turned down the small lane and onto the little spot on Zuma Beach that had once been my favorite place. Then I'd shut off the car and cried for a good ten minutes straight.

The tears had passed, but I still couldn't wrap my head around the idea that my parents were splitting up. Never in a million years would I have believed it was possible. They'd never fought. They'd never seemed even a little unhappy. They'd never once hinted that something like this could happen. But there must have been signs, right? A marriage doesn't fall apart overnight and they'd said it was a long time coming. Yet I hadn't seen any problems at all. How could I have been so incredibly blindsided by this?

Of course, it wasn't the first time I'd been wrong about love, so maybe my instincts couldn't be trusted at all. Just last week I'd been shocked to find my boyfriend of almost two years screwing some other girl. I'd let myself into his apartment, hoping to surprise him when he got off work, and instead I'd found a naked blond riding him cowgirl-style on his bed. Now I couldn't close my eyes without picturing her bouncing up and down on him, or hear the way he'd said "baby" over and over while he gripped her hips—like he'd once done with me.

I'd never seen his betrayal coming, despite countless warnings from my friends. They'd never liked Daryl, but I'd always insisted he was a good guy. How wrong I'd turned out to be.

After the blond had grabbed her clothes and left, Daryl reluctantly admitted he'd cheated on me before. In fact, there had been *many* other women in the time we were together. He'd claimed he got lonely when I traveled for work, that he had a sex addiction, that the others meant nothing and he loved only me. He'd rattled off a dozen excuses and had even got down on his knees and begged, but I was done with him.

My friends hadn't even been surprised, though they'd kindly refrained from saying, "I told you so." I was the only one who was shocked, and I'd spent the past week bawling my eyes out. I'd thought I was in love with Daryl. He was supposed to move with me to New York. He was an important part of my five year plan. And now it was over.

Maybe the signs had been there all along, and I was the one who'd been blind —with Daryl, with my parents...and with Ryan.

My gaze swept over the dark waves lapping at the pale shore. Last time I'd been at this beach, I'd read the situation all wrong. I'd missed the signs and thrown myself at Ryan, confessing that I loved him, that I had *always* loved him. And then I'd kissed him.

Big mistake.

Now I was back at the scene of the crime, and for what? To remind myself of the pain of my first heartbreak? To really drill it in my head that I couldn't trust my feelings when it came to relationships?

I gripped the steering wheel of my Mustang and sighed. Ryan's return must have triggered some masochistic side of me that made me want to relive it all again. Maybe because the faded pain of the past seemed more manageable than the current pain of the present.

Except it wasn't. I couldn't even get out of the car. If I did, all the memories and emotions from six years ago would come rushing back, and I didn't need those on top of my current misery. My parents and my ex-boyfriend were enough to send me to tears without the added bonus of seeing Ryan again.

Why had he picked tonight, of all nights, to return?

Suddenly, I just wanted to be back in my apartment. I would open a bottle of wine with my roommates Maddie and Becca and they'd make me feel a hundred times better. Coming to the beach had been a stupid idea. I should've gone straight home instead.

I turned the key in my ignition, but it made a few pathetic sounds and then died. *Don't do this to me. Not now.* I tried again, with the same result. Okay, deep breaths. Maybe the third time was the charm?

Nope.

My head fell forward against the steering wheel. Seriously, universe? As if my night wasn't bad enough already, now it threw this at me too? Was I being punished for something I'd done in a past life?

No, I refused to be beaten. I was the daughter of a mechanic and I'd grown up with a wrench in my hand and oil running through my veins. I could fix whatever was wrong with my car.

I popped the hood and checked the engine, but it was so dark out I couldn't see much of anything. With my phone as a flashlight, I poked around as best I could, but I suspected the timing chain had snapped. I'd have to replace it, which meant there was nothing I could do out here. The car would have to be towed to my dad's shop.

I slammed the hood shut and took stock of my situation. I was on a deserted road next to an empty beach and my car was dead. I didn't even have my sweater because I'd left it at my parents' house. I was truly screwed.

I pulled out my phone, but hesitated. I could call Dad—he had a small fleet of tow trucks available and would be happy to get me, but I didn't want to talk to him or Mom. I was too upset with them. I considered calling my roommates, but then remembered their band had a show tonight. Great. I'd have to suck it up and ask my brother for help.

I called Daniel and told him what happened, then listened to him berate me for five minutes about going to the beach alone at night.

"Stay inside the car with the doors locked until help arrives. Call 911 if you see anything. *Anything*, okay?"

I sighed. "Yes. I'll be fine though. Really."

"Carla—"

"My phone's dying. Gotta go." It wasn't dying, but I hung up before he could launch into another lecture.

I parked my butt against the hood of my Mustang and crossed my arms while I waited for Daniel to arrive. Getting in the car and locking the doors was probably good advice—not to mention it was getting really cold out here—but I stubbornly refused. I was tired of the way my brother always treated me like a fragile little child who needed someone to take care of her. Ever since I'd gotten cancer, Daniel had taken overprotective to extreme levels. It was bad enough having a mom who took me to the ER every time I got a papercut and a dad who wouldn't let me date a boy without giving him a lot of not-so-subtle threats with a baseball bat. I didn't need this kind of parenting from my older brother too.

After about five minutes my annoyance with my brother faded. I'd never been able to stay mad at anyone for long, and Daniel was just looking out for me, showing me he cared in his own annoying way. He was picking me up, after all. I couldn't be too angry at him.

But when a black Ducati motorcycle pulled up, it wasn't my brother who'd come to my rescue.

It was Ryan.

FIVE

Ryan

Carla did *not* look happy to see me.

"What are you doing here?" she asked, as soon as I took my helmet off. Despite her height, she looked small standing beside her car with her arms wrapped around herself. God, she was beautiful. I was overcome with relief knowing she was okay. What if I hadn't gotten here so fast? What if something had happened to her?

I stormed over to her, suddenly furious that she had put herself in such a vulnerable position. "What the hell were you thinking? Coming out here by yourself in the middle the night?"

Her lips pressed into a tight line, but it didn't make her any less stunning. "I already got this lecture from my brother. I don't need another from you."

"He has a point, you know. You shouldn't come to places like this on your own. It's not safe."

"Since when do you care? You show up after six years and think you can tell me how to live my life?" She shook her head, her glorious curls bouncing. "You're not my brother, Ryan."

Didn't I know it. I couldn't stop staring at the spot where her tank top strap had fallen down one arm, revealing a smooth, dark shoulder just begging for me to press my mouth against it. Nope, I definitely didn't see myself as her brother.

"I *don't* care. I'm only here as a favor to Daniel." I forced my gaze away. To her car, to the ocean, to anything but her body. Jesus, the second we were alone together I couldn't stop thinking about kissing her. This was exactly why I'd avoided her all these years.

"I've been perfectly safe here this entire time. I didn't need you to show up and rescue me like some kind of white knight." With that, she turned away from me and stalked toward the beach. Where was she going now?

I stared after her as she reached down and plucked off her flip flops, temporarily paralyzed by the sight of those long legs under her shorts. She dropped her shoes on the curb before stepping into the sand and walking with purpose toward the dark water.

I had no choice but to follow her. My heavy motorcycle boots were clunky in the sand, but I didn't stop to take them off. She paused near the black waves, which crashed with a soft spray then lazily slid close to her toes before retreating again. I thought of the last time we were here, and how her mouth had pressed against mine, and how for a second I'd had everything. Before I'd pushed her away. Before I'd lost her forever.

I wondered if she was reliving the same memory.

––––––

"I'm going to grab another drink," I told Daniel, who was sitting on the beach with Paula in his lap. He nodded and went right back to kissing her. Paula's friend Maria gave me a hopeful look as I stood up, but I ignored it. She'd be more than happy to climb into my lap, but I wasn't feeling it. What was the point when I was leaving tomorrow?

Besides, the girl I wanted to talk to was the one standing all alone at the edge of the party, just outside of the bonfire's light. She was two years younger than everyone else here and wasn't celebrating high school graduation like the rest of us. She was only at the party because Daniel and I had invited her.

"You okay?" I asked, as I approached her.

She turned toward me with a sad smile. "I'm fine. I just wanted to get away for a moment."

I nodded. Carla had always been shy and this wasn't her group of friends. She was probably counting the minutes until she could leave. "Need anything? A drink?"

"Can we go for a walk?" she asked, her dark eyes shining under the bright moonlight.

"Sure." She looked hot tonight, in an off-the-shoulder sweater over tiny cutoff shorts. It was impossible to say no to her. Especially when I knew this was probably the last time I would see her in a while.

We strolled down the beach, leaving our friends and the bonfire behind us, while the waves strained to reach us but never quite made it to our feet. We walked close enough that sometimes our bare arms or fingertips would brush against each other. That slight, innocent touch of skin was enough to drive me crazy, to make me wish I wasn't leaving for another state tomorrow. And that I hadn't promised her brother I would never touch her.

In the past few months I'd started to notice Carla as more than my best friend's little sister. Ever since she'd turned sixteen, she'd suddenly become a young woman with curves I couldn't stop staring at and a mouth made for kissing. It was a good thing I was leaving, because I wasn't sure how much longer I could hide how badly I wanted her.

She sat on a patch of sand near a group of rocks that completely blocked the rest of my friends from view. I took the spot beside her and we stretched our legs in front of us. Hers were long and bare under her tiny shorts. I wanted so badly to slide my hands along them, to see if her skin felt as soft and smooth as it looked. Instead, I leaned back, planting my hands behind me in the sand.

She gazed across the beach at the water, where the moon lit up the night, casting the dark waves in silver. It was beautiful, but none of it captivated me the way she did.

"I can't believe you're leaving tomorrow," she said, with a soft sigh.

"Me neither."

"And Daniel too. I'm losing my two favorite guys in the whole world at the same time. What am I going to do?"

"Hey, it won't be so bad." She sounded so miserable that I wrapped my arm around her, pulling her against me. She immediately leaned in like she belonged there. "We'll both come back and visit you all the time. I promise."

"Will you really though?"

"How else are we going to fight off all the boys who will be clamoring for your attention?"

"Ha. What boys?"

I swallowed the jealous lump in my throat. "A girl as beautiful as you who also fixes up cars? Guys will be lining up outside your door soon, I guarantee it."

"I doubt that." Her hands tugged on the end of her shorts, like she was nervous.

"It's true. And Daniel and I won't be around to protect you from them." I slid a finger under her chin, tilting her face toward me, and heard her intake of breath. "Be careful, okay? I don't want you to get hurt."

"I don't want guys lining up at my door," she whispered. "And I won't get hurt."

"No?" My hand had somehow slid from her chin to her cheek, like it had its own mind. I couldn't help but stroke her, and yes, her skin was even smoother than I'd imagined. I never wanted to stop touching her.

She covered my hand with hers, pressing it to her cheek. "There's only one guy I want and I know he would never hurt me."

With those words, she touched her lips softly to mine. A quick brush of her mouth, so tentative and hopeful, as if she was searching for a response.

I gave her one, without a second thought.

I dragged her against me and found her mouth again with my own. She moaned softly as I slid my tongue across her lips, and then she opened for me, letting me take the kiss deeper. She was so sweet, so good, and kissing her was like tasting sunshine itself. Her body pressed against mine and her fingers dug into my shirt and I was lost, my control snapping as I finally gave in to the thing I'd been craving for months but never let myself have.

"Ryan," she breathed, and there was nothing sexier than my name on her just-kissed lips.

But then the reality of what I was doing hit me like a truck. I was kissing Carla, my best friend's little sister. Carla, who had always been off-limits. Carla, who I would be leaving tomorrow for four years.

I tore myself away from her. She looked dazed, licking her lips like she wanted more, and god how I wanted to give it to her. I was half-tempted to lower her down onto the sand and cover my body with hers, to capture her mouth again and slide my fingers across her skin. It took everything in my power to hold myself back, before we both made a huge mistake.

"I'm sorry." I stood up quickly, adjusting my jeans to hide what was going on there. "That shouldn't have happened."

She blinked up at me slowly. "Why not?"

"Because I'm not the guy for you."

"Yes, you are." She stood up too, moving closer to me, but I took a step back. "Ryan, I... I love you."

I cringed, knowing I would have to hurt her even more now. I had to end this fast, before it went any further. "You don't love me. You have a childhood crush on me and I'm a jerk for taking advantage of that." I ran a hand through my hair, hating every second of this. "I promise it won't happen ever again."

Her face fell, her eyes watering, and I was the biggest asshole in the entire world. I wanted to take it back, to tell her how much I cared about her, to tell her I didn't want any other girl but her, but it was better this way. Daniel had made me swear that I would never touch her, especially once it became obvious Carla had a crush on me. Besides, I was moving to Seattle tomorrow for four years of college. I couldn't get involved with anyone right now. Especially with my father breathing down my neck to go work for him at his company. The scholarship I'd gotten was too good to pass up, and I had to get out of the city and go after my own dream before I was trapped in a life I didn't want.

Turning her down was the best thing for both of us. I just wish it didn't hurt so fucking bad.

"But you kissed me," she said.

"It was a mistake."

"I…I don't understand."

"I've been drinking and I got carried away. It doesn't mean anything. You're like a sister to me, you know that."

"Like a sister. Wow." She wiped at her eyes. "I'm so stupid. I thought maybe you felt the same about me. I guess I was wrong."

I opened my mouth to tell her she wasn't wrong, but then slammed it shut. It was better she think that I wasn't interested in her. That way, once I was gone, she'd move on and never look back. She'd forget about me, writing me off as a stupid crush she'd had on her older brother's friend, and then she'd find some other guy who could make her happy in all the ways I couldn't. Even if the thought of her with someone else made me want to punch something.

"I don't see you that way. I'm sorry."

She nodded slowly. Her face turned away from me, her arms crossed, her body folding in on itself. The silence between us became almost painful, but there was nothing more to be said.

I gestured down the beach. "We should get back."

She still wouldn't look at me. "I'll be right there. I need a minute."

I hesitated, trying to think of something else I could say, but I would only make it worse. I walked down the beach, back to our friends, and left her behind.

———

That was the last time I'd spoken to Carla, until tonight.

My memory was broken up by her voice, jolting me back to the present. "What are you doing here, Ryan?"

"Daniel's been drinking, so he asked me to pick you up. He'll send one of your dad's trucks to get your car tomorrow morning."

"That's not what I meant. Why are you in town?"

I stiffened. I didn't want to talk about that. Not when Carla had enough problems on her mind. She didn't need my shit to add to it. That was my burden and no one else's. "Visiting family."

"And you thought you'd show up at our dinner table out of the blue? Now, after all these years?" Her voice was angry. Good. It was easier for both of us if she hated me. I should encourage that.

"Daniel invited me."

She gazed across the waves, rubbing her bare arms. I shrugged off my leather jacket and moved toward her, but she gave me a look of pure disdain and took a step back.

"You're freezing," I said. "Put this on. I won't bite."

"I'd rather be cold."

I held out the jacket again. "I realize I'm the last person in the world you want to be with right now. Trust me, this isn't how I'd prefer to spend my night either. Put the damn jacket on and we'll get out of here and go our separate ways."

"Sorry for ruining your night," she said sarcastically. "What, do you have a hot date? One of your blond actresses maybe? What was the last one's name? Heidi?"

My eyebrow darted up. "You sure know a lot about my sex life."

"You're not exactly subtle about it."

"Why would I be?" I gave her a sly grin that I knew would infuriate her.

She looked like she wanted to drown me in the ocean. I'd never seen Carla like this before. When we were younger, she rarely got angry, and when she did it passed almost instantly. She was always kind to everyone, even people who were rude to her, and she left every room brighter than when she'd entered it. What happened to the sweet girl I used to know? Had she really changed so much over the years?

No, I didn't think that was it. I remembered a picture from last Thanksgiving I'd seen on Facebook, when she'd gone to feed the homeless at a nearby shelter. In the photo, she'd been smiling at the person she was serving and her eyes had lit up with that inner glow that made her so incomparable. She was still the same person…with everyone except me.

She rubbed her arms again, then made an annoyed huff. "Fine. I'll take your stupid jacket."

Finally. I stepped close and helped the jacket onto her arms. My fingers brushed against her skin with an electric jolt. Her breath caught and she turned her head toward me, the anger fading from her eyes. It was the first time I'd touched her since our kiss.

I didn't move. My hands lingered on her arms over my jacket. I had the strongest urge to pull her closer and relive that moment on this beach six years ago. Despite my harsh words, I burned with the need to show her how much it killed me to stay away from her all this time. Her lips parted like she wanted the same thing, and I imagined how soft they would be against mine. My head lowered toward hers.

She stepped back abruptly, breaking the connection between us. My brain woke up again. Shit, that had been close. Another second and I would have kissed her. What the fuck was I doing?

She gripped the edge of the jacket, pulling it tighter around her so it hugged her body. "Let's go."

I exhaled sharply. "Right."

We headed back across the sand to the parking lot. We were the only people on the beach and it was pitch dark except for the tiny sliver of a moon overhead. Once again I felt a rush of protective anger at the fact that Carla had come out here alone tonight—and at myself too, because I suspected I was part of the reason why. Did she visit this beach a lot? Or was my presence at dinner the spark that caused her to flee here?

She stopped beside my motorcycle, giving it a long once-over. "You came to pick me up on *that?*"

I looked down at my gleaming black Ducati. She made a good point. I'd rushed to the beach as fast as I could, not even considering that she might not be comfortable riding my bike. She would be safe with me though. Daniel would kill me if something happened to her, but more than that, I would never forgive myself.

"I brought a second helmet, but if you're too scared, I can call us a car." I made my tone flippant on purpose. I'd come too close to kissing her once tonight already. Time to rebuild those walls between us and fast.

She put her hands on her hips, the annoyance back in her eyes. "I'm not nervous. I've been on Daniel's bikes many times before."

"You sure? I wouldn't want you to mess up your hair."

Her eyes narrowed to slits. "I need to get my things."

She unlocked the Mustang and grabbed a bag from the passenger side. I examined the car, admiring how much it had changed since I'd last seen it. I'd spent hours working on that car with her in her father's shop, back when it barely ran.

"What's wrong with your car?" I asked.

"I think it's the timing chain. It's too dark to tell for sure, but the engine's been making a weird rattling noise for a couple weeks."

"A couple weeks? Seems unlike you to let it go so long."

"I've had a lot going on. Not that it's any of your business."

"Hmm. Can I look?"

She glared at me, but popped the hood. I leaned over the car, admiring the engine. Like she'd said, it was hard to see much in the dark.

"I think you're right about the chain. Should be an easy fix, at least." I slammed the hood shut, then ran my hand over the paint job.

She'd gotten the car for her sixteenth birthday. Her parents had wanted to get her something new, but no, she'd fallen in love with a beat-up '67 Mustang with a rusted paint job, broken headlights, and a million things wrong with it. She'd spent all her free time repairing it, spending every dime she earned on parts. I think she enjoyed the restoration process even more than actually driving it.

And now? It was a thing of pure beauty, inside and out. Just like her.

I handed her the extra helmet and she squished it on over her dark curls, then I put on my own helmet and climbed onto the bike. She got on behind me, her movements smooth, like she had done it a hundred times before. Her body tensed against mine as I started the engine. Her arms reluctantly slid around my waist, making her breasts press against my back and her thighs tighten around me. We were closer than we'd ever been before. Body to body. So damn right and so damn wrong at the same time.

Taking the bike was a huge fucking mistake. Now I'd have to drive her home while rocking some major wood, and then try to forget the feel of her body against mine. I had to forget it. Carla was my best friend's little sister and she was completely off-limits. And no matter how much I wanted her, I wouldn't risk losing what little I had left of a family.

SIX

Carla

My Mustang was already waiting for me in Dad's shop by the time I arrived the next afternoon. None of the mechanics had dared to touch it after it was towed in. They knew better than that. It was my baby and no one worked on it except me.

But first, I needed to have a serious talk with my brother. I found him in the back office doing paperwork. He'd started working for Dad while going to business school and he knew how to run the place at this point. Dad relied on him a lot now that the business had expanded recently, especially with the new location opening soon. Daniel loved both cars and business, so working here was the perfect fit for him. One day he planned to take over so Dad could retire, but we all knew that wouldn't be anytime soon.

I shut the door to the office and crossed my arms. "What was that last night?"

He looked up at me with a scowl. "What, when you took off and left me to deal with the fallout of our parents' marriage by myself?"

"No, when you sent Ryan to get me."

He gave a slight shrug. "I was drunk. I couldn't have picked you up even if I wanted to."

"But you didn't want to."

"Not really, no." His eyes narrowed. "I can't believe you just walked out during dinner."

I unfolded my arms and sighed. "I'm sorry. I shouldn't have left you like that."

"No shit. We're supposed to have each other's back when it comes to this kind of stuff." He slammed the desk drawer shut and stood up. "And what were you thinking going off by yourself to that beach? It was late and you shouldn't have been there alone. Especially since your car was having problems."

"I was fine. I've been to that beach a hundred times before."

"Not alone." He ran a hand along his shaved head. "It's probably better Ryan picked you up and not me, 'cause I would have let you have it. All I can say is, thank god Ryan got to you quickly before something happened."

"Nothing would have happened! I just... I had to get away, okay? I needed to be alone. That was the only place that made me feel better." My eyes welled up with tears thinking about dinner last night, replaying the moment when my parents said they were splitting up. I swiped them away with the back of my hand.

Daniel walked around the desk and gave me a big hug. "Hey, don't cry, baby sister. Everything is going to be okay."

"No it isn't. Mom and Dad…"

"They'll work it out. They're just going through a rough patch."

"Do you really believe that?"

He hesitated. "I have to."

I nodded and wiped at my eyes, feeling silly for crying in front of my brother. He'd seen it before though and he always made me feel better. Even if we bickered sometimes and he made me crazy with his over-protectiveness, he was always there for me when I needed him.

Daniel wrapped an arm around me and led me out the door. "Come on, let's figure out what's wrong with your car."

Together we headed back to my Mustang, but I stopped abruptly when I spotted Ryan pulling into the shop on his bike. What was he doing here? I'd planned to avoid seeing him again before I left for New York, but now every time I turned around he was there. Couldn't he just leave me alone?

By the time Ryan had dropped me off in front of my apartment last night, every one of my nerve endings had been on fire from sitting behind him with my arms wrapped around his waist, feeling his broad shoulders and hard back against my chest, watching his strong arms handle the bike. I'd burned with both annoyance and desire, a confusing mix of emotions I wanted to extinguish as fast as possible.

Now he was here and every inch of me flared with heat at the sight of him in his black leather motorcycle gear. It was like the universe was taunting me with something I'd once wanted badly but couldn't have. Something I'd tried to forget, but apparently my body still craved as much as ever.

How dare he come back into my life after six years of silence? How. Dare. He.

"Hey, man," Daniel said. "Didn't know you were coming by. You here to work on Carla's Mustang?"

"I actually came by to clean the chain on my bike and change the oil." Ryan began pulling off his motorcycle gloves. "But I'm happy to help if Carla needs me."

"I don't want your help." My voice came out steelier than I intended, and Daniel glanced back and forth between the two of us. He didn't know about what happened six years ago or how uncomfortable it was for me to be in Ryan's presence now.

"My bike could use an oil change too." Daniel clasped Ryan on the shoulder with a grin. "The three of us here, just like old times, eh?"

"Yeah, great," I muttered.

I popped the hood on the Mustang and leaned over it, examining the engine compartment while the two guys talked about their bikes. Like I'd suspected, the timing chain in my car had snapped and needed to be replaced. Luckily that was an easy fix and the car would be running smoothly again in a few hours.

I didn't say a word to Ryan while we worked, but it was impossible not to look at him. My eyes were thirsty for glimpses of him, as if I'd been in a visual drought until he'd arrived back in my life. Today he wore a soft black t-shirt that hugged his toned frame, and when he reached up to grab something off a top shelf, it slid up just enough to give me a peek of his abs and the hint of his hips disappearing into his jeans. I imagined resting my hands there and how I'd be torn between sliding my fingers higher or lower.

His eyes cut to mine, like he could feel my gaze on him. He scowled and I looked away. The daydream evaporated.

My phone started ringing in my purse and I'd never been more glad for a distraction. I fished it out and saw Giselle Roberts' name flash on the screen.

I stepped outside the garage area and onto the sidewalk, away from the noise of the shop. "Hello?"

"Hey, Carla. How are you doing?"

"I'm good," I said, even though I'd been anything but good in the past week. But I wasn't about to unload all my drama on my future boss. "How are you?"

"I've had better days." There was a pause before she spoke again. "Carla, I'm very sorry to tell you this, but *American Supermodel* has been cancelled by the network."

"W-what…?"

"I know, it was a total surprise to me as well. Completely out of the blue. They green-lit us for another season but now they've pulled the plug at the last minute. Those assholes." She sighed. "I'm really sorry."

The world was crumbling under my feet. I rested a hand on the chain-link fence to keep me steady. "I understand," I said, but inside my head I was silently screaming. This couldn't be happening, not now of all times.

"I know this puts you out of a job and I feel terrible, I really do. Especially with the situation with your mom…" She cleared her throat. "That's why I wanted to tell you about another opportunity I have available."

"What is it?" I asked, reaching for any spark of hope. Without the spot on *American Supermodel*, I had nothing lined up for the summer. No job. No apartment. No boyfriend. Absolutely nothing at all.

"I could use you on our other show, *Road Trip Race*."

That spark of hope burst into a giant flame. No way. A job on *Road Trip Race*, my favorite show? "As the host? Is Chuck Bannon leaving?"

"No, sorry. As a contestant."

Just like that, my hope flame was extinguished, leaving only a smoky trail behind. I didn't answer. I'd had a permanent position on a show and now she wanted me to be a *contestant* on one? Seriously?

"I know it's not nearly the same, but you would get paid a stipend for every week you're on the show, plus the winner of each challenge gets five thousand dollars. And if you make it to the end, you and your partner would win a million dollars."

I couldn't find my voice. I couldn't believe she was even offering me this after she'd just told me all my dreams for my career had been crushed. Even though I loved *Road Trip Race*, going on it wasn't a job. What would I do when my time on the show was over?

"I think viewers would love to see you on the show since you were previously on *Behind The Seams*. And you have a boyfriend, right? Maybe he could go on as your partner? If not, I'm sure we could find someone to pair up with you."

I'd always daydreamed about going on the show with Daniel and using our car knowledge to win, but I'd never been serious about the idea. I'd never once thought we would actually do it. I wasn't sure he would even be interested in being my partner, especially with the new location opening soon and this drama with my parents.

"Carla? Are you there?" Giselle finally asked, when the silence became overwhelmingly awkward.

"I'm here."

"What do you think?"

My hand shook as it held the phone up to my ear and the pressure in my throat became unbearable. "I... I can't. I'm sorry. I'm grateful for the chance, but it's not for me."

"I understand. Again, I apologize for what's happened. It was completely out of my control. But if you change your mind, give me a call in the next day or two. The show starts filming next Monday."

"Okay. Thank you."

I hung at the phone and stared at nothing. The summer after graduating from college was supposed to be the best time of my life. I'd planned everything perfectly, but now it was all turning to dust. Within the space of a week I'd lost *everything*. What was I supposed to do now?

I clicked my phone screen on and off while trying to make a new plan. I could call my agent and see if he could whip up some modeling jobs for me to make sure I could eat. But where would I live? My roommates and I were moving out of our apartment at the end of the week. One option was to move in with my brother, except Ryan was staying with him for the time being. I could live with my parents —or my dad, anyway—but I couldn't deal with them right now. I'd have to find a new apartment, but that took time and money and I was short on both right now.

I'd never felt more lost in my life.

Maybe going on the show really was my best option. For a moment I considered it. Daniel and me in a car, cruising along the highway, looking for scavenger hunt items. Visiting all sorts of different places and working together to try to win money. But then I shook that fantasy away and got back to reality. Going on the show was not an option.

After a quick phone call to my agent, I wasn't in any better shape. According to him, every decent job was already booked for the summer. He could schedule me some spots for fall or winter, but otherwise I'd have to wait around and see if any last minute modeling jobs popped up. No, I'd have to figure out some other way to make money. Or I'd have to go to my parents and beg them for help.

I took a deep breath and attempted to regain my composure, then headed back inside the shop. The guys were both working on their bikes, but they looked up when I walked in with nearly identical worried expressions.

"What's wrong?" Ryan asked.

I blew out a long breath of air. I supposed there was no reason to hide it at this point. "*American Supermodel* got cancelled. I'm out of a job. I'm not moving to New York after all." My voice trembled a little at that last bit and I ducked my head in case the tears came. I would *not* cry in front of Ryan.

"Oh shit. I'm sorry. I know you were excited about that job." Daniel stepped forward like he wanted to hug me but I shook my head.

"Yeah, I was. I don't know what to do now. And the craziest part is that she asked me to go on *Road Trip Race* instead."

He frowned. "Like, as a contestant?"

"Yep." I laughed, a pathetic sad laugh, and leaned against the side of my car.

"Are you going to do it?" Ryan asked.

"No, of course not." I shook my head. "I've had my fill of being on a reality TV show as a contestant already. I don't need to go through that again."

"You love *Road Trip Race*." Ryan wiped his hands on a rag and tossed it aside. "You should do it."

Daniel shot him an incredulous look. "No way. She can't go on the show."

"Why not? She might have fun."

"Yeah, why not?" I didn't want to do it, but it annoyed me that my brother was so adamant against it.

Daniel shook his head. "It's not a good idea. Driving across the country on your own? Hell no. That's way too dangerous."

I crossed my arms. "It's not dangerous. You've seen the show as many times as I have, and you know there are cameras everywhere and people from the show around at all times. Plus I'd have a partner."

Daniel scoffed. "But who would your partner be?"

"Um. You?"

He laughed sharply. "Yeah, right."

"Come on! We've always said we wanted to go on the show. Now's our chance." I wasn't sure where the words were coming from. A second ago I'd been determined not to go on the show, but with Ryan saying yes and Daniel saying no I suddenly wondered, why not? It wasn't like I had anything else going for me right now.

"This is the worst possible time for me to leave with the new location opening soon. Especially since Dad is so distracted by this mess with Mom. He needs me here more than ever now." Daniel waved his hand dismissively. "But if you're so determined to go, ask that boyfriend of yours."

My eyes dropped to the oil-stained floor. "I can't. We... I broke up with him."

"Oh yeah? Finally!" Daniel let out a sharp whoop. "What'd he do? Did you catch him with another girl or some shit?"

He was joking, but my cheeks flushed and I turned away. Toward Ryan, whose gaze was as intense as the sun on a hot day. I couldn't tell if he wanted to grab me in a hug or punch someone for me.

"Oh shit," Daniel said, quickly sobering up. "He really was cheating on you? Son of a bitch. I'll murder him."

"Yes, he was," I said quietly. "He had been for a long time. With multiple girls."

Ryan moved to my side, his hands clenched and his body tense like he would defend me with his life. "Where is this guy now?"

"That asshole." Daniel straightened up to his full, massive size. "He's going to pay for hurting my baby sister."

I held up my hands. "No one is making anyone pay. I handled it."

Daniel paced back and forth, like an angry panther. "I always knew he wasn't good enough for you. If I ever see him again, I swear to god…"

"I'm fine, really. I'm over it already. Although it'd be nice if he would stop texting me."

"He's texting you?" Ryan asked, his voice quiet but hard as steel. "Tell me where he is. I'll get him to leave you alone."

"I don't need you to protect me," I said, looked up at his eyes. They were such a dark brown that they looked almost black. If I let myself, I'd get lost in them forever.

He set his hand on my shoulder for a brief moment. It sent a little thrill through me, and at the same time it annoyed me. My brother took overprotective to the next level, but Ryan was just as bad. It didn't mean anything though. If he cared about me at all, it was like a sister, nothing more. I didn't need *two* over-bearing big brothers.

Daniel wrapped an arm around me. "I don't like the idea of any guy messing around on my little sister. What kind of idiot would cheat on you anyway? You're a fucking model!"

"I seem to have a habit of falling for guys who don't return my feelings." I didn't look at Ryan when I said it, but from the corner of my eye I saw him stiffen.

"Some guys are assholes." Ryan's voice was so quiet I almost didn't hear him. My eyes lifted to his and he stared at me with such force that my heart skipped a beat.

"See, this is exactly why you can't go on the show," Daniel said. "You're too nice. The other contestants will take advantage of you so they can win."

"I'm not that nice." I yanked away from my brother's arm. His words stung, probably because there was a hint of truth in them. I always tried to be positive and to see the best in people, at least until they proved me wrong. But that hadn't worked out for me very well so far, had it?

"I just don't want you to get hurt. Or, god forbid, what if you got sick during the show?"

Ah, there it was. The real reason Daniel didn't want me to go on the show. He was worried I'd relapse. Like our parents, he still saw me as that frail teenager who almost died, even though that was a long time ago.

"I'm not going to get sick."

"Carla." He reached for my arm but I stepped back.

"You think I'm some weak, fragile girl who needs to be protected at all times. You don't think I can win because I'm 'too nice.' But you're wrong. I know that show inside out, and I know cars and maps, and I bet I could win."

"Of course I think you could win. You're not fragile or weak or any of that. But you do need someone to look out for you on the show. Everyone does. And the only person I trust to protect you on the show is me." He paused and glanced at his best friend. "Or Ryan."

Ryan stiffened. "That's not an option."

"No, definitely not." Like I'd want Ryan as my partner. *Anyone* but him would be better. Except my choices were pretty limited. I didn't know a single other person who was free this summer and who would go with me. "I guess the show could assign me a partner."

"Not going to happen," Ryan said, his face stern.

"No way," Daniel added. "You can't go on the show with some stranger. Our parents would never let you, anyway."

"You don't control me and neither do they. I'm twenty-two years old. I can make my own decisions." I threw up my hands. "Forget it. I'm not going on the show anyway so this entire conversation is pointless."

I grabbed my purse and headed for the door. I hated abandoning my car when I wasn't finished working on it, but I couldn't stand being around those two for another minute. Maddie's car was parked down the street and I made my way toward it. She'd let me borrow it for the day, since she would be with Becca at practice.

Rushed footsteps sounded behind me. "Carla, wait."

I stopped, took a deep breath, and turned to face Ryan. "What is it?"

"I'll go with you."

I blinked. "What?"

"On the show." His gaze held mine, dark and hypnotic. "I'll be your partner."

SEVEN

Ryan

I couldn't believe I'd just said that. What the fuck was I thinking? I couldn't go on a reality TV show. I had a company to run. My father was sick. And Carla couldn't stand me.

"You want to go on the show…" Her eyebrows slowly lifted up. "With me."

"I do."

She regarded me skeptically. I'd never been obsessed with the show like she and Daniel were, although I'd watched it with them a few times. Not in many years though. But after she'd told us how she'd lost her job and how her boyfriend had been cheating on her, she'd looked so lost and alone it made me want to take care of her, to do whatever I could to make things better. And even though she was far more capable than Daniel gave her credit for, she was way too nice of a person for her own good. She needed someone to protect her on the show, to make sure no one took advantage of her, to watch out for her both emotionally and physically. She needed someone she could trust. Someone like me, who wasn't a good person, who could insulate her from all the bullshit so she could have a fun time and maybe win some money too.

After the shitty summer she was having, she needed something good to happen to her. I wasn't it, but I could help. Besides, like Daniel, I didn't trust anyone else to go on the show with her. The thought of some stranger driving across the country with her made me see red. No, it had to be me.

She swatted back a stray curl that had fallen over her eye. "Why would you offer to do this?"

I gave a casual shrug. "You need help and I need to get away for a while."

It wasn't a lie. I'd gone back to my father's house this morning, but was told by my stepbrother that Dad refused to see me. Then he'd slammed the door in my face like he had more right to be in that house than I did, the little prick.

I'd gone to visit my father's office after that, to see how things were holding up.

Dolores was running the place by herself, but it seemed like it was doing well even without Dad around. I'd tried to picture myself working in the place, running the construction company, dealing with housing projects and permits and construction crews, and felt sick. I'd never wanted that life and I never would.

But the moment I'd gotten on my bike to leave, I'd caught sight of the Evans Construction sign and felt the guilt like a punch to my gut. If I sold my company to Slade Industries, I'd be able to run the family business. It was a good deal Slade was offering too. I'd be compensated very well, my employees would keep their jobs, and I could make my father proud for once in my life. If it was his dying wish for me to continue the family business, could I really turn him down? Even if doing so made me miserable?

There was no good answer. No matter what I did, I would hate myself for it.

"I don't need your help," Carla said. "I don't want your help."

"No?" I looked around us in an exaggerated way. "I don't see anyone else lining up to offer."

She crossed her arms. "I have other people I can ask."

"Like who? That cheating ex-boyfriend of yours?" My hands clenched into fists. "Over my dead body."

"No, not him."

"Who then?"

She huffed. "It doesn't matter. You are the absolute last person on my list."

Of course she wouldn't want me as her partner after what I'd done, after the way I'd treated her. She hated me, and I didn't blame her. But I also wasn't letting her go on the show with anyone else.

I stepped closer, lowering my voice. "I'm going with you. Consider this my way of making it up to you for being a complete asshole all this time."

Her eyes widened and she looked away quickly. When she spoke again, her voice was rough. "Ryan, I'm grateful for the offer, but you and I... after what happened..." She shook her head, making those dark curls bounce. "It's not a good idea. And it doesn't matter anyway. I'm not going on the show."

I wanted to slide my fingers into her hair so badly. I wanted to lose myself in those curls forever. "Why not?"

"It's not a good fit for me. I should be looking for a new job and a new place to live. And Daniel's right. I'm not the type of person who'd do well on that show."

"Ignore him. He's trying to look out for you, but he wants you to be happy too. If this is what you want, then he'll be on board with it, as will your parents."

"They'll only agree if you come as my partner."

"And I offered to do that."

She studied me like she was trying to figure me out. "I'll think about it."

She got in a car I didn't recognize and drove off, quickly vanishing down the road. I was tempted to get on my Ducati and follow her to make sure she got home safely, but I forced myself to give her some space.

I returned to my bike to finish the oil change, but Daniel immediately started in on me. "What the fuck, man?" he asked. "I thought you had my back."

"What are you talking about?"

"She can't go on that show!"

"It'll be good for her. She needs this, especially after all the shit that's happened to her. She deserves to be happy."

He gave me a look like I was a complete idiot. "She won't be happy when some asshole screws her over, and you know someone will."

"Not if I go with her."

He paused. "You'd do that?"

"I told her I would. Like you said, I don't trust anyone else to go."

His eyes narrowed. "What's going on with you two?"

"Nothing. Absolutely nothing."

He crossed the room until he was right in front of me. "Promise me you'll protect her on the show."

I met his gaze without backing down. "I promise. I'd never let anything happen to her."

He squinted at me. "You don't have a thing for her, do you?"

"No. Hell no. Like you said, she's not my type."

"Don't bullshit me. If you have feelings for my sister, tell me right now."

"No. She's like my own sister. I'd just as soon kiss you."

"Keep your mouth to yourself, pretty boy." He poked a finger at my chest. "Fine, go with her on the show. Just swear to me you won't touch her or get involved with her."

"I swear it. Just like I swore it years ago."

"Good." He dropped his hand. "After that fucker cheated on her, the last thing she needs is to get involved with someone like you. I'd hate to have to kill my best friend."

I bristled. "What the fuck is that supposed to mean?"

"Man, I love you like a brother, but you don't exactly have a good track record with the ladies. What was your longest relationship—a week? If even that?"

His words cut deep, but I smirked instead of showing how much they hurt. "If they're lucky."

"That's exactly my point. Carla is way too good for you."

"That's the damn truth," I muttered. "But who is ever going to be good enough in your eyes?"

"No one. I keep hoping she'll wake up and decide to become a nun, but it hasn't happened yet."

I remembered the way Carla had kissed, passionate and sensuous, and shook my head. "Fat chance of that ever happening."

EIGHT

Carla

When I stepped into the apartment, music hit my ear—a common sound when you lived with two rock stars. My roommates Maddie and Becca were hanging out in the living room with an acoustic guitar in each of their laps, but they both stopped when I came in.

"I need some wine, stat." I threw my stuff on the dining room table without a care for where it went. My purse skittered across the table and knocked a candle over. Oh well. What did it matter anyway? Our apartment was a disaster zone already. Everything in it was being packed up. Maddie and Becca were moving in with their boyfriends, and I was supposed to be heading to New York. In a week this apartment would be someone else's, and I'd have nowhere to live.

They each looked at me and my mess and jumped to their feet, their guitars forgotten. "What's wrong?" Maddie asked.

I shook my head. "Wine first."

"Shit, it must be really bad if she's drinking," Becca said. "I'll make some emergency cookies."

Maddie nodded and patted the couch. "Come sit down and relax. I'll open a bottle."

"Thanks." I crashed onto the sofa in a sideways heap, while the two girls disappeared into the kitchen for a few minutes. When they returned, they had wine and three glasses and they tucked in beside me.

"Cookies will be done in ten minutes," Becca said. She'd discovered a newfound love of baking ever since she'd moved in with us, and Maddie and I were definitely not complaining. I'd only known her a few months, but she'd already become a good friend. After our previous roommate Julie had moved to New York to work in fashion, we'd needed another roommate. Becca had just joined Maddie's band (for the second time) and needed a place to stay, so it worked out perfectly. She had a tough-girl exterior with her choppy blond hair and piercings, but I'd discovered she was really a big softie inside.

Maddie, on the other hand, looked exactly like the warm, geeky girl she was, with her long brown hair and black-rimmed glasses. I'd met her in my freshman year of college, along with Julie. They'd quickly become my new best friends, and even though I'd had friends in high school, it was nice to hang out with people who didn't know me as "the girl who almost died of cancer." I'd never told Maddie or Julie about the time I was sick, about the years of chemo and other treatments, about the months living in a hospital. They never knew that my hair, my wild, untamable, glorious hair, had all fallen out and then took forever to re-grow.

Those years were a dark spot in my past that I tried to put behind me as much as possible, even if my parents reminded me about it all the time. Ryan was another reminder of that past. He'd been with me through the entire thing, from the first moment I'd gotten sick to the time the doctors had told me I was in remission. He'd sat with me during hours of chemo. He'd shaved his head with my brother in solidarity when I'd lost my hair. He'd brought me books and played video games with me to cheer me up. Was it any wonder I'd fallen in love with him? And that I'd thought he'd felt the same about me?

Now I knew better. Just like I knew he wasn't offering to come with me on the show because he had romantic feelings for me, but because he wanted to act like my big brother again.

Maddie poured the Merlot into the glasses and passed them out to us. "Okay, spill. What happened? Something with your parents?"

"Was it Daryl?" Becca asked. "Cause I swear, I will punch him right in the balls."

I choked on my wine with a sad little laugh. "No, it's not Daryl." If nothing else, my parents and Ryan had distracted me from *that* drama. "I mean, Daryl is still the worst, but so much else has happened in the last twenty-four hours. First, I found out last night my parents are splitting up."

"Oh no." Maddie rushed forward to give me a hug. "I'm so sorry."

"That blows," Becca said, giving my arm a squeeze.

"I don't understand it at all." My eyes watered up. Maddie grabbed a nearby tissue box and handed it to me, just as the tears started to roll. "They always seemed so happy. But after twenty-five years of marriage they're just…done. How can they do that?"

"I don't know," Maddie said. "Did they say why?"

"Sort of. My mom is taking a job as the host of *Behind The Seams* in New York and she's moving there and Dad isn't going with her. She said they needed space or something, that she wanted to focus on her career again. I don't get it. If they love each other why can't they make it work?" I wiped at my eyes with another tissue.

Becca refilled my wine glass. "Whoa. That's big. She's moving to New York?"

"And hosting a TV show, like you are?" Maddie asked.

I sobbed a little into my tissue. "Well. That's the other thing that happened. I lost my job."

They listened while I explained about my phone call with Giselle and her subsequent offer, although I left out everything about Ryan. They had no idea who he was and were clueless about our complicated past.

"So she fired you from one show, but invited you to compete on another show?" Maddie scrunched up her nose.

"Something like that."

"That's bullshit," Becca said. "She should have offered you the job she gave your mother."

"No, I wouldn't want to take that away from my mom. She seemed so excited about it."

"Are you going to go on *Road Trip Race* then?" Maddie asked.

"I don't think so. I need to spend the summer finding a job and a new place to live."

Becca jumped to her feet. "Screw that. You should go on the show."

I blinked up at her. "Really?"

"Definitely. I fucked up and missed my chance to go on *The Sound* with the band, and I'll regret it forever. Don't make the same mistake."

"It worked out in the end though," Maddie said to Becca with a smile, before turning to me. "But I agree with her. You love that show. It sounds like you could use an escape right now, and you can look for a job and an apartment when you get back. You should do it."

"Hang on," Becca said, before running into the kitchen. I blew my nose, while Maddie patted my back softly and let me ponder their words. Becca returned a few minutes later with a plate full of hot, gooey chocolate chip cookies that looked and smelled like pure heaven.

"You two are the best," I said, as I took a cookie. They knew exactly what I needed after the rough week I was having. "But I haven't even told you the other thing."

"What, there's more?" Becca asked.

"It's stupid, really." I shoved a cookie in my mouth and let the warm chocolate melt. I didn't know why I'd brought up Ryan. He was a part of my life from before I'd met them, and he would be gone from my life again soon. But I knew if I didn't talk this out with them, I'd be up all night obsessing over it. "My brother's best friend Ryan showed up at dinner last night out of the blue. I haven't seen him in six years, and I once had a huge crush on him when I was a teenager, but he didn't feel the same about me. Now he's back and he's the only person I can get to go on the show with me."

"Do you still have feelings for him?" Maddie asked.

"No, definitely not. Last time I saw him I kissed him and said I loved him and he rejected me, telling me he saw me as a little sister and nothing more. I put him out of my mind after that and moved on. Seeing him again brought back all that old humiliation and made it fresh again." I took a big gulp of wine. "Not to mention, he seems to be a complete asshole now. I probably won't see him again for a long time anyway. He's only in town a short while."

"They say you never get over your first love." Becca waved around her wine glass. "I think that's bullshit, but maybe it's true for some people."

"I *am* over him! Really. It's just that I'm a bit emotional after what happened with Daryl, and then my parents splitting up. I didn't need the reminder of my first heartbreak to top it all off." I gave them both a warm smile. "Thanks for listening to me."

"We're here for you, whatever you need," Maddie said.

I took another cookie instead of pointing out the obvious—that even though they said that, they were both leaving in a few days and then I would be truly, completely alone.

A year ago, Maddie, Julie, and I had been roommates all going to UCLA and life had seemed full of possibilities. Now we'd all graduated and everyone was moving on but me. Julie had moved to New York to start her fashion career with her hot British boyfriend. Maddie and Becca were in a famous rock band that was going on tour this summer to promote their new album. And then there was me.

Don't get me wrong. I was incredibly happy for my friends and wanted nothing but the best for them. They deserved every bit of success they'd worked so hard for and it warmed my heart knowing they had amazing futures ahead of them. But they'd all found their soul mates and now they were leaving, while I was stuck here by myself with no career, no home, and no boyfriend. Was there a word that meant when you were both incredibly envious of a friend but also incredibly happy for them? If so, it would perfectly sum up my emotional state right now.

I glanced around at all the half-packed boxes. "What am I going to do?"

"I still think you should go on the show," Becca said.

I groaned. "I'm not going on the show."

Maddie gave me a sympathetic smile. "I totally understand. Julie's going to be sad you're not moving to New York, but it's not the end of the world. Most of your friends and family are here in LA and we'll help you however we can. You can stay with one of us for a while. In no time at all you'll find a new apartment and a new job."

"And a new guy," Becca added.

"No guys," I said. "I'm glad you've both found perfect boyfriends, I really am. But I'm done with romance and relationships for the time being. I think it's best if I was single for a while until I get my life back on track."

Becca grinned. "I'll raise a glass to that. You need to have some fun! You've been in nothing but serious relationships for so long, and you need to get over Daryl and his dirty dick. Preferably with some other dicks."

Maddie gasped. "Becca!"

"What? The girl needs to get laid by someone really hot. Like this Ryan guy who just came back to town. What about a quick fling before he goes home? Just to get him out of your system."

I shook my head vigorously. "No way. Definitely not. Every time I talk to him I want to strangle him."

Becca shrugged. "Hey, if that's what gets you off."

Maddie shook her head. "I'm not sure Carla is the type for a quick fling."

Becca leaned forward and her voice dropped, like she was conspiring with us. "The old Carla wouldn't have one. But the new Carla who has nothing to lose? She can sleep with a guy once and move on." She sat back with a naughty smile on her lips. "C'mon, you know you're curious what he's like in bed. Have you ever seen him naked?"

I felt my cheeks burn. "Um. Not since I was eleven and he was thirteen."

"Okay, probably not a good idea to bring up that mental image. But listen. You want to get over this guy once and for all? You bang his brains out and use him to get over Daryl at the same time."

I fell back on the couch with a groan. "I wish it was that easy, but I don't think I could separate sex and emotions. I'm just not made like that. When I date a guy, and especially when I sleep with him, I have to believe it can last. I want…" But I couldn't finish the sentence.

"What do you want?" Maddie asked softly.

I stared into my empty wine glass. "I was going to say I want what my parents have. That's all I've ever wanted—a marriage like theirs. But now it's over, so maybe Becca's right. Maybe I should just sleep around and enjoy myself and not worry about the future, because it's not like relationships last anyway."

"You know you don't believe that." Maddie threw her arms around me. "Your forever guy is out there somewhere, I promise."

"But until you find him, think about what I said." Becca winked. "Nothing wrong with having a little short-term fun sometimes."

Could I really do that—sleep with Ryan and then move on? No, probably not. I didn't think it would be something a girl could ever forget. But the idea was tempting, assuming he would even be interested.

The girls played me part of a new song they were practicing in preparation for their upcoming tour this summer with their band Villain Complex. I loved watching them get lost in the songs, but it also reinforced how much of an outcast I was. Maddie and Becca had music. Julie had fashion. I had nothing anymore.

Maybe I *should* go on the show. What did I have to lose at this point? Getting away for the summer while going on a fun reality TV show would be the perfect escape from all my real life drama.

I grabbed my phone and—after ignoring another text from my ex-boyfriend begging me to take him back—sent Ryan a message. *Still want to be my partner on the show?*

Within a few seconds he texted back: *I'm in.*

NINE

Carla

One week later, I stared across the bustling Santa Monica Pier at the crisp blue ocean and took a deep breath of salty air. The warm, sunny day felt ripe with possibilities and new beginnings. I was ready for anything.

I turned to Ryan with a mix of nervousness and excitement swirling in my gut. "Do you have everything?"

"You mean, did I follow your extensive color-coded packing lists?" He raised an eyebrow at me. "Yes, I have everything."

"I was just trying to help. Preparation is key in a competition like this."

The show had given us a short list of items we should bring, such as sunblock and shampoo, along with a list of things we weren't allowed like maps or computers. I'd taken those lists and then made my own much longer one with all the things I would need, from toothpaste to tampons. Then I'd sent Ryan a list too, for his convenience of course, along with some suggested episodes for him to watch and study. If he didn't want to use them, that was his loss. Some people went on reality TV shows without doing any planning, but I was not one of them.

"Your notes were helpful," Ryan grudgingly admitted. "But none of that will matter if they take all our gear during one of the challenges, like in the episode where the mom and son won by using that off-road shortcut."

My mouth split into a huge smile. "So you *did* watch the episodes I suggested!"

He hefted his backpack onto his shoulders and gave me a lazy smirk. "Maybe."

Butterflies fluttered through my stomach at the knowledge he'd done his homework, along with that smirk. Under the bright sunlight, his jet black hair shined like onyx and looked so thick and inviting I wanted to run my fingers through it. He wore a dark blue dress shirt that was so perfectly tailored to his body I knew it had to be expensive, along with black jeans that made it hard not to stare at his long legs and perfect butt. Remind me again how I was supposed to keep my hands off him—and keep my heart intact—for the next few weeks?

Nothing to do but get on with it. I threw my backpack on and we started toward the commotion in front of us. We were allowed only a single bag each, but I was a pro at packing and over the past few days I'd spent hours plotting out all of my outfits for the show. I'd made sure to bring clothes that mixed and matched with each other, wouldn't get wrinkled, and could be easily washed.

One end of the parking lot was fenced off and we had to show our IDs to get past security. Once we were inside, a guy in a *Road Trip Race* shirt directed us to one of the red tents that had been set up. Other people milled about with backpacks on, who I assumed were our competition. We stepped inside the tent and walked toward a woman who was checking people in, with a backdrop behind her that said *Road Trip Race: Couples Edition.*

Wait…what?

Hang on. That couldn't be right. No one had mentioned anything about this season being for couples only. Maybe we were in the wrong place or something. I glanced around, checking out our competitors again, and they *did* look like couples. The signs were all there. Wedding rings. Holding hands. Standing a bit too close to each other.

Oh *no*. What had I signed us up for?

"Couples edition?" Ryan asked.

Before he could get any more out, Giselle Roberts herself swept over to us, wearing dark shades and a sun hat. She was an older, curvy black woman who always managed to look both completely gorgeous and totally professional. I had a lot of respect for her since she had produced so many successful TV shows over the past few years, especially in an industry that wasn't always supportive of women or people of color.

"Carla!" She gave me a quick hug. "So good to see you. I was just talking to your mom actually."

I smiled and tried to ignore the reminder that Mom was on her way to New York and I wasn't. "It's great to see you too. Thank you for inviting me on the show."

"I'm so happy you could make it. And I see you brought your partner." She offered her hand with a smile. "I'm Giselle Roberts, creator of *Road Trip Race.*"

"It's an honor." He shook her hand. "Ryan Evans."

"Lovely to meet you. Carla told me you were together and I'm delighted you're coming on the show. Viewers will *love* it. My son is a huge fan of your game, by the way. I can't go a day without hearing him talk about Outerworld."

"Sorry about that," Ryan said, sounding not sorry at all.

I took another glance at the *Couples Edition* logo behind her, my head still spinning. "Um, I didn't realize the show had a special focus this season…"

"Didn't I mention that on the phone?" Giselle asked. "We're trying something new to spice up the show and boost ratings. This season it's couples only and all the challenges will be romantic and sexy. Fun, right?"

No, no, no. That couldn't be right. Why hadn't she warned me?

But it all made sense now. When I'd called to tell her I was going on the show, she'd asked, "With your boyfriend?"

"No, we're not together anymore," I'd said. "I'm bringing someone else—Ryan Evans."

"The Meta Entertainment guy? Wow, nice catch. I heard he's a hard one to pin down."

I'd thought she was joking around at the time and had laughed it off, but now I knew what she meant—she'd thought we were *together* together.

"It won't be a problem, will it?" Giselle glanced back and forth between us with a frown. "You *are* dating, aren't you?"

Well, that was it. Our time on the show was over already. I opened my mouth to confess that we weren't a couple, when I felt Ryan's arm slide around my waist, tugging my hip against his in a possessive way. "Yes, we are."

A ripple of shock ran through me, but Giselle didn't seem to notice. Her frown disappeared. "Perfect. How did you two meet, anyway?"

Ryan jumped in with an answer, his voice smooth. "We've know each other since we were kids, but we fell out of touch and recently reconnected after six years apart. It's new, so we've been keeping it quiet until now, but we're excited to be going on the show together."

If this was how he talked in boardrooms, no wonder his company was dominating their industry. His hand was on my hip, his thumb sliding just under my shirt and brushing against my skin, and every one of my nerve endings seemed to alight. I leaned against him, smiling at Giselle like one-half of a happy couple, while my heart was doing an erratic tap dance all over the place. Good thing he was doing all the talking, because all I could think about was how it felt to have his arm around me and how much I wished everything he said was true.

"Good luck to you both. I hope you win!" Giselle gave a little wave and left the tent.

I pulled out of Ryan's grasp. "I am *so* sorry. I had no idea, I swear. Do you still want to do this? Because I completely understand if you want to back out now."

"Of course I still want to do it."

"But the whole couples thing..." My stomach did somersaults just thinking about those sexy and romantic challenges Giselle had mentioned, wondering what they might involve. Kissing? Touching? *Nudity?*

"Don't tell me you want to back out already."

"No, of course not." I stood up a little taller at his cynical voice.

"We both know it's not real, so it won't be a problem. Or will it?" His eyes seemed to bore into mine, peeling away all my layers.

"Not a problem at all," I said quickly.

He frowned, glancing at the *Couples Edition* sign again. "Daniel is going to lose his shit when he watches the show."

"Not if we warn him in advance that we were pretending the whole time. It won't air until mid-September, so there's plenty of time to explain it to him."

Ryan nodded and we let the subject drop. I wasn't sure how I was going to make it through days or even weeks of pretending to be a couple with him though. Being around him was exhausting. My emotions boomeranged from wanting to kiss him to wanting to slap him and back again in a flash. I reminded myself that Ryan had no interest in me and nothing would ever happen. Anything that *did* happen would be fake. But if all of America thought I was dating a handsome billionaire genius? Well, it wouldn't be the worst thing to happen to me.

The real danger was that I'd forget it wasn't real—and get my heart broken all over again.

———

Over the next hour we were given surveys to answer and then we were interviewed on camera, while we played our roles perfectly with big smiles and bright eyes. At one point we even held hands. Everyone bought it without question. Turns out it wasn't that hard to convince people that we were a new couple, filled with the hope of true love.

Once we were done, we made our way down the rickety wooden pier toward the camera crews that were set up, past the tourist shops, the roller coaster and Ferris wheel, and all the restaurants. At the very end of the pier the other couples were gathering to wait for the host of the show to arrive and for the cameras to start rolling.

I studied the competition. There were all types of couples there—old, young, gay, straight, from all different races and cultures. I tried to size up who would be our toughest competition, but it was hard to tell at this stage. One blond husband and wife pair stood out because they reminded me of bulldogs—big, muscular, and good looking. When they spoke they had charming Southern drawls, but they eyed everyone with a predatory hunger. We'd definitely have to watch out for them.

I overhead another couple mention they were a flight attendant and a mechanic and made a mental note to keep tabs on them too, since travel and car skills were a dangerous combo in this game. There was also an older lesbian biker couple who I guessed the other teams might underestimate, but I suspected they'd prove to be one of the better competitors.

Ryan's gaze followed mine across the crowd. "What do you think? Do we have a shot at winning?"

I tried to sound more confident than I felt. "Of course we do. I spent two days studying maps to prepare for this."

"I bet you had a dozen color coded lists too."

"Not a dozen." Okay, maybe half a dozen.

He leaned against the pier railing, his shirt stretching over his hard chest, and the reflection of the ocean made his dark eyes sparkle. "What happens when the show throws a curveball and it's something you haven't prepared for? Or life, for that matter?"

I gave a casual shrug. "I'm still working on that."

"Exactly. That's why you need me. To come up with a Plan B."

"Oh please. You know I always have a Plan B, C, D, and E."

"I'll settle for handling Plan F then." He gave me another sexy smirk. "It does sound a lot more dirty."

Whoa, was he flirting with me? No, that couldn't be right. He thought of me as a little sister, after all. And ever since he'd come back, he'd been a total jerk to me.

Even so, I was relieved when the *Road Trip Race* crew told the contestants to line up at the end of the pier with the ocean behind us. After a few minutes, the host of *Road Trip Race*, Chuck Bannon, moved to stand in front of the cameras, facing us. He was a middle-aged white guy with a shaved head and he wore his usual outfit on the show, a polo shirt with long shorts over hiking boots.

"Welcome to the twelfth season of *Road Trip Race!*" he said to the camera. "This year we're trying something different: a couples theme. Each of the 10 pairs competing this season are romantically involved. Some of them have only been dating for a few weeks, some of them have been together for years, and some of them have been married for decades. Each couple will attempt to travel from Santa Monica to New York in a car while hunting for scavenger list items and competing in fun, romantic challenges. Which couple will make it to the end and win one million dollars? And more importantly, which couples will be broken up by then?"

He grinned at the camera, while my pulse stuttered and a million bees buzzed around inside my stomach. The show was starting and I wasn't ready at all. I was overcome with the feeling I'd forgotten to pack something important before going on a trip, but couldn't remember what it was. But no, I hadn't forgotten anything— I'd checked my lists and my bag a hundred times. It was just that none of my planning could have truly prepared me for actually living in this moment.

Chuck turned to speak to the contestants. "At the end of the pier there are ten cars waiting for you. Each one is fitted with interior cameras and microphones, along with a speed logger that will track your GPS and let us know if you travel above the speed limit. You'll find the keys in the glove box, plus a camera and your first scavenger hunt list. You'll need to take photos of four out of six scavenger hunt items before you reach the next location. If you don't, you'll be sent off to finish before you can attempt the challenge."

I knew all of this from watching the show, but it was a good refresher anyway. Three of the scavenger hunt items were always landmarks or other pit stops, while the other three were things you might encounter on the road, like a broken-down truck. On previous seasons I'd seen contestants go to every one of the locations and travel so far out of their way that they ended up last at the destination and got kicked off. But I'd also seen contestants only go to one location, then fail to find enough of the chance scavenger hunt items, forcing them to backtrack. Those kind of mistakes could cost you the win. The trick was to map out the best way to a few of the locations and hope you got lucky along the way with the other items too.

Chuck glanced up and down the row of contestants. "Once you complete the scavenger hunt, you'll have to finish a challenge before getting the location of the final destination for the night. The first team to reach the final destination gets a special romantic evening, plus five thousand dollars each. They also get to start the next part of the race first in the morning, with each other team leaving in order, five minutes apart. The last team that arrives each night will be eliminated from the game. The team that makes it all the way to the end will win a million dollars."

The prize money wasn't really why I was on the show, but winning it would make me feel a whole lot better about not having a job lined up. Half a million dollars would give me a huge buffer until I decided what to do next with my life. Ryan, of course, didn't need the prize money. I still wasn't sure why he was even here.

"Are you ready to get started?" Chuck asked all of us. We all cheered and yelled, our energy level high. Many of the competitors leaned forward, like they were about to burst into a run at the start of a race.

"I said, are you ready to get started?" he yelled. To the side of us, a bunch of crew members waved at us to cheer. We yelled back, "Yes!" and some of the others stomped their feet. I bounced on my heels, ready to sprint off as much as they were.

"Ready? On your mark… Get set… Go!" Chuck stepped back, gesturing for us to head for the cars.

The line of contestants burst forth in one big, excited rush, speeding forward as if the two seconds they might gain on the other teams would make or break the game for them. Not that I was any better. I ran at full speed too, with Ryan at my side.

Our long legs came in handy and we were one of the first teams to reach the cars. Ten black Chevy Malibu sedans waited for us, and I knew from previous seasons they'd get tons of product placement during the show when it aired.

We claimed one of the cars in the front, threw our bags in the trunk, and slammed the doors shut. Ryan took the driver's side. I popped open the glove compartment. Everything was happening so quickly, but all I could think of was grabbing that scavenger hunt list and getting out on the road.

Ryan started up the car. "What do we have to find?"

I scrambled to open the envelope and pull out the list. It had all the rules we already knew on the back, along with this list on the front:

Challenge Location: Las Vegas
    1) Cabazon Dinosaurs
    2) Bottle Tree Ranch
    3) World's Tallest Thermometer
    4) Tumbleweed
    5) Person with a beard riding a motorcycle
    6) "Wash me" written on a vehicle

I read off all of the items while Ryan drove out of the lot. Some of them seemed pretty easy, like typical things you would find on a road trip. Tumbleweed was so common on the road to Las Vegas you couldn't throw a rock without hitting it. We'd visited the dinosaurs once before, and I was pretty sure I'd passed a sign for the thermometer on the way to Vegas. But the rest? I wasn't sure.

We were the third ones to leave, but the other teams were right on our tail. I took a moment to study the interior of the car we were in, which would be our home for the next few days. It had a sunroof, light gray leather seats, and that new car smell I'd always loved. Tucked away in each corner were small black cameras to capture everything we did while we are on the show, along with hidden microphones to record everything we said. The dashboard looked standard, except for the special speed logger. The show tracked the location of each car with GPS and if you went over the posted speed limit for too long, usually more than a few minutes, you would be penalized on time at the end of the day.

If you did it multiple times you'd disqualified from the show. They didn't want anyone getting into accidents or getting tickets, so while speed was a factor on the show, it wasn't the biggest one. The teams that won did so with a combination of luck, quick thinking, and the ability to navigate a map and plot out their journey.

Ryan drummed his fingers on the steering wheel. "If I remember correctly, it will take four or five hours to get to Las Vegas, depending on traffic."

"That sounds about right. Once we get out of Los Angeles we should pick up a map. Right now we want to put as much distance as we can between us and the other teams." I checked the scavenger hunt list again. "We should go to the Cabazon Dinosaurs first, since it's the nearest location."

His brow creased. "That's not on the way to Vegas. We'll lose too much time by going there. No, we'll skip it and head straight for the next one."

"But what if we can't find the random items on the list?" I shook my head. "We need to photograph four things to finish the hunt, which means at least one location and possibly all three of them. I don't want to have to backtrack if we don't see any bikers with beards."

"We won't need to backtrack, because the other items are easy." His voice left no room for argument and I guessed he was used to getting his way all the time. Well, too bad.

I sat up straighter and faced him down. "I know what I'm talking about. I've watched every single episode of *Road Trip Race*. The best strategy is to always go to the first location, even if it's a little out of the way. That way you know you won't have to backtrack to it. It's the safest bet."

"You can't always play it safe in a game like this. Not if you want to win."

"And you can't always take stupid risks unless you want to be kicked off in the very first episode."

He clenched his jaw, but finally nodded. "Fine. We'll go with your plan and visit the dinosaurs. Let's hope we don't encounter any traffic, or this detour of yours will cost us a lot of time."

Victory! I sat back in my seat. Except now that we'd agreed to my plan, I worried it wasn't the correct decision. Maybe Ryan was right and we'd be better off skipping this location. Ugh, the thought of that made me even more anxious. No, playing it safe was the best bet, at least for this challenge. We didn't need to win this one, we just needed to stay in the game.

At this time of day there shouldn't be too much traffic on the freeway, but I had no way to check. We'd given our phones to the crew during our interview and we weren't allowed to use any sort of technology while on the show, including computers, phones, or tablets. All we could use were directions from other people or paper maps, which we had to buy ourselves. We weren't allowed to use our own money either. We'd been given a credit card to charge things to, and each day one hundred dollars would be added to take care of gas, food, and other necessities. Whatever we didn't use would get carried over to the next day.

I gestured up ahead. "You can get on the freeway up here."

"I remember."

"Do you?" I tried to keep my tone neutral. "Have you been back to the city even once since you left for college?" What I was really asking was, "Since you left me that day?"

"A few times."

I stared out the window to avoid looking at him. Of course he'd come back. Over the years he'd visited with my brother and my parents, from what I'd heard, but not once had he even said hello to me. Another reminder that once he'd left for college everything between us—even our friendship—had ended.

Ryan

It took way too much time to get to Cabazon. I spent the entire drive counting the minutes and miles we'd gone off course, annoyed that Carla hadn't listened to me. This was going to be a huge mistake when we ended up last and got kicked off the very first episode.

But once we parked and got out of the car, Carla's face lit up with a big smile at the sight of the dinosaurs. It was the first smile of hers I'd seen in years. I changed my mind about this detour being a mistake.

"I remember this place," she said, her eyes sparkling under the bright sun.

Just off the side of the road, the army green T-rex statue towered over us and dwarfed the palm trees next to it. Another life-size brontosaurus stood nearby and a few tourists milled about taking photos.

"We came here once late at night," I said. "With Daniel."

She nodded, smiling up at the T-rex. "We got someone to buy us beer and took photos until 2 AM and then got lost on the way home. My dad grounded me and Daniel for a week."

"He gave me a pretty stern talking to also."

I remembered it well. Carla had recently gone into remission and had begged us to take her out for the night, but we'd stayed out way past curfew, plus we'd each had a beer. Henry had sat me down after he'd sent the other two up to their rooms. "Son," he'd said, "I'm disappointed in you."

It was the worst thing he could have said to me. My own father was disappointed with me all the time, if he ever even remembered I existed, so that was nothing new. But Henry? He'd always treated me like I mattered. Hearing I'd failed him killed me a little. "It won't happen again," I'd promised him.

"Good." He'd paused, his warm brown eyes studying me. "I know I'm not your real father and I can't ground you or anything, so I'll just say this. I need you to look after Daniel and Carla. They both look up to you. They'd follow you anywhere."

I'd frowned hearing that. If anything, I was the one who'd latched onto them. They'd had everything I'd ever wanted in life. But Henry asking me to do something for him gave me a swell of responsible pride, and I'd stood up a little straighter. "I will."

He'd patted me on the shoulder. "I know you will. You're a smart kid, smarter than you give yourself credit for. If you put that mind of yours to good use you could really make something of yourself. Heck, I bet you could get a scholarship and go to any college you wanted."

His words had lit a fire in me. I'd always been somewhat reckless and hadn't cared much about school, although I'd done well in it without even trying. After that? I'd started trying. From that night on, I studied my ass off and did whatever it took to get ahead, to change my fate to something of my own choosing instead of the life my father had picked for me.

Carla gestured for me to join her under the T-rex. "Come on. We need a photo!"

I groaned. "Do we have to be in it?"

"Yes!"

As I walked toward her, I spotted a camera crew from the show off to the side, filming us. They would likely be at all of the scavenger hunt locations, which mean we'd have to keep the couple act up at all times. Shit. Why had I agreed to this again?

I moved next to Carla and slid my arm around her waist, pulling her against my side. I caught a glimpse of dark cleavage in her low-cut top, before dragging my eyes away. She was warm and soft and smelled like vanilla. I wanted to bury my face in her breasts and breathe her in, but I restrained myself.

"Smile!" she said, and took a selfie of us under the dinosaur. We were teenagers again, both of us looking into the camera with goofy grins. Then she slipped away from me and the moment ended.

"Happy now?" I asked, clutching the keys too tight. "Let's go."

I stormed back to the car and she skipped after me. Once inside, Carla grabbed a pen and cross off number one on our list: Cabazon Dinosaurs.

We stopped at a nearby gas station before hitting the freeway again. After rushing around to get everything we needed, including sandwiches for our lunch on the road, we were back in the car in less than ten minutes.

Before I could pull out of the gas station, Carla grabbed my arm. "Wait!"

I slammed on the brakes. "What? Did we forget something?"

She fumbled for the camera and then snapped a photo of two older men pulling up at the gas pumps next to us. Both were riding Harleys and had long beards.

"Our second scavenger hunt item!" She crossed off item number five on the list: person with a beard riding a motorcycle. "Only two more to go." She sat back and grinned. "See, I told you visiting the dinosaurs was a good idea."

———

Over the next few hours I drove while Carla navigated and watched for items on the scavenger hunt list. The landscape became more and more desolate the farther we moved from Los Angeles. At this time of year it was all hard dirt and dead shrubs and little else. Nothing like where I lived now in Seattle, and yet I oddly missed this view. I'd spent hours driving these freeways when I was younger, always with Carla and Daniel at my side. We'd ventured all over Southern California, to remote places and tourist traps and spots we'd only found by getting lost.

Doing it again with Carla now brought back a rare yet pleasant feeling of nostalgia, except for the heavy silence between us. In fact, Carla barely even looked my way at all. At first, I figured she was focused completely on the race, but after an hour of driving I realized she just didn't want to talk to *me*.

This was going to be a long journey.

We rolled past a car that had "Wash Me" written on the back in scraggly, dusty lines. Carla took a photo and crossed it off the list. "That's three!"

"Nice one."

She settled back in her seat. The pointed silence crept across the car again. I'd kill for some music right now, but we weren't allowed to play any because it would interfere with the mics. But a road trip without music wasn't right at all.

I cleared my throat. "Tell me about your life while I was gone." My eyes left the road to glance at her. She stared out the window at the bleak landscape, her arms crossed over her breasts. She wore a pale orange dress that had ridden up to her thighs. Smooth, curvy, very tempting thighs. I forced my eyes forward again. "Daniel hasn't told me much."

She didn't answer at first, but then uncrossed her arms. "There's not much you don't already know. I graduated from high school, went to UCLA, majored in theater, and worked as a model on the side." She gave a slight shrug and I got the feeling I wouldn't get much more out of her without some prying.

"Who'd you go to prom with?"

She turned toward me with her mouth open, but quickly recovered. "Um. Brad Johnson."

"Brad Johnson? *That* guy? No way."

"What's wrong with Brad Johnson?"

"He was head of the chess club."

"So what? That just meant he was smart."

"You *hate* chess. And he was a full head shorter than you, last I remember."

"I don't care about that." She crossed her arms again. "He was a nice guy."

"Nice." My hands gripped the steering wheel so hard I was surprised it didn't break. "He wasn't your type at all."

She huffed. "What do you know about my type?"

"I thought I was your type."

The look she gave me could have melted the skin off of a lesser man. I pointedly raised my eyes to the cameras filming everything we said and did. She took the hint and her fierce expression dropped down a notch.

"Of course you are," she said, in a monotone that wouldn't convince anyone.

Only a few hours in and we were already doing a shit job pretending to be a couple. I hoped they'd edit all this out later.

"Surely there was a better choice than Brad Johnson." Why was I bringing this up again? I had no fucking clue. I was a dog with a bone and couldn't let go of it.

"He was the only one who asked me."

I gave her a skeptical look. "You expect me to believe that?"

"Believe it. I wasn't exactly Miss Popular in school."

"Bullshit. You should have had boys falling all over you. What kind of idiot wouldn't want a model who can fix cars?"

"I don't know, you tell me," she said, her voice razor sharp.

"That was different. You and I—"

She turned toward the window again, her posture stiff. "It's fine. We don't need to talk about it."

"No. I handled it all wrong and—"

"Please, let's just drop it." Her voice wavered, almost like she was about to cry.

Shit. I had to fix this. But nothing I said could make up for or explain what I'd done six years ago or how I'd avoided her ever since. I scrubbed a hand over my face and tried again. "Carla—"

She suddenly jerked up, grabbing the camera. "Look! Tumbleweed!"

A big clump of dead sticks and weeds rolled across the freeway in the wind, like something out of an old west movie. Carla snapped a couple photos and then turned to me, our argument forgotten for now. "That makes four! Now we can head directly to the challenge and skip the other locations."

———

We crossed the Nevada state line and came upon Buffalo Bill's immediately, a casino with a roller coaster and flashing neon signs, before we were driving through endless desert again. The sun beat down on us and we cranked the air conditioning up even higher. And then, finally, we made it to the sparkling city in the middle of nowhere, Las Vegas.

"Remember when we went to Vegas with your parents?" I asked.

"Of course." A tiny smile touched her lips. "That was a fun trip, even though we were too young to do much beyond stuffing our faces at the buffets."

"We rode the roller coaster at New York-New York eight times."

Her face was full of memories. "You and Daniel kept trying to convince bartenders you were both 21, but it never worked."

"Can't blame us for trying."

"You were fifteen!"

"Hey, I looked at least eighteen."

The smile on her lips died and she looked away again. "Then we had to end the trip early."

I'd tried to bury that memory. Carla had started throwing up on our second night in Vegas. Her parents thought it was the stomach flu and they took us all home, but she didn't get better. A few days later she was diagnosed with leukemia.

My chest clenched up at the remembered pain of hearing the news and of all the hours spent in the hospital with her, staring at her ashen face and trembling hands, watching her glorious curls disappear, seeing her bright eyes dim. I'd thought I would lose her during those long months and came to realize how much I cared for her. Not as the little sister I'd never had, but as something more. Once she got better, those feelings only grew, even though I could never act on them. I thought going away for a few years would fix that problem, but obviously not. Years and distance had done nothing to dilute the strength of the attraction between us.

Carla checked the map again. "Get off at this exit."

I followed her directions, and within minutes we found ourselves in a parking lot. Only after I'd turned off the car did I spot the sign in front of us.

Oh hell no.

"Are you sure this is the place?"

Her mouth hung open. She checked the scavenger hunt, then looked at the map again, and then nodded slowly. "This is the right address, but..."

Another black car identical to ours pulled up and a couple—the intense blond ones—jumped out and ran toward the building at full speed. My competitive nature kicked in and I unhooked my seat belt, throwing open the car door. "This must be it. Hurry."

Carla didn't hesitate and launched out of the car. We ran for the bright white building labelled with a flashing neon sign that proclaimed it as the Desert Magic Wedding Chapel.

Once inside, a guy in a cheap-looking suit with a pink bowtie smiled at us and handed Carla a card. "Welcome to Las Vegas and your first challenge."

There was no sign of the other couple. I leaned over Carla's shoulder and read the top of the card, where it listed the name of the challenge: Race To The Altar.

Oh shit.

Carla read the rest out loud, while a camera crew filmed us from the side. "For this challenge, you'll need to get dressed up as bride and groom and undergo a wedding ceremony worthy of Las Vegas. Don't worry, it won't be a real one."

"Thank god," I muttered.

She ignored my comment and kept reading a list of things we had to do to receive the location of tonight's final destination: get dressed, get hitched, carry the bride down the aisle, and eat wedding cake. When she was done, she let her hand with the card fall and looked up at me, panic in her eyes. "I don't know if I can do this."

I was right there with her. What kind of fucking comedian thought this fake wedding would be a good idea? I'd known we would face some romance-themed challenges, but I hadn't expected *this*. But there was no time to stress over that now. We were playing a game and we had to get it together or we'd get left behind. I was not going to let Carla get kicked off in the first challenge, no matter what it took. Even if that meant getting married.

I took Carla's hand. "Will you do me the honor of being my pretend wife?"

An unexpected laugh burst out of her. "Yes!"

We were sent to a room where different wedding dresses and tuxedos hung on racks. Without hesitation, Carla and I ran to the racks and began searching for something in our size. My options were tuxedos with sequins, pastel colors, or hearts all over them. The cheap fabric was even more offensive than the outdated styles. In the end the only one that would fit me was a baby blue polyester suit with bell bottom trousers.

Kill me now.

Carla's wedding dress choices were just as over the top and her options were limited even more because she was so tall. Still, she managed to grab a dress and ran behind the privacy screen. I caught a glimpse of her pretty feet under it as she kicked off her shoes, and then her orange dress hit the floor. It was enough to make my mouth go dry. I imagined her behind that screen as she changed: her long legs, her smooth skin, her delicious curves. I shoved those thoughts aside with a flash of guilt and rushed behind the other screen to change.

When we emerged, we looked like something out of an eighties romantic comedy. Me, with my baby blue bell bottoms and a jacket cut that hadn't been fashionable since before I was born, plus a purple sequined bow tie and red cowboy boots. And Carla, wearing a giant poof of a dress with tulle, sequins, and massive bows that lit up with white LED lights in a pattern that threatened to give anyone attending the wedding a seizure. She still looked good though. The neckline of it was low, giving me a flash of her ample cleavage. Even in the hideous dress she was the most gorgeous woman I'd ever seen. If anything, it only made her beauty shine even brighter.

"Oh my gosh." She burst out laughing. "Your tux!"

I scowled. "Don't even start. Your dress has more lights than your mom's Christmas trees." She clasped a hand over her mouth, but couldn't stop giggling. I offered her my arm. "Shall we go get hitched, my twinkling princess?"

"Yes, my pastel prince." She slid her arm into mine.

A woman handed Carla flowers before sending us into the chapel. Loud music rang out all around us as we walked down the aisle toward—I shit you not—an Elvis drag queen who stood under an arch decorated with neon lights and fake roses. The whole thing was fucking surreal, and before I knew it, I was at the altar facing Carla.

Elvis launched right into the ceremony without breaking character once. Carla's eyes met mine, still dancing with amusement, and even though it was all fake and over the top, something inside me stirred.

I'd never once wanted to get married. Never thought I was the type. I'd decided long ago I wasn't going to tie myself to one person, to open myself up to heartbreak like my father had. Especially if I couldn't have the one girl I wanted.

With Carla in front of me in a white dress, looking at me with those big brown eyes while a few stray curls fell around her face, a part of me wondered, what if? I allowed myself a short daydream while Elvis rattled on about love. Waking up next to Carla every morning. Sharing our lives and our home. And one day, maybe even having kids. It was impossible, but it was a nice fantasy.

Drag Queen Elvis turned to me. "Do you, Ryan Evans, take Carla Jackson to be your partner on *Road Trip Race* in sickness and in health, across thousands of miles, as long as you're both on the show?"

"I do."

Elvis asked Carla the same questions and then said, "I now pronounce you... partners on *Road Trip Race*. You may kiss the bride."

Shit, what? I hadn't thought this through obviously. Of course there would be a kiss at the end of a fake wedding. I hadn't kissed Carla since we were teenagers. That had been a disaster, and I was pretty damn sure she wouldn't want me to kiss her now. But there was no time to hesitate. We needed to get out of the chapel and on to the final destination already.

I took Carla by the waist with one arm and brought her lips to mine. It was supposed to be a quick kiss, just enough for the camera so we could be on our way. But the second our mouths met, six years of longing rushed through me. The dam burst open, and the kiss turned into more.

She didn't stop me. No, she pulled me closer instead, sliding her arms around my neck, pressing her body against mine. When her tongue touched my own I was lost. My fingers caressed her soft cheek and I couldn't stop kissing her, didn't *want* to stop kissing her. Not now, not ever.

Elvis made an impatient sound and I pulled back, releasing Carla. She looked dazed, her lips full and lush, ready for more. I wanted more too, but as soon as we stopped touching all the reasons this was a bad idea came back to me. Shit, that kiss was going to be aired on TV in a few months and Daniel and everyone else would see it. He was going to *murder* me. It was one thing to fake being a couple, it was another to practically devour his sister on TV.

No time to stress over that now. I'd deal with it later. Carla tossed her bouquet and I bent down and swept her off her feet, like we'd been instructed to do. She let out a soft cry and grabbed onto my shoulders. Her face was right by mine again, but I couldn't let myself focus on her pretty lips or we'd never get out of here.

"Sorry, but we need to hurry," I said, as I carried her out of the chapel room.

She nodded, biting her lip. "You better not drop me."

"Never."

We were sent to a table with all different kinds of cake and instructed to feed each other an entire slice. I picked a chocolate cake with purple frosting and Carla picked a vanilla and strawberry one. We grabbed forks, but she hesitated. I lifted a bite of her strawberry cake to her mouth. She opened for me, her eyes never leaving mine. I watched her lips close around the fork, before I slowly slid it out of her mouth. Her tongue wiped away the faint trace of white frosting left on them. I wondered if she could still taste me on her lips. I wondered if her tongue would taste like cake now. I wanted to test the theory.

She fed me next, but I could barely stay still. I was so hard I was uncomfortable, and had to keep subtly adjusting myself. I swallowed the bite and didn't taste it at all. We had to get out of here before I swept all the cake off that table and pushed her down onto it. I'd wrap her legs around me, thrust into her, and suck cake crumbs off her pouty lips.

I tried to hurry the next bites and Carla sped up too. On the third one, she missed and got frosting all over my face. "Oops."

Was that on purpose? I scowled and shoved the next bite at her face, getting frosting all over her mouth. She gave a mock gasp and thrust a bite at me, leaving frosting all over my nose. She looked at me and giggled, and soon it became a game of not only how fast we could eat the cake, but who could make the other more messy. I got frosting on her neck, she got it on my jaw. I got it on her cheek, she got it on my forehead.

When we were done, we were both panting and completely covered in sticky, sweet frosting. I wanted to lick every inch of it off her. Her eyes made me suspect she wanted to do the same. Instead, she stuck one frosting-covered finger in her mouth and sucked. Jesus. Was she *trying* to kill me?

We might have jumped each other right then and there, if not for the man in the pink bowtie. He handed us a card with the final destination for the day: a hotel in the town of Laughlin, Nevada.

We changed quickly, cleaned ourselves up, and returned to the car for the final stretch of today's journey. Carla drove this time. As the sun set and darkness descended, neither one of us mentioned the kiss or what happened with the cake. But I knew it would come up later. A kiss like that couldn't be ignored for long... and then I'd have to break her heart a second time.

ELEVEN

Carla

He kissed me.

I knew it was only because of the show, because he had to do it, but it felt so real. So right. He could have given me a quick peck and then been done with it. But he'd lingered. He'd used his hands. His tongue. His entire *body*.

His kiss had felt like the start of something.

Okay, I needed to calm down. His kiss had felt real six years ago too. I'd already learned I couldn't trust my instincts in these situations. He was just a really damn good kisser, that was all. I was too much of a romantic and always wanted to believe something was there, even if it wasn't. Which was how I ended up with a boyfriend who'd cheated on me for a year right under my nose.

No matter how real it seemed, Ryan was just putting on a good show for the camera to keep up our couples act. The intense sexual attraction during the cake-eating was part of the same thing. It didn't mean anything. I knew that, but I couldn't stop myself from desperately wanting him to kiss me again anyway. I wished he'd say something to make me angry so I could extinguish that desire.

As I drove to Laughlin, all those thoughts tangled with the worry that we hadn't been fast enough today. There were nine other teams and I had no idea how many were ahead of us or behind us. The thought of getting kicked off now, in the first episode, made me so anxious I thought I might throw up.

Luckily, I got us there without barfing. Laughlin was like a mini Las Vegas right on the Colorado River, with desert behind it and mountains in the distance. Our destination was one of the river-front casinos, and we parked and ran straight into the lobby. I was hit with a blast of cigarette smoke, flashing neon lights, and the ringing of slot machines, but I didn't slow down.

Chuck Bannon stood with a camera crew near the casino floor and grinned at us when we approached. "Congratulations! You're the fourth team to arrive, which means you're moving on to the next challenge."

"Yes!" I turned to Ryan and gave him a hug, overwhelmed with relief.

"Tomorrow you'll set out from this location to the next destination," Chuck continued. "Since you were fourth, you'll have a fifteen minute delay."

That wasn't too bad. We could easily make that up with good planning and some luck. We might even win a future challenge.

We were swept off by a petite brunette crew member named Luisa to do quick interviews about what we thought of the first challenge. I talked about how exciting it was to be on the show after watching it for years. Ryan said little, but all he had to do was sit there and look handsome and everyone loved it.

I tried to imagine the show when it finally aired on TV in a few months, and how every time I was on screen there would be a caption on the bottom: Carla, 22, Los Angeles, Model. What would Ryan's say? Billionaire CEO? Wealthy tech genius? Video game mogul? He was ratings gold and they would milk that however they could. I could already see how the show would spin him and our supposed romance. The young, handsome genius who'd clawed his way up from nothing, now finally reunited with his long lost love. Ah, if only that last part was true.

Once we were done, Luisa handed us two hotel room keys. "Feel free to enjoy anything in the hotel, but remember you're not allowed to leave the premises at any time. Doing so will result in disqualification. Please arrive back here in the morning at 7 AM. Enjoy!"

We grabbed the keys and took the elevator up to our floor. I couldn't wait to get to the room so we could unwind and have some time to ourselves off-camera. But we soon discovered there was a big problem with the room.

There was only one bed.

A large one, sure, but just one. Were we going to sleep in that bed *together?* Sharing a hotel room was bad enough, but I'd figured they would give us two beds at least.

But why would they? This season was supposed to be romantic, of course they'd get us only one bed. The show got the best ratings when there was sex or fighting. If there was both, even better.

At least the room was a decent size and had a couch, plus a view of the river. It was too bad we weren't allowed to leave the hotel, because I'd love to be able to explore this slice of Nevada. I'd never been to this city before.

Ryan dropped his bag on the floor and surveyed the room. "I'll take the couch."

I started to protest, but then stopped myself. Everyone said I was too nice, so even though my first reaction was to tell him that wasn't necessary, I slammed my lips shut. The idea of sharing a bed with him was too much for me to handle. I wouldn't be able to get any sleep, I'd just replay that kiss over and over a million times. Oh, who was I kidding? I was going to do that anyway. But it'd be even worse if he was in the bed next to me.

"Thanks." I kicked off my shoes and flopped onto the bed. The second I hit its soft duvet, I let out a moan that was way too loud.

Ryan turned toward me. "Are you okay?"

"Sorry. Bedgasm."

"What?" He looked at me like I had lost my mind.

"That's what my friend Julie calls it. You know, that feeling of euphoric release when you finally climb into bed after a long day." I kicked off my shoes. "I've been up since the crack of dawn and we've been driving for about eight hours. I never want to get out of this bed again."

He grabbed the room service menu and tossed it on the bed next to me. "Order something to eat. I'm going downstairs."

He was leaving? "Wait." I scrambled off the bed. "I'll come with you."

We found a Mexican restaurant on the first floor of the hotel, which had the bonus of cheap margaritas. We couldn't afford anything nicer anyway, not on the hundred dollars we got per episode to spend on food, gas, maps, and other supplies. We'd already spent about half of it, but we'd get more tomorrow and whatever we didn't spend would carry over to the next day.

At first, we both stared at our menus in silence. I read mine three times before I realized I had to do something or this would be a very long, very awkward dinner. If we were going to keep working together on the show, we needed to get along. I'd have to stick to safe topics. No discussion of kissing or the past. Talking about family was off the table too. That left work.

"What's your favorite thing about your job?" I asked.

He looked surprised and set his menu down. "Developing a new project, like an app or a game, from the ground up. At first it seems like it will never work, but when it comes together, there's no better feeling."

"That must be amazing, to be able to create something like that. Especially when millions of people use it."

"Yes. Too bad my father doesn't agree with you."

The waiter came and took our orders, then left us with a basket of chips and salsa. Ryan took a chip and asked, "What do you like about modeling?"

"The travel, the makeup and clothes, some of the people..." My voice trailed off. I didn't want to talk about myself. "What's your least favorite thing about your job?"

"Having every random person I meet tell me they have an idea for an app. What's your least favorite thing?"

I dipped a chip in the salsa. "Having everyone judge my appearance constantly. Too fat. Too tall. Too black. Not black enough. It's exhausting. And I'm so tired of always watching what I eat." I shoved the chip in my mouth as if in protest.

"I can see how that would be frustrating."

"I'm sorry, I know it's dumb. I hate when girls complain about being pretty. But it'd be nice to be praised for something other than my looks once in a while."

The waiter brought our margaritas and I took a huge sip of mine, which resulted in an immediate brain freeze. "What's the worst app idea you've ever heard?"

He tilted his head, considering. "Most of them are ideas for weird dating apps. But there was one... This guy wanted to make an app that he pitched as car sharing for dogs. Basically, you'd put out a notice your dog needed walking and some random stranger would pick it up on their way to work or wherever they were going."

"That sounds terrible! How would you know the person wouldn't let your dog run into the street or something? Or just keep it?" I shuddered at the idea. I'd grown up with the best dog ever, a corgi named Hamster (blame Daniel for the name), and one of my dreams was to get another one someday when my life was settled. I couldn't imagine letting someone I didn't trust walk my dog.

"Exactly. And there was no return system. So the person would walk the dog to work, and then what? Leave it there? Let someone else take it?" He shook his head. "It would never work. Even if there was a way to verify the people, there wouldn't be enough of a demand for such a thing to sustain the costs." He took another chip. "He called it Woofer."

"Woofer?" I laughed. "Seriously?"

"Yep. He wanted to do a cat version too called Meowist."

I nearly spit out the margarita I was drinking. "That's the most ridiculous thing I've ever heard!"

That lazy smirk was back. "Now you see what I have to put up with."

"You definitely have it rough." I giggled again. Warmth pooled in my stomach and our eyes locked. My gaze fell to his mouth. My lips were heavy with the taste of him.

He looked away first. "What are you going to do once the show is over? Go back to modeling?"

"I'm not sure." I played with the salt on my margarita glass. "I had everything planned out with that job in New York and now I feel...lost."

"Hmm." His dark eyes regarded me. "What would you like to do?"

"Nope. You already asked me a question. Now it's my turn."

His head tilted. "Is this a game, then?"

I pointed at him with a chip. "That's also a question."

"Both questions were addendums to the original question. You did the same thing earlier."

"Fine, I'll allow it." Dammit, this game sucked. "I don't know what I want to do. I guess I can keep modeling for a while, but..."

He gestured for me to continue. "But..."

"I was hoping to move on from that into something more stable. There's not much long-term career potential in modeling once you get older. I want a career I know will last. I'm just not sure what that is yet."

The waiter brought our food out. A tostada for me, and an enchilada and taco combo for him. When the waiter left, it was my turn for a question.

"Have you had anyone serious in your life these past years?" The words tumbled out of my mouth and I immediately regretted the question.

Ryan's expression hardened. "No. I don't have serious relationships. I have no interest in being tied down."

"Is that why you have a new girl on your arm every other week?" Oh my gosh, I needed to stop talking. What had they put in this margarita?

Something shifted on his face. A tiny crack. A slight peek at emotion. Then it was gone. "Yes." He stabbed his fork at his rice. "When we were kids you wanted to be an engineer. What happened to that plan?"

I shoved a huge bite in my mouth so I wouldn't have to answer right away. "I don't know. Pass."

"You can't pass. I answered all of your questions, including the two about my sex life. Would you rather I asked you about that?"

"No!" I took a long breath and smoothed out my napkin. "Okay. I guess things changed when my mom's talent agent recruited me in high school. After getting sick and losing my hair and all the other things my body went through, modeling made me feel beautiful and confident again. It let me be in control of my life for the first time in ages." I stared into my tostada bowl so I wouldn't have to look at him. "It's stupid, I know."

"It's not stupid." He reached across the table and took my hand. I was so surprised I jumped. Heat raced from his touch to every part of my body.

"Thanks." I squeezed his hand once, before letting go. "I do sometimes wish I'd majored in engineering, like I'd originally planned. It's too late for that now though."

"You could still go to graduate school."

"No way. My major was in theater. I'd have to take a ton of classes to get the right prerequisites and that would take ages. Not to mention how much it would cost." I shook my head. "I'll have to figure something else out."

"It would take some time, yes, but you're one of the smartest people I know. You've always been good at math and science. You'd whip through those classes easily."

His praise gave me a tingly feeling all over, or maybe that was from the margarita I'd already finished. Either way, I couldn't help but smile at him. "I'll think about it."

I got up to use the restroom and found one of the other competitors, the blond Barbie girl whose husband seemed to be her matching Ken doll. She reapplied her lipstick and gave me a big smile.

"Having fun so far?" she asked, with her slight Southern drawl. Or Texan, maybe?

"Very much. I've always loved the show, so it's amazing to be on it now."

"I hear ya." She held out her hand, which had long pink nails. "I'm Brenda."

I shook her hand and smiled. "Carla. Nice to meet you."

"It's a pleasure." She practically beamed at me and I felt bad for judging her so harshly before. "Is that your boyfriend with you?"

Her question caught me off-guard and I didn't have a ready answer. "Y-yes. Sort of. We just got together so we haven't really used that label yet."

"Ah, I know what you mean. My husband Ron didn't want to call me his girl for months. Finally I told him if I wasn't his girl then I was going to date some other guys on the side. That fixed that problem right quick." She winked.

"I'll keep that in mind, thanks." I wiped my hands and headed for the door. "Have a good night."

"Thanks—and good luck tomorrow!"

"You too."

I returned to Ryan with a smile on his face. "I just met that blond contestant from the South in the bathroom. She was really sweet."

Ryan scowled. "Be careful. She could be trying to play you."

I rolled my eyes. "She's not trying to play me."

"Maybe not, but every other couple on this show is our enemy. Don't forget that."

"There's no harm in being polite to someone." My good mood was gone now. Why did Ryan have to be such a grump?

We finished our meal, then walked back to the elevator. Once in the lobby, Ryan stopped. "I'm going to ask if they have another room available."

Wow. Was sharing a room with me *that* bad? "We don't have the money for that."

"I'll put it on my company's account."

He went to the front desk and I turned away with an ache in my chest. Perhaps it was for the best. I'd loved him for years, and then I'd avoided thinking about him for years, and now I couldn't escape him for more than five minutes. We were stuck together for as long as we were on the show. Separate hotel rooms would make this all easier.

Outside it had begun raining, one of those wild summer storms that promised thunder and lightning. I so rarely saw rain in Los Angeles that it captivated me and drew me closer. I moved toward the giant window at the end of the lobby bar and stared out at the downpour, my palms on the glass.

"Beautiful, isn't it?" A dark-haired man at the bar asked me. He swirled a glass of amber liquid in his hand.

"Yes, very."

"Not nearly as beautiful as you."

I stiffened. Ryan appeared out of nowhere, resting his hand on my lower back protectively. "Don't call her that." His voice could cut through diamonds.

"Sorry, man. Thought she was alone." The guy scurried off to the other side of the bar, followed by Ryan's gunfire eyes.

"You don't need to scare away every guy who talks to me."

His hand dipped lower, nearly brushing the top of my butt. "Yes. I do."

Thunder rolled through the hotel, so loud it made me jump. Three seconds later, a huge crack of lightning split across the sky, so big and bright it left spots in my eyes. For an instant, I saw the river and the flat land across it. Then it all faded to black again.

"There are no rooms available." His fingers traced faint patterns against the back of my dress. "You're stuck with me."

His words made me shiver. "Too bad," I said, though I was secretly relieved.

We returned to the hotel room. In the bathroom, I changed into an old t-shirt and sleep shorts and got ready for bed. I took longer than I needed to, anxious about being alone in the room with him again. What would happen when I walked out? I pictured different scenarios, ranging from us getting into another heated argument and climbing into our separate beds angry, to him grabbing me by the waist and kissing me senseless before we tumbled into bed and tore each other's clothes off. I was secretly hoping for the latter.

When I finally did emerge, Ryan was already lying on the couch with the spare blanket pulled up to his chest. Okay, so neither one of my scenarios was going to happen.

"That couch is way too short for you," I said.

He scowled and adjusted his pillow. "It's fine."

"Maybe it's a pull-out couch?"

"No, I already checked." He shifted again. Most of his legs hung off the end of the sofa. It was definitely not built for tall people to sleep on.

I sighed. "You can't sleep like that."

"I'll manage."

"Don't be silly. We can share the bed."

His jaw clenched. "That's not a good idea."

"The bed is huge. There's plenty of room for both of us. If you sleep on this couch you'll be sore tomorrow, and I need you at your best. We have a lot of driving to do."

I could tell he was about to stubbornly refuse, so I grabbed his arm and yanked him up. He rose to his feet and the blanket dropped away, revealing that he wore only black boxer briefs. I could see the outline of him through them. My mouth went dry. I forced my eyes to travel up, but then I met his naked chest, all muscles and ridges and smooth skin. Scenario number two played through my head on a loop with porn music in the background.

I couldn't seem to let go of his arm and we stood so close I felt the heat coming off his bare skin. He looked down at me, traveling slowly from my eyes to my lips, and I got the feeling he wanted to kiss me again.

"Only if you're sure." His voice sounded rough, like he was in pain.

"We'll pretend you're sleeping over, like in the old days."

"Except there's no Daniel this time."

"No Daniel," I whispered.

The words were barely out before his mouth came down on mine. A soft moan escaped me as our bodies fitted together and my heart danced to the tune of *yes, yes, yes*. Ryan was kissing me again and we weren't teenagers and there were no cameras and I didn't know what it meant and I didn't care. Maybe the alcohol made me bolder, or maybe it was Becca's words about how I should have some fun, but I wanted to touch him all over, every dirty inch of him. My hands traveled down his firm chest. My fingers dipped into the elastic at his waist.

He jerked away like he'd been hit by the lightning outside. "Fuck."

Yes, please, I thought. I reached for him, but he backed away.

"No," he said. "This isn't happening."

My stomach began to freefall. He was turning me down. Again. "But—"

"No." He grabbed his jeans and tugged them on his long legs. "*This* is why we need separate rooms."

I should have known scenario number one would win out in the end. "You were the one who kissed me."

"A mistake. Won't happen again."

"Why not?"

He pulled his shirt on. "We've both been drinking. We're not thinking clearly."

I sat on the edge of the bed, my throat tight. "Ah, that excuse again."

He shot me a dark look and moved toward the door.

I jumped to my feet. "Where are you going?"

"I'll be back soon. Get some sleep."

"Wait! Tell me why at least."

He turned to face me, his expression like granite. "Carla, you need to get over this silly crush you have on me, because this is never going to happen. *Never.* Got it?"

Humiliation made tears touch my eyes and I wiped them with the back of my hand. I tried to keep my voice from trembling. "When did you become such an asshole?"

He walked out the door without another word.

TWELVE

Ryan

I went down to the bar and got a drink, then stood at the window, the one she'd been at earlier. I moved to the glass and pressed my forehead against it, felt it vibrating from the intensity of the storm outside. Or the storm inside me.

Her words kept replaying in my head. *When did you become such an asshole?*

That was easy. The day I left her behind on the beach.

I downed the rest of my whiskey and slammed the glass on the counter. The bartender, a cute, pale blond girl, gave me sex eyes. Any other time, I'd take her home with me. I'd use her to try to erase the dark goddess who always drew me back with her siren call.

There was no escaping Carla this time. My first night alone with her and I'd already fucked it up. There went my promise to Daniel. How the hell was I supposed to get through the rest of this show? Or face him afterward?

I returned to the room an hour later, after doing three laps of the hotel grounds. The lights were off and she was in bed, but I knew from the way she was breathing that she was awake.

I lay down on the couch. I wouldn't be sleeping much anyway.

———

We didn't speak at all the next morning. We didn't even look at each other. She'd been right, of course. I was sore as hell from lying on that too-small couch all night.

Carla snatched the keys off the table. "I'm driving."

We waited in the lobby with the other teams until it was our turn to go, exactly fifteen minutes after the first team left. Chuck handed us our scavenger hunt list, wished us luck, and we set off.

Challenge Location: Petrified Forest
    1) London Bridge
    2) Meteor Crater
    3) Standin' On The Corner Park
    4) Tire on side of road
    5) The letter Q
    6) Someone picking their nose while driving

Carla drove away from the hotel while I studied the map. There was actually a bridge in Arizona called the London Bridge. Who knew?

I folded the map up. "We need to skip the London Bridge. It's too far out of the way."

Her hands tightened on the steering wheel. "It's the first location. We talked about this yesterday."

"Yes, I know. The safest thing is to visit the first location, but not this time. It will take us an hour and a half longer if we go there, at least. We can't afford to lose that much time."

"No, we can't afford to skip it." Her voice was angry, her tone suggested she wasn't backing down on this. But I wasn't going to back down either. Not when I was right.

"Doing it your way worked out the first time, but you can't always stick to the plan if you want to get ahead."

"Plans work! That's why we make them!"

"And how has that worked out for you so far?"

She was practically seething now. "Fine! We'll do it your way this time. But if we don't come in third or better, we're going back to my plan next time."

"Fine."

We sank back into tense silence. She was pissed with me, but I was okay with that. Hell, she probably hated my guts after last night. Fine with me. Her anger was easier to deal with than her desire. She had no idea, *no idea*, what it was costing me to keep my distance.

For the next hour we drove through the stark desert and it seemed like we wouldn't see a single scavenger hunt item. Carla tapped her nails on the steering wheel in an irritated pattern. I refused to admit that skipping the first location was a mistake, but I grew more stressed with each passing minute. Shit, what if I'd made a huge error by taking this risk? She'd never let me live it down.

I spotted something ahead that made me sit up straight. "Get off here."

"Here? Now? Why?"

"Just do it!"

She quickly changed lanes and got off at the exit at the last moment, barely making it. Right off the side of the road was a gas station called the Quickee Mart. I snapped a photo of the Q on the sign. Finally, one item on the list down.

"Good catch," she grudgingly said.

"Might as well refill the tank and grab some snacks while we're here."

She parked the car in front of one of the gas pumps. "Thank goodness. I've had to pee for the last half hour."

"Why didn't you say anything?"

"I didn't want us to lose any time."

The blond Barbie couple was refueling their car a few aisles over. Carla waved at them and they waved back with big smiles.

I held out my hand for the keys. "Go. I'll take care of this."

She tossed them to me and took off. I got the gas rolling, then hit the bathroom myself. Inside the shop, I bought her favorite snacks (Fritos and sour gummy worms) and some bottled water, plus a better map of Arizona and New Mexico. I made it back to the car first and turned it on so we could drive off immediately. The blond couple's car drove away, getting ahead of us, but we wouldn't be far behind.

When Carla didn't return after a few minutes, I began to wonder if she was okay. Maybe her stomach was upset or she'd gotten her period or something. Maybe she was avoiding me because I was such a dick. I checked the time and got out of the car to clean the windshield, which was covered in bugs and dirt.

Ten minutes later and she still wasn't back. Something was definitely wrong. I went into the store and looked around, but didn't see her. I poked my head into the bathroom and called her name, but no one was in there. I asked the clerk if he'd seen her and he shook his head.

What. The. Fuck. Where the hell was Carla? Had she ditched me? No, she'd never do that. We'd be disqualified. I'd watched every one of the episodes she'd sent me for research and that had happened on one of them. Besides, no matter how mad I made her, Carla would never leave a friend behind.

I stood outside and looked around the dusty old gas station, but there were no other cars in sight. A cold lance of panic struck me. Had someone *taken* her? Oh fuck no. If she'd been kidnapped, I didn't know what I would do. No, that wasn't true. I'd track her down no matter where she was or how long it took. I'd find her somehow.

I ran around to the back of the building, searching everywhere for clues. I was in a total frenzy now, my adrenaline spiking. Then I heard banging.

"Carla?" I yelled, spinning around.

"Ryan!" Her voice was muffled and came from behind a plain metal door. A shiny new padlock was on it. The area smelled of piss, rotten food, and trash. I yanked on the padlock but it wouldn't budge. Then I spotted a bright silver key in the dirt near my feet.

I bent and grabbed the key. "Hang on, I'll get you out of there."

"Hurry, please." She sounded like she was on the verge of tears.

The key unlocked the padlock and I flung the door open. Carla rushed out of a pitch black room and into my arms with a choked sob. A profound feeling of relief settled over me and I ran my hands over her hair and down her back. Carla wasn't injured or kidnapped or in danger. She was here with me. She was safe.

"Ryan." She buried her face in my shoulder, crying and trembling against me.

I held her tighter and stroked her head softly. I was shaken too. This was all my fault. I should have protected her better. "It's okay, I've got you. I'm here."

For a few minutes I simply comforted her, rubbing her back as she clung to my shirt. Once she calmed down and stopped shaking, she looked up at me. "I'm sorry for crying on you. It was just so dark and small in there, and I was so upset with myself."

"What happened?"

"Brenda and Ron asked me for help reading their map, then said they'd show me a scavenger hunt item they'd found as their way of thanking me. I followed them back here and they shoved me in that room and locked me in."

"Those assholes." Red hot rage replaced my relief. My hands turned to fists. If I saw those fuckers again… "They wanted us to fall behind."

"Brenda seemed so friendly last night. I never thought she would try to trick me." Carla ducked her face into my shirt again. "I'm too nice, just like you and Daniel said. Now we're going to lose the game because of it."

I took her by the shoulders, looking her in the eye. "Your kindness is one of the most admirable things about you. Never let anyone make you feel bad for being a good person. And we are *not* going to lose."

She stared at me, clearly surprised by my words, and then took a long breath. "How did you unlock the door?"

"They left the key in front of it. Probably knew they'd get in trouble with the show if we couldn't get you out right away."

She straightened up and wiped at her eyes, putting on a look of determination. "We can't let them win."

"We won't."

We returned to the car and Carla found the snacks I'd bought for her. "You remembered my favorites after all these years?" She ripped open the bag of Fritos immediately. "Thank you."

"You're welcome." I paused before starting the car. I was supposed to keep making her hate me, but I couldn't stop myself from blurting out, "I'm sorry about last night."

I couldn't look at her, but I could tell she was watching me. I held my breath, waiting for her response.

"I'm sorry for calling you an asshole," she said.

"I deserved it."

"Yeah, you did." She smiled faintly. "Apology accepted. Now drive."

———

W hile we traveled down what used to be Route 66, Carla was vigilant about looking for scavenger hunt items. By the time we got near the next location, she'd already found both the tire on the side of the road and caught someone picking their nose while driving. We decided to skip the Meteor Crater since it was farther off the freeway and hit the Standin' On The Corner Park instead.

We entered the small town of Winslow, Arizona, and I pulled over so Carla could get a photo. The tiny park was surrounded by a wall of bricks with a huge mural made to look like a reflection of the street, including the red flatbed Ford parked in front of it. There was also a statue of a guy with a guitar, under a road sign that said "Standin' On The Corner."

I squinted at the statue. "I don't get it."

Carla snapped another picture. "I think it's from a song. I'd look it up, if I had my phone." She sat back and sighed. "I miss the internet."

"And music," I added, as I navigated us back to the highway.

"Yes. That's definitely one of the worst things about this road trip. I'd kill for anything at this point, even country music."

"Damn, you must be really desperate. You hate country music."

We launched into discussions about music and she talked about how both of her roommates were in Villain Complex. The band had really taken off in the last year. I bet if we turned on the radio right now we could find one of their songs on there.

"They have impromptu gigs in the apartment all the time. It's amazing." Her face fell. "Except all of that is over now. We've each moved out. Someone else is probably living in our apartment already."

"You'll find a new place to live after we win the million dollars."

"I hope so." She rested her head on the window, staring out at the endless blue sky. I thought that was the end of the conversation, but then she turned back to me and asked, "Why did you come on the show with me?"

I shot her a sharp look, then raised my eyes to the cameras watching and recording everything. "You know why."

"I know you came on the show to help me," she said slowly. "But I think there's another reason too. Something you haven't told me."

I didn't answer for some time. The show would capture all of this and I wasn't sure I was ready for my personal business to be aired on TV. But maybe I needed to talk about it or something, because the next words out of my mouth were, "My dad has cancer."

Her hands covered her mouth, barely hiding her gasp. "Oh no. I'm so sorry, Ryan."

I nodded. "Lung cancer. From the smoking. Stage two."

"Did you just find out?"

"Yeah. He didn't even tell me. Can you believe that? My stepmother had to call me and let me know. That's why I went to LA." My jaw clenched up at the memory of him yelling at me to get out of his house. "But he didn't want anything to do with me."

"That's so sad. I know you've never had a great relationship with him, but I can't imagine why he wouldn't want to see you now."

"The usual shit." I was close to breaking the steering wheel with my grip. I forced my fingers to relax. "He's pissed I won't take over the family business. He'll never forgive me for starting my own company. All the same things he disowned me for before I left for college."

"He can't blame you for wanting to follow you dream."

"He can and he does."

She reached across the center console and took my hand. I nearly jumped at her touch, but my stiff fingers relaxed into hers. This was dangerous, letting her get this close to me again, but I couldn't pull away.

"You came on the show to escape," she said.

I shrugged. "I already had the time off work."

"I understand. I came on the show to escape too." She squeezed my hand. "When this is over, you should try again with your dad."

"It's too late. Things between us can't be repaired."

"That's not true. As long as he's still alive, it's not too late."

I wasn't sure about that, but I let it go.

We lapsed into silence, but our hands remained joined together until we made it to the challenge location.

———

We parked at an RV camp near the edge of the Petrified Forest and people from the show led us into an area they'd taken over with camera crews and *Road Trip Race* signs. Desert stretched on either side of us, broken up by jagged brown mountains, huge rocks, and chunks of petrified wood. The sun beat down on us with an angry, dry heat and sweat soaked through my shirt.

In the middle of it all stood an obstacle course with three pools and raised platforms over them, connected by wobbly rope bridges. The first pool was full of thick, dark mud, while the other pools had water in them. At the end of the obstacle course there was a huge plastic pot, like the kind you'd plant a large tree in. I stared at it all, wondering what we had gotten ourselves into…and why it involved mud.

A man wearing a bandana handed me a card with the information. I groaned when I saw the name of the challenge: Rub One Out. It got even worse when I saw what we were about to do. One person had to roll in the mud, climb to the other person and rub mud all over them, and then that person had to fill the giant pot with mud. Once it was full, we could move on.

So much for keeping my hands off Carla.

There was no time to worry about that now because we had to hurry. The challenges were meant to slow us down and we were already behind. Carla shot me a nervous look, before splitting off to the women's restroom to change. I headed into the men's and threw on my swim trunks quickly.

When I emerged, it was all I could do to not outright ogle Carla. She wore a pale yellow bikini that showed off every inch of her curves. I'd thought last night with her tiny shorts and thin t-shirt had been torture enough, but this was worse. My gaze ran over it all. The swell of her breasts. The tightness of her ass. The curve of her hips. The smooth plane of her stomach. Those long legs that went on for miles. How was I supposed to get through this challenge, or hell, the rest of the night, without jumping her?

Remember Daniel, I told myself, conjuring the memory of her brother telling me to stay away from her. But that image vanished when I saw her eyeing my chest like she wanted to take a bite. Fucking hell.

I climbed to the middle platform, while Carla stood in front of the mud pit. A horn sounded and she dove in without hesitation. I stared, completely transfixed, as she rolled around in the mud, getting her entire body covered. She'd need a good shower after this. So would I. A cold one.

Once she was completely soaked in mud she ran across the rope ladder toward me. I stood in the middle of the platform, cringing as she swayed and nearly fell, then offered her my hand when she got close enough. I pulled her off the bridge and she smacked against my chest, mud flying. There was a second where she looked up at me, each of us taking a breath, and then she began rubbing against me. Her muddy skin slid against mine, wet and hot and slick. Within seconds I was both covered in mud and more turned on than ever.

I tore myself away from her and ran across the other rope bridge, which was difficult to do with a raging hard-on. When I made it to the platform I leaned over the pot and pushed as much mud into it as possible. Once it was suitably disgusting, I went back to the middle platform to do it all over again. I estimated we'd have to do this three times, without falling, before we could leave.

Easier said than done.

Carla fell off the rope bridge and into the water on the second attempt and had to start all over. She got herself muddy once again and made it to the platform safely this time, and we repeated the rubbing, sliding, and panting. Whoever came up with this challenge was seriously cruel.

We broke apart and I got as much mud in the pot as I could, then we began again. This time when she reached my platform, her foot slipped in all the mud and she nearly fell. I caught her easily, drawing her into my arms, and we locked eyes. She took my slick face in her hands, her mouth so close to mine I could feel her breath on my lips. As she pressed her body against me, her soft curves meeting my hard ridges, all I could think about was how I wanted to wrap her legs around me and have my way with her right then and there, even with this mud all over us.

By some act of god, I managed to restrain myself, despite her heavy breathing and the look in her eyes like she was hungry for something only I could give her. I pulled away and scrambled to the last platform, then scraped off enough mud to completely fill the pot. The horn sounded and we were finished. Thank god.

We climbed off the obstacle course and were sent to the outdoor showers they'd set up. I wasn't sure where the other teams were, but we were alone when we stepped into the wet, muddy shower area. I switched the water on and stood under the spray.

Carla moved under the shower next to me and let water run down her body. I watched as she lifted her mass of curls to wash away the mud. Water poured down her graceful neck and shoulders and between her plump breasts. She turned and I got a view of her perfect ass, barely concealed by those tiny yellow bottoms.

Christ. This shower was not nearly cold enough.

She turned around again and caught me watching her. Her eyes did a slow perusal from my mouth to my chest to my shorts. Her expression was downright filthy, her body shiny, slick, and wet. One hand slid across her breast, over her bikini top, taunting me. I was this close to saying fuck it and crossing the distance between us, when she switched off the shower, grabbed a towel, and walked away.

I watched her go and took long, even breaths. That was the most erotic shower of my entire life and we hadn't even touched.

Oh yeah. I was screwed.

THIRTEEN

Carla

W e were declared fifth when we reached the final location of today's journey, a campground in Bluewater Lake State Park, shortly past the border into New Mexico. I could have rubbed it in Ryan's face that he'd lost the bet and we would be going with my plans from now on, but I kept quiet. We would have been even farther behind if it wasn't for his idea to skip the first location. The only reason we'd lost time was because I'd been locked in a gas station shed by Brenda and Ron, who I'd now dubbed the Blond Menace.

It was getting cold at the campground now that the sun was touching the horizon, but the sight of scraggly trees and the glistening dark lake was a relief after two days of endless, barren desert. A bonfire raged nearby, along with a barbeque and some picnic tables. Beyond that, eight tents were set up for the teams to sleep in. The crew told us not to leave the camp area and advised us to pick a tent, get some food at the barbeque, and relax for the evening. We'd be setting off early again the next morning.

Ryan and I shuffled across the dusty ground until we found an empty tent and left our stuff in it. He stretched his arms and his back while my eyes lingered on him. We'd changed back into our regular clothes and he wore a soft gray t-shirt that hugged every muscle. I wanted to tear it off him with my teeth. His eyes landed on me, and I quickly checked out everything *but* him. How did he always catch me looking at him?

As we headed to the bonfire, Brenda stuck her head out of another tent, a much larger and nicer one. "So sorry about earlier! We had to make sure we won the challenge—which we did. No hard feelings, right?" She laughed and disappeared back into the tent before I could answer.

I stomped across the dirt. "I hate them."

Ryan easily kept pace with my angry strides. "You don't hate anyone. Except me, perhaps."

"I don't hate you." We got in line for food behind one of the other couples. "We should prank them tonight. Put rocks in their shoes. Steal their clothes while they're showering. Sneak into their tents and draw moustaches on their faces."

"Remind me to never get on your bad side."

I sighed, the anger already leaving me. "You know I would never actually do any of those things."

The people in front of us turned around, the lesbian bikers who always wore leather jackets covered in metal. They were probably in their sixties at least and complete opposites: one was tall and wide with short white hair, the other was short and thin with long black hair.

"Who are you plotting against?" the white-haired one asked.

"Oh, um." My cheeks warmed. "Do you know Brenda and Ron?"

"Unfortunately," the other one said.

Ryan placed a protective hand on my lower back. "They locked Carla in a gas station today."

"They did *what?*" the first one asked, putting a hand on her hip.

I told them the whole story while we got our food and sat down at a nearby picnic table to eat. Ryan gave me the side-eye the entire time, but kept his mouth shut. Even so, I could feel him mentally telling me to be careful about what I said. I mentally told him to zip it.

"What little weasels," Judy, the black-haired one, said once I'd finished my tale.

Sally nodded sternly. "We'll keep an eye out for more of their tricks."

As we ate, I learned that they'd come in second today. The two of them were from Portland, they had six cats, and were both retired. They'd met thirty years ago at a book club and had a wedding the day that gay marriage became legal.

"We didn't want to wait another second," Judy said, taking Sally's wrinkled hand in her own. My heart warmed and I smiled at both of them.

After dinner, Ryan and I walked back to our tent, our shoes kicking up dust. Everything here was so dry. I'd been slathering myself with lotion and lip gloss so my skin didn't crack and peel off, but it was never enough.

"You can't trust these people," Ryan said. "Don't forget they're our competition."

Ah, I knew this lecture would be coming. His dark eyes had been judging me all throughout dinner while he'd stabbed at his food. "It doesn't hurt anything to be friendly. I really like Judy and Sally."

"You said that about Brenda too. Look where that got you."

I huffed. "I can't go through life assuming everyone is going to screw me over." I gave him a wry look. "I'm not you."

"Good thing I'm here then. Someone has to keep you out of trouble."

I pressed a hand to my heart. "My loyal protector. What would I ever do without you?"

He lifted his eyes to the sky with a long sigh before following me back to our tent. It was barely big enough for two people to lie in and not nearly tall enough for us to stand in. No wonder everyone was hanging out around the bonfire.

I ducked into the tent and flopped onto the sleeping bag. "Are you tired?"

"No." He crawled beside me, filling the space with his masculine presence. The air in the tent grew thick, laced with our unspoken chemistry. It didn't matter how much I tried to ignore it, the connection between us was always there.

"We could go back to the bonfire," I suggested.

"I'd rather not."

I nodded. I didn't want to go back either. Something had shifted between us today. I wasn't sure if it was because of the gas station incident, the mud challenge, or the talk about his dad, but the walls between us had cracked. All they needed was one hard push and they'd come tumbling down.

"What should we do?" I asked, my voice breathless as ideas ran through my head. I pictured our kiss last night, when my hand had dipped in the elastic of his boxer briefs. I imagined the mud challenge earlier, with his hard arousal pressing against my thighs. I remembered those hours in the car, when we'd held hands for so long I'd forgotten where my skin ended and his began.

But he didn't think about me that way. Or did he? I wasn't sure of anything anymore.

"Let's go for a walk," Ryan said.

"Now?" I gestured into the night. "It's pitch black out there."

"I have a flashlight. Number twenty-one on your packing list, if I remember correctly."

So he really had paid attention. I smiled faintly. "It was, yes. I have one in my bag too. But what if there are bears out there?"

"I doubt they have many bears in New Mexico."

"Okay, coyotes then. Wolves. Snakes." My eyes grew wider with each word. "Raccoons. Owls. Spiders."

"You're just listing random animals now." He got out of the tent, rising to his full height, and offered me his hand. "I'll keep you safe."

I grabbed my flashlight and took his hand, letting him pull me to my feet. "They told us not to go far. What if we get caught?"

"We won't get caught." He started walking away from the tent, his flashlight bobbing ahead of him. "I bet you haven't broken a single rule since we were teenagers."

I rushed after him. "I break rules all the time!"

"Name one."

"Um." I wracked my brain. "I came on the show with you, even though we're not a real couple."

"That doesn't count. You didn't even know about that rule and you would have blabbed the truth to Giselle if I hadn't jumped in and saved us."

He was right, of course. I tried to think of something else as we walked through the darkness, but finally threw up my hands. "Fine, you got me. I'm a rule follower and a planner. I'm too nice and too honest. I'm basically the most boring person ever."

He stopped abruptly and I almost crashed into him. He brushed a curl away from my cheek, his thumb grazing my skin. "Carla. You are anything but boring."

Before I could respond he turned around and kept walking through the sparse trees. I hurried after him, the feel of his touch still burning up my skin.

We carefully climbed up a hill that overlooked the lake, using our flashlights to make sure we didn't lose our footing. By the time we reached a clearing at the top my blood was rushing and my legs twitched. I usually ran an hour every morning, but I'd been cooped up in a car for the past two days. I was refreshed and invigorated in a way I hadn't felt since starting on the show.

We moved to the end of a bluff overlooking the bonfire and the lake. The moon was a perfect crescent overhead and the air was crisp and hummed with the sound of crickets. I took in a deep breath, my lungs clearing out. "A night hike was a good idea."

Ryan stood at my side, gazing across the dark forest. "Even if it meant breaking the rules?"

I smiled at him. "I'll allow it this once."

"Too bad, because I broke another rule." He pulled something out of his jacket: a small fleece blanket he unfolded and set on the ground. "I borrowed this from Brenda and Ron's tent on my way to the bathroom earlier."

A short laugh escaped me. "You did not!"

He shrugged, with the hint of a sly grin on his face. "You wanted to prank them."

"We have to give it back! They're going to be cold."

"Later." He sank onto the blanket, stretching his long legs out, and patted the spot next to him. I sat down, drawing my knees up to my chest. For a few minutes we sat in companionable silence, taking in the beautiful, crisp night while the stress of the day faded away.

His low voice broke through the quiet. "Remember when we would go hiking in the Santa Monica Mountains?"

"Of course I remember." I'd been thinking about that too, ever since he'd brought out the blanket. "Daniel hated it."

"He did. He stopped coming after he twisted his ankle."

"After that it was just the two of us. We would bring a blanket and stretch out on it and eat sandwiches." Those hikes were some of the few times we'd been alone when we were younger. On every one of those hikes, I'd silently wish Ryan would kiss me. He never did.

"I didn't bring any sandwiches, sorry."

"Good thing we already ate." I liked this Ryan, the one who wasn't being a total jerk to me all the time, who remembered my favorite car snacks and stole blankets for us to sit on like the old days. I wanted to keep him. It would never happen, but my silly heart couldn't help but wish for it anyway.

With a bittersweet sigh, I leaned back and took in the vast, incomprehensible sky above us. Millions of stars left shiny pinpricks across the black expanse. I'd never seen a night this clear or so close to us. I could almost reach out and take a star in my hand, or climb up and slide down the curve of the moon.

"It's so beautiful. The stars, the moon. You never see a night like this in LA." I glanced over at Ryan, but he was staring at me with his dark, intense eyes. I nudged him, feeling self-conscious. "You're not looking!"

"I'm looking at the most beautiful thing here." His gaze never left me. "You outshine the moon and all the stars."

My mouth fell open. I couldn't form words. Ryan, who'd rejected me time and time again, was now telling me I was beautiful. Was he drunk? Was I dreaming? Had I stumbled into a parallel universe?

At my silence, he looked away. "Sorry. I know you don't like being called beautiful. Forget I said anything."

He actually sounded hesitant. This was definitely unusual. Ryan exuded confidence. It was one of the things that made him so sexy and so successful at everything he did.

"I don't mind when it comes from you." Warmth rushed through me from his compliment and I leaned against his side. "I was just surprised. I thought I wasn't your type."

"You're not," he said quickly. "But I'm not blind."

The warmth immediately vanished. Nothing between us had changed after all. I was reading too much into the moments we'd shared and the things he'd said. It wouldn't be the first time.

A shooting star dashed across the night. "Look," I whispered.

Ryan's voice was at my ear. "Make a wish."

"I don't know what to wish for."

"I don't believe that for one second."

I wish you wanted me the way I wanted you, I thought. *I wish you would kiss me again.*

I waited, but it didn't happen. So much for wishing on shooting stars.

Ryan rose to his feet, a blur of dark movement, then reached down to help me up. "Come on. We're going to play a game."

"Like the questions game last night?" I tried to keep the disappointment out of my voice. Right now going back to the tent and trying to forget this day ever existed sounded like the best plan.

"Something like that." He bent down and grabbed something off the ground, which he clenched in his fist. "Find a rock."

"A rock?" I asked skeptically.

"Just do it."

"Fine." I searched with my flashlight until I found a decent-sized rock of my own. "Got one."

"Now throw it off the hill into the darkness, and yell out something you want."

"What? I can't throw a rock here! What if it hits someone?"

"It won't hit anyone. There's no one out here but us."

I shook my head, my stomach swirling with anxiety, and not just from the idea of accidentally injuring someone. "This is silly. What's the point of this game?"

"The point is for you to yell at the world about what you want." I could practically hear him rolling his eyes as he said it, like it was incredibly obvious.

"But I never yell."

"Which is why you need to do this more than anyone. Besides, you have no problem yelling at me."

"That's different. You're infuriating."

"So pretend you're throwing the rock at my head."

I bit my lip. The only thing I knew for sure I wanted was him and I wasn't about to yell that out loud. Everything else was up in the air at the moment. For once, I didn't have anything in my life planned out and it terrified me.

"Fine, I'll start." He raised his arm and launched the rock off the bluff. "I want us to win *Road Trip Race*!"

The rock disappeared into the night with a soft thump and the rustle of leaves. No one screamed or cried out in pain. No coyotes jumped out of the darkness to have their revenge.

"Your turn," he said.

"I don't think I can do this."

"Yes, you can. You can do anything."

He had such faith in me. I raised the rock with a shaking arm. "I want—"

"No, you have to yell it."

"I want us to win *Road Trip Race* too!" I shouted the words as the rock flew from my hand and vanished.

"That wasn't so bad, was it?"

"No." It was kind of fun actually.

"Again. But this time you can't copy me." He picked up another rock and threw it far in front of us. I watched the muscles in his arm and shoulder move with precision. "I want to keep my company!"

"That's easy. Turn down the offer from Slade Industries."

"It's not that easy. They're offering a lot of money. It would make things better with my father too. But stop trying to distract me. It's your turn now."

I carefully selected my rock, testing the weight in my hand. "I want my parents to get back together!"

He tossed his rock next. "I want your parents to get back together too!"

"Hey, no copying!" I grabbed another rock. "I want my ex-boyfriend's balls to shrivel up and fall off. No, wait, that's too horrible. I want someone to punch him in the balls!"

"I can definitely arrange that," Ryan said. "I owe that guy a beating."

Ah, it was time for the overprotective big brother part of the evening. Daniel would be so proud. "No, you really don't."

"I'm shocked Daniel didn't do it. He's slacking on his brotherly duties."

"Only because I wouldn't let him." I nudged Ryan in the side. "It's your turn."

He picked up another rock and stared at it for a long moment. Then he let it fly and yelled, "I want my father to be proud of me!"

"Oh, that's a good one." I lightly touched his tense shoulder. "I know it's not the same, but I think what you've done with Meta Entertainment is amazing."

"Thanks." His shoulders seemed to relax a smidge. "Your turn."

"Um." I toed the dirt with my shoe and searched my head. "I can't think of anything else I want."

"Yes, you can. Here." He took my hand and set a bunch of smaller rocks into my palm, then closed my fingers over them. "Just yell everything that comes to mind. Even if it's silly."

"All right." I took a deep breath and then threw the pebbles one by one, letting it all out. "I want to go back to school! I want to dye my hair a crazy color my mom would never approve of! I want to get a corgi!"

"I miss Hamster too."

"Best dog ever."

He moved behind me, resting his hands on my waist, surprising me with his touch and how close we were. "Do you feel any better?"

"Yes. But I have one more rock." Uncertainty nearly held me back, but I knew exactly what I wanted now. And if I didn't say it in this moment, I never would.

"Go on then."

I threw the rock as hard as I could. "I want us to be friends again!"

My words echoed in the night and I held my breath, waiting for his response. I teetered between embarrassment and hope and fear, glad he stood behind me so he couldn't see my face.

"Carla," he said softly.

I turned around in his arms, gazing up at him, but he didn't say more. A battle was being waged behind his eyes, like shadows dancing in the dim light.

"It's your turn now," I finally said, when his silence grew uncomfortable.

"Carla," he said again, and this time I heard the pain in his voice. "We *are* friends. We've always been friends."

"Then why didn't you speak to me for six years?" Emotion shook my voice, but I couldn't hold back any longer.

"Because I'm an idiot."

"You were my best friend and then you were *gone*. You said you'd be back. You said you'd watch over me. You *lied*. And now I don't know what this thing between us is anymore. Are we friends?" A single tear slid down my cheek. "I really don't know."

He took my face in his hands, his touch gentle yet firm, and his thumb slowly wiped away my tear. "I'm sorry. I thought I was doing what was best for you."

My knees grew weak and I grabbed onto his shirt to steady myself. "I missed you. I missed you so much."

"I missed you too. Every damn day." His thumb moved down to run over my lower lip. "I told myself you didn't want to hear from me. That it would be easier for you to move on and find someone else if I stayed away. But I never stopped thinking about you."

"I tried to move on. I thought I'd succeeded, too. And then you showed up at dinner."

He rested his forehead against mine, our mouths only a breath apart. "Do you wish I'd never returned?"

"No." My fingers tightened on his shirt, pulling him closer. "*No*. I'm really happy you came back."

"Me too." His eyes dropped to my lips and I thought for sure he was going to kiss me. Instead, he tilted my head down and pressed a kiss to my forehead. Then he pulled away. "It's late. We should get back to the tent before anyone notices we're missing."

"*Now* you care about following the rules?" I wrapped my arms around myself, cold from the loss of his body warmth.

"I care about making sure you stay on the show." He took my hand and began leading me down the hill. His movements were deliberate and his grip was strong and steady as we made our way back to our tent. He never let go of my hand even once.

I stole glances at Ryan, but his face was too hard to read. Even though I was disappointed he hadn't kissed me, I did feel a lot better after opening up to him. Maybe we could be friends again now. That would be enough. It had to be.

The camp was quieter now, with most of the teams in bed already. Ryan discreetly returned the blanket he'd stolen while I changed and got ready for bed. I slid into the sleeping bag, wondering what would happen between us now. There was nowhere to escape in this tiny tent.

Ryan returned and I saw a split second of hesitation before he sat on the sleeping bag beside me. He tugged off his shirt and I tried not to stare at his hard chest. His jeans came off next, leaving him in only his boxer briefs again. Did he sleep like that every night?

I rolled onto my side, facing away from him to stop torturing myself with something I couldn't have. It wasn't long before he slid into the large sleeping bag beside me. His bare skin brushed against mine as he got comfortable, and I held my breath as each touch sent little shocks through me. He switched off the flashlight.

"Try to get some sleep," he said.

Impossible. All I could think about was how close our bodies were. If I adjusted just a tiny bit, or rolled over a little too far, we'd meet in a tangle of limbs and skin. I was hyper aware of every inch of myself and every slight movement he made.

He shifted again. He was facing me now.

I turned toward him, my heart racing. My eyes had adjusted to the darkness and I saw the outline of his head and shoulders, but couldn't make out the details. It didn't matter. I knew them all by heart, even with my eyes closed. I wanted to close the distance between us so bad I nearly trembled with it.

How was I supposed to sleep like this?

The minutes passed by and I was convinced I would be awake all night. Memories of his nearly naked body and of the way his mouth tasted kept flashing through my head. I grew so warm I wanted to throw the sleeping bag off me. I couldn't tell if he was sleeping either, but I didn't think so.

"Ryan?" I whispered.

"Yes?" He was still awake. In fact, he didn't sound sleepy at all.

"Thank you for coming on the show with me."

"You're welcome."

I rolled over again, trying to put some distance between us. No matter how much I twisted and turned, I couldn't get comfortable. Finally, I gave up. "I can't sleep."

"Come here."

He was lying on his back with one arm folded above his head. I slowly moved closer to him, unsure what he wanted of me. He wrapped his other arm around me, tugging my body against his side, so that I curled up around him. With a soft sigh, I rested my head on his shoulder, placing my hand over his heart. Every inch of my soul whispered, *yes, this is where you belong.*

We'd never been so close to each other before, never before shared a moment so intimate and so right. It should have made me even more wound up, but after the first few seconds, a strong sense of calm settled over me. As I listened to his heart beat steadily and felt his chest rise and fall under me, my busy brain finally began to settle down.

I closed my eyes. I was exactly where I was supposed to be.

FOURTEEN

Ryan

I'd never slept with a woman before. Sure, I'd had sex with plenty of them. But I'd never fallen asleep with one in my arms, and never woken up with one still beside me. It was one of my rules.

Until last night.

I'd nearly kissed Carla again, too. My plan to keep her mad at me had failed spectacularly. After only a few short days she'd worn down my resolve to keep my distance, and soon I would be helpless against her. But if I gave in to the sexual tension between us, what would happen to us? What would we do when the show was over? And how would I face Daniel afterward?

I pondered all of these questions as we drove to our next challenge. We had to travel from western New Mexico to Colorado.

    Challenge Location: Desert Flower Hot Springs
        1) Rio Grande Gorge Bridge
        2) RoboCop Miner Statue
        3) UFO Watchtower
        4) Billboard with picture of food
        5) Car carrier carrying cars
        6) Dog with head out of window

We found item number four almost immediately on a McDonalds sign by a freeway exit. Carla crossed it off, but then puzzled over the list and the map, making a lot of noises along the lines of, "Hmm."

"What do you think?" I sipped my coffee with a grimace. I hadn't wanted to get out of our tent this morning, thanks to the gorgeous woman who'd been curled up against me. I hadn't wanted to do much of anything except roll her onto her back and give in to what we both wanted. Instead, I'd dragged myself to a cold shower at the crack of dawn, gotten dressed in one of my last pairs of clean clothes, and grabbed this coffee that tasted like piss. All because I wanted Carla to win this stupid show.

"The map we have only shows the bridge, and it seems like it might be something of a detour to get to. I have no clue where the other two locations are." She chewed on her lip, her eyes darting over the map again. "I think we should stop in Albuquerque to ask someone about these other two places."

"Agreed."

We rolled into Albuquerque a little over an hour later. The mountains shadowed the city on the east and many of the buildings had a distinct Southwestern feel, with boxy shapes and sandy hues. We got off the freeway and stopped at one of the first restaurants we saw, a retro diner that sported a historic Route 66 sign with pink neon lights. Inside it looked like something right out of the 1950's, with a black and white checkered floor, turquoise-colored booths, and an old jukebox in the corner. The sizzling smell of burgers and the sound of "Rock Around The Clock" filled the air.

We sat at the counter and both ordered old-fashioned milkshakes, burgers, and fries. When we told the waitress we were in a hurry, she said they could put it in carry-out boxes for us.

"No salad today?" I asked Carla.

"Nope. In a place like this, it would be a crime to not have a burger." She pulled out our map of New Mexico and poured over it, chewing on the pen in her hand.

The waitress returned with our milkshakes—vanilla for me, strawberry for Carla. "Need some help, hon?"

Carla explained what we were doing and the waitress provided a tourist brochure for the area. The two of them bent over the map and made marks on it for all the scavenger hunt locations and then Carla began to work out all the possible routes. One of the chefs came out and gave his opinion while we sipped on our milkshakes. I nodded along, but mostly I let Carla handle it. In every other area of my life I enjoyed being in control and taking charge of the situation. Most of the time I didn't trust anyone else to do as good a job as I would. Letting Carla take over was freeing, and I never doubted for a second that she would plan the best route for us. Plus, watching her use that brain of hers was sexy as hell.

By the time our food was ready, Carla had figured it out. She explained everything while we walked back to the car, milkshakes and take-out bags in hand. "We have a couple options. We can try to hit up every location, but it would take us something like ten hours, at best guess."

"Ten hours? It'll be the middle of the night by the time we finish the challenge."

"I know. Another idea is to visit two of the stops—the bridge and the UFO Watchtower—which will take us about seven hours. That's probably our best bet."

"Seven hours is still a really long time."

We got in the car and strapped ourselves in. "The last option is to only go to the RoboCop Miner Statue, which will take between five and six hours. It's a much faster route, but it's also the most risky plan."

"You already know which one I'm going to pick."

She nodded slowly, looking at the map again. We were fifth yesterday, which meant this morning we'd started out twenty minutes after Brenda and Ron, who'd gone first. There were only eight teams left and another would be eliminated tonight. We couldn't afford to get any farther behind—but if we screwed up this challenge, we could be the ones kicked off.

I saw Carla's indecision written all over her face and knew she was torn between the safest route, the middle path, or the riskiest one. I started up the car and stayed silent, letting her decide. Finally, she drew in a long breath and set the map down. When her eyes turned to me, they danced in the sunlight. "Let's do it. Let's take the shortest route."

Surprise washed through me, along with something else, some feeling I wasn't ready to identify. This decision felt big, like it was about more than just which route we took. "I thought for sure you'd pick the safer route."

A sly grin lit up her face. "Must be your bad influence."

"Must be." I touched her cheek, stroking her soft skin. "You're sure about this?"

She placed her hand over mine. "Yes. I'm ready to take a risk."

———

A few hours later we arrived in the small town of Raton and parked in a lot between a motel and a medical center out in the middle of the endless desert. A discreet camera crew filmed us as we got out of the car and walked over.

"Is that it?" I asked, squinting in the bright light. The sun beat down on us, making sweat drip down my back immediately.

Carla walked around a raised platform in the middle of the lot, which featured a metal statue with a coal mining cart next to it. "I think so. But I'm not sure why they called it a RoboCop statue. This just looks like a weird tribute to coal miners."

The statue was about ten feet tall and depicted a shirtless man with a mining helmet and a menacing pickaxe in his hand. Parts of his body, including his ribs and most of his back, looked like they had been blasted away, leaving nothing but the sunlight filtering through it.

"He's a cyborg miner from the future," I suggested. "He lost most of his body in an 'accident' and now he's more machine than man. He's traveled back in time to seek revenge on those who caused the so-called accident."

She giggled, but then covered her hand with her mouth and pointed. "Look at his spine! It's made out of tiny faces!"

"Of course it is. Those are the faces of the people he plans to track down one by one."

She smiled, amused by my story. "But why did they name him RoboCop?"

"Probably to get stupid tourists like us to come look at it." I pulled at my shirt, which clung to my chest now. "It's hot as balls out here. Let's get a photo and get back on the road."

Carla took a selfie of us in front of the statue while we both made confused faces for the camera. She laughed when she saw it and I kissed her on the cheek, aware of the camera filming us the entire time. We got back in the car, cranked up the air conditioning, and set off for the next destination.

"That's two items down," Carla said. "Now we need to get lucky and find a dog with its head out the window and a car carrier. What if we don't see them?"

"We'll find them."

"You sure I can't drive?"

"No, you're much better at spotting scavenger hunt items than I am."

"As long as you're not tired..."

"I'm fine. Once we get four items, then you can drive."

We passed a fully loaded car carrier about thirty minutes later and crossed it off the list, then stopped to refuel at a gas station. Carla groaned when she saw Brenda and Ron already there. They stood in front of their car, arguing over their map with loud voices, but looked up at us as we parked.

"I'm not falling for that trap again," Carla muttered, as we walked inside the store. We took care of business and were out the door in less than five minutes.

Brenda came rushing over to us, her blond ponytail bouncing behind her. "I know we're the last people you want to help, but we've been looking all over for this RoboCop thing and we can't find it anywhere. Do you know where it is?"

I figured Carla's innate goodness would make her give up the location with a smile. Me, on the other hand? I would rather lie and give them false directions after what they'd done. I was one second away from throttling the woman for locking Carla up in that gas station as it was.

Carla gave Brenda a little wave with a smile. "Sorry. We're in a hurry. No hard feelings, right?" She dropped into the car and closed the door in Brenda's face.

I suppressed a laugh as I got into the driver's side. "I thought for sure you were going to tell her where to find the statue."

"I thought about it. I also thought about giving her false directions so they would get lost, but I couldn't lie. But after what they did to me yesterday, I couldn't help them either. They're on their own." She relaxed into the seat with a little smile while I drove us out of the gas station. "They do seem terrible with maps. They really were confused when they asked me for help yesterday."

"If only they had a map wizard on their team like we do."

"I'm not a wizard. I've just done a lot of research and preparation. But I would have helped them if they hadn't been so horrible to me already. Fool me once and all." She suddenly slapped my arm and bounced in her seat. "Look! A dog! Pull us up beside that car!"

I sped up and she leaned across me to take a photo of a golden retriever with its head out of the front window, tongue lolling and ears flying back. Carla's arm brushed my thighs, and I shifted uncomfortably.

She sat back with a laugh. "That's four! We did it!" She touched me on the arm again, smiling. "My turn to drive."

———

Wearrived at the Desert Flower Hot Springs, where there was nothing around us but flat, barren land with a dry shrub here and there, except for the mountains in the distance and the shimmering blue pool in front of us. Chairs and lounges were set up all around the hot spring with umbrellas overhead, and a small building provided bathrooms, towels, and a gift shop. A statue of a naked woman and a colorful set of metal chimes topped it all off.

"Welcome to the Desert Flower," an older woman said to us, her skin tanned and leathery. She wore a long, flowery sack dress and handed us a card. "Changing rooms are to the left. Bathing suits are optional."

Optional? Oh shit. I was already dreading what the challenge would involve. According to the card, this one was called Let's Get Wet and all we had to do was get in the pool and answer a few questions about our partner. Hmm. That sounded too easy.

"I hope you're keeping your bikini on," I said, while we walked to the changing rooms. As much as I'd enjoy seeing her naked, I didn't want that aired on TV. Daniel would slaughter me.

"Actually, I was planning to go *au naturel* this time." She shrugged. "Why not?"

I took her arm and spun her toward me. "Seriously?"

She laughed and pulled her arm away easily. "Of course not. It's just so easy to get you riled up." Her fingers grazed the stubble on my jaw and she flashed me a smile before walking into the women's room. I stared after her, temporarily frozen from her touch, before stumbling into the men's room.

When we were finished changing we walked out to the pool and I pointedly did not look at her tiny yellow bikini or her long dark limbs or her delicious curves. Much.

None of the other teams were in sight, but other hippies hung around the lounge chairs while holding clipboards. We slid into the pool, which was comfortably warm but not hot, and Carla let out a soft moan as the water enveloped her. I had to admit, it was pretty refreshing after a long day on the road, especially with the sun setting over the horizon and the sound of the chimes in the breeze. Too bad we weren't alone here.

An older man with long white hair and a braided hemp necklace stepped forward and raised his clipboard. "Hi there. I'm Jim and I'm going to ask you some questions about your partner, based on the surveys you filled out at the beginning of the show. If you get an answer wrong, you'll have to do two laps around the pool. Once you each get three questions right, I'll give you the location of the final destination. Ready to begin?"

"We got this," I told Carla. This challenge was perfect for us. We'd grown up together, after all. These questions would be a piece of cake.

"First question is for Ryan. What's Carla's favorite color?"

"Yellow." Like her bikini.

"Correct! Carla, what was Ryan's first job?"

Carla smiled faintly. "He worked at Best Buy in the Geek Squad."

A memory of her coming by the store popped into my head. I'd gotten the job to save some money for college, since I knew my father wouldn't help me. That day she'd pretended to be interested in buying a laptop so she could talk to me for a few minutes without my boss getting mad. Then she'd slipped me a Snickers—my favorite—to tide me over until the end of my shift.

"Correct! You two are good at this, I can tell." Jim grinned at us and checked his clipboard. "Ryan, who was Carla's first kiss with?"

Hell, how was I supposed to know that? Thinking about Carla kissing some other guy made me want to punch something. While I bobbed in the warm water I searched through my memories, trying to recall any guys she'd been interested in, but couldn't come up with a single one. Either I'd been blind to all of that, or I'd blocked it out completely.

I did vaguely remember a boy she'd hung out with once, right before the cancer had taken over her life. "Jason Heilig?"

"Wrong. Er…" Jim looked up at me quickly. "You were her first kiss."

"What?" I quickly looked over at her, but her head was turned away from me. How could *I* have been her first kiss?

How could I not have known that?

"Sorry Ryan, but that means you have to do two laps around the edge of the pool," Jim said.

I dove into the water without hesitation, doing the breaststroke as I swam around the pool. It was a relief to use my body again after a long day in the car and it helped get my mind off the memory of our kiss on the beach all those years ago. I'd never suspected I was her first kiss. It made me feel even more guilty for walking away from her, but also oddly pleased in a primitive caveman kind of way. I was glad I was her first. I wished I could be her last.

After two laps I moved beside Carla, who stood in the center of the pool with her breasts bobbing in the water. Her dark skin practically glowed under the fading sunlight, and the urge to go to her, to pull her into my arms and kiss her, was almost too strong for me to resist. I nearly gave in, but movement behind her caught my eye. While I'd been swimming, Judy and Sally had arrived and were now climbing into the pool in their bathing suits. Shit. They'd been together for thirty years, these questions would be a walk in the park for them. We had to hurry.

I slicked my wet hair back and nodded to Jim that I was ready for another go.

"Next question for you, Ryan. What is Carla's favorite song?"

I had to get this right or we'd be in trouble. It was an Alicia Keys song, from what I remembered, but which one? What if it had changed in the past few years? Dammit. It had been so long since we'd seen each other, maybe we didn't know each other as well as I thought. Maybe Carla had changed more than I realized in the six years I was gone.

I went with my gut and prepared for another swim. "'If I Ain't Got You' by Alicia Keys."

Jim paused and gave me a long look. "Correct."

I let out a long breath. Thank god. I still knew Carla pretty well after all. Now we only had a few more questions to go and we could get back on the road.

"Carla, what is Ryan's favorite animal?"

She tilted her head and considered. Her wild mass of curls was tied back to keep her hair from getting wet, but stray pieces of it had escaped and now framed her thoughtful face. I resisted the urge to reach over and tuck them away. "Dog."

"Correct! You're both doing great. You each need to get one more question right before you can go."

Judy and Sally began answering questions behind us and I tried to block their voices out. Carla reached across the pool and took my hand under the water. Immediately I felt better, stronger, calmer. Until yesterday, we'd never held hands before. Hell, we'd barely ever touched until going on the show. Now we couldn't seem to stop. Being linked with her felt as right as breathing.

"Ryan, what is Carla's favorite season?"

"Spring—no, wait, summer." She squeezed my hand and I nodded. "Yeah, summer."

"Correct. Carla, what does Ryan wear to bed?"

I could practically feel her blushing from over here, and her fingers tightened even more around mine. "Boxer briefs and nothing else."

"Correct! Good job! You can both move on to the final destination now."

I yanked Carla into a hug, sliding my hand down her back as her wet nearly-naked body pressed against mine. Her mouth brushed my cheek, my lips touched her jaw, but we were clumsy, excited, and rushed, so it wasn't a real kiss. We broke apart and climbed out of the pool as fast as we could.

Jim gave us the location we needed to head to next, a hotel in Colorado Springs that he said was only about forty-five minutes away. We threw our clothes over our wet swimsuits and rushed back to the car with the lesbian bikers right on our tail.

As we strapped into our seat belts, I watched Carla with an odd mixture of exhilaration and satisfaction. We'd defeated the challenge and we still knew each other well, even after my six year absence. She still wanted to be friends with me. Maybe I hadn't ruined everything between us after all.

FIFTEEN

Carla

"Congratulations," Chuck said. "You're the first team to arrive, which means you've each won five thousand dollars!"

I let out a gleeful scream and covered my mouth with my hands. "No way!"

"You'll also be treated to a special romantic dinner and a stay in the honeymoon suite tonight, plus you'll be starting first tomorrow."

I couldn't believe it. We'd actually won this episode. A giddy laugh escaped me and I flung myself into Ryan's arms. He picked me up and swung me around with a grin, then gave me a quick kiss as he set me back down. It was barely anything more than a light touch of his lips, but it still sent a rush of electricity through me.

"We did it!" I laughed again, gazing up at him. "We actually won!"

"All thanks to you."

I couldn't stop bouncing. I was about to burst from all the happy energy inside me. "You drove. You helped."

"You figured out the best route."

"I couldn't have done it without you." No one else could have convinced me to throw out my safe plan for a risky one, and no one else would have gotten all those questions about me right. Ryan deserved this win as much as I did.

Sally and Judy ran into the lobby of the hotel and their faces deflated a little when they saw us already there. But then their disappointment faded and they offered their congratulations with big smiles that I could tell were genuine.

"See, I told you they were nice," I said to Ryan as the elevator lifted us to the penthouse floor. He gave an unconvincing sound of agreement.

We found our room at the end of the hall, and when we opened the door, I gasped. The suite had high ceilings and was decorated with classic elegance and luxury in a way that reminded me of the 1920s. Plush couches and overstuffed chairs framed a marble fireplace in the sitting room, and double doors opened to a large patio that offered amazing views of the lake and mountains.

"I've never stayed anywhere so fancy before." I spun around, taking it all in. The place even smelled nice, like lavender or violet or something luxurious and purple. "I bet you have though. This is probably a normal hotel room for you."

He watched me as I twirled and examined everything. "You deserve this kind of luxury all the time."

I laughed. "I doubt I'll ever have that kind of lifestyle, but it's definitely fun for one night."

I moved to the bedroom, where a giant four-poster canopied bed awaited us opposite a wall-to-wall mirror, then entered the bathroom. It was huge, with a walk-in closet, a separate sitting area for doing hair and makeup, and a massive shower that could easily hold at least two people.

I never wanted to leave the place, but we had a romantic dinner waiting for us. I took a few minutes to change out of my half-dried bikini and into the nicest dress I'd brought, a tight sheath in midnight blue.

After I finished touching up my makeup and doing the best I could with my unruly hair, I found Ryan waiting for me in the sitting area. He'd changed too, into a pair of black slacks and a crisp white button-down shirt that framed his strong back and broad shoulders. His shirt alone probably cost more than my entire wardrobe, but his fine clothes couldn't hide the raw, masculine power of his body.

He leaned in the doorway that led out to the patio and gazed across the stunning night view. As I approached, he turned toward me and drew in a sharp breath. His eyes traveled slowly down my body with a hunger I recognized from the other night. For a second I thought he might pick me up and carry me into the bedroom, but then he offered me his arm. "Shall we?"

The restaurant was just as elegant as our hotel room, with views of the mountains and lake from every window. We were taken to a dark, private room lit by candles and decorated with red roses on the table. Soft music played in the background and wine was poured as soon as we sat down. The waiter discreetly left us alone as soon as he'd taken our orders.

I took a sip of my wine. "Wow. They weren't kidding about this romantic dinner."

He watched me with eyes so dark they looked as black as his hair. "It's definitely a step up from last night's campfire barbeque."

"True, although I had fun last night."

"I did too." His voice dipped low and husky. A memory of sleeping next to his nearly naked body in the tent popped into my head. Was he thinking about that too?

It was impossible not to drink in the sight of him while we ate. He hadn't shaved since the day we came on the show and now his jaw had a perfect dusting of dark stubble, making him look even more roguish. His collar was open a little, giving me a glimpse of his smooth neck and a hint of his strong chest. I squirmed in my chair, remembering when he swam laps in the pool and how the water had dripped off his hard muscles when he'd finished.

We kept conversation light during dinner and I got the feeling both of us wanted to get out of there as quickly as possible even though the food was amazing. All I could think about was getting back to our hotel room so I could be alone with him. I conjured up a dozen fantasies of everything I wanted to do, although I still wasn't sure he felt the same way I did. One second he'd tell me I was beautiful and act like he wanted to kiss me, and the next he'd say I wasn't his type and push me away again. Which was the truth?

I was determined to find out tonight.

In the elevator, I leaned against him while his hand slid leisurely up and down my back, over the tight fabric of my dress. His gaze dropped to my mouth and the chemistry between us flared so intense I thought the carpet might burst into flames. Yet he still didn't kiss me.

Once in the hotel room, I set down my purse and drifted to the window to gaze at the view. "My favorite thing about being on this show is all the different places we get to visit. I've always wanted to go on a road trip across America, visiting states I've never traveled to before, like New Mexico and Colorado. Now I get the chance." He moved beside me and I turned to face him with a smile. "What's your favorite thing about it?"

He answered without hesitation. "Spending time with you."

"Really?" Every time he said something nice like that I could barely believe it.

"Why are you so surprised?"

"You left for six years and didn't contact me in all that time. When you came back, you didn't seem to want anything to do with me. I was shocked you offered to go on the show with me at all."

He stared out the window so long I thought he wouldn't answer. "I tried to contact you. I wrote so many emails I never sent. I started and deleted a million texts. I picked up the phone a hundred times but couldn't do it. Nothing I tried to say was ever good enough. When I returned to LA for my dad's wedding, I decided I had to apologize to you in person."

"I had no idea." My knees felt like they might give out at any moment. What was he talking about? He'd never come to see me, not in all those years. "When was this?"

"Three years ago."

"But…"

"Daniel told me where your apartment was and I rushed over as soon as I could escape the wedding. I couldn't bear another minute without seeing you. I was still wearing my tuxedo and I brought you flowers. Yellow roses."

"My favorite," I whispered.

"I got out of the car and walked toward your apartment. You stood outside. It was the first time I'd seen you in years." He stared at nothing, completely lost in the memory, but the emotion in his voice tore at my heart. "You wore a white dress and looked like something out of a dream. But you weren't alone. You'd moved on." He looked over at me, his face anguished. "I turned around and walked away."

My head spun from this revelation, from the memory I'd forgotten until now. If I hadn't been on a date that night, would everything be different between us now? "I thought I saw you, but then you were gone. I told myself it was someone else, because why would Ryan Evans be on my street in the middle of the night holding yellow roses and wearing a tuxedo? I assumed it was my mind conjuring up some silly fantasy."

His gaze held me captive. "It was me."

I reached up to trail my fingers down his face. He was so handsome, it was almost painful to look at him. "What were you going to say to me that night?"

"That I was a fool for ever leaving you on that beach."

Ryan took my face in his hands and pressed his mouth against mine. *Finally*, my heart whispered. I softened against him, melting into his embrace, opening myself to him completely. He caressed my cheek and tilted my head, all the while kissing me with a hungry, relentless passion. With each slide of his tongue and every taste of his lips, I was pulled deeper and deeper under his spell.

His touch skimmed slowly down my dress, traveling along parts of me he'd never dared explore before. He palmed my breasts, brushing against my nipples, and I gasped against him, light-headed with lust. His large hands were everywhere —circling my waist, spanning my hips, cupping my butt—and I gripped his shirt tighter. If I let go now, I would surely fall.

Then his hands were on my thighs, sliding my short dress up and up. It was almost too much, too intense, too unbelievable, but he didn't stop. I didn't want him to. With the dress bunched around my hips, his fingers tightened on my bare skin and he lifted me up, wrapping my legs around him, bringing his hard arousal against me.

He carried me into the bedroom like that, never breaking away from my mouth, and lowered us down onto the covers. His body sheltered mine and his warm, heavy weight sent hot pulses between my legs. I was dizzy with anticipation of what was to come.

"We can't do this," he said, in the brief space between his mouth and mine.

"Don't stop." I tugged at his hair, pulling him back to my lips. We got swept away again, this thing between us too strong to be halted.

"Carla, we can't. We need to stop." But he didn't stop. His lips left burning imprints on my skin. His fingers tore at my dress with an urgent, hungry need.

"Why?" I managed to get out.

"Because it's you."

He gave me one last, desperate kiss before drawing a shuddering breath and rolling off me. The sudden absence of him was like being doused in a bucket of cold water. All I could do was lie there, motionless, as I slowly returned to the real world. The world where Ryan was just a fantasy and would never be mine.

I pushed myself to a sitting position and pressed a hand to my forehead. Ryan stared at the ceiling, his chest moving up and down with each breath. A horrible, sinking dread spread through me. This was turning out exactly like the other times we had kissed. He was going to push me away, reject me, tell me I meant nothing to him and then walk away. If he did, I wouldn't be able to handle it. If he turned me down now, it would be the last time. I'd have to leave the show or find a new partner. I'd never speak to him again if he told me that kiss meant nothing.

"Carla, we can't be together." To his credit, he sounded miserable.

"Why not?"

He sat up and scrubbed his hands over his face. "Daniel would kill me."

My brother? What did he have to do with this? "I don't care what he thinks."

"*I* care. Daniel's like a brother to me. And you and I, we're practically family."

My throat was tight and my eyes began to burn, but none of that was as bad as the ache in my heart. He was using *that* excuse again. When would I ever learn? "I get it. I'm not your type. I'm like a little sister to you." My voice shook. "You don't want me."

"Carla, no." He reached for me, but I scrambled away, pressing my back against the pillows. "Do you think I could kiss you like that if I only had brotherly feelings for you?"

"But you said before—"

"I lied."

SIXTEEN

Carla

His words fell like a heavy weight, but I couldn't wrap my brain around them. "You lied?"

He ran a hand through his silky black hair, his face tormented. "Carla, you've always been my type, and I've always wanted you."

"Always?" My voice tripped over the word. I took a deep breath, struggling to mentally adjust to this new information. What he'd said painted our entire past in a new light. If it was true, it meant that I hadn't been wrong all this time about us. But if he wanted me, then why did he push me away every single time we got close? "Even when we were younger?"

"Even then."

"Why did you walk away that day on the beach?"

"You were only sixteen. I was leaving for college in another state the very next day. There was no future for us." He shook his head. "There still isn't."

"We're not teenagers anymore. Things are different now."

He stared at me with a grim set to his mouth. "Nothing is different. You're still my best friend's little sister, and I'm still the guy who promised him I would protect you."

"I don't need your protection!" I was so fed up with his nonsense, I wanted to scream. I jumped off the bed and headed for the door, but he moved after me.

"You do." He took my wrist, halting my escape. "You need protection from *me*."

I wrenched my arm away from him, and he let me go. "Stop treating me like some princess who needs to be rescued. If you don't really want me, just tell me that. Be honest with me for once."

"I want you. You know I do." He closed in on me and I moved backward, until I was pressed against the mirrored wall. He placed his hands on either side of the mirror, caging me in without even touching me. His face turned into my hair and he breathed me in like he needed me to survive. "I want you so bad I can't think straight. But I'm terrified of hurting you."

All anger fled from me at the sound of vulnerability in his voice. I touched his rough, masculine jaw and gazed into his dark eyes. "You won't hurt me."

"I broke your heart once. I won't do it again."

He began pulling away from me, like he always did. But I refused to let him retreat this time. Now that I knew he wanted me, I wasn't going to let him go so easily.

I gripped the collar of his shirt and spoke the next words before I could lose my courage. "We both want this, and we're going to be spending every night together for the rest of the time we're on the show. The way I see it, we can either go crazy trying to keep our distance from each other, or we can have some fun together over the next few days. We get whatever this is between us out of our system."

His brow creased. "Is that what you want?"

"Yes. Definitely. You don't do relationships, and I just got out of a bad one. Neither one of us wants something serious right now." It was a lie, one that my mind desperately wanted to believe even if my heart told me this was a bad idea. I wanted Ryan forever, but if all I got with him was a few days, then I would take what I could get. It was better to have him for a short time than not at all.

"And after the show ends?" he asked.

"We'll go home and go back to the way things were before."

He frowned. "What about Daniel?"

"My brother doesn't need to know. As far as he's concerned, everything on the show is an act, right?"

I could see the conflict written all over his face, along with the lust he was barely keeping in check. "Carla…"

"You're always trying to get me to take risks." I pressed soft kisses against his neck while my fingers began to pull at the buttons on his shirt. "Take this one with me."

His hand slid into my hair, tangling in my curls. "God, you're so hard to resist."

"Then stop resisting."

I saw it in his eyes, the moment his control snapped. With a groan, he hauled me against him and captured my lips with his. If I'd thought his kisses before were amazing, this one blew every other kiss out of the water. He must have been holding back the other times we'd kissed, because the full intensity of Ryan's desire was nothing I could have imagined. He was an expert, his tongue sliding against mine, his teeth grazing my lower lip, his mouth taking and giving all at once. I had to hold on to his shoulders to keep myself steady, to stop the surge of emotions from pulling me under.

Just when I thought I would die from his kiss, that I would give up my last breath to Ryan and happily surrender to him forever, he moved his lips to my neck. He kissed my collarbone, my pulse point, the spot just below my ear, all with such fervent tenderness that I was totally undone. I moaned softly, sliding my fingers into his thick, beautiful hair. I prayed this would never end, that I would never wake up from this impossible dream.

He spun me around so that I faced the mirror. Our eyes met in the reflection. I couldn't help but notice how good we looked together, both of us tall, dark, and wild-eyed. I gathered my hair to one side and he unzipped the back of my dress so slowly I worried he would stop, that he'd put an end to this like he had every other time, but the look on his face told me he was as lost as I was.

His forehead was creased in concentration and his eyes devoured every new inch of skin that was revealed. When the zipper hit the bottom, he pressed his mouth to the back of my neck and a tremor ran through me. His lips trailed along my spine, following it down, down, down while he eased the dress off me.

I wasn't wearing a bra. My shoes had slipped off somewhere between the sitting room and the bed. All that was left was the thin fabric of my tiny black panties. I wasn't shy about my body. As a model, you got over that pretty fast. But with my bare breasts and dark nipples completely on display in the mirror, heat rushed to my cheeks and I had to fight the urge to cover myself.

Ryan rested his hands on my shoulders and his eyes devoured me for what seemed like an eternity. When he finally spoke, his voice was rough. "You're the most stunning woman I've ever seen. I could look at you forever."

Forever. The word echoed in my head, but then his hands and lips were on me and I lost all thought. I turned around and pulled his mouth back to mine, desperate to kiss him again. We slammed back against the mirror so hard I was sure it cracked, but I was too far gone to care.

My world narrowed to his touch, his taste, his scent. His fingers traced circles around my nipples until they were so hard they almost hurt, while I tugged his shirt open and slid my hands across his solid wall of muscle. His shirt hit the floor and I pulled at the front of his pants, trying to get them off him. My hands were clumsy and he reached down to help me, then his pants hit the floor.

With both of us in only our underwear, he picked me up like he'd done in Vegas at the altar. His eyes never left mine as he carried me across the room and set me down on the bed. I slid my arms around his neck and dragged him on top of me and back to my mouth. He lingered there, devouring my lips, before moving lower and lower. His hands slid down me, claiming every inch, and his mouth followed. To my neck. My shoulders. My breasts.

When his tongue flicked against my nipple, my back arched and a moan escaped me. He explored each one thoroughly, figuring out what made me gasp, while his hands continued their journey downward. Across my stomach. Along my hips. Between my thighs.

When his finger pushed my panties aside and slipped inside me, I cried out from the sheer pleasure of it. I yanked at his boxer briefs, trying to tug them off him.

"Ryan, please," I gasped, while he stroked me inside and out.

His mouth curved into a dangerous smile. "Please what?"

"Please, I need you." My hips lifted, straining for him, sending him even deeper.

His lips descended along my body until they hit the edge of my panties, which he then pulled down my legs with his teeth. Once they were off, he kissed his way up my thighs slowly, making me part for him. I needed him against me, around me, inside me. I gasped out his name and tried to tug him back up to my lips.

He reluctantly broke away and slid up my body with agonizing slowness, showing way more restraint than I'd like. His firm body covered mine, fitting against me, skin to skin. I held my breath while his fingers stroked my cheek and he searched my eyes, like he couldn't believe this was real either. Then he eased off me and stood up.

"Where are you going?" I asked, panic rising in my throat. Was he stopping *now*? Had he decided this was a terrible mistake?

He went to his bag and pulled something out of one of the front pockets. "Condom."

I blinked. "That wasn't on the packing list."

"No. A terrible oversight on your part."

He was the one thing I couldn't prepare for. My mouth fell open when he slid his boxer briefs off. All I could do was gape at his naked body. He was all hard lines, rugged masculinity, and raw, primal lust. Looking at him made me thirsty. I wanted to take a nice, long drink of him.

He gripped my legs and dragged me down to the edge of the bed, spreading my knees to either side of his waist. I watched as he slipped the condom on, while standing just in front of me. I was practically exploding with desire, so turned on I was delirious with it. Ryan was my favorite "what if," the guy who'd starred in every one of my fantasies, my first love and the man I could never get over. I'd tried to move on a dozen times, but it always came back to him.

Now I would finally have him.

With his eyes locked on mine, he lifted my legs up until my toes rested against his broad shoulders. He wrapped his fingers around my thighs, bringing my hips right to the edge of the bed, and then entered me slowly, inch by amazing inch. He was so much bigger than anyone I'd ever been with before. My breath left me in a rush at the feel of him sliding inside, filling me up, going deeper and deeper until he was fully sheathed.

He paused, letting me adjust to his size, while we both stared at each other with something like amazement. Nothing in my fantasies could have prepared me for this moment. The reality of it was so much better than anything I'd conjured up.

The words slipped out before I could stop them. "You don't know how long I've wanted this."

"I know," he said. "Because I've wanted it that long too."

His lips brushed against my ankle and he began to move. Slowly at first, sliding in and out with long thrusts that made me gasp and beg for more. In this position he was entirely in control, putting me at his mercy, completely exposing me to him. I was sure he could see every one of my secret fantasies about him playing across my eyes even as he brought one of them to life. But this position gave me a front row seat to his gorgeous body too, and I let my eyes drown in the sight of him until I could barely breathe anymore. Everything about him was familiar and yet somehow new. I'd known Ryan for most of my life, but I'd never know him like *this*.

As he continued his slow, measured torment, I raised my hips, trying to get every last inch of him. He sensed my need and began to move faster, harder, rocking into me in a delicious rhythm, reaching deep places that had never been stroked before. When he tilted me up and hit a spot that made me arch off the bed,

I truly thought I might die from extreme pleasure. When he thrust there again, a whimper escaped me and my eyes fluttered shut.

He took my chin and forced me to meet his gaze. "Look at me," he said. "I want you to know who's inside you when you come. I want to hear it on your lips."

"It's you, Ryan," I gasped out, as he hit that spot again and again. "It's always been you."

No other guy had ever made me feel this way, and he knew it. He saw what he did to me. How I came unraveled at his touch. And still he demanded more.

He slipped one hand between us to rub me in a way that sent me higher and higher, while his other hand gripped my hips to get exactly the right angle for his relentless pace. His skin gleamed golden in the light and his name tumbled from my lips over and over as the pressure built to a dizzying peak. I didn't want this to end. Not now, not ever. But he was too good, and I couldn't hold out forever against his firm fingers or his skilled movements, and then it was impossible to hold back any longer. I broke into a million pieces, losing all control of my body, becoming a wild, primal creature. I tore at the sheets, my back arched up, my voice made sounds I'd never heard before. Ryan joined me only seconds later, his shoulders straining as he surged inside me, and we were both lost. Truly, completely lost in each other.

All we could do was look at each other and breathe, while the reality of what we'd done sank in. Finally, after all these years, after all the distance between us, we'd given in. And there was no turning back now.

He pulled us both onto the bed and we curled together. We wrapped each other in arms and legs and skin, our bodies fitting together so perfectly it was clear we'd been designed as a pair by some higher power. He gently stroked my cheek as our breathing slowed, and he whispered my name as I tucked in tighter against him. And I knew, without a doubt, that I'd made a terrible mistake, because how was I ever going to get over Ryan after *that*?

SEVENTEEN

Ryan

I was well and truly fucked.

Not just in the literal sense, although yes. Definitely that.

Sex with Carla was unlike anything I'd ever experienced before. I'd been with countless women, but nothing, *nothing*, compared to the feel of being inside her, or the taste of her desire on my tongue, or the sound of her pleasure in my ears. But we both knew this couldn't last.

We had another week or so on the show before we'd go back to our regular lives. I'd have to face Daniel and either lie to him or hide the truth about what I'd done to his sister. I'd broken my promise to him and if he ever found out, he'd kill me. I couldn't let that happen. I couldn't lose the last remaining family I had left, but I didn't want to lie to him either.

Shit.

As Carla stirred in my arms, the sun peeked through the curtains, highlighting her smooth skin and shiny curls. I ran my fingers along her side slowly, tracing every curve. I'd forbidden myself from touching her for so many years, it was pure heaven to be able to do it so freely now. I never wanted to stop.

She nuzzled into me, her lips finding my neck, and I was instantly rock hard and ready to go. I claimed her mouth and stroked her breasts, making her moan softly. Her leg came up around me, making me nudge against her soft warmth. I rubbed against her folds and she was wet and eager for me, just begging for me to slip inside. Yes, a long, slow, sleepy fuck, that was exactly what we needed right now. If I'd already messed everything up by sleeping with her, doing it again wouldn't make anything worse, right?

Carla pulled out of my arms with a sigh. "We need to get ready. We only have an hour and we both have to shower and get dressed."

The one benefit of her getting up was that now I had a full view of her glorious naked body. I ran a hand along my shaft and her eyes stared at it hungrily. "Then we'll have to continue this in the shower."

I gave her gorgeous butt a light slap and she giggled and ran into the bathroom to turn on the shower. I searched my bag for a condom, but I must have only had the one. No problem, we could have fun in other ways, then pick up a box once on the road.

For a minute I simply watched her as she moved under the water, letting it drip down her dark body. She was like something out of a Victoria's Secret ad: tall, curvy, and impossibly sexy. I wanted to fall to my knees and worship at the altar of her beauty. If we had more time, I would do exactly that, with my head between her legs and her fingers in my hair, until she came on my mouth and my tongue. Next time.

I opened the shower and stepped inside, moving under the water with her. She turned toward me, fitting her body against mine, drawing me in for a kiss. I ran my hands along her wet skin, down her forbidden curves, imprinting the feel of her in my memory forever. All traces of guilt were replaced with reckless desire as I touched her. She was off-limits, but I was going to have her anyway, damn the consequences. Her lips were my sin, her touch my redemption. I couldn't resist her, no matter how hard I tried.

Her hands stroked along my chest as we took the kiss deeper, our mouths locked together, our hips rocking against each other with a slow yet urgent need. I pulled back to look at her, taking her all in, from her hungry eyes to her full lips to her round breasts, and even lower, to her flat stomach, wide hips, and that dark triangle between her long legs. I'd never wanted anyone as much as I wanted her. No, *needed* her.

"You have the most perfect breasts I've ever seen," I said, before pulling one dark nipple into my mouth. Back and forth I lavished attention on them until she was clawing at me like a cat, her back pressed against the shower, beautiful moans coming from her lips.

Her hand reached between us to grab hold of me, and in return I slid my fingers deep into her wet heat. We stroked each other in tandem, in and out, up and down, getting off on touching each other as much as being touched. Harder, deeper, our mouths devouring each other, our wet bodies slipping and sliding against each other.

"Please, Ryan," she gasped out.

"I'm out of condoms. We'll just have to get each other off like this."

She gripped me tighter. "I'm on the pill and I got tested after my ex. We don't need condoms as long as you're clean."

My throat tightened at the idea of entering her bareback. I'd never done it with any other woman, but Carla was different. "You're sure?"

"I trust you."

I turned her around so she faced the wall and gripped her hips, lifting her round ass toward me. She set her hands against the tile and rested her foot on the small seat in the corner, lifting her leg to spread her nice and wide. I admired the view while I eased myself inside her, with nothing between us this time.

God, there was nothing better than sliding into her warm, tight embrace. I wanted to go slow to savor every second of it, but we had a time limit. The second I was sheathed all the way inside her, she pressed back against me and took me even deeper, making a guttural growl escape my throat. I dug my fingers into her hips and guided myself in and out of her. The sight of her long, smooth back and her hands pressed against the tile filled me with a primal urge to claim her hard and fast. I wanted to fuck her so good she felt it for days, for weeks, for *years*, so that no guy after me could ever compare.

I palmed her breasts, tilting her back so I could force a kiss from her lips. She was tall enough to straighten up while keeping me buried inside her, a perfect match for my height. With her back pressed against my chest and my hands covering her wet breasts, I pumped into her from behind. She used the wall to steady herself and I slid one hand between her legs, rubbing her there as I increased my pace. I could tell I was hitting her somewhere good by the way she started trembling and how loud her whimpers became.

I both heard it and felt it when she came. Her head dipped down, her voice erupted with a long cry, and her body clenched around me. I wanted her orgasm to be nice and long, so I rode through it until she was weak in the knees and practically sobbing from the unrelenting pleasure, and then I finally let go of all control, releasing inside of her with a few last, hard thrusts.

I rested my head against the back of her neck, burying myself in her curls, pressing quick kisses against her skin. We were both breathing heavily and she turned her head and caught my mouth with hers. The look on her face of pure release was the best thing I'd ever seen.

How the hell was I going to make it through this week? Carla had said it herself, neither one of us wanted anything serious, and that worked for me. Usually. But this time I wasn't sure I could keep this casual.

I'd have to make sure I never showed just how much she meant to me. I'd keep it about sex. I'd harden my heart. And then, somehow, I'd walk away from her at the end of our time on the show.

I had to.

EIGHTEEN

Carla

Our quick round of shower sex was totally worth being a few minutes late for, even with Chuck Bannon giving us an annoyed huff. I didn't mind. We were still the first team to leave that morning and my spirits were higher than ever. I had everything I wanted within my reach. Ryan. The grand prize. A new life.

I took the first shift driving and we quickly worked out the day's plan together. We had to drive to a farm near Topeka, Kansas while searching for our four scavenger hunt items.

    Challenge Location: Miller Family Farm
        1) Giant Van Gogh Painting
        2) Giant Ball Of Twine
        3) Giant Coke Can
        4) Feather
        5) Out of date political sticker
        6) Someone taking a selfie

The Giant Van Gogh Painting was on the way to everything else, so that was a no-brainer. The feather would be easy to find. The Giant Coke Can was more of a detour than the Giant Ball Of Twine, so we decided to skip the former and hope we got one of the other items along the way to the latter. I had a good feeling about it all.

Even better, Brenda and Ron were nowhere to be seen this morning. When I'd asked one of the show's crew members, they'd told me the Blond Menace had come in last during the previous episode and were sent home. For a split second I'd felt guilty, but then I remembered they'd brought it upon themselves. If they hadn't tricked me, I would have helped them find that RoboCop statue and they'd probably still be on the show.

"Good fucking riddance," Ryan had said. Without the Blond Menace, I thought we had a good shot at winning at this point. Our biggest competitors were Judy and Sally, but it was hard for me to be upset about that since they were good people. If we didn't win, I hoped they did.

We drove for the first hour without saying much and I took the time to admire the landscape around us. The endless desert had ended and now wheat fields and prairies stretched under the widest blue sky I'd ever seen.

Ryan casually rested his hand on my thigh, surprising me. I glanced over at him, but he was looking out the window at a field of cows. I reached across and placed my hand on the identical spot on his leg, unable to conceal the grin on my face. Touching Ryan was still so new and thrilling, like I was about to get caught with my hand in the cookie jar.

Without turning toward me, his hand moved an inch higher. I copied him exactly. A wry smirk crossed his mouth. Now it was a game. His hand kept sliding up, dipping under my skirt, moving so slowly I thought I'd die with anticipation. Everything he did, I did to him in return, although it wasn't as fun since he was in jeans while he touched my bare skin.

I checked the cameras, wondering if they could see any of this. It would definitely be difficult to explain away to my brother. Luckily, the cameras didn't point low enough to film below our chests. As long as we were careful, no one would know.

Ryan's fingers dipped between my thighs to stroke along the edge of my panties. I inhaled sharply and cupped the hard bulge at the front of his jeans, giving it a little squeeze. He began rubbing slow circles along the fabric of my now very wet underwear. I stroked his erection in the same way through his pants. Neither one of us looked at the other the entire time. We both tried to act casual, my expression schooled to boredom. Only our increased breathing might give it away to a careful viewer.

I could barely concentrate on the road, but luckily the highway was straight and there were few other cars in sight. Ryan's fingers were talented and I was tempted to move my hips to demand more from him, but that would surely be caught on camera. Instead I squirmed a little in my seat, spreading my legs a little wider. What had he done to me? Being fingered while driving was so outside my normal comfort zone, yet Ryan brought out this wild side of me.

He pushed aside my panties and slipped his fingers inside me and I couldn't help but let out a little moan. He gave me a sharp look and paused his movements. I slammed my mouth shut. Only when I was quiet did his fingers start to move again.

It wasn't fair that he could touch me and I couldn't touch him. I eased the fly on his jeans open and slipped my hand inside to grip his hard length. He sucked in a ragged breath as I began stroking him up and down. My fingers matched his as they moved in and out of me. I wanted to throw my head back and close my eyes, but I couldn't. How was I going to keep driving like this? Should I pull over?

His thumb rubbed me in just the right way and the friction became too much. I exploded with a silent moan, clenching around his fingers, my legs clasping shut around him. He groaned and let go a second later, pulsing against my hand, while he gripped the car door with white knuckles.

He looked over at me for the first time since we'd started touching each other and I gave him a little smile. He leaned across and kissed me hard and fast, then sat back with a smug look on his face.

That guy was trouble, no doubt about it. And I didn't mind one bit.

He cleaned himself up with a napkin from the glovebox and handed me one so I could do the same. Good thing I always saved some in the car, just in case. You never knew when you'd need an extra napkin. Of course, I never expected to use it because I'd been finger-banged while driving, but there was a first time for everything I supposed.

Just when my pulse was beginning to return to normal, we heard a sharp pop and the car suddenly veered to the right. I regained control immediately, hitting the brakes, and heard the tell-tale *flop, flop, flop* of a busted tire.

"Shit," Ryan said. "Pull over up here."

I eased the car onto the side of the highway. We got out and I took a second to yank down my skirt to make sure I was decent.

A quick inspection showed that the back left tire had blown out, probably from some debris on the road. My good mood immediately disappeared and a sinking feeling settled over my stomach, but I pushed it away.

"Okay, it's just a flat tire. I'll get the kit, you grab the spare."

Ryan gave me a quick kiss. "Don't worry. We've got this."

I nodded, but I was still worried. We popped the trunk and pulled out the extra tire back there, then we got to work changing it. We'd both done it many times before on other cars, so we got the new one on without a problem. But even with how fast we were, I still saw at least one other black Chevy Malibu pass us by in that time. We were no longer first.

We got back on the road and found the first scavenger hunt location after another hour. Only a short detour off the highway stood an eighty-foot high easel with a reproduction of Van Gogh's "Three Sunflowers In A Vase." We got out of the car, walked over to the viewing area, and took a quick photo of the two of us with the painting in the distance behind us. There was no one else around, unfortunately. I was hoping to cross off the selfie scavenger hunt item while we were at it, but no such luck.

We got back on the road, but soon had to stop for gas—except none of the credit card machines worked at the only gas station in the area. The show hadn't given us any cash to use, so we had to get back on the road and head to the next exit to try again. Another delay.

With each minute wasted a sense of dread began to spread through me, but no other disaster befell us for the next few hours. Just when I'd started to relax and had convinced myself we wouldn't be the last team, trouble brewed in the form of a terrible traffic jam.

"What's going on?" I asked, as we came to a stop behind a long line of cars.

"No clue." Ryan leaned out of the window to get a better look. We'd had good luck so far with traffic on the show, only hitting a few short slow-downs while in big cities. Nothing like this stop-and-go traffic now.

"The good news is, if we're stuck in it then so is everyone else." I forced a smile, but I didn't sound convincing, even to me. My smile fell. "Unless they took a different route."

An hour later we'd moved barely ten feet, but finally made it to the car accident. A pick-up truck had rear-ended a black car, and my first thought was that it was someone from the show. As we got closer I saw that it wasn't the right kind of car, and breathed a sigh of relief.

We made it to Cawker City and followed the twine stripe painted on the sidewalk on the small main street, passing quaint little shops with postcards, paintings, and other souvenirs. A huge mound of brown thread sat under a roof with no walls, along with a sign that proclaimed it to be the World's Largest Ball of Twine. I rolled down the window to get a photo and caught the pungent smell of mildew.

I quickly closed the window. "According to the sign, we can come back in August for the annual twine-a-thon."

"Hard pass." Ryan pulled the car back onto the road.

"What's with all the giant stuff in Kansas? The painting, a ball of twine, and next a Coke can?"

"Must be all this wide open space. People want to fill it with something big."

I gave him a sly grin. "I know how they feel."

"Dirty girl." He smirked at me. "Tonight."

I sat back in my seat and reached for the map, but as I checked our location, a heavy dose of worry hit my veins. According to the map we were almost to the challenge at the farm, but we only had three scavenger hunt items. We'd found a feather keychain in the gas station, but we hadn't seen anyone taking a selfie or an out-of-date political sticker. Now we were almost out of time. We had to make a decision.

"We're almost to the challenge," I said. "We need to go to the final location."

We'd never visited all three locations before because it was such a huge time suck. We'd always gotten lucky with the other scavenger hunt items. Not today though.

Ryan frowned. "How do we get there?"

I chewed on my lip as I tried to figure out a route. "We have to either backtrack, or go past the challenge to Topeka and then go south, then come back again. Either way, it would be a long detour that would cost us a lot of time. What do you think?"

"Backtrack."

I told Ryan how to get to the location, hoping we were making the right choice. Maybe we'd get lucky and spot one of the items on the way there. But with each passing mile I knew that wasn't going to happen.

Even with the long summer days, the sun was already low in the sky by the time we made it to the Giant Coke Can at the end of a little gravel road. There wasn't anything else around, just a huge monument to the classic soda rising out of the flat lands of Kansas. We snapped a photo from the car and quickly drove off.

The challenge was located on a farm outside of Topeka and we spotted three other teams already there. One couple got in their car and left the minute we pulled up.

I got out of our car. "Okay, so we definitely won't be first for this challenge."

Ryan glanced over at the other teams. "It's fine. We don't have to win every challenge. We got this. Come on."

A guy in overalls and a cowboy hat handed us the card with the challenge info. I groaned as I read the title on the card. "This one is called 'Playing Farmhouse.'"

Ryan read over my shoulder. "We have to wear cowboy hats, milk a cow, and herd some sheep. Easy enough."

"Let's just get this over with."

"Already ahead of you."

Five minutes later I knew why I worked on cars and not a farm. I looked across the stall at Ryan as he finished. "You're done already?"

He tipped his cowboy hat and gave me a wicked smile. "What can I say, I'm good with breasts."

Despite the cow's leathery teat in my hand, I laughed as I filled my bucket to the line. "Done!"

"Come on, let's go wrangle some sheep." Ryan sporting a cowboy hat was way more of a turn-on than I'd thought it would be. He looked rugged and masculine and I wanted him to throw me on the back of a horse and ride off with me into the sunset.

I stood and stomped hay off my shoe. "I think you like that hat a little too much."

His head dipped down to my ear. "I think *you* like me in this hat a little too much."

Desire shot up my spine. "You might be right."

He took my hand and led me to the sheep pen. Another guy in a cowboy hat told us we had to move the sheep across the field to the opposite pen, then left us to it without a single clue as to how. He didn't give us sheepdogs or whistles or anything. Now what?

Ryan scanned the length of the field. "How hard can it be to get some sheep from point A to point B?"

There were five sheep total, all white and fluffy, including one small lamb. They were cute but also smelled pretty bad, plus they were much dirtier than I expected —more of a light brown than the pristine white I'd seen in photos and movies.

I stepped into the pen. "What do we do?"

"No clue. My business card says CEO, not sheep whisperer."

"Go sheep, go." I waved my hands, but they just stood there, baaing at me while they munched on the grass. Almost like they were mocking us. "Shoo!"

Ryan burst out laughing. "*Shoo*? Is that the best you got?"

"Let's see you do it then, Mr. CEO."

"Watch and learn." He put his hands on one sheep's rear and gave it a shove. It turned and snapped at him.

I bit back a smile. "Is that how you manage your employees? You push them around?"

"No, I take them out to drinks or surprise them with pizza." Ryan scowled as the sheep went back to eating grass.

"I don't think pizza's going to work here."

He swept his hand out in arc. "Then please, by all means, show me how it's done."

I took a run at them, but they scattered like startled chickens, going in every direction. "Shoot!"

"If there was ever a time that called for 'shit,' it would be now." He checked the bottom of his shoe with a frown. "In fact, I think I just stepped in some."

"You know I don't swear."

"Yes, it's adorable. Don't worry, I'll swear enough for the both of us."

"Well, don't just stand there!" I ran at one of the sheep. "Help me scare this one toward the pen." I clapped my hands at it and it started to move. Fast.

Ryan jumped out of its way, just in time. We both ran after the thing, me clapping my hands and waving my arms like complete fool, while Ryan lunged at it and swore loudly. The sheep ran right into the pen across the field.

"Daniel is never going to let me live that down." Ryan shook his head but I could see the smile he held back.

"One down, four to go."

We herded the rest of the sheep across the field by waving our arms around while standing on either side of the group to direct them. When we latched the pen, we were both covered in sweat and exhausted.

I took my hat off and fanned myself with it. "I never want to see another farm animal again."

Ryan wrapped his arm around my shoulder. "Too bad. You looked pretty sexy in that hat too."

The guy with the cowboy hat gave us our final destination of Kansas City and we rushed back to the car. Night had fallen and there were no other teams in sight. Every one of them had moved on already.

Silent tension filled the car while Ryan drove as fast as he could to Kansas City. By the time he parked in front of the tiny motel, my anxiety had ratcheted up. I threw my door open. "We need to—"

"Run!" Ryan barked, rushing around the front of car and not even bothering to close his door.

I broke out in a sprint. *Please don't let us be last. Please don't let us be last.*

We dashed into the lobby and screeched to a halt in front of Chuck Bannon and the cameras. My heart raced, but I held my breath.

"I'm sorry." Chuck looked sympathetically between us. "You're the last team to arrive and have been eliminated from *Road Trip Race.*"

NINETEEN

Ryan

"No," Carla whispered. Her face fell, and I wrapped an arm around her. The cameras turned off and the crew herded us to the side. Production assistant Luisa explained something to us, but it all went over my head. All I could see was the look of defeat on Carla's face. Fuck. I'd failed her. I had to fix this somehow.

Luisa gave us back all our personal belongings, including our phones, then gestured toward the parking lot. "That van will take you to the airport for your flight to Los Angeles in two hours and—"

"No," I interrupted. "It's almost midnight and Carla needs to rest. We're not leaving tonight."

"But—"

"I don't give a shit if I have to pay for it myself. We're flying out tomorrow."

Luisa shrank a little at my tone, but then went to check with her boss. I wrapped my arms around Carla and said, "I'm sorry." She didn't answer.

For the next twenty minutes I argued with the crew until they finally agreed to switch our tickets to tomorrow. Then I got us a room in the motel for the night. This place wasn't the nicest, but I didn't think Carla was up for traveling anywhere right now.

As soon as we got inside the room, she dropped her bag on the floor and sank onto the bed, face down. She was one of those people who wore every emotion on her face, and for the last few minutes she'd been draped in despair.

I hated it. I wanted to fix any problem she had, to give her everything she wanted, to make the world a better place for her. Instead I took a few minutes to sort our bags and then persuaded her to change into her sleep clothes. She made me do most of the work, all her energy depleted, her dark eyes staring at nothing while I removed her clothes and slipped on new ones.

Once changed, she sat on the edge of the bed and I kneeled in front of her, taking her hands in mine, desperate to coax some warmth back into her.

"It's over," she finally said. "We lost."

"I'm sorry. I really thought we might win the whole thing."

She shook her head slowly, looking down at our hands. "I don't understand how this happened. It doesn't make sense. We were first in the previous episode. How did we come in last this time?" A single tear slid down her cheek. "It isn't fair."

"You're right, it isn't. And if I could go back and change things, I'd do whatever I could to keep you on the show." I moved to sit beside her, wrapping an arm around her. "But life isn't fair. Things happen that don't make any sense. Sometimes no matter how hard you work or how prepared you are, you fail anyway. And sometimes the biggest achievement is that you pick yourself up and keep going anyway."

She gave a choked laugh. "What do you know about failure? You look like a movie star. You're a billionaire. You could have anything you want."

I tightened my arm around her. "Trust me, I've failed. Many times. I only got where I am now through a lot of painful trial and error." I paused. "Did you ever hear of Tormented Shadows?"

"No. What is that?"

"It was the game I put out before Outerworld. Let's just say there's a good reason you've never heard of it."

Her voice softened. "Was it that bad?"

"Not really. It was rushed and could have been a lot better, but it wasn't a terrible game by any stretch. I worked my ass off on it, spending countless days and nights poring over the game. I thought it would be my big break and that everything would take off from there. But then it tanked."

Her face turned toward me and she wiped at her eyes. "How come?"

"Who can say? Maybe because another game came out around that time with a similar premise. Maybe we didn't market it well. Or maybe the game simply wasn't good enough." I rubbed her back in slow circles while I spoke. "I lost so much money and years of my life on that game. I thought for sure it was the end, that my career was done for and I would never be able to create anything as good in the future. But a month later I got the idea for Outerworld. I took everything I'd learned from Tormented Shadows and used it to make the best game I could. So even though Tormented Shadows was a complete failure, I don't regret a single minute I spent on it. One day you'll look back and think the same thing about this experience."

She sighed. "I know what you're saying. You're probably right, but at the moment I can't possibly see how this could be a good thing. We've been kicked off the show and I still have absolutely nothing waiting for me when I get back home. I don't even *have* a home."

I pressed a kiss to the top of her head. "You're upset now, but soon it will pass and you'll figure out what to do. You'll make a new plan, because that's what you're good at, and later you'll be see the bright side of all this, like you always do."

"Not this time. There is no bright side."

"Then I'll stay in the dark with you, as long as you need me."

She buried her face against my shoulder, her fingers digging into my shirt. "I was wrong. The bright side is you."

The way she said it made my throat constrict. I pulled her tighter against me, holding her in my arms. "It's going to be okay. You're stronger than you think you are, and you'll get through this. I promise."

We sat like that for some time, until she was no longer on the verge of tears. Eventually I got Carla under the covers and she fell asleep on her side. She was completely exhausted. So was I, actually. I curled against her back, my arm wrapped protectively around her, and closed my eyes.

When I stirred, it was still dark out and Carla was sitting up in bed, looking at her phone. The alarm clock read 3:08 AM. I reached for her, sliding a hand along her leg. "You okay?"

"I have so many messages. My parents. My brother. My ex." She fell back on the pillow with a sigh, covering her face with her arm. "I can't face any of them right now."

My stomach turned at the reminder that this was the end. In a few hours we'd get on a plane and head back to LA, back to our normal lives, where the two of us couldn't be together. The deal had been for no-strings-attached sex while we were on the show, but now that was over and we'd have to walk away and pretend it never happened. I'd had a single day of heaven and now I had to give it up forever.

Back in LA, we'd have to deal with all the things we'd come on the show to escape. My father's cancer. Carla's parents' separation. A best friend I'd broken a promise to. We both had decisions to make about our futures too. Neither one of us was ready for that—or to say goodbye to each other.

"What if we keep going?" I asked.

Her eyes snapped to mine. "What?"

"We were supposed to be on the show for another week, right? No one knows we've been kicked off. I don't know about you, but I'm not ready to go back yet."

"I don't want to go back either."

"We'll drive to New York like we originally planned, except now we do it our way. We go where we want, do what we want to do, stay where we want to stay." I took her hand and brought it my lips. "What do you say? Want to finish this road trip with me?"

"Yes!" She flung herself into my arms, looking up at me with so much warmth I felt like I was lying on a beach under the sun. "Let's do it. There are so many more places I want to visit before we go home." Her eyes shifted to the clock and she frowned. "But we're supposed to be at the airport in a couple hours. We have plane tickets. And no car."

"I'll handle it." I grabbed my phone. I hadn't looked at the dozens of notifications on it yet, but now I quickly scrolled through them. Lots of messages from my assistant Olivia, a few invitations to events, two texts from Daniel, but little else. There was nothing from my father or Dolores. Nothing at all.

Carla moved behind me and wrapped her arms around my chest. "Thank you, Ryan. I wasn't sure how I was going to make it through today, but you've made everything better. I'm so glad you came with me on the show. I'd be completely lost without you."

Her words kicked me in the chest, making me feel things I shouldn't be feeling. I turned to catch her lips and teased a slow kiss out of them. One more week with Carla before we returned to reality and I was going to make every minute count.

"Get some rest. In the morning, we'll start the next part of our journey."

TWENTY

Carla

When I woke up, Ryan was gone.

I sat up in bed and looked around, blinking sleep from my eyes. The motel room was small and from here I could see every inch of it, including the inside of the bathroom. There was no sign of Ryan anywhere. His backpack was gone too. It was like he'd never been here at all.

My heart sank and anxiety choked my throat. He'd changed his mind about continuing our road trip together. He'd decided it was too much, too fast, too serious, and then bailed on me. He'd walked out of my life *again*.

No, I told my panicked brain, *Ryan wouldn't do that*. He wouldn't abandon me in the middle of Kansas. He cared about me as a friend if nothing else, and he was too good of a guy to ditch me like that. There had to be some explanation for why he was gone so early in the morning.

I took a deep breath and forced myself to calm down. Ryan was probably out getting us some food. I'd take a shower and by the time I got out, he'd be back.

But when I got out of the shower, he was still gone. Now what?

I re-packed my bag so I was ready to go. I ate a granola bar and drank some bad hotel coffee. I paced in the tiny room, trying to figure out what to do, telling myself he would return any moment now. With each minute that passed it grew harder and harder to convince myself he was coming back. I finally caved in and turned my phone on again, ignoring all the notifications from a life I wasn't ready to return to, and sent him a text. No response.

We were supposed to be at the airport in thirty minutes. Maybe it was time to give in and admit that this thing between us had meant nothing. He was gone and it was time to go home.

I grabbed my backpack and went to the lobby to check out. After handing in my key, I stepped outside to get in a taxi. A sleek yellow Porsche 911 pulled up in front of me and stopped. I took a second to check out the car, barely noticing the tall man getting out of the driver's side.

"Leaving without me?" Ryan asked.

Relief washed over me at the sight of him. He hadn't left me after all. "I woke up and you were gone. I thought you…" I shook my head. "Where did you go? Whose car is this?"

He took my hand and set the keys inside it. "It's yours."

My mouth fell open and I glanced between him and the car. "What?"

"It's in both of our names, but I'll get it transferred to you alone when we get back to LA."

"But this… You bought this? For me?"

He took my chin and tilted it toward him, then brushed his lips across mine. "I told you I would take care of everything."

I clutched the keys to my chest. "No, I can't accept this. I know how expensive these cars are."

"It's a gift. Let me spoil you for once. Please."

I bit my lip and debated back and forth. I wanted the car, no doubt about it, but taking such a huge gift felt wrong, especially since we were supposedly just having fun together. A car like this felt like a present you'd give your wife, not your friend with temporary benefits. Then again, I kept forgetting how rich he was now, so maybe this was nothing big to him. Maybe he gave his assistant expensive sports cars for Christmas, so giving one to me seemed normal.

I set my hand on his chest and looked up at his near-black eyes. "I really appreciate this, I do. It's so thoughtful and kind of you, and you even got it in my favorite color. But I can't accept a present like this. We can both drive the car for the next week, but then it will be yours when our road trip is over."

He gave me one of those infuriating and way-too-sexy smirks. "I'm pretty sure you'll change your mind after you take it for a spin."

I shook my head, but let it go. "What about our flight to LA?"

"Already got it refunded. All you need to do is figure out where we're going next." He opened the driver's side door for me and I reluctantly slid inside. As the soft leather seat molded to my body and I set my hands on the steering wheel, I knew he was right. This car would be hard to give up.

Then again, so would he.

———

We headed east, to St. Louis. We'd already lost half the day while Ryan was getting the car, so I figured we'd hit the next big city and figure out the rest of the plan once we got there. The ultimate destination hadn't changed—we were still going to New York—but now we could go at any pace we wanted, see the things we wanted to see. The freedom was exhilarating.

Ryan's hand rested on my knee as I drove, like it was the most natural place for it to be. We didn't have to worry about being filmed or what anyone else would think. We didn't have to look for scavenger hunt items or try to beat the other teams. We could even listen to music.

I switched the radio on and changed stations until I heard a familiar song, one of the new ones off Villain Complex's second album. "Finally! Music!"

"Isn't this your roommate's band?"

I nodded. "They're on tour right now. I'm so happy for them."

"Are they playing a show near here? We could go see them one night."

I glanced over at him. "You'd want to do that?"

"Sure. I'd like to meet your roommates."

Huh. I hadn't expected that. Meeting my friends seemed a bit serious for our casual fling, but I wasn't going to argue. "I can check their tour schedule when we stop."

The next song that came on was "Get Lucky" by Daft Punk and Pharrell, which always reminded me of my ex-boyfriend Daryl because it was playing when we'd first met at a typical drunken college party. How strange—it had been days since I'd thought about him at all. Before going on the show I'd been upset about him, but now I didn't miss him one bit. That aching heartbreak was gone, wiped away by Ryan's presence. Now all I felt was anger at myself for staying with a jerk for so long. I quickly switched the radio off, then let out a long, relieved breath.

Ryan glanced at me. "You okay?"

I kept my eyes straight ahead on the road. "Yeah. I was just thinking about my ex."

His voice went flat. "I see."

"Not like that." I looked over and smiled at him. "I was thinking that I was with him for over a year, but never really loved him. When he cheated on me, I was more hurt by the betrayal than anything else." I shook my head. "I should have broken up with him a long time ago."

"Why did you stay with him for so long?"

"I don't know. There were things about him I liked, but mainly I was too much of a coward to break up with him. It seemed easier to stay with him instead of making a big, scary change. But I'm not living my life like that anymore."

"Good." He was quiet for a moment, but I felt his eyes on me. "What did you see in him?"

"He was really smart. An engineering major. That probably made him more interesting to me because we could talk about that stuff for hours. I used to hang out at his place and read his textbooks for fun. He would use me to help him study, even said I was the best tutor he could have found. Maybe it was my way of living vicariously somehow." I bit out a harsh laugh. "Looking back, it seems so stupid now."

"It's not stupid, but he obviously didn't deserve you." Ryan's hands were in fists on his lap. He slowly made them relax before speaking again. "If you went back to school, what would you do with your engineering degree?"

"I was thinking…" I shot him a quick, hesitant look. "Maybe I would work in car safety."

He stared at me, but didn't respond. His face was unreadable.

I shifted in my seat and kept talking. "Your mom's death never should have happened. I can't do anything about that, but maybe I can save some other people from a similar tragedy."

"Carla." He reached across to touch my cheek. "I don't deserve you either."

I took his hand and squeezed it tight. "That's not true."

We never talked about Ryan's mom or what happened to her. She'd died in a car accident when he was seven due to a known problem with the airbags. The car company should have recalled the cars long before the accident, but they'd decided it wasn't cost effective. Many people had died because of their greed, and Ryan's father became involved in a long, drawn-out battle with them for years with the other families. In the end all they got was a settlement. I wanted to do my part to prevent something like that from happening ever again.

The worst part was that Ryan had been in the car with her. He claimed to not remember the accident, but I knew it must weigh heavily on him. Especially since his relationship with his father was never the same after that.

"Do you ever think about her?" I asked softly.

"All the time." His voice was strained. I thought that would be the end of it, but then he spoke again. "Sometimes I wonder what she'd think of me now, or what things would be like if she'd never died. If my father would..." He shook his head and pulled his hand away. "It doesn't matter."

"Your mom would be so proud of you. I hope you know that."

"Yeah." He rested his head against the window, staring across the fields outside. Ryan had once told me that before his mom died their family was full of love and close like mine was. Only after her death did his father become cold and absent, spending all his time at work and completely ignoring his own son. I suspected it was one reason why Ryan never had serious relationships now. He couldn't imagine loving someone that much and then losing them.

The silence weighed heavily between us. I switched the radio on again, but it had gone to commercials. I tried to find another good station, but I didn't know any of the local channels and we were too far out of a city to get many of them.

"I should have sprung for satellite in this car," Ryan muttered.

I waved it away. "It's fine. We don't need music."

"Yes, we do." He pulled out his phone. "If we're going to have a proper road trip, we'll need to make some playlists."

"Good idea."

For the next couple hours we came up with three new playlists. The first was Endless Road, featuring our favorite songs about driving, including two songs called "Night Drive," one by Jimmy Eat World and the other by The All-American Rejects. The second was Quarter-life Crisis, where every song was about being in your early twenties, with "22" by Taylor Swift, "What's My Age Again?" by Blink 182, and "Pardon Me" by Incubus. And then there was my personal favorite, Childhood Lost, which featured songs we'd loved as kids and now realized were super dirty, such as "Touch Myself" by Divinyls, "Shoop" by Salt-N-Pepa, and "Genie In A Bottle" by Christina Aguilera.

We made it to St. Louis by sunset, giving us plenty of time to relax in the evening. Ryan had taken care of arranging our hotel, which meant we were staying in the most expensive, luxurious place he could find. He refused to let me pay for anything either. I couldn't decide if I was flattered or annoyed by it all.

"I'm going to pay you back for all this someday," I told him during dinner.

He'd booked us a table in a restaurant on the 42ⁿᵈ floor of a building that offered views of the Gateway Arch and Mississippi River, along with fine Italian cuisine. I was forced to wear my blue sheath dress again, since it was the only nice thing I'd brought with me and most of my other clothes were dirty from wearing them on the show.

He gave me a stern look. "No. You're not."

I sighed and took another sip of red wine. I had the five thousand dollars we'd won on the show, plus the refund for my plane ticket, but that didn't even come close to what Ryan was spending on this road trip already. Besides, I'd need that money when I got back to LA to find a new place to live. "I appreciate your generosity, I really do, but I still feel guilty."

"Don't feel guilty. You know I'm a billionaire, right?"

"Yes, but…"

He reached across the table and took my hand. "Carla, let me take care of you for a few days. Consider it my way of making up for being a terrible friend over the past six years." He brought my fingers to his lips and kissed my knuckles one by one. "You're doing your part by figuring out our route. I assume you have it all planned out already?"

"Mostly. I'm leaving a little room for spontaneity and risk taking." I smiled at him. "I learned that from you."

He gave me a wry grin. "Nice to know I'm rubbing off on you, and not just in a sexual way."

"You definitely are. Right now the plan is to arrive in Chicago tomorrow and maybe even spend two days there. I'd like to visit the Museum of Science and Industry. I've heard it's great, and they have an exhibit about transportation I'd love to see."

I laid out the rest of my plan for the next week, culminating in us arriving in New York and spending a few days there before going home. Ryan watched me the entire time with hooded eyes, but I couldn't tell if he was bored or if he found it all fascinating.

"What do you think?" I asked, once I'd finished.

"I think your mind is sexy as hell."

A surprised laugh escaped me. "Is that so?"

"Mm. I get turned on by a girl who does her research."

Warmth fluttered in my stomach. "That might be the best compliment anyone has ever given me."

He tilted his head with a smirk. "So I should stop buying you fancy cars and just tell you how smart you are?"

"Something like that." I traced the edge of my wine glass and smiled. "Why did you choose the Porsche 911 anyway?"

"When you were fifteen you said you wanted one."

"You remember that?"

"Of course. I remember everything about you. I would have gotten all the other answers in that swimming pool trivia challenge correct. What your favorite Disney movie is—*Lady And The Tramp*. What your Hogwarts house is—Hufflepuff. How you got all your scars—hell, half of them were my fault."

I pointed my fork at him. "You didn't know you were my first kiss."

His expression turned serious. "No, I never knew that."

"Would it have changed anything if you knew?"

He hesitated. "No."

"I thought you would be my first...my first in other things too." I shook my head, my cheeks warming from the confession. "I was so young and stupid."

"I should have been your first. I would have taken care of you."

I leaned close and whispered, "So take care of me tonight."

The intense look in his eyes sent a shiver of desire down my spine. "I'm planning on it."

TWENTY-ONE

Carla

W hen we got back to the hotel room—a penthouse suite decorated in blue and gold, with a whirlpool tub and windows overlooking the city—I found an unexpected surprise: all of our clothes had been washed, ironed, and folded.

"Did you arrange this?" I asked Ryan.

"I thought we'd both feel better with clean clothes. We can go shopping tomorrow too, if you need some more."

"Thank you. I think I have enough to get me through the rest of our trip now."

Strong arms went around me and tugged me against his chest. He rested his forehead against mine, our mouths close but not touching. "Anything you need, I'll get for you."

"You're too good to me."

"No. I'll never be good enough."

His kiss was slow and absolutely decadent, a promise that we had all night and he was going to take his time. I was an expensive box of chocolate and he was going to savor each piece and lick his fingertips to get every last taste.

He lifted me up onto the edge of the dining table and ran his hands up my knees and thighs, pushing my dress up to my hips. While his tongue lazily stroked mine, his fingers hooked around the edge of my panties and pulled them down slowly. By the time they finally hit the floor, the anticipation was killing me.

He kneeled in front of me, spreading my knees wide, then kissed up my thighs in a slow, deliberate path. But as he moved his head between my legs, I squirmed away, heat rising in my cheeks.

"Ryan, you don't have to—"

He looked up at me and clamped his hands around my hips, holding me in place. "I want to."

"But—"

All words left me as his face disappeared between my thighs. His mouth lingered there, his tongue sliding along my wet heat. I dug my fingers into his hair and it was so good I couldn't believe it was real. Then I pushed his head back. "Stop. I…"

"What's wrong?" he asked, looking up at me with his brow creased.

"You don't need to do that. I know it's not, um…" I pressed a hand to my forehead, drowning in humiliation. Trust me to turn a sensual moment into an awkward one.

"You don't ever have to feel shy around me."

"It's not that." I blew out a long breath. "My ex-boyfriend Daryl, he um… He only went down on me once and it was disappointing. He said it was disgusting for guys and never did it again."

Ryan's fingers tightened on my thighs. "That guy is an asshole."

"It's fine. It wasn't anything special anyway. I figured if he didn't like it and it wasn't that good for me, what was the point? I don't want you to feel like you have to do it either."

Ryan stood up, his eyes flashing dark and angry. "First of all, that guy couldn't be more wrong. Going down on a woman is fucking amazing. There's nothing better in the world. And trust me, it should be just as good for you. Second, he sounds like a selfish prick who didn't know what he was doing down there. Let me guess, he still wanted you to blow him?"

I pressed my legs together, ready to crawl under the table and hide. "Um. Sometimes. Yeah."

"That guy better hope I never run into him." He took my hand, tugging me off the table. "Now I'm going to show you how good it can be with someone who knows what the fuck they're doing and cares about nothing more than your pleasure."

"Really, this isn't necessary." I was so embarrassed about the whole thing, I wasn't sure how I'd ever get back to feeling sexy. Maybe we could go watch a movie or something and forget any of this ever happened.

Ryan gave me a stern look and led me into the bedroom, then began unbuttoning his shirt with his strong fingers. My throat went dry as the shirt parted and revealed his hard chest underneath, igniting my lust again instantly. It seriously wasn't fair how drop dead gorgeous he was, or how quickly my body responded to him.

I slid my hand along his firm stomach, feeling every ridge. "How do you look like this? Don't you sit behind a desk all day?"

"I have a personal trainer."

I laughed softly. "Of course you do."

He lay back on the bed, propping his head on the pillow with one arm. "Take off your dress."

I slowly slid the dress off me while he watched with a predatory look in his eye. His slacks had a massive tent, but he made no effort to remove them.

"Good." He crooked one finger at me. "Now get over here and sit on my face."

I blinked at him, my mouth hanging open. "Sit where?"

"You heard me." His voice was commanding and left no room for argument.

I eased myself onto the bed beside him, but hesitated. "Won't I crush you? How will you breathe?"

"Let me worry about that." He slid an arm around my waist and yanked me up to his shoulders. I moved forward until my knees were on either side of his head on the pillow, then hovered over him. I couldn't believe I was really about to do this. I felt so open. So *exposed*.

He dug his fingers into my butt and pulled me down to his face, making me cry out from the sheer shock of it. His tongue slid along my folds, slowly at first, just a tease. He licked, sucked, and tasted me, making the rest of the world completely disappear. I sank down even further and grabbed hold of the wooden headboard in front of me.

Ryan showed me exactly what I'd been missing out on all this time. With expert skill, he used his mouth and tongue and even his breath to tease pleasure out of me in ways I'd never known were possible. My fingers tightly gripped the headboard, breathing became a challenge, and I couldn't stop the whimpering sounds coming from deep in my throat no matter how hard I tried.

When he slid his fingers into me, I couldn't help but buck my hips in time with his movements. His mouth devoured me, his fingers thrust into me, and I rose up and down on him, wanting—no, *needing*—everything he could give me. It wasn't long before I came completely undone, caught in the waves of the most incredible orgasm in my life, one that never seemed to end.

He pressed soft kisses on my thighs as the tremors faded. "You taste so good. I don't think I'll ever get enough of you."

"You were right," I said with a shaky laugh. "My ex had *no* idea what he was doing."

Low laughter rumbled through his chest. "Don't move and I'll give you a repeat performance."

"Now?" I rested my head against the headboard. "I might die."

"No, you won't."

"Wait." I turned around on him so I was facing down the bed. "At least let me take care of you too."

I reached for his waist, dragging the zipper down, tugging his very hard shaft out of his slacks. I'd never sixty-nined with a guy before, but I was doing all sorts of new things with Ryan. Somehow he brought out my adventurous side, maybe because I always felt completely safe with him.

"Naughty girl, what are you doing?" Ryan asked.

In response, I leaned over his body, hands on either side of his hips, and ran my tongue along his long length.

"Christ," he gasped.

I explored him thoroughly with my mouth and my hands, learning every inch of him, memorizing what he liked best and what made him even harder. I loved the taste of his skin, the way he responded to my touch, the way he sucked in a breath as I took him deeper into my mouth. In return, he did the most amazing things with his tongue, discovering what made me fall apart over and over again.

After another mind-shattering orgasm, he flipped me over on the bed, taking control again, and moved up my body with a trail of kisses. When his hard length nudged between my legs, his mouth caressed my neck. "The other night, you said you'd wanted this for a long time."

"Yes," I whispered, closing my eyes.

"You thought about me. About what it would be like if we were together."

"Yes."

"You fantasized about it. And then you touched yourself here." He rubbed himself against me, a perfect mix of hard and soft against my most sensitive skin.

"Yes," I gasped.

"Tell me."

I buried my face in his shoulder, breathing in his warm, masculine scent. "I can't."

"Just one. Tell me one of your fantasies."

"When we were younger you would sleep over in that extra bed and I would…" I swallowed. I'd never told anyone this. "I would imagine climbing into bed with you while Daniel was asleep. You would confess you'd always wanted me, and then you'd slip inside me from behind, covering my mouth so I wouldn't wake up Daniel or my parents."

A low, husky laugh escaped him. "God, Carla. There were so many nights when I would lie awake all night thinking about the same thing. I figured I was just a horny teenage boy. I had no idea you'd wanted the same thing."

"I guess I was a horny teenage girl too."

"Mm. If I'd known that, I would never have been able to resist you." He wrapped my legs around his waist and just the tip of him entered me. I raised my hips, trying to get more of him, but he held back.

His dark eyes never left me, never gave me a break from his delicious interrogation. "And when we were older. After I left. Did you still think of me when you touched yourself?"

"Yes. Always." I dug my fingers into his butt, trying to bring him closer, but still he resisted.

With his mouth at my ear, he sank an inch into me. "When your other boyfriends were inside you, did you wish it was me fucking you?"

"Yes," I confessed. "Every time."

"Tell me." He pushed a little deeper inside me before retreating again. He was such a damn tease. "Tell me what you imagined."

I closed my eyes, lost in both the memory and the reality of him. "I imagined we'd meet again and when you saw me you'd realize you'd made a mistake. You'd get me alone—a bathroom, a closet, sometimes an elevator—and you'd be overcome with desire. You'd lose control and shove me against the wall. You'd push my clothes out of the way and take me right there, hard and fast."

He let out a low, primal growl. "You have no idea how hard it's been to not do exactly that every single minute since I came back into your life."

I took his face in my hands, staring up at him. "You don't have to hold back anymore."

He picked me up, with my legs around his waist and my arms around his neck. He walked over to the bedroom door, kicked it shut with a loud *thud*, then shoved my back against it, hard. His mouth devoured mine in a demanding kiss, while my fingers slid into his hair, pulling at his scalp. He grabbed my wrists, forcing my arms above my head, against the wooden door.

"Is this what you imagined?" he asked. I nodded, too far gone to form words.

He slammed into me, so big and rough I cried out against his lips. I was still so sensitive from all the times he'd made me come with his mouth, it would take barely anything to set me off again.

He buried himself inside me with hard, deep thrusts. Claiming my body with his, caging me against the wall like a prisoner. Except if I was his prisoner, I never wanted to escape my cell. True freedom was giving myself up to him completely, surrendering without a care for what happened between us tomorrow or the day after that.

"You wanted to see me lose control?" he asked, his voice rough and dirty.

"Yes." I tightened my legs around his hips. "Do it. Let go."

He pressed his face to my neck with a soft groan, making my skin vibrate. His pace became relentless, making the door rattle as he went faster, deeper, all his tightly-held control falling away to an animalistic frenzy. The friction between us became too much and I threw my head back and closed my eyes as the orgasm rushed through me, strong and sharp. I tightened up around him and I could tell he felt it because his thrusts became more powerful. His back arched, his fingers tightened around my wrists, and my name slipped from his lips. It was the most beautiful thing I'd ever heard.

He released my wrists and I wrapped my arms around him. We were still connected, my body tingling and warm. He rested his forehead against mine, his chest rising and falling, a sheen of sweat on his golden skin. "Was it as good as you imagined?"

"Better."

"You're the only one who could make me lose control." His mouth brushed against mine. "The *only* one."

I wanted to stay forever in the breath between his lips and mine, in the space between now and tomorrow. As long as I held him here, I would never have to give him up.

TWENTY-TWO

Ryan

Every day with Carla was better than the last. And every night…every night she made it harder for me to leave her at the end of our time together.

We set out for Chicago after a long brunch, taking turns driving the Porsche and singing songs from our playlists at the top of our lungs. Once it was my turn to drive, I pulled off the highway and into a small shopping center.

"What are we doing here?" Carla asked, as I parked outside a beauty salon.

"Being spontaneous. Taking risks. Checking off one of the things on your list."

"I don't understand."

"In the forest, you said you wanted to dye your hair a color your mother wouldn't approve of. I had my assistant find a highly rated salon on the way to Chicago and made an appointment for you."

She bit her lip, looking between me and the salon. "We're going to dye my hair today? *Now?*"

"Only if you want to. If not, we'll leave. I'd never make you do anything you didn't want to do."

She drew in a long breath and studied the people inside the salon. Many of them had brightly colored hair and unusual cuts. "Okay, I'll do it."

I gave her a quick kiss. "That's my risk-taker."

An hour later, Carla's beautiful curls were bright purple and the smile on her face was huge. "I love it so much," she said, checking herself out in the mirror from different angles. "And my mom is definitely going to hate it."

"Yes, she is."

As we walked back to the car, a long, happy sigh escaped her. "I feel so free. For the first time in my life I don't care what anyone thinks about how I look." Her eyes slid to mine and a shy smile crossed her lips. "Except you, maybe."

"I think the only thing more beautiful than your body is your mind. But you knew that already."

"When you say things like that…" She ducked her head, looking away.

"What?"

"Nothing." She slid her arms around my neck and gave me a kiss that made me instantly hard. "Thank you so much. This was a great idea."

"It was your idea. I simply made it happen." I tried to hand Carla the keys, but she shook her head.

"You drive. My heart is still racing and my hands are shaky from the excitement."

"All right. Let me know when you want to switch. It's your car after all."

"No, it's not." She gave me a heated look once we'd gotten into the car. "Besides, you're sexy when you drive."

I raised an eyebrow at her. "I'm not sexy the rest of the time?"

She rested her hand on my thigh and leaned across the seat to place a kiss on my neck. "You are. You know you are."

I grinned and started up the car, even though her lingering fingers on my leg were driving me wild. I navigated us back onto the highway, but traffic was bad due to an accident up ahead. Her nails traced patterns on my jeans while we sat there waiting to move forward. The pattern got bigger and bigger, until it was moving dangerously close to my growing erection.

"What do you think you're doing?" I asked.

"Just passing the time," she said in an innocent voice while her hand cupped the large bulge in my jeans.

"Are we playing this game again?"

She tugged on my zipper. "No, because now there are no cameras filming us this time."

"Just cars all around us." Not that I cared. I was enjoying this side of Carla too much. Fuck, if I'd known she was so dirty before, I'd never have been able to keep my hands off her all this time.

"No one will see us. It's getting dark out."

She finished sliding the zipper down and slipped her fingers inside to grip my length. I filled her hand completely and she gave me a soft squeeze. I nearly jumped off the seat. I reached for her, but she swatted away my hand. "You keep your hands on the wheel."

I scowled, but then we drove past the accident and the traffic let up. I put distance between us and the other cars, just as she pulled me all the way out of my pants and began stroking. My fingers tightened on the steering wheel until my knuckles were white. "You're going to make it impossible for me to drive."

"Hey, if I can drive while you get me off, you can do it too."

I smirked at her. "Is that a challenge?"

She didn't answer, but gave me a naughty smile and leaned across the seat, lowering her head to my lap. Her mouth closed around me, and it took every ounce of control I had not to run us off the road. I glance down quickly to catch a glimpse of her pouty red lips along my shaft, and then forced my eyes back on the road. Fucking hell. I'd never seen anything more erotic than Carla giving me a blow job while I drove a Porsche.

Her mouth worked me up and down, her tongue sliding around the head. I groaned and shifted in the seat, giving her better access. She took me deeper between her lips and I gripped her hair with one hand, tangling my fingers in her purple curls, while keeping the other hand on the steering wheel. She bobbed up and down on me while I pressed her head even lower, making her take more and more. I could barely stop from coming in her mouth, but I worried I wouldn't be able to keep driving if I did that. Jesus, she was going to kill us both like this.

"Enough." I pulled off the side of the highway and turned off the car, then slid my seat back as far as it would go. Carla sat up and looked at me with slick lips and lusty eyes. I patted my lap. "Get over here."

She wiggled out of her underwear and tossed it on the floor of the car, then climbed across to straddle me. I pushed her skirt up enough to palm her ass as I slid between her folds. God, she was already wet as hell and I hadn't even touched her yet.

She sank down onto me slowly and we both breathed a sigh of relief, like it had been years instead of hours since we'd been connected like this. She set her hands on my shoulders and looked me right in the eye as she began to move. Night had fallen around us, giving us some cover, but I could still see the pure lust in her eyes, along with something else. Something neither of us wanted to say out loud. Something she probably saw in my eyes too.

I slipped my hand under her shirt to stroke her lush breasts, then captured her lips with mine. My tongue licked at her mouth while she rode me, rocking her hips under me leisurely. She set the pace, controlling all of it, and the minutes faded away. We were right on the side of the highway where anyone driving by might see us, but there was no one in the world but us.

She moved faster, bouncing up and down on me, her breath escaping her in little throaty gasps. My fingers dug into her hips, encouraging her, urging her on. I watched her face, studying every slight change as she brought herself closer and closer. When she was almost there her eyes fluttered shut, but I gripped her chin and made her look at me again. I needed to see it when she came. I wanted to be right there with her.

She took my face in her hands, her fingers scraping against the stubble on my jaw, and then she gasped my name. I watched as the orgasm took her, her body clenching tight around me, her nails digging into my skin. I slid my fingers into her curls, holding her there as I thrust up into her pulsing warmth. My name tumbled from her lips over and over like a chant as she rode through the last tremors. With my hand locked on the back of her head, her mouth consuming mine, I finally gave myself up to her.

I held her against me, feeling her heart beat against my chest with the same fast pace as mine. Emotions I'd never felt before choked my throat, threatening to come tumbling out at any second. Shit, shit, shit. It was just sex, I reminded myself. Amazing sex, unlike anything I'd ever experienced before, but that was it. It didn't mean anything. It couldn't, no matter how much I wanted it to.

"Carla," I said slowly. "What the hell are we doing?"

"We just had sex in a car on the side of the road. Which is probably illegal." She laughed and buried her face in my neck, kissing me below my jaw. "You wanted me to take more risks, after all."

"No, I meant…this. Us."

She looked at me with her warm brown eyes, but her smile faltered. "We're having fun. Right?"

"We are." I drew in a ragged breath. "Is that what you still want?"

"Yes, definitely." Her fingers coiled in my shirt. "Don't you?"

"Of course."

That settled it. She wanted something temporary, some fun, casual sex while we were on the road together, nothing more. Why would I ever think she'd want to continue this after it was over? She'd just gotten out of a long-term relationship with a total asshole. She'd had a crush on me forever, and now we were "getting it out of our system," according to what she'd said the other night. The problem was, I never wanted her out of my system. I wanted to breathe her in until she filled every pore of my skin, every gap between my cells, every strand of my DNA.

I told myself there were a dozen reasons why it would never work between us. We lived in different states. We had totally different lives now. She deserved someone better than me, who could commit to her without hesitation. I'd made a promise to her brother.

That last one sat heavy on my shoulders, weighing me down with guilt. I didn't want to lie to my best friend or keep secrets from him once Carla and I returned to our normal lives. I couldn't live that way.

"We need to tell Daniel," I said.

She sighed. "We will. As soon as we get back."

I nodded. He'd be pissed as hell at me for screwing his sister, but maybe if I told him it was a temporary fling he'd forgive me. He had to. I couldn't imagine losing both him *and* Carla—the two people who meant more to me than anyone else on this planet.

———

We made it to Chicago late and decided to order room service and eat it on the couch while watching TV. It felt like something a real couple would do, a glimpse of how easy and right it would if we were really together. When she fell asleep with her head on my shoulder, I repeated to myself that it didn't mean anything, but it was getting harder and harder to convince myself of that with each passing minute.

We spent the next day in the Museum of Science and Industry like the total geeks we were. The best part was watching Carla's face light up as we studied the transportation exhibits. We took hours discussing the things we saw there, until I worried the security guards might kick us out. I didn't care. I could listen to her talk science all day and all night.

When the museum closed, we continued our conversation over dinner. I was determined, more than ever, to get her to go back to school so she could pursue her dream. I couldn't give her everything she'd yelled that she wanted that night in the forest—we'd already lost the show, and her parents' relationship was out of my hands—but I'd try to make everything else happen for her.

While we waited for our food, she showed me tomorrow's journey on the map in her phone. "It's so much easier planning all this now that we have GPS again."

"We're only a few days away from New York." I sat back in my chair and studied her. "Have you figured out what you're going to do when you get back to LA?"

She set her phone on the table. "No. Have you figured out what you're going to do about your company?"

"No."

We eyed each other for a moment, but neither one of us was willing to back down. Finally, Carla took a sip of wine. "How did you get the idea for Outerworld anyway?"

"My roommate in college would run Dungeons & Dragons games and sometimes I would join in. One day I thought, what if a world of magic existed over our own and we just couldn't see it? I got the idea to use augmented reality to overlay the game onto the real world, so that everyone could be Harry Potter, basically."

"Genius."

"Have you ever played?"

She shrugged. "A little…"

"If I look on your phone, am I going to see a level 50 sorceress on there?"

"I don't play *that* much."

"I don't believe you." I snatched her phone from the table and opened up the game app. "Holy shit. You're a level 100 healer." I raised an eyebrow at her. "So when you said you don't play that much, what you meant was, you play way *more?*"

"No! I mean, I enjoy the game, and when I'm on photo shoots there's a lot of downtime…" She tried to grab her phone back but I held it away, clicking on her inventory.

"Damn, your character has some nice stuff. The Staff of Twisting Shadows? That was a rare drop during the last Halloween event. The Cloak of Infinite Light? Shit, even I don't have that."

"I've been lucky, that's all. What class do you play, anyway?"

"I've played all of them in testing, but my main character is a rogue. Ooh, you have a Purple Mechanical Dragon. Somehow this doesn't surprise me at all."

She shrugged. "I wanted a yellow one, but it didn't come in that color."

"I'll make sure they add one in the next update."

A small smile tugged at her lips, but then her phone buzzed. A notification popped up on the screen, showing a text from her mom. *Giselle told me you're not on the show anymore. Where are you? Are you okay? Call me!*

I handed it over to her and her face dropped. "I better call her before she sends a private detective to track me down."

I nodded and she slipped outside to make the call. Through the window, I watched her pacing back and forth while she talked to her mom, sometimes gesturing wildly or rolling her eyes. Then her eyebrows pinched together and she stopped in her tracks, before finally hanging up the phone.

She walked back inside and sat down at the table. "Sorry about that."

"What did she say?"

"That she's worried about me, but she feels a lot better knowing you're with me."

"Does she know we're…together?" Eva had never made it a secret that she'd always wanted me and Carla to get married and give her a dozen grandchildren. She was probably planning our engagement party already.

"I'm pretty sure she figured it out." She sighed and slumped down into her chair. "So much for keeping it under wraps."

A new, horrible thought occurred to me. "Will she tell Daniel?"

"I asked her not to say anything. My hope is that she's too busy with her new life to talk to him before we get back."

"How does she sound?"

"Miserable. I think she misses my dad a lot." Carla sighed, resting her chin on her fist. "I don't understand why they can't make it work. It's just distance, right?"

"Maybe it's more than that. Your mom said she needed some time to find herself again."

"I suppose. She wanted us to have dinner with her in New York, but I told her no. I'm too upset with her still. Is that terrible of me?"

"No. It's okay to need some time and space. Their separation was a big shock for you."

She rubbed the bridge of her nose, closing her eyes. "I don't want to go home and deal with any of it. I just want to keep driving. With you."

"I know what you mean." I didn't want to go back either and face reality, but we both knew this journey would have to end eventually. In a few days, it would all be over. I'd go back to my life and she'd go back to hers, and we'd have to find a way to live without each other all over again.

TWENTY-THREE

Carla

The next few days were a whirlwind of cities. From Chicago we visited Indianapolis, Columbus, Pittsburgh, and Philadelphia, exploring each city for one night before moving on the next morning. We explored each other too, for hours and hours. We had sex in hotel beds, in fancy whirlpool tubs, on countertops, on the floor. I'd never had so much amazing sex in my life, but neither one of us could get enough of each other. We were insatiable, craving each other like a drug we'd die without. I didn't understand how I could want someone so badly when he was already mine. Or at least temporarily mine.

But it wasn't all sex either. We had a great time even when we kept our clothes on and our hands off each other. We loved driving together, visiting touristy places, going to science museums, watching movies in hotel rooms, eating at unique restaurants, and just generally spending time with each other. I'd forgotten how easy it was to relax and be myself around him. Now that we were together again it was like I finally had my best friend back.

I wished the week could last forever.

Arriving in New York was bittersweet. I'd planned it so we arrived a few days earlier than we would have if we'd stayed on the show, so that way we could do some sightseeing and relax after days of driving. As we approached the buildings shining in the distance, I watched the horizon with a sad smile. I was excited to be back in one of my favorite cities and to share it with my favorite person, but it also meant the end of our time together was quickly approaching.

On our first night there, Ryan treated me to a surprise showing of *Hamilton*, which he somehow got front row tickets to—one of the perks of being super rich, I supposed. I'd listened to the music a thousand times, but it didn't compare to seeing the show in person. Ryan and I were both children of immigrants, our biracial heritage evident in our skin and our hair, and seeing people on stage who looked like us was a rare, thrilling experience.

The next day we went to the Statue of Liberty and then it was my turn to take Ryan out. First, we met my former roommate Julie and her boyfriend Gavin for dinner at a BBQ restaurant she swore was amazing. Laughter burst out of me as Julie, a petite Korean-American girl, threw her arms around me in a tight hug. Her head only came up to boob level, but I gave her a tight squeeze anyway.

"Your hair!" she said. "I love it! And I can't believe you're in New York. Or that you went on *Road Trip Race!* You need to catch me up over dinner. I need to know *everything.*"

Gavin grabbed me in a hug next. He was as tall as Ryan, which made him tower over Julie, but the height difference had never seemed to bother them. "Carla, always a pleasure," he said, with his sexy English accent.

"I'm so happy to see you both." I turned to smile at my date. "This is Ryan Evans, my partner on the show and…a family friend."

Ryan arched an eyebrow at me, but I wasn't sure how to label our relationship. He wasn't my boyfriend, after all.

Julie, of course, never missed anything. She shook Ryan's hand and looked back and forth between us with a knowing smile. "I get the feeling there's more than friendship going on here. I'm going to need all the details. And I do mean *all* of them."

Gavin clasped hands with Ryan. "Nice to meet you, mate."

"Thanks. It's great to meet some of Carla's friends."

Julie frowned and studied Ryan. "Hang on. If you're an old family friend, how come we've never met before?"

"We were out of touch for the last few years," I said. "Now we're reconnecting."

"Yeah, I'll bet you are." She gave me a nudge and a sly grin. "I'm just happy you moved on from that loser Daryl already. God, he was the worst."

"So I've heard," Ryan said.

We sat down for dinner and I told them all about our time on the show, which led to Julie and Gavin telling Ryan about when the three of us had been on *Behind The Seams.* They caught me up on what the other designers were doing, then told us about getting their new line ready for New York Fashion Week in September.

Julie leaned forward, her hands flat on the table. "You should see our place. It's like a hurricane swept through it and scattered fabric everywhere. I'm honestly not sure how we'll get the collection done in time for the show."

"I'm sure you'll manage," I said. "The two of you are unstoppable."

Gavin rested his tattooed hand over Julie's. "She is. I just try not to get in her way."

"The collection is a perfect blend of both of us. You two must come to our studio and see what we have so far. In fact…" She glanced at Gavin, before turning back to me. "If you're free in September, we would love to have you as our lead model on the runway."

Gavin nodded. "Yes. Just like old times. Ryan, you would of course be invited too. Have you ever seen Carla walk the runway before?"

"No, I haven't."

"She's incredible," Gavin said. "I couldn't have won the show without her."

I glanced at Ryan, squirming in my seat. In September he'd be back in Seattle, I'd probably be in LA, and we wouldn't be together anymore. But Ryan simply gave them a casual smile. "Thanks for the offer. I'll see if I can make it. Assuming Carla is interested, of course."

I hesitated. I wanted to go back to school someday, but it would take time and money. My best option was to keep modeling for a few years to pay the bills. "I'd love to be in your show in September. You know I could never turn you two down."

"Excellent," Julie said.

We finished dinner and took the subway to the venue for the next part of our evening. It was so good to see Julie and Gavin again, and they were so obviously happy, even after almost a year of living together. My heart clenched—I wanted that too. With Ryan. We only had two more days together. Could I convince him to extend what we had after that? I'd have to find a way to ask him tomorrow. Tonight we had a concert to see.

The venue was already packed by the time we got there, but we got right in with our VIP tickets, which also allowed us into the backstage area. The show was about to start, so we quickly took our seats while the crowd went wild.

I gave Ryan's hand a squeeze as the lights went down and the music began to play in the darkness. The haunting sound of Maddie's guitar rang across the theater, followed by Jared's deep, unforgettable voice as he sang the opening of "Behind The Mask," one of their older but most popular songs. Julie and I both burst into cheers as the lights came up, showing the two of them on stage along with Hector on drums, Becca on bass, and Kyle on keyboard.

Jared stood in the center of the stage, clutching the microphone like a lover as he crooned into it, while Maddie strummed her guitar beside him. It was hard to believe a year ago she'd been too shy to play guitar in front of anyone except me and Julie, or that she'd never believed a rocker like Jared could fall for a geeky, glasses-wearing girl like her. Now they were performing every night to sold out shows across America, their songs were playing non-stop on the radio, and she and Jared were completely in love.

The other band members had all found love too—Kyle, with his high school girlfriend Alexis, Hector, with his online best friend Tara, and Becca with, of all crazy things, Tara's ex-boyfriend. I felt that twang of jealousy plus happiness again, until Ryan pulled me in close for a kiss during one of the slower songs. I didn't need to be jealous anymore, because I'd found the same thing they had.

I couldn't deny it any longer. I was in love with Ryan, in an all new way. This wasn't the puppy-dog love I'd felt when we were kids, or the unrequited love of our teenage years. This wasn't the bittersweet love when I knew he was leaving for college, or the heartbroken love after he was gone. This was a new love, a mature love, a love based on the real Ryan and not some fantasy of him.

I wanted to tell him, but I worried it would only scare him away. But he'd told me to take risks, hadn't he? And there was no greater risk than giving him my heart.

Tomorrow, I thought. In the morning, when we were in bed. I'd tell him then.

The band disappeared before their encore and I leaned into Ryan's arms. "Are you having fun?"

"When I'm with you? Always. But yes, they're even better live than I thought they'd be."

"I told you they were amazing! No one does a show like Villain Complex."

The shouts from the audience got louder and louder, until finally the band returned to the stage. A spotlight highlighted Jared, who took the microphone and faced the audience.

"Thank you all for coming tonight. This is an especially exciting concert for us because today marks exactly a year since we performed 'Bad Romance' on the finale of *The Sound*." He looked over at Maddie with a smile, no doubt remembering how he'd professed his love for her on live TV in front of millions during that episode.

The band began playing the first notes from that unforgettable cover, turning the well-known pop song into something dark and sensual. But Jared didn't start singing. Instead he stood in front of Maddie and got down on one knee. My mouth dropped open. Was he…?

"Maddie, a year ago I got down on my knees and begged you to come on *The Sound* with us. Then I got down on my knees and told you I loved you on live TV in front of millions. Now I'm on my knees again in front of all these people because I have a very important question to ask you." He pulled a box from his black jeans and opened it, revealing a huge diamond ring. "Maddie, will you marry me?"

"Oh my god." Her hand covered her mouth as she stared at him, her eyes wide in shock behind her black-rimmed glasses. "Yes. Of course I will. Yes, yes, yes!"

He stood up and they fell into each other's arms, while the audience went totally wild. Beside me, Julie let out a happy squeal and grabbed my arm. I clutched her tightly, my heart pounding. On stage, the rest of the band was clapping too, grinning from behind the happy couple, who were wrapped up in each other. The huge screen captured their kiss in giant size, before they finally broke apart and began playing "Bad Romance."

After the concert ended, we headed for a room backstage where the band was supposed to meet us. When we stepped inside, Maddie and Becca were lounging on one of the couches in the room, which also had a TV and a small kitchen.

"Congratulations!" Julie and I yelled at the same time, grabbing Maddie in a tight hug.

"Thank you," she said, laughing.

"Did you have any idea that was going to happen tonight?" I asked.

"No, not a clue."

"The rest of us knew it was going to happen," Becca said. She was reclining on the couch with her boots propped on the table in front of her. "I had to keep it a secret all day from Maddie, but it was totally worth it to see the shock on her face when Jared got down on one knee."

"I can't believe you didn't give me a hint at least," Maddie said, shaking her head with a big smile. Her eyes caught sight of the guys behind us and her smile got even bigger. "Oh, there's Gavin!" She gave him a hug and then smiled at Ryan. "Hi, I don't think we've met before."

"This is Ryan. We've been um…spending the last couple days traveling around together." I ducked my head with a shy smile. "And having fun."

Becca let out a loud whoop. "Yeah you are. Finally someone listens to my advice around here."

"What advice are you giving?" Julie asked. "Or do I not want to know?"

"I told Carla she should get some action, that's all." She took a long look at Ryan and licked her red lips. I blushed even more, but Ryan just smirked at her. "I can see why you took my advice."

Her boyfriend Andrew emerged from another room, holding a bottle of champagne. He wore a button-up shirt with a tie, black glasses, and had perfect blond hair, like some kind of all-American actor playing the part of "boy next door." He was so completely opposite of the punk rock look that Becca sported, yet they somehow worked together. "Who are you eyeing up? Should I be jealous?"

"Nope." She grabbed his tie and pulled him down for a kiss. "You're the only one I want."

The rest of the band entered the room and we all hugged each other while I introduced everyone to Ryan. First there was Kyle, with his dyed black hair, piercings, and tattoos, along with his girlfriend Alexis, who had fire engine red hair and a camera around her neck at all times. Then there was tall, dark, and handsome Hector and his sweet, blond girlfriend, Tara, who wore a t-shirt from their comic book *Misfit Squad*. And finally, there was Jared, with his perfectly tousled dark hair, tattooed arms, and sinful blue eyes. He'd changed out of his concert attire and now wore one of his signature villain t-shirts, this one with Kylo Ren on it. Even among all of these good-looking people Jared stood out, his charisma like a beacon drawing all attention to him.

"The gang's all here," Jared said, grinning at everyone. "I knew I'd picked the right night to propose."

It *was* pretty amazing, since we so rarely all got together anymore. Alexis and Tara explained that they'd flown out to surprise the band for the show. Andrew managed PR for the band, which meant he was often on the road with them. Julie and Gavin lived here, of course. Ryan and I just had good timing.

"I can't believe we're all in New York at the same time," Tara said, giving Hector a knowing look. "Must be fate."

"Go on," he said. "Tell them."

Tara flushed, looking down. "No, it's Maddie and Jared's big night."

"Yes, tell them," Alexis said, with a huge smile. She clearly knew whatever the big secret was already. A year ago, Tara had moved to LA for work and to be with Hector, but she hadn't known anyone else really. She and Alexis had immediately hit it off and soon become best friends. Now they were practically inseparable.

Jared slid his arm around Maddie's shoulders and grinned at Tara. "Yep, you have to tell us now."

"We just found out…I'm pregnant." Tara looked up at Hector, who smiled down at her like the luckiest man in the world. Hector sometimes came across as grumpy, but he was really like a big teddy bear, especially around the woman he loved.

"Oh my god!" Maddie said, then grabbed Tara in a hug. Jared clasped his best friend in a tight embrace, muttering quiet words to Hector that made them both smile.

"When's the wedding?" Andrew asked, hugging Tara next. He'd once dated her for a year and had even proposed to her, but he didn't seem upset in the slightest that she was now happy with Hector. Having Becca at his side probably had something to do with it.

"Hmm, guess we need to have one soon," Hector said.

"All right, it's definitely time for some champagne," Jared said. Andrew opened up the bottle and served everyone other than Tara, who was stuck with soda. We all toasted and drank to our new beginnings, while warmth spread through me that wasn't entirely from the bubbly champagne.

Ryan slid his arm around my waist and brushed my ear with his lips. "I like your friends."

I leaned against him. "Me too."

We spent the rest of the night drinking, laughing, and catching up with everyone. It was the best thing in the world to be back with all of my friends, and even better was watching Ryan fit right in with them. I'd been so worried about all of us moving on with our lives, scared we'd drift apart, but now I realized we'd always be connected to each other. No matter how many miles there were between us, we'd always find our way back together again. We were family, after all.

TWENTY-FOUR

Ryan

By the time we got back to the hotel room, it was way too late, or rather, too early in the morning, to do anything but crawl into bed. I woke up the next day with a dryness in my mouth and a slight headache. I rubbed my eyes. Damn, how much champagne did we have?

It was the middle of the afternoon already and Carla was still asleep. Not that it mattered what time we got up. According to her schedule, we had nothing planned for the day except spending time with each other. As my eyes skimmed over her naked skin, I had an idea for how I wanted to start.

While I waited for her to wake, I went onto the balcony and checked my messages. There was one from my assistant with her daily update on what I was missing at Meta Entertainment, along with an email from Slade Industries stating they were getting impatient and wanted a response about their buyout offer. I had to make a decision by Monday afternoon or they'd walk away.

Dammit. I really had to get back to the office. But what about the situation with my father? Should I return to LA and check in on him, or was that door closed for good?

I called Dolores for the first time since I'd left for the show. She answered on the third ring. "Hello?"

"Hey, it's Ryan."

"Hi Ryan." She sounded exhausted.

"Sorry, did I wake you?" It was three hours earlier in LA, after all.

"No, I'm just tired. How are you doing?"

"I'm good." I paused and steeled myself. "How's my father?"

"He's been coughing a lot but otherwise no different. We're going back to the doctor on Monday."

"Do you need me to go with you?" I'd postpone going back to work and get

Slade Industries to wait another few days somehow, if it meant being there for my father.

"No, we're fine. That's sweet of you to offer though."

"Okay." I gripped the phone tightly. "Can I talk to Dad?"

"Hang on, let me get him."

I heard shuffling and then silence. While I waited, I stared at the tall buildings of New York, at the city all around me full of people going about their daily lives, dealing with their own problems, going after their own goals. The heat and humidity was already intense, but that didn't seem to slow the city down at all.

A few minutes later she came back on the line and sighed. "I'm sorry, Ryan. He says he doesn't want to talk to you."

I swallowed the lump in my throat. "Thanks anyway."

As soon as I hung up, Daniel's name popped up on my phone. My already tense shoulders tightened up even more. Fuck, what *now*?

I braced myself. This had to be bad. Daniel wasn't a phone call kind of guy. "Hey."

"You asshole," he practically shouted. "Are you screwing my sister?"

Shit, shit, shit. "Let me explain."

"No need. Mom told me everything. You got kicked off the show and you've been with Carla this entire time. Did you think I wouldn't find out?"

I could imagine the expression on his face perfectly: the veins in his neck standing out, a bead of sweat on his forehead, murder in his eyes. I'd seen the same look when some guy had gotten handsy with Carla when she was fifteen. Except back then, I'd had the exact same look on my face too. We'd scared the shit out of the kid, but I'd always considered him lucky that I hadn't torn off his head.

"We were going to tell you." *Eventually*, I silently added.

"When? After you'd ditched her and moved on to the next girl?"

I drew in a sharp breath. "It's not like that."

"No? So tell me what it's like then. You going to marry her?"

"God, no. We're just having fun." Except as soon as I got the words out of my mouth, I wasn't sure they were true anymore.

"Maybe *you* are, but Carla's not like that. You're going to break her heart again, just like you did before." He paused, letting the words sink in. "What, you thought I didn't know about that? I'm not stupid. She was in love with you and you didn't give a damn about her. Why do you think I told you to stay the fuck away from her?"

"You're wrong." My hands gripped the railing, squeezing tighter and tighter. "I care about Carla a lot. I'd never do anything to hurt her."

"Bullshit! If you actually cared about her, you'd end it now before this goes too far. Before she falls in love with you again." His voice shook. I'd never heard him so upset before. "Christ, man. She's my baby sister. You're my best friend. How *could* you?"

I couldn't swallow the guilt clogging my voice. "I'm sorry. I fucked up, okay?"

"Keep your apologies. You broke your promise. You *lied* to me. And when you're gone, I'll be the one taking care of Carla, as usual. So have your fun or whatever the fuck you're doing, then walk away. But you and me? We're done. You're not my brother anymore."

The line went dead.

I swore loudly, then rested my elbows against the railing and covered my face with my hands. Every ugly emotion I could imagine reared up inside me. In one morning, everything had gone to shit. My company was slipping away. My father wouldn't talk to me. My best friend hated me.

The worst part was, everything Daniel had said was true. I'd lied to him and broken my promise. I'd failed to protect Carla and I'd been careless with her heart for the second time. She deserved so much better than me, someone who could give her everything she needed without hesitation, someone who actually believed in love and marriage and happily-ever-afters. That wasn't me. I was only going to hurt her again.

Daniel was right. The best thing I could do for her was end it now—even if it killed me to walk away from her.

I sent my assistant some instructions and then stepped back into the hotel room to begin re-packing my things. Carla stirred, her long, dark limbs stretching out across the duvet. A pang of lust broke through and I debated climbing back into bed, kissing her until I forgot everything that had just happened, but I knew that would only delay the inevitable. I opened up the closet.

"What are you doing?" Carla sat up in bed, her voice still laced with sleep and her hair wild.

I grabbed my bag and yanked it open. "I need to get back to Seattle."

"Now? We have another two days scheduled in New York." Her full lips pulled into a frown. "Is something wrong?"

I tossed my clothes into my bag, not caring if they were folded or not. "I have a company to run. I can't keep trying to escape from my life."

"I understand. But what does that mean for us?"

"It means we had our fun, but this is over now."

She didn't respond, but I could feel her eyes on me. I couldn't look at her face. If I did, I wouldn't be able to finish packing. Fuck, this was hard. But she had to know this was coming, right? Wasn't this what she wanted?

"We both knew this was going to end after we reached New York," I said, but it sounded like I was trying to convince myself too. "The plan was always for us to reach the final destination and then walk away."

She crawled to the edge of the bed, wearing nothing but one of my shirts, the fabric brushing against her thighs. "Maybe the journey doesn't have to end now. We can take another week, go to DC, tour the White House, visit the National Air and Space Museum…"

"I can't. I need to get back." My jaw clenched and I turned away. If I kept staring at her thighs, I'd take back everything I'd just said. "If you're ready to head back too, I can get you a flight to LA. We'll ship the car back. I'll handle everything."

"I'm not ready to go back." She grabbed my hand, trying to pull me back to her. "I don't think you are either."

I held my ground, staring at the door. "It's time to face reality again. This fling, or friends-with-benefits, or whatever the hell we were calling it, was never going to work."

"What if it wasn't a fling? What if it was…more?" She sounded like she was holding her breath. Waiting for my answer.

"It wasn't," I lied.

She stood up, moving in front of me so I couldn't help but look at her. "So now you'll walk away again, like you did before, like none of this meant anything. Like you did with all the other women."

"No." None of this was going the way I'd intended. I took her face in my hands, stroking her lower lip with my thumb. "Things with you were different, Carla. But I can't give you what you want. It's better if we end this now before I hurt you again."

She took my wrists, holding me in place. "I don't want this to end."

I got caught under the spell of her brown eyes and all my resolve crumbled. How could I walk away from the one girl I'd ever cared about? How could I say goodbye to the person I couldn't imagine living without?

A reckless, wild feeling rushed through me and I let it voice the next words. "Then come with me."

She blinked. "To Seattle?"

"My flight leaves in four hours. I can get you a seat beside me in First Class."

Her gaze drifted to my bag. "And then what?"

"Then you stay with me for a few weeks until you figure out your next move. We'll keep having fun until things settle down for you in LA."

Her mouth twisted. "Fun. Right."

"That's all I can offer." This was the best I could do. I couldn't make her any promises. She wanted to extend this thing between us another week, and I was suggesting we take it even further. Hell, I was inviting her to live with me for a while, which I'd never done with any other girl. So why did she look so damn upset?

She turned away from me and grabbed her bag, throwing her stuff inside. She put on some clothes, leaving my discarded shirt on the bed. Then she walked across the room and grabbed the car keys off the table.

"Where are you going?" I asked.

"I'm taking the car for a drive. I need to think."

I crossed my arms. "Fine, it's your car."

She threw her bag over her shoulder and headed for the door. I was suddenly hit with the feeling that this was it. If I didn't do something right now I might never see her again.

I went after her. "Wait."

She turned around. "Don't. I want to be alone right now. I need some space to figure things out on my own."

Dammit. She was right, I had to let her go. "If you want to come to Seattle with me, meet me at the airport in two hours. And if you decide not to join me…" I had to force the next words out. "Then enjoy the car."

I took her face and slanted my mouth across hers in a desperate, rough kiss, aware that it might be the last one. My hands gripped her waist, her fingers tangled in my hair, and a soft moan escaped us both. I kissed her deeper and deeper, like maybe I could show her how much I needed her. Like I could convince her to stay.

She pulled away, her eyes damp. After one long, achingly beautiful look, she walked out the door.

"Carla!" I yelled, but it was too late. The door slammed shut.

I pressed my back against it. For a few minutes I waited, hoping she would come back. Then I picked up my bag, booked a car to the airport, and wondered what the hell I'd just done.

TWENTY-FIVE

Carla

I drove.

North, out of the city, along some route I'd found on my phone and had barely paid attention to before putting it into my GPS. Now the robotic voice told me to turn and I turned, letting everything else fade away except the car and the road. But still, there was no escaping Ryan.

My thoughts couldn't move an inch without bumping into some piece of him. Everything about this car felt like him, even *smelled* like him, and the endless road only reminded me of all our days spent driving together.

Something had changed in him this morning, but I wasn't sure what it was. He'd mentioned needing to get back to his company, but I got the feeling there was more to it than that. His father, maybe? Had he gotten worse? But if that was it, why wouldn't Ryan tell me?

No, it had to be something else. I'd hoped Ryan would open up about it, but he'd kept whatever the problem was locked tight inside him. Then he'd pushed me away, saying it was the end between us, before changing his mind and inviting me back to Seattle with him for a few weeks. Now I wasn't sure what he really wanted at all.

As for me? I wanted to go with him, desperately. It wasn't like I had anything back in LA tying me down there. I could fly with him to Seattle today, and this thing between us wouldn't have to end for another few weeks. Or I could keep driving and let him go back to his life, while I figured out what to do with mine.

The problem was that we didn't really want the same thing. He wanted to keep things casual between us, to keep it "just sex" and nothing more. Maybe he could do that, but I couldn't. He'd offered a few weeks, but I wasn't interested in a relationship with an expiration date. My heart would get broken at some point, why delay the inevitable?

I loved him. So much it made my chest ache at the thought of not being with him anymore. There were a few times over the last couple days where I'd thought maybe he felt the same way for me. I'd planned to tell him how I felt today and suggest we continue our relationship somehow. We were both smart people, we could find a way to make it work no matter the distance or whatever else was in our way.

Now I wasn't sure what he felt. Maybe I was wrong when I'd thought he loved me. After all, my track record in that area wasn't great. I'd believed in love many times before and I'd always gotten burned. By now I should know better than to trust my instincts when it came to relationships.

Everyone said I was too nice, too trusting, too optimistic and naïve. I could only imagine what they'd think of me after this. Poor, sweet Carla, living in her fantasy world, believing Ryan would finally love her after all these years. I'd convinced myself he had changed, but the reality was that Ryan and I would never work. My feelings for him would always be unrequited.

I'd gambled my heart on Ryan again. And I'd lost. Again.

My phone rang and I sighed, but pulled over to answer on the third ring. My brother. "Hi Daniel."

"Hey. Are you okay?"

I wasn't sure how to answer him, but something in his voice made me suspicious. "Why do you ask?"

"Are you with Ryan?"

He knew about us. Thanks a lot, Mom. "No. He's flying back to Seattle."

Daniel exhaled loudly. "Good. You should come home too."

"I'm not ready to come home yet."

"Then go see Mom. You shouldn't be alone right now."

"What are you talking about?"

"After Ryan, you know, dumped you."

"He didn't dump me." Or at least, I didn't think he did. And how would Daniel even know if he had? I sat up straighter, heart pounding. "Oh no. What did you do?"

"I had a talk with Ryan this morning. I told him to end things now before you got hurt."

My hands started shaking and I gripped the steering wheel to keep them steady. "Why would you do that?"

"Carla, don't be mad. I was just looking out for you. You've always had feelings for Ryan, but he isn't the kind of guy who sticks around. That's why I made him swear not to touch you. Not that he listened."

"You *what*? When was this? Before we went on the show?"

"Yeah, before the show. But also when we were younger."

My mouth fell open. When we were younger? So when Ryan rejected me on the beach, it wasn't because he was moving away or anything else, it was because of my *brother*?

Shock gave way to anger, making my voice shrill. "I can't believe you! You have no right to get involved in my love life like that!"

"Of course I do. You're my little sister and he's my best friend." He paused before adding, "Well, former best friend. I'm done with him now. That asshole can't treat my sister like another of his hookups and get away with it."

"Don't blame him for this! It wasn't like that between us at all." I blinked back angry tears. "No wonder he acted all weird this morning. How could you do this to me?"

"I was just trying to protect you!"

"I don't need your fucking protection!"

My yell echoed into the phone and got only silence in response. He was probably too shocked to speak. I never swore, but damn, that felt really good. I was so tired of everyone in my family treating me like the little girl who still had cancer, but that was going to end now. It was time to stand up for myself and go after what I wanted.

I took a long breath and spoke evenly. "I'm a grown woman and who I date is none of your business. If I want to get my heart broken by Ryan, that's my decision. You will stay out of it. Got it?"

"Got it," he said, his voice quiet.

"One more thing. If you throw away your friendship with Ryan, you're a bigger idiot than I thought. No matter what happens between me and him, he's your best friend. No, he's *family*."

I hung up before he could respond. When the phone went blank, I closed my eyes and rested my forehead against the steering wheel. My head spun with everything I'd just learned, but it all made sense now.

Daniel, my own brother, was the reason Ryan had pushed me away all this time, both when I was sixteen and now. I should have realized it all along. Ryan was practically an orphan—after his mother died, his father wanted nothing to do with him anymore, and my family had taken him in. Daniel became like a brother to him, but I became something more.

I wasn't wrong about his feelings for me, I knew that now. He'd confessed the other night that he'd always wanted me. But he hadn't been willing to risk his friendship with Daniel to go after me, not when he'd swore to never touch me. No wonder he'd been so conflicted once we did finally get together. He'd been torn between his duty to my brother and his feelings for me.

I started the car up and made an illegal U-turn at full speed, pushing the car to its limits. I had to get to that airport before it was too late. I wasn't going to let Ryan walk away without telling him how I really felt about him, or explaining that I'd talked to my brother and convinced him to stay out of my love life.

I imagined it in my head as I raced down the highway. It'd be like one of those cheesy movies, where I'd run into the airport shouting Ryan's name. Our eyes would pick each other out of the crowd, and then he'd sweep me off my feet and kiss me. We'd both confess our love and live happily ever after. With a dog, naturally.

A car suddenly cut in front of me, breaking my daydream. I slammed on the brakes to avoid hitting it, my tires shrieking against the pavement.

Something hit me from behind, hard. My head snapped forward. Airbags burst into my face. The Porsche spun out of control. I tried to scream, but couldn't get air in my lungs.

With a loud crash, everything went black.

TWENTY-SIX

Ryan

I waited at the airport as long as I could. I hovered outside the gate until every other person was on the plane and the airline employees threatened to leave without me. I texted Carla, but she didn't answer. I thought about going after her, but she'd asked me to give her some space, and I had to respect her wishes.

The airline employee wrung her hands. "I'm sorry, sir. But we really need to take off."

I glanced around the terminal one final time before turning away. "I'm ready."

I had to accept the truth. She wasn't coming. It was over between us.

―――――

The flight from New York to Seattle was six and a half hours long. I thought about Carla for every single minute of it.

A driver was waiting for me once I landed. He reached to grab my bags, but I'd taken so little with me on the show that all I had with me was a carry-on. I shook my head.

I didn't even register the drive back to my condo. Once I got there, I dropped my bag on the floor in the middle of the entryway. The place was spotless, gleaming white and silver, all hard lines and sharp edges. I'd always liked the modern simplicity of it, but now it looked lifeless. Colorless. It didn't feel like home.

Neither did the city. I moved to the floor-to-ceiling windows and looked out at the night sky, but Seattle had become a stranger to me. I didn't belong here anymore.

If I was honest, the only place that had ever truly felt like home was Los Angeles, and that was only because the people I cared about were there. Carla. Daniel. Even my father.

I'd lost all three of them now. My father was dying and he wouldn't even talk to me. Daniel said he wanted nothing to do with me anymore. And Carla… she'd decided not to come back to Seattle with me. This time, she'd been the one who had walked away.

Losing her was like someone had turned all the lights off. I'd told myself I could go back to my previous life after our time together, but that was impossible. She'd changed me, made me a better man, made me want something more. I should have fought harder for her. I should have told Daniel to mind his own fucking business.

All my life I'd avoided serious attachments. I wasn't an idiot—I knew it was because of my father. Before my mother's death, things had been perfect. My mom was loving, my dad was warm, and we did everything together, just the three of us. But after she died, everything changed. My father began to look at me with disgust and anger. I figured he resented me for surviving the accident, or somehow blamed me for what happened. For years, I convinced myself her death must have been my fault somehow, because why else would he treat me like a stranger after that?

When I was older, I realized that was bullshit. The truth was that he'd fallen apart after losing my mother, the one person he truly cared about in the world. He became a broken man, stuck with a kid he never wanted, forced to work long hours to pay the bills, sucked into a brutal lawsuit that never ended.

I swore to myself I would never let myself become like that. I'd never fall in love, never get married, never open myself up to that kind of heartbreak. I'd already lost enough.

Carla was the only one who'd ever made me want to change my mind. But loving her had always meant losing Daniel, the only brother I'd ever had. When I'd been lost, he'd taken me under his wing. When I'd believed no one would ever accept me, his family had proved me wrong. When I'd felt alone, they'd always been there.

Leave it to me to screw it up and lose them both.

All I had left was my company. For a little while longer, anyway. Fuck, maybe I should give that up too. It'd probably be better off with Slade Industries running it. But then what would I do? Who would I be without my work?

I slammed my palm against the glass. No. I wouldn't give up. I'd never backed down from anything before in my life, why would I start now? I'd told Carla she had to pick herself up when she failed, and now it was time for me to do the same. Starting with Carla. I'd track her down in New York or wherever she was. I'd win her back, somehow. I'd tell her I loved her and couldn't live without her. Then I'd somehow fix everything else.

My phone rang. I stared at Daniel's name on the screen, wondering why he would call me again. Did he want to yell at me some more? Remind me of how I'd had everything for a short while and thrown it all away?

Finally, I answered. "What is it?"

"Carla's in the hospital."

"*What?*" My heart jumped into my throat. Oh fuck, was the cancer back?

"She got in a car accident outside New York."

"Jesus. How bad is it?" I closed my eyes and pressed my head against the glass.

God, not a car accident, please, anything but that. I couldn't handle it, not after my mom. What if I lost Carla too now, *really* lost her? What if she died without ever knowing I loved her?

"I don't know." Daniel sounded stressed. "Mom says she has a concussion, maybe some broken bones. I'm about to get on a flight to New York now."

I grabbed my bag off the floor and headed for the door. "I'm on my way."

Carla

"Ryan…" I coughed. My throat felt like it was full of glass shards. "She's waking up!"

That was my mom. What was my mom doing here? Wait, where was I?

My eyes snapped open to bright lights, mint green walls, and chemical smells that triggered too many bad memories. I was in a hospital. I was sore all over and my left wrist was in a cast. My first thought was that the cancer was back, but no, that wasn't right.

The accident.

I squeezed my eyes shut. I didn't remember everything, but I remembered enough.

I drifted back into sleep. When I opened my eyes again, Mom stood beside the bed, her face paler than usual. "Angel, how are you feeling?"

"Sore," I admitted.

"You were unconscious for a few hours. You have a broken wrist and a concussion. They want to keep you here overnight to do X-rays and make sure there's nothing else wrong." She took my hand, the one not in a cast, and held it tight. "I rushed over as soon as they called me, and Daniel and your father are both on the plane over here now."

"They don't need to do that. I'll be fine."

"They're worried about you. They want to make sure you're okay."

There was no point arguing about it. We were a family of worriers—I knew I'd be on the first flight out if either of them had been in a car accident too.

"What about Ryan?" I asked.

She looked down at our hands. "I don't know. Should I call him?"

I hesitated. "No."

"If you change your mind, let me know." She smiled at me. "I always knew the two of you would be perfect together."

"We're not together, Mom."

She shrugged. "I'm sure he would want to see you anyway."

I wanted to see him too, but not like this. It would only bring back bad memories for him, of his mother's accident and of the previous time I'd been in the hospital. As soon as I got out of here, I'd go after him.

My hospital room had one window and outside it was dark. Probably the middle of the night. I sat up and studied my mom. Her eyes were puffy, her dark curls a bit wild. I wasn't positive, but it looked like her blouse was on inside-out. It was a true sign of how upset she was that she hadn't mentioned my purple hair at all so far.

"How are you doing, Mom? Besides all of this, I mean. Last time we talked you didn't sound very happy."

She forced a smile. "I'm fine, don't you worry about me."

"You're not fine. Is it work? Is it Dad?"

She sighed. "I do miss your father. I wanted to go back to work and have a life again, a career that fulfilled me like my old one did. And I like my new job, I do. But it isn't the same without Henry to share it with."

"So what's the problem?"

She picked at a loose strand on the blanket covering me. "The problem is that he won't move to New York to be with me, and I have to be in New York for the show."

"Can't you work something out?"

"I don't know. Your father... He is very stubborn." She smiled. "But then again, so am I."

"You love each other. You've been married twenty-five years. That must mean something."

"Oh, angel. I wish you were right." She touched my cheek, then touched my curls "Now, tell me why you did this to your beautiful hair."

I sat back and groaned.

———

My mom and I talked for an hour and she caught me up on everything. My Porsche was a mess and she didn't know if it could be fixed. I wasn't sure how to repay Ryan for it, but I'd figure it out somehow. If nothing else, I'd work on the car myself until I got it running again, no matter how long it took.

Road Trip Race had ended, and my mom got the scoop from Giselle that our lesbian biker friends Sally and Judy had won the million dollar prize. I was so happy for them. I didn't even care anymore that I hadn't won. I would always be grateful to the show for bringing me and Ryan together, but I was even happier that we'd gotten kicked off and had spent all those days together, just the two of us.

After we finished talking, I fell back asleep and only woke up when a nurse took me to get X-rayed. When I got back, my brother and my dad were in the room, but there was no sight of my mom. They both looked exhausted after their cross-country flight, but they hugged me and fussed over me anyway, with only a few comments about my hair. I told them a hundred times I was fine.

Then I asked Daniel if I could speak to Dad alone. He nodded and left the room.

"Are you really okay, sweetheart?" Dad asked.

"Yes. The doctor says I'm going to be fine."

"You know I can't help but worry." He sat on the edge of the hospital bed. "What did you want to talk about?"

"Mom."

His shoulders tightened. "What about her?"

"She's miserable, Dad."

"Did she say that?"

"Sort of. She misses you so much. You have to talk to her."

He frowned. "She left me. What am I supposed to do?"

"Fight for her!"

He sighed, folding his hands in his lap. "I only want your mother to be happy. She wanted to move to New York and follow her dream, so I let her go. What else could I do?"

"You can follow her! Let Daniel handle the business for a while. You know he can do it." I grabbed his arm. "Dad, you both love each other. You can't give up on your marriage."

"Look at you, giving me advice." He patted my hand with a smile. "How did you get so smart?"

I smiled at him. "I had the best parents."

He chuckled softly. "All right. I promise I'll talk to her."

"Good."

He kissed my cheek. "You get some rest now."

He left the room, and Daniel came in next. He sat beside me, his eyes dark and brooding as he stared at my cast. "God, Carla. I'm so sorry. This is all my fault."

His voice broke and he looked like he might burst into tears at any second. It shocked me more than anything to see Daniel, my big, tough older brother, reduced to a crying mess over me. I wrapped my arms around his broad shoulders. "No, it's not."

He hugged me back, hard. "Yes, it is. You got in that accident right after we spoke. If I hadn't made you angry…"

"That doesn't make it your fault. Just bad timing."

We broke apart and he sat back, but wouldn't meet my eyes. "About Ryan—"

I held up my uninjured hand to stop whatever he was going to say. "It's fine. Just don't be upset with him. He tried really hard to keep his promise to you."

"I shouldn't have gotten involved. I just didn't want either one of you to get hurt."

"I know." When it came down to it, my brother was just trying to look after the two people he cared about most. Even if he'd gone about it all wrong, I couldn't be mad at him for doing what he thought was best. "It's okay."

He ran an anguished hand over his shaved head. "Was he good to you at least?"

"Yes." I closed my eyes, remembering everything he'd done for me. I missed him so much, it made every ache in my body feel like nothing compared to the pain of losing him.

He cleared his throat. "Do you love him?"

"Yeah. I do."

He nodded slowly, and that was the last we spoke of it.

I didn't know if I would ever be able to get Ryan back, or if he loved me in return. But as soon as I got out of here, I was going after him. Even if he turned me down, at least I would have tried.

Getting into the accident had reminded me that life was too short. I couldn't wait around for things to happen to me—I had to *make* them happen. Not just in my love life, but in every area. After today, I was going to gather up all my shattered dreams and build the life I wanted. With or without Ryan.

TWENTY-EIGHT

Ryan

I rushed through the hospital toward Carla's room, but stopped in my tracks when I saw Daniel outside it. Oh shit.

I'd known he would be here, but I'd been so caught up in worrying about Carla I hadn't thought about how hard it would be to see my best friend again after our fight. He'd called me when Carla got in the accident, but I wasn't sure where we stood with each other. Would he still be pissed? Would he yell at me some more? Or would he treat me like a stranger?

"Ryan," he said, rising to his full height, his eyes hard.

He could try to intimidate me all he wanted, but I wasn't leaving. Not until I saw Carla and told her what I had to say. "Is she okay?"

"Yeah, she's fine."

My breath escaped me in a rush. "Thank god."

We eyed each other for a long moment, but then his face cracked. "Look, man. I'm sorry for what I said."

"I deserved it."

"No, I shouldn't have made you promise me anything to begin with. Who Carla sleeps with is none of my business, even if it's you." He scowled as he said it, like the words left a bad taste in his mouth. "I just wish I'd heard it from you first."

"We were going to tell you as soon as we got back."

His arms crossed over his chest and he looked away. "It's just… It was always the three of us, you know? We did everything together. Then I found out the two of you were keeping this secret from me." He pinned me with his eyes again, eyes that looked so much like Carla's. "We don't keep secrets from each other. You're my *brother*, man."

A hard lump of emotion clogged my throat. "Still?"

"We're family. Nothing will ever change that."

I nodded, my jaw clenching. "I'm sorry. I didn't mean to fuck things up so badly."

He studied me. "You love her?"

I refused to look away. "Yeah. I do."

"For how long?"

"Always."

If that surprised him, he didn't show it. "You promise to treat her well?"

"I swear it."

He poked a finger at my chest. "If you don't, I'll be coming for you. You know that."

"I wouldn't have it any other way."

Daniel nodded. "Then go get her."

I stared at him, speechless.

He clasped me on the shoulder. "She's in there waiting for you. Don't mess it up."

TWENTY-NINE

Carla

The door opened and there, in the doorway, stood Ryan. He looked more worn out than I'd ever seen him before, with messy hair and dark circles under his eyes, and he was still wearing the same clothes as when I'd left the hotel all those hours—days?—ago. But he was *here*.

"Carla." He rushed toward me. The door shut behind him and he grabbed my hand, then lightly touched the one in a cast. "How bad is it?"

"Concussion, broken wrist, bruised ribs, and a whole lot of aches and pains, but otherwise I'm okay. Really." None of that mattered, because I was so happy to see him again. He'd come back for me. He really did care.

"I got here as soon as I could." He sat on the edge of the bed, cradling my hand in his like he worried he might break it. "Seeing you here, like this…" He visibly shuddered and closed his eyes. "It brings back a lot of things I never wanted to relive."

"I'm going to be fine. I promise." I stroked his silky black hair. This had to be so hard on him. "You look tired. Have you slept at all?"

"No. When you didn't show up at the airport, I thought you didn't want to be with me anymore, so I flew to Seattle. Then Daniel called and said you'd been in a car accident and I immediately got on the first flight back to New York."

"I was on my way back to you when I got in the accident. I was going to say yes, that I would go with you to Seattle, that I didn't want this to end."

He looked surprised. "You were?"

"Daniel told me everything, how he made you promise not to get involved with me, and how he called you that morning and told you to end it. I realized you were pushing me away all this time because of him."

"That was partly why, yeah." He glanced at the closed door. "He and I talked in the hallway. I think we're okay now."

"Good. I told him my love life was none of his business." I sat up, adjusting the pillow at my back, trying not to wince. "What was the other reason?"

"I thought I could protect your heart if I kept you at arm's length. I was so scared of hurting you again that all I did was hurt you even more." He drew in a long breath. "Maybe I was trying to protect myself too. After what happened with my parents…"

His face was pained. I traced my fingers along the dark stubble on his jaw. "I understand."

"I tried to convince myself what we had didn't mean anything, but it didn't work. When I went back to my place in Seattle, everything about it seemed wrong. It wasn't my home anymore, because you weren't with me. Even before I knew about the accident, I'd decided to fly back to New York or wherever you were and beg you to take me back. To tell you I wanted to give this relationship thing a try."

My heart was pounding so fast I was sure it would set the monitor off. "I thought you didn't want a serious relationship."

"Before, I didn't. With any other girl, I couldn't. But with you, I can. I will."

His words were like the sun breaking through the clouds after a rainy day. I couldn't contain the smile spreading across my lips. I took his face in my hands and kissed him, feeling his rough stubble against my fingertips and the softness of his mouth against mine. He opened for me with a groan, sliding his arms around my back, kissing me like I was as necessary to him as breathing.

He pulled back, staring into my eyes. "Carla, I love you. I've loved you from the time we were kids and every year since. You've defined the word 'love' for me since I first understood it's meaning."

Happiness filled me with warmth and I pressed soft kisses to his lips, his cheeks, his jaw. This was the opposite of falling in love. This was soaring, floating, *flying* in love. "I've waited so long to hear you say those words."

"It took me far too long to say them."

"I love you too, Ryan." I pressed another kiss to his lips. "I've loved you forever. It's always been you, and only you."

He closed his eyes, like he was soaking my words in. When he opened them again, his face looked more relaxed than I'd ever seen it. "I'm not good at this, but I'll try to be. For you."

"You're doing pretty well so far."

"No. I should have brought you flowers or something. Isn't that what boyfriends do?"

Boyfriend. I liked the sound of that. "I don't need flowers. You've bought me enough already." My spirits sank as I remembered something. "I'm sorry I wrecked the car."

"That's okay. I'll just get you another one."

I laughed softly, but it made my head hurt. "Please don't." I pressed a hand to my forehead. "Ow."

His brow creased in concern. "Do you need anything?"

"No. I'm just ready to go home already." I drew in a long breath. "Speaking of home… I've decided what I'm going to do when I get back to LA."

"Oh?"

"I thought I would look into what classes I'd need to take to apply to graduate school."

"An excellent idea. You might be able to take some of them online this summer."

"Maybe. If not, I'll take some this fall. I'm going to get an apartment with the money we won on the show, and I'll ask my agent to line up some modeling jobs to help pay for it all."

"Or…" He paused. "Maybe we can get an apartment together."

I was pretty sure my heart stopped. Any second now the nurses would come in with one of those defibrillators to revive me. "Together? Does that mean…?"

"I'm moving back to LA. It's time Meta Entertainment opened an office there."

"So you're not selling it to Slade Industries?"

His wry smile was everything. "No. I'm not."

"Oh, thank goodness." I relaxed back against the pillow, weaving my fingers into his. "But what about your father?"

Ryan looked down at our joined hands. "That I don't know."

"You need to fix things with him before it's too late. For yourself, if not for him."

"I'm not sure if things can be fixed, but I'll try. I promise."

THIRTY

Ryan

____

Holy shit. This was the hardest thing I'd ever done. Harder than leaving for college. Harder than facing Daniel after he found out I was screwing his sister. Harder than telling Carla I loved her.

I knocked on the door.

Dolores opened it and gave me a sad, tired smile. "You know he doesn't want to see you."

"Too bad. I'm not leaving 'til I speak with him."

She stepped back, then touched me on the shoulder briefly. "Good luck."

My father was watching TV in the back room, just like he was the last time I'd visited him. This time I grabbed the remote and turned it off, earning an angry look in return. I gave the same look right back at him.

"Dad, I need to talk to you."

"Who do you think you are, walking in here like that?"

"I'm your *son*."

He scowled. "What do you want?"

"I have some things to say to you, and I'm not leaving until I get them all out." I drew in a breath, standing up straighter. "First, I'm not taking over your company. I have my own, and it's pretty damn successful. Mom would be proud of what I've accomplished, even if you'll never be. But that's okay. I don't need your approval anymore. I do what I do because I love it and because I'm good at it."

"You've always done what you want." My father said, waving his hand dismissively. "You never cared about our family's business."

"That's not true. I want it to be successful, even if I'm not the one running it. Which is why I'm going to create an app for your company that I think will bring in more business."

"Great, an app," he said, dripping with sarcasm. "But who the hell's gonna run the place after I'm gone?"

"You're going to give the company to Dolores and her son. They're running it right now anyway."

He sniffed. "They're not blood."

"They're family, and real family has nothing to do with blood. Family is about the people who are there for you, no matter what." Daniel and Carla had taught me that. "Dolores and Jay have been more of a family to you these past few years than I've been. More than that, they want to work there. They'll do a good job with it and I'll help them however I can."

He crossed his arms, staring at the silent TV like I wasn't even there. Damn, this was harder than I'd thought it would be. I pictured Carla giving me a kiss this morning and telling me that I was doing the right thing. Her belief in me was the only thing getting through this. She'd even offered to come with me, but I'd told her I needed to do this on my own.

"Second, I'm not going anywhere. I'm moving back to LA and I'm going to be with you through all of this, right up until the end. You don't want my money or my help? That's fine. You can hate me. You can yell at me. You can ignore me. I don't care. But you're my father and I'm not leaving you."

He looked at me then, his eyes squinting. "You're moving back here?"

"Yes. I already have an apartment." Carla and I had signed the lease last week and we'd already moved most of our stuff in.

He grunted. "About damn time."

It was the closest thing to approval I'd ever gotten from him. "I'm taking you to your next doctor's appointment too."

"Yeah. Fine."

That was it then. My father might never love me or be proud of me, but I was done running away from him. I was going to keep showing up, for however long he had left, because that's what family did. We stuck together.

I headed for the door, but then his voice called me back. "Ryan."

It had been so long since I'd heard him use my name. I turned around, gripping the doorframe for support. "Yeah?"

"I know I was a shit father. After your mother died, I couldn't…" He wouldn't meet my eyes and each word sounded like it was being dragged out of him. "You looked so much like her. Still do." He coughed. "It's good to have you back in town."

The anger on his face had melted away and for the first time in years I saw him, *really* saw him. He was no longer the huge, intimidating man who'd ignored me for most of my life. Nor was he the warm, smiling man from before my mother had died. Instead he looked frail and sad, maybe even a little lonely. Maybe I'd mistaken his disinterest and disgust all these years, never realizing what it truly was: grief.

My chest tightened up and I nodded. It was as much of an apology as I'd ever get out of him, but at least it was something. A step in the right direction. "I'll see you next week."

———

W hen I got back to the apartment I now shared with Carla, I found her sitting on the couch with textbooks spread out all around her. It had only been a month since her car accident, but she'd already started taking some classes at a local community college. I had no doubt she would get through them easily and then she could apply to any graduate school program she wanted.

She looked up at me with a hopeful smile, her hair escaping from its ponytail in an adorably sexy way. "How'd it go?"

"Not too bad, actually. There was no yelling this time, at least."

"Oh, good." She threw her arms around my neck and gave me a quick kiss. I took her chin and held her there longer, taking my time with her lips, before finally releasing her.

"I got something for you."

Her eyebrows shot up. "You did? What is it?"

"Wait here."

I returned to the hallway and opened the kennel to pick up the little guy inside. He licked my hand as I carried him over to Carla. The look on her face when she saw what was in my arms went from curiosity to surprise to absolute delight. Her hands covered her mouth.

"Is that a corgi?" she asked, her voice rising into a high-pitched squeal. "You got me a *corgi puppy*?"

"Rescued him, yes. Can you believe someone turned him in to the shelter because they said he was too much work?" I held the puppy up to her and his big wet nose brushed against her cheek. "You're not too much work, are you little guy?"

She took the tawny-colored dog in her arms. He immediately put his paws on her and covered her face with kisses, which made her giggle uncontrollably. "Oh my goodness. This is the best present I've ever gotten. I love him so much." She looked up at me with shining eyes. "I can't believe you did this for me."

"That night in the forest you said you wanted a corgi. It was the only thing you didn't have yet."

In the last month, Carla's parents had gotten back together, after her dad decided to semi-retire and move to New York. Now Daniel was pretty much running the company. As for her ex-boyfriend, he'd shown up at her dad's shop while we were there one day and begged Carla to take him back. When he'd realized she and I were together, he'd called her a "dirty whore." Really, he'd brought the ball-punching on himself.

She buried her face in the puppy's fur. "I didn't actually expect you to get me all of those things."

I sat beside her on the couch, rubbing the puppy's back. "Maybe not. But I'm madly in love with you and I will never stop trying to give you what you want. I plan to spend the rest of my life making you happy."

"I want you. That's all I need."

"Not a corgi?"

She snuggled up against me, squeezing the dog between us. "Okay, maybe him too."

"Good. Because we've bonded and we're kind of a package deal now."

Her smile was the most beautiful thing I'd ever seen. She was sunshine itself. "So I get to keep you both?"

"As long as you want us."

"How about forever?"

"Forever sounds good to me. Maybe we can even make it official." I reached into my coat pocket and pulled out a small black box. As her eyes widened, I got down on one knee in front of her. "Carla, I love you more than I could ever say. There's nothing I want more in the world than to be with you for the rest of my life. You're my home. My family. Will you marry me?"

She set the puppy down on the couch and pressed her hands to her chest. A tear ran down her cheek but her smile was huge. "Oh, Ryan. Yes, I will marry you. I love you so much."

Overwhelming relief and happiness washed through me. I slid the ring onto her finger. "This ring was my mother's. I know she'd want you to have it."

"Thank you. I love it." She held it up to the light and smiled. Then she practically leaped into my arms, knocking us both down onto the floor. I laughed, wrapping my arms around her, then covered her mouth with mine. We kissed long and deep, until the puppy jumped down and nudged us with his nose. When we broke apart, he climbed all over us, wagging his tail.

I chuckled softly. "I can't tell who's more happy, me or the dog."

Carla giggled. "You know who's *really* going to be happy? My mom."

"She already knows, and yes, she was ecstatic. She's expecting a phone call from you any minute now, I'm sure."

"How does she know?"

"I called to ask for your dad's blessing yesterday. He was also thrilled."

"Of course he was. They both adore you."

I got up and put the puppy back in his kennel, then scooped Carla into my arms, like I'd done in Vegas. "I talked to Daniel too."

Her arms tightened around my neck. "No way. What did he say?"

"That he was glad I would be an official part of the family."

Now she was really crying, but they were happy tears. I kissed them off her cheeks, then carried her into our sparse bedroom. We were still decorating and unpacking, but soon this would be a real home. Once Carla got her master's degree, we'd buy a house and make our family even bigger. I could see it all clearly, like the future was mapped out in front of us.

Everything was changing, but this wasn't the end of our adventure. Love was the ultimate journey, and ours was just beginning.

Bonus Epilogue

I hope you enjoyed More Than Distance! Read on for a bonus epilogue - exclusively in this box set!

———

This scene takes place one year after the end of More Than Distance.

CARLA

Everything was perfect, exactly as I'd planned.

The sun hung right at the horizon, splashing the blue sky with pink, orange, and purple, and the fading light made the waves sparkle as they slowly lapped at the shore. The sand practically glowed under my white rhinestone-covered flip flops, and my thin veil swayed in the cool breeze, which carried the scent of roses, lavender, and lilac from my bouquet. All around me were my favorite people in the world. My friends. My family. Ryan.

He stood in front of me wearing a black tux, looking every inch the perfect combination of rugged masculinity and handsome elegance. Behind him stood Daniel in a matching tux, holding the leash to Bandit, our one-year-old corgi, who calmly sat at our feet with his tongue hanging out. Next to me was Julie, holding a bouquet and wearing an ocean blue dress she'd designed, along with my dress.

"You may now kiss the bride," the officiant said.

Ryan swept me into his arms, then slanted his mouth across mine. A dizzying, bubbly feeling swept through me as he kissed me, while everyone clapped and cheered. But then all of that faded away and it was just me and him, bound together for the rest of our lives.

It was hard to believe that seven years ago we'd stood in this exact spot when he'd kissed me for the first time, or that a year ago we'd almost kissed here before going on the adventure of a lifetime. Now we would forever remember this as the place we'd kissed as husband and wife for the first time.

Bandit barked and we broke apart, laughing. Daniel reached down and pet the dog's head.

"Ready, Mrs. Evans?" Ryan asked, then bent down to sweep me off my feet before I could answer. I wrapped my arms around his neck, while my dress flared out around us. It was off-white and gorgeous—much better than the dress I'd worn when Ryan and I had gone through that fake wedding in Vegas.

"You better not drop me," I said, echoing my words from back then.

"Never."

He carried me down the aisle, his feet sinking into the sand, while people blew bubbles toward us. In the front row, my mother cried happy tears while clutching my dad's arm, and Ryan's stepmother Dolores and her son smiled at us warmly. I knew Ryan was sad that his father had passed away a few months before the wedding, but it was some comfort to know his remaining family was here—and that Ryan had reconciled with his dad before the end.

Behind them sat all our other friends. Gavin, smiling up at his girlfriend Julie, my maid of honor. Jared and Maddie, who had gotten married a few months ago in the wedding of the century, befitting two rock idols. Becca and Andrew, who had their own wedding coming up this winter. Alexis and Kyle, who had run off to Las Vegas and eloped earlier in the year. Tara and Hector, happy and content with their baby. Even Daniel had a new girlfriend sitting in the audience, looking gorgeous and completely smitten with him.

When we reached the end of the aisle, Ryan gave me another kiss, and everyone behind us cheered some more. I gazed up at him, so happy I thought I might burst from it. A year ago I'd sworn my life was falling apart, and now everything was exactly as it should be.

"I can't wait to get you alone." Ryan's voice was low in my ear as he carried me into the nearby tent where I'd gotten ready. "I want to claim my wife in the most primal way possible."

Desire spread through me and I pressed a kiss to his neck. "Tonight."

He made a soft, guttural growl, then set me down in the sand and captured my mouth in a hot, demanding kiss. My fingers wove into his thick black hair, pulling him closer to me, and his hands skimmed all over my dress. He fisted handfuls of fabric and yanked the skirt up to my hips. "How about now?"

"Now? But—"

"I don't want to wait any longer to make you mine."

He grabbed my waist, lifted me up, and set my butt on the edge of a nearby table. With my wedding dress pushed up around my waist, his hands stroked the white garters on my legs, eyeing my thighs with hunger.

My eyes fluttered shut as his mouth went to my neck. "We're supposed to take photos with the wedding party and our family now."

"They can wait." His fingers slipped between my thighs, finding my white lace panties, and yanked them off me. They hit the sand at our feet.

"What if someone walks in?" I asked, as I reached for his black slacks and tugged them open.

"We'll make it fast." One finger slid inside me and he smirked. "You're already wet for me."

"It's the sight of you in this tuxedo." I grabbed the tie at his neck and pulled his body closer, moving him between my legs. We were both still dressed and we didn't have time for foreplay, but we didn't need it. He pushed inside me easily and we both sighed in relief.

"I love you," he said, his voice rough. "I love you so damn much."

"I love you too." I was just as breathless as he was. "Forever."

We clung to each other as he rocked into me, finally joined in every way possible. I dug my fingers in his hair, devouring his mouth while he buried himself deep inside me. Being with him was so right and I knew I'd never stop feeling this way about him. No matter how many years had passed or how much distance we'd put between us, our feelings had never dimmed. And they never would.

The friction between us grew with his deep, fast thrusts, and soon we were both close to the edge. His hands slid under my butt, lifting me off the table, pulling me even harder against him. It was too much, too good, and the orgasm burst out of me, making me tighten up around him. I clung to his shoulders and he came inside me with a low groan, burying his face in my hair.

I pressed my forehead against his as our breathing slowed. He took my face in his hands and kissed me softly. "Forever," he said.

"That was a beautiful wedding—Oh!" Alexis said, behind us. "Sorry! Not looking!"

We broke apart quickly and Ryan zipped up his slacks, while I yanked down my dress. Alexis stood at the entrance to the tent, covering her eyes with her hands. Her camera was around her neck—she'd offered to do all the photos for our wedding for free as a way for her to build her portfolio. Not that she really needed to build it more, with all her photos of Villain Complex and other bands performing and on the road.

"Sorry," Ryan said, with a naughty smirk. "I couldn't resist."

"Of course not. I mean, look at her in that dress." Alexis winked at me. "We're ready for photos by the water whenever you are."

"We'll continue this later," Ryan promised me, before following Alexis out of the tent. I took a moment to check my hair and makeup, then went after them.

———

Hours later, when the sky was black and stars were twinkling overhead, our wedding reception finally began to wind down. We'd taken over this entire section of the beach, with round white tables set up on the sand in front of a stage where Villain Complex had performed a few songs earlier. The cake had been demolished, the bouquet had been tossed, and now a DJ played slow, romantic songs while a few couples swayed across the dance floor.

One of them was Hector and Tara, holding their baby Miguel between them as they danced and smiled at each other. They'd gotten married in a small, casual wedding shortly after they'd announced she was pregnant, and I had a feeling more babies would be on the way soon. On top of that, Tara's TV show had taken off and was now starting its third season.

I crashed next to Julie and Gavin at their table, happy to be off my feet after standing and dancing for hours. They both looked gorgeous in clothes they'd designed themselves, of course. Their fashion empire had completely taken off, and they'd recently hired a huge crew to help them expand their line. They'd even gotten their clothes into Nordstrom and Bloomingdale's, which was a huge success.

"Lovely wedding," Gavin said, raising a glass of champagne with his tattooed hand.

"Thanks." I gave them both a sly grin. "Looks like the two of you are next."

Julie coughed into her champagne. "Just because I caught the bouquet doesn't mean I'm next."

I laughed. "You're the only one of us who hasn't gotten hitched yet. It's your turn!"

Julie shrugged casually. "Not all of us are meant for marriage. We're focused on work right now."

"Is that so?" Gavin asked, arching an eyebrow. "So if I got down on one knee right here and asked you, you'd say no?"

Julie blinked. "I...um..."

"I think you should test this theory," Ryan said, moving behind me. He placed his hands on my shoulders and I reached up and took one with a smile.

"Good idea, mate." Gavin dropped to one knee in the sand, then whipped out a box from his coat jacket. "Julie, love, will you marry me?"

Julie gasped, her eyes widening. "Oh my god! Really? I never expected this!"

Gavin grinned. "I wasn't going to propose tonight, but you look as lovely as ever, the stars are shining, and you caught the bouquet, so it seemed like a sign. Besides, I'm tired of waiting. Let's get married already."

"Yes, of course!" She grabbed him in a hug and then kissed him. "But which one of us is going to design the dress?"

He slid the ring onto her finger. "It'll have to be a collaboration, of course. Everything is better when we do it together."

All of our friends had gathered to watch and now broke out into cheers, clapping loudly. Julie laughed and kissed Gavin again, her eyes wet. I couldn't think of anything better than my best friend getting engaged on my wedding night.

"C'mon, let's grab everyone some champagne," Jared said, draping an arm around Gavin. The guys all went to the bar together, chuckling at something Jared said.

Maddie sank into the chair beside Julie and grabbed her in a tight embrace. I leaned in and wrapped my arms around them both, in one big group hug like we used to have when we were roommates. Our days of college were long over now, but we would always be best friends for the rest of our lives.

"We've come so far in the last two years," Maddie said, wiping at her eyes.

"I know," I said, smiling. "I can't wait to see what happens next."

"Actually, there's something I have to tell you two. I wanted to let my best friends know first. But remember how I told you the band isn't touring this summer and are working on a new album instead? That's only half the truth. The other thing is… I'm pregnant."

"That's wonderful!" I said, hugging her again.

"I knew it!" Julie yelled, with a huge smile. "I thought your champagne glass looked a little too full!"

"Jared's been drinking for the both of us." She smiled as he came up to us with the other guys, who began passing out champagne.

"This calls for a toast," Ryan said, raising his glass. "To new beginnings."

"Here, here," everyone said, toasting each other before taking a sip. Except Maddie, of course. Jared drank hers and downed it with a wink.

I glanced around at all of my friends, every one of us happy and in love. It seemed almost too good to be true. Somehow, against all odds, we'd all found our perfect soul mates, while also going after our dreams. Sure there were bumps along the way, but the road forward looked smooth.

As for me and Ryan? He was finally an official member of my family, much to my mother's delight. My brother seemed pretty happy about it too, surprisingly. Ryan and I were living here in LA while he worked at the new office of Meta Entertainment and planned the launch of an all new game. Meanwhile, I was starting graduate school in the fall to get my engineering degree. We were planning to buy a house next, and soon we'd get to work on adding some *new* members to our family.

I couldn't wait to get started.

More Than Exes

A CHASING THE DREAM PREQUEL STORY

Chapter One

ONE MONTH BEFORE MORE THAN MUSIC

I f there was one thing I'd learned, it was that good guys never got the girl. Even if the good guy was covered in tattoos and piercings and wore an old Joy Division shirt with the sleeves cut off. Nope, the ladies would still recognize him (or in this case, me) for what he was and ditch him for the guy who practically screamed, *I'll break your heart.* Usually that guy was my brother, Jared.

My Saturday night had just begun, and I'd already had the lesson drilled into my head. We'd unloaded all our gear and stashed it backstage but had hours to spare before we were scheduled to go on. It seemed pointless to arrive at the club so early, but the organizers of the UCLA vs. USC Battle of the Bands had told us to show up at 6:30 PM, and Jared would sooner slit his wrists than be late.

With so much downtime before our 10:30 PM set, I headed for the bar to grab us a couple of beers. On the Rocks was a small club in Hollywood that held a few hundred people. The place was almost empty now, but we were the last band to perform and I figured it would fill up by then. The few who'd arrived early stood around in the big, dark room either at the bar along the back wall or in front of the small stage where the first band was setting up. I didn't recognize them, so they must have been from USC.

At the bar, a girl with a red plastic cup in each hand nearly crashed into me. She took a quick step back, but one of the drinks slipped from her grasp. I managed to catch it without even a spill. Not bad, if I said so myself.

"Wow, great save," she said, taking the drink from me. "Thanks."

"No problem. Sorry I almost knocked you over."

"Totally my fault." She looked me up and down, checking out the ink on my arms. "Hey, you look familiar."

The girl was hot, with bleached hair and a low-cut, black dress showing off a small butterfly tattoo between her breasts. Definitely my type. I didn't want to get too excited, but damn, it had been way too long since I'd gotten laid. Or gone out with anyone. Tonight might finally be my lucky night.

"Do you go to UCLA?" I asked. I didn't recognize her, but it was a pretty safe bet most people at the show either went to my school or to our rival. "Maybe we have a class together."

"I do." She cocked her head and studied me again. "Are you in Villain Complex?"

A fan of the band? This was getting better and better. "Yeah. I play keyboard."

"That's how I know you!" She laughed a little, and her chest bounced, making it look like the butterfly was flapping its wings. *Must not stare, must not stare.* "I saw you play last week at that parking lot show. You guys were amazing! I went home and bought all your songs from your website."

"Thanks." I offered her my hand and smiled. "My name's Kyle, by the way."

She juggled the drinks into one hand and slipped the other into mine. "Tiffany."

She liked our band, she seemed interested in me, but now what? I couldn't offer to buy her a drink since she had two already. Why did she have two? Was she going to meet someone? No, she was giving off that single vibe so probably here with a friend. I needed to make a move but had to keep it cool, too. *Think, think, think.* Man, I sucked at this pick-up-line stuff. Oh, I could ask her about her major. That was always a pretty safe bet.

Before I got the chance, she asked, "So I guess you know Jared Cross?"

And just like that, any hope I had of getting some action suffered a swift and violent death. *Womp womp.* "Yeah. He's my brother."

"Really?" She glanced around, like she hoped Jared would pop out from behind me. I could tell the second she saw him because her breath got fluttery and her cheeks turned pink. What was he doing? Serenading random strangers with his shirt off? It wouldn't be the first time.

I turned and spotted him leaning against the wall, talking to our drummer, Hector. Not half-naked, thank god, but even fully clothed Jared had this crazy effect on women. As if to prove my point, he looked over and gave us that lazy smile that girls could never resist. And then, to top it off, he winked.

I hated it when he winked.

I rolled my eyes and turned back to Tiffany, but she was a goner already. She made a little sound like a gasp, and her eyes flitted back to me. "Could you introduce me?"

I should have seen this coming. Why would I think she would ever be interested in me when my stupid brother was only feet away? I didn't get it. We shared a lot of the same DNA, but I must have been missing the "come-hither" gene. Even though Jared looked like a toned-down version of me—fewer tattoos, natural hair color, and no piercings—girls somehow had this radar that honed in on him. It's like as soon as they heard him sing they decided, *Yes, this guy is trouble. I must go after him.* And they all thought they could fix him, like they'd be the one girl who could make him settle down and change his ways.

Keep dreaming, ladies. I guaranteed that tomorrow morning I'd be patting Tiffany —or some other girl—on the back as I walked her to her car and wished her a nice life. Jared didn't do relationships, and no girl was going to "fix" him because he wasn't broken. He just liked women. Lots of women. All the time.

Like I said: good guys never got the girl.

I'd already lost Tiffany's interest. No point in continuing with this. I led her over to Jared, who raised his eyebrows at us, and Hector, who shook his head like he knew where this was going already.

"Jared, this is Tiffany. She's a fan of the band and wanted to meet you." My voice sounded flat, but then, I'd given this speech quite a few times before.

My brother flashed that same annoying smile, the one he only used when he was on stage or flirting with someone. "Nice to meet you, Tiffany. Thanks for coming to the show."

I turned away—I didn't need to see or hear the next part—but I still caught Tiffany saying, "I love your band *so* much. Here, I got you a beer."

So that's why she had two drinks. I'd never stood a chance. Rejection always sucked, but being passed up for your older, better-looking, more talented brother every single time?

Yeah, that got old real fast.

Hector joined me as I made my way back to the bar. He was perpetually single, too, so at least we could stick together and roll our eyes at Jared and his harem of groupies.

"He's starting early, I see," Hector said.

"He probably figures he can hook up with this one now and then find a second girl for later." I kicked at a plastic cup on the floor. Bitter? Me? No, definitely not.

"That must be it." We ordered two beers, and then Hector turned to me. "Where's Becca?"

"She was supposed to meet us here at 6:30." I checked the time on my phone. 7:00 PM. "She must be running late. I'll text her."

"She better not bail on us," Hector said, removing his Villain Complex baseball cap and then shoving it back over his dark mop of curly hair. He always did that when he was stressed or pissed about something. Hector had been Jared's best friend since high school, and he'd become almost like a second brother to me over the years. It was usually my job to calm him down when he got like this.

"She wouldn't do that," I said. "Don't worry. She'll be here."

"I don't know, man. She's been acting weird."

Now that he mentioned it, Becca had been late to practice all week, and she'd seemed especially moody, too. But Becca was often like that. She'd never taken our practices as seriously as the rest of us did, so I figured she'd been having an especially bad week.

Becca was the latest in a long string of short-term bassists. She'd joined the band a couple months ago after Jared met her at a party. We'd lost our previous bassist when Jared had kicked him out of the band for stealing money from us to buy meth. So far we hadn't had too many problems with Becca, and I'd hoped that our bad luck was over.

I sent her a text asking if she was almost here and took a sip of my beer. "I'm sure she's on her way. There's plenty of time before our set."

The first USC band started playing, but the singer shrieked like a parrot being strangled and the rest of the band sounded like they'd learned how to play their instruments a week ago. The feedback blasting through the speakers was the best part of the song.

"My ears are bleeding," I yelled at Hector over the noise. "Make it stop."

"It's not that bad," Hector said, but he cringed when the drummer dropped one of his sticks and had to stop playing to pick it up. "Nope, I take that back."

"I don't know if I'll be able to get through all fifteen minutes of their set without my head exploding."

"Let's pray the other USC bands are as bad as they are." He gestured across the room with his beer. "I'm going to say hi to the guys from Twisted Regime. I'll catch up with you later."

He took off toward one of the UCLA bands we often played with, and I decided I'd had enough of this torture. I walked past Jared, who was still leaning against the wall, now with Tiffany pressed against him. He held the drink she'd given him in one hand and trailed the other up and down her back. She tilted her head up and said something that made him grin, and then he kissed her right there in front of me.

Ugh. My brother always worked fast, but it'd be nice if I didn't have to see it all the damn time. The worst part was there were other girls hovering nearby, hoping for their chance with him soon. Hello, I was right there and available. But no one looked at me as I brushed past them and through the door.

It wasn't much quieter backstage, and worse, it reeked of piss, weed, and cheap cologne. The area was tiny—little more than a hallway, really—and filled to the brim with the other bands standing around waiting for their sets. Graffiti had been scrawled across every inch of the walls underneath faded and ripped posters of bands like Bad Religion and the Sex Pistols. Dim lighting barely concealed the empty plastic cups, used ticket stubs, and god only knew what else that littered the floor.

I slipped off to a corner to sip my beer in peace and check out our competition. Tonight four bands from each college would compete against each other to win a $1,000 prize and a gig next month at a bigger club on Hollywood Boulevard, along with a $1,000 donation to the winning college's music program. USC had won the last two years, so the pressure was on for us to end their streak. Not to mention, we really wanted that gig. This was our chance to finally break out, to move beyond playing frat house parties and underground shows in the UCLA parking lot.

One band stood out from the others in pastel-colored shirts, khaki shorts, and shoes that looked more suited to taking daddy's boat for a spin than going to a club like this. With their frat boy looks and entitled smiles, I could almost guarantee they were from USC, and in the middle of them was Todd, another one of our former bassists.

Had Todd joined a new band? He went to USC so it was possible, but I couldn't imagine anyone actually putting up with the guy. Maybe he'd only recently joined and his bandmates hadn't yet realized what a dick he was. They'd find out soon enough like we had.

A girl showed up and started talking to Todd with one hand on her hip, her long, bright-red hair trailing down her back. Not natural red, but Starburst red.

Hot Tamale red. Like candy I'd like to take a bite of. She had her back to me but wore a black leather jacket and jeans tight enough to show off her perfect ass. She tucked her hair behind her ear, and I caught a glimpse of a tattoo on her wrist. Hot. Too bad she was with Todd.

She raised a professional-looking camera and peered through it, taking shots of Todd's band. Maybe she wasn't actually with him, but a photographer for the show. My theory seemed to be confirmed when she turned to snap a few photos of the chaos around us.

I kept my eyes on her as she moved through the crowd, trying to get a glimpse of her face. But when she lowered her camera, the entire world stopped.

I recognized her.

I hadn't seen her in years and she looked completely different now, but I'd know that face anywhere. Those bright green eyes, those lush red lips, that smooth pale skin with the hint of freckles across her tiny nose. The girl I would never forget, the girl I could never get over.

Alexis Monroe.

Chapter Two

What was Alexis doing here? She was supposed to be at Princeton, not here in LA and definitely not at our show tonight. Maybe she was with Todd's band. He was exactly her kind of guy, living off daddy's money and taking the private jet on vacations. But still, it was Todd. I thought she had better taste than that.

For a split-second, I debated whether I could duck out or hide or something, but she paused with her camera half-raised to her face, her eyes wide and her lips parted. She'd seen me. It was too late to escape.

We stared at each other for the longest minute of my life. She looked so different it was hard to believe it was actually her. Gone was her preppy image, with the stuffy cardigans and sensible shoes. In her leather jacket and studded boots, she looked like she belonged with our band, not Todd's. And her hair…it had always been red, but when we were in high school, it had been natural red. A soft ginger color. Copper and bronze. The color of the sun as it set over the horizon. I'd spent hours running my fingers through it and watching the strands glow as the light hit them. Now it was Maraschino cherry red, but still just as beautiful.

And that was definitely a tattoo on her wrist, though I couldn't tell what it was from this distance. She'd told me she would never get another tattoo, not after the ones we'd gotten together. What had changed in the past three years?

Of course, I looked different, too. My hair was dyed black now and longer, with an annoying tendency to fall in my eyes instead of sticking up like Jared's did. I'd added round black gauges to my ears, and I had more tattoos—not just on my arms, but across my chest, up my neck, and down my fingers. We'd both changed. My change just hadn't been quite as dramatic as hers because I'd already been halfway there when we'd broken up. Hell, that was one of the reasons she'd dumped me: that we were too different from each other and I wouldn't fit in with her new Princeton lifestyle. Kind of ironic that she had now fallen to the dark side herself.

Everything else faded away until it was only Alexis and me and all of our history stretching between us. Memories flashed through my mind like a slideshow. The first time we'd talked in tenth grade English class, when I'd finally worked up the courage to say hello to the girl so completely out of my league. The first time we'd kissed, in front of my piano after I'd tried—and failed—to teach her to play it. The first time we'd had sex, in her room surrounded by pink walls while her parents were out of town. Sneaking out to concerts using fake IDs. Practicing with the band while she watched and did her homework. Studying for the SATs together. Prom night. And finally, graduation—the last time I'd seen her.

What was I supposed to do? Walk over and say, *Hey, how's it going? How have you been since you ripped out my heart, tore it into a thousand pieces, and stomped all over it?* I could ignore her and walk away before things got weird, try to avoid her for the rest of the night. No, hiding would seem weak, like I wasn't over her or something. That was out, which meant I had to man up and talk to her.

I pushed off the wall and made my way through the throng of people, and she ditched Todd's band to meet me halfway. She stood a little straighter as I neared but was still a few inches shorter than me. The perfect height for our bodies to fit together. I moved to hug her, either out of habit or because it seemed the natural thing to do, but I shoved my hands in my pockets instead.

"Alexis," I said. "Long time, no see."

"Kyle," she said, in that breathy voice I knew too well, the one she used when she was excited. I'd heard her say my name like that many times—along with, *Oh god* and *Don't stop* and *Yes!*

I quickly pushed those memories aside. Thinking about Alexis like that would get me both turned on and depressed, and that combo couldn't lead to anything good. Especially since her body was as amazing as I remembered, with large, round breasts and curvy hips I wanted to run my hands over. I tried not to stare, but she gave me a dazzling smile that reeled me back in.

"It's so good to see you," she said, and I could tell from the way her face lit up that she meant it.

"What are you doing in LA? I thought you were at Princeton."

"I was for the first two years, but I transferred to USC for my junior year."

She'd been back in LA for months and hadn't contacted me all this time? I wasn't surprised exactly. She'd made it clear that we were done and she wanted nothing to do with me. But it still hurt a little.

I started to ask her why she'd come back to LA, but then it would seem like I cared and I didn't want that. "You look different. Your hair…I like it."

"Oh, thanks," she said, smoothing a loose curl. "My parents hate it."

"I bet."

"You look different, too. The hair, your tattoos…" Her lips quirked up, and her gaze traveled below my waist and then back to my face. "You look really good."

There went my plan of not getting turned on. I coughed and adjusted my weight, trying to hide the growing bulge in my jeans. "What are you doing here tonight?"

"I'm taking photos for the school paper." She gestured behind her at Todd and his friends, who were chugging drinks and pumping their fists like they were at a football game.

"You know those guys?" I asked, hoping she'd say no.

"Yep, they're one of the USC bands. Rubber Horse."

I cringed. Their name was an obvious play not just on the USC mascot, but also the condom brand and the Trojan horse from myth. Exactly the kind of thing Todd would choose.

"I didn't know you were going to be here," Alexis blurted out. "I didn't see Cross Paths listed on the lineup."

Wow, I'd forgotten how bad our original band name had been, back when Jared and I were dumb kids who thought using our last name was a good idea. "We're called Villain Complex now."

Her head tilted as she considered it. "Villain Complex.... I like it."

"Jared came up with it."

"Why am I not surprised?" She laughed. "How's he doing? Is he here? And Hector?"

"They're both by the bar. They're…good." I tried to think of what else I could say about them. When you haven't seen someone in years, it's hard to know how much info to give about everything they'd missed. "Jared graduated last year, and now he manages the band and works as a bartender. Hector finished art school and has a graphic novel coming out later this month."

"That's great. I'd love to see them again."

"Um, that might not be such a good idea."

"Oh…" Her face fell, her smile vanishing. "They probably hate me, huh?"

"They're…not your biggest fans, no."

"I guess I understand that." She took a step closer, looking up at me with hopeful eyes. "What about you? Do you hate me, Kyle?"

She smelled faintly of strawberries, and I had to look away before I did something stupid—like kiss her or push her away, I wasn't sure which. Did I hate her? Maybe once, but the anger was long gone now. After I'd started college, I'd moved on and tried to forget her. I thought I'd succeeded, too, until tonight. Now all the old scabs had fallen off and started bleeding again.

"No, I don't hate you."

She exhaled in a rush. "Good. Because I was hoping we could get a drink and catch up."

A part of me jumped to say yes, but I forced it down. I needed this conversation to end so I could escape and then avoid her for the rest of the night. The longer I was in her presence, the more I ached to touch her, the more I remembered how good she'd felt in my arms, the more I wanted to kiss her again. The nostalgia for what we'd once had was so strong it was almost crippling.

"Look, Alexis, I…" I trailed off, trying to find the right words. "It's just not a good idea. I'm sorry. But it was good to see you again. Really."

A flash of pain crossed her face. "Oh. Okay. Yeah. Maybe some other time."

The look in her eyes as I walked away made me feel like a total ass, but what else could I do? Spending even these few minutes with her had been torture. There were too many memories between us, both good and bad, and I didn't need to relive them again. Three years ago, I'd have done anything to make it work with her, even long distance, but she'd said no. I'd wanted forever, but she'd told me it was over, that she didn't love me anymore, that she was too good for someone like me.

And no matter how different she seemed or how hurt she looked, when she rejoined Todd and his friends I knew nothing had changed.

Chapter Three

I finished my beer outside in the parking lot behind the club. It was quiet there or as quiet as it could be with the sounds of traffic and palm trees crashing in the wind. The Santa Anas were kicking up again tonight, drying out my eyes with warm gusts that blew trash everywhere. Still, it was better than being inside where my options were to listen to that band butcher their instruments, watch Jared make out with someone, or talk to my ex-girlfriend. I couldn't stay outside all night, but this seemed the safest way to avoid Alexis for as long as possible.

I kept picturing her face when I'd turned her down, how vulnerable and hurt she'd looked. Maybe I'd made a mistake saying no so fast. Her sudden appearance had completely thrown me off and scrambled my brain, and even now I could barely accept that she was really here. I just needed some time to process that she was back in my life. Once the shock of it wore off, I could figure out what to do about her.

Besides, I had bigger things to worry about. It was 7:25 PM, and Becca hadn't texted me back or arrived yet. I tried calling her, but it went straight to voicemail. I hung up without leaving a message. Where the hell was she? We still had three hours before our set, but I was starting to get a bad feeling. I texted her again, just in case.

The back door banged open, and Todd came through, followed by his other band members. I turned in the opposite direction and played on my phone, hoping they wouldn't bother me.

"I thought I saw you in there, emo boy," Todd said with that shit-eating grin that never left his face. "Don't tell me your band actually got into this thing?"

I took a deep breath, trying not to let him get to me. "Top spot for UCLA, actually. You?"

"Same, for USC."

Each band had been ranked by the Battle of the Band organizers based on talent and popularity, with the top band from each school playing at the end of the night when there would be more people to vote for the winner. Todd's band must be pretty good to get the highest ranking for USC. Then again, based on that other band I'd just heard, maybe not.

"Where's Jared?" Todd asked. "I know you never go anywhere without your big brother's permission."

"Hilarious." I gestured at his entourage. "How'd you convince these guys to play with you? Did you have to pay them?"

"I got my own band together after I left yours. Turns out I was better off without you losers holding me back." He laughed, and his cronies behind him joined in with identical chortles. I wanted to punch each of them in the face to wipe off those arrogant smirks.

"After you *left*? More like after we kicked you out."

We'd tried to work with Todd—we really had. He was a good bassist, but after a few weeks, we'd all had it with his entitled attitude and dickish behavior so Jared got rid of him before things escalated. Good thing, too, because I doubted Hector could have refrained from bashing his head in much longer. Really, Todd should be thanking us.

"Do you even have a bassist now?" Todd asked. "I heard you've gone through a bunch since me. Guess I'm a tough act to follow, huh?"

"We have one. She's better than you, actually."

"A chick? Let me guess, Jared's screwing her on the side, too?" He made exaggerated humping motions, and all the other guys joined in, adding sounds to go with their movements. In case anyone around us had missed what huge douchebags they were. I felt dirty just standing near them.

"Real classy," I said. "And no. He's a professional. But you wouldn't know anything about that, obviously."

Hector walked out before Todd could piss me off any further. He quickly sized up what was going on and moved to my side, crossing his arms. "Hello, Todd."

He smirked. "Hey, *amigo*. Good to see they haven't shipped you back to Mexico yet."

Every muscle in Hector's body tensed. "What the fuck did you just say to me?"

Wow, I'd thought I couldn't hate Todd any more, but he'd just proven me wrong. It wasn't the first comment he'd made like that—once he'd asked Hector if he had swam here from Mexico—but it shocked me every time. This one was especially bad, though, because Hector's parents had been deported when he was a kid, leaving him with his grandmother and his three little sisters. I doubted Todd knew that, but that didn't excuse him being a racist shit.

He was an idiot if he wanted to mess with Hector, even with his three friends at his back. Hector worked out a ton to keep up his stamina for shows, and he'd been in plenty of fights before. He could probably take all four of these guys and not even break a sweat.

"Just messing with you, bro." Todd did that arrogant laugh again. This time his friends didn't join in.

Hector's hands clenched into fists, and a vein in his neck throbbed. I was tempted to let him knock Todd out—hell, I was pretty close to joining in myself—

but we couldn't afford to get in a fight and risk getting kicked out of the competition.

I put a hand on Hector's shoulder. "Let's go inside."

"Yeah, run back to big brother!" Todd called as we headed for the door. Hector stiffened and I thought he would turn back, but he shook it off and we made it inside without throwing any punches.

"I hate that guy," Hector muttered.

"Who doesn't? Todd wins Asshole of the Year every year. Don't let him get to you."

We returned to the main room where our friends, Twisted Regime, were on stage doing an AFI cover. I didn't see Alexis anywhere. Not that I was looking for her.

Okay, I was totally looking for her. But only so I could avoid her. That was it. Really.

I checked my phone again. Still nothing from Becca. I sent her yet another text, this time with a lot of exclamation points, but I didn't think that would get answered, either.

Jared joined us, and I was relieved to see he was alone. "Is Becca here?"

"I tried calling and texting, but she won't answer," I said.

"Shit." Jared ran a hand through his spiked-up hair, stress starting to peek through on his face. He was good at keeping it hidden, but I knew what to look for. "She knows how important this show is. She's coming, right?"

"She's probably running late." I didn't believe that, but I didn't want Jared to freak out. I quickly changed the subject. "Todd's here, though, with a new band. They've got the top spot for USC."

Jared's eyebrows shot up. "Who did he blow to get that?"

"Who knows? Probably paid someone off. Hector nearly took his head off outside."

"I'm sure he deserved it."

"Damn straight," Hector said.

"Oh, he did," I said. "He made another racist comment to Hector and said you were screwing Becca. What a jackass."

Jared coughed. "He said that?"

"Yeah." I rolled my eyes, but something about Jared's expression made me pause. He looked almost…guilty. "Oh, hell no. Don't tell me he's right?"

"I'm not *screwing* her…" He trailed off and rubbed the back of his neck.

I finished the sentence for him as it all came together in my head. "But you did."

It wasn't a question, and yet I hoped he would deny it. Every part of me wanted to believe my brother wouldn't be stupid enough to hook up with Becca, not when we'd finally found a good bassist, scored a decent gig, and had a shot at winning an even better one. But he looked away, and I knew the answer.

That's it. I was going to kill my brother.

"What the fuck, Jared?" Hector asked, echoing my thoughts exactly.

He held up his hands in surrender. "It was last week, after the parking lot show.

We were drunk, she started taking her clothes off, one thing led to another.... I didn't mean for it to happen, I swear."

"That doesn't make it okay!" I couldn't believe he'd do this. Yes, Jared got around, and yes, it had been obvious to everyone that Becca wanted him. But the band *always* came first to Jared, and he must have known this would only mess things up.

"It was a stupid mistake, and we both agreed it was just a dumb hook-up and didn't mean anything. I thought she was fine with it. But at that party last night, she caught me making out with another girl and nearly took my head off, so I guess she's not as fine with it as she said."

"You think?" I snapped. No wonder Becca hadn't shown up.

"I'm sorry, okay? I didn't think it would be a problem."

Hector glared at him. "No because you never think with anything other than your dick."

Jared frowned but didn't answer. Probably because he knew Hector was right. I rubbed my face, trying to wipe all of this away. How was I going to fix this?

"If Becca doesn't show up soon, we're fucked," Hector said.

Jared sighed. "I'd call her, but I doubt she'd listen to me."

"Let me handle it." I wanted to strangle my brother, but that wouldn't solve anything. He'd gotten us into this mess, and as usual, it was my job to get us out of it. I checked my phone. 7:40 PM. Only a few hours to find Becca before our set. I had to try. "Any idea where she is right now?"

"No clue. You could try her apartment, I guess."

"Where is it?"

He gave me the address, and I put it into my phone. Luckily she lived fairly close. As long as traffic wasn't too bad, I'd make it back with plenty of time to spare. Assuming she was at her apartment. If not, we were screwed.

"I'll go with you," Hector said.

"No, stay with Jared. If I run late, you two will have to set up all our gear. And if she does show up while I'm gone, you might need to stop them from killing each other."

Hector grunted. "Fine."

I held out my hand. "Keys."

Jared reluctantly dropped the keys in my palm. "Maybe I should go..." He didn't like anyone else driving the band's van, but tough shit.

"Hell no. You've done enough. Just stay here and try not to piss anyone else off." I gave Hector a look that I hoped conveyed, *Keep him out of trouble.* He nodded, so he must have gotten the gist.

I fumed the entire way to the van. How could Jared do this to us? How could Becca? I was pissed at my brother, but she was partly to blame, too. They both must have known what a bad idea sleeping together was at the time. I didn't care how drunk or horny they'd been; they should have thought about how this would affect the rest of us. But clearly they hadn't, and now I was cleaning up after my brother once again. Not exactly how I wanted to spend my Saturday night.

At least it got me out of having to avoid Alexis for the next hour or so.

I got in the van and put the key in the ignition, but when I turned it, nothing happened. What the...? I tried it again, and this time got a few pathetic noises from it but not much else. This must be a mistake. The van had worked fine when we'd arrived. I checked the dashboard but didn't see any warning lights, and we still had gas. It *should* work. I tried again. And again. Still nothing. Dammit!

I banged on the steering wheel, accidentally honking the horn. Could this night get *any* worse?

"Car trouble?" Alexis asked from outside my window.

And just like that, it did.

Chapter Four

I'd been so distracted trying to get the van to start I must not have noticed her approach. She leaned through the window to glance at the dashboard, giving me a glimpse down her shirt. "Need some help?"

I tilted my head back and closed my eyes, trying to block out the image of her impressive cleavage. That was the last thing I needed to deal with right now. Maybe if I waited a minute, everything would be fixed when I opened my eyes. The van would work, and Alexis would be gone. Or, even better, Becca would be standing there instead of Alexis. I held my breath and waited for a miracle.

"Where are you going, anyway?" she asked. "Aren't you on soon?"

She was still there. The eyes-closed plan was a total fail. Damn.

"Not until 10:30. Our bassist is missing and I need to track her down, but our fucking van won't start."

I tried it again, hoping the fifth time would be the charm, but it just made that pathetic sound. I considered popping the hood and checking the engine, but I'd have no clue what to look for. Cars weren't my thing, and Jared and Hector were just as useless with them as I was.

"I don't suppose you picked up anything about fixing cars at Princeton?" I asked.

"No. But I could drive you."

I'd been avoiding looking at her as much as possible, but now my gaze snapped to her face. "Don't you have work to do here?"

She shrugged and tossed back a lock of her fiery hair, revealing a view of her graceful neck. "I have all the photos I need for the moment. I'm just waiting around until Rubber Horse goes on stage. We should be back by then, right?"

"We better be. We're on right after them."

I tapped my fingers on the steering wheel and tried to think of some other option. I could call AAA, but it would take them too long to get here and they'd probably want to tow the van to a mechanic, anyway. Public transportation in LA was such a joke I'd never get to Becca's place and back in time. If there was anyone else I could ask for help, I would have, but Alexis was my only hope. Still, I hesitated. I wasn't sure I wanted to be alone in a car with her. I had a feeling if I did this I'd be starting down a path I wasn't sure I wanted to travel.

I wracked my brain for any other solution, but in the end, it was my only option. "Are you sure?" I asked, giving her one last chance to change her mind.

"I'm sure." She laid her red-tipped fingers on my arm, over my phoenix tattoo. "I want to help you."

I swallowed as heat rushed through me, like she'd ignited the inked flames she was touching, and hopped out of the van. "Okay. Thanks."

"My car's over here," she said, leading me to the other side of the parking lot.

"The same one as before?" We'd spent so much time in that old Mercedes back in high school. Truth be told, I was kind of excited to see it again.

"No, that one died a year ago. I have a MINI now."

"Too bad. We had some good memories in that car."

"We did." She gave me a sly smile. "Some *very* good memories in the backseat."

I coughed and tried to steer the conversation back to something less dangerous, but all I could think about was when we'd been together. "Remember that time we got lost on our way home from a concert in Pomona? And we ran out of gas in a shady part of LA and had to wait for Jared to come get us?"

"I remember. I was scared we were going to get carjacked, so you helped… distract me." She met my eyes. "You were so very good at distracting me."

Suddenly, all I could think about was how I'd like to distract her now. First, I'd tangle my fingers in that long, thick hair, getting a good hold of it. Then I'd tilt her head back so I could press my lips to her neck, to that spot just below her ear. She'd moan my name, and I'd work my way down, lower and lower, dipping inside the V of her shirt to taste every inch of skin I'd seen earlier. She'd reach for the front of my jeans and—

Whoa there. None of those things could happen. I could not get involved with Alexis again, and the only way I'd get through the night was to banish those thoughts entirely. Why was she even bringing all of that up again? Earlier she'd mentioned wanting to catch up, and now she was flat-out hitting on me. Did she want to get back together or something?

We stopped at a black MINI Cooper with white racing stripes across the hood. Not a car I'd ever picture her driving. Hmm, maybe she *had* changed.

"Nice car," I said. "Not much room in the backseat, though." Wait, why had I said that? It's like I couldn't stop myself from flirting with her, either.

"I bet we could still fit."

Her eyes swept over me again, and it took all my energy not to press her back against the side of the car and devour her. I was so, so tempted to make a move, even though it was a terrible idea. Being around Alexis was causing my brain to not function properly. I wanted to blame my growing hard-on for rendering me stupid, but that wasn't the entire reason. All the memories of being with Alexis, combined with seeing her again, were turning me into a sentimental fool.

I cleared my throat and tore my gaze away. "Let's just find Becca, okay?"

"Sure," she said, but she sounded disappointed. Hell, I was, too. I wished I was more like Jared and could do random, meaningless hook-ups, but that wasn't me. If I got a taste of Alexis, I would only want more and more. I had to stop this now before it went any further.

Once in the car, I pulled up the directions on my phone, and we drove out of the parking lot in silence, save for the perky, robotic voice of the GPS. I tried to picture the most disgusting things I could to calm my raging sex drive. Dead cockroaches. Moldy sandwiches. Old people in hospital gowns.

"So…how have you been?" she asked.

Did she actually care or was she making small talk to pass the time? When someone asked a question like that, they never wanted a real response. They just wanted to hear that you were fine. I didn't know what to tell her.

She glanced at my face and laughed.

"What?" I asked.

"I know that look."

"What look?"

"That one where you're trying to figure me out. It's just a simple question, Kyle."

Simple. Sure. Let's see, last time we'd spoken she'd broken up with me and moved across the country, taking my heart with her and turning me into a puzzle with pieces missing. Since then, I'd gone to UCLA, dated a couple girls I could barely remember, and drowned myself in the band with Jared and Hector. And somewhere along the way, I'd tried to find another girl to replace Alexis and failed over and over again.

But I just said, "I've been good. You?"

"Me too. I guess. Princeton wasn't really my scene. Too stuffy and uptight. Too much like my parents."

"Sounds familiar…"

"Yeah, yeah, you told me so and all that. I knew it would be like that, but I didn't realize just how much I would hate it. Or how much I would miss LA." She glanced at me, long and full of meaning, like I was a part of what she'd missed. "I'm still glad I went, though. It made me realize who I really was—and how much I wasn't like those people."

"That explains the new look."

She dressed now like she had when she'd sneaked out with me on dates. She'd leave her house in her floral dresses and pink heels, giving her parents some lie about going to a friend's house, and then would change into a tight black dress, fishnets, and combat boots in the car. I liked that she wasn't hiding that side of her anymore.

"I was tired of pretending to be someone I wasn't," she said. "As soon as I got back to LA, I tried to make the outer-me match the inner-me."

"It suits you. And the new ink, too."

She lifted up the sleeve of her leather jacket, revealing the tattoo I'd glimpsed before—a black aperture symbol on her wrist. "I got this once I decided on my major."

"What happened to psychology?"

She shrugged. "It wasn't for me. I can barely understand my own head half the time. Who am I to try to get inside someone else's? But one semester, I took a photography class and fell in love. I'm planning to go into photojournalism. What about you?"

"I'm a music major, mainly studying sound engineering and mixing."

"That's what you always said you wanted to do," she said, smiling. "And you got some new ink, too. I like them."

"Thanks." When we'd been together, I'd had a few already, but after I'd turned eighteen, I'd gotten full sleeves—a phoenix on one arm and a water dragon on the other, surrounded by flames, waves, and stars. Recently, I'd gotten the words *LIVE LOUD* across my knuckles, too.

"What's the story with the triangles?" she asked.

I had a triangle tattooed on each wrist, the left one all black and the right one hollow and inverted. "Jared and I got them not long after..." I was about to say, *not long after you left,* but that didn't seem very nice. "After I started college."

"You got matching tattoos?"

"Yeah. His are mirror images of mine. They symbolize brotherhood, duality, dark and light, inner and outer selves..." I shrugged. "That sort of thing."

It sounded stupid when I said it all out loud, but they were my favorite tattoos. Once, Jared had been the golden boy, the one who could do no wrong, who'd gotten everything he wanted and made our parents proud. Growing up, I'd been the one who'd gotten tattoos and sneaked out to goth clubs, who'd been caught stealing booze from a liquor store and barely gotten away with a warning, who'd nearly been kicked out of school for smoking pot. And Jared had been there to rescue me time and time again. But over the last few years, we'd switched places. Or maybe we were both stumbling through the dark together, looking for the light to find our way again.

"I like them," Alexis said. "Do you still have our tattoo?"

"Of course."

"Me too." We stopped at a red light, and she lifted the hem of her shirt, revealing the infinity symbol peeking out above her jeans. Damn, she was sexy, showing off that tiny glimpse of bare skin. Was she *trying* to make me crazy?

Two could play at that game. I raised the bottom of my shirt, flashing the matching tattoo on my hip. It must have worked because she reached across to brush the ink with her cool fingers. I held still as she traced the symbol slowly, like she couldn't stop herself. Even the slightest touch from her awakened parts of me I'd thought long dead. I was frozen in place, wishing she would smooth that hand up across my chest. Or even better, dip those fingers inside the waist of my jeans and move lower...

The light changed, and she yanked her hand away. "Sorry."

"It's fine." It was so not fine.

"No, I shouldn't have done that. I just couldn't resist."

"Don't worry about it." I adjusted in the seat, trying to get comfortable again. It was unfair how easily she excited me. All she'd done was touch me, and I'd instantly turned into a horny, single-minded male. Pathetic. I wasn't sixteen anymore. I needed to get control of myself before I did something I'd regret.

I stared out the window, willing my body to relax. I'd known this car ride would be a bad idea. We hadn't arrived at Becca's place yet, and I was already losing my damn mind. Not because of the lust—though that was definitely a problem—but because of all the memories that kept coming back to me. Like when we'd gotten the tattoos and how we'd held hands the entire time, helping each other be strong through the pain, believing we would be together forever. The infinity symbol had been a promise to each other, the kind only stupid kids in love for the first time would make. I'd thought about covering it up many times, but I'd never been able to go through with it. Maybe a part of me was still hoping for forever.

And Alexis still had the tattoo, too.

Chapter Five

It took us a good ten minutes of circling the area before we found a parking space we could squeeze into near Becca's place. The wind had gotten worse, and palm fronds were scattered across the sidewalk, forming an obstacle course on the way to her apartment building. We headed up stairs with peeling paint and a broken handrail. I checked the address on my phone again and rang the doorbell.

No one answered. What would we do if she wasn't home? I had no backup plan. Going to her place was all I'd come up with. I rang the doorbell again. And again.

A girl with a nose ring finally opened the door, and with her came the strong smell of clove cigarettes. "Yeah?"

"Hey, I'm Kyle. I'm in a band with Becca. Is she here?" I tried to peek into the dark room behind her, but I didn't see Becca's blue hair anywhere.

"Nope," the girl said, sounding bored.

"Do you know where she is?"

"Nope."

Wow, could she be any less helpful? "Could you text her or something? Do you have *any* idea where she could be?"

The girl huffed. "How should I know? I'm not her babysitter."

She started to close the door, but Alexis slammed her palm against it, holding it open. "We need to find Becca *now*, and we're not leaving until you tell us where she is."

The girl chewed on her lip while Alexis stared her down. She shrugged. "Becca won't answer my texts, but she's probably at the bar on the corner. That's where she likes to hang out when she's in one of these moods."

"See, that wasn't so hard, was it?" Alexis asked. She released the door and stepped back, flashing me a triumphant grin. She'd never looked sexier.

"If you find Becca, tell her she owes me money for rent." The girl mumbled something else under her breath and then shut the door in our faces.

"Thanks for the help," I said to Alexis as we walked down the stairs. She'd always been confident, but she had never been this bold before. I liked it. I just prayed Becca was actually at this bar, or we'd be in big trouble.

"You were being too nice," she said.

"Yes, that is a problem I have."

She took my arm, turning me around. She stood a step above me, putting us at the same height. "Maybe it's time to be not so nice for a change."

"Oh, yeah?" I moved close enough to feel her breath on my cheek. I knew I was flirting with her again, but I couldn't help myself. "And what would a not-so-nice guy do right now?"

"Hmm…try to kiss me?" she suggested, with that breathless, excited voice I knew so well.

Her parted lips were an invitation, and I trailed a finger down her cheek, unable to stop myself. It would be so easy to lean in and press my mouth to hers, to slide my arms around her waist and pull her against me, to feel her body along mine. Every inch of me strained to close the distance between us.

I didn't know if I could let her into my heart a second time, but that didn't stop me from wanting her. If anything, I wanted her more because of the danger. Alexis was an open flame, and I was drawn to her deadly beauty. I wanted her to burn me all over again.

I traced my thumb along her bottom lip, but when her eyes fluttered shut, I dropped my hand and turned away. "Good thing I'm a nice guy then."

She sighed but didn't say another word as we walked down the block in search of the bar.

I had to stay focused. My goals were to get Becca, return to the club, and win the Battle. I repeated those three things in my head like a mantra, trying to distract myself from Alexis's far-too-tempting body beside me.

I spotted Becca as soon as we turned the corner. She was leaning against the outside of the bar, smoking a cigarette like she had all the time in the world, like we weren't all waiting for her or spending our entire night tracking her down.

"Hey, Kyle." She took a long drag. "I heard you used to be able to smoke inside bars in LA. Wouldn't that be nice?"

"Where the hell have you been?"

She shrugged. "Here and there."

I wanted to yell at her, to shake her and ask her why she'd abandoned us tonight, but something in her face stopped me. I had a feeling yelling at her wouldn't help. "How are you doing?"

"How am I *doing*?" She snorted. "I'm great. Don't I *look* great?"

Not in the slightest. Her short, blue hair stuck out all over the place, her eyes were bloodshot and dripped black like a goth clown, and her tank top and jeans were ripped and barely hanging together with a few choice safety pins. On second thought, her clothes always looked like that.

But the thing that alarmed me most was that her words were slurred like she was drunk. I had never seen her flat-out drunk before, and I wasn't sure if she could play like that. I wasn't willing to risk it, not with a gig this important. I'd have to get her sobered up fast, assuming I could even convince her to come with us.

I took a minute to consider my words while she blew smoke in my direction. "Becca, I get why you're upset. Jared told me what happened, and the way he treated you sucks. It really does. But we can't go on stage without you. If you don't come to the show tonight, we're *all* screwed."

She flicked ashes toward the street. "I know. Don't care."

"I don't believe that."

After all the hours practicing together, she had to care a *little*. She'd been a part of Villain Complex for a few months, and I'd thought we were becoming something close to friends in that time. But even if she didn't care, I was desperate. If I had to resort to begging on my knees in the middle of the street, so be it.

"Look, whatever this thing is with Jared, we'll work it out. I promise. Just come with us to the club. Please, Becca."

"There's nothing to work out. Your brother's a dick. I'm done with the band. End of story."

I tugged on the gauges in my ears, trying to hold on to my last remaining slivers of calm. I couldn't be too mad at her when part of this was Jared's fault, but she'd known what my brother was like and had still gotten involved with him. They were both to blame for this mess, and I was stuck in the middle. Leave it to Kyle to fix everyone's problems—again. But I got the feeling, no matter what I said, Becca would never come to the show. She didn't care that she was screwing over me and Hector; she was too mad at my brother to see beyond anything else. And time was ticking away while we argued about it.

"Jared *is* a dick," Alexis said. I scowled at her—yes, he was a dick sometimes, but he was my brother, too—but she ignored me and continued. "But Kyle's *not*. He came all the way out here to make sure you were okay. He's a good guy, and he doesn't deserve this. Quit the band tomorrow if you have to, but do this one show tonight...for him."

"Who the hell are you?" Becca asked.

"Alexis." Her eyes flicked to me for a second. "I'm Kyle's...friend."

I fully expected Becca to tell Alexis to piss off, but she just stared at the passing cars while she smoked. Finally, she said, "I thought things would be different, you know? After we hooked up."

I'd never heard her be so open before about anything, but maybe the alcohol was loosening her tongue. I placed a hand on her shoulder. "I'm sorry, Becca. But you know how Jared is. He doesn't do relationships."

"I know. I *know*." She slumped against the wall, eyes closed. "I only joined your stupid band to get close to him, and now I can't even look at him. Or you, Kyle." She took another long drag off her cigarette. "God, I wish he was more like you."

I wanted to say, *If Jared was more like me, you wouldn't have slept with him.* But I think we both knew that, even without saying it. "Becca, it doesn't matter why you joined the band. You're a damn good bassist, and we don't want you to leave. Please do this show with us tonight."

I was about to give up and resort to full-out begging, but she put her cigarette out on the wall behind her and pushed off with a kick of her combat boots. "Fine. Let's go."

"Thank god." My shoulders sagged with relief. "I mean, thanks."

"Yeah, well, I was planning on coming to the show eventually," Becca said. "I just wanted Jared to sweat a little first."

I wasn't sure I believed that, but my good-guy status was working in my favor for once, so I wasn't going to argue. As long as we got through the Battle, I'd deal with everything else later. Even if it meant finding yet another bassist.

Chapter Six

We stopped at Becca's place to pick up her gear (while her roommate yelled about the rent again), and then she squeezed into the backseat of Alexis's car. I was starting to think we'd actually make it back to the club in time —or even be early—until Becca burped behind us, making the car reek of alcohol.

"We need to get her sobered up fast," I said to Alexis.

"I'm *fine*," Becca said. "I just had a couple beers. And some tequila. Not a problem. I can totally play like this."

"She needs some carbs and coffee, stat," Alexis said. "How about that Denny's on Sunset Boulevard? The one we used to go to after concerts?"

I couldn't help but smile at the memory of all those late nights, but I shook my head. "That would take too long. Let's just hit a drive-thru."

"One drive-thru coming up."

She returned my smile, and all the reasons why I couldn't get involved with her again started to dissolve. I placed my hand on hers when she went to shift gears, to silently thank her for all her help. Without her, I'd still be stuck in that parking lot yelling at our stupid van.

"So what's the deal with you two?" Becca asked, ruining the moment. "Are you dating?"

"No," I said, jerking my hand back.

"We did, once," Alexis said, as she pulled away from the curb.

Becca leaned between us, and the whiff of beer and cigarettes made me almost gag. "Ooh, are you getting back together?"

"No!" I didn't want to discuss my love life with a drunken Becca, of all people. "Alexis just happened to be at the show tonight taking photos for USC."

"Actually…that's not *entirely* true," Alexis said.

My head snapped back to her. "What?"

She gave me a hesitant look before focusing on the road again. "Promise you won't get mad?"

"No, that question pretty much guarantees that whatever you say is going to upset me."

"Okay, here goes." She sucked in a breath, like she was steeling herself for what might come next. "Earlier I said I didn't know you'd renamed the band, but that wasn't true. I've been following you guys this entire time. I thought, if I came back to LA, we might be able to start over again, and when I saw you were doing this show, I had to come. Taking photos for the school paper was just an excuse I made up." She blurted out the words, like she had to get them out before she lost her nerve. "I know it sounds crazy, but I had to try at least. I had to see you."

"But…why?" I wasn't sure if I was asking why she'd lied or why she'd been following the band or why she'd had to see me. Option D: all of the above.

She bit her lip, giving me another quick glance. "I…I missed you."

"You *missed* me?" My voice grew louder, filling up the small car, but I couldn't help it. "You were the one who broke up with me!"

"I know. And I'm sorry." She gripped the steering wheel harder. "God, I'm an idiot. I don't know why I thought you'd be happy to see me."

"So Kyle was the one who got dumped," Becca interrupted. "Very interesting."

"Shut up, Becca!" I stared at Alexis, studying her face. She seemed sincere, but did she really think she could show up tonight and apologize and I'd be cool with everything? That we could pick up where we'd left off? She said she missed me, but why would anything be different this time? "Look, Alexis. Things have changed a lot since high school and—"

"You know, this all makes sense now," Becca continued, leaning over my shoulder. "Kyle hasn't had a girlfriend the entire time I've known him. Can you believe that? He's a good-looking guy, so I thought maybe he was gay or something, but then I caught him checking out my boobs so I knew *that* wasn't the case. Or, at least, I figured he swung both ways. But I guess he just wasn't over you."

"He does like boobs," Alexis agreed.

Becca snorted. "Don't all guys?"

"That is *not* true," I got out through gritted teeth. I didn't want Alexis to think I'd been pining over her all this time. Yes, I'd been going through a dry stretch lately, but that happened sometimes. Totally normal.

"What—that all guys like boobs?" Alexis asked.

"I guess some *are* probably ass men," Becca said with a drunk giggle. "Or, you know, into other guys."

I banged my head against the window, hoping it would knock me unconscious and get me out of this conversation. What would Jared do in this situation? Probably do his stupid wink and say something that convinced both girls to get into bed with him. Me? I was not that smooth.

"I've just been busy with school and the band," I muttered. Becca giggled again, and I seriously considered opening the car door and throwing myself into the street. "I've had other girlfriends, okay?"

"Of course," Alexis said, but she fidgeted in her seat and frowned. "So you've dated a lot of girls since me?"

Talk about a loaded question. There was no safe answer to that. "Why do you care?"

"I don't. I just…" She shook her head. "Never mind."

"No, really, what kind of question is that?" I asked, getting even more riled up. "If I say no, will that make you happy? Or do you want me to say yes so you won't feel guilty? Do you *really* want to hear about the other girls I've been with?"

"Oh, this is getting good," Becca said, wedging her head between us again.

"Shut up, Becca!" Alexis said.

She leaned back, raising her hands. "Hey, just pretend I'm not here. You two clearly have a lot of issues you need to work out."

"It was a stupid question," Alexis said to me. "Forget it."

This was so not the time to have this discussion, but I couldn't stop now. I'd held onto this shit for three years. It felt damn good to finally let it out. "At graduation, you told me you didn't love me anymore. That we were too different and I wouldn't fit into your new, perfect life at Princeton. You *broke* my heart, Alexis, so you're not allowed to be jealous of who I slept with after you left."

"I didn't *want* to leave you! You could have come to New Jersey with me! Even though you didn't get into Princeton, there were other colleges nearby—"

"But that was never my dream! My place was always here, with the band, with my brother. I couldn't leave them behind."

"So I should have given up *my* dream and stayed behind with you?"

"No, of course not! I never asked you to do that, but you didn't even want to go to Princeton. That was your father's dream, not yours!"

"That's not true! It had nothing to do with my dad—"

"It had *everything* to do with him and with your good-little-rich-girl image! You broke up with me because I wasn't part of his plan for you. I didn't fit into that lifestyle, with the country clubs and boat parties and fancy cars."

"That's not why I broke up with you!" She drew in a ragged breath. "Kyle, it never would have worked out between us."

"What's that supposed to mean?"

She sighed. "We would have tried to do the long-distance thing at first, but over time we would have talked less and less as we made other friends, experienced new things, chased different dreams. Eventually, our lives would've no longer overlapped and we wouldn't have anything to say to each other. I couldn't stand the idea of going through that, of us slowly growing to resent each other and our love fading away into nothing. That's why I lied and said I didn't love you—to save us from all of that heartache. I figured one quick moment of pain would be better than four drawn-out years of it. I thought I was doing the right thing for both of us."

"What about forever, Alexis?" I asked, touching the tattoo on my hip. "What's four years out of forever? I would have waited for you. I would have done *anything* to make you happy. But you gave up on us!"

"And I'm admitting that I made a mistake!"

"Damn, your make-up sex is going to be *awesome*," Becca said.

"Shut up, Becca!" we both yelled.

The car dropped into silence, with only the sound of the engine and the traffic around us to play a score for our thoughts. For years, I'd wondered what had changed between us at the end, why Alexis had stopped loving me. Or if she had ever loved me at all. I'd often dreamed of her running into my arms and telling me she'd made a mistake, but now that it had happened, I wasn't sure how I felt.

Yes, long distance would have been hard. Being thousands of miles apart for four years would have been torture, but I would have done it gladly. She'd *always* been the one, from the moment I'd seen her in English class. Like a fool, I'd meant it when I'd said forever, but I wasn't lying now when I said things had changed since high school. I wasn't the same stupid kid who believed in things like soul mates and love that lasted forever.

Even if I still loved her, I wasn't sure love was enough anymore.

Chapter Seven

We pulled into a Jack In The Box, and Becca groaned. "I don't feel good."

Alexis shot her a warning glance. "Don't you dare throw up in my car."

I scanned Becca's face, which had taken on a color only a few shades away from her hair. "We better go inside."

Alexis abandoned the drive-thru line and pulled into a parking spot. I hopped out and moved the seat up, but Becca didn't budge.

"C'mon, Becca," I said.

She moaned and then flopped to the side and practically rolled out of the car. I caught her arm to help her up, and she leaned against me while I led her inside. Everyone stared at us, either because of our kaleidoscope of hair colors or because Becca looked like she might hurl at any moment. How was she going to play tonight if she was like this?

"I'll get some food," Alexis said. "You stay with her." She got in line behind one of those guys with big, bushy beards that made you wonder whether he was homeless or just a hipster.

I dumped Becca into a booth and sat across from her. "Are you going to be sick?"

"I need a cigarette," she mumbled.

"Is that a no?"

She jumped up and ran into the bathroom, covering her mouth. I heard gagging sounds just as the door shut, so I guessed that answered my question.

Alexis was still at the counter, so I texted Jared to let him know the situation and then got up to knock on the bathroom door. "Becca, you okay in there?"

"Go away!" she yelled.

Well, at least she wasn't passed out on the floor. "Can I get you anything?"

"No!"

The sound of vomiting continued, and I raked my fingers through my hair. "All right. I'm out here if you need me."

I dropped back into the booth as Alexis returned with a tray of food. She slid in next to me, her arm brushing against mine. I tensed up but didn't move away, waiting to see if she would bring up our conversation from the car. I wasn't ready yet. The wound was still too raw and tender.

"How's she doing?" Alexis asked, and I relaxed.

"Not good."

"Maybe she'll feel better after she throws up."

"Maybe…" Or maybe we were completely screwed.

"I got her a breakfast meal. Pancakes, hash browns…. She'll be sober in no time." Alexis started arranging the food on the table. "Have you eaten anything?"

"No. Haven't had time."

"Here, I got you something." She slid a cheeseburger over to me, along with curly fries and a coffee. The cheeseburger even had bacon on it. All of my favorite things—she remembered.

"Thanks," I said as I took a bite. "Mmm…. Bacon makes everything better."

She unwrapped one of those tiny, crunchy tacos, and I burst into laughter. "What?" she asked.

"You're still eating those nasty things?"

She gave me a playful shove on the shoulder. "They are not nasty! Just because you once ate so many of them you got sick doesn't mean they're not delicious."

"Don't remind me," I said with a groan. "Damn, I can't believe you remember that."

"Of course I do. I remember everything, babe."

For a second, it was like we were in high school again on some crazy, late-night adventure. We'd always ended up in one food place or another, drunk on love and music and youth, and she'd always called me "babe."

We resumed eating, but my every sense was completely tuned to her body next to mine. I didn't taste any of my food; there was only her, living and breathing and real. No longer a ghost haunting my memories, but beside me again. Despite all the heartache, sitting so close to her felt natural, like the world had clicked back into alignment. Like I'd taken a big gulp of air after holding my breath too long.

I wanted to bring up our conversation from the car, but I wasn't sure how to ease back in without it turning into another fight. "Were your parents mad that you left Princeton?" There. That was relatively safe.

"They were disappointed, especially my dad, but they were happy I was back in California, too. Until they saw the tattoos and the hair, anyway. Then they wanted to disown me."

"Bet they would have loved to blame me for that one." Her parents had always hated me—for being in a rock band and having tattoos and generally being a "bad influence."

"I'm sure they wished they could have. What about your parents?"

I crumpled the empty burger wrapper in my fist. "I barely talk to them."

We'd been in high school when my parents had split up, and Jared and I had gotten stuck in the middle of their nasty divorce. Our parents fought over custody, over money, over the house, over everything down to a broken lamp in the garage. They each tried to get us to turn against the other parent, to give up information, to make us choose, but we wouldn't. Jared had taken it better than I had, of course. I'd been so angry, so willing to rage at anything and anyone, so eager to do anything to forget for a little while.

After I'd gotten caught stealing and almost gotten my dumb ass arrested, my parents had made me see a shrink. Then my dad had tried to get the shrink to testify that my actions showed that my mother was unfit to have custody over me. My mom had retaliated by bringing up my father's cocaine addiction and all his affairs. I'd spiraled lower and lower, hating them both, hating myself, wanting it all to end. One night, I'd tried to make the pain stop with pills and alcohol. That's when Jared had somehow convinced my parents to let him have custody of me until I turned eighteen. To this day, I still don't know how he did it, but I wouldn't be alive today without him. He'd helped me redirect my anger, and music became my savior.

And then I'd met Alexis and the world had truly seemed worth living in again. Like Jared, she'd believed in me, even when I was at my worst. With my history, I'd never expected to go to college, but she'd convinced me not to give up on school. She'd spent hours tutoring me to make sure my grades got better, making me take a hundred SAT practice tests until I got my scores up and helping me write entrance essays about how I'd turned my life around with the power of love and music and all that bullshit. It was only due to her tireless efforts that I'd gotten into UCLA at all.

"I'm sorry," Alexis said. "I know that's a sore subject."

I shrugged. If anyone knew what I'd been through with my parents, it was Alexis. "Their divorce went through finally. My mom moved to New York last year, but my dad's still in LA. I'm just glad they're not dragging us into court every week anymore."

"That's good." She pushed around a stray curly fry. "And Jared, he's…better?"

"Sort of. I mean, he's not drinking as much or getting into fights these days, at least. But he still has a new girl in his bed every other night."

At eighteen, Jared had given up his spot at Columbia and switched to UCLA at the last minute to take care of me. And yeah, he'd been a terrible cook, he'd sucked at keeping the house clean, and he'd shrunk all our laundry, but he'd also made sure the bills got paid, that I'd gotten to school every day, and that I'd had someone looking out for me, all while going to college himself. That was more than I could say for our parents.

So when Jared caught his long-term girlfriend sleeping with Ben—our first bassist and my best friend at the time—and snapped, I'd been there for him, too. For a year after that, it was a rare night when he hadn't stumbled home at 4 AM either drunk, with bloody knuckles and a black eye, or on the arm of some new girl. Or all of the above. He'd been a mess, and I couldn't have left him to go to college with Alexis. Jared had always been there when I'd needed him, so I'd done the same for him when he'd fallen apart. That's what brothers did: we stuck together, no matter what. Even if it meant giving up what we wanted.

Even if it meant losing the girl I loved.

"Same old Jared, then." A sad smile touched her lips. "I miss the Jared before all that, who'd help us with our homework and then make us popcorn and let us stay up all night watching horror movies."

"Me too. I think that Jared is gone for good, though. You saw what happened with him and Becca." I let out a bitter laugh. "You seem to be the one girl who can resist him."

She wrinkled her nose. "Oh, gross. He's like my big brother."

I couldn't help but smile. "Good."

"Trust me, you don't have anything to worry about there." She rested her hand lightly on mine, like she wasn't sure if I would pull away. "Kyle, it's *always* been you."

I missed this. The simple things, like holding her hand. The way she flipped her hair over her shoulder. The glint in her green eyes when she laughed at something I said. The freckles on her cute nose peeking out from under her makeup. The softness of her red lips, the delicate curve of her neck, the swell of her breasts...

I looked away, clearing my throat. "Alexis, what do you want from me?"

Her hand tightened around mine. "Three years ago, I made a huge mistake. It *killed* me to break up with you, and I've regretted it ever since. I should have tried to make it work long distance, but I messed up." Her voice trembled, but she went on. "I know you'll probably never forgive me for what I did, and I don't blame you. All I want now is a second chance to try to make it up to you. To do something different this time. To prove I never stopped loving you."

Her words woke up something within me—a memory of what we used to be and a spark of hope for what we might be again. "I *am* happy to see you," I admitted, referring to what she'd said in the car. "But why should I believe anything will be different this time?"

She raised her free hand to my cheek. "Because I've changed. I'm not afraid to be who I am anymore. I'm not afraid to fight for what I want. *Who* I want."

I wanted, more than anything, to believe her. I leaned into her touch, staring at the girl I had always loved, who said she still loved me. I didn't take my eyes off her as she trailed her fingers down, along my stubble, tracing my jaw. Her touch was soft but direct, like she was exploring the changes in my face since she'd last seen me. I held completely still. I didn't blink. I didn't breathe. If I moved, I'd break the spell over both of us.

Her fingers skimmed down my neck, and she laid her hand against my chest, digging her fingers into my Joy Division T-shirt where it said, *Love Will Tear Us Apart.* She was already so close, her thigh pressed against mine in the tiny booth, her strawberry-and-spice scent tickling my nose with each breath. Being with her again was so familiar, so comfortable, so *right.* I couldn't stop myself from moving closer, resting my hand on the curve of her shoulder, lowering my head to hers. I closed my eyes, savoring that instant before our mouths met, before everything changed between us and there was no going back.

But I never got to kiss her because Becca slumped down in the booth across from us and groaned. I jerked away from Alexis, and the fog in my head cleared a little.

"You're back," I said, like an idiot.

Becca reeked of vomit and alcohol, but at least she'd returned to a normal color. She grabbed the coffee in front of her and started chugging it. "Were you two making out?"

"I wish," Alexis said with the hint of a smile.

Damn, we *had* been about to make out, right in the middle of a Jack In The Box with the hipster/homeless guy watching us from another booth. I needed to get a grip.

I reminded myself of my priorities: get Becca, return to the club, win the Battle. Becca. Club. Battle. Alexis was a distraction I didn't have time for at the moment, no matter how tempting she was.

"Are you feeling better?" I asked Becca. "'Cause we need to get going."

"Fine, let's go, but I'm taking this with me." Becca scooped up her breakfast meal as she stood up.

"Just don't get syrup all over my car," Alexis said.

"Deal."

She headed for the door, and for a moment, Alexis and I were alone in the booth again. Our eyes locked, and the electricity of our near-kiss crackled between us. If we touched, we'd surely set off sparks. I almost reached for her, anyway. It was so damn hard to leave her alone.

Focus, Kyle. Becca. Club. Battle. Later I'd figure out how I felt about Alexis and what I would do about it. Later I could kiss her for hours, if I wanted. But not now. I had to get my band back together first.

Chapter Eight

The LA traffic gods smiled on us for once. We got back to the club with a little over an hour to spare. Hector and Jared were already in the parking lot, watching while our van was hooked to a tow truck. Getting our gear home tonight was going to be a pain, but I added that problem to the list for later. I mentally crossed off *get Becca* and *return to the club*. Time to focus on item number three: win the Battle.

I let Becca out of the car, and she immediately lit up another cigarette. I stared over the hood at Alexis. We'd been quiet on the drive back, too conscious of Becca behind us, and in the silence, all my doubts had crept back in. Being around her was intoxicating, but when I stopped to think about getting involved with her again, my heart wanted to don battle armor to protect itself. I didn't trust her not to break me again.

I moved around the car to stand in front of her. "Thanks for helping me find Becca. I would have been screwed without you."

She smiled up at me with those dark red lips I'd so wanted to kiss. "It was my pleasure."

"About what we said..." I rubbed the back of my neck, unsure how to continue. I was tongue-tied and awkward, like I was sixteen all over again and asking Alexis out for the first time. "I need to think about it, okay?"

She bit her lip but nodded. "I understand."

I hated seeing her look so disappointed. "Maybe we can talk about this after the show. Or some other night. I just have a lot to deal with right now."

"Of course. The Battle. I can't wait to see you perform again. It's been a long time."

"Yeah." I glanced behind me in the direction of the other guys. "Um, I better go sort things out with the band before the show. I'll see you later, okay?"

Before I could think better of it, I wrapped my arms around her in a hug. She slid her hands up my back, pulling me closer, tucking her face into my neck. Her breasts flattened against my chest, and I buried my nose in her hair, savoring the feel of her against me, how perfectly we fit together, how amazing it was to hold her again. The wind kicked up around us, tearing at our hair and our clothes, and we pulled apart.

As she walked away, I admired the view from behind, resisting the urge to run after her. I shook it off and gestured for Becca to come with me. She groaned but tagged along, and we joined Jared and Hector on the other side of the parking lot as the van was being towed out of the lot.

"Hey," I said. "What's going on with the van?"

Jared ignored me and scanned Becca. "Where have you been?"

She waved her cigarette at him. "Don't even start."

His eyebrows shot up. "What's that supposed to mean?"

"Nothing," she snapped.

"No, what exactly is the problem? Is this about that night? 'Cause we both agreed that was a mistake. You said you were fine with it."

"I am fine with it! I'm just tired of your shit!"

I stepped between them, giving them each pointed looks. "Hey, as far as I'm concerned, you both messed up, but that's over now. It's done, it's in the past, and you both need to move on. We're a band, and we have to stick together if we want to win this thing. Can you two handle that?"

Jared's face went blank, putting his cool mask on again. "Of course."

Becca flicked ashes on the ground and said nothing. Hector took a sip of his beer and shook his head, like he was disappointed in all of us. So much for my rousing speech.

I sighed. "At least for tonight, let's try to keep it professional, okay?"

"Not a problem," Jared said, practically spitting the words out.

"Whatever." Becca dropped her cigarette and took off without another word, her heels clicking on the pavement.

"That went well," I muttered. If Jared and Becca got through the night without killing each other, it would be a miracle.

Behind us, someone sniggered. Todd leaned against a nearby parked car, looking like a cat who'd just caught a mouse. "Told you he was screwing her."

"What do you want, Todd?" I was too tired to deal with him on top of all the other shit going on.

"Oh, that's easy. I want to watch you lose. I want the three of you to walk off that stage with your tails between your legs, knowing I beat you."

"Keep dreaming," Jared said, crossing his arms. "We're going to crush you."

"Guess we'll see, won't we?" He flashed that cocky smirk and headed back to the club.

Hector downed the rest of his beer and crumpled his red cup. Probably pretending it was Todd's head. "I want to snap that guy in half."

"Pretty sure that would get us kicked out of the Battle," I said.

Hector shrugged. "Worth it."

"Forget him," Jared said, though he still glared in the direction Todd had gone. "We're going to win tonight, end of story."

"You mean, as long as Becca doesn't ditch us or pass out?" Hector asked.

"She'll be fine," I said and prayed I was right.

"Hey, who was that girl who gave you a ride?" Jared asked. "With the red hair?"

His question instantly put me on alert. "Why, you want to screw her, too?"

Jared arched an eyebrow at me. "No, I was just curious."

Hector snorted, and I looked at the ground, feeling like an ass. Maybe my question had been a bit harsh, but I was already pissed at my brother for everything else and the thought of him eyeing Alexis like one of his conquests made me crazy. And yeah, I had neglected to mention in my texts to Jared who I had gotten the ride from. I told myself it was because it hadn't seemed like the right time to bring it up with so much other shit going on, but mostly I didn't want to hear Jared give me a hard time about it. But I couldn't hide it from him forever.

"It was Alexis."

"No fucking way," Hector said, under his breath.

Jared stared at me, his mask slipping for an instant. "Alexis is here?"

"Yeah. I was shocked, too."

Hector shook his head. "Damn, she looks totally different. Nice car, though."

"She's not at Princeton?" Jared asked.

"No, she transferred to USC." I gave them both a quick rundown of the night so far, describing how Alexis had given me a ride and helped me find Becca, though I left out the part where we'd almost kissed. That was none of their business.

"Wow." Jared paced back and forth, like he had to walk this news off. "Alexis. I can't believe it. Why is she here? Oh, man, I bet she wants to get back together with you, doesn't she?"

I stared at the ground and said nothing.

He stopped in his tracks. "She *does*? What did you tell her?"

"I said I had to think about it."

"What is there to think about? Nothing. It's a bad idea. The end."

I knew he'd get on my case about this. He couldn't just trust me to make the decision on my own, like an adult. "Wow, thanks for the tip. But after this shit with Becca, I don't think you get to give me girl advice."

"He does have a point," Hector said to Jared.

Jared shot him a stay-out-of-this look and turned back to me. "That's different. Becca was a one-time mistake. Alexis is your Kryptonite. You need to stay away from her."

"He also has a point," Hector added to me.

I gave him an identical look to Jared's. "I'll figure this out, okay? I just need some time. But trust me, I know the risks. Better than anyone."

Jared's face softened, and he wrapped an arm around my shoulder. "I'm sorry. I'm just trying to look out for you. I don't want you to get hurt again. But I know you'll sort it out."

"Thanks." I rubbed the all-black triangle on my wrist. Jared had been the one who put me back together after Alexis left the first time. I had finally gotten to a place where I could move on from her, but now she was back, tempting me again. A part of me wanted to give her another shot, to believe that this time would be different if I only gave her a chance, but I didn't know if Alexis had actually changed. Had I, really?

Jared touched the black triangle on his own wrist, and I knew he understood. After all, he'd had his own heart broken, too, by two of the people he'd trusted most. The tattoos were a reminder of what we'd been through together, of what we'd survived, of how—no matter what happened—we always had each other to rely on. As much as Jared drove me crazy, he did only want the best for me.

"Hey, what about your friend Maddie?" he asked. "Isn't she coming tonight? Maybe you should ask her out. Get out of your dry spell."

"We're not like that. We're just friends." Maddie was also a music major, and for all of freshman year, I'd had a thing for her. I'd sat beside her in every class we'd shared and made sure to get paired up with her on every duet or project. But I'd been too much of a chicken to do anything more. Alexis had taught me that good girls like Maddie weren't compatible with messed-up, tattooed guys like me. So I'd let it go. And over time, I'd realized Maddie and I were better as friends, anyway.

"You sure? 'Cause you talk about her all the time…"

"Seriously. We're friends. That's it." This wasn't the first time we'd had this conversation. He'd never met Maddie, but he was always telling me to go after her, like the "just friends" thing made no sense to him. As usual, Jared's advice involved thinking with his dick and not his head. I couldn't listen to any more of it. "I need a beer. I'll see you guys later."

The club had filled up a lot since I'd left, though the crowd thinned near the back around the bar. On stage, another band was playing bad heavy metal that made my ears bleed. I spotted Maddie at the edge of the crowd at the same moment she saw me, and I instantly felt a hundred times better at the sight of her smile. She wore a plaid shirt and jeans, her dark hair loose around her shoulders, her black-rimmed glasses framing her cute face.

She said something to the guy she was with—white button-up shirt, khaki shorts, and enough hair gel to be a fire hazard—and ran over to me. "There you are! I've been looking for you!" she yelled over the music.

"Hey, Maddie. Sorry, I ran out for a few minutes." I gave her a hug, and she felt nice in my arms but without the rush of desire that accompanied touching Alexis. Being with Maddie was easy, effortless, uncomplicated. If I was smart, I would have asked her out ages ago, like Jared had told me to, but it wasn't like that between us.

She grinned up at me. "This is so exciting! I can't wait to see you play."

"You've seen me play hundreds of times before," I said with a laugh.

"Not like this. Not with the whole band." She bounced on her heels a little. "You know I'm Villain Complex's biggest fan."

"You are. I'm really glad you're here."

I'd given her our album a few months ago. Our band had put it out ourselves once we'd had enough songs written. We'd rented a studio for a few hours to record them all, and then I'd done all the mixing and stuff in our home studio, while Jared had handled things like production and promotion. It had been the first time I'd used the skills I'd learned at school on our own music, and I'd worked hard to make it as good as possible. It meant a lot to me that Maddie, who was basically a musical prodigy, had approved of it.

I glanced behind her at Hair Gel Guy, who was playing on his phone. "Who's that with you?"

She looked back at him and sighed. "I'm on a date, but it's not going well."

"How come?"

"He already wants to leave. And he's just…boring."

"He can't be any worse than Chad." That was her last serious boyfriend. I'd had the urge to drive over to his place and smack some shit into him every time she'd mentioned what a dick he was.

"He's basically Chad 2.0." She adjusted her glasses. "Where's the rest of your band?"

"They're around here somewhere." As I said it, Jared appeared in the crowd, heading for the bar. I nodded in his direction. "Speak of the devil, there's my brother."

Maddie followed my gaze, and her eyes widened. "*That's* your brother?"

Oh, hell no. I'd seen that look a hundred times before. If this were a cartoon, little red hearts would be floating out of her eyes. She was caught in Jared's Death Star tractor beam, and there was no escape for her. That was exactly why I'd never introduced them before. I couldn't believe Maddie had succumbed so easily, too.

"That's him. Do you want to meet him?" *Please say no*, I thought.

"Oh, um…" Her cheeks flushed, making her look even cuter. "I should get back to my date. Maybe next time."

"Sure. Next time." Hopefully, there would be no next time. The last thing I wanted was for Jared to sleep with Maddie and leave me to deal with the fallout when he moved on the next day. Maddie was way too good for him, and I'd hate to have to strangle my brother. It's too bad, though, because if Jared wasn't such a prick, they'd be perfect for each other. They both lived and breathed music like it was a fundamental part of them, written into their very DNA. It was all so easy for them, too. I didn't have that gift, and I'd always envied them for that.

"I'll see you in class on Monday," she said. "Don't forget we're doing that piece from *The Dark Knight* score. And good luck tonight!"

We hugged again, and with a lingering gaze at Jared, she slipped back through the crowd to rejoin her date. I prayed she hadn't fallen under my brother's spell already. Maybe Chad 2.0 would turn out not to be a total loser. I doubted it, though. He didn't even glance up from his phone when she returned. What a punk.

Maddie didn't look back at me. Or at her date. No, she looked at my brother one last time. Just like every other girl, Maddie wanted the bad boy. She'd never once looked at me like that. No girl had…except Alexis. But even she'd said I was being too nice earlier. Her words replayed in my head: *Maybe it's time to be not so nice for a change.*

She was right. What had being nice gotten me, anyway? Nothing. Jared got all the girls, and I was forever alone. But the girl I wanted was here somewhere in the club, waiting for me. I just had to find the courage to go after her.

Screw it. Being the good guy had never worked out for me all these years. It was time to take a chance, to be more like my brother, to do something stupid for once.

It was time to be a little bad.

Chapter Nine

Alexis stood alone in front of the bar, watching the band on stage. Her leather jacket had been left in her car, and in her tight jeans and tiny, V-necked top, she radiated a cool, sexy confidence I found irresistible. She'd had that same confidence when we were younger, too, but now it had an edge, like she wasn't afraid to be herself. It made me want her even more.

I moved behind her, fitting myself against her back, and whispered her name in her ear. I didn't need to say anything else. She turned her head and met my eyes with a look of desire that matched my own. Her hand reached up to circle my neck, drawing my head down to hers, and I gave in to her siren call.

Our lips touched for the first time in three years. It was everything I remembered and more. Like waking from a long coma. A bright sunrise over a dark sky. The first hint of spring after a long winter. I was truly living again, in the way I normally only felt when I was on stage.

The kiss started slow, an awakening, an exploration, a forgiveness of our past mistakes. I teased at her mouth with my own, opening her wider, wanting more, wanting everything. Her lips were amazingly soft and sweet, like candy I'd tasted long ago and had finally rediscovered. I wrapped my arms around her hips, holding her flush against me. She groaned and dug her fingers into the back of my hair, pulling me even closer.

She turned in my arms to face me. "I guess this means you're giving me a second chance."

"I guess it does." I lowered my lips to hers again.

Our bodies fit together perfectly, like when we'd hugged except this time we didn't hold back. I slid my hands down to cup her butt, pressing her against the front of my jeans. Our kiss deepened, mouths hungry for each other, bodies desperate to be together again. We couldn't get close enough, couldn't get enough of each other. She clung to me like I was her savior, and I kissed her harder, flicking my tongue across hers, nibbling at her lower lip. Her fingers gripped the top of my jeans and tugged on them, like she wanted them gone. If she kept this up, I would rip her clothes off and take her right there on the bar counter.

This was all moving so fast, but I didn't care. This was exactly the kind of thing my brother did, and after being apart from Alexis for so long, I didn't want to go slow.

"Let's go to my car," she said, breathless. "The backseat…"

"My thoughts exactly."

We broke apart, and the rest of the club came into focus again. The crowd pressing around us in the dark. The clink of bottles behind the bar. The music blasting from the speakers. The lights illuminating the band on stage. I checked the time. About an hour before our set. No one would miss me if I slipped out for a few minutes.

I took Alexis's hand, the action so familiar I could almost believe we'd never broken up. She gave me a knowing smile and let me lead her through the club, weaving between other couples and head-banging fans. I couldn't get us out of there fast enough. My brain had shut off and my body had taken over, with only lust and primal urges controlling me now.

This might only last one night. I didn't care. I'd take one night with Alexis. As long as I reminded myself it was just sex and nothing more, I'd be fine. If Jared could do it, so could I.

Alexis slid her hand up my arm, pressing her body against my side as we walked, and all rational thought disappeared again—except for one warning flashing through my head, reminding me that I didn't have any condoms. We had some in the van, but the van was gone.

I stopped and turned to Alexis. "Wait. Do you have a condom?"

Her eyebrows jumped up. "That's a bit presumptuous of you."

Oh, shit. I was the biggest ass in the entire world. I was literally the worst guy ever. "I'm sorry, I'm such an idiot. I didn't…um, I just thought…"

She laughed and nudged me with her hip. "I'm kidding! We totally need a condom. Or five."

A slow grin spread across my face. "We don't have *that* much time before my set…"

"For later, then."

There was going to be a later? Now I couldn't *wait* to get to her car. "Give me one minute."

She gave me a long, lingering kiss that I didn't want to break away from. "I'll meet you at the car."

I found Jared backstage, sipping a beer and staring off into space. For once, he was alone. Where were all his groupies? He looked so lost in thought I almost hated to disturb him, but he snapped out of it when he saw me. "Hey, Kyle."

"Hey." I leaned close to him, lowering my voice. "I, uh…" Damn, this was embarrassing. I'd never had to ask my brother for this before. "I need some condoms."

His eyebrows show up. "You need some right now?"

"Um…yeah."

He laughed and wrapped an arm around my shoulders, yanking me close. "No way! Who's the lucky girl?"

"It's not that big a deal," I muttered, pulling away from him. It wasn't *that* rare for me to get laid.

"I'm just proud." But then his grin faded away. "Hang on. Who *is* the lucky girl?"

"Alexis." I stared him down, preparing for another lecture. I already knew everything he would say, and I didn't care. Yes, it was a mistake. Yes, I might get my heart broken again. Yes, I knew the risks.

Yes, I wanted to do it anyway.

But the lecture never came. Jared reached into the inside pocket of his leather jacket and yanked out a long strip of condoms. Way more than I would ever need tonight. Could he possibly use all those in one evening? No wonder he was so popular with women.

"Just be careful," he said.

"You gave me plenty of condoms for that."

"Not what I meant." He shook his head and opened his mouth like he wanted to say more, to give me older brother advice that I'd likely ignore, but then he seemed to change his mind. "Have fun."

"Thanks."

I shoved the condoms in my jeans and headed for the exit, but just outside the door, I was stopped by Todd. He moved in front of me, trying to block my path.

"Emo boy," he said. "Where you running off to?"

"None of your business." I didn't have time for his shit. I brushed past him, but he grabbed my arm hard.

He smirked, digging his fingers into my skin. "Almost time for us to go on. You ready to get your ass handed to you?"

I yanked my arm away. "Fuck off, Todd."

He got right up in my face. "You think you're so fucking cool, with your tattoos and your black clothes, but you're not. You're a loser, and tonight I'm going to prove it to everyone."

He started laughing, like his words were hilarious, and I had that urge to rip his head off again. When I was in middle school, kids like him had bullied me because I'd been the weird, scrawny kid who always wore black and didn't really talk to anyone. Jared had always defended me, and now I made a fist the way he'd once taught me.

"Get out of my way."

"You're *all* losers," he went on, like he hadn't heard me. "Like Hector. He should be mowing my lawn, not playing drums. And Jared? He's the biggest loser of them all. He works as a bartender! Talk about a waste of a college education."

That was it. I could put up with him talking shit about me, but once he'd brought the other guys in, it was over. I'd ignored all his other crap this evening, but I'd had enough. Normally, I'd walk away or try to smooth things over. Good guys didn't get in fights.

Unfortunately for Todd, I'd just decided to stop being a good guy.

I slammed my fist into his eye. It hit with a loud *smack*, and pain shot through my hand. It'd probably be harder for me to play keyboard tonight, but it was worth it to see Todd stagger back, clutching his pretty-boy face.

"You son of a—" Todd lunged for me but stopped when Hector appeared at my side.

"You don't want to do that," Hector growled, the muscles in his arms flexing.

Todd stood up straighter, holding one hand over his eye. "Whatever. It's almost time for my set, anyway. I'll deal with you two later."

He stalked off, and Hector snorted. "Coward."

"Where did you come from?" I asked as I massaged my hand and stretched out my fingers.

He gestured across the parking lot. "I was sketching over there when I heard you two arguing. Nice shot, by the way."

"Thanks." I'd thought about hitting Todd many times before but had always stopped myself. Somehow that only made it sweeter now.

"I'm just sad I didn't get to punch him myself."

"Don't worry, there's still time."

He grinned and slapped me on the back. "You okay?"

"I'm good." My hand hurt and I was a little shaky from the adrenaline, but that would wear off soon. Mostly I just felt *alive*.

I could get used to this being-bad thing.

Chapter Ten

Alexis had parked at the very end of the lot under a broken streetlamp, giving us a tiny bit of extra privacy. She sat on the hood of her MINI, leaning back with one foot propped on the front bumper, and a rush of lust flooded me at the sight. She crooked a finger at me, beckoning me to her.

I took Alexis in my arms and kissed her like I was making up for all the years we'd been apart. Her nails grazed up my arms, along my tattoos, and she kissed me back even harder, like she needed to show me how much she regretted leaving me. And with my lips I showed her that I forgave her, that I wanted this as much as she did.

For tonight, at least, she was mine again. I wanted to taste every inch of her.

I started with her neck, kissing my way down the smooth, pale skin. I stopped just below her ear, focusing on a spot that had always driven her wild. She moaned and leaned back against the hood, pulling me down against her, spreading her legs around me. I loved hearing her make those noises, knowing I did that to her. I loved feeling her body underneath mine again.

I dipped lower, kissing along her collarbone, down the V of her shirt, across the top of her soft breasts. She gripped my hair hard, holding me to her chest, and for once, I was thankful I'd let it grow so long. I wanted to yank her top off, but we were still out in the open, where anyone could see us. Not that I cared much at the moment.

I moved back up to claim her lips and slipped a hand under her shirt. She gasped against my mouth as I slid my fingers across her smooth stomach up to her lacy bra, cupping each breast in my palm and tracing her nipples through the fabric. She arched up, legs wrapping around me, drawing me closer, grinding her body against my hips.

Her little, breathless cries did more to turn me on than she could ever know. I was harder than I'd been in years, practically bursting through my jeans to get to her. Her hands slid down to finger my studded belt, like she knew what I needed. She undid the buckle, and it made a soft *clank* as it hit the hood. Then she reached for my jeans, popping them open, relieving a little pressure there.

Someone whooped behind us, and we froze. I lifted myself off Alexis and glared at the two guys walking past, ogling us like they'd never seen two people making out on the hood of a car before.

Alexis slipped out from under me. For a second, I worried those guys had ruined our night together, but then she opened the car door and climbed into the backseat.

"You coming?" she asked in a teasing voice.

I grinned at her. "Soon, I hope."

She laughed, and I followed her inside. The backseat of the MINI was bigger than you'd expect from the outside, but there still wasn't a lot of room to move around in. At least the windows were tinted, giving us some privacy. I sat beside her on the dark leather seats but hesitated. This wasn't my style, hooking up with someone for a quickie in the back of a car.

But this wasn't some random girl I'd just met in the club. This was *Alexis*. We'd been each other's firsts. We'd learned how to please other people by practicing on each other. I knew her, inside and out—or, at least, I had once. I wanted to know her again, in every sense of the word.

"If we're going too fast…" she started, her face etched with concern.

"No," I said. "I want this. I want you."

"Good." She put her hands on my jaw and pulled me to her, kissing me hard. And just like that, my brain shut off again.

I gripped the hem of her top and yanked it off her. My eyes devoured her delicate, bare shoulders, her chest rising and falling with each breath, and that lacy bra teasing at what was underneath. God, she was the sexiest girl I'd ever seen. But that bra had to go.

I unhooked it and tossed it into the front seat. Her breasts were even more beautiful than I remembered, round and lush, with large, taut nipples just begging for me to suck on them. I cupped them in my hands and kissed each one, using my mouth and tongue to make her sigh. I knew what she liked, what drove her mad with pleasure, what made her gasp and cry my name. And I did it all.

"Kyle," she pleaded and tugged on my shirt.

I released her and sat back, letting her take over. She pulled my shirt off, and her eyes swept over me, taking in the sight of my inked skin, of everything that had changed since she'd last seen me. Her lips quirked up in a smile, and I knew she approved.

She leaned forward and kissed me again, her bare breasts crushing against my naked chest. I wrapped my arms around her, and she moved onto my lap, straddling me. I loved the feel of her like this, her skin against mine. Now if only our jeans weren't in the way.

Her lips brushed across my neck, along the flames and waves dancing along my skin, and up to my earlobe. She traced the round black gauge with her tongue, and I dug my fingers into her hips to steady myself as twangs of hot pleasure shot through me.

"These are new," she whispered. "I like them."

She took my earlobe into her mouth and sucked, and I thought I might pass out from the sensation. And then she repeated it with the other ear, and I nearly did.

"Alexis," I groaned, but she didn't stop. Her mouth moved to my shoulders, to kiss the tattoos on my arms and chest, and finally to the small metal rings through my nipples. She dipped a finger through each, tugging a little, and I gasped.

"These are new, too." She flicked my nipple and the piercing with her tongue, and I cried out, nearly jolting out of the seat. "Oh, I *love* these."

I couldn't handle any more of this. I needed her, naked and sweating and on top of me. We didn't have much time, but even if we had all night, I didn't think I could wait any longer. Not after being apart so long.

She must have had the same thought because she started yanking at my jeans. I let her have at it, watching the way her red hair fell over her face as she tugged my clothes down. Not all the way off, but enough to get the job done. Then she shimmied her own jeans down, followed by pink lacy panties that matched her bra. I watched with hungry eyes and couldn't stop myself from touching her. I slid my hands along her shapely legs and up her thighs, but she pushed me back in the seat, taking charge again.

She climbed onto my lap, her knees on either side of my hips, rubbing herself against me. I looked up at her, pushing the hair away from her face. This was our last chance to back out of this, but I saw in her eyes that she wanted it as much as I did.

"Condom," I said, my voice strained. "In my jeans."

She grabbed one and ripped it open with her teeth, and wow, that was hot. She rolled it over me herself, her deft fingers working quickly but making me moan at the same time. She was much better at that than I remembered. How many guys had she been with since me, anyway? I pushed the thought away as she got the condom on and squeezed once, sending throbbing pleasure through me.

"Keep that up and I won't last long," I said through gritted teeth.

She laughed and placed her hands on my shoulders. I gripped her hips as she moved over me and then slid down, down, down, taking me in so slowly I thought I would die from the delicious agony of it. I filled her completely, her body sheltering me inside her. It was like coming home, and for a moment, neither of us moved, just enjoying the feeling of being one again. This was where we belonged: together.

"Kyle," she whispered. "I've wanted this for so long."

"Me too," I said into her red hair. It was so good I wanted to cry out, to shout to the heavens, to scream it across the parking lot.

She began to move, slowly at first, rocking over my hips, gliding up and down. Our mouths met again, our tongues dancing together, our lips sucking on each other. Her breasts rubbed against my chest as she increased her speed, and I groaned. I loved letting her take over like this, letting her be in control, letting her find her own pleasure.

I dug my fingers into her hips, urging her on as she pulsed on top of me. One of her hands pressed against the window of the car, leaving an imprint in the steam we'd created. She moved faster and faster, her movements growing wilder, and it was hard not to explode inside her. But I held back, focusing on pleasing her first.

I took each of her nipples in my fingers and teased them, and she rode me harder, bucking like a cowgirl, losing control. Her hands moved up to the ceiling, steadying herself as she angled her hips so I went even deeper. I clutched her back, helping her along, lifting my own hips to thrust into her.

Just when I thought the pleasure was too much and I couldn't hold back any longer, she cried out and closed her eyes, tightening around me. Feeling her body tremble, watching her face as she lost herself, it was too much for me. I let go, shuddering as I spilled myself into her, giving myself up to her completely.

She collapsed against me, and I held her close while we caught our breath. As our heartbeats slowed, I touched her cheek, stroking her soft skin. It was hard to believe she was really here with me, after so long. Being with Alexis was even better than I'd remembered, and there was no point fighting my feelings for her. I was already too far gone.

She took my hand and kissed each of the letters tattooed across my knuckles, spelling out the word *LIVE*. She went to kiss the *LOUD* on the other hand, but I flinched. It was still sore from punching Todd.

"You okay?" she asked.

"Yeah. I hurt my hand earlier. It's nothing. Don't worry." I pulled her close again and kissed her, hoping she'd drop it. I wasn't ashamed of punching Todd or anything, but I didn't want to bring it up with her, either. I had a feeling she'd be disappointed, even though she seemed to like the badder, bolder me.

When the kiss ended, she stroked my stubble and smiled. "I never thought.... I mean, I hoped this would happen. But I wasn't sure you'd ever take me back."

Me either, but I'd been deluding myself thinking I'd be fine with just one night together. "Alexis, I can't make any promises. I still need some time to figure things out." I paused, tracing her lips with my thumb. "But I do want to give this a shot."

"Oh, Kyle." She buried her face in my neck, resting against me, and for a few minutes, we just held each other. I'd missed Alexis so much and been heartbroken for so long, but that was over. Time and distance may have kept us apart, but we were together again…and maybe this time it would last.

Chapter Eleven

We returned to the club only minutes before Todd's band went on stage, and the place had filled up so much we had to squeeze our way through the crowd to get a good view. My band was up next and I had to find the others soon, but I wanted to check out our competition first. Plus, I was curious if Todd had a black eye already.

"Perfect timing," Alexis said, adjusting her camera. "I need to get photos of Rubber Horse's set."

"I thought that was just an excuse to come to the show tonight."

"Yes and no. I don't have an official assignment, but I did promise to take photos of them for their website."

Did that mean she was friends with them? Or was she just doing them a favor? I hated the idea of her doing anything for Todd and his entourage. Hell, I hated the idea of him even talking to her.

They walked out on stage in their pastel shirts and boat shoes, and Alexis cheered. Not just polite cheering with the rest of the crowd, either, but loud, arms-in-the-air, full-out-rooting-for-their-band kind of cheering. Like she was a Rubber Horse fangirl or something.

"What are you doing?" I asked, horrified.

She peered through her lens at the stage. "What do you mean?"

"Forget it." I shouldn't blame her for cheering for a USC band since she went there and all, but a bad feeling seated itself in my gut that I couldn't shake off.

Alexis gasped. "Oh, his eye! Did someone hit him? And now he has to play like that. Poor guy."

He did have a shiner over half his face, which made me a little proud. Jared had taught me well. But Alexis was acting like she was actually concerned about Todd. "Are you friends with him or something?"

"Yeah, I've known him since we were kids. Our parents are good friends. Now that I'm at USC, we hang out sometimes."

That explained it. One of her friends from that other part of her life that had never included me. I bet they played golf together and hung out on their families' boats wearing nautical-themed pashminas. Even though the thought made me want to set fire to something, I knew I should drop it. It wasn't my business who she was friends with or which band she cheered for. Even if it *was* Todd.

But then he grabbed his bass and flashed that cocky smirk, and I couldn't let it go.

"How can you be friends with a guy like that?"

She shrugged. "Once you get past the frat boy clothes, he's not so bad."

"Are you kidding me? Todd once asked Hector if he swam here from Mexico!"

"He said that?" She frowned, eyeing me closely. "Hang on—how do you even know him?"

"Todd was our bassist for a while, but Jared kicked him out."

"Ah," she said, like that explained everything.

"What?" I asked. She didn't answer, and that made me even more annoyed. "No, seriously, what was that 'ah' about?"

"Just that it makes sense now why you hate him."

"I hate him 'cause he's a dick!"

She rolled her eyes. "No, you hate him because Jared hates him. And Jared hates him because he's not Ben."

I stared at her, trying to make sense of her words. "That's ridiculous. We kicked Todd out because he's an asshole. End of story."

"He's not an asshole! He's kind of an idiot sometimes, but he's not that bad, really."

"Are we talking about the same Todd? The one on stage right now? Holding the bass?"

She propped her hands on her hips. "Kyle, I've been following your band all these years. I know you've been through a lot of bassists. No one will ever be good enough for Jared, not after Ben betrayed him, and you always go along with whatever Jared does because Ben was your best friend and you feel guilty. Admit it—this isn't about Todd at all."

"You've been gone for *three years*! You have no idea what we've been through in that time!" People around us were starting to stare, but I didn't care. Alexis was wrong. Yes, maybe I'd felt guilty about Ben once, but that was years ago. And maybe we'd gone through a ton of bassists, but only because they did shit like never showing up for practice or stealing money from us. We'd had bad luck, that's all.

"I know enough," she said. "I know you still look at guys like Todd and judge them without giving them a fair chance, just like you always did."

I took a step back, her words stinging. She was accusing *me* of caring about image? After she'd dumped me for not fitting into her life? After admitting she had changed her look to stop hiding who she was? Yes, I'd judged Todd, but on his words and his actions, not on anything else. How could she not see the real him? He must have her completely fooled.

Or maybe she just didn't *want* to see it.

I was about to argue with her, but Rubber Horse started playing and the music blasting from the speakers drowned out any words I might say. The worst part was they were pretty good. They sounded sort of like Sublime or 311, a mellow stoner jam with a hint of reggae, and they even had a white-boy rapper. Not my kind of music, but they made it work.

Alexis snapped photos as they played, and I realized nothing had changed between us. Yes, she looked different and she'd come back to LA, but underneath she was still the girl who hung out with guys like Todd and then sneaked off with guys like me to hook up in the back of cars. I couldn't go through that again.

"Be honest. Who do you want to win tonight?" I asked, yelling over the music.

Her mouth dropped open. "That's not fair! I go to USC and they're my friends, too—"

That said it all. "I figured. God, this is just like Princeton all over again."

"What's that supposed to mean?"

"You choosing your perfect, father-approved friends over me, just like before. It will never end, will it?"

She huffed. "I'm not choosing them over you! I want *both* of your bands to win!"

"But only one of us can!" I shook my head, and my hair fell in front of my eyes. I pushed it out of my face, and Alexis caught my hand, making me yelp.

Her eyes widened. "Oh my god, you're the one who hit him!"

I rubbed it, trying to smooth out the ache. "Trust me, he deserved it."

"For what? For not fitting into your scene? For saying something you didn't like? I can't believe you'd do that!"

"*I* can't believe you're taking his side!"

"I'm not taking his side!"

"You don't know what he's like! He's been harassing me and the other guys all night. He—"

"I don't care what he did! That's not who you are! Or, at least, that's not the Kyle *I* used to know. That Kyle was a good guy. Not the kind of guy who went around punching people he didn't like." She sucked in a long breath. "I'm sorry. I just… I'm not sure I like this new version of you."

As the song ended, she stared at me like she'd never seen me before, like I was a stranger, and that hurt more than anything. Maybe I'd been wrong to hit Todd, but she wouldn't even listen to me explain why I'd done it. No matter what I said, I would never be good enough for Alexis and she would never be on my side.

"This was a mistake," I said.

"What do you mean?"

"You and me." I tried not to let my voice shake, hiding how hard it was to say those words. "It's never going to work. We tried but…we're just too different."

"But…" Her lip trembled, and she looked away. "Maybe you're right."

The next song started, and she turned back to the stage to take another photo. I'd expected her to fight harder, to beg me to change my mind, but maybe she'd realized we were still as messed up as we'd always been. If we couldn't make it through one night without fighting, what kind of chance did we have for the future?

There was nothing else to say. I left her there, letting the crowd swallow me up, just another tattooed guy in black. A guy who'd just walked away from the only woman he'd ever loved.

Chapter Twelve

Jared found me outside, sitting on the ground against the side of the club. He sank down beside me, and for a few minutes, we watched the palm trees blow under the handful of visible stars in the LA night sky.

Finally, he broke the silence. "I really fucked things up, didn't I?"

It took a second for me to realize he was referring to the Becca drama. I'd been so wrapped up in my own screw-up, I'd momentarily forgotten about it. "We all do stupid things sometimes."

"Yeah, but I'm the only one who nearly ripped the band apart." He ran a hand through his hair, his telltale, stressed-out move. "We're going to lose another bassist, and it's all my fault."

"If that happens, we'll deal with it. And it's not entirely your fault. Becca's partly to blame, too."

"No, I really screwed up this time." He leaned his head against the wall and closed his eyes. "I can't keep doing this, Kyle. I can't keep being this guy. I need to get my shit together."

I hated seeing him like this. This Jared was different from the one on stage, the one all his groupies saw. Even though he acted the part of the bad boy, deep down he was a good guy, too. Problem was he didn't believe it himself. As much as I wished he would go back to the old Jared, I wasn't sure he ever would. He enjoyed being the villain too much.

I draped an arm across his shoulders. "Hey, it's going to be okay. We'll figure it out."

"Yeah." He slumped against me. "What happened with Alexis?"

I picked at a tiny hole in my jeans, debating how much to tell my brother. "I messed everything up with her. We, uh, hooked up and I thought things were going well, but then I punched Todd. Turns out he's one of her friends."

"You punched Todd?" He laughed. "Well, I'm sure he deserved it."

"Exactly! I tried to tell her that, but she wouldn't listen."

Except…Todd hadn't *really* deserved it. He'd insulted the band, but I didn't care what Todd thought about us. He'd grabbed my arm and gotten in my face, but I should have walked away. I should have let it go.

"You were doing the world a service," Jared said. "I wanted to punch him myself for that terrible Bob Marley cover his band did."

"I must have left before that."

He shuddered. "Trust me, it was painful. You don't mess with a classic like that."

"I shouldn't have punched him. I let him get to me. It was stupid."

He elbowed me. "Hey, what did you just tell me? We all do stupid things sometimes."

Except, I wasn't allowed to do stupid things. I was the one who was supposed to have it together. Jared was our leader, the mastermind who wrote most of the music and took care of the management stuff the rest of us didn't have time for. Hector was the one who challenged Jared on his bullshit, the rock who was always there to support us through everything. And I was the mediator, the one who held us all together, who smoothed things over and fixed our problems. I couldn't afford to make mistakes, not when the other guys were counting on me.

"Don't be like me, Kyle," Jared said. "Quick hook-ups in cars, punching people…. That's not you. You're better than that."

I dropped my head. His words hit a little too close to home. I'd been so hung up on being "bad" that I'd forgotten who I really was. I'd thought I had to be more like my brother to get the girl. I'd thought Alexis wanted me to be that kind of guy. But I was wrong. She'd loved me for who I was.

I'd blown it with her, but maybe that was for the best. Did I want to be with someone I didn't trust not to break my heart again? Who hung out with guys like Todd? I wasn't sure.

I sighed. "You were right. I should have stayed away from Alexis."

"No, *you* were right. I'm the last person who should give relationship advice." Jared toed a rock with his boot. "All these years you've never gotten over Alexis, and now you have a chance to start over with her. You have to try. Just talk to her again."

"I don't know. Maybe we're too…broken."

"You're not broken, just…bent. Like that P!nk song with the guy from fun."

He started singing "Just Give Me a Reason," and I jabbed him in his side. "Stop that."

"Sorry," he said. "Seriously, though. She's here and she wants you back. She even helped you find Becca. So she has bad taste in friends. No one's perfect. But isn't she worth fighting for?"

I wasn't sure why Jared had changed his mind about Alexis, but maybe I should listen to him for once. I hadn't exactly given her a real chance tonight. I'd made a mistake by punching Todd, but instead of owning up to it, I'd used it as an excuse to end things with her. All because I was scared of getting hurt again.

But if I continued this way, I'd never open myself up to anyone. Alexis was my first love. My *only* love. She was worth fighting for.

I stood up and brushed off my jeans. "Thanks for the pep talk. I'll go find her."

"Any time." He checked his phone. "But it'll have to wait. We only have ten minutes before our set."

We hurried backstage to where our gear was being stored. Hector was already there, waiting. "About time," he said. "Where's Becca?"

Oh, shit. Not this again.

"She's not here?" I glanced around the backstage area. All of the other bands had already performed and were in the main part of the club, so it was nearly empty. No sign of Becca's blue hair anywhere.

"I haven't seen her since you came back with her," Hector said.

Jared frowned. "Me either."

"We still have a few minutes," I said. "She'll show up." *Please show up, Becca.*

Hector took off his Villain Complex hat, raked his hand through his curly hair, and shoved it back on again. "And if she doesn't?"

I didn't need to answer because we all knew what would happen. We couldn't play without a bassist. Okay, technically we could, but it wouldn't sound right. We might as well hand the prize to Todd right now.

"Let's start setting up," I said. "If she's not here in the next five minutes, we'll…figure something out."

As I said it, Todd and his band walked off stage, carrying their gear and laughing. They stopped and glared when they saw us, their laser beam eyes seeming to hone in on me. I didn't blame them for being pissed at me for punching their bassist. I'd be pretty mad, too, if I was in their shoes. But this could only lead to trouble.

"There you are." Todd set down his guitar case and cracked his knuckles. "Payback time."

"We're a little busy at the moment," Jared said, hefting his own case. "Rain check, maybe?"

"Looks like the perfect time to me." Todd and his entourage moved closer, like sharks circling in for the kill. "If you're too fucked up to play afterward, not our problem."

How nice of Todd to pick the moment right before our set to try to beat us up. We were outnumbered, but Hector counted as at least two guys on his own, which evened it out. Our two bands stared each other down, like cowboys about to get into a shootout. We were all tense and ready to reach for our guns, but no one wanted to make the first move. I almost expected a tumbleweed to roll past us.

Hector smacked his fist into his other palm. "Bring it on."

"Wait." I couldn't let our bands fight each other over my one lapse in judgment. Jared and Alexis were both right—that wasn't who I was.

I wasn't that kind of guy. I wasn't like my brother. But maybe that wasn't a bad thing.

Besides, we didn't have time for this shit.

"I'm sorry I hit you, Todd. I've been having a rough night, and I took it out on you. It was inexcusable, and I apologize."

Todd blinked, and then he burst out laughing. I thought we might be okay until it turned into a mocking kind of laugh.

"Damn, it's going to feel even better when I pound your face in after that pathetic speech." A wide, evil grin spread across his face. "You know, I saw you with Alexis earlier. But she's coming home with me tonight 'cause you're such a pussy. And when I'm balls-deep in her, it'll be even sweeter knowing I'll have won the Battle *and* the girl."

He laughed again, and Jared took a step forward, fists clenched. I put a hand on his arm to stop him. The thought of Todd sleeping with Alexis made me want to punch him again, to beat him until he couldn't move—let alone *think* of touching her—but I wouldn't let him get to me this time.

I shrugged, like his words didn't affect me at all. "She can go home with whoever she wants, but hey, how about I buy you all a round of drinks after the show? What do you guys think?"

His eyes narrowed, like he didn't understand why I wasn't coming at him, fists flying. The other guys in his band looked confused, too.

"I could go for a drink," the rapper said, and the others nodded.

"No." Todd got up in my face again and poked a finger in my chest. "We're settling this right here, right now."

Well, I'd tried. I really had. But being nice to Todd only seemed to make him angrier, and Becca was still MIA. If we weren't going to perform tonight, we might as well go out with a bang. I sucked in a breath and readied myself. I wouldn't throw the first punch this time, but I wasn't going to let him beat the shit out of me either.

"Kyle was right about you, Todd," Alexis said from behind me. "You *are* an asshole."

I spun around at the sound of her voice. She glared at him like she might shoot fire from her eyes and burn him down where he stood. Becca was at her side, her arms crossed. They looked like they could take on all four guys themselves.

"Hey, baby," Todd said, flashing Alexis his pretty-boy smile. "You know I was just joking about all that. You're still coming to my party tonight, right?"

"No, I'll be celebrating with Villain Complex after *they* win."

"Huh?" His face twisted, shifting from surprise to anger. "You're going to pick these losers over us?"

"I am," she said. "And I suggest you get out of here before I tell the guy running this show what's holding up the final band."

Alexis moved to stand beside me and flipped her red hair over her shoulder, looking like some kind of warrior princess ready to do battle. God, I loved this woman.

Todd's buddies hesitated, dropping their shoulders, backing off. Maybe because they didn't want to have to fight a girl. Maybe because they were outnumbered now. Or maybe I'd appealed to their decent sides earlier and they were starting to question if listening to Todd was such a good idea.

"Let's go," one of them said. The rest agreed, and they took off down the hallway, grabbing their gear as they went. Todd growled at us, but after one final look of pure hatred directed at me, he turned on his heel and followed.

As soon as they were gone, we all seemed to collectively relax, the tension vanishing from the air. My brother turned to Alexis and pulled her in for a hug. "It's good to see you again."

"You too, Jared." I detected a little quiver in her voice as she hugged him back. He whispered something to her that I didn't catch, but she bit her lip and nodded.

Hector brought her in for a big bear hug next. "Damn, it's been a long time, girl."

"Yay, we're all best friends again," Becca said, rolling her eyes. "Can we get on with the show already?"

"Oh, now you care?" Jared asked. "Where were you five minutes ago?"

"I was about to take off, but Alexis convinced me to stay," she said, glaring at him. "So let's do this before I change my mind again."

She grabbed her bass and stomped out to the stage. That one was a ticking bomb that I'd never be able to diffuse. At least for tonight, she was still part of the band—thanks to Alexis.

Jared and Hector grabbed their gear and headed after her. We were already running late, but I had to say something to Alexis before I could go.

I stared at her while a million emotions rushed through me at the speed of light. She'd convinced Becca to stay and had chosen me over Todd. She'd taken my side, and she was rooting for me to win. I just hoped she could forgive me for the things I'd said to her. I hoped she could see I was still the good guy she loved.

"Thank you," I said. "For Todd and for Becca and for being here tonight. And I'm sorry about earlier. I was totally out of line and—"

Alexis raised a hand to stop me. "No, I was the one who was out of line, and I'm sorry, too—"

"Kyle, come on!" Jared yelled.

She kissed me on the cheek. "Go out there and win this thing, babe. I'll be here when you're done."

I gave her a quick hug and then ran after the rest of my band. I wanted to do so much more—to kiss her and tell her how much she meant to me and how I wanted to start over—but there was no time. We had a Battle to win. Because no matter what else happened tonight, we were *not* losing to Todd.

Chapter Thirteen

Being on stage was unlike anything else in the world. Every show was a spiritual awakening, a moment of enlightenment when all my daily troubles faded away and left only the roar of the crowd and the lights and the music. Performing was magic, an act of creation that controlled the emotions of those who heard the music, forming a shared experience between everyone in the room.

And being part of a band—with each person contributing, harmonizing, and creating magic together—was a true rush. We weren't individuals anymore; we were one voice, one breath, one heartbeat. The only thing that came close was having sex, and even then, only those really good times or with the person who made it truly special. Like Alexis.

I knew she was out there in the audience somewhere, cheering for me, and that made the moment even better. Maddie was out there, too. My brother was at my side, and Hector was at my back. Even Becca had pulled it together. I was surrounded on all sides by people I cared about, and I channeled that energy into my performance.

My fingers flew across my keyboard, my head banging along to the music. Unlike other instruments, with keyboard, there was no specific role you took on for every song. Each one was different, and I filled in where I was needed—sometimes accentuating another instrument, sometimes adding something extra here and there, sometimes providing a background ambiance for the entire song. I brought together Jared's hard guitar riffs, Becca's pulsing bass line, and Hector's steady beat. I picked up the slack. I smoothed any rough spots. I held them together and boosted them up. They could have performed the songs without me, but I made each one a hundred times better.

Our set was only fifteen minutes, so we played the catchiest tunes off our album. In the middle, we did a cover of "Karma Police" by Radiohead, with Jared's vocals making the audience swoon. The song's lyrics struck a nerve with me tonight after everything I'd been through. I really had lost myself for a few minutes, but here on stage, with my favorite people all around me, I knew exactly who I was.

We finished the set with one of our best songs, "Behind the Mask." As the last note died, the crowd went wild and Jared spread his arms out as if to embrace them. The sound filled me up, sustaining me like air, and I closed my eyes and breathed it in. And then I ran backstage. I had a beautiful girl waiting for me, after all.

Her eyes lit up when she saw me. I walked right up to her, took her face in my hands, and kissed her. Her fingers dug into my shirt as she kissed me back, and I slid my arms down to circle her waist. My heart was already pounding from the show, but she made it speed up even more as her body pressed against mine and her tongue slipped into my mouth. I nibbled on her lower lip and felt her smile. The rest of the band walked off stage, but they wisely left us alone.

"You were amazing," she said, breathless. "You were always good, but now…it was epic."

"Thanks." I kissed her again. "But there wouldn't have been a show without you."

"I barely did anything." She ran her thumb across my jaw, her eyes fixed on the tattoos on my neck. "I'm sorry I didn't listen to you about Todd. I've never seen that side of him before, I swear. He's always been a decent guy around me, but I should have trusted you."

"No, you had every right to stick up for your friend. I'm the one who messed up. I shouldn't have punched him in the first place, and I shouldn't have used him as an excuse to pick a fight with you. I was just scared. I barely survived when you left me last time, and I'm terrified of going through the same thing a second time."

"I'm so sorry, Kyle. I thought if I ended it we would both be better off, but I was wrong. I'll never make that mistake again."

"No regrets," I said, brushing hair away from her face so I could stare into her green eyes. "As much as it hurt, being apart for three years was good for us. We've both grown and changed, and we'll be stronger together because of it. But I don't want to go another day without you."

"Good because I want to make it last this time. Whatever it takes." She slid her arms around my neck. "I love you, Kyle."

"Still?"

"Always."

We kissed again, losing ourselves in each other until Jared told us it was time for the audience to vote for a winner. The entire band, plus Alexis, rushed into the main part of the club, blending into the crowd and looking up at the stage. The Battle of the Bands organizer stood up there, an older guy who looked like he was straight out of an '80s metal band with hair down to his waist, an old AC/DC shirt, and leather pants.

"We're going to vote by school first," he said into his mic. "I have an app here on my phone that measures sound levels, so when we get to the band you think should win, scream your heart out. I want you to make some fucking noise!" The audience cheered in response. "Exactly like that. Okay, ready? USC first!"

He ran through the list of USC bands, with each name flashing on a screen behind him. Rubber Horse easily won, which didn't surprise me. What did surprise me was that Alexis didn't cheer for any of her school's bands.

The guy checked his phone. "Rubber Horse is our USC winner! And now it's time for UCLA!"

He called out each of the bands that had performed, and the sound from the crowd grew louder with each one. When the Villain Complex logo flashed on the screen, the audience's roar took over the room. We joined in, too, yelling and clapping, and it felt good to let it all out after everything I'd been through tonight.

It felt even better when the guy said, "Villain Complex is the UCLA winner!"

"Yes!" I gave Alexis a squeeze, and she laughed. Next to us, Jared and Hector were hugging and thumping each other on the back. Even Becca looked slightly less sullen than normal.

"Time for the final vote," the guy said. "Rubber Horse versus Villain Complex. USC vs UCLA. Only one of them can be crowned the winner of the Battle of the Bands and get the prize: a show next month, plus one thousand dollars for themselves and another thousand for their school's music program. Will USC win again for the third year in a row? Or will UCLA finally take it home?"

This was it. The moment we'd find out if everything we'd been through tonight had been worth it. Jared wrapped an arm around me and Hector, and I grabbed Alexis's hand. We tried to pull Becca in, too, but she rolled her eyes and crossed her arms.

The cheers for Rubber Horse were loud, but when our band's name was called out, the response from the audience was almost deafening. The club filled with the sound of the crowd voting for us with their voices and their bodies. Yelling. Clapping. Whistling. Stomping their boots. Alexis was part of it, screaming louder than anyone. I was too shocked by the reaction to even cheer for us myself. Jared's eyes met mine, and I could tell he felt the same.

"Villain Complex is the winner of the third annual UCLA vs. USC Battle of the Bands!"

We collapsed in on each other in one big group hug, laughing and shaking from the adrenaline, from the relief and exhilaration of victory. Becca even joined in this time. We'd done it. We'd beaten Todd, won the prize for our school, and scored a gig for ourselves at the same time. And we'd done it together, as one big, sometimes-dysfunctional, family. None of us could have done it without the other —and that included Alexis.

I pulled apart from the rest of the band and kissed her in the middle of the audience while they continued to cheer for our win. I would never forget this night, marking a fresh start and a new beginning. For the band, and for the two of us.

Chapter Fourteen

I woke with Alexis in my arms. I might have written last night off as a really great dream, except the proof that it was real slept beside me, wearing only my old Ramones T-shirt. Alexis was in my bedroom, her bare legs tangled up with mine, and we'd won the Battle. Every time it hit me, it felt too amazing to be true, like it must have happened to someone else and not me. But no, this was my life.

Alexis looked so beautiful. I wanted to kiss the freckles on her nose and breathe in the strawberry scent of her hair. Her half-naked body felt so good against mine I wanted to do more than just kiss her, but I let her be. I could save all of that for when she woke up. It was Sunday, and my plan was to spend the entire day with the girl I loved, learning her body all over again.

I slipped out of bed, careful not to disturb her, and threw on a pair of boxers. It was still early, barely past dawn, so I moved quietly through the house to get some water from the kitchen. I paused when I heard a noise coming from our garage-turned-studio. The room was soundproofed, but the door was open.

Inside, Jared was sprawled on the couch with his laptop, wearing a shirt with *Lex Luthor for President* on it. My brother was obsessed with villains, hence our band name. We even had a wall of quotes by and about villains on the wall above where he sat that Hector had painted for us in comic book style.

Seeing Jared awake before noon was a rare occurrence. Even more shocking, he hadn't brought a girl home with him last night. Maybe he *was* trying to get his shit together.

"What are you doing up this early?" I asked.

"Oh, hey," he said, looking up from his screen. "The show recorded all of the different sets last night and posted them online. I got the video, and I'm using it to apply for *The Sound.*"

I rubbed my eyes, still not entirely awake. "The reality TV show?"

On *The Sound*, a bunch of different bands competed against each other on four teams led by famous musicians. The winning band got a recording contract with a major label, plus a tour across the country. It was a big deal, but thousands of bands auditioned for it every year. Our chances of getting on were pretty slim.

He nodded. "I know it's a long shot, but I don't see a reason not to try."

"Might as well." I didn't think anything would come of it, but it always made Jared feel better when he had something to do for the band. "We'll have to deal with Becca, though."

"I'll talk to her."

I started to argue that I should do it, but then I closed my mouth. Jared needed to start fixing his own problems. As much as I loved my brother, I couldn't clean up after him for the rest of his life.

I yawned. "I'm going back to bed."

Jared grinned at me, like he knew exactly what I had in mind for the rest of the day. "Have a good time."

I crawled into bed with Alexis, and she stirred, opening her eyes with a sleepy smile. We wrapped around each other, so close we were almost one person, and it was pure heaven having her in my arms again. She'd come back to me, and she still loved me, proving that sometimes the good guy *did* get the girl. We'd gotten a second chance, and this time we were going to make it last.

I touched the tattoo on her hip and kissed her, and her lips tasted like forever.

Bonus Content

I hope you enjoyed More Than Exes! Read on for a bonus scene from Alexis's POV - exclusively in this box set!

THREE YEARS BEFORE
ALEXIS

I stood with Kyle on the football field under the scorching sun, holding my cap and gown while waiting for the ceremony to start. Our new lives were about to begin, which meant I had to end this first.

I drew in a breath and forced out the words. "Kyle… I can't do this."

He turned to me, still smiling. "Do what?"

My chest tightened. This was my last chance to see that smile. He was so handsome, with that dark hair and those warm blue eyes that always made me melt. How was I going to live the rest of my life without ever seeing him again?

I closed my eyes, steeling myself for what I had to do, hating myself for what I was about to say. "This. Us."

He didn't answer, just stared at me like he couldn't believe what I was saying. I continued even though each word was like a knife stabbing me in the gut. "I'm moving across the country for four years. And then who knows what will happen after that? It will never work out between us."

His face fell, but then he shook his head. "No. *No.* I refuse to accept that. Not after everything we've been through." He took my hands in his and stared into my eyes. "Alexis, we can make it work, even long distance. If anyone can, it's us. What's four years out of forever?"

His words gave me a slight glimmer of hope. Maybe I could convince him to change his mind this time. "It's not too late. You could still apply for late admission to one of the schools near Princeton…"

He dropped my hands and the hope vanished. "I've already accepted at UCLA. I *want* to go there. Their music program is perfect for me, and the band is starting to take off. I can't leave now. You know that. Especially with Jared the way he is…"

I bit my lip. "But Jared's doing better, and the band will still be here when you get back."

"He's *not* better. And the band is my life. That's my dream, and I won't give it up. I can't."

We'd had this argument a hundred times since we'd opened our college acceptance letters, but neither of us had ever swayed. We had different dreams, different futures, and after today they wouldn't overlap anymore. Every time we'd fought about it we'd cry and hold each other and swear we'd figure it out later. But now there was no later.

I had to end this and set Kyle free.

"You're right." I shook my head, my copper curls glinting in the sunlight. My mother had made them especially bouncy today. "And let's face it. It would never work between us anyway. We're too different. I mean, look at us."

I gestured at my yellow flower-print sundress and at his Ramones t-shirt and ripped jeans like it was obvious why I was breaking up with him. I actually loved the contrast between us, the preppy girl and the emo boy. I loved that he was in a rock band and that my father hated him. And Kyle loved being the guy who brought out my inner bad girl when we were alone. But he'd always been sensitive about our differences, and I had to convince him that I really wanted to end this somehow.

"Since when do you care about that?" he asked. "Is that you speaking, or your parents?"

I glanced behind us, where my parents were waiting. "It has nothing to do with them. I'm going to Princeton and things will be different there. It's time I got serious about my future. And that means ending it with you." I was proud of myself for not letting my voice falter as I said that last line.

"But this isn't you! You don't even *want* to go to Princeton! You're only going because your dad expects you to!"

"That's not true!" A tear slid down my cheek, despite my best efforts to remain strong. "This isn't about my dad, or your brother, or anything else. It's about you and me. Things have changed, Kyle. It's…it's just not the same as it was."

"What's not the same?" he asked, his voice desperate. "What changed? Tell me!"

Once I said these next words there would be no going back. I didn't *want* to say them. I'd resisted so far because I knew they'd break me, too. But I realized now that this was the only way to break it off with him. Otherwise he'd never let me go.

"I don't love you anymore," I lied, and this time my voice did tremble.

He stepped back, like I'd slapped him in the face. "What?"

Another tear fell, down my other cheek. I wiped my face, brushing it away. "I don't love you anymore. It's over."

"No, Alexis, please…" The look on his face nearly killed me. I actually *saw* his heart breaking.

"Goodbye, Kyle."

I couldn't stand the pain in his eyes and had to turn away. I walked back to my parents, the tears flowing freely now. I wanted to retract every single thing I'd said, but I couldn't. This was for the best. We both had to move on with no regrets or we'd spend the next four years pining away for each other and never really living our own lives.

I loved Kyle too much to do that to him. Which is why I had to let him go.

PRESENT DAY

I surveyed the crowd backstage, but didn't spot the one face I wanted to see. Maybe Kyle was in the main part of the club. Villain Complex was scheduled for the last set of the night so I knew he must be here, somewhere.

God, what was I doing? Maybe this was all a big mistake. I could leave now and he'd never even know I was at the show tonight.

No, I had to find him. I drew in a long breath, forcing myself to calm down. I'd been back in LA for months and had nearly contacted Kyle a hundred times, but always chickened out in the end. When I'd heard about tonight's UCLA vs. USC Battle of the Bands I knew it was the perfect chance to see him again. No matter how scary it was, I had to talk to him.

I said hello to my friend Todd and his band, who were competing on the USC side, and took a few photos of them before turning away to look for Kyle again. I peered through my camera, snapping a few shots, using it as an excuse to study people without them noticing. That was the beauty of a camera, you could hide behind it in the middle of a crowd and no one thought it was odd.

And then I saw him. His hair was dyed black and longer than I remembered, falling into his eyes a little. He had more tattoos and round black gauges in his ears, but otherwise he looked so similar to the boy I'd known in high school that my heart felt like it was about to burst open. He looked more beautiful than ever, and I loved him just as much as I had then.

I felt it when he spotted me. His eyes widened a touch, his lips parted, and surprise flickered across his face. He'd always been easy to read—unlike Jared, Kyle wasn't very good at keeping his emotions off his face. He was definitely shocked to see me—and not entirely pleased.

Of course he wasn't pleased to see me. What was I thinking, coming here tonight without any warning? He probably had a girlfriend. This was a terrible idea, and now it was too late to hide behind my camera. Not that I wanted to hide —I was here to see him, after all. But I should have planned this better.

We both began moving through the crowd toward each other, drawn together by some invisible force. I'd rehearsed what I wanted to say to him, but now the words slipped from my mind. I'd have to wing it and hope for the best. I could do this. I had to.

Three years ago I broke Kyle's heart. Tonight I was going to win it back.

About the Author

Elizabeth Briggs is the *New York Times* bestselling author of paranormal and fantasy romance. She graduated from UCLA with a degree in Sociology and has worked for an international law firm, mentored teens in writing, and volunteered with dog rescue groups. Now she's a full-time geek who lives in Los Angeles with her family and a pack of fluffy dogs.

Visit Elizabeth's website: www.elizabethbriggs.com

www.ingramcontent.com/pod-product-compliance
Lightning Source LLC
Chambersburg PA
CBHW070225200726
48293CB00005B/1471